THE REAPER OF ST. GEORGE STREET

THE ADVENTURES OF FLAGLER'S FEW
ST. AUGUSTINE'S GHOST HUNTERS

WRITTEN AND ILLUSTRATED BY
ANDRE R. FRATTINO

Pineapple Press, Inc.
Sarasota, Florida

Inquiries should be addressed to:

Pineapple Press, Inc.
P.O. Box 3889
Sarasota, Florida 34230

www.pineapplepress.com

Library of Congress Cataloging-in-Publication Data

Frattino, Andre R., 1984-
The Reaper of St. George Street : the adventures of Flagler's Few, ghost hunters of St. Augustine / written and illustrated by Andre R. Frattino. -- 1st ed.
     p. cm.
ISBN 978-1-56164-517-6 (alk. paper)
1. Ghosts—Comic books, strips, etc. 2. Parapsychology—Investigation—Comic books, strips, etc. 3. Saint Augustine (Fla.) —Comic books, strips, etc. 4. Graphic novels. I. Title.
PN6727.F697R43 2012
741.5'973—dc23
          2011046792

First Edition
10 9 8 7 6 5 4 3 2 1

Design by Andre Frattino
Printed in the United States

IN MEMORY OF...

MY GRANDFATHER, WHO ALWAYS TOLD HIS OLD WAR STORIES WITH SUCH FLAIR.

MY COUSIN, WHO, DESPITE BEING MILD-MANNERED, WE ALL BELIEVED WORKED AS AN INTERNATIONAL SPY!

MY FATHER, WHOSE CHARACTER AND SPIRIT HAVE GONE UNMATCHED AND KEEP ME ON THE HUNT...

PROLOGUE

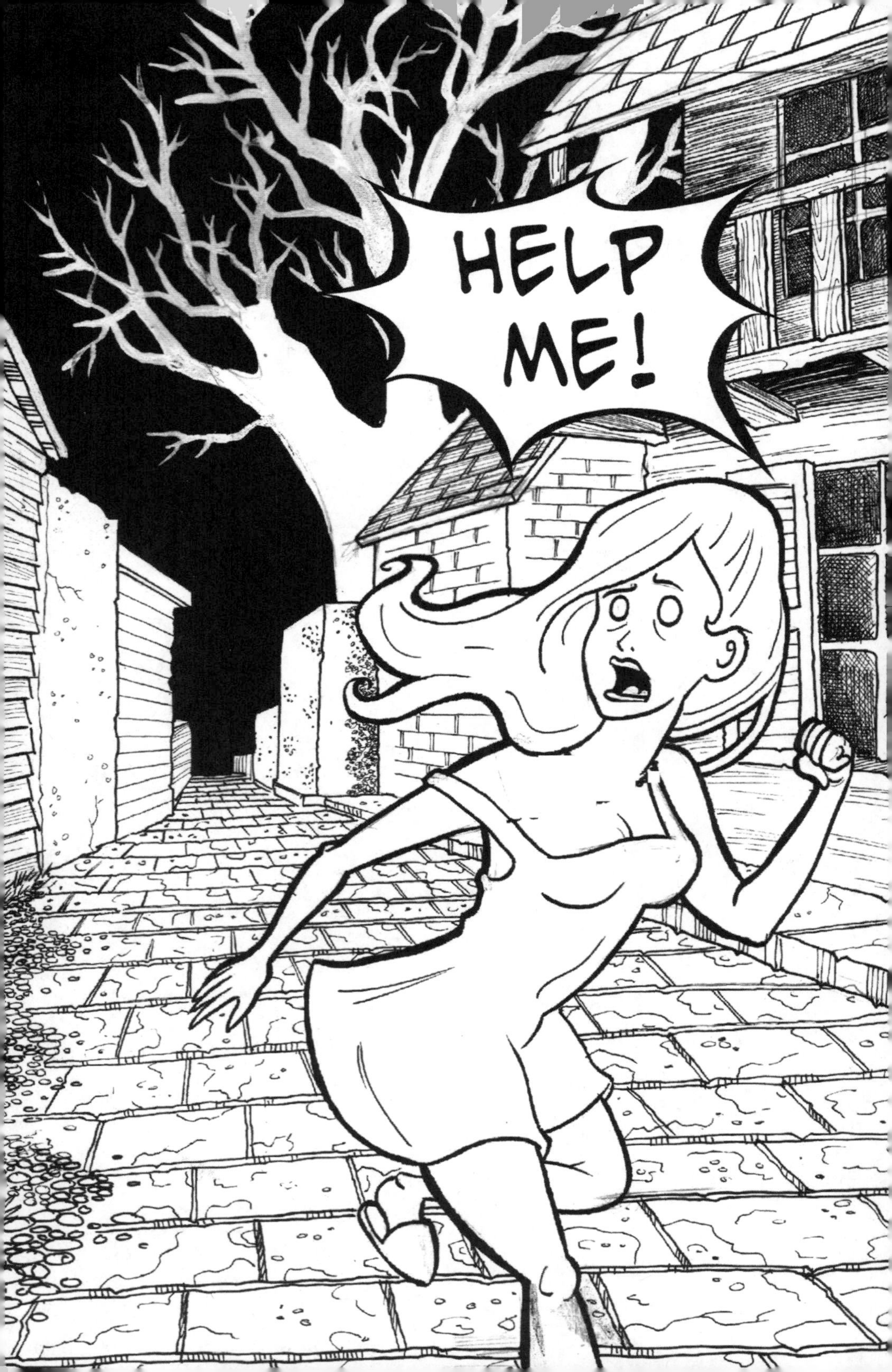
HELP ME!

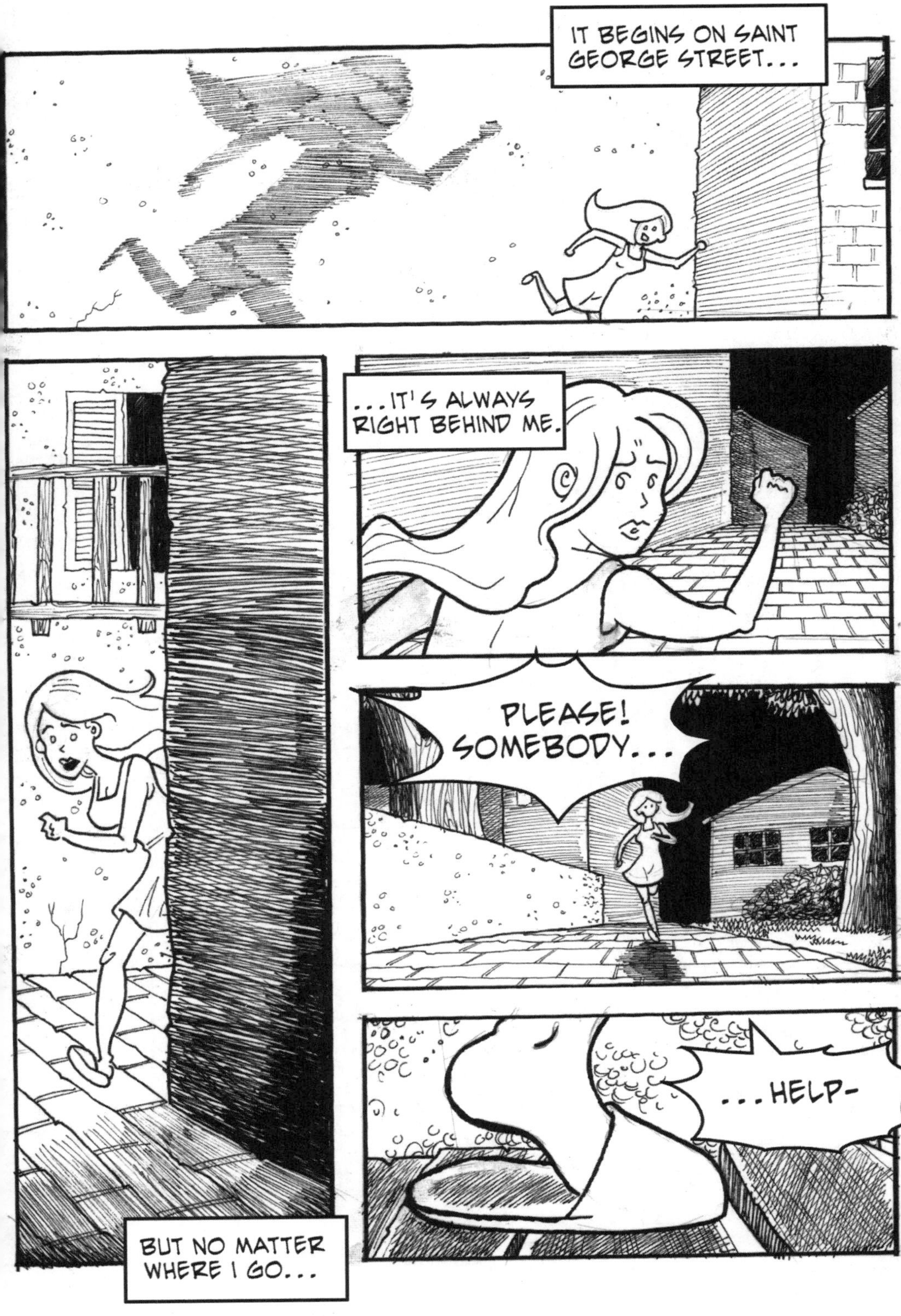
IT BEGINS ON SAINT GEORGE STREET...
BUT NO MATTER WHERE I GO...
...IT'S ALWAYS RIGHT BEHIND ME.
PLEASE! SOMEBODY...
...HELP-

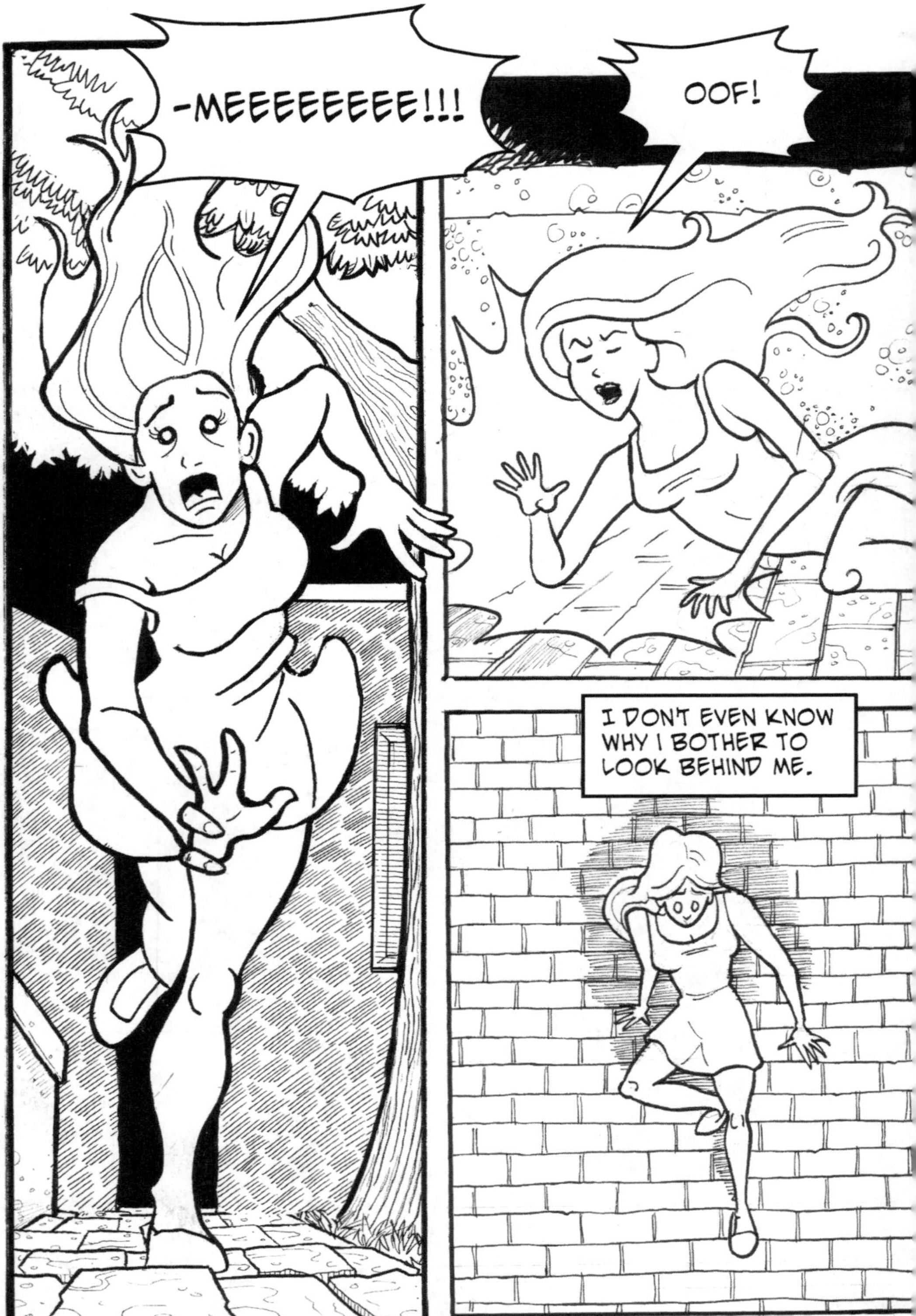
-MEEEEEEEEE!!!
OOF!
I DON'T EVEN KNOW WHY I BOTHER TO LOOK BEHIND ME.

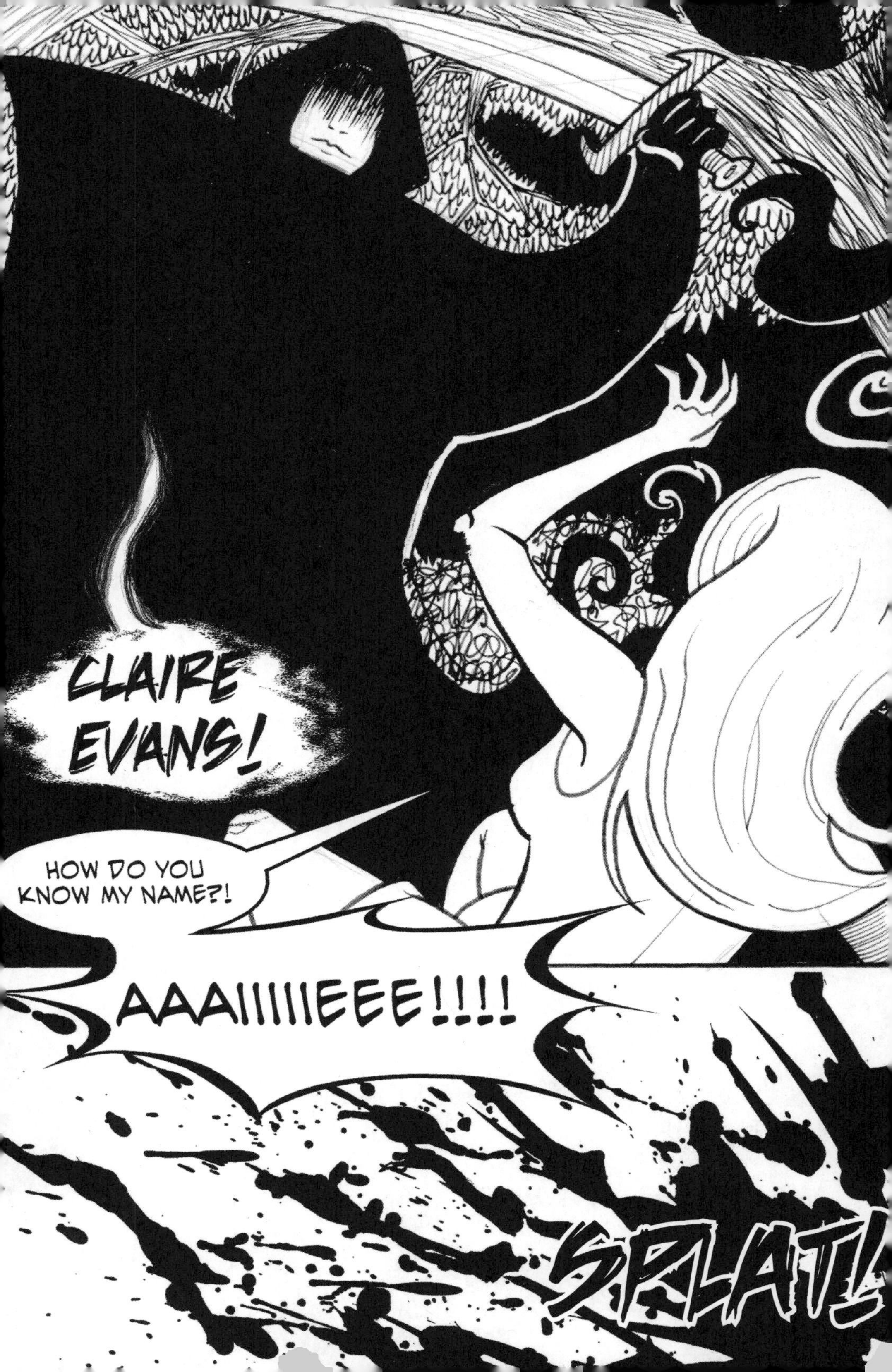
CLAIRE EVANS!
HOW DO YOU KNOW MY NAME?!
AAAIIIIIIEEE!!!!
SPLAT!

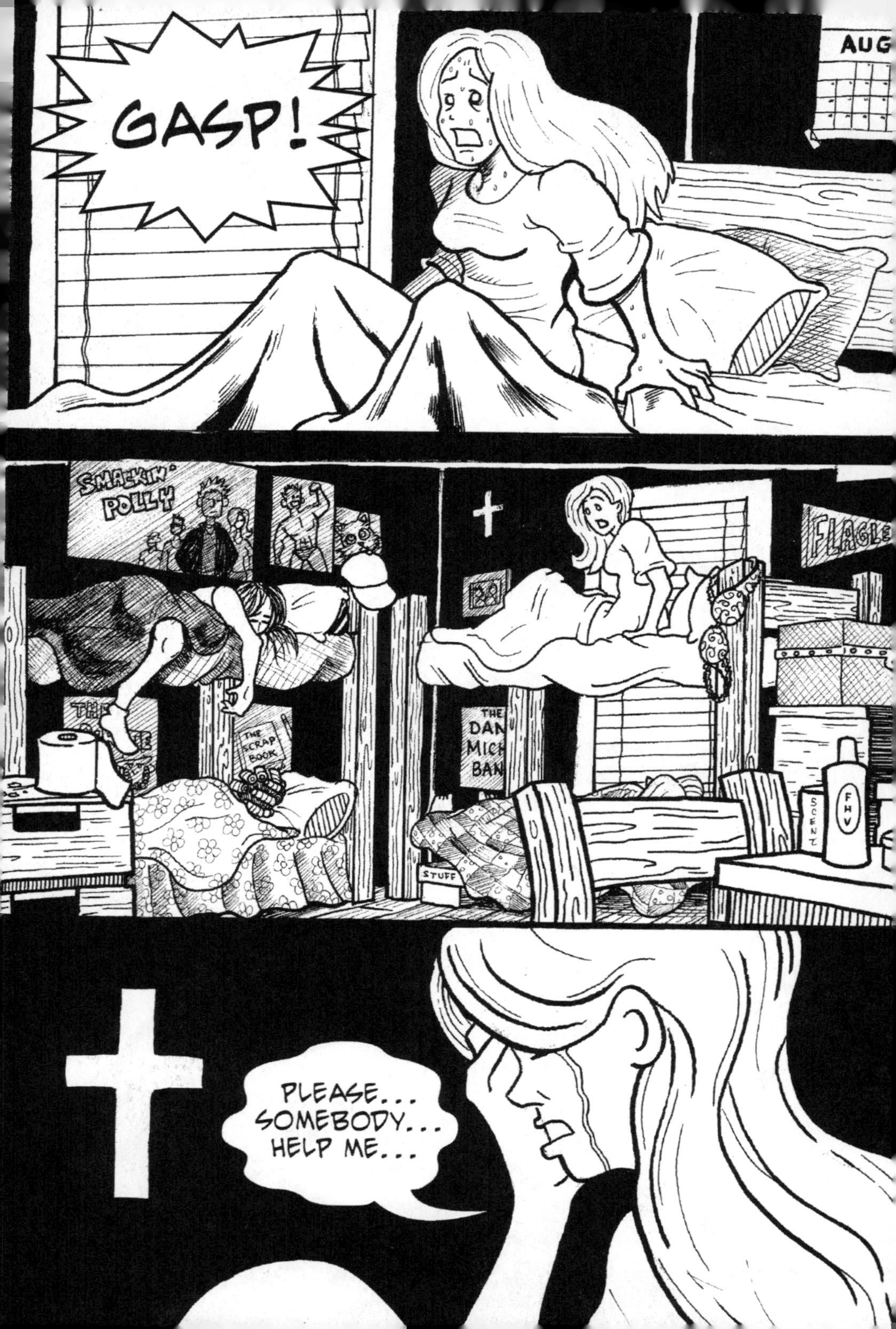

GASP!
AUG
SMACKIN' POLLY
FLAGLE
THE SCRAP BOOK
THE DAN MICH BAN
STUFF
SCENT
FHV
PLEASE... SOMEBODY... HELP ME...

CHAPTER
1

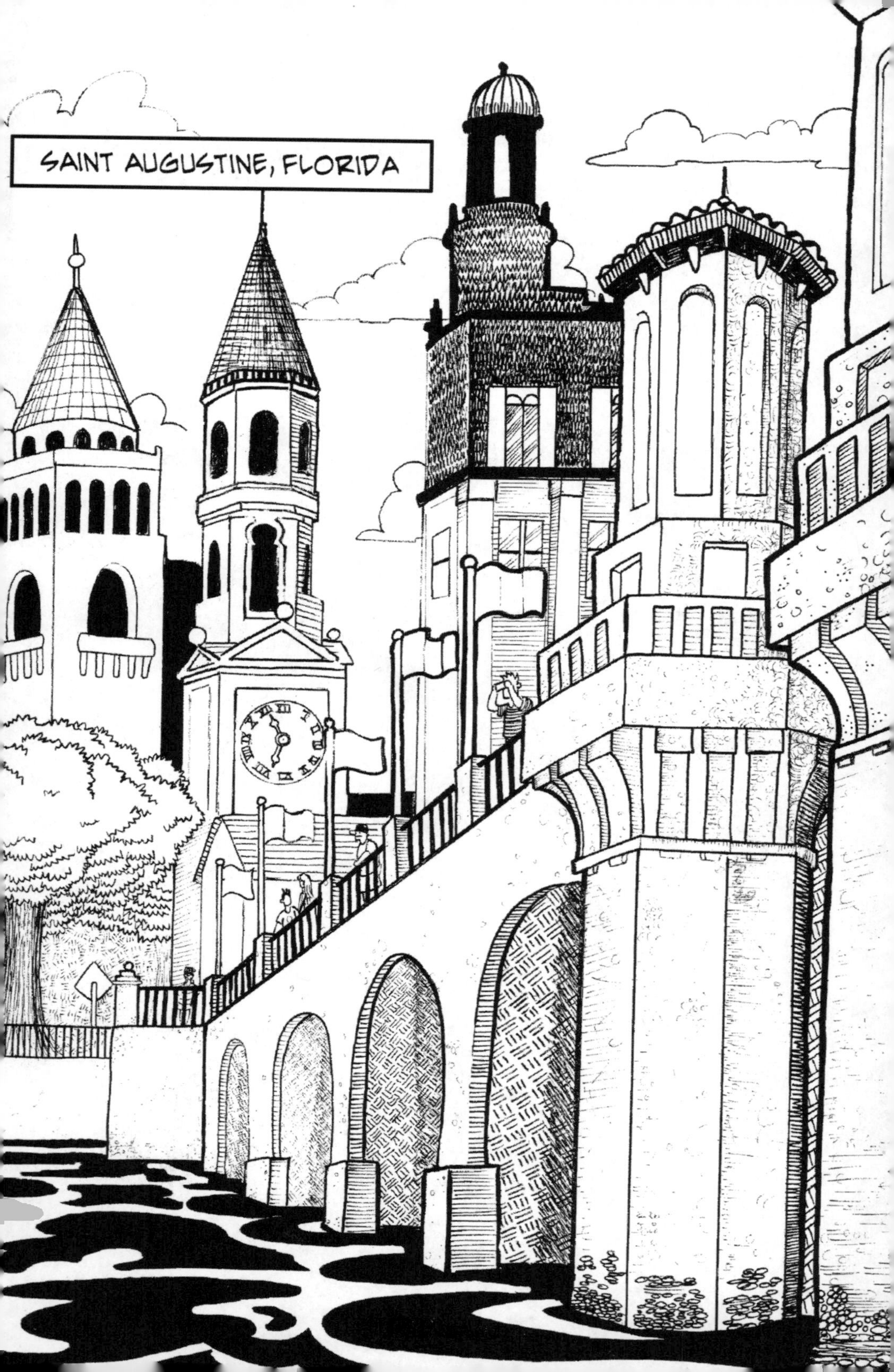
SAINT AUGUSTINE, FLORIDA

FOUNDED IN 1565 BY THE SPANISH EXPLORER PEDRO MENEDEZ DE AVILES.

WHILE MANY OTHER COLONIES CAME BEFORE ITS CONSTRUCTION ...

...SAINT AUGUSTINE WAS THE FIRST SUCCESSFULLY FOUNDED CITY IN THE NEW WORLD.

THE SPANISH RULED FROM 1565 TO 1763.

THEN THE BRITISH TOOK CONTROL IN 1763, BUT RELINQUISHED CONTROL BACK TO SPAIN IN 1784.

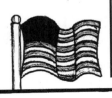

IN 1821, THE UNITED STATES BECAME ITS CURRENT OWNER.

SAINT AUGUSTINE BECAME MUCH MORE IMPORTANT AFTER THE ARRIVAL OF HENRY M. FLAGLER, A WEALTHY INDUSTRIALIST WITH BIG PLANS.

FLAGLER OPENED UP A STREAM OF HOTELS IN THE EARLY 1900S, HOPING TO MAKE IT A HIDEAWAY FOR THE RICH.

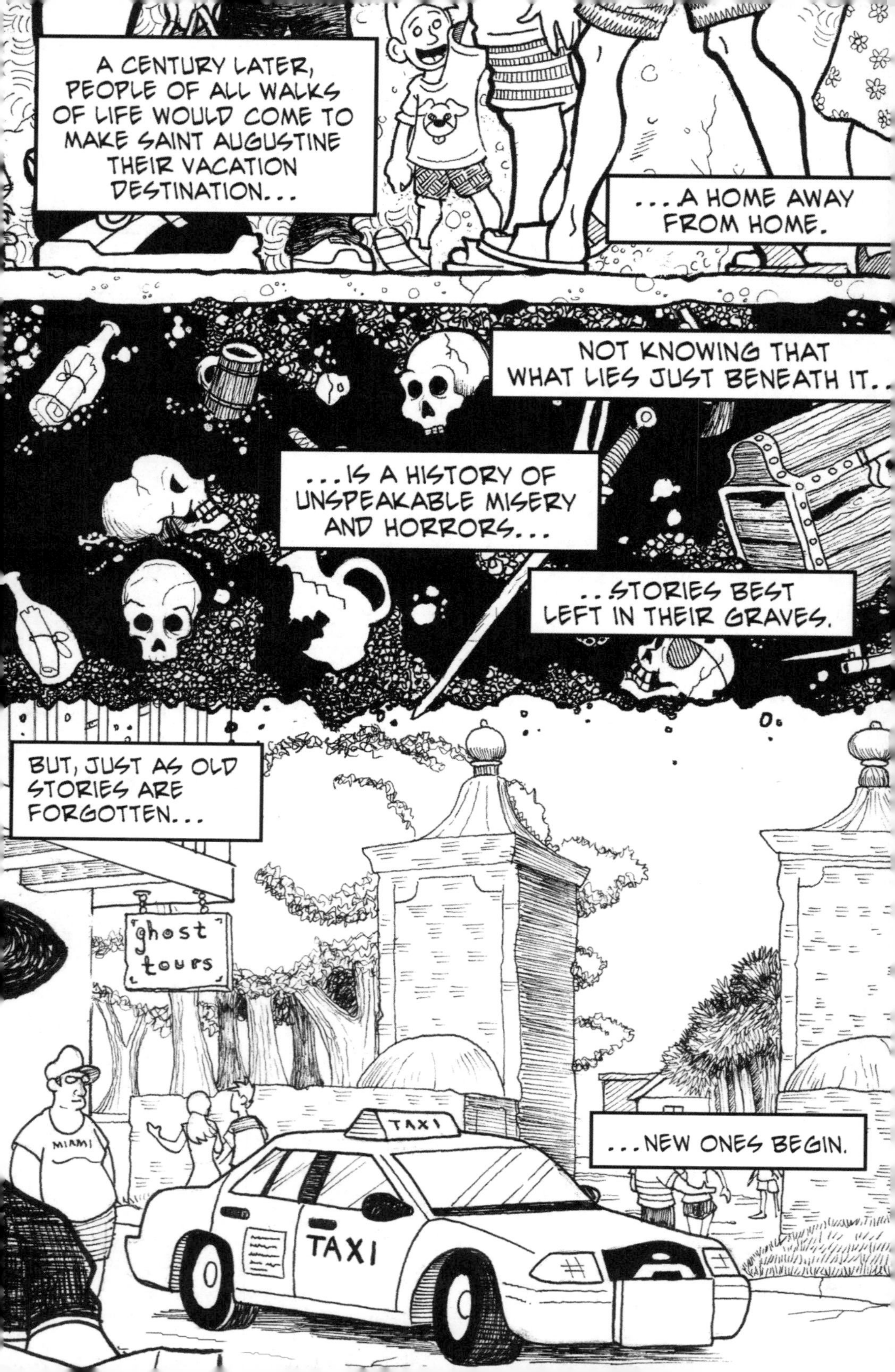
A CENTURY LATER, PEOPLE OF ALL WALKS OF LIFE WOULD COME TO MAKE SAINT AUGUSTINE THEIR VACATION DESTINATION...
...A HOME AWAY FROM HOME.
NOT KNOWING THAT WHAT LIES JUST BENEATH IT...
...IS A HISTORY OF UNSPEAKABLE MISERY AND HORRORS...
..STORIES BEST LEFT IN THEIR GRAVES.
BUT, JUST AS OLD STORIES ARE FORGOTTEN...
ghost tours
MIAMI
TAXI
TAXI
...NEW ONES BEGIN.

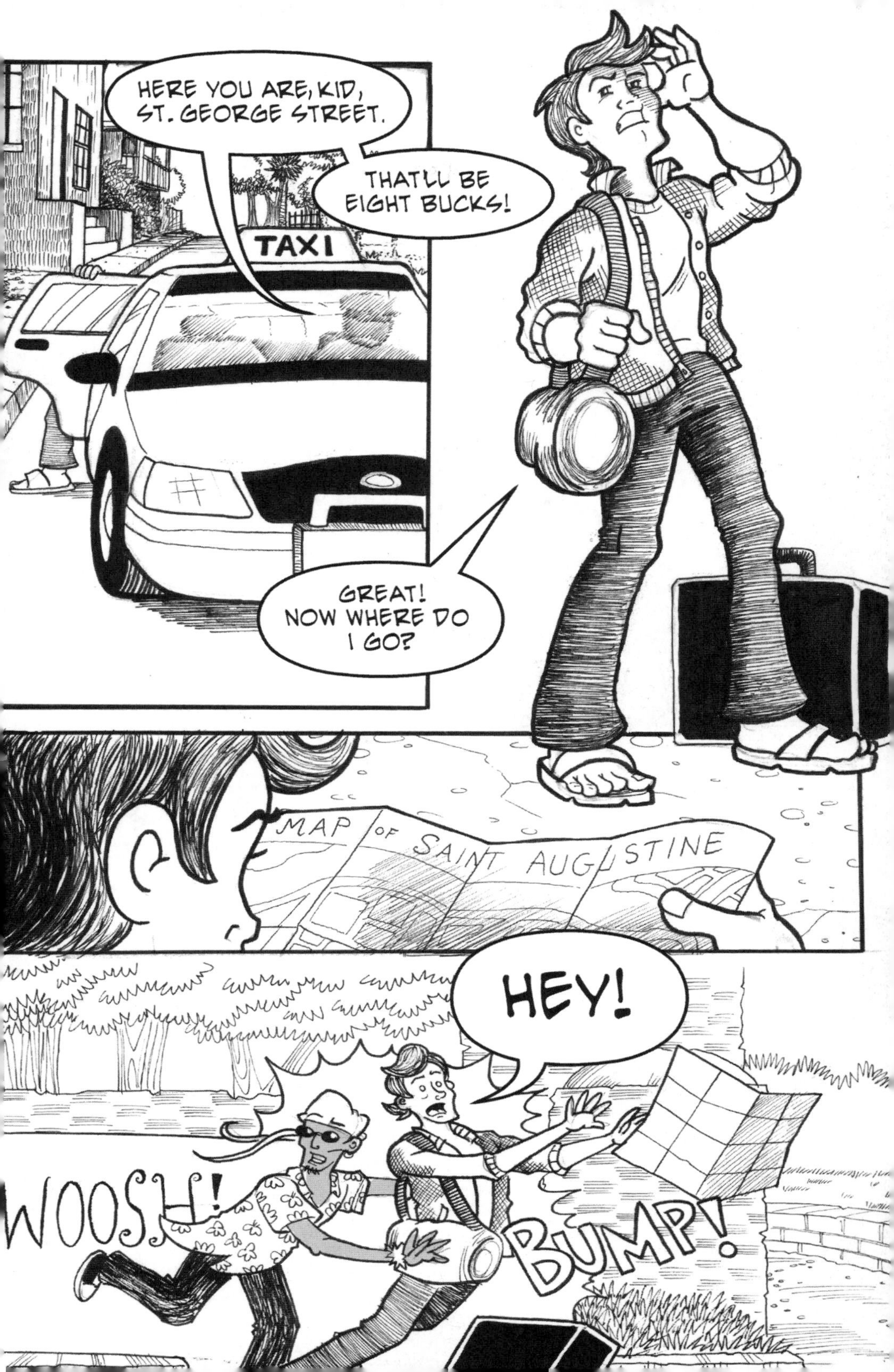
HERE YOU ARE, KID, ST. GEORGE STREET.
THAT'LL BE EIGHT BUCKS!
TAXI
GREAT! NOW WHERE DO I GO?
MAP OF SAINT AUGUSTINE
HEY!
WOOSH!
BUMP!

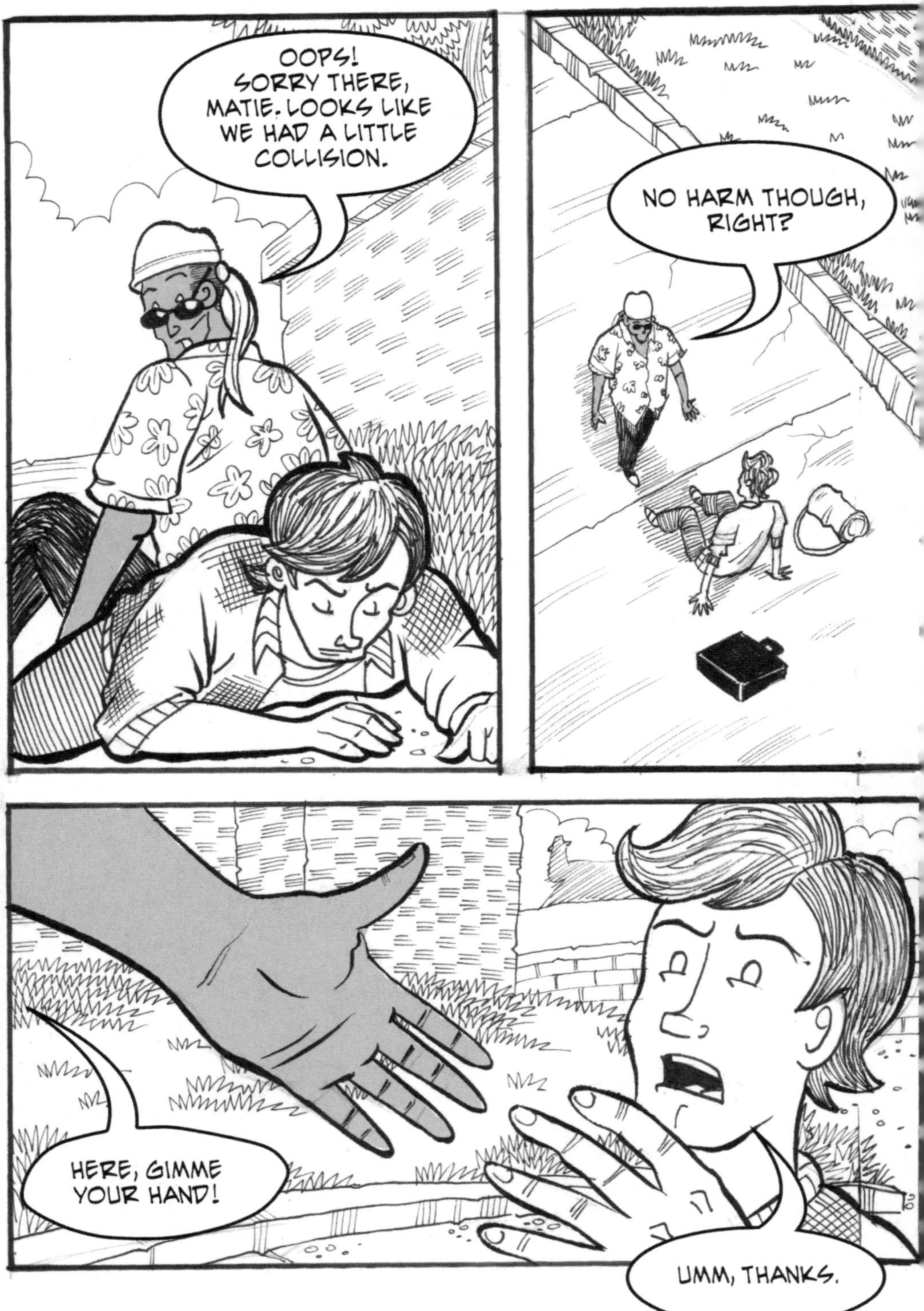
OOPS! SORRY THERE, MATIE. LOOKS LIKE WE HAD A LITTLE COLLISION.
NO HARM THOUGH, RIGHT?
HERE, GIMME YOUR HAND!
UMM, THANKS.

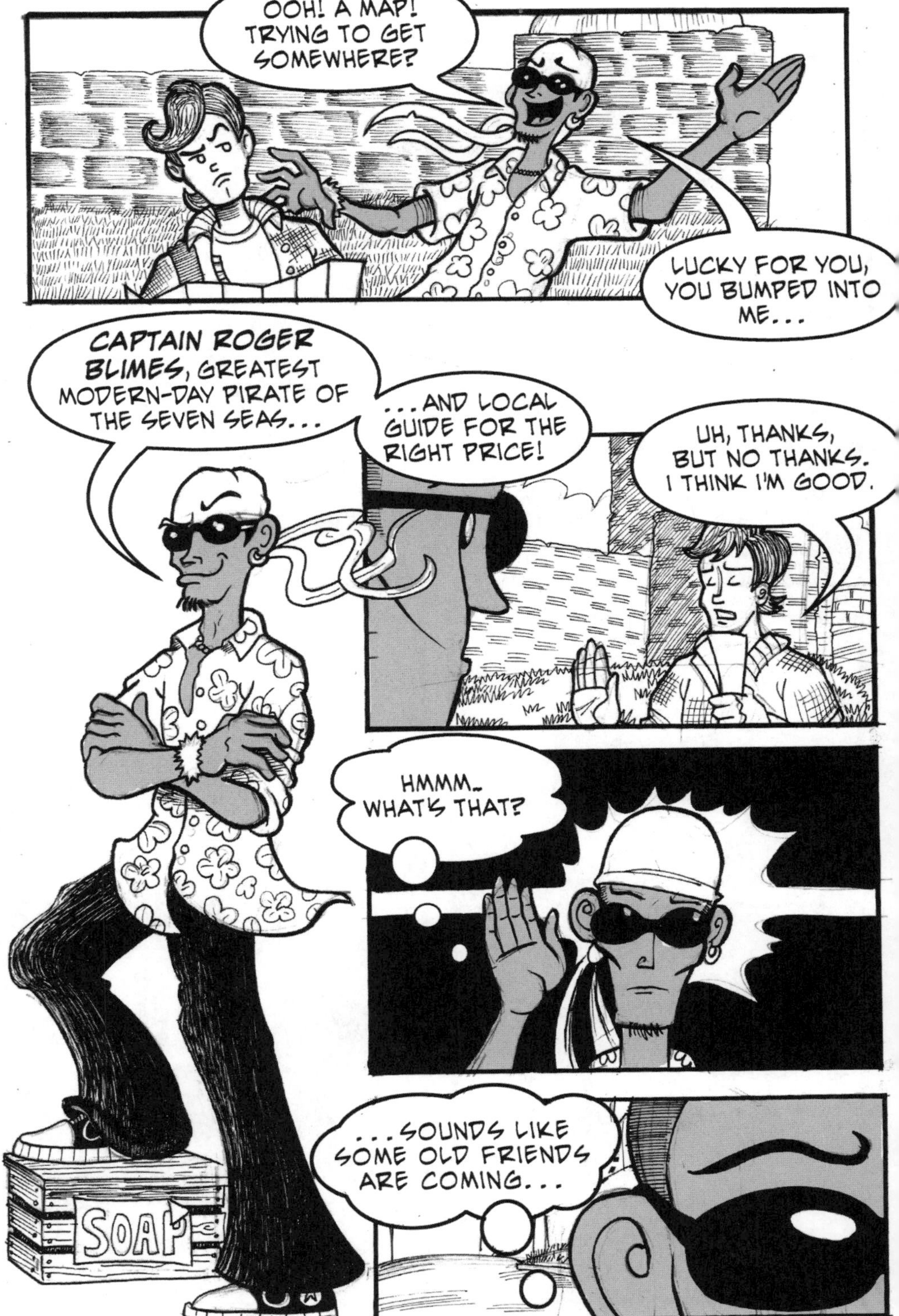
OOH! A MAP! TRYING TO GET SOMEWHERE?
LUCKY FOR YOU, YOU BUMPED INTO ME...
CAPTAIN ROGER BLIMES, GREATEST MODERN-DAY PIRATE OF THE SEVEN SEAS...
...AND LOCAL GUIDE FOR THE RIGHT PRICE!
UH, THANKS, BUT NO THANKS. I THINK I'M GOOD.
SOAP
HMMM.. WHAT'S THAT?
...SOUNDS LIKE SOME OLD FRIENDS ARE COMING...

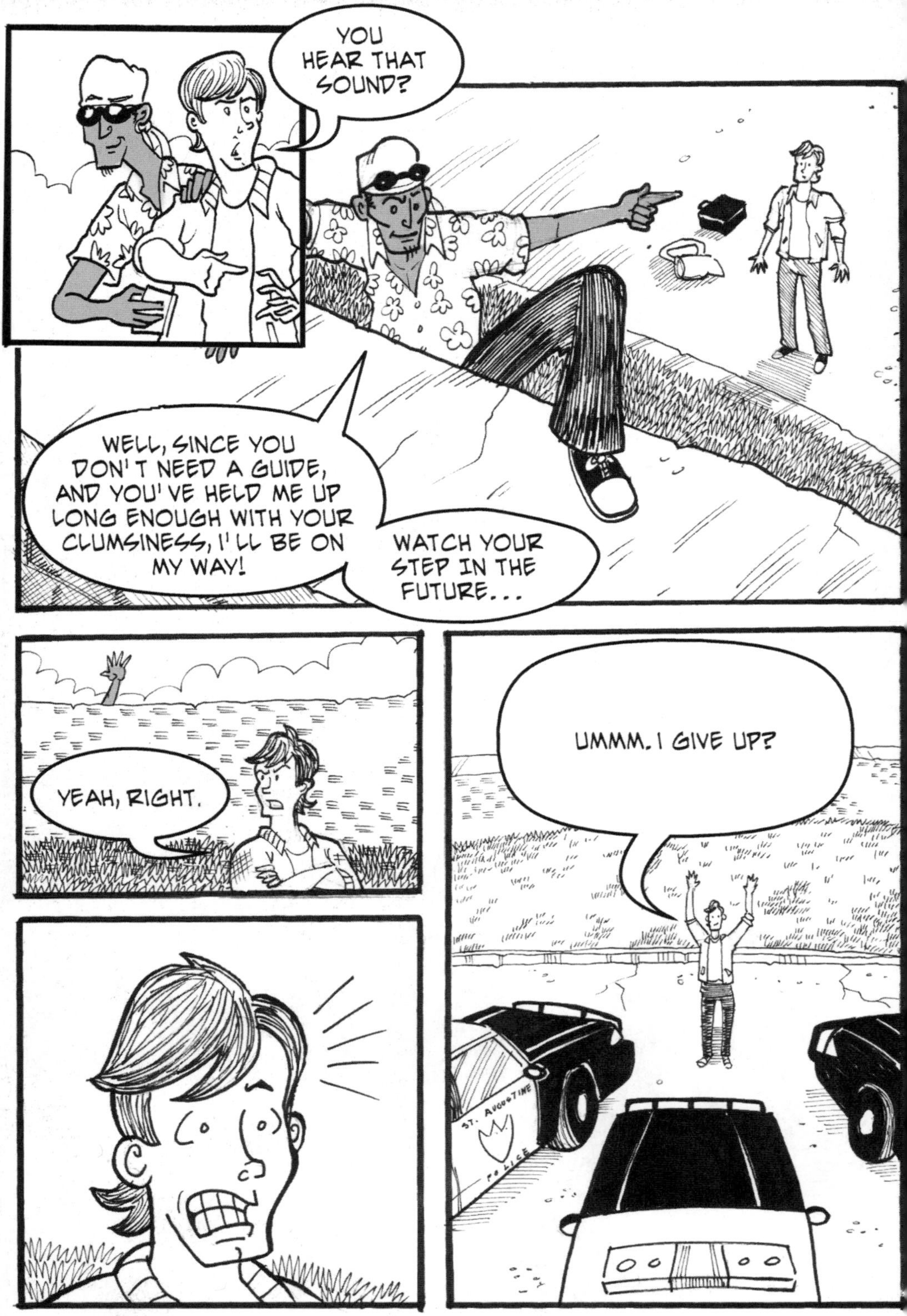
YOU HEAR THAT SOUND?
WELL, SINCE YOU DON'T NEED A GUIDE, AND YOU'VE HELD ME UP LONG ENOUGH WITH YOUR CLUMSINESS, I'LL BE ON MY WAY!
WATCH YOUR STEP IN THE FUTURE...
YEAH, RIGHT.
UMMM. I GIVE UP?
ST. AUGUSTINE POLICE

CHAPTER

2

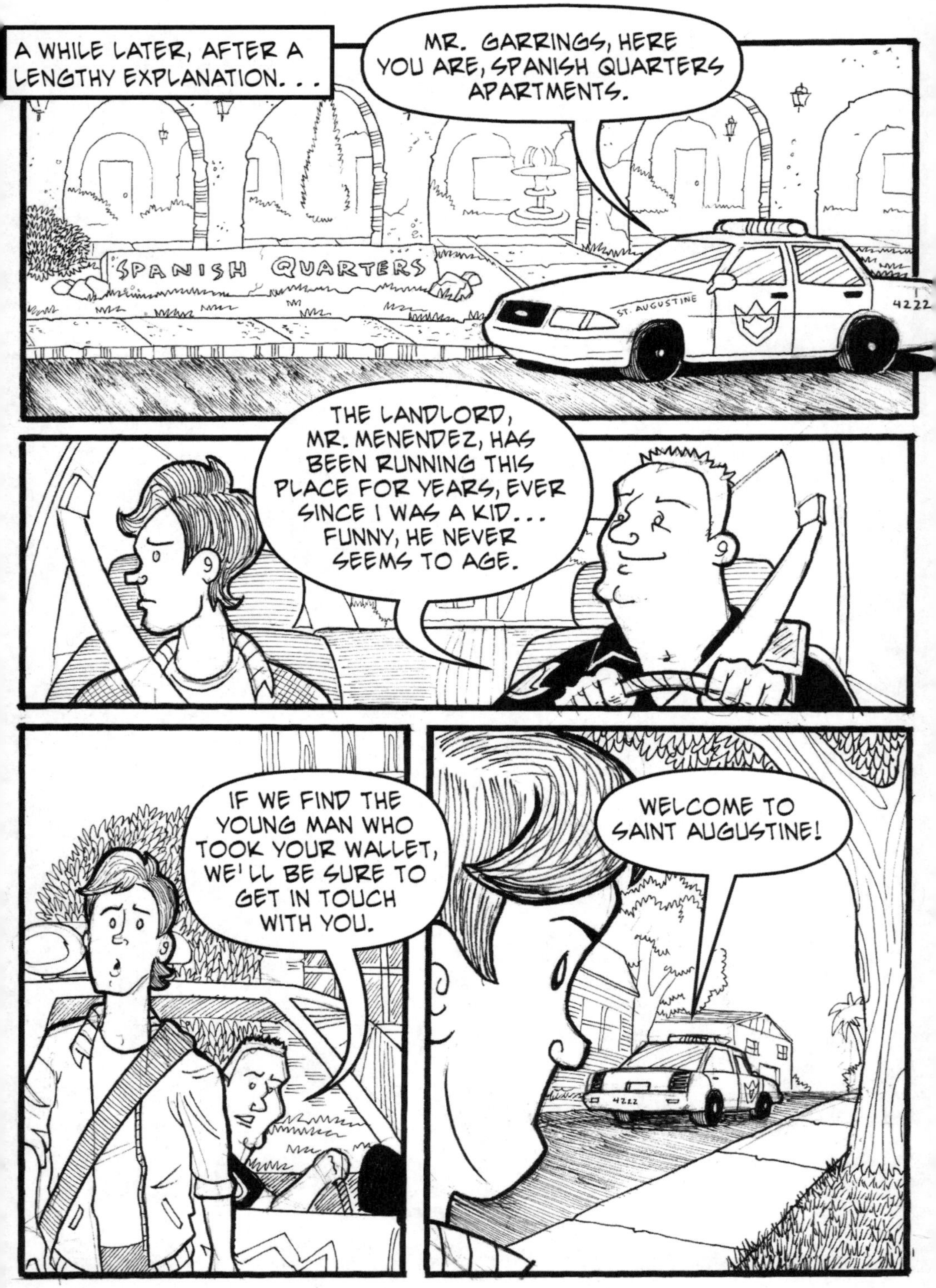
A WHILE LATER, AFTER A LENGTHY EXPLANATION. . .
MR. GARRINGS, HERE YOU ARE, SPANISH QUARTERS APARTMENTS.
SPANISH QUARTERS
ST. AUGUSTINE
4222
THE LANDLORD, MR. MENENDEZ, HAS BEEN RUNNING THIS PLACE FOR YEARS, EVER SINCE I WAS A KID... FUNNY, HE NEVER SEEMS TO AGE.
IF WE FIND THE YOUNG MAN WHO TOOK YOUR WALLET, WE'LL BE SURE TO GET IN TOUCH WITH YOU.
WELCOME TO SAINT AUGUSTINE!
4222

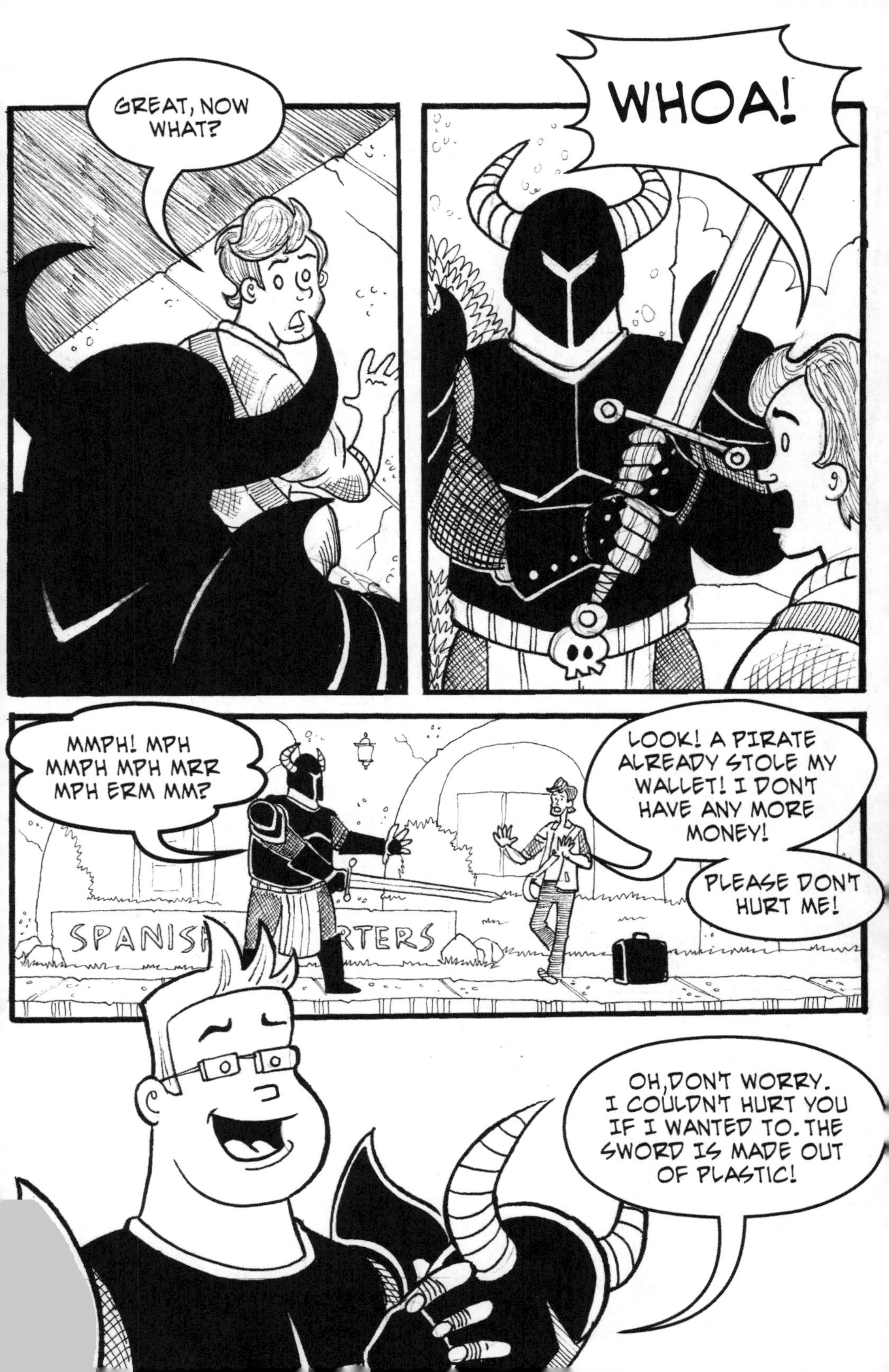
GREAT, NOW WHAT?
WHOA!
MMPH! MPH MMPH MPH MRR MPH ERM MM?
LOOK! A PIRATE ALREADY STOLE MY WALLET! I DON'T HAVE ANY MORE MONEY!
PLEASE DON'T HURT ME!
SPANISH ...RTERS
OH, DON'T WORRY. I COULDN'T HURT YOU IF I WANTED TO. THE SWORD IS MADE OUT OF PLASTIC!

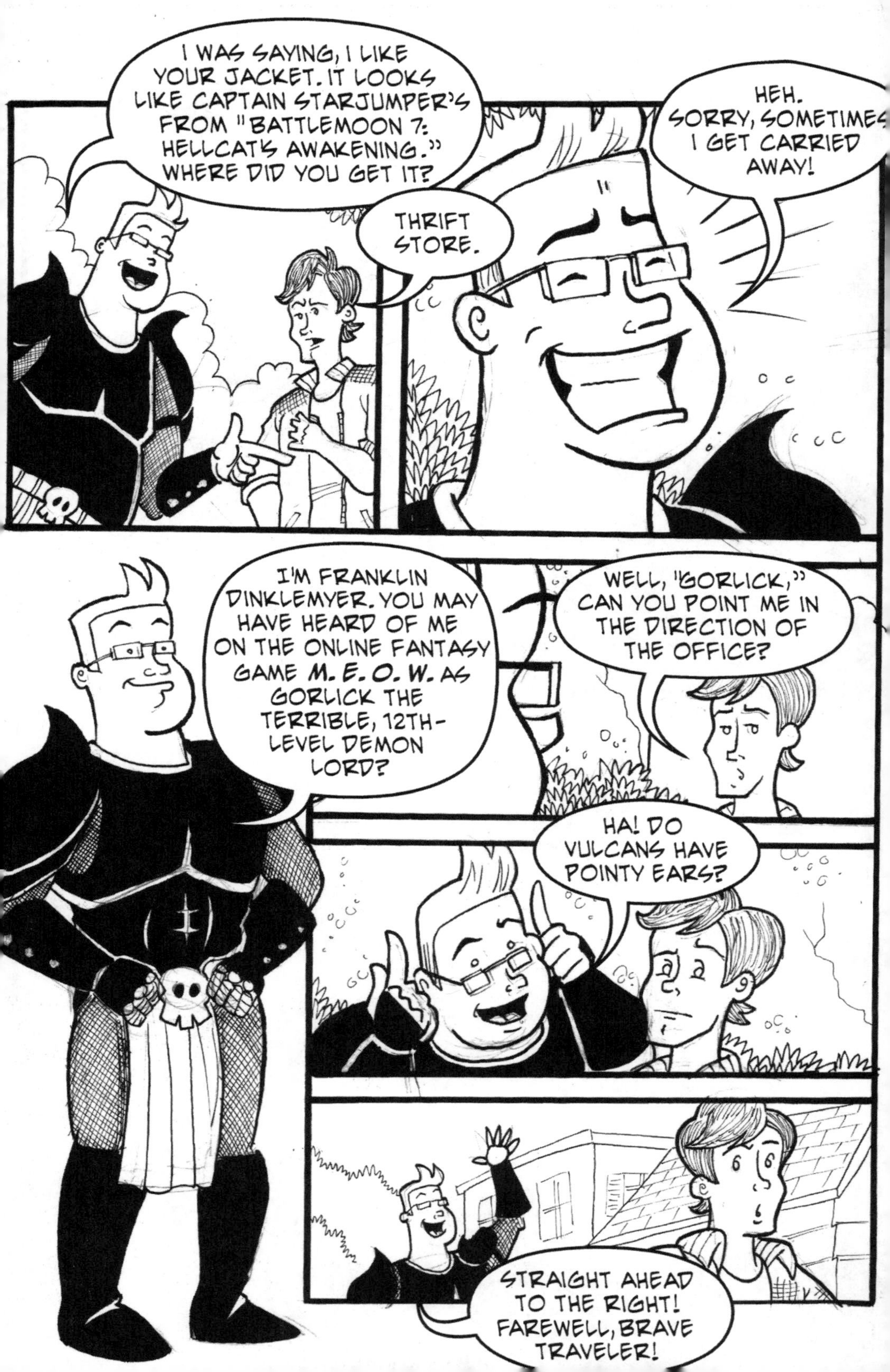
I WAS SAYING, I LIKE YOUR JACKET. IT LOOKS LIKE CAPTAIN STARJUMPER'S FROM "BATTLEMOON 7: HELLCAT'S AWAKENING." WHERE DID YOU GET IT?
THRIFT STORE.
HEH. SORRY, SOMETIMES I GET CARRIED AWAY!
I'M FRANKLIN DINKLEMYER. YOU MAY HAVE HEARD OF ME ON THE ONLINE FANTASY GAME M.E.O.W. AS GORLICK THE TERRIBLE, 12TH-LEVEL DEMON LORD?
WELL, "GORLICK," CAN YOU POINT ME IN THE DIRECTION OF THE OFFICE?
HA! DO VULCANS HAVE POINTY EARS?
STRAIGHT AHEAD TO THE RIGHT! FAREWELL, BRAVE TRAVELER!

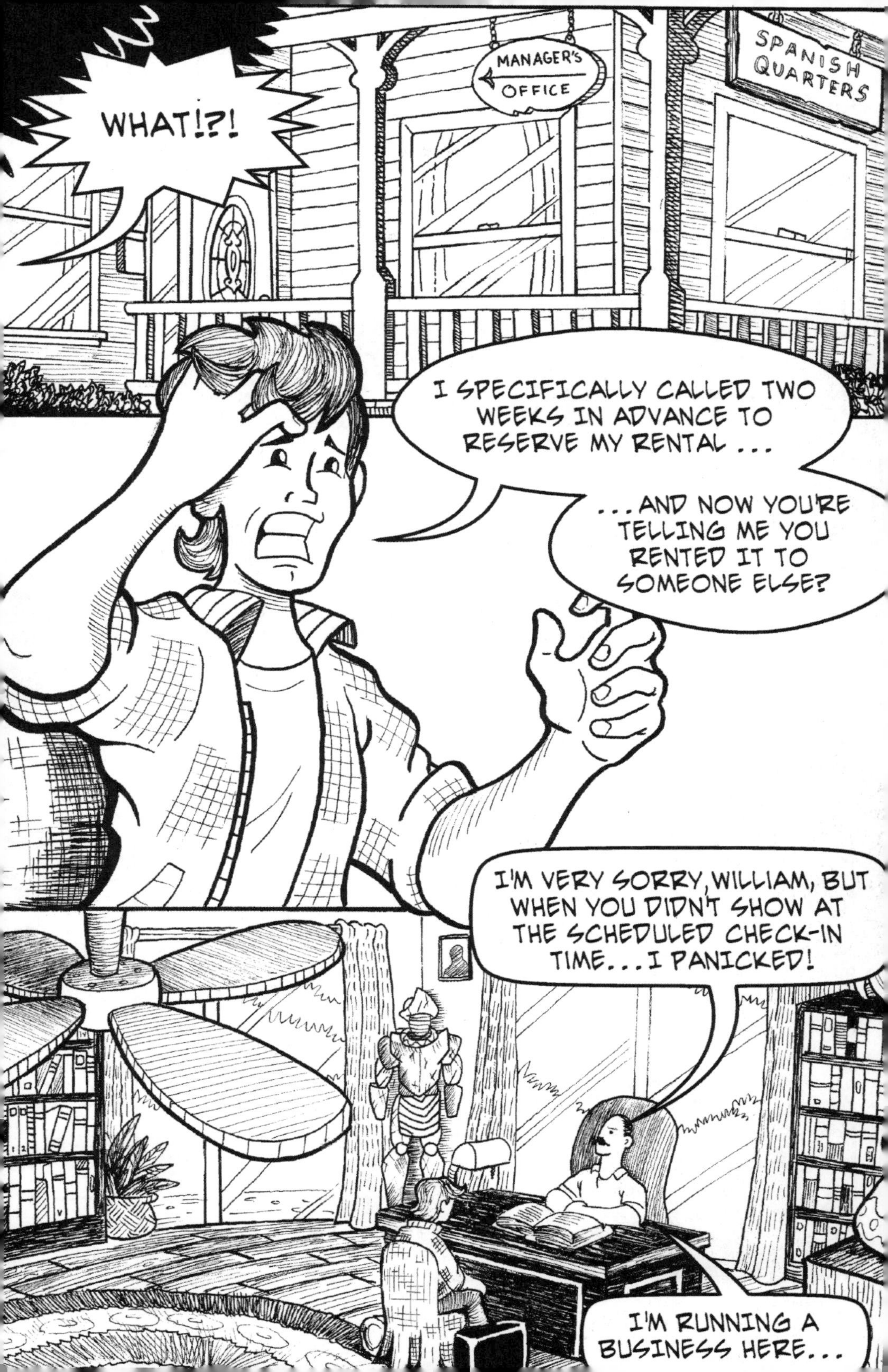
MANAGER'S OFFICE
SPANISH QUARTERS
WHAT!?!
I SPECIFICALLY CALLED TWO WEEKS IN ADVANCE TO RESERVE MY RENTAL . . .
. . . AND NOW YOU'RE TELLING ME YOU RENTED IT TO SOMEONE ELSE?
I'M VERY SORRY, WILLIAM, BUT WHEN YOU DIDN'T SHOW AT THE SCHEDULED CHECK-IN TIME. . . I PANICKED!
I'M RUNNING A BUSINESS HERE. . .

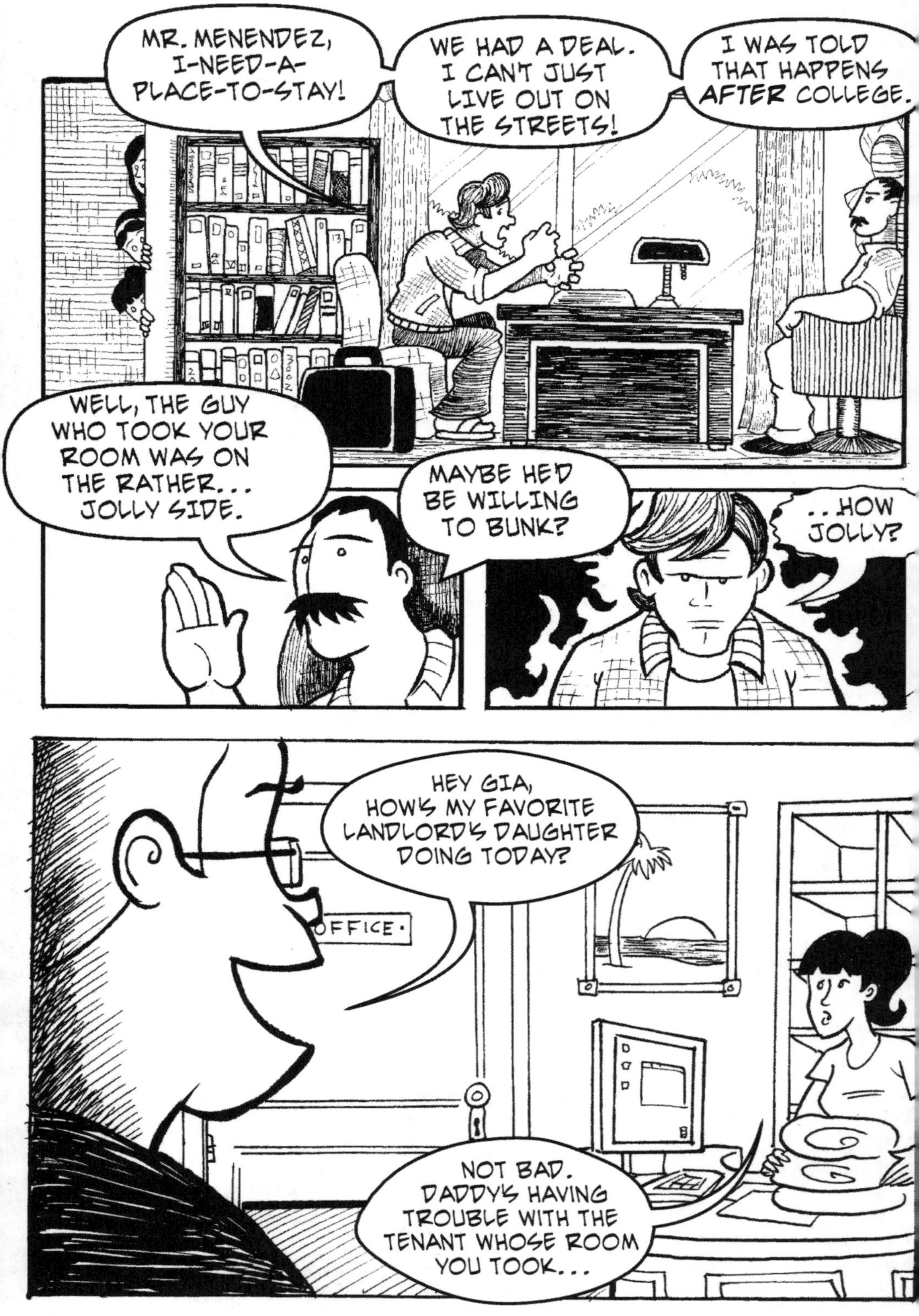
MR. MENENDEZ, I-NEED-A-PLACE-TO-STAY!
WE HAD A DEAL. I CAN'T JUST LIVE OUT ON THE STREETS!
I WAS TOLD THAT HAPPENS AFTER COLLEGE.
WELL, THE GUY WHO TOOK YOUR ROOM WAS ON THE RATHER... JOLLY SIDE.
MAYBE HE'D BE WILLING TO BUNK?
..HOW JOLLY?
HEY GIA, HOW'S MY FAVORITE LANDLORD'S DAUGHTER DOING TODAY?
OFFICE
NOT BAD. DADDY'S HAVING TROUBLE WITH THE TENANT WHOSE ROOM YOU TOOK...

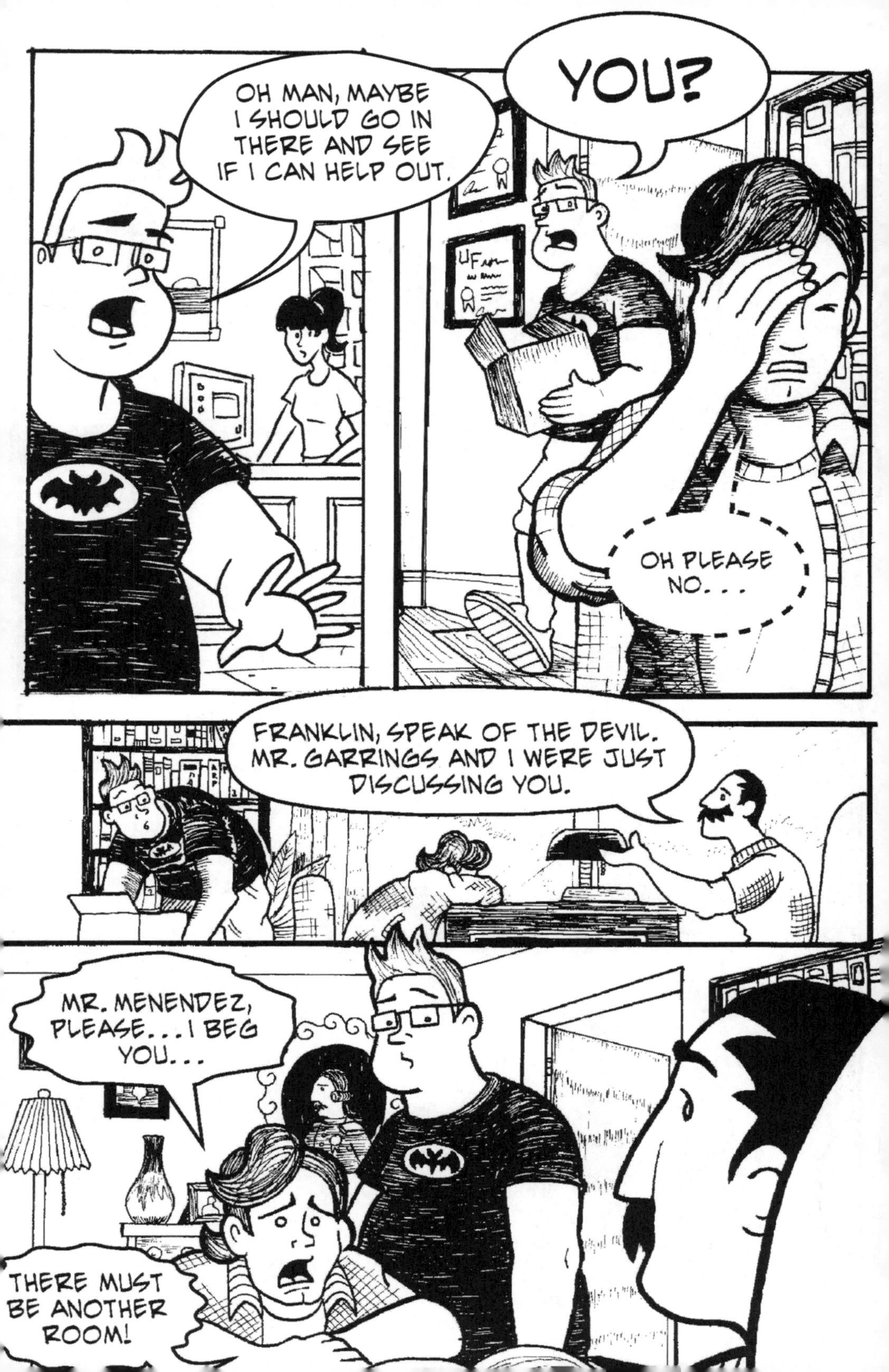
OH MAN, MAYBE I SHOULD GO IN THERE AND SEE IF I CAN HELP OUT.
YOU?
OH PLEASE NO. . .
FRANKLIN, SPEAK OF THE DEVIL. MR. GARRINGS AND I WERE JUST DISCUSSING YOU.
MR. MENENDEZ, PLEASE. . . I BEG YOU. . .
THERE MUST BE ANOTHER ROOM!

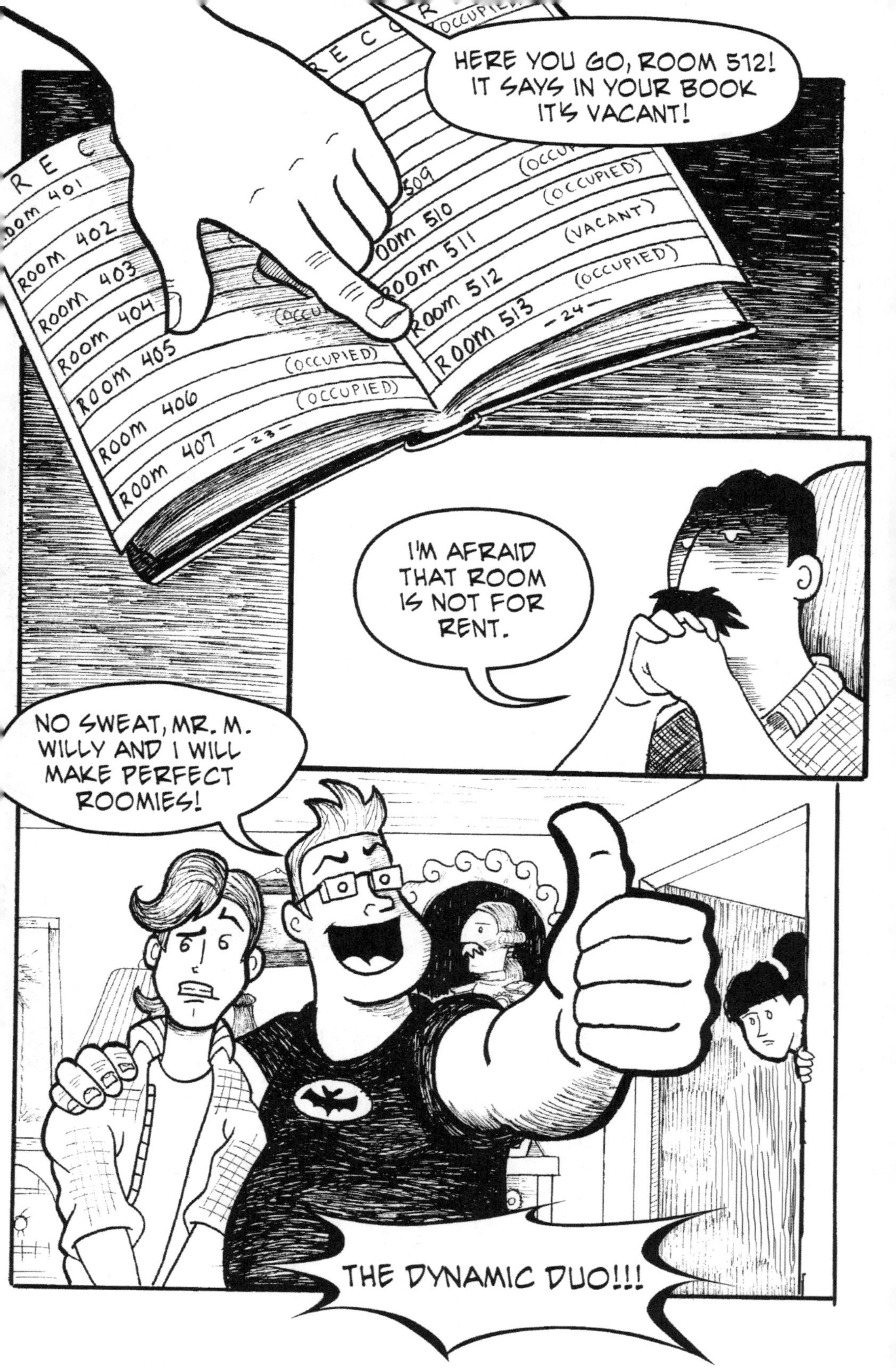
HERE YOU GO, ROOM 512! IT SAYS IN YOUR BOOK IT'S VACANT!
ROOM 402
ROOM 403
ROOM 404
ROOM 405 (OCCUPIED)
ROOM 406 (OCCUPIED)
ROOM 407
-23-
ROOM 510 (OCCUPIED)
ROOM 511 (VACANT)
ROOM 512 (OCCUPIED)
ROOM 513
-24-
I'M AFRAID THAT ROOM IS NOT FOR RENT.
NO SWEAT, MR. M. WILLY AND I WILL MAKE PERFECT ROOMIES!
THE DYNAMIC DUO!!!

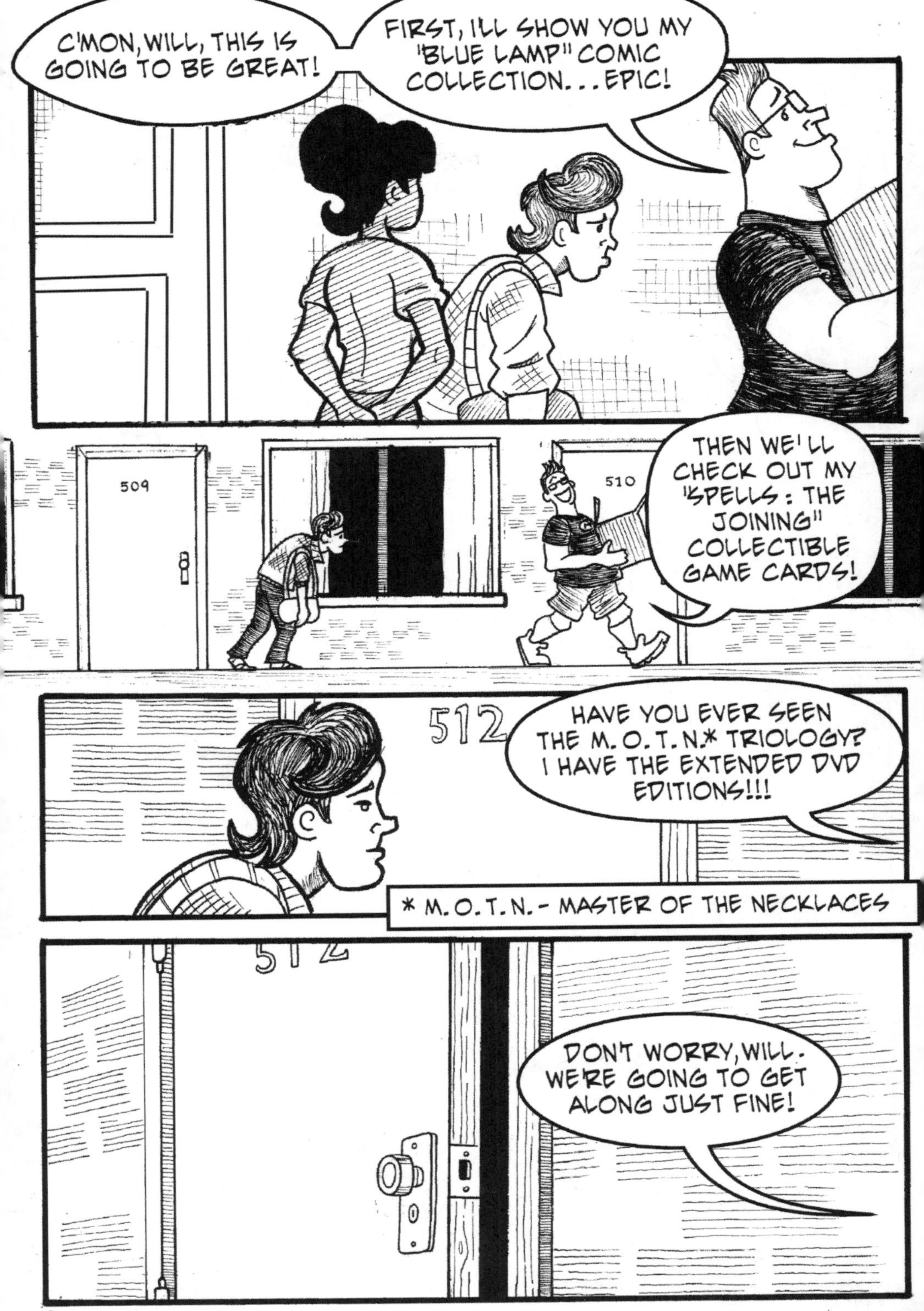
C'MON, WILL, THIS IS GOING TO BE GREAT!
FIRST, I'LL SHOW YOU MY "BLUE LAMP" COMIC COLLECTION... EPIC!
509
510
THEN WE'LL CHECK OUT MY "SPELLS: THE JOINING" COLLECTIBLE GAME CARDS!
512
HAVE YOU EVER SEEN THE M.O.T.N.* TRIOLOGY? I HAVE THE EXTENDED DVD EDITIONS!!!
* M.O.T.N. - MASTER OF THE NECKLACES
512
DON'T WORRY, WILL. WE'RE GOING TO GET ALONG JUST FINE!

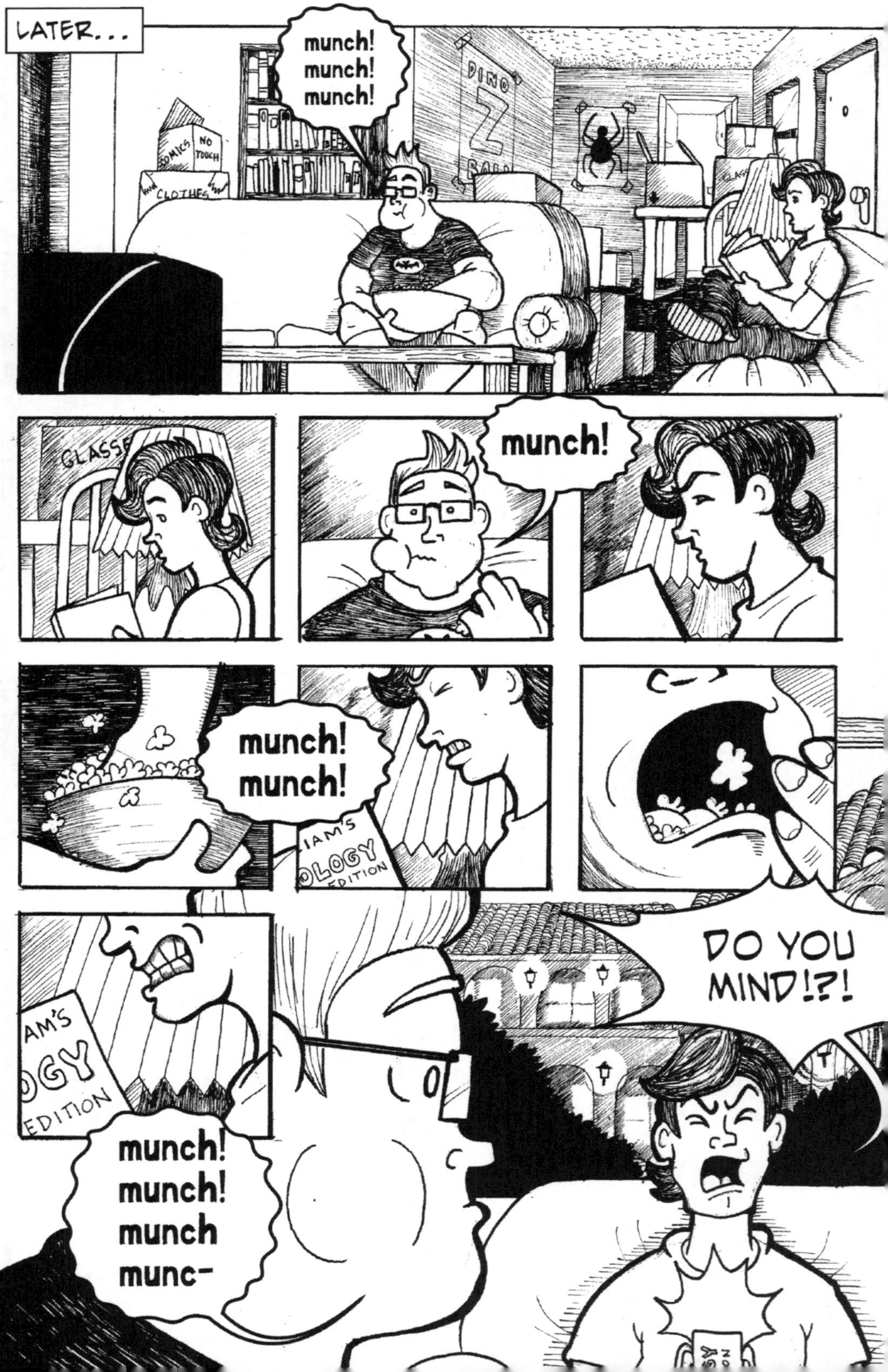
LATER...
munch! munch! munch!
DINO Z BALL
COMICS NO TOUCH
CLOTHES
GLASSES
munch!
munch! munch!
IAM'S OLOGY EDITION
AM'S OGY EDITION
munch! munch! munch munc-
DO YOU MIND!?!

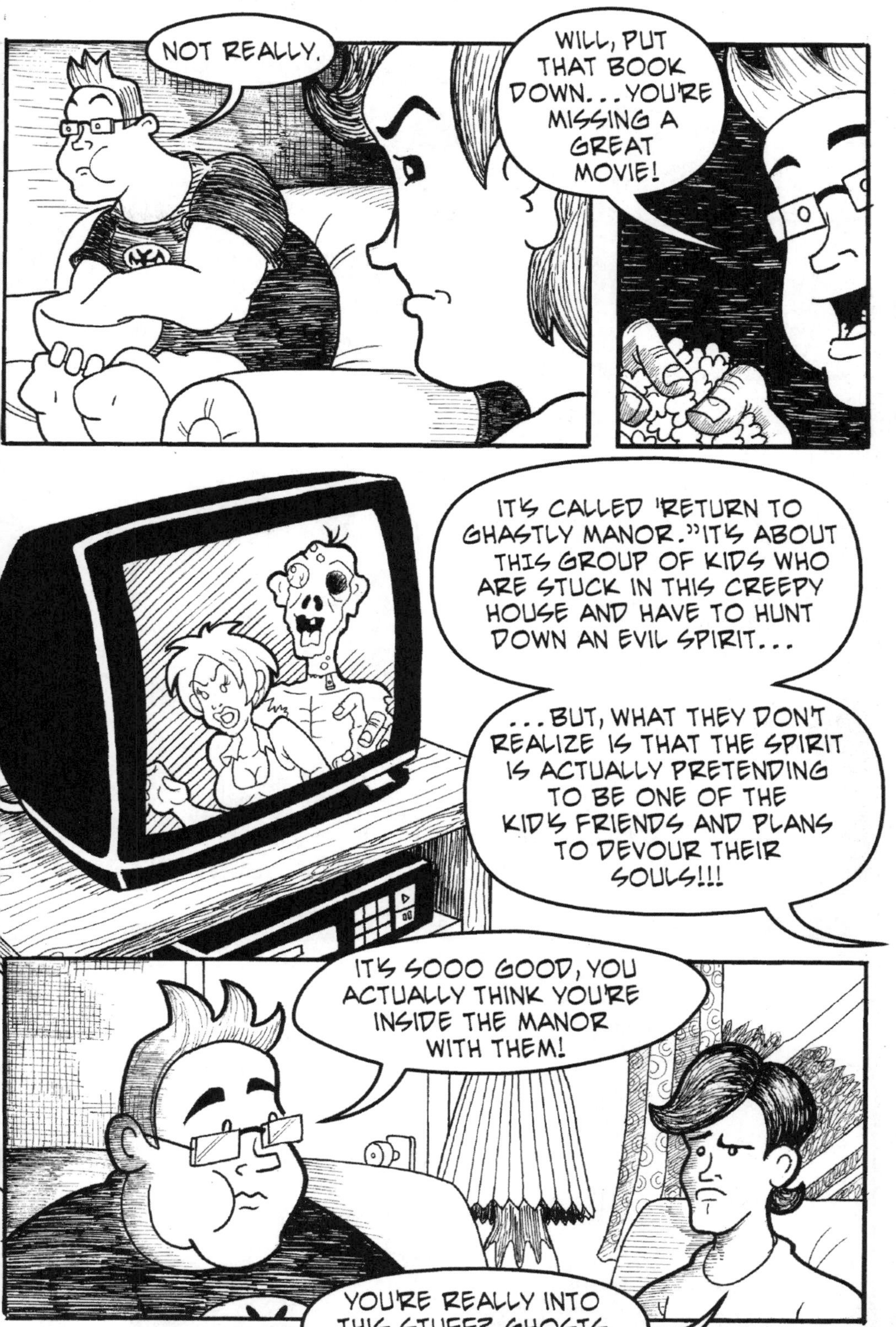
NOT REALLY.
WILL, PUT THAT BOOK DOWN...YOU'RE MISSING A GREAT MOVIE!
IT'S CALLED "RETURN TO GHASTLY MANOR." IT'S ABOUT THIS GROUP OF KIDS WHO ARE STUCK IN THIS CREEPY HOUSE AND HAVE TO HUNT DOWN AN EVIL SPIRIT...
...BUT, WHAT THEY DON'T REALIZE IS THAT THE SPIRIT IS ACTUALLY PRETENDING TO BE ONE OF THE KID'S FRIENDS AND PLANS TO DEVOUR THEIR SOULS!!!
IT'S SOOO GOOD, YOU ACTUALLY THINK YOU'RE INSIDE THE MANOR WITH THEM!
YOU'RE REALLY INTO THIS STUFF? GHOSTS AND GOBLINS?

[redacted]

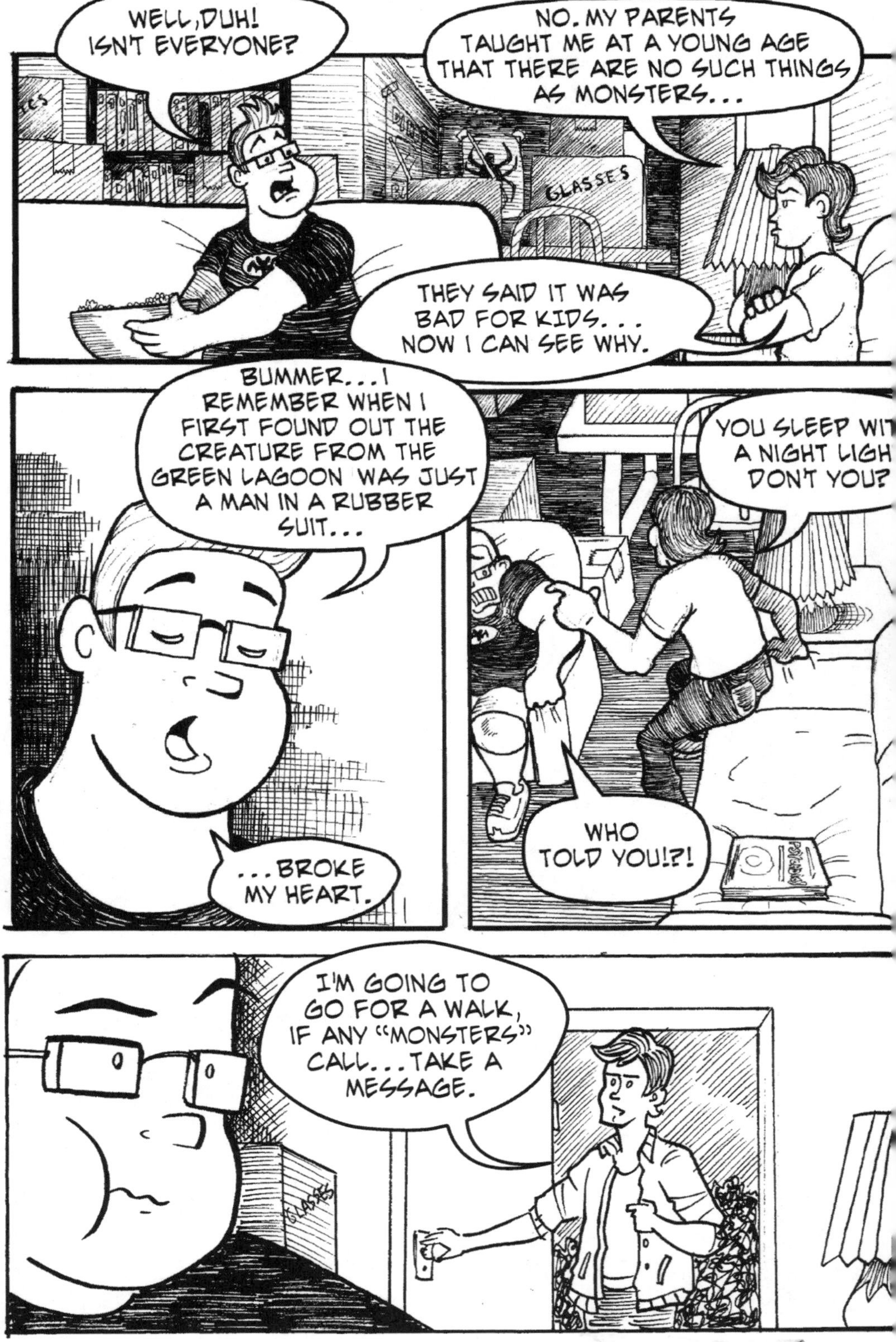
WELL, DUH! ISN'T EVERYONE?
NO. MY PARENTS TAUGHT ME AT A YOUNG AGE THAT THERE ARE NO SUCH THINGS AS MONSTERS...
GLASSES
THEY SAID IT WAS BAD FOR KIDS... NOW I CAN SEE WHY.
BUMMER... I REMEMBER WHEN I FIRST FOUND OUT THE CREATURE FROM THE GREEN LAGOON WAS JUST A MAN IN A RUBBER SUIT...
...BROKE MY HEART.
YOU SLEEP WIT A NIGHT LIGH DON'T YOU?
WHO TOLD YOU!?!
I'M GOING TO GO FOR A WALK, IF ANY "MONSTERS" CALL...TAKE A MESSAGE.
GLASSES

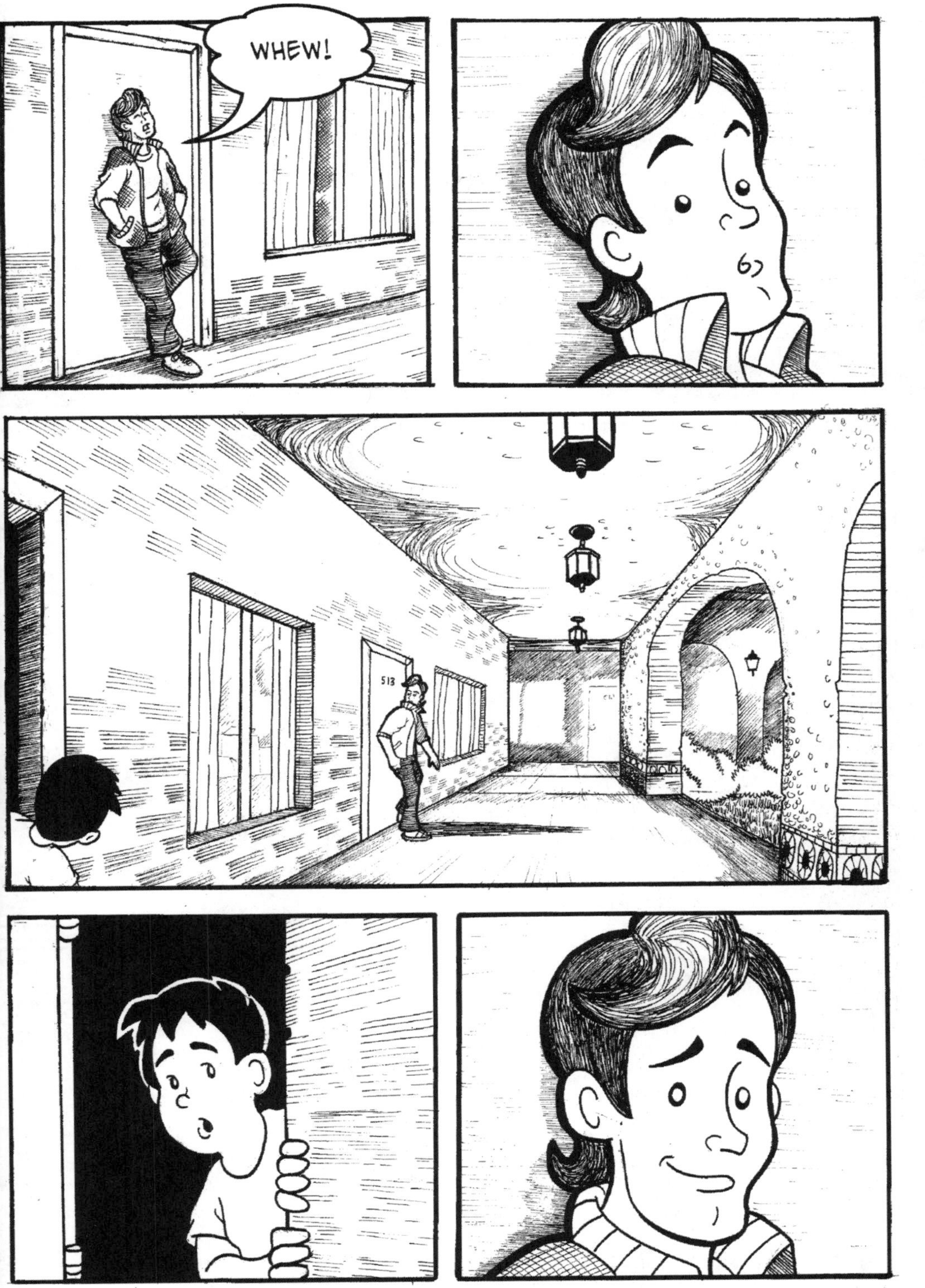
WHEW!
513

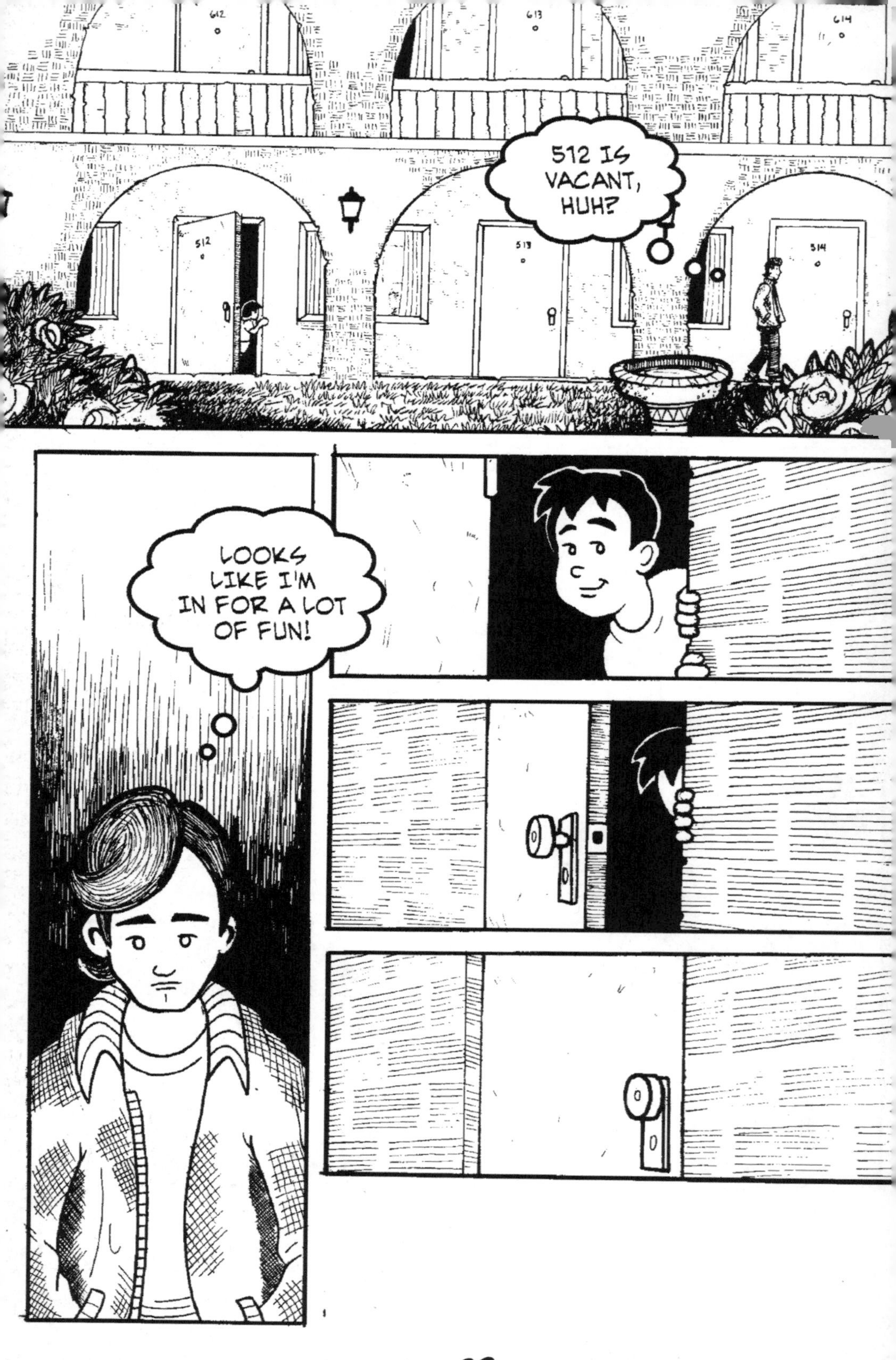
512 IS VACANT, HUH?
LOOKS LIKE I'M IN FOR A LOT OF FUN!

CHAPTER

3

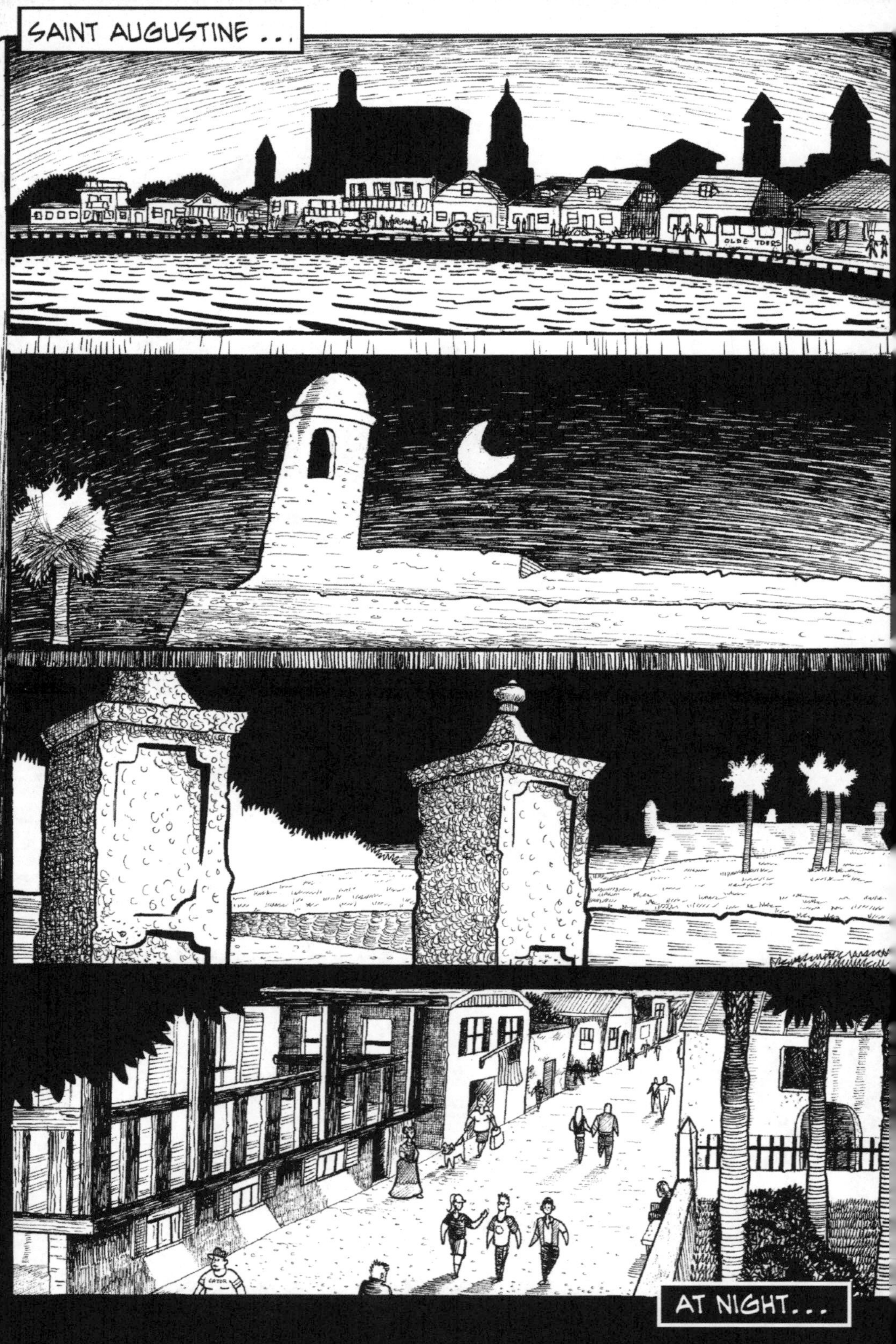
SAINT AUGUSTINE ...
AT NIGHT...

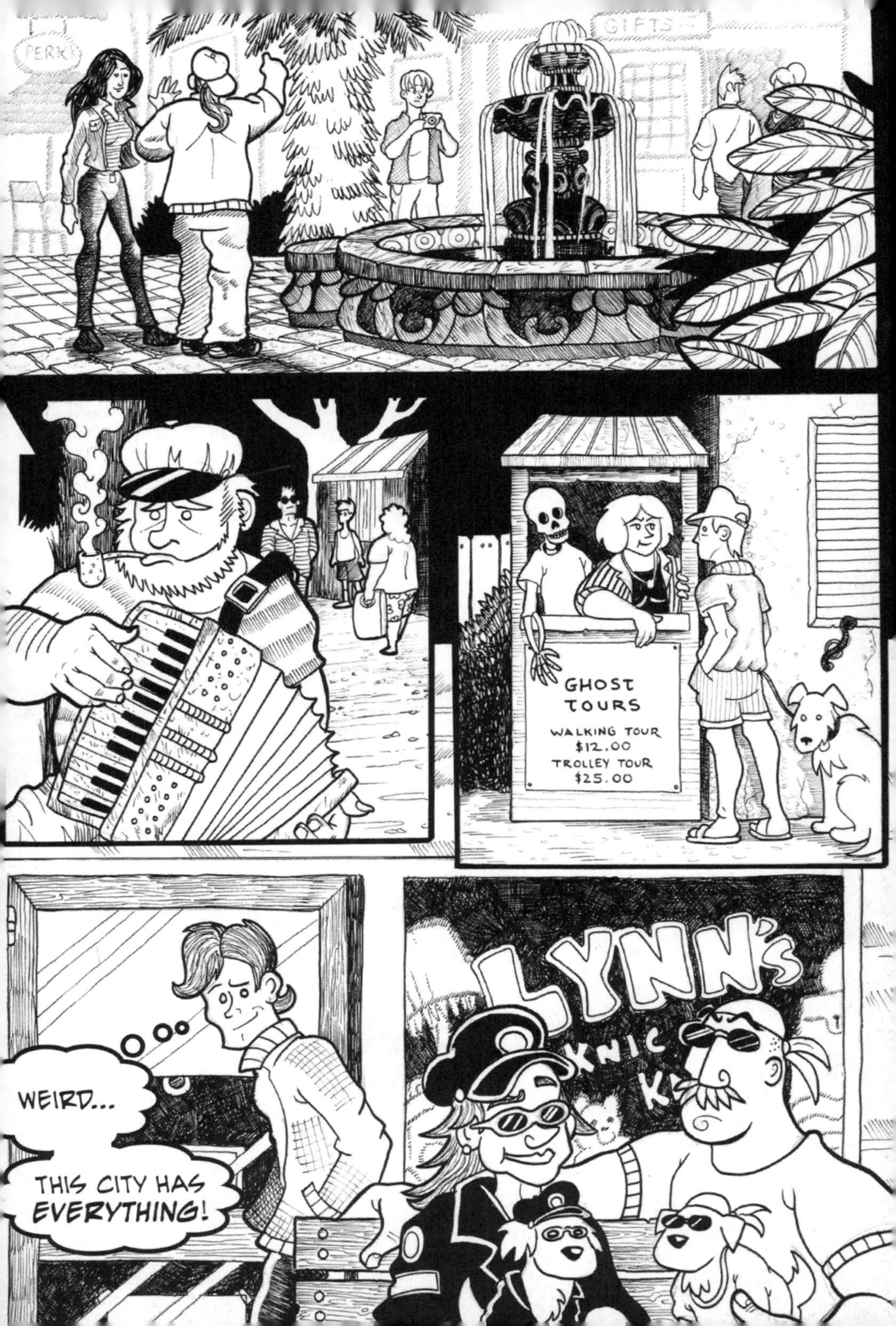
PERK'
GIFTS
GHOST TOURS
WALKING TOUR $12.00
TROLLEY TOUR $25.00
LYNN'S
WEIRD...
THIS CITY HAS EVERYTHING!

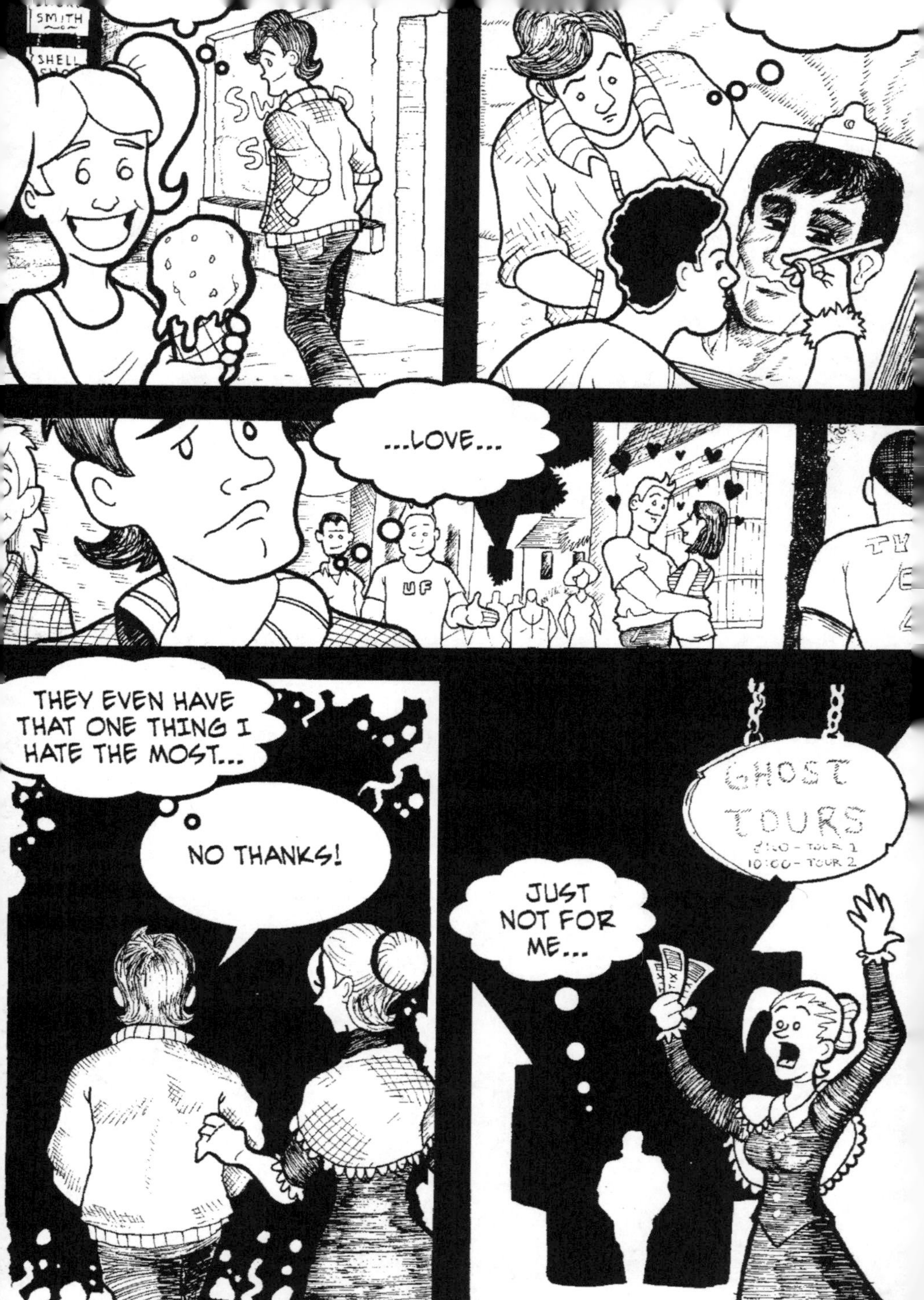
SMITH
SHELL
...LOVE...
UF
THEY EVEN HAVE THAT ONE THING I HATE THE MOST...
NO THANKS!
GHOST TOURS
10:00 - TOUR 2
JUST NOT FOR ME...

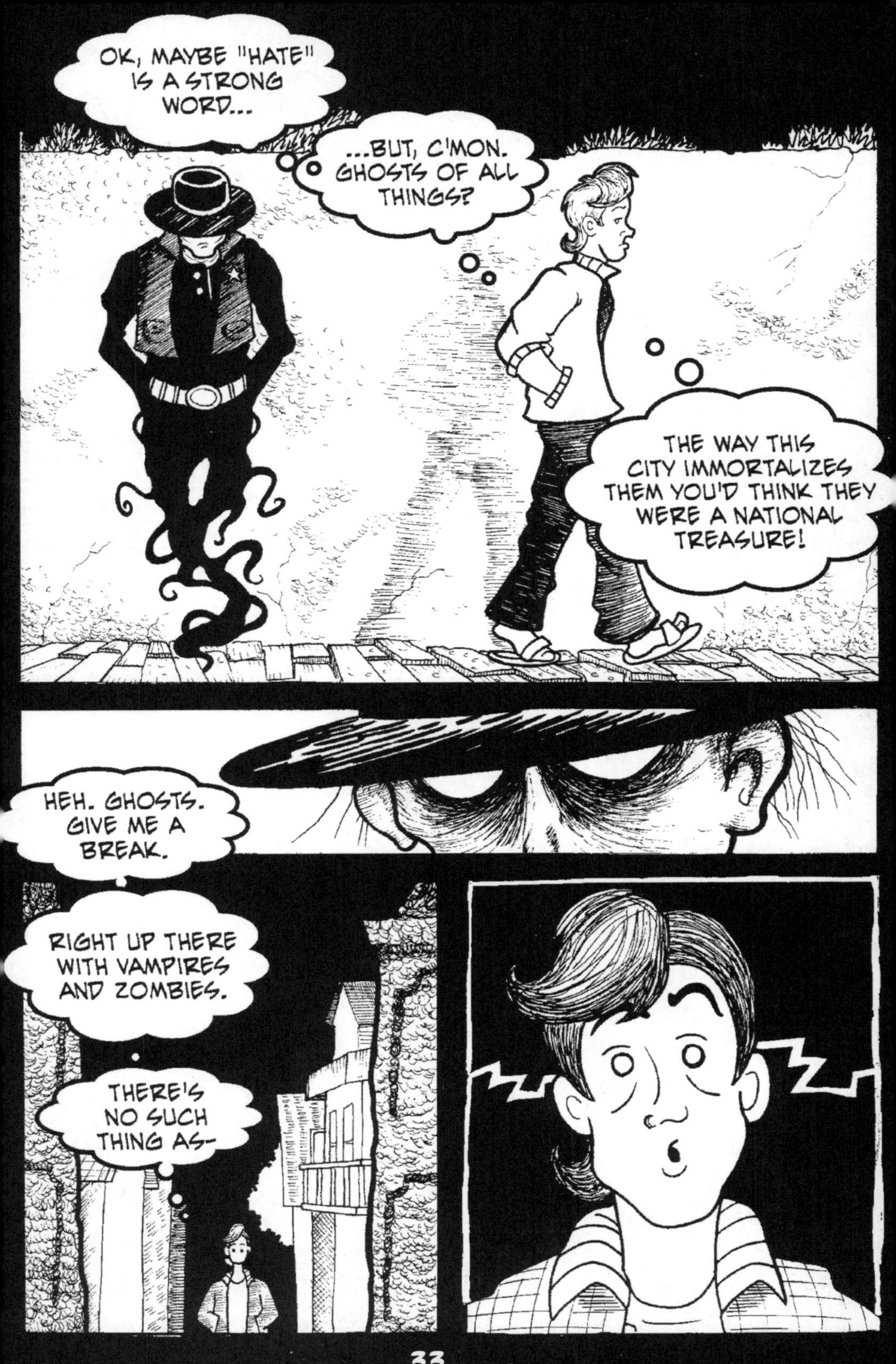
OK, MAYBE "HATE" IS A STRONG WORD...
...BUT, C'MON. GHOSTS OF ALL THINGS?
THE WAY THIS CITY IMMORTALIZES THEM YOU'D THINK THEY WERE A NATIONAL TREASURE!
HEH. GHOSTS. GIVE ME A BREAK.
RIGHT UP THERE WITH VAMPIRES AND ZOMBIES.
THERE'S NO SUCH THING AS-

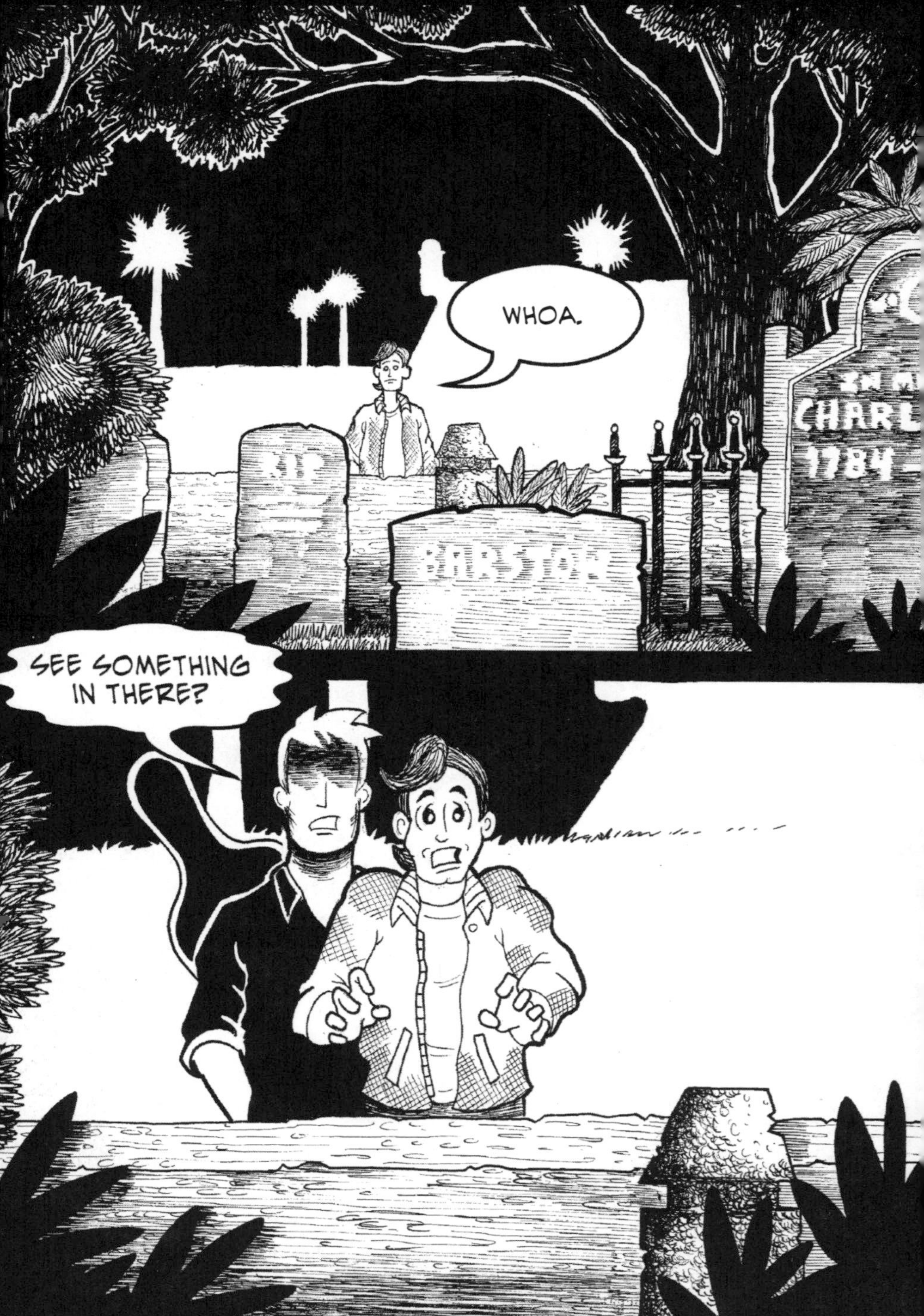
WHOA.
BARSTOW
SEE SOMETHING IN THERE?

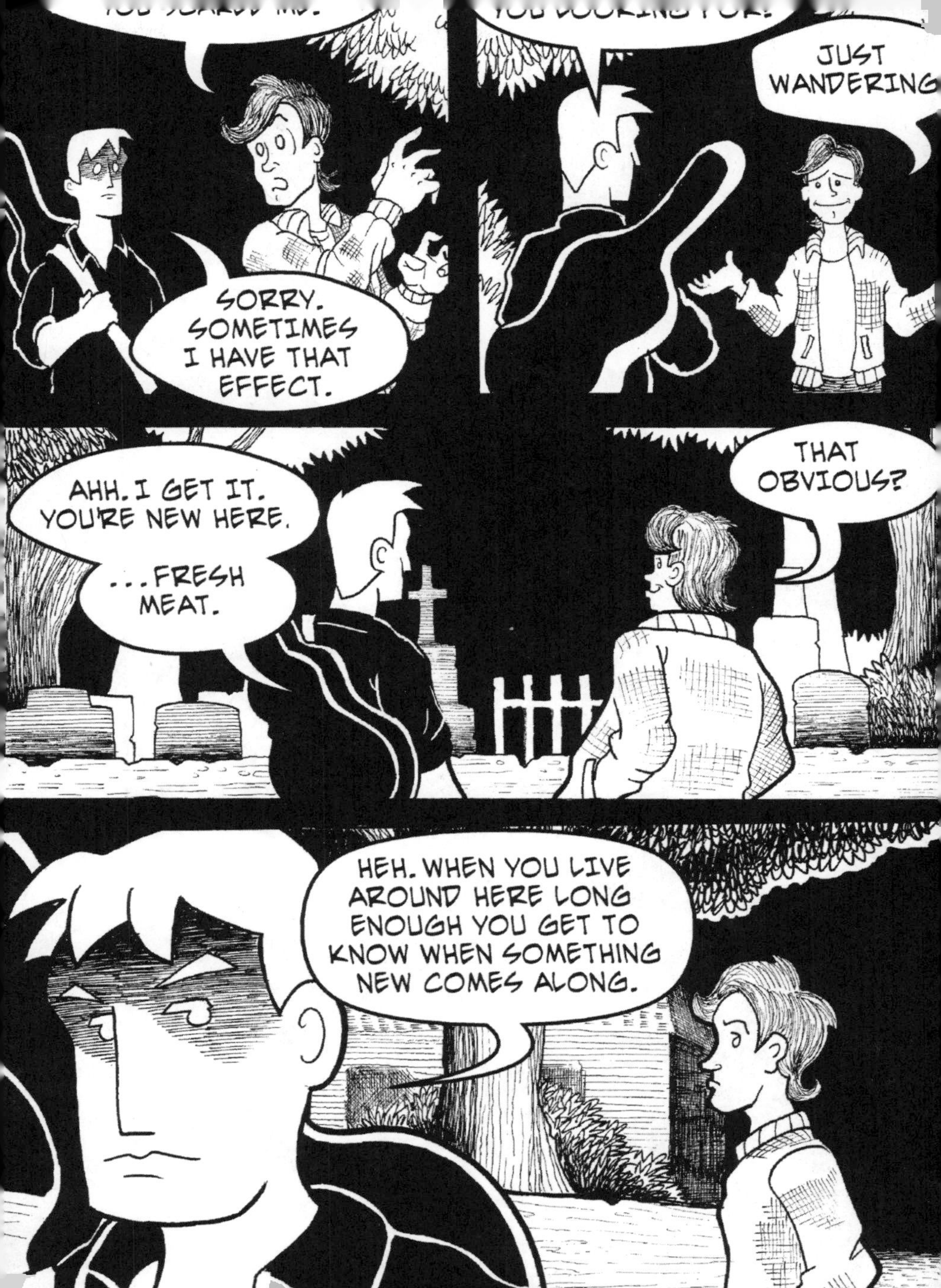
SORRY. SOMETIMES I HAVE THAT EFFECT.
JUST WANDERING
AHH. I GET IT. YOU'RE NEW HERE.
...FRESH MEAT.
THAT OBVIOUS?
HEH. WHEN YOU LIVE AROUND HERE LONG ENOUGH YOU GET TO KNOW WHEN SOMETHING NEW COMES ALONG.

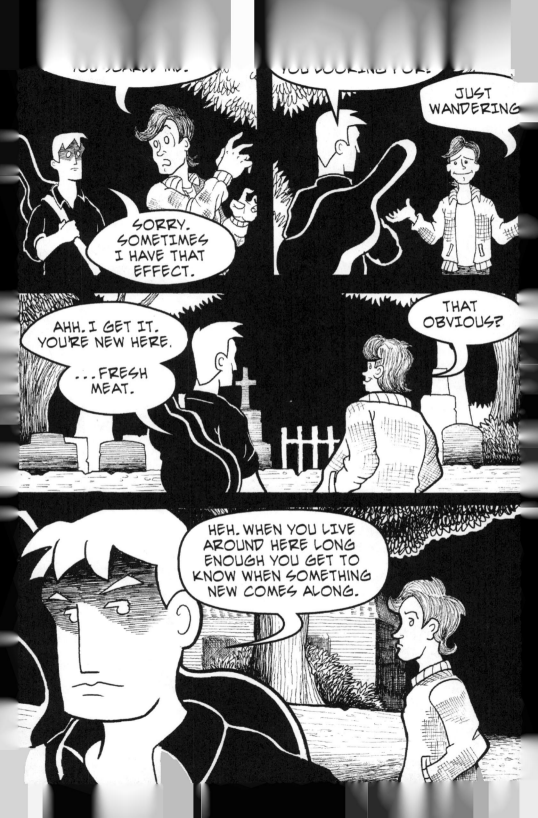

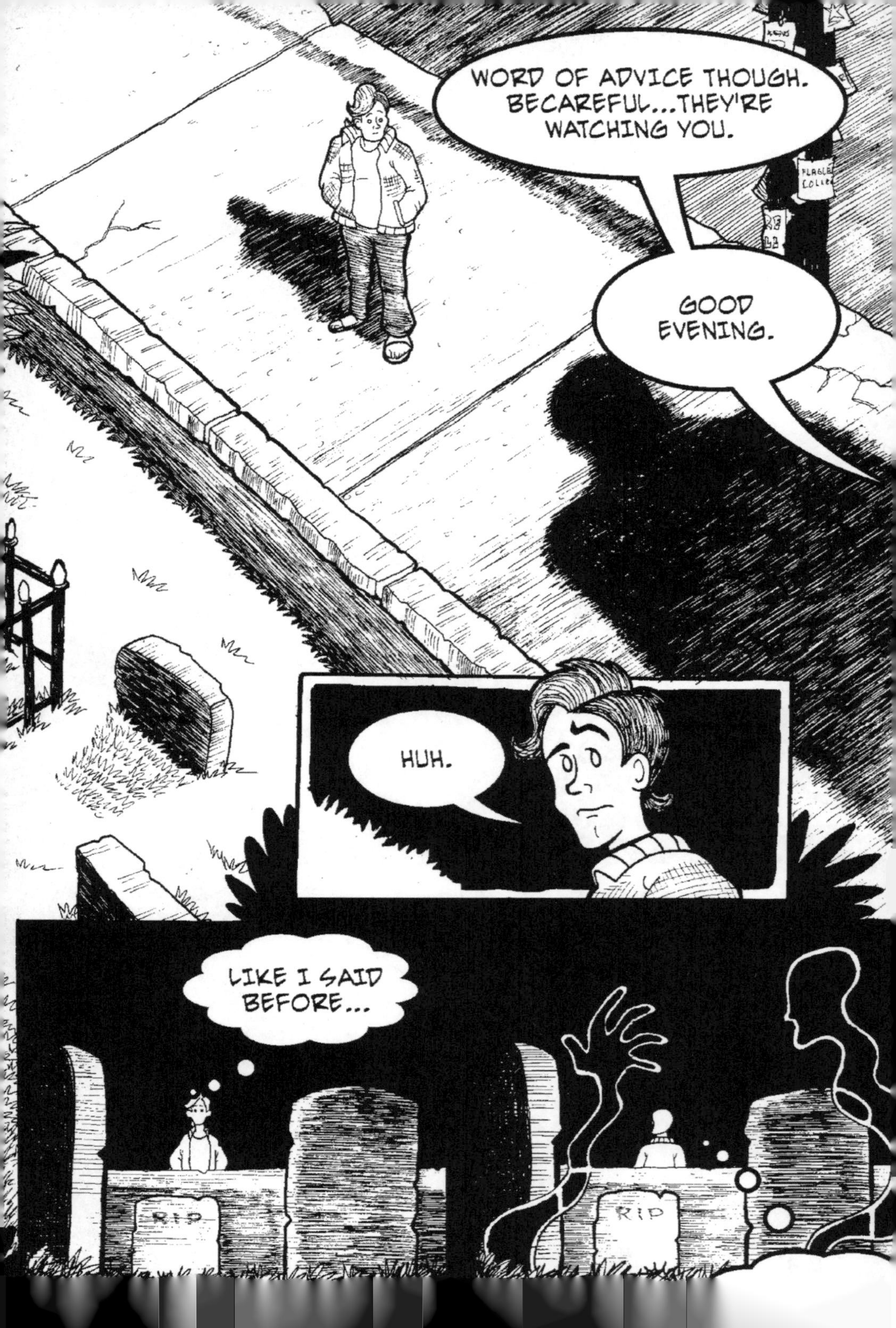
WORD OF ADVICE THOUGH. BECAREFUL...THEY'RE WATCHING YOU.
GOOD EVENING.
HUH.
LIKE I SAID BEFORE...

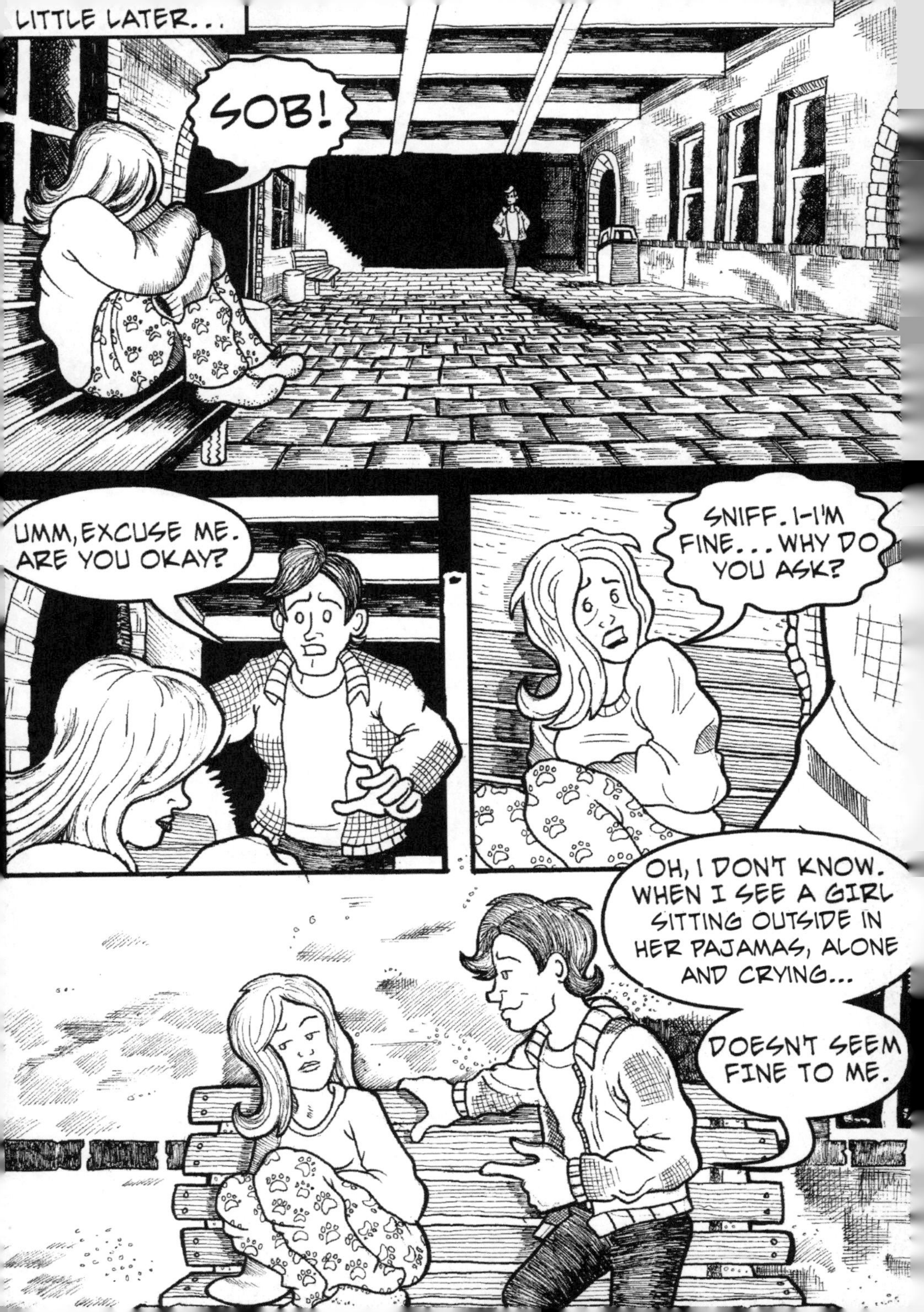
LITTLE LATER...
SOB!
UMM, EXCUSE ME. ARE YOU OKAY?
SNIFF. I-I'M FINE... WHY DO YOU ASK?
OH, I DON'T KNOW. WHEN I SEE A GIRL SITTING OUTSIDE IN HER PAJAMAS, ALONE AND CRYING...
DOESN'T SEEM FINE TO ME.

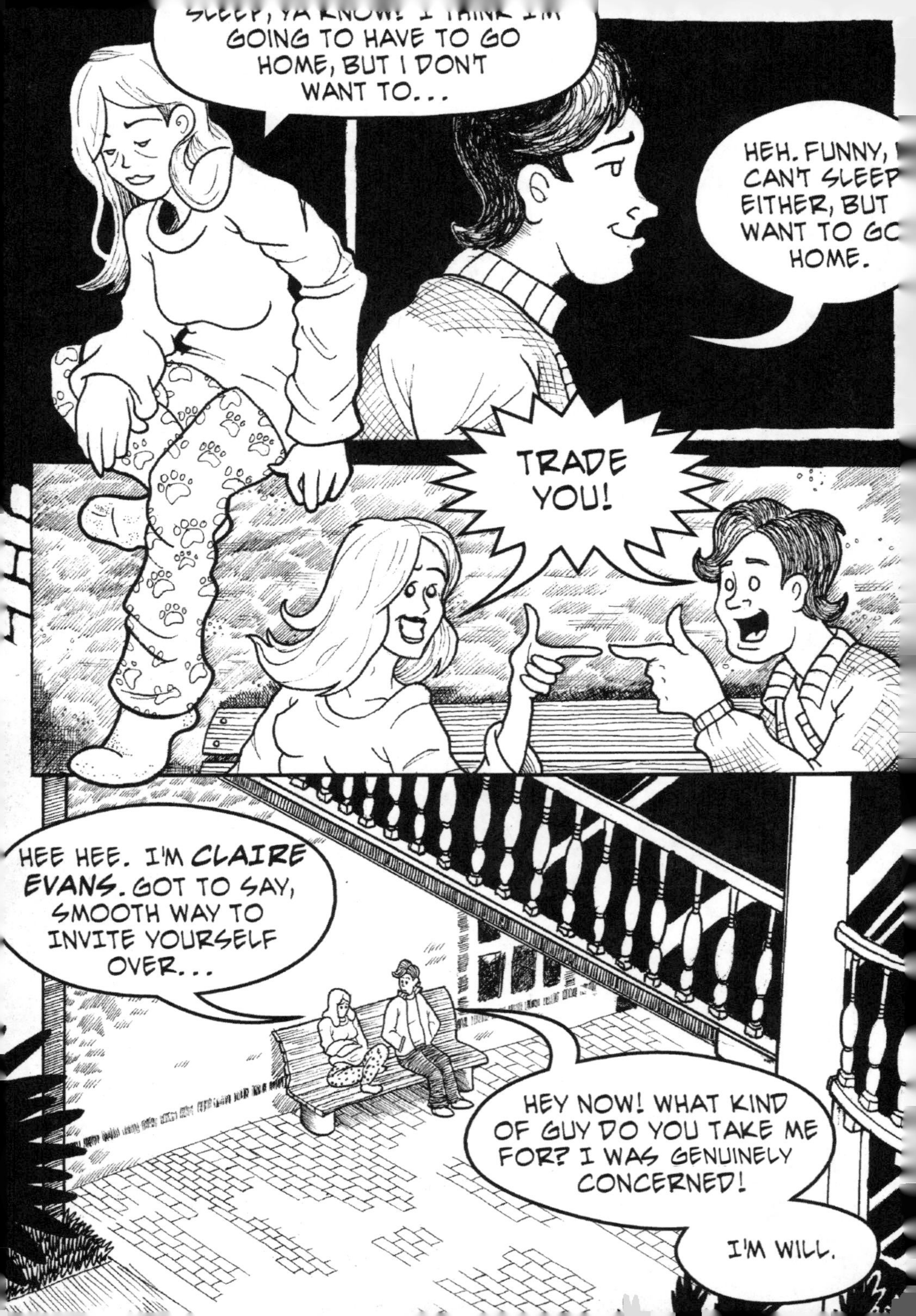
GOING TO HAVE TO GO HOME, BUT I DON'T WANT TO...
HEH. FUNNY, CAN'T SLEEP EITHER, BUT WANT TO GO HOME.
TRADE YOU!
HEE HEE. I'M CLAIRE EVANS. GOT TO SAY, SMOOTH WAY TO INVITE YOURSELF OVER...
HEY NOW! WHAT KIND OF GUY DO YOU TAKE ME FOR? I WAS GENUINELY CONCERNED!
I'M WILL.

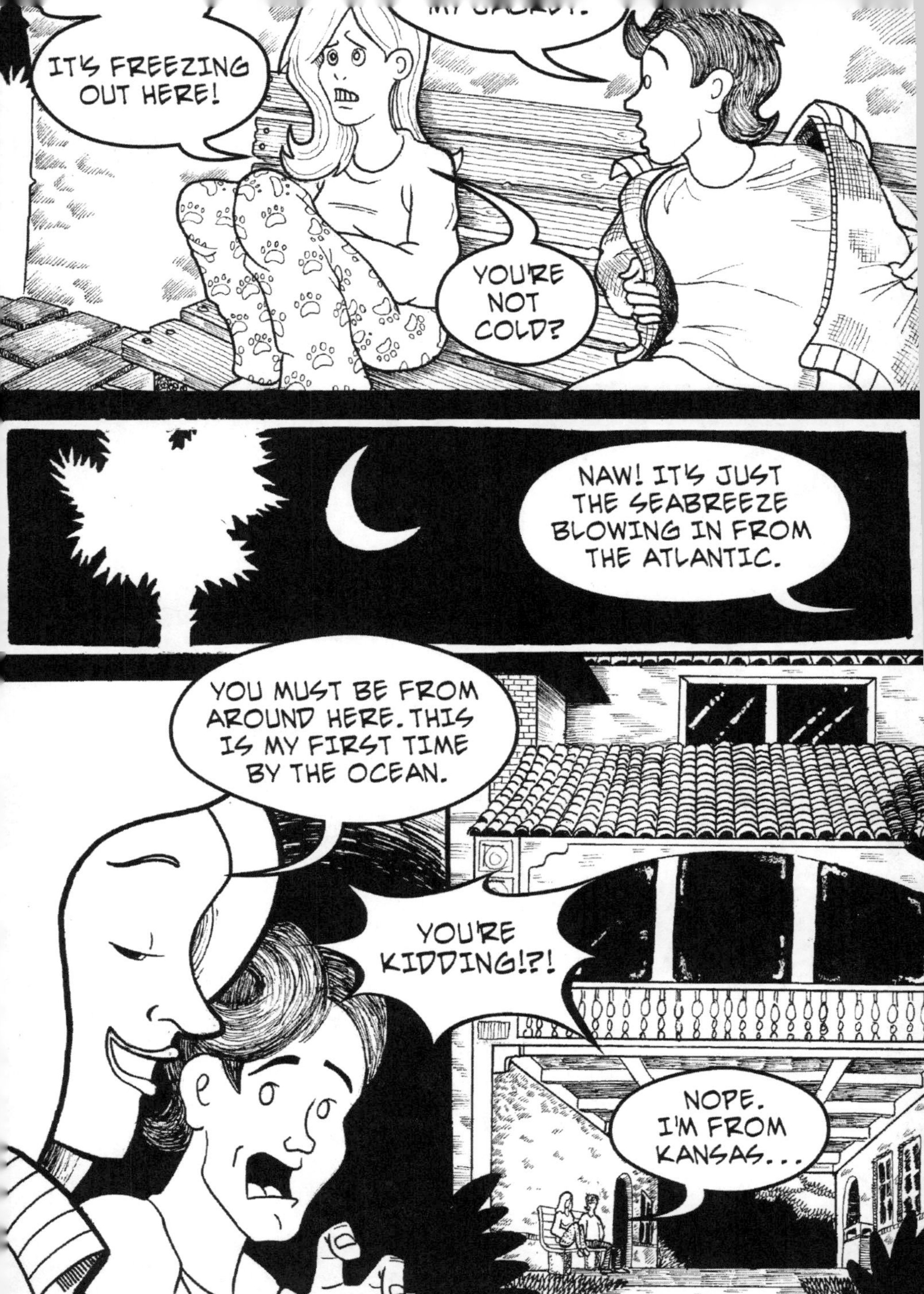
IT'S FREEZING OUT HERE!
YOU'RE NOT COLD?
NAW! IT'S JUST THE SEABREEZE BLOWING IN FROM THE ATLANTIC.
YOU MUST BE FROM AROUND HERE. THIS IS MY FIRST TIME BY THE OCEAN.
YOU'RE KIDDING!?!
NOPE. I'M FROM KANSAS...

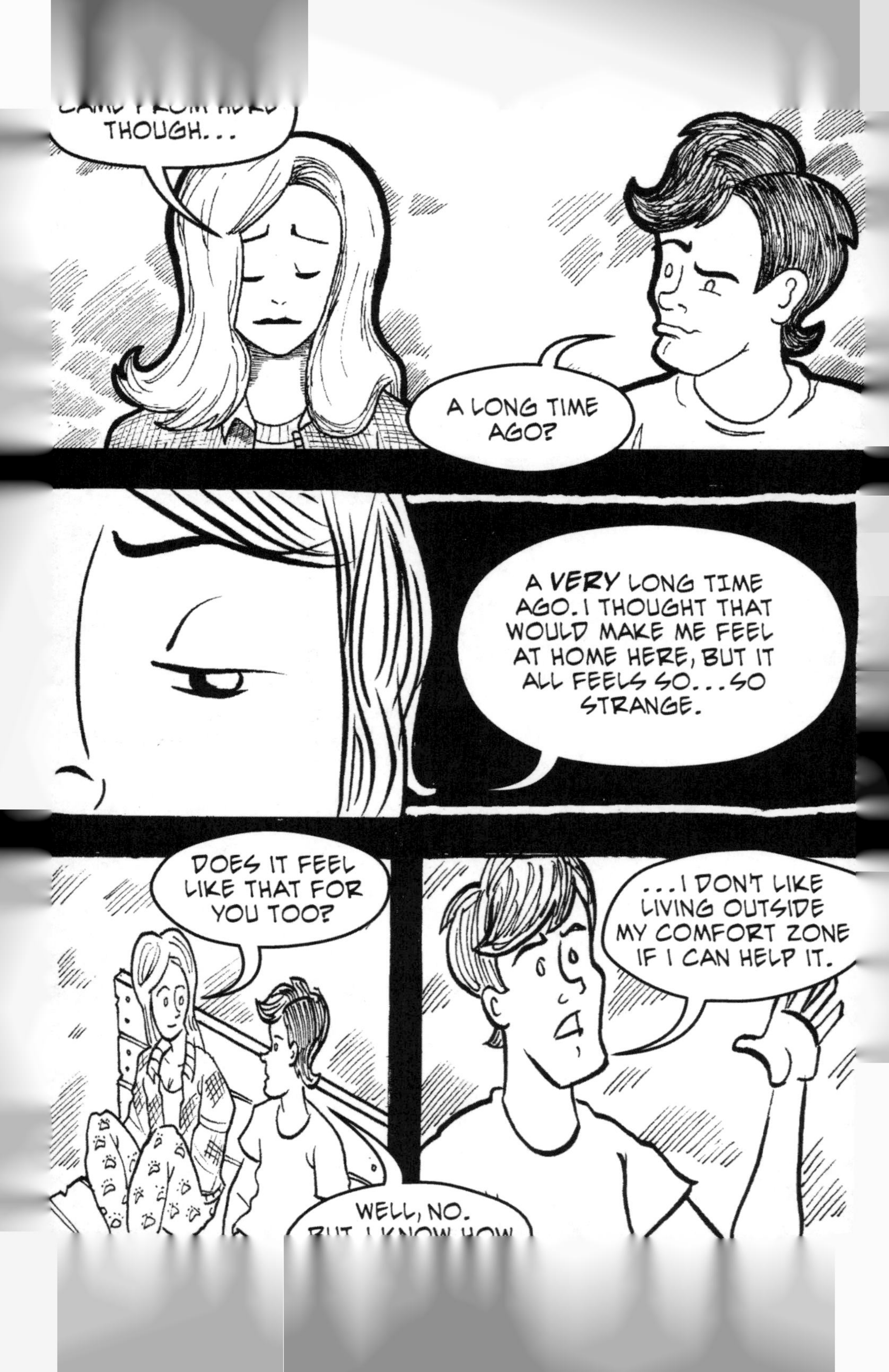
THOUGH...
A LONG TIME AGO?
A **VERY** LONG TIME AGO. I THOUGHT THAT WOULD MAKE ME FEEL AT HOME HERE, BUT IT ALL FEELS SO... SO STRANGE.
DOES IT FEEL LIKE THAT FOR YOU TOO?
WELL, NO.
...I DON'T LIKE LIVING OUTSIDE MY COMFORT ZONE IF I CAN HELP IT.

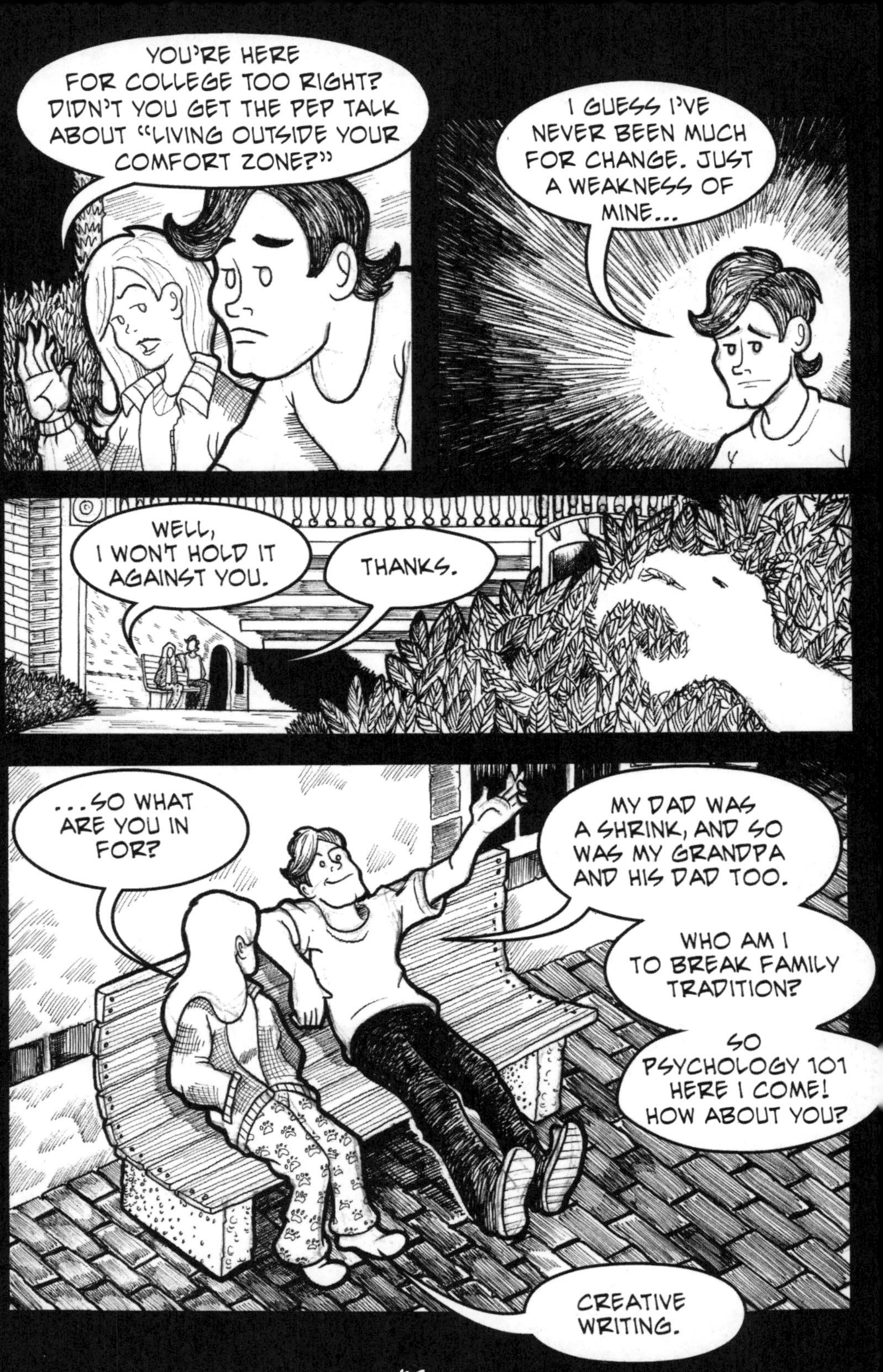
YOU'RE HERE FOR COLLEGE TOO RIGHT? DIDN'T YOU GET THE PEP TALK ABOUT "LIVING OUTSIDE YOUR COMFORT ZONE?"
I GUESS I'VE NEVER BEEN MUCH FOR CHANGE. JUST A WEAKNESS OF MINE...
WELL, I WON'T HOLD IT AGAINST YOU.
THANKS.
...SO WHAT ARE YOU IN FOR?
MY DAD WAS A SHRINK, AND SO WAS MY GRANDPA AND HIS DAD TOO.
WHO AM I TO BREAK FAMILY TRADITION?
SO PSYCHOLOGY 101 HERE I COME! HOW ABOUT YOU?
CREATIVE WRITING.

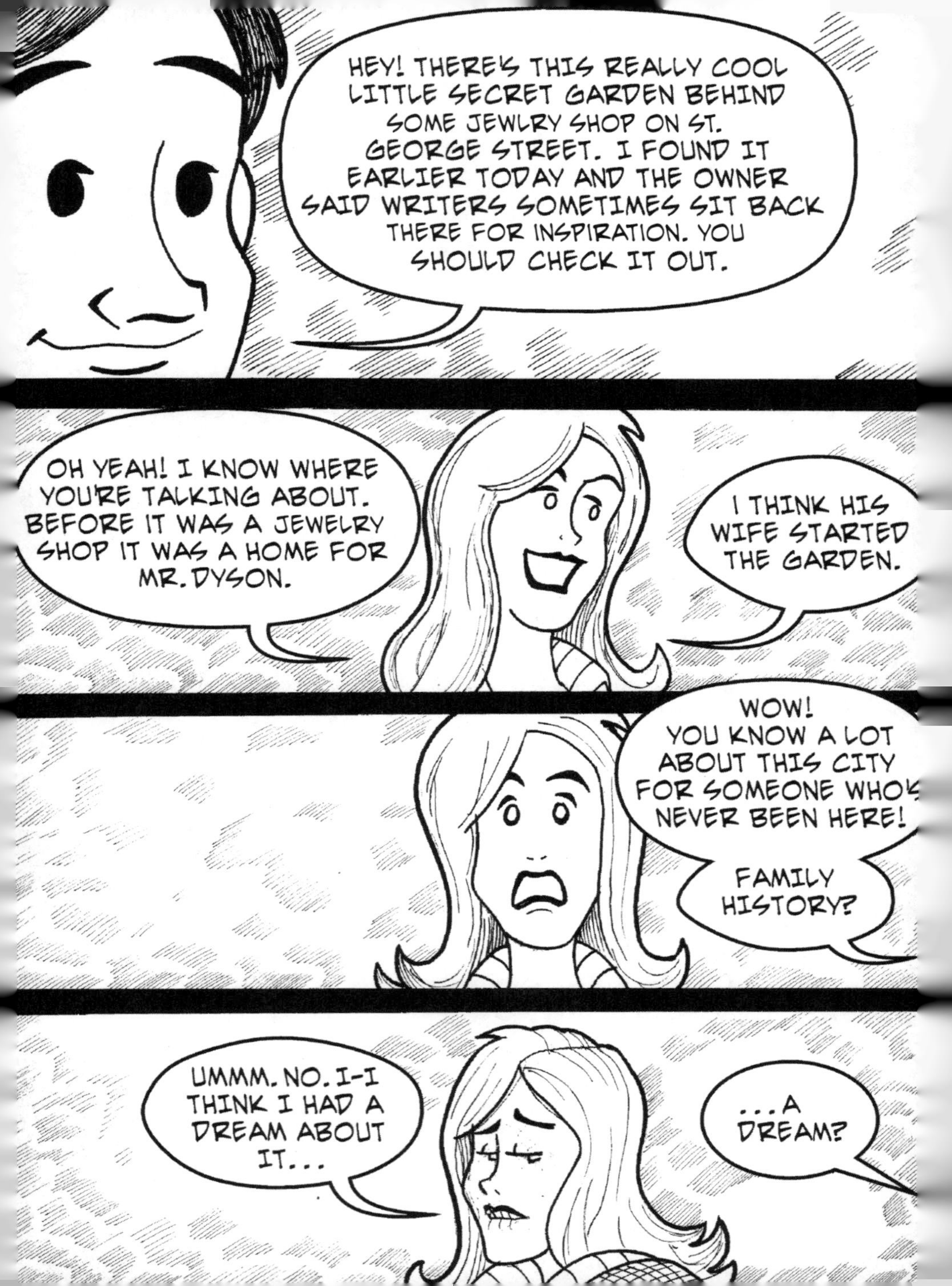
HEY! THERE'S THIS REALLY COOL LITTLE SECRET GARDEN BEHIND SOME JEWLRY SHOP ON ST. GEORGE STREET. I FOUND IT EARLIER TODAY AND THE OWNER SAID WRITERS SOMETIMES SIT BACK THERE FOR INSPIRATION. YOU SHOULD CHECK IT OUT.
OH YEAH! I KNOW WHERE YOU'RE TALKING ABOUT. BEFORE IT WAS A JEWELRY SHOP IT WAS A HOME FOR MR. DYSON.
I THINK HIS WIFE STARTED THE GARDEN.
WOW! YOU KNOW A LOT ABOUT THIS CITY FOR SOMEONE WHO'S NEVER BEEN HERE!
FAMILY HISTORY?
UMMM. NO. I-I THINK I HAD A DREAM ABOUT IT...
...A DREAM?

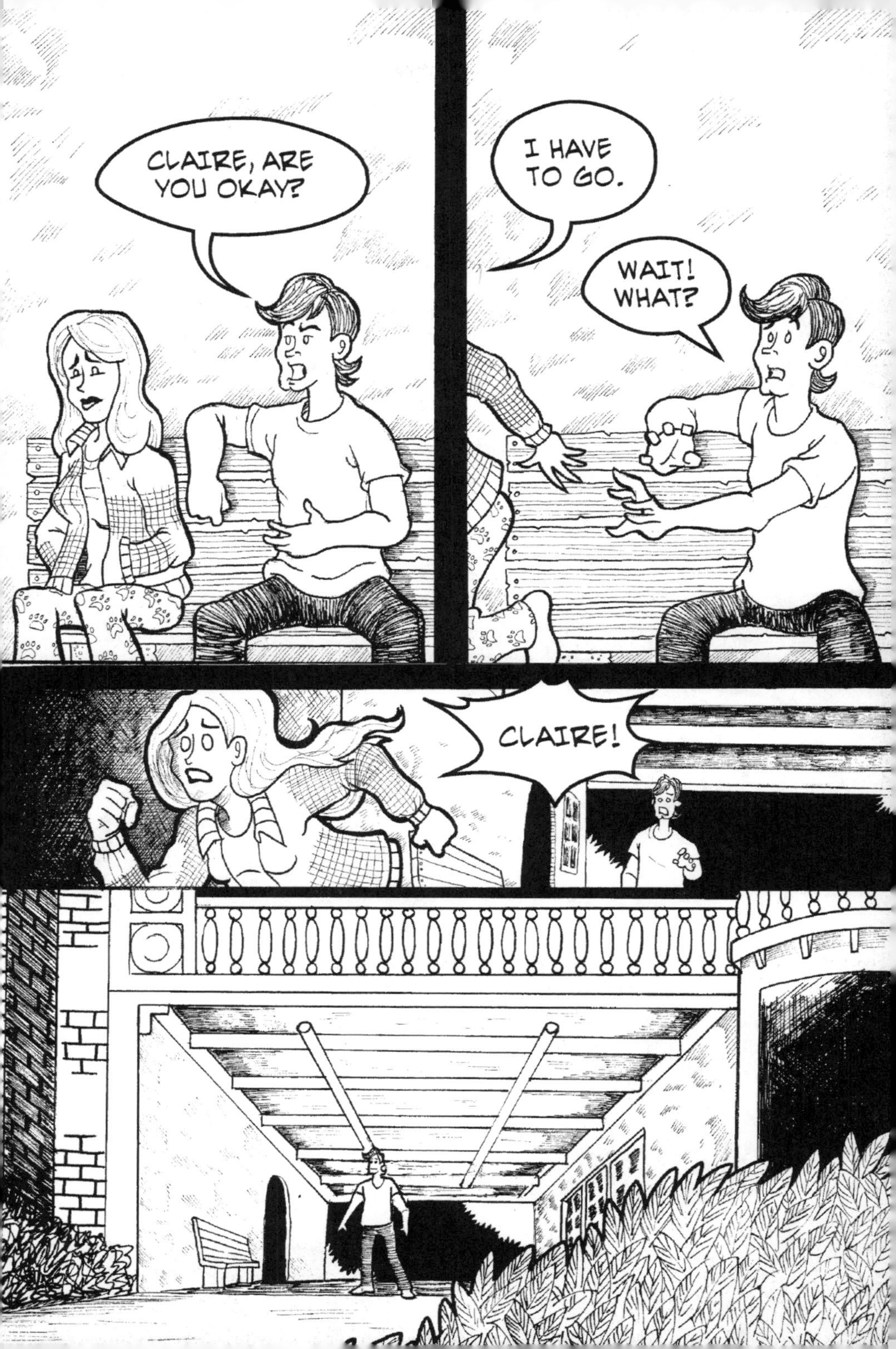
CLAIRE, ARE YOU OKAY?
I HAVE TO GO.
WAIT! WHAT?
CLAIRE!

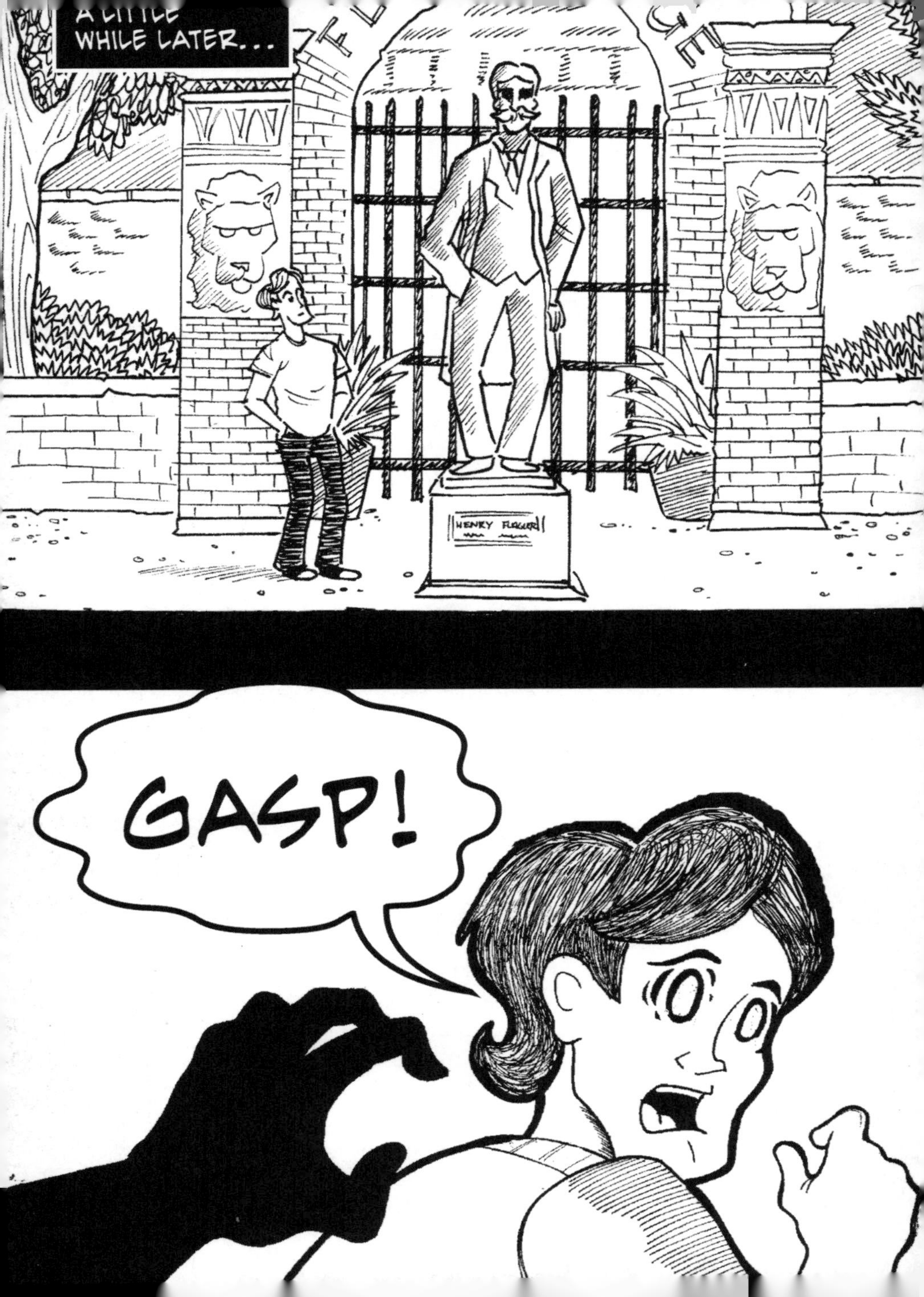
A LITTLE WHILE LATER...
HENRY FLAGLER
GASP!

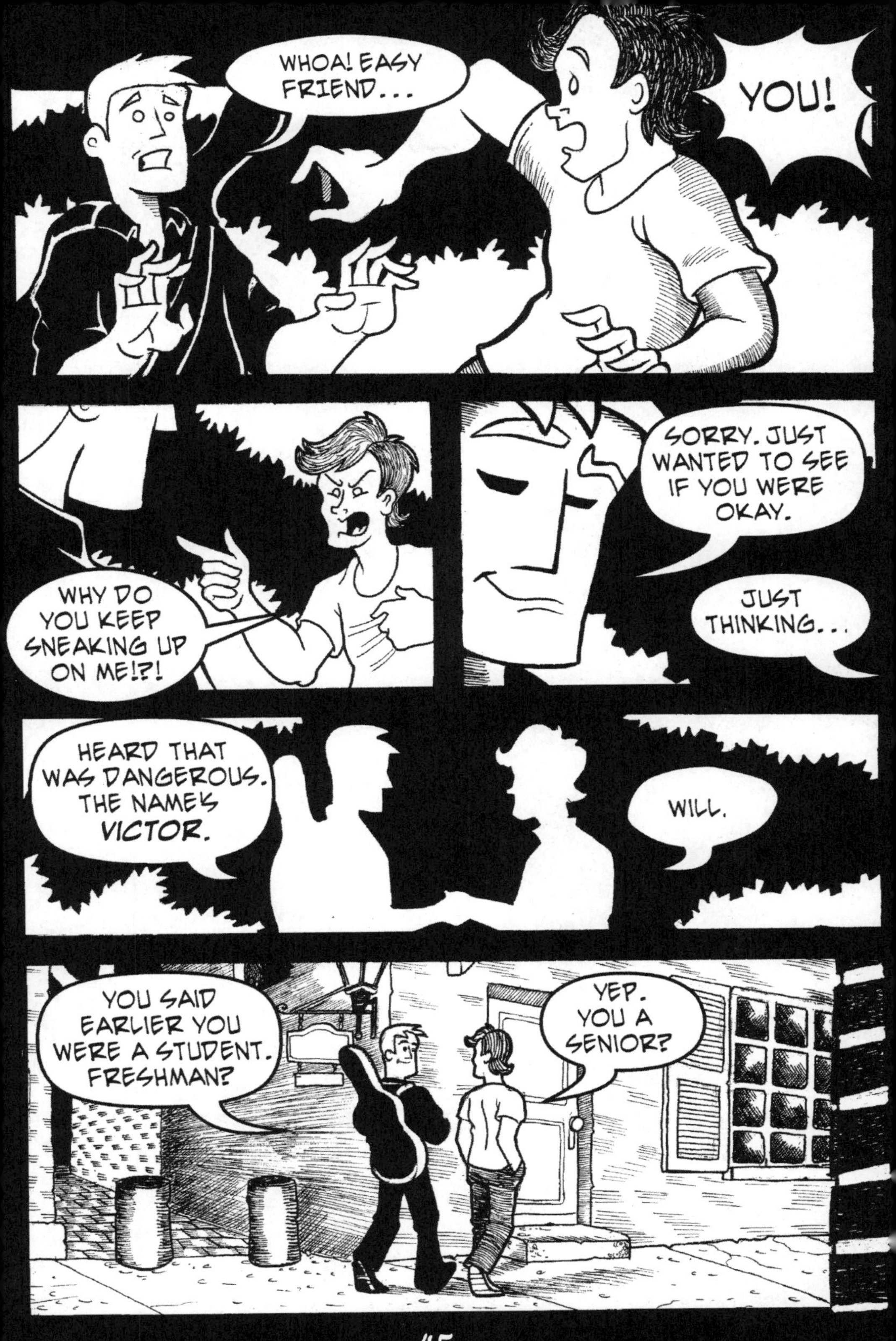
WHOA! EASY FRIEND...
YOU!
WHY DO YOU KEEP SNEAKING UP ON ME!?!
SORRY. JUST WANTED TO SEE IF YOU WERE OKAY.
JUST THINKING...
HEARD THAT WAS DANGEROUS. THE NAME'S VICTOR.
WILL.
YOU SAID EARLIER YOU WERE A STUDENT. FRESHMAN?
YEP. YOU A SENIOR?

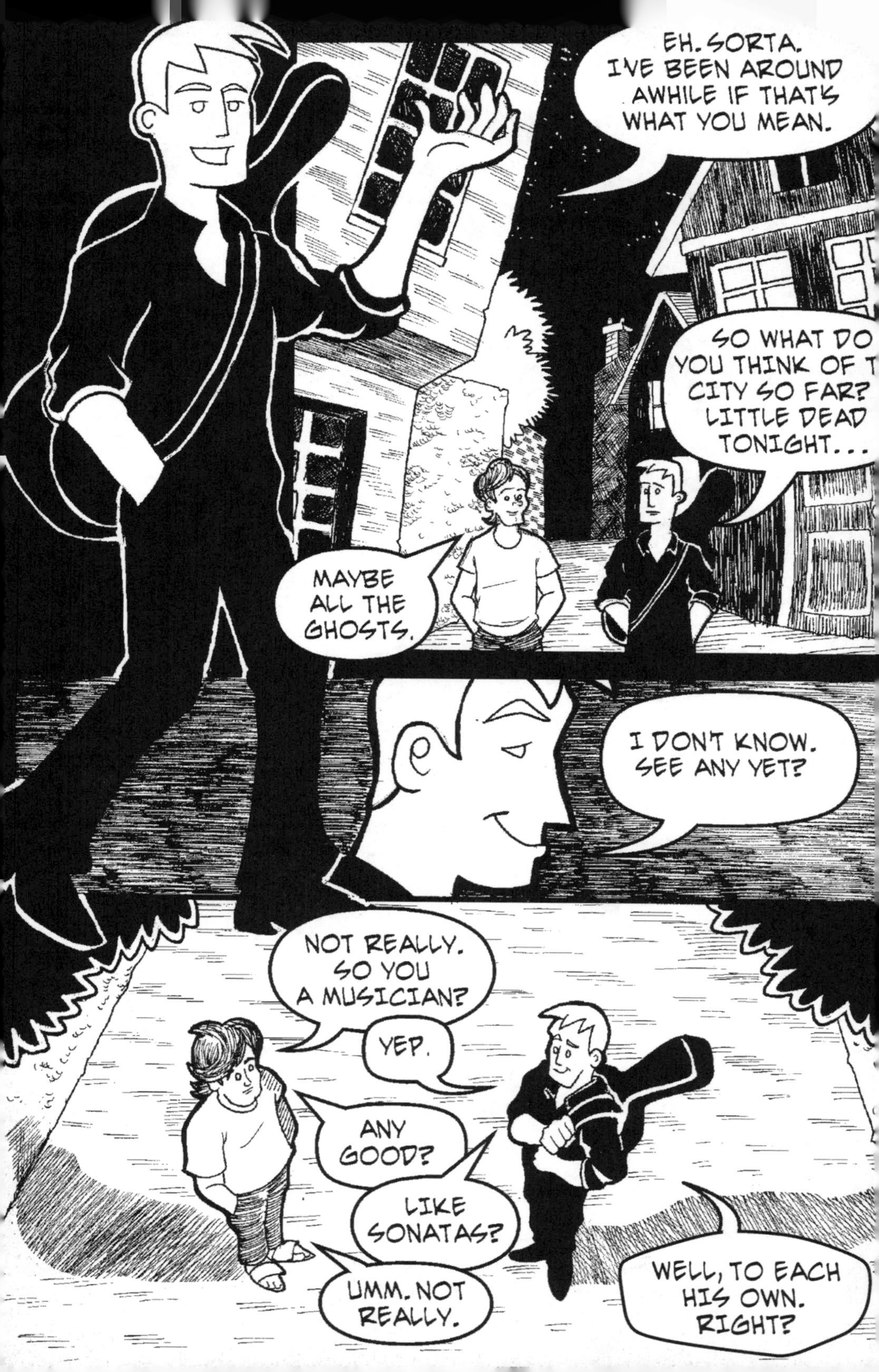

EH. SORTA. I'VE BEEN AROUND AWHILE IF THAT'S WHAT YOU MEAN.
SO WHAT DO YOU THINK OF T CITY SO FAR? LITTLE DEAD TONIGHT...
MAYBE ALL THE GHOSTS.
I DON'T KNOW. SEE ANY YET?
NOT REALLY. SO YOU A MUSICIAN?
YEP.
ANY GOOD?
LIKE SONATAS?
UMM. NOT REALLY.
WELL, TO EACH HIS OWN. RIGHT?

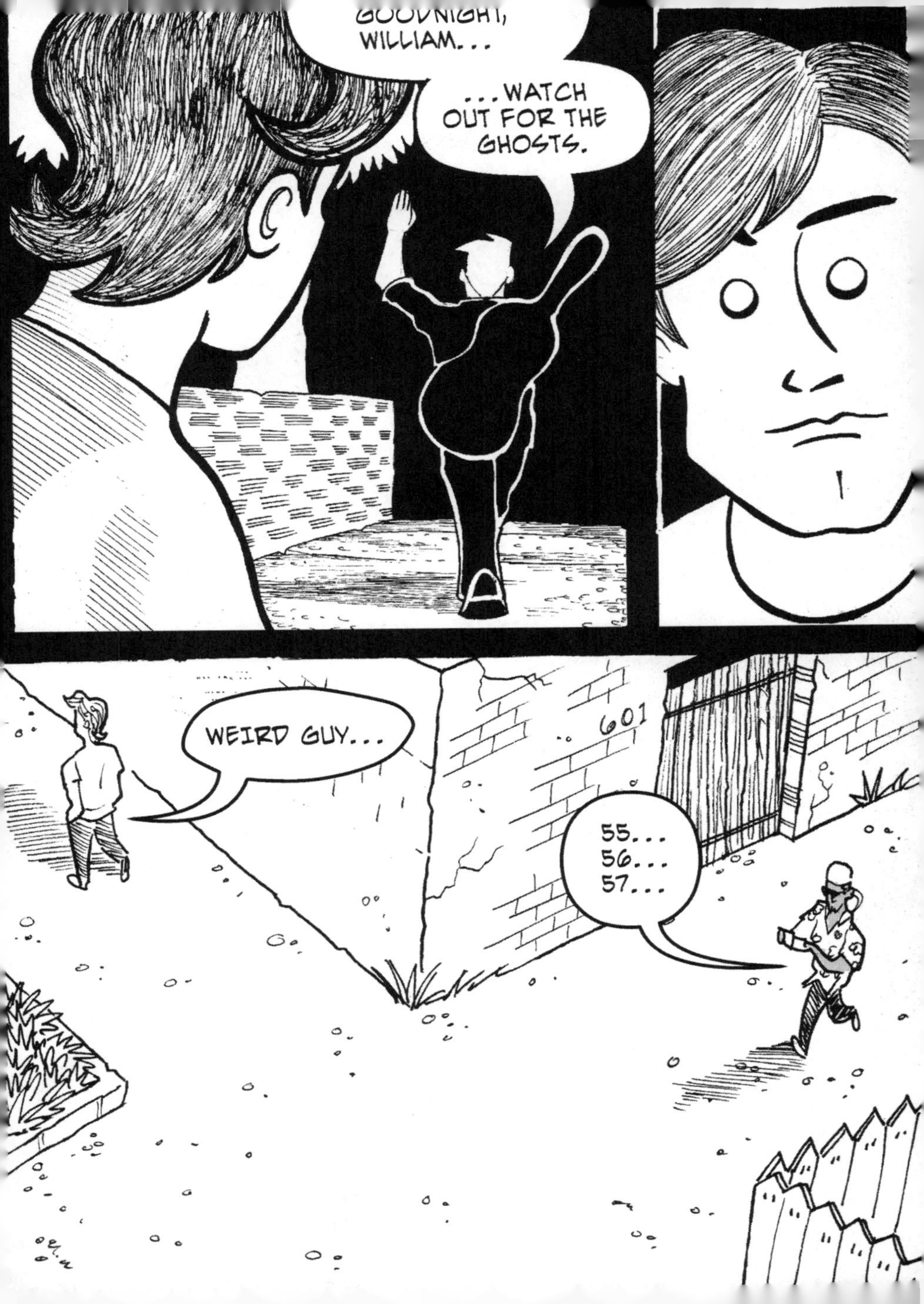
GOODNIGHT, WILLIAM...
...WATCH OUT FOR THE GHOSTS.
601
WEIRD GUY...
55...
56...
57...

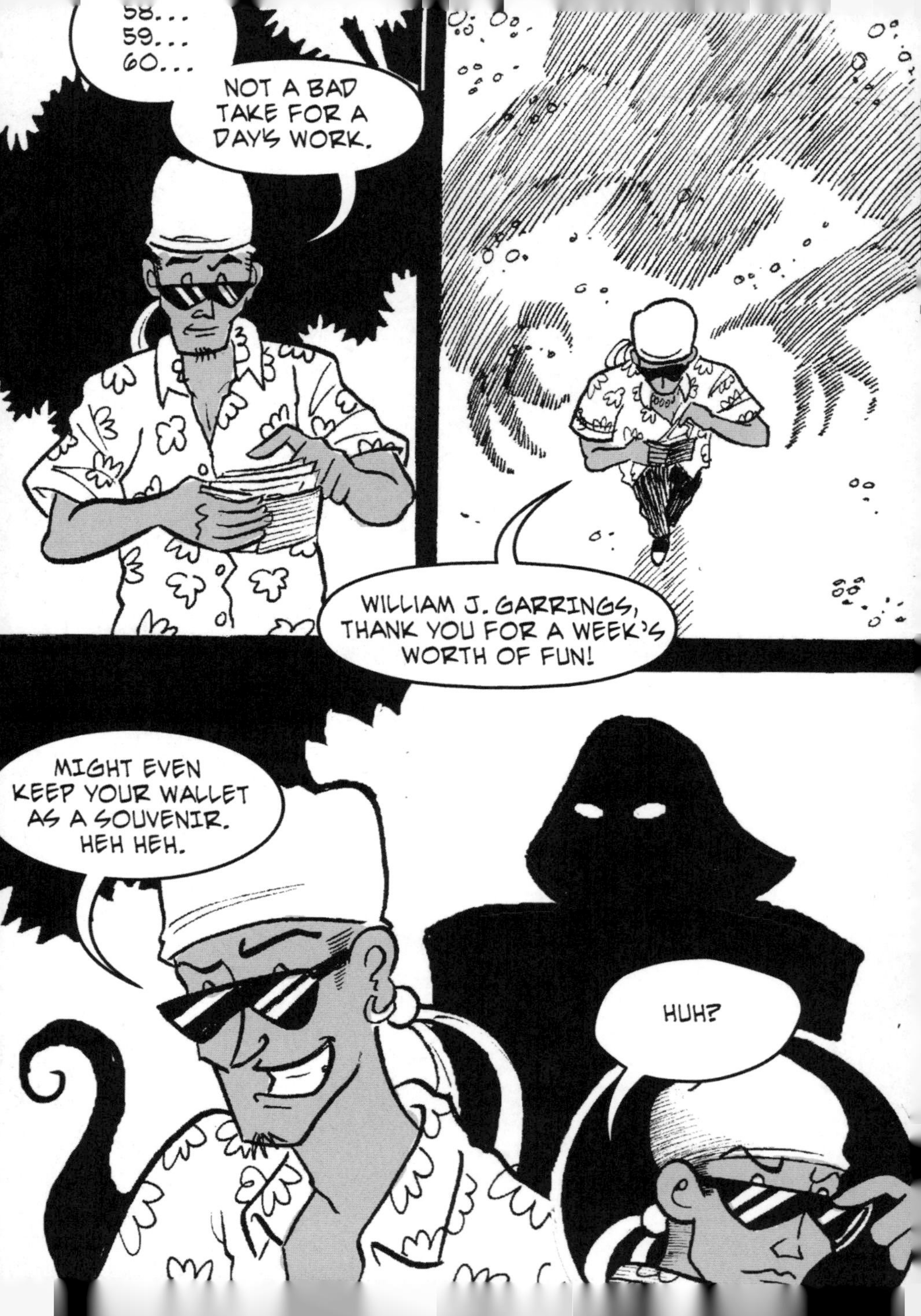
58...
59...
60...
NOT A BAD TAKE FOR A DAY'S WORK.
WILLIAM J. GARRINGS, THANK YOU FOR A WEEK'S WORTH OF FUN!
MIGHT EVEN KEEP YOUR WALLET AS A SOUVENIR. HEH HEH.
HUH?

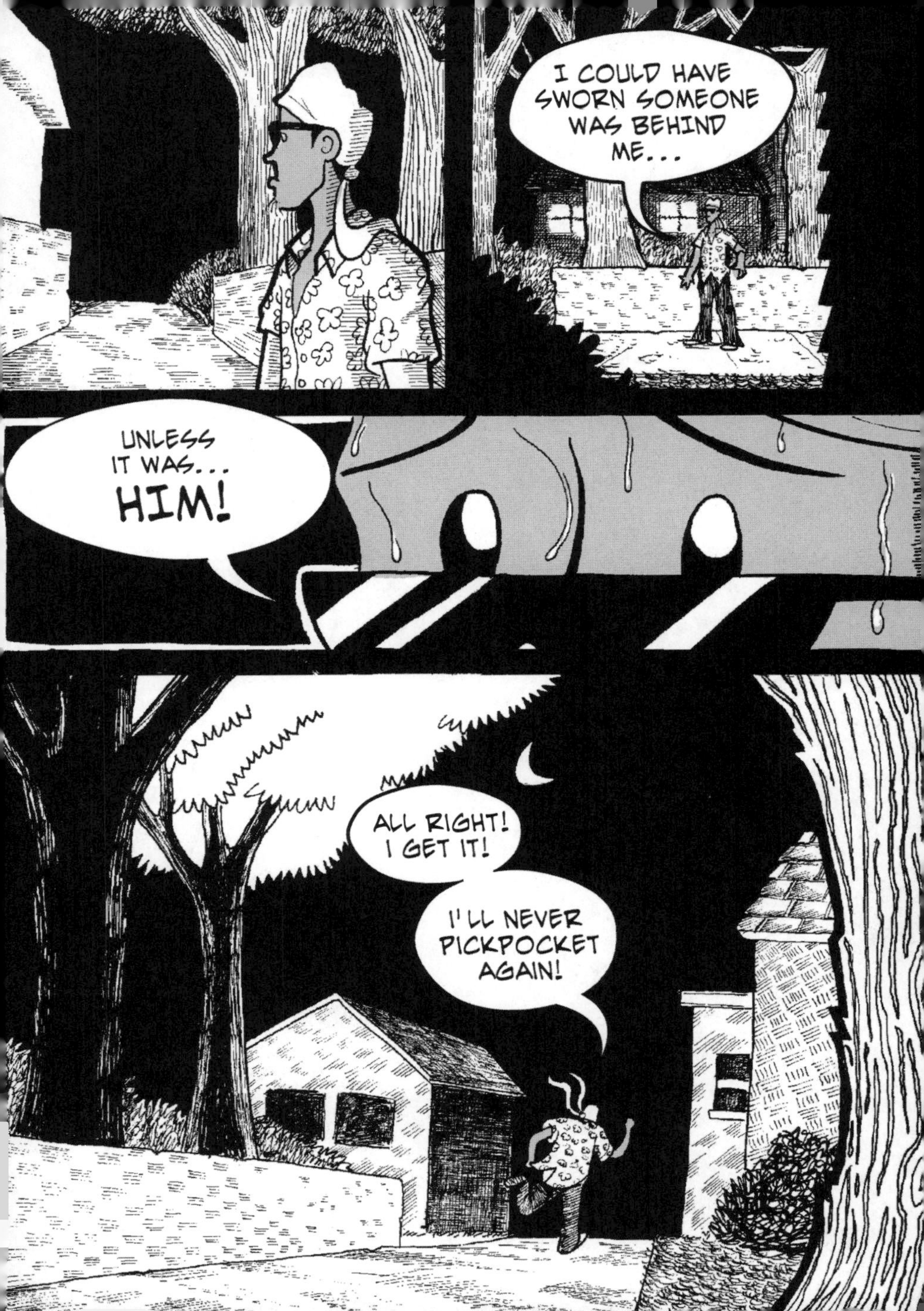
I COULD HAVE SWORN SOMEONE WAS BEHIND ME...
UNLESS IT WAS... HIM!
ALL RIGHT! I GET IT!
I'LL NEVER PICKPOCKET AGAIN!

CHAPTER
4

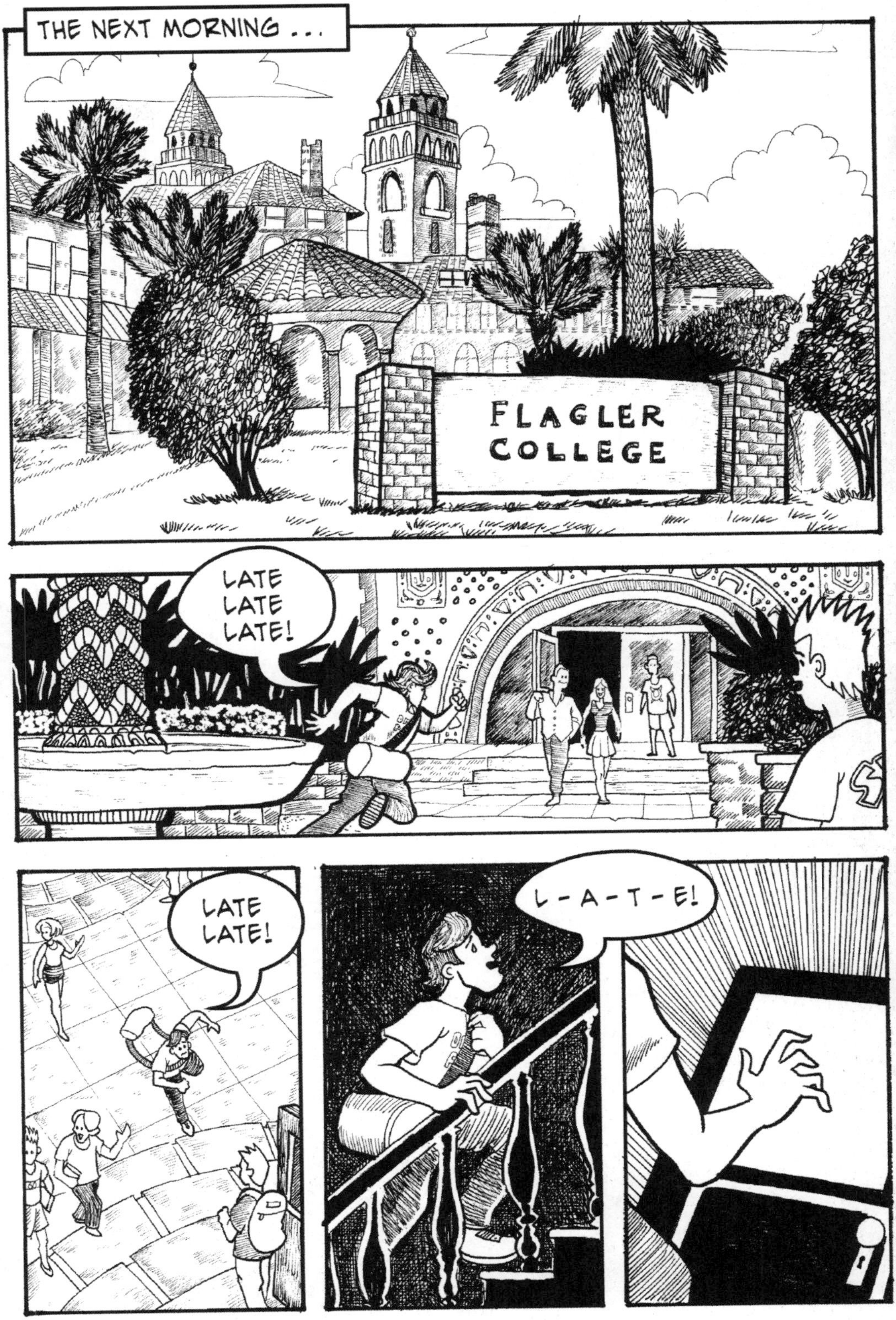
THE NEXT MORNING ...
FLAGLER
COLLEGE
LATE
LATE
LATE!
LATE
LATE!
L-A-T-E!

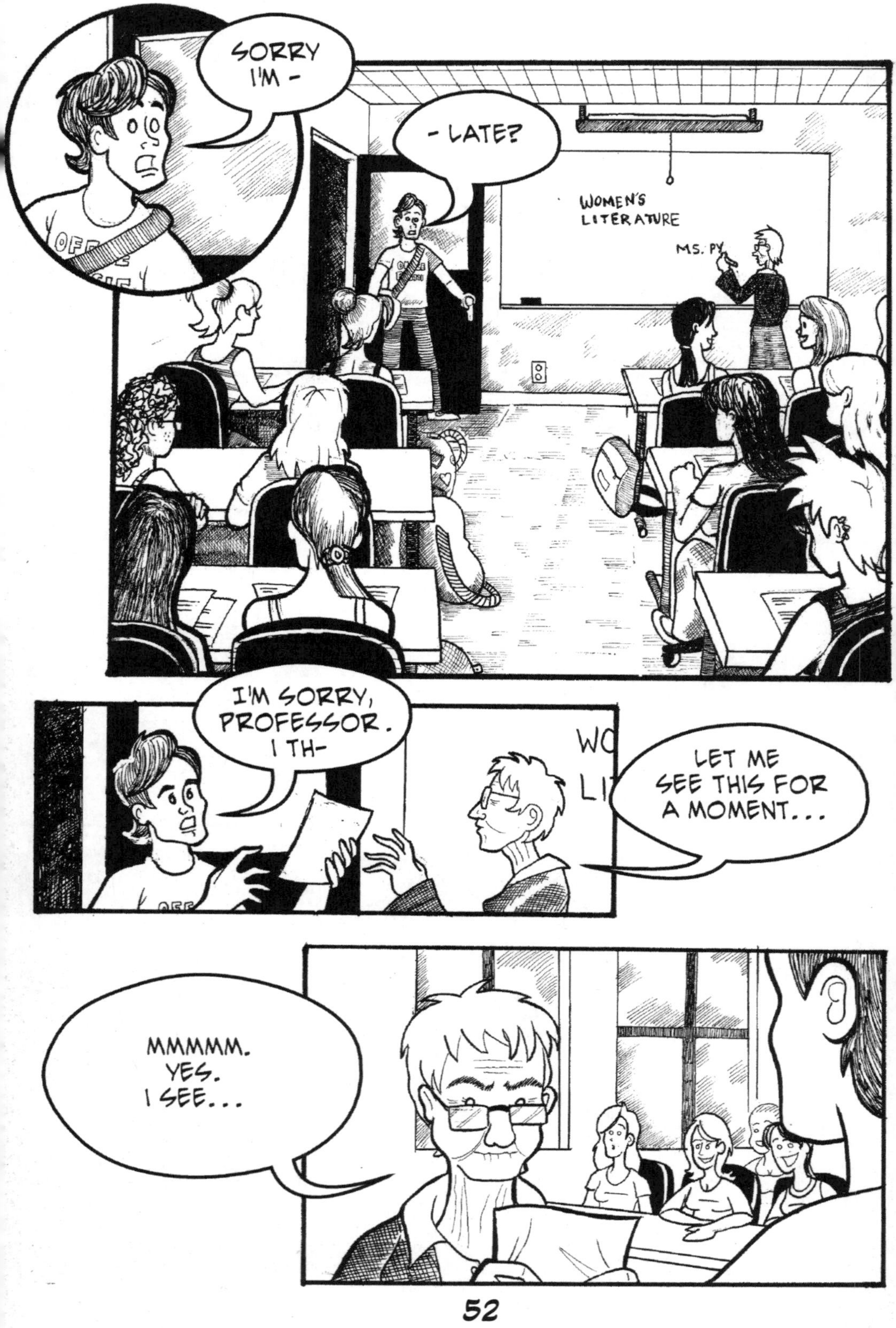
SORRY I'M -
- LATE?
WOMEN'S LITERATURE
MS. PY
I'M SORRY, PROFESSOR. I TH-
LET ME SEE THIS FOR A MOMENT...
MMMMM. YES. I SEE...

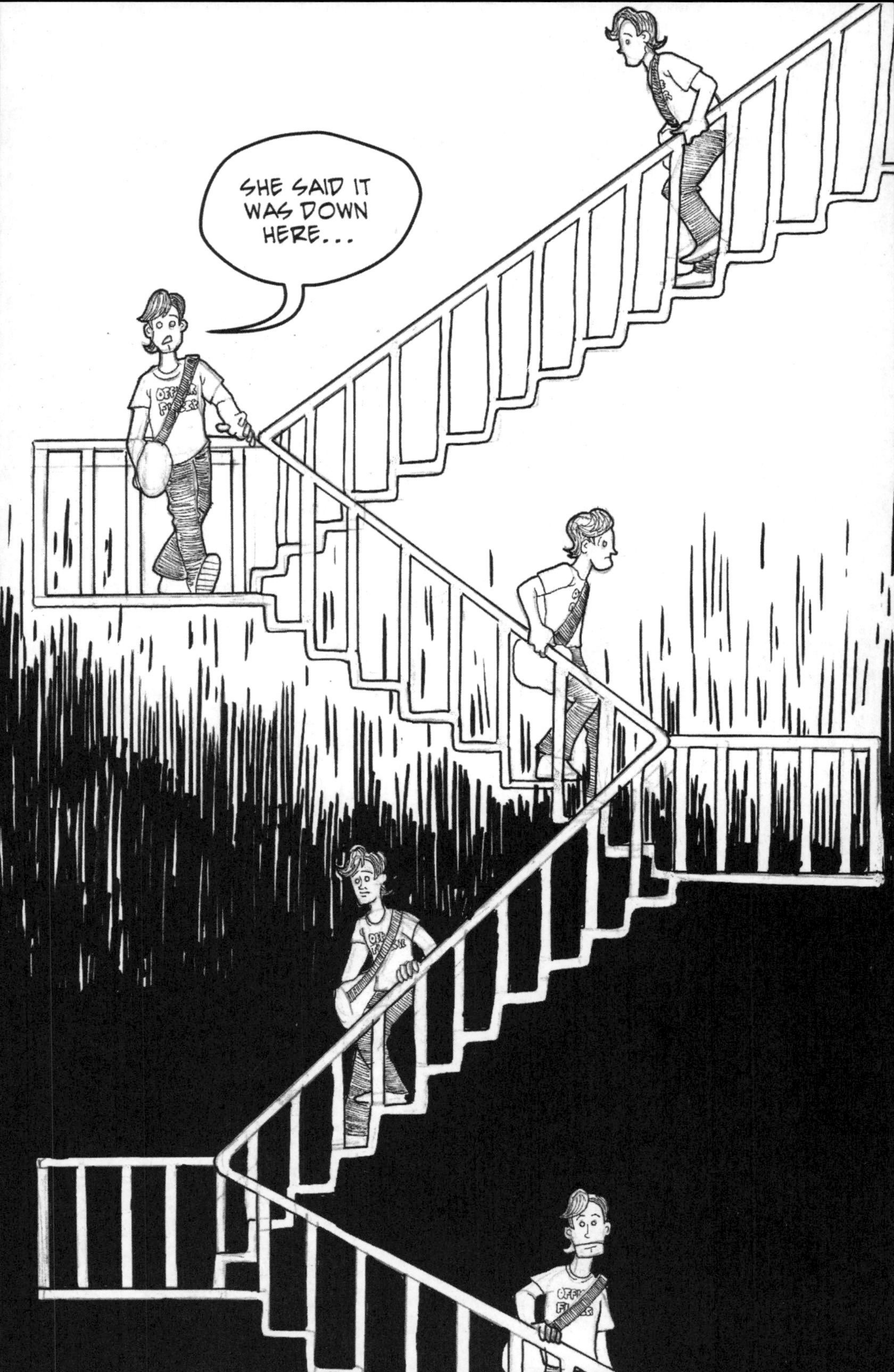
SHE SAID IT WAS DOWN HERE...

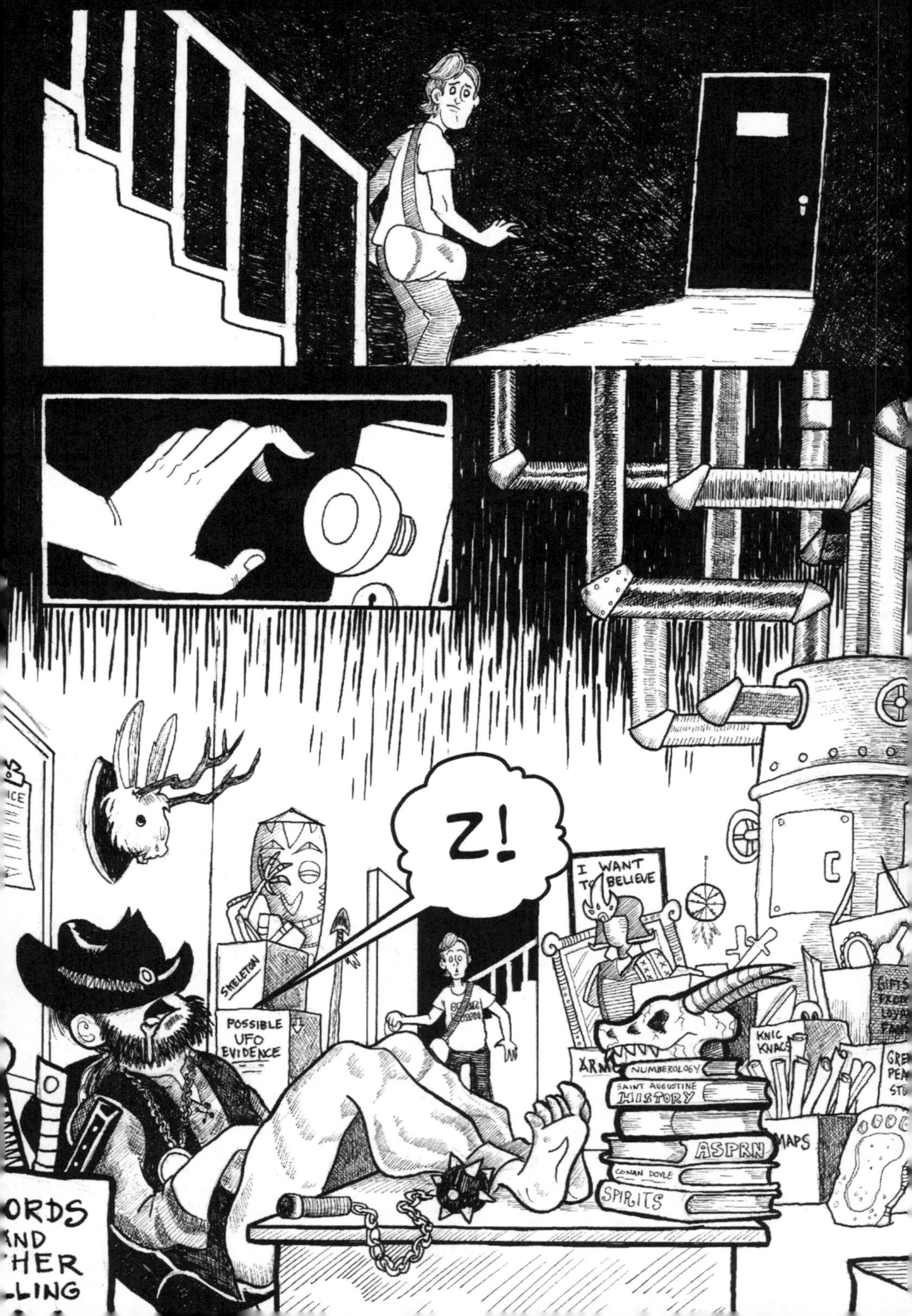
Z!
I WANT TO BELIEVE
SKELETON
POSSIBLE UFO EVIDENCE
NUMBEROLOGY
SAINT AUGUSTINE HISTORY
ASPRN
CONAN DOYLE
SPIRITS
KNIC KNACS
MAPS

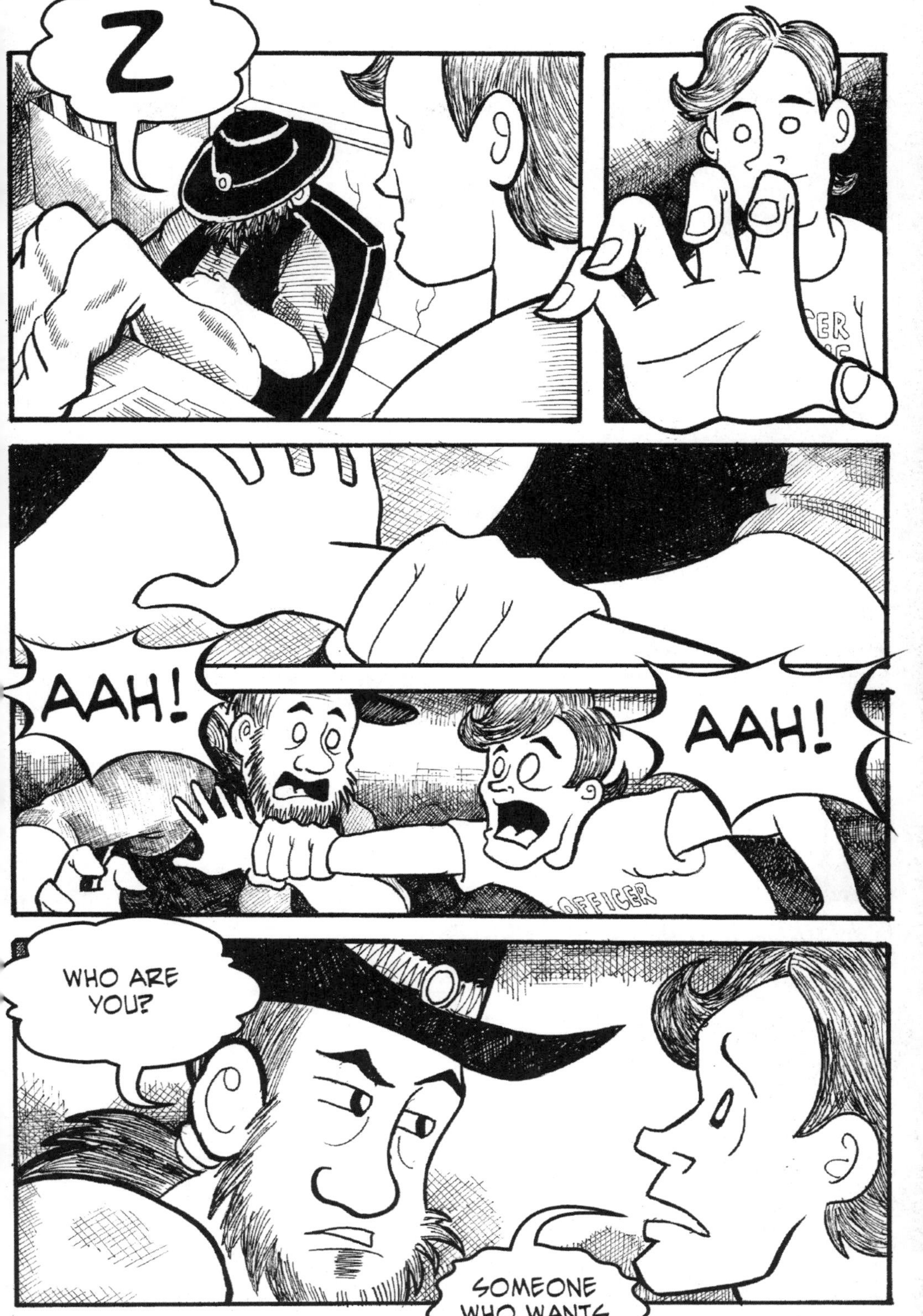
Z
AAH!
AAH!
OFFICER
WHO ARE YOU?
SOMEONE WHO WANTS TO LIVE...

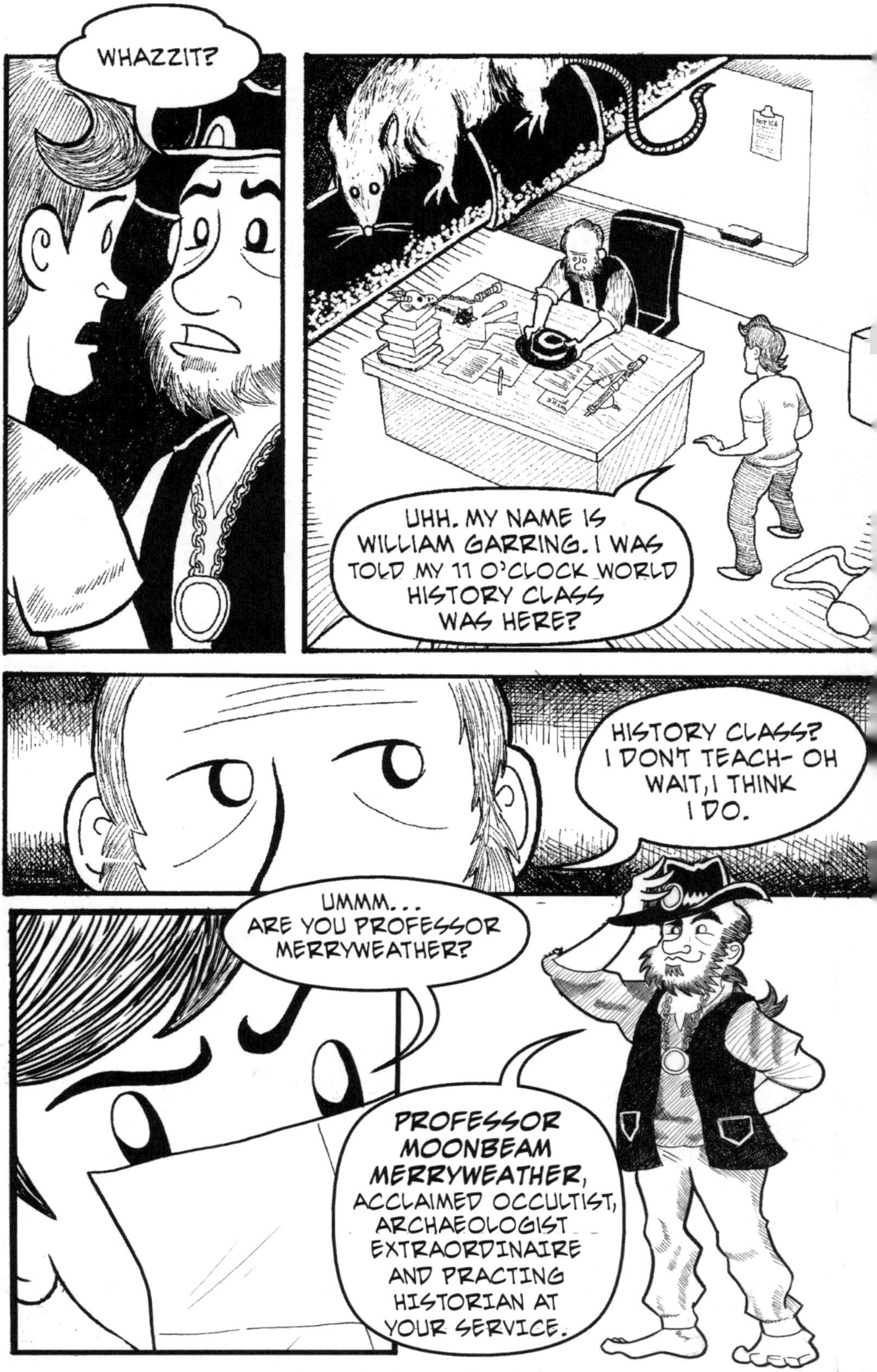
WHAZZIT?
UHH. MY NAME IS WILLIAM GARRING. I WAS TOLD MY 11 O'CLOCK WORLD HISTORY CLASS WAS HERE?
HISTORY CLASS? I DON'T TEACH- OH WAIT, I THINK I DO.
UMMM... ARE YOU PROFESSOR MERRYWEATHER?
PROFESSOR MOONBEAM MERRYWEATHER, ACCLAIMED OCCULTIST, ARCHAEOLOGIST EXTRAORDINAIRE AND PRACTING HISTORIAN AT YOUR SERVICE.

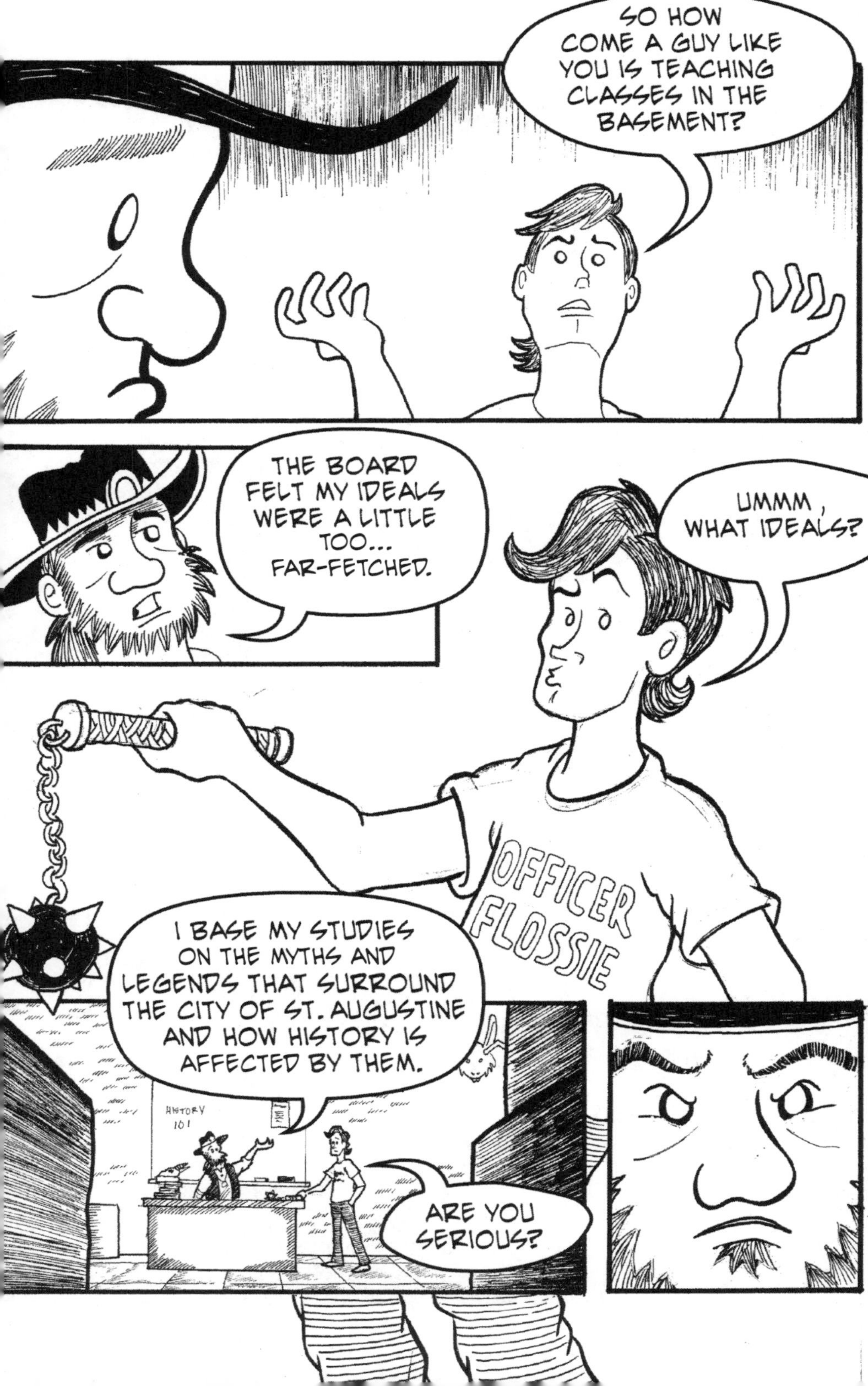
SO HOW COME A GUY LIKE YOU IS TEACHING CLASSES IN THE BASEMENT?
THE BOARD FELT MY IDEALS WERE A LITTLE TOO... FAR-FETCHED.
UMMM, WHAT IDEALS?
OFFICER FLOSSIE
I BASE MY STUDIES ON THE MYTHS AND LEGENDS THAT SURROUND THE CITY OF ST. AUGUSTINE AND HOW HISTORY IS AFFECTED BY THEM.
HISTORY 101
ARE YOU SERIOUS?

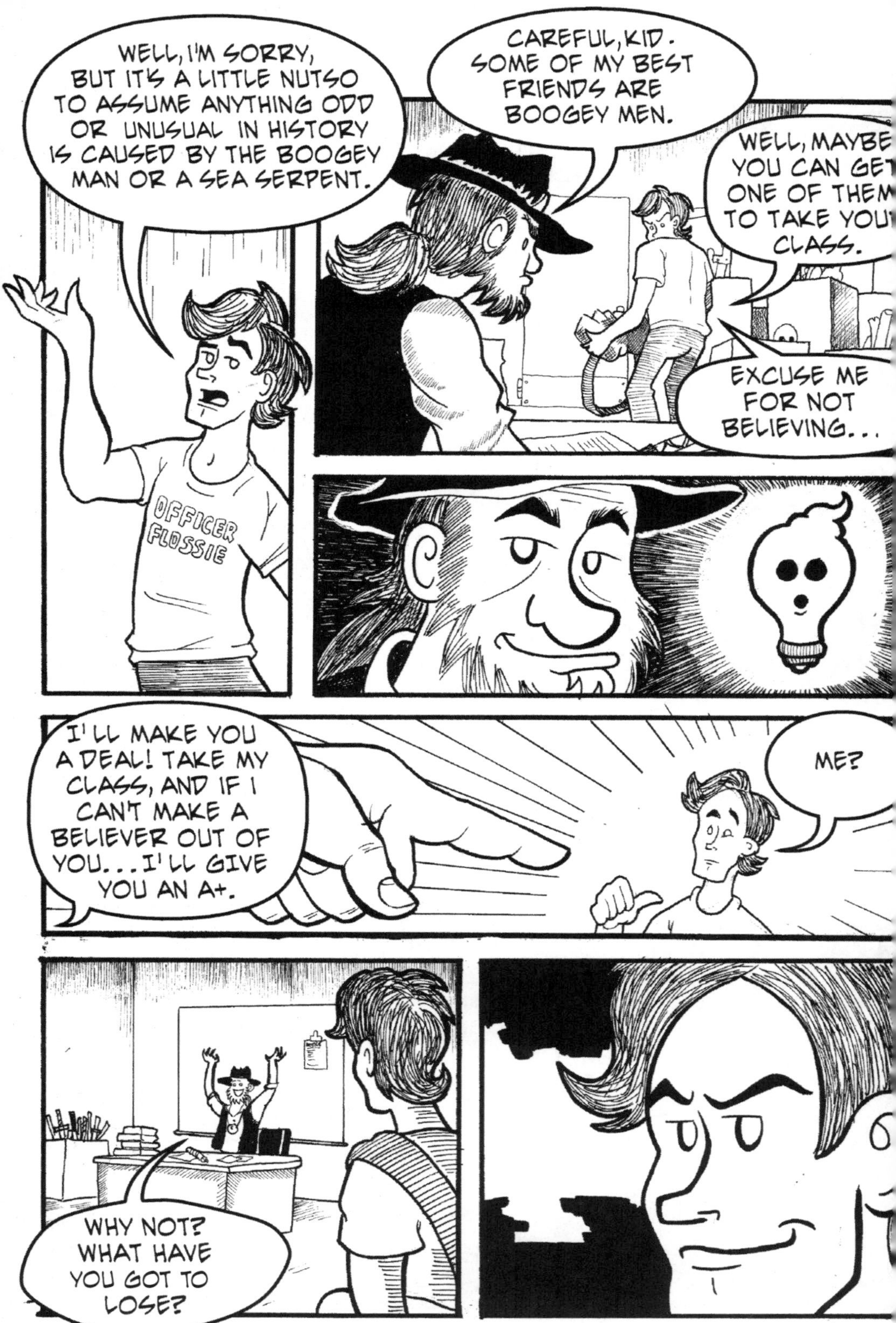
WELL, I'M SORRY, BUT IT'S A LITTLE NUTSO TO ASSUME ANYTHING ODD OR UNUSUAL IN HISTORY IS CAUSED BY THE BOOGEY MAN OR A SEA SERPENT.
CAREFUL, KID. SOME OF MY BEST FRIENDS ARE BOOGEY MEN.
WELL, MAYBE YOU CAN GET ONE OF THEM TO TAKE YOUR CLASS.
EXCUSE ME FOR NOT BELIEVING...
OFFICER FLOSSIE
I'LL MAKE YOU A DEAL! TAKE MY CLASS, AND IF I CAN'T MAKE A BELIEVER OUT OF YOU...I'LL GIVE YOU AN A+.
ME?
WHY NOT? WHAT HAVE YOU GOT TO LOSE?

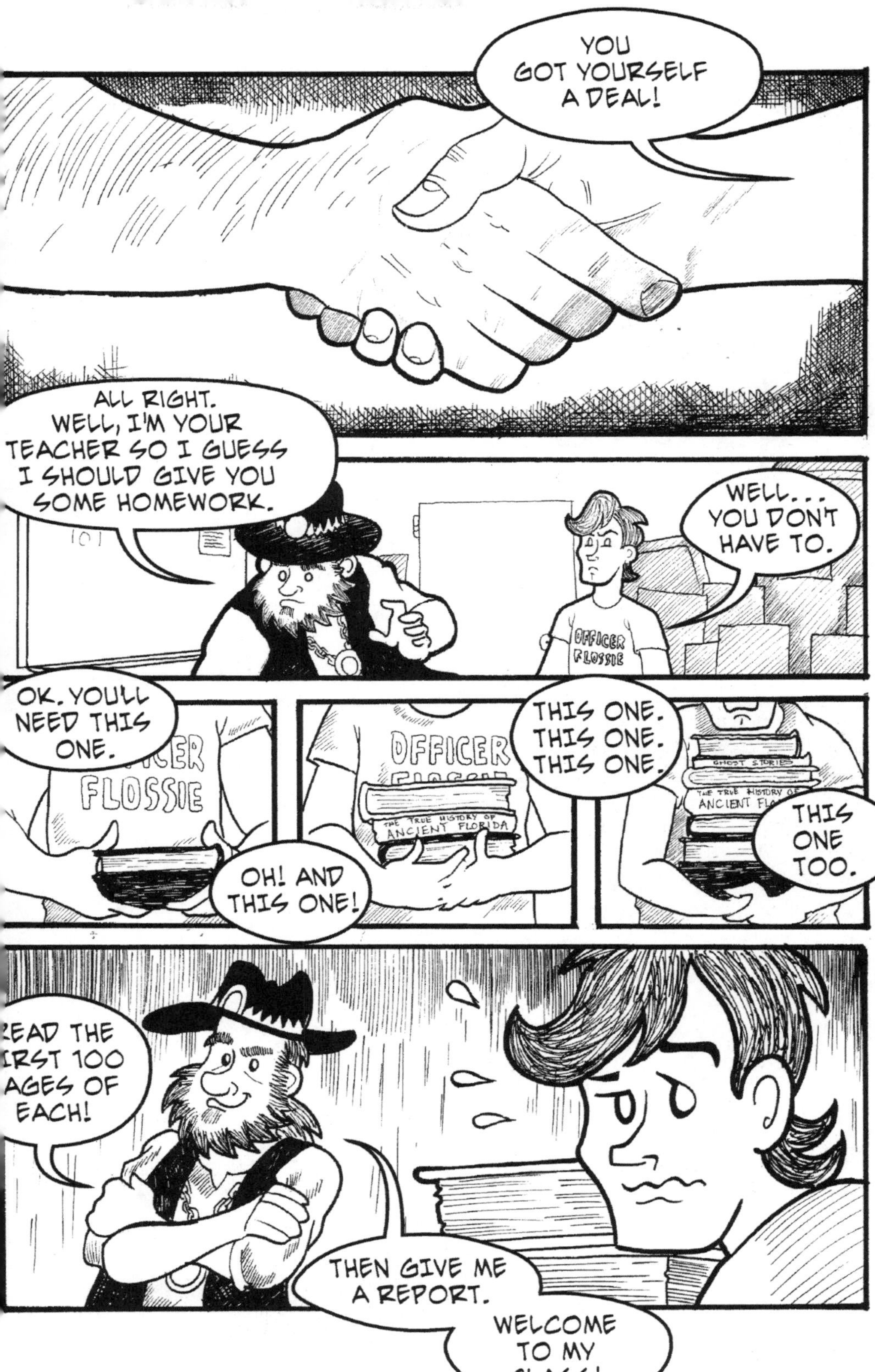
YOU GOT YOURSELF A DEAL!
ALL RIGHT. WELL, I'M YOUR TEACHER SO I GUESS I SHOULD GIVE YOU SOME HOMEWORK.
WELL... YOU DON'T HAVE TO.
OFFICER FLOSSIE
OK. YOU'LL NEED THIS ONE.
OFFICER FLOSSIE
OH! AND THIS ONE!
THE TRUE HISTORY OF ANCIENT FLORIDA
THIS ONE. THIS ONE. THIS ONE.
GHOST STORIES
THE TRUE HISTORY OF ANCIENT FL
THIS ONE TOO.
READ THE FIRST 100 PAGES OF EACH!
THEN GIVE ME A REPORT.
WELCOME TO MY CLASS!

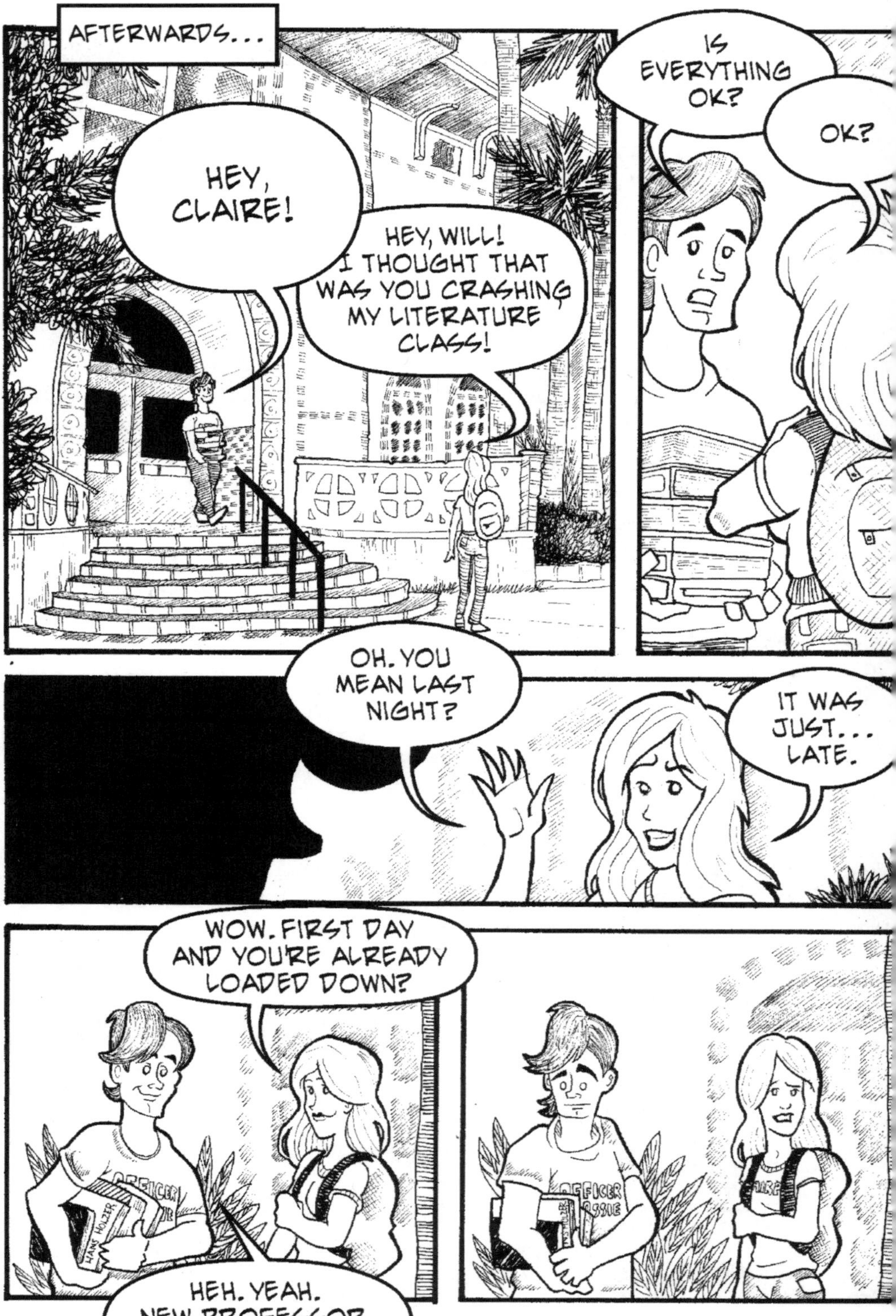
AFTERWARDS...
HEY, CLAIRE!
HEY, WILL! I THOUGHT THAT WAS YOU CRASHING MY LITERATURE CLASS!
IS EVERYTHING OK?
OK?
OH. YOU MEAN LAST NIGHT?
IT WAS JUST... LATE.
WOW. FIRST DAY AND YOU'RE ALREADY LOADED DOWN?
HANS HOLZER
OFFICER
HEH. YEAH. NEW PROFESSOR. ...HE'S THOROUGH.

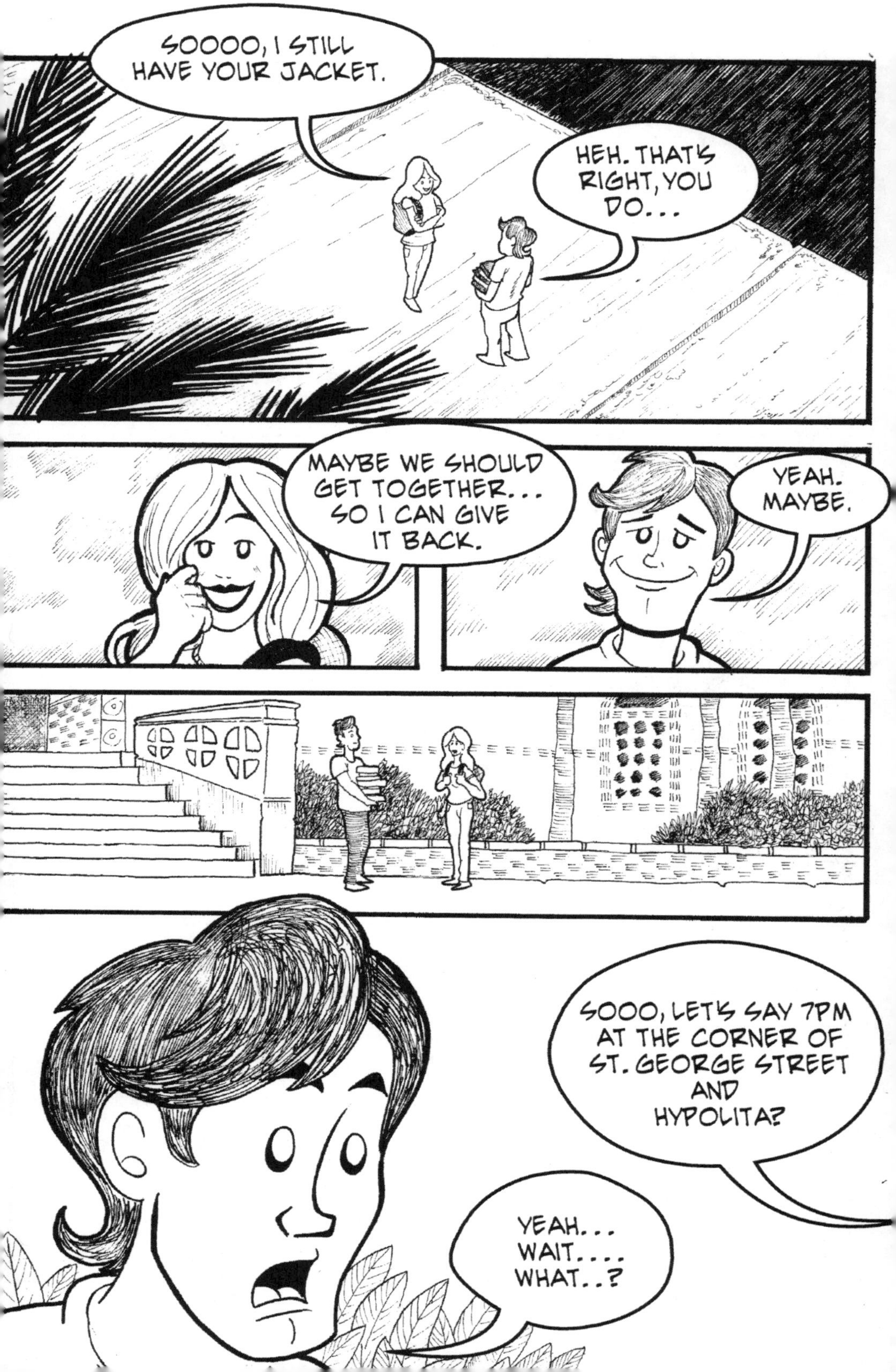
SOOOO, I STILL HAVE YOUR JACKET.
HEH. THAT'S RIGHT, YOU DO...
MAYBE WE SHOULD GET TOGETHER... SO I CAN GIVE IT BACK.
YEAH. MAYBE.
SOOO, LET'S SAY 7PM AT THE CORNER OF ST. GEORGE STREET AND HYPOLITA?
YEAH... WAIT.... WHAT..?

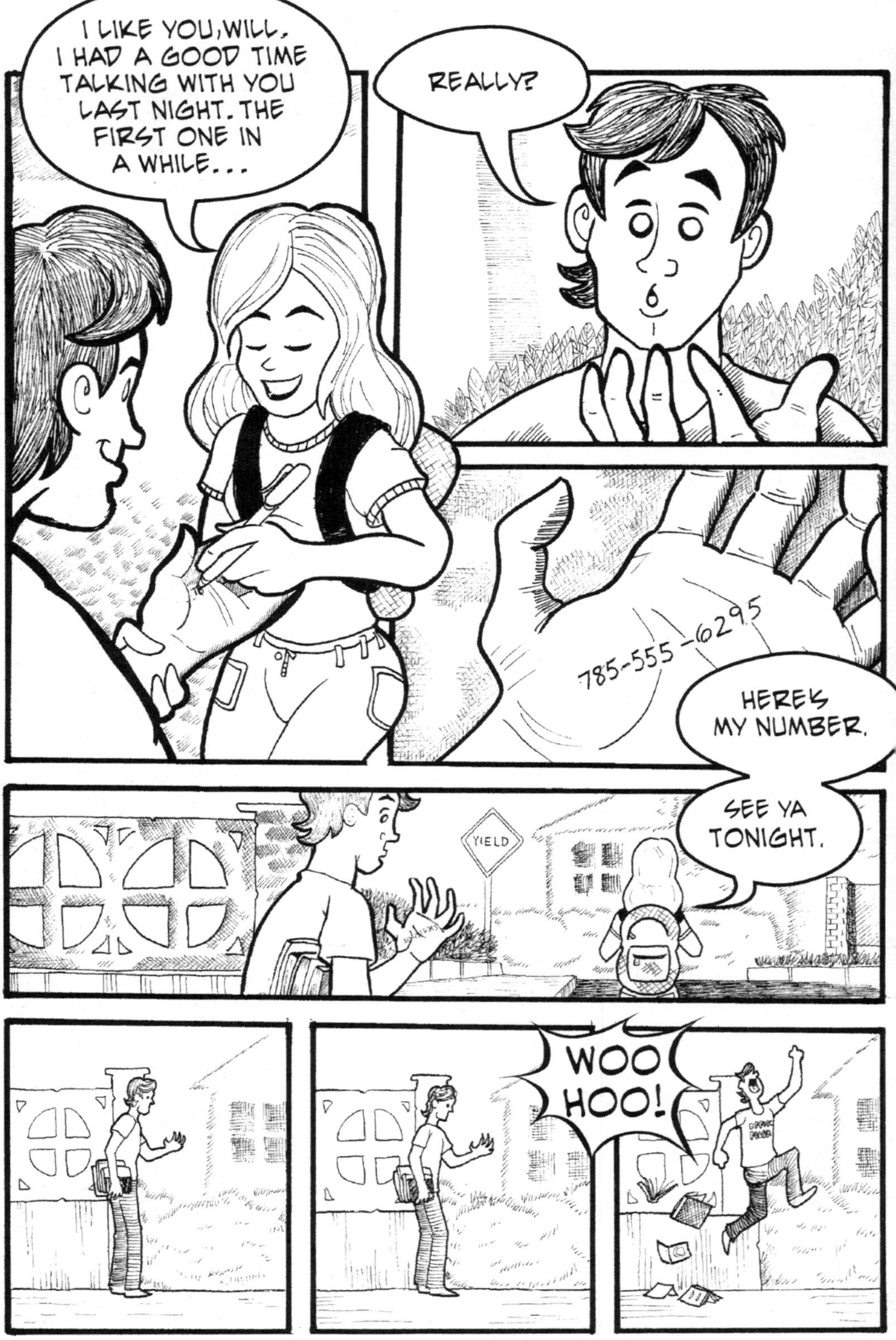
I LIKE YOU, WILL. I HAD A GOOD TIME TALKING WITH YOU LAST NIGHT. THE FIRST ONE IN A WHILE...
REALLY?
785-555-6295
HERE'S MY NUMBER.
YIELD
SEE YA TONIGHT.
WOO HOO!

CHAPTER
5

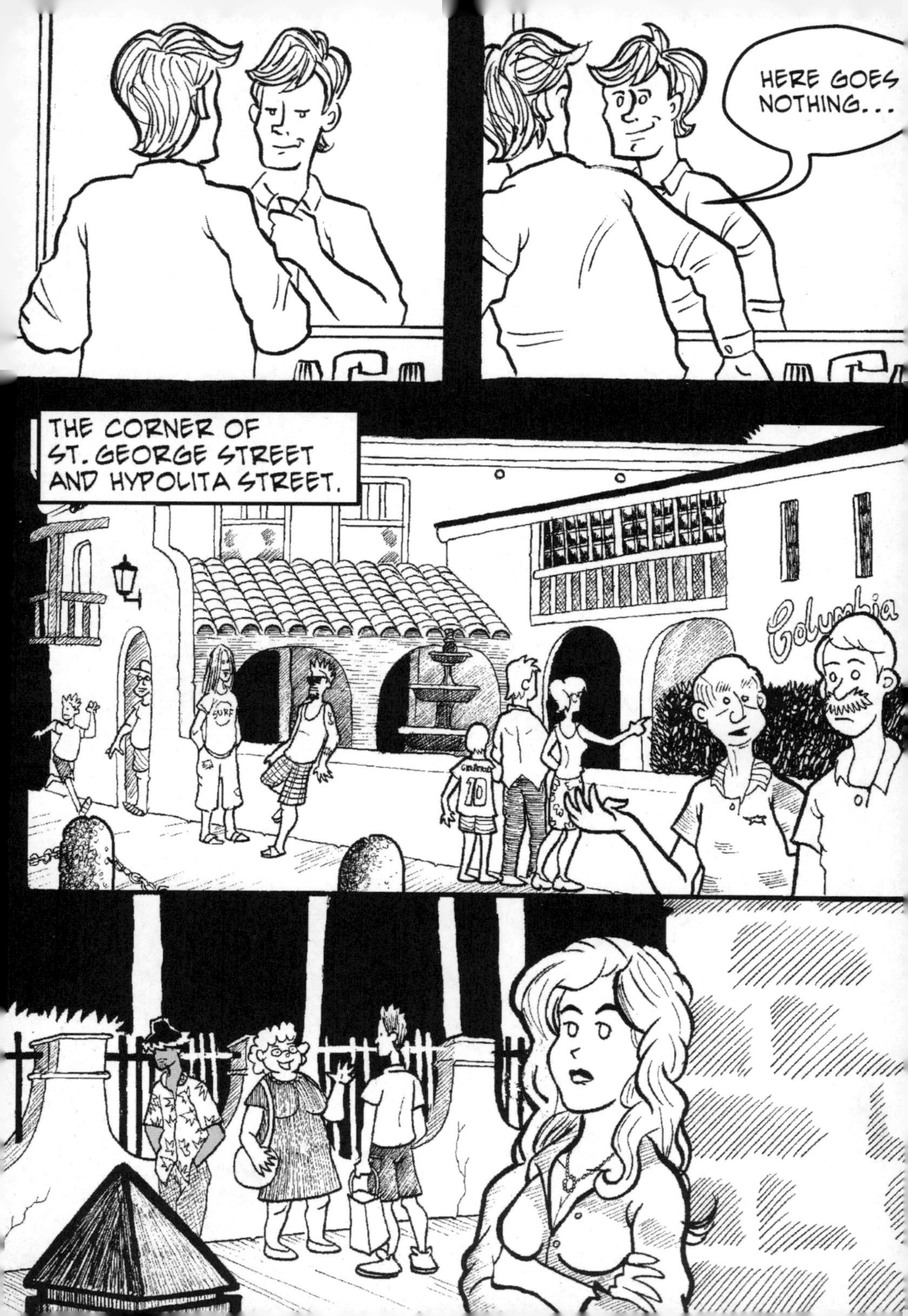
HERE GOES NOTHING...
THE CORNER OF ST. GEORGE STREET AND HYPOLITA STREET.
SURF
10
Columbia

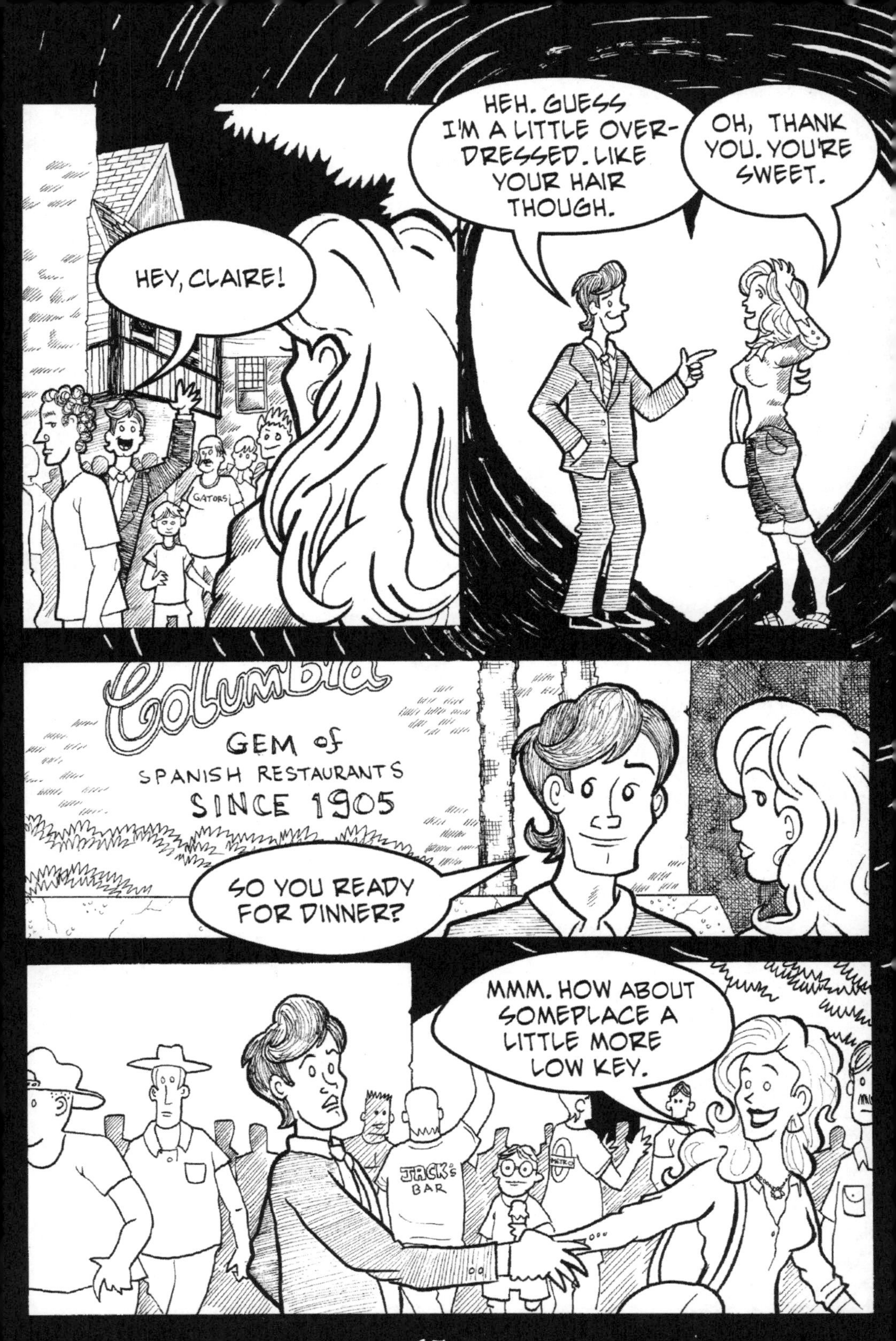
HEY, CLAIRE!
HEH. GUESS I'M A LITTLE OVER-DRESSED. LIKE YOUR HAIR THOUGH.
OH, THANK YOU. YOU'RE SWEET.
GATORS
Columbia
GEM of SPANISH RESTAURANTS SINCE 1905
SO YOU READY FOR DINNER?
MMM. HOW ABOUT SOMEPLACE A LITTLE MORE LOW KEY.
JACK'S BAR
METRO

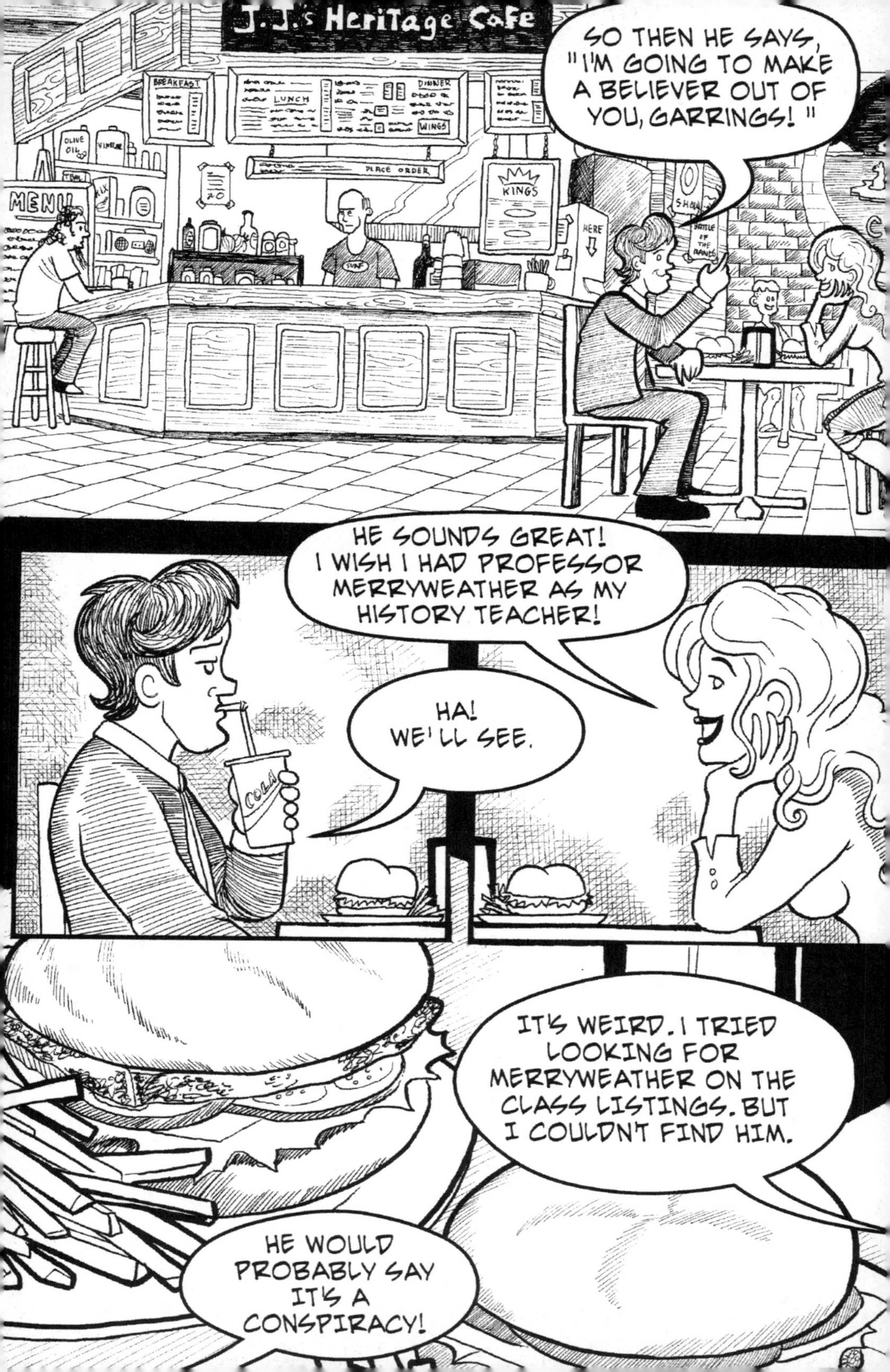
J. J.'s Heritage Cafe
SO THEN HE SAYS, "I'M GOING TO MAKE A BELIEVER OUT OF YOU, GARRINGS!"
HE SOUNDS GREAT! I WISH I HAD PROFESSOR MERRYWEATHER AS MY HISTORY TEACHER!
HA! WE'LL SEE.
COLA
IT'S WEIRD. I TRIED LOOKING FOR MERRYWEATHER ON THE CLASS LISTINGS. BUT I COULDN'T FIND HIM.
HE WOULD PROBABLY SAY IT'S A CONSPIRACY!

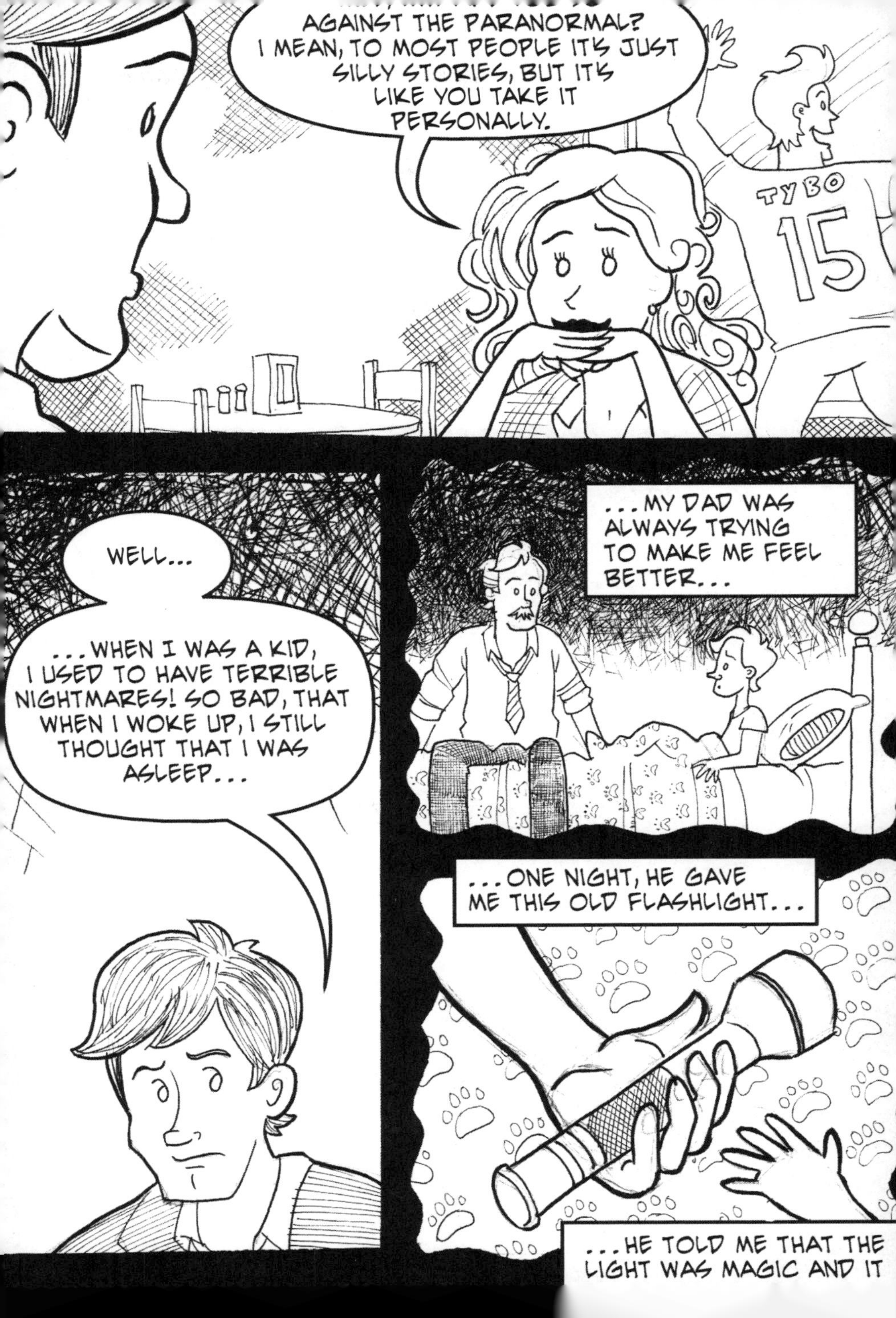
AGAINST THE PARANORMAL? I MEAN, TO MOST PEOPLE IT'S JUST SILLY STORIES, BUT IT'S LIKE YOU TAKE IT PERSONALLY.
TYBO
15
WELL...
...WHEN I WAS A KID, I USED TO HAVE TERRIBLE NIGHTMARES! SO BAD, THAT WHEN I WOKE UP, I STILL THOUGHT THAT I WAS ASLEEP...
...MY DAD WAS ALWAYS TRYING TO MAKE ME FEEL BETTER...
...ONE NIGHT, HE GAVE ME THIS OLD FLASHLIGHT...
...HE TOLD ME THAT THE LIGHT WAS MAGIC AND IT

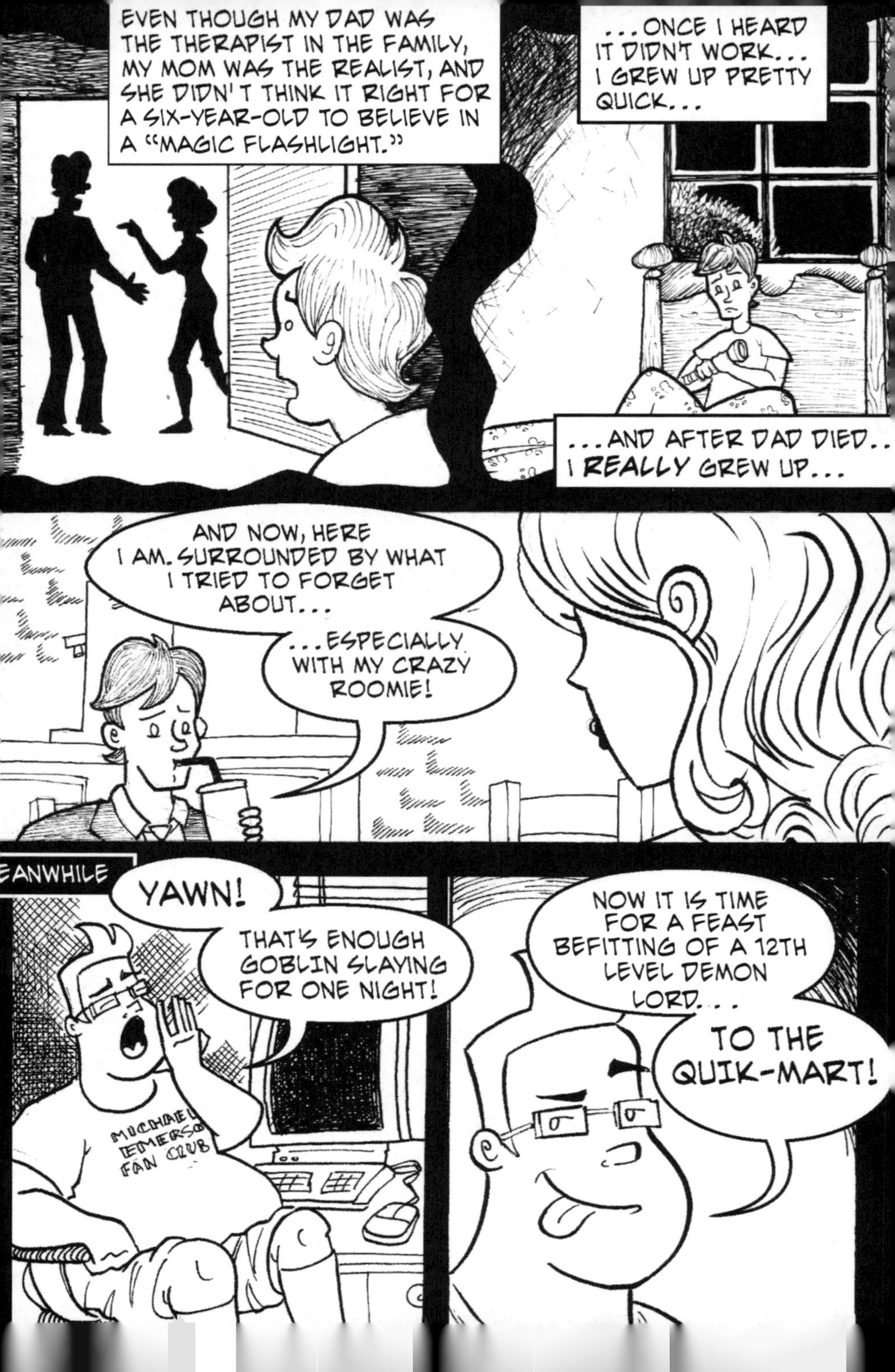

EVEN THOUGH MY DAD WAS THE THERAPIST IN THE FAMILY, MY MOM WAS THE REALIST, AND SHE DIDN'T THINK IT RIGHT FOR A SIX-YEAR-OLD TO BELIEVE IN A "MAGIC FLASHLIGHT."
...ONCE I HEARD IT DIDN'T WORK... I GREW UP PRETTY QUICK...
...AND AFTER DAD DIED... I REALLY GREW UP...
AND NOW, HERE I AM. SURROUNDED BY WHAT I TRIED TO FORGET ABOUT...
...ESPECIALLY WITH MY CRAZY ROOMIE!
EANWHILE
YAWN!
THAT'S ENOUGH GOBLIN SLAYING FOR ONE NIGHT!
MICHAEL EMERSO FAN CLUB
NOW IT IS TIME FOR A FEAST BEFITTING OF A 12TH LEVEL DEMON LORD...
TO THE QUIK-MART!

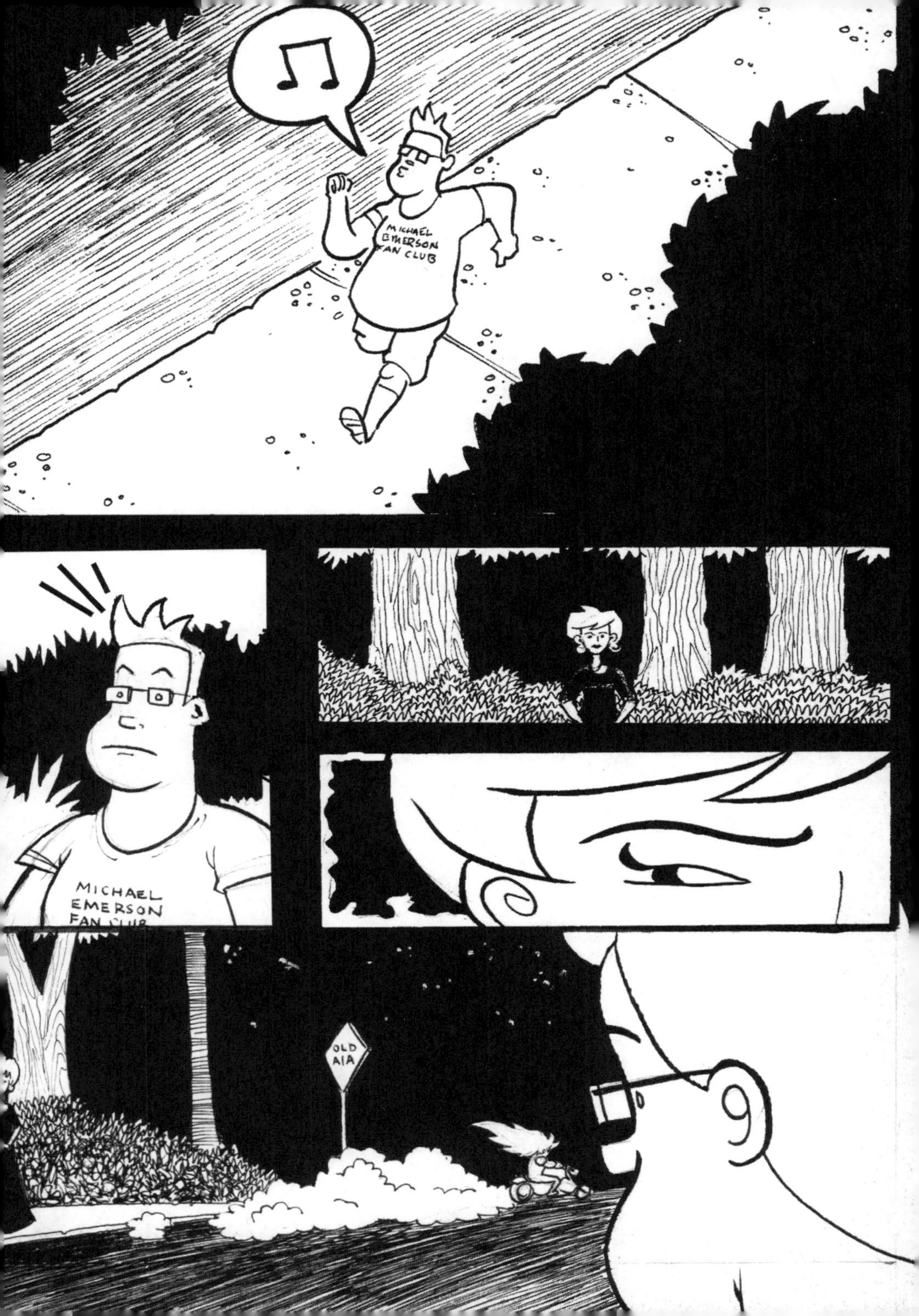
MICHAEL EMERSON FAN CLUB
MICHAEL EMERSON FAN CLUB
OLD A1A

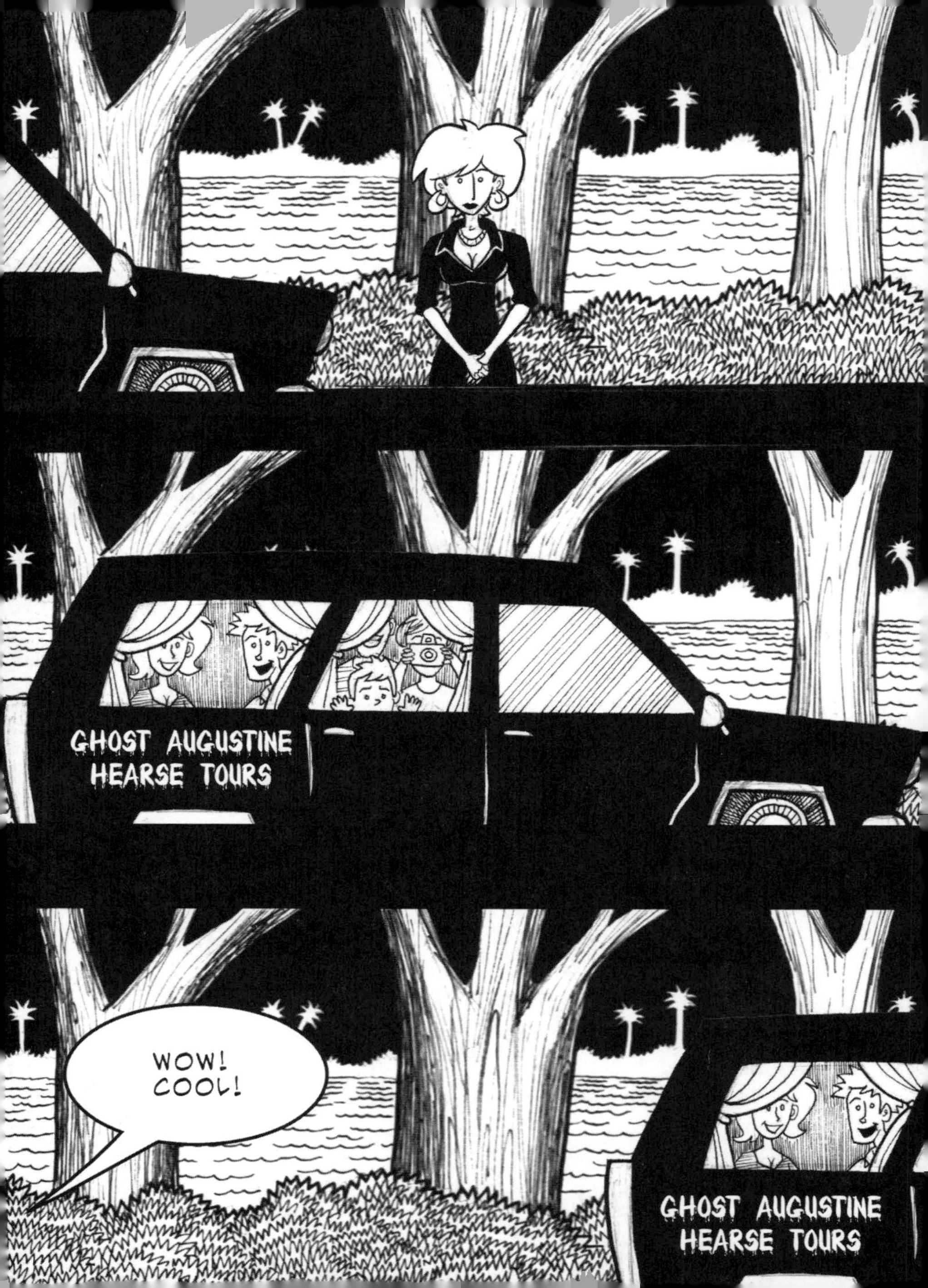
GHOST AUGUSTINE HEARSE TOURS
WOW! COOL!
GHOST AUGUSTINE HEARSE TOURS

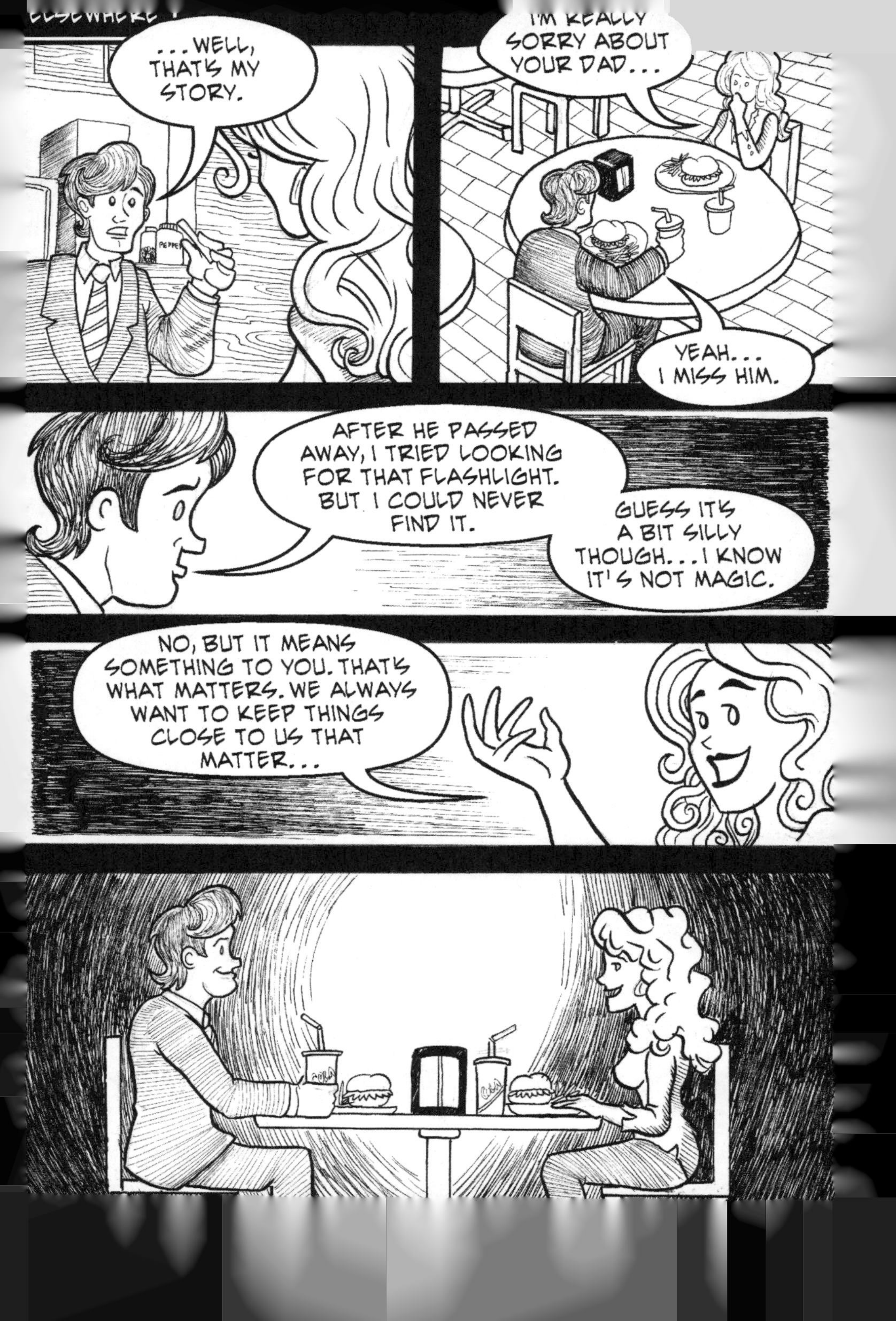
...WELL, THAT'S MY STORY.
I'M REALLY SORRY ABOUT YOUR DAD...
PEPPER
YEAH... I MISS HIM.
AFTER HE PASSED AWAY, I TRIED LOOKING FOR THAT FLASHLIGHT. BUT I COULD NEVER FIND IT.
GUESS IT'S A BIT SILLY THOUGH... I KNOW IT'S NOT MAGIC.
NO, BUT IT MEANS SOMETHING TO YOU. THAT'S WHAT MATTERS. WE ALWAYS WANT TO KEEP THINGS CLOSE TO US THAT MATTER...

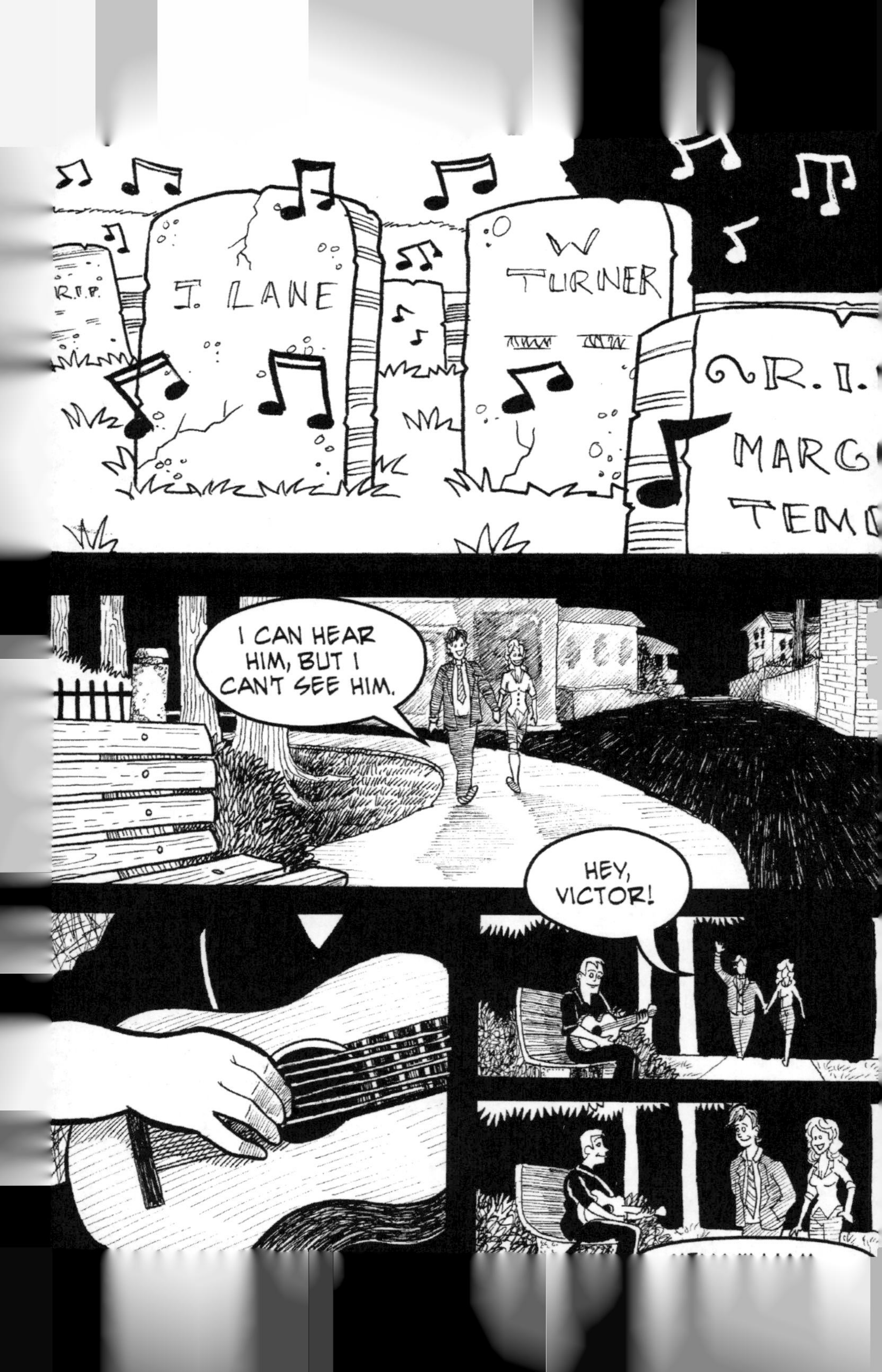
R.I.P.
J. LANE
W TURNER
R.I.
MARG
TEM
I CAN HEAR HIM, BUT I CAN'T SEE HIM.
HEY, VICTOR!

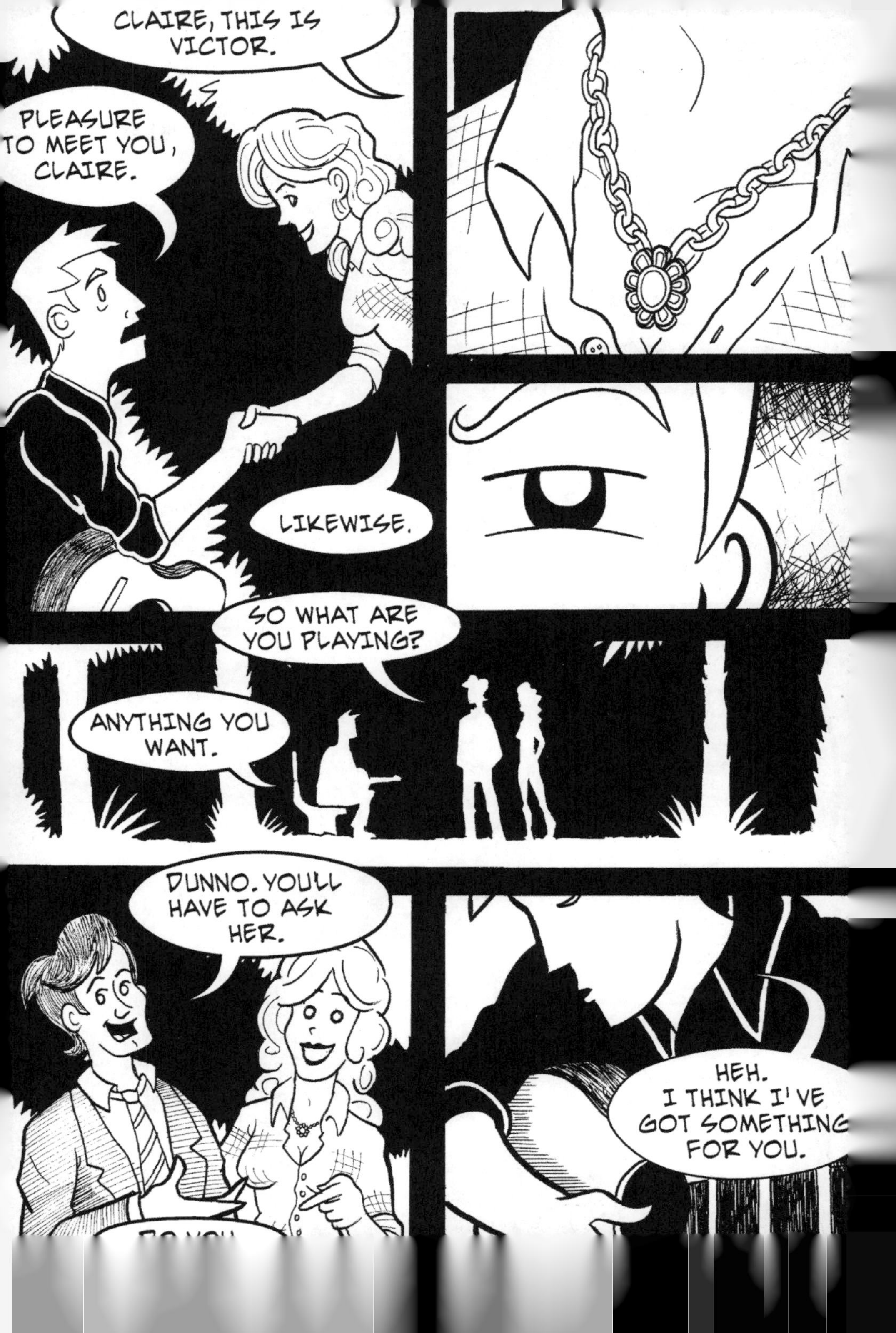
CLAIRE, THIS IS VICTOR.
PLEASURE TO MEET YOU, CLAIRE.
LIKEWISE.
SO WHAT ARE YOU PLAYING?
ANYTHING YOU WANT.
DUNNO. YOU'LL HAVE TO ASK HER.
HEH. I THINK I'VE GOT SOMETHING FOR YOU.

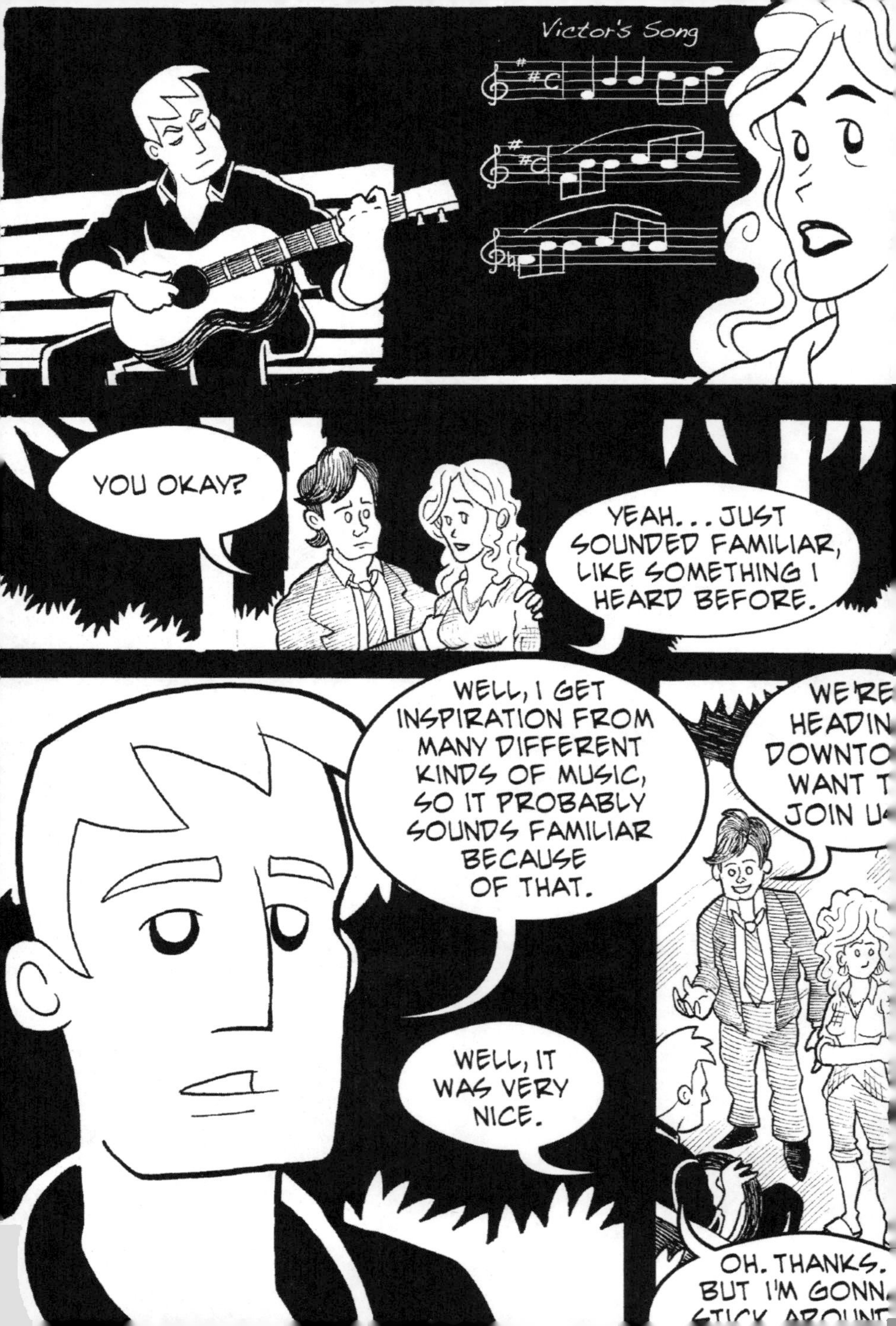
Victor's Song
YOU OKAY?
YEAH...JUST SOUNDED FAMILIAR, LIKE SOMETHING I HEARD BEFORE.
WELL, I GET INSPIRATION FROM MANY DIFFERENT KINDS OF MUSIC, SO IT PROBABLY SOUNDS FAMILIAR BECAUSE OF THAT.
WELL, IT WAS VERY NICE.
OH. THANKS. BUT I'M GONN

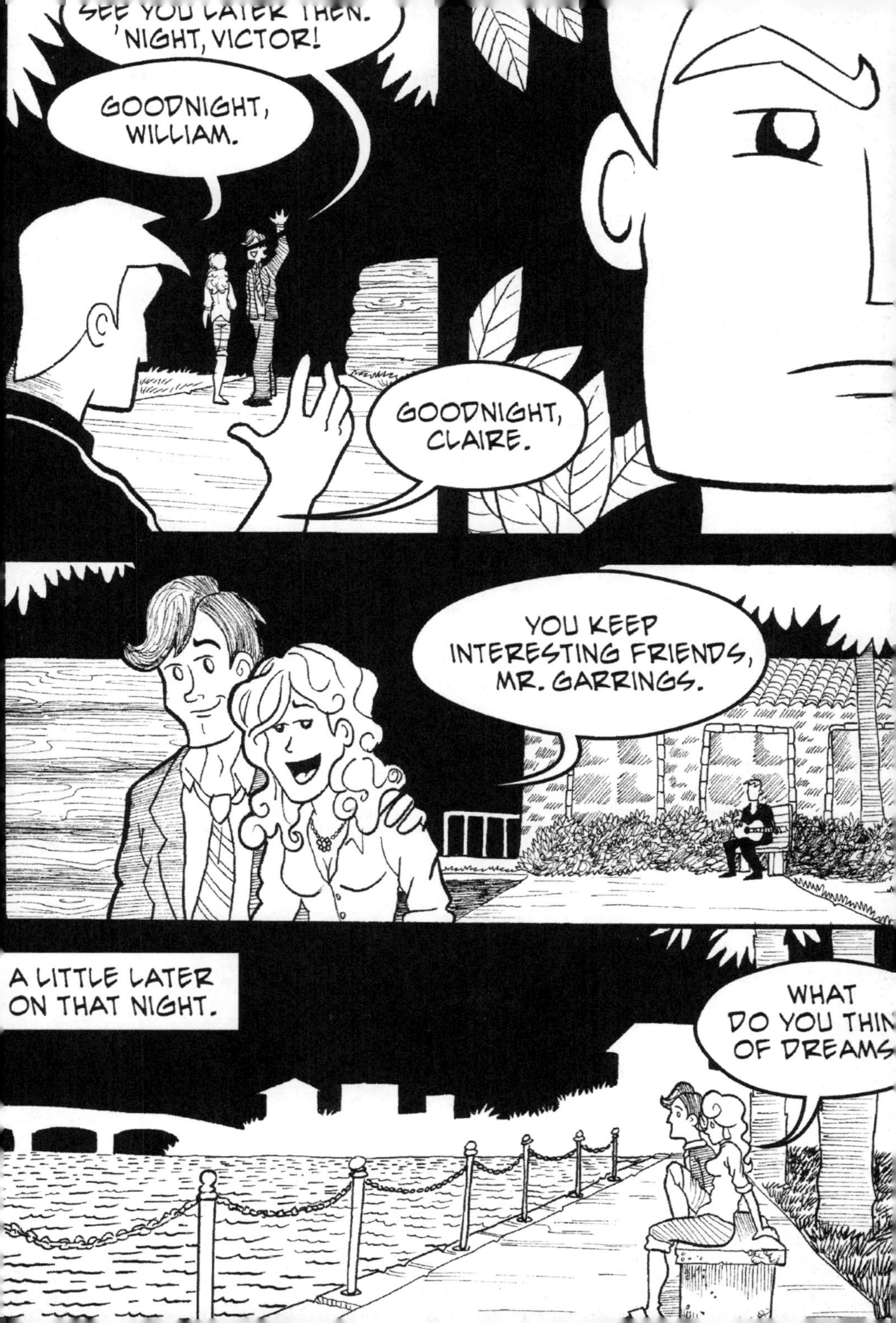
SEE YOU LATER THEN. 'NIGHT, VICTOR!
GOODNIGHT, WILLIAM.
GOODNIGHT, CLAIRE.
YOU KEEP INTERESTING FRIENDS, MR. GARRINGS.
A LITTLE LATER ON THAT NIGHT.
WHAT DO YOU THIN OF DREAMS

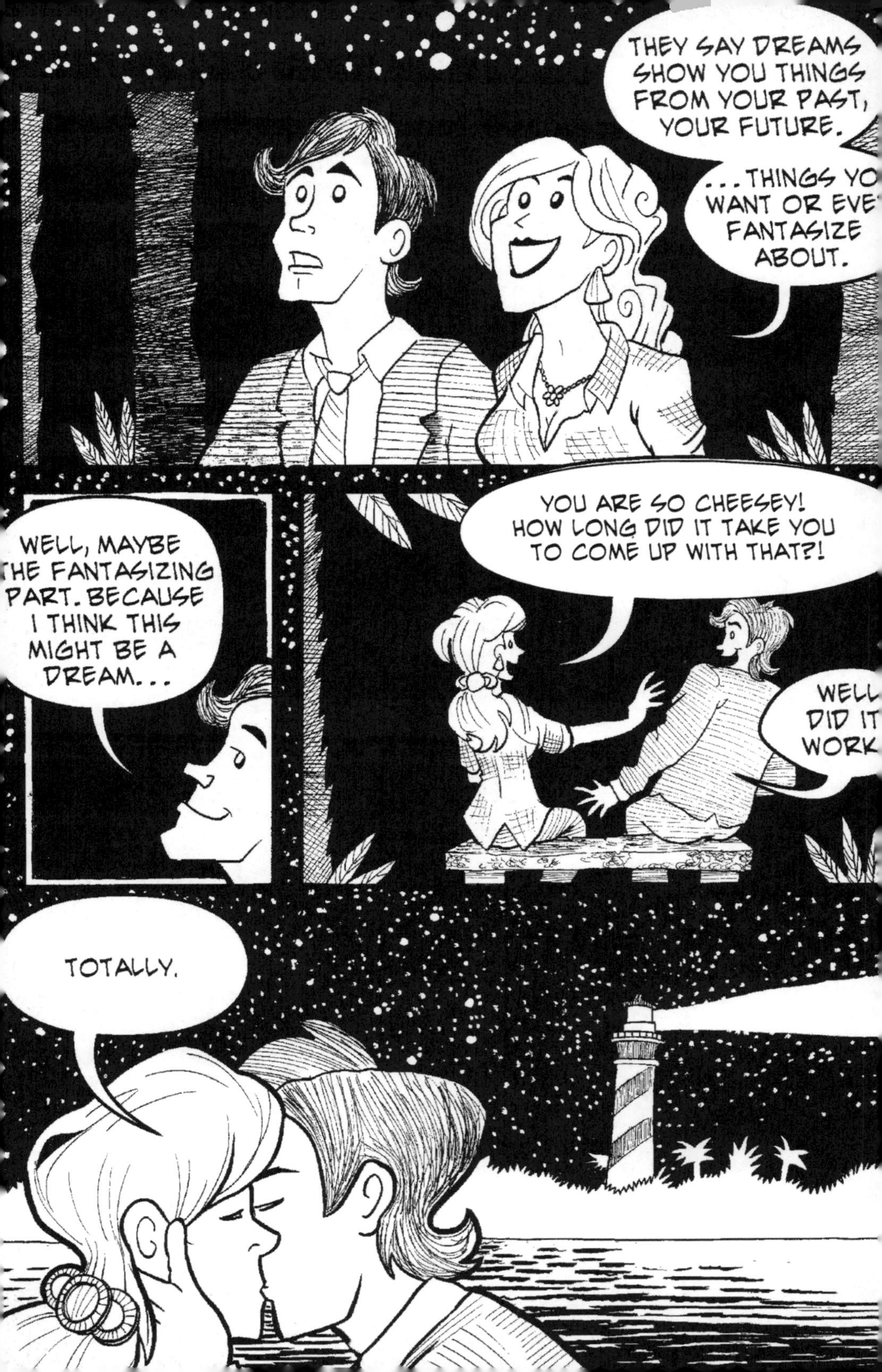
THEY SAY DREAMS SHOW YOU THINGS FROM YOUR PAST, YOUR FUTURE.
...THINGS YO WANT OR EVE FANTASIZE ABOUT.
WELL, MAYBE THE FANTASIZING PART. BECAUSE I THINK THIS MIGHT BE A DREAM...
YOU ARE SO CHEESEY! HOW LONG DID IT TAKE YOU TO COME UP WITH THAT?!
WELL DID IT WORK
TOTALLY.

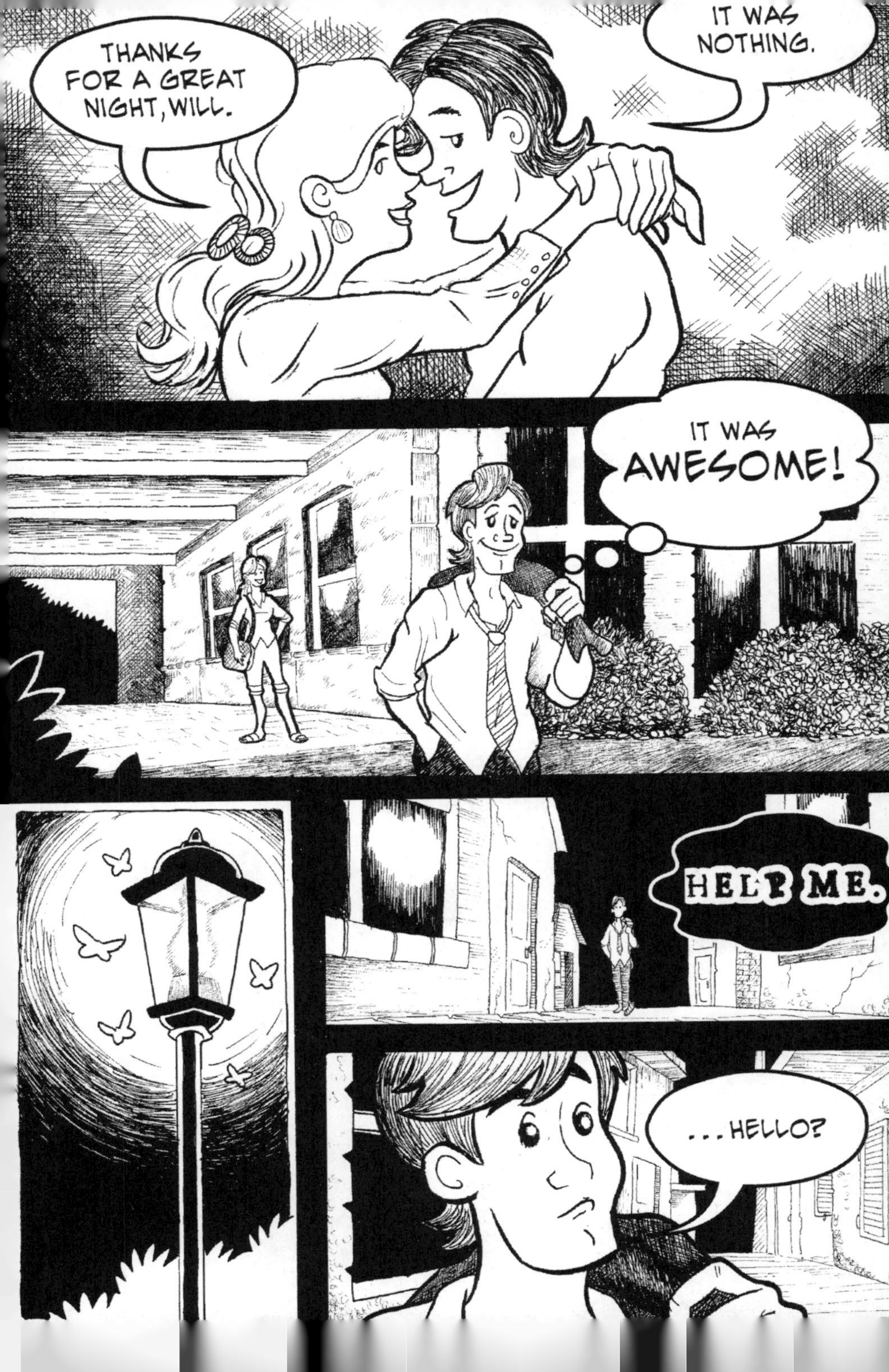
THANKS FOR A GREAT NIGHT, WILL.
IT WAS NOTHING.
IT WAS AWESOME!
HELP ME.
...HELLO?

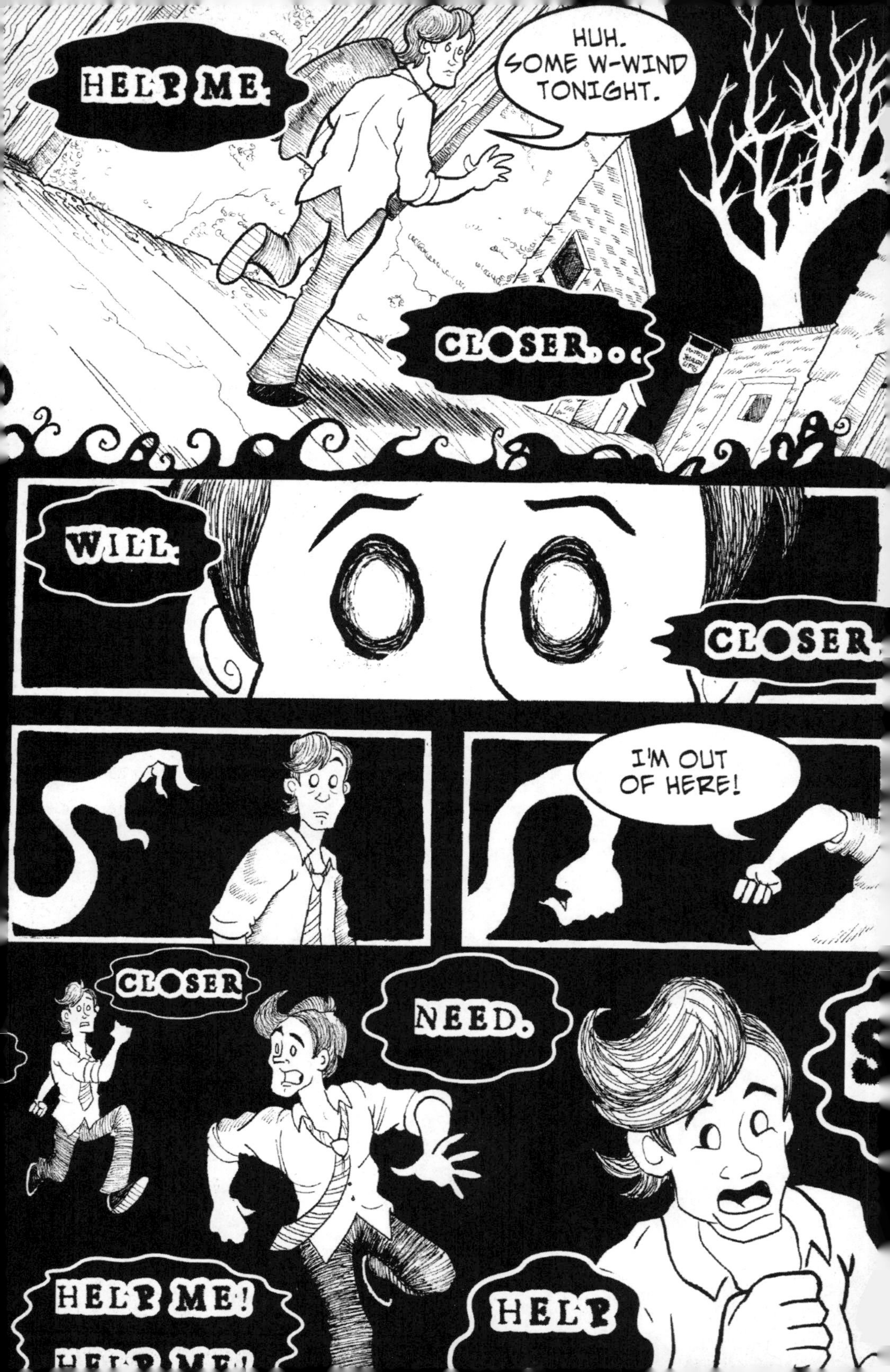
HELP ME.
HUH. SOME W-WIND TONIGHT.
CLOSER...
WILL.
CLOSER.
I'M OUT OF HERE!
CLOSER
NEED.
HELP ME!
HELP

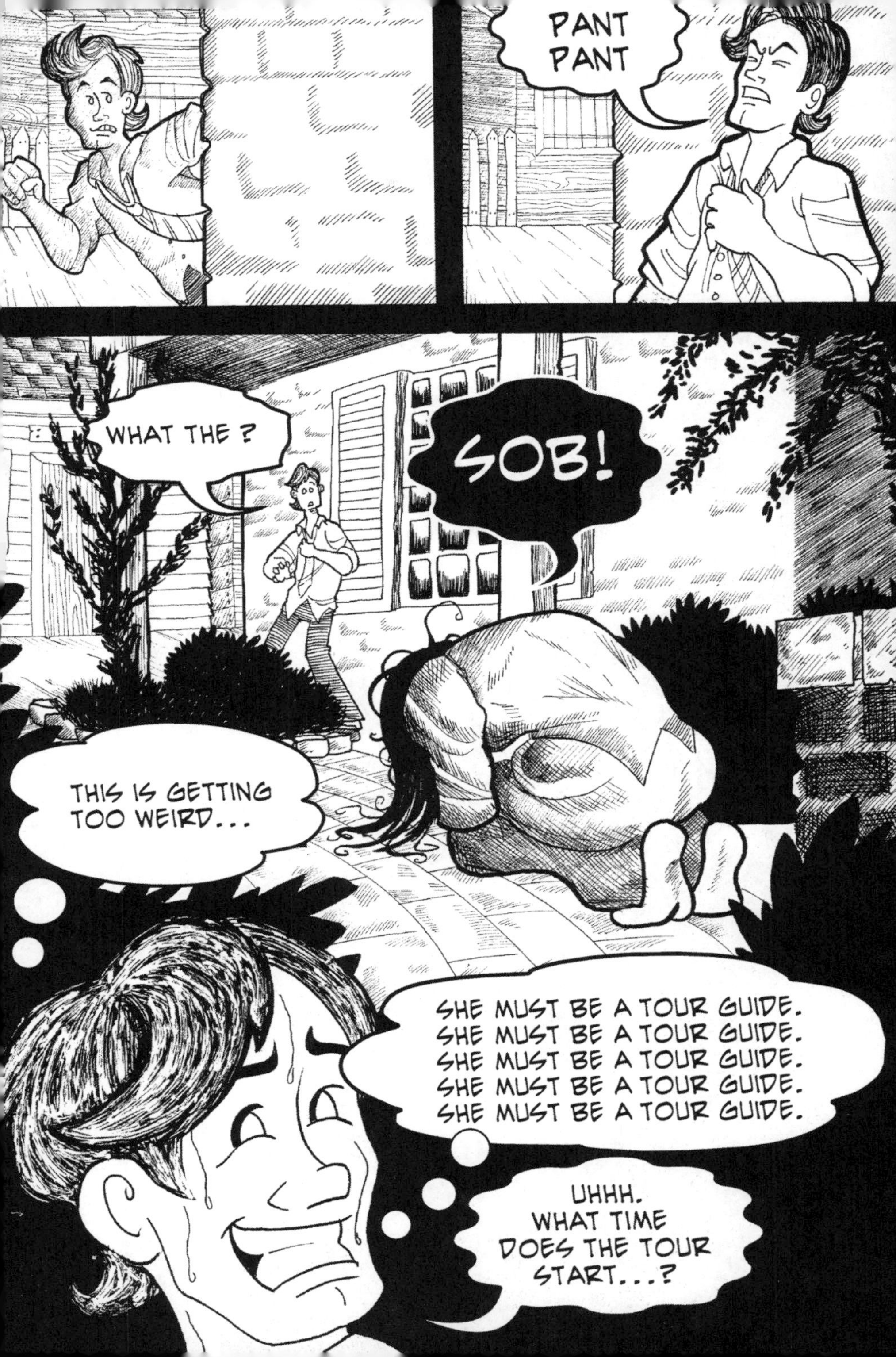
PANT PANT
WHAT THE ?
SOB!
THIS IS GETTING TOO WEIRD...
SHE MUST BE A TOUR GUIDE. SHE MUST BE A TOUR GUIDE. SHE MUST BE A TOUR GUIDE. SHE MUST BE A TOUR GUIDE. SHE MUST BE A TOUR GUIDE.
UHHH. WHAT TIME DOES THE TOUR START...?

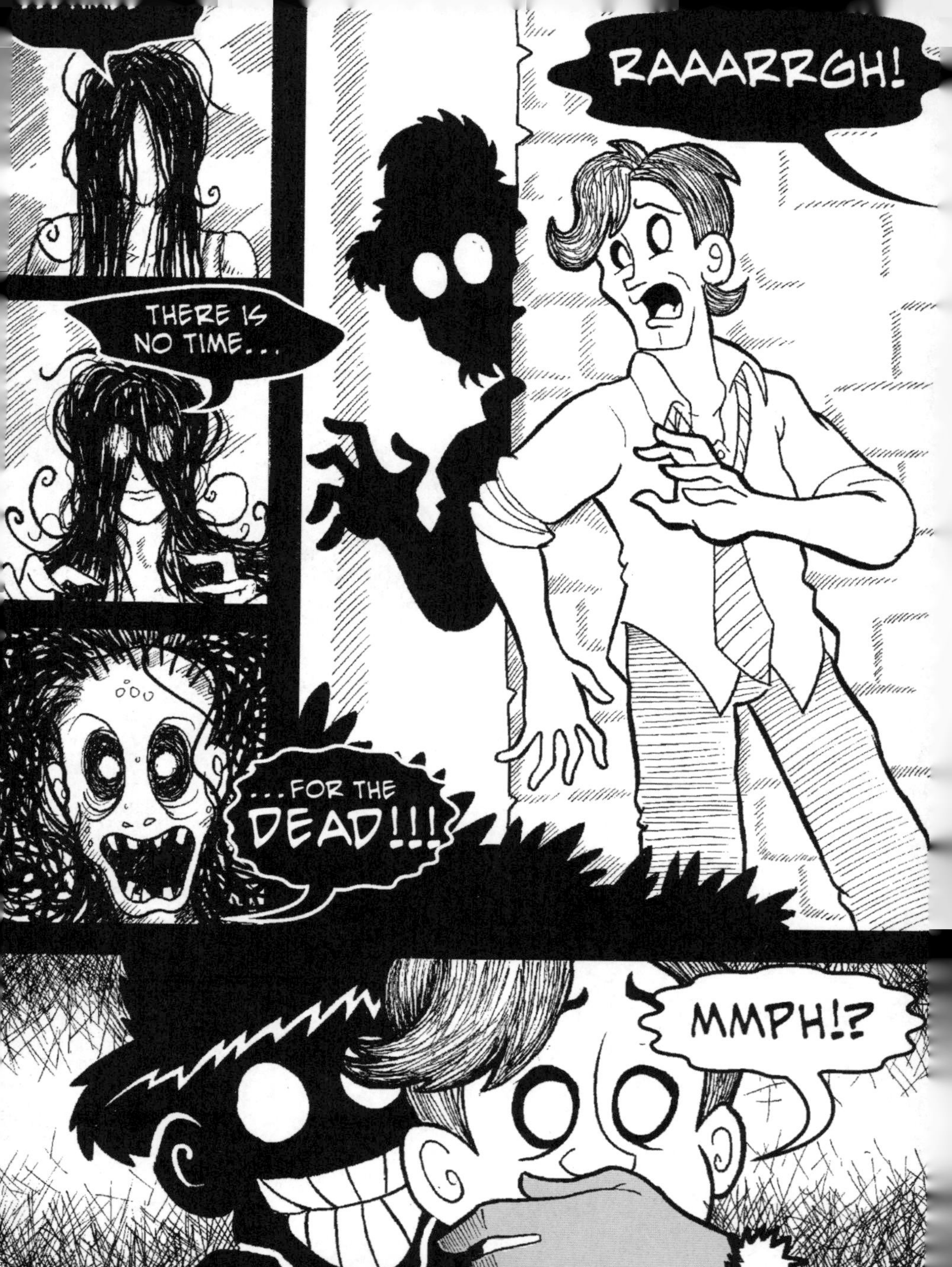
RAAARRGH!
THERE IS NO TIME...
...FOR THE DEAD!!!
MMPH!?

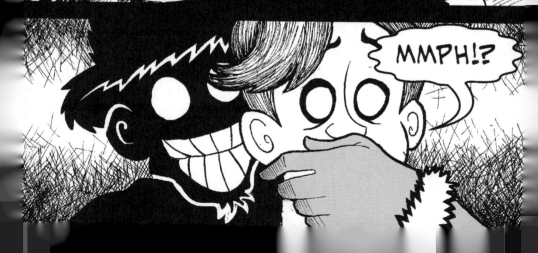

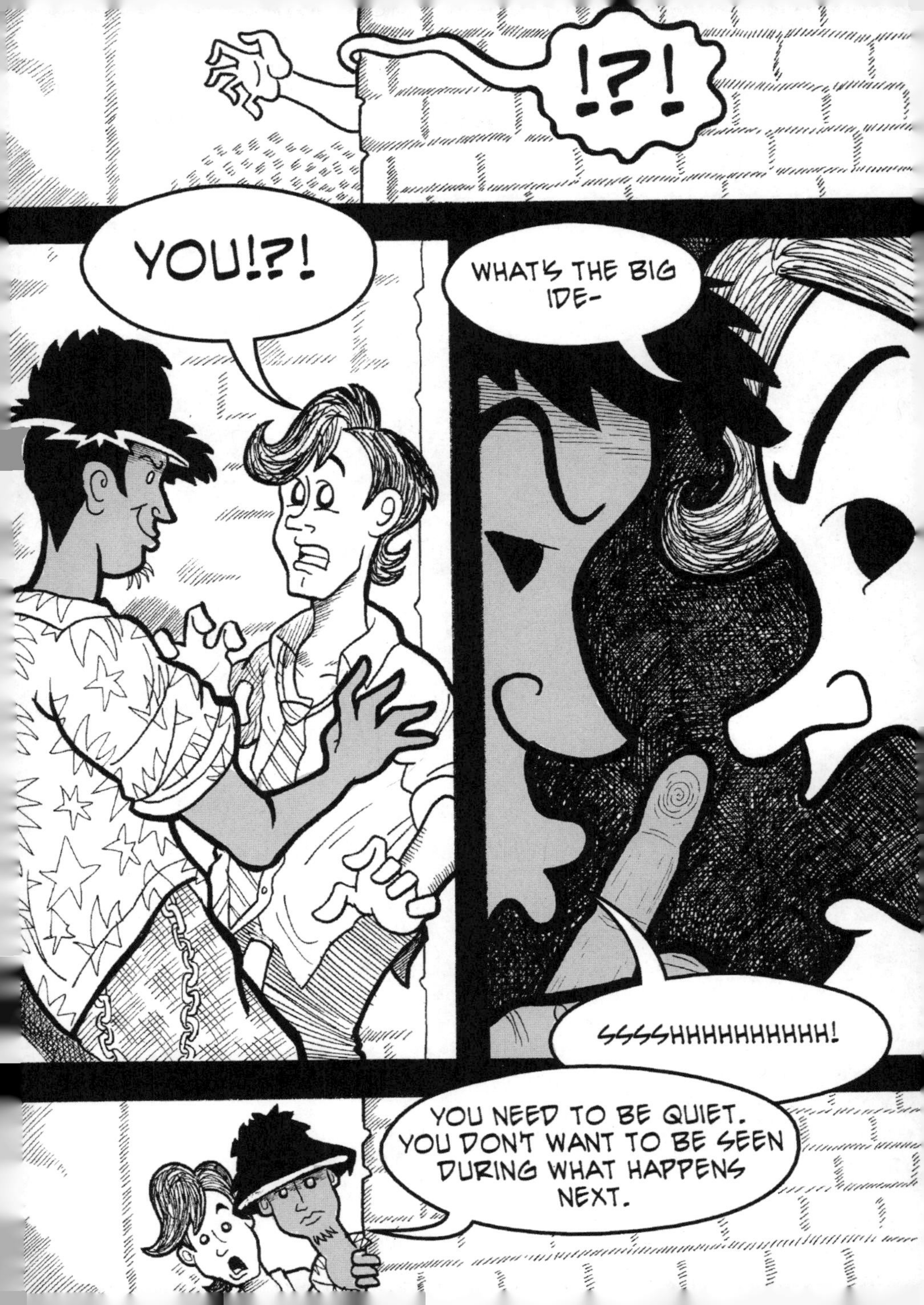
!?!
YOU!?!
WHAT'S THE BIG IDE-
SSSSHHHHHHHHHH!
YOU NEED TO BE QUIET. YOU DON'T WANT TO BE SEEN DURING WHAT HAPPENS NEXT.

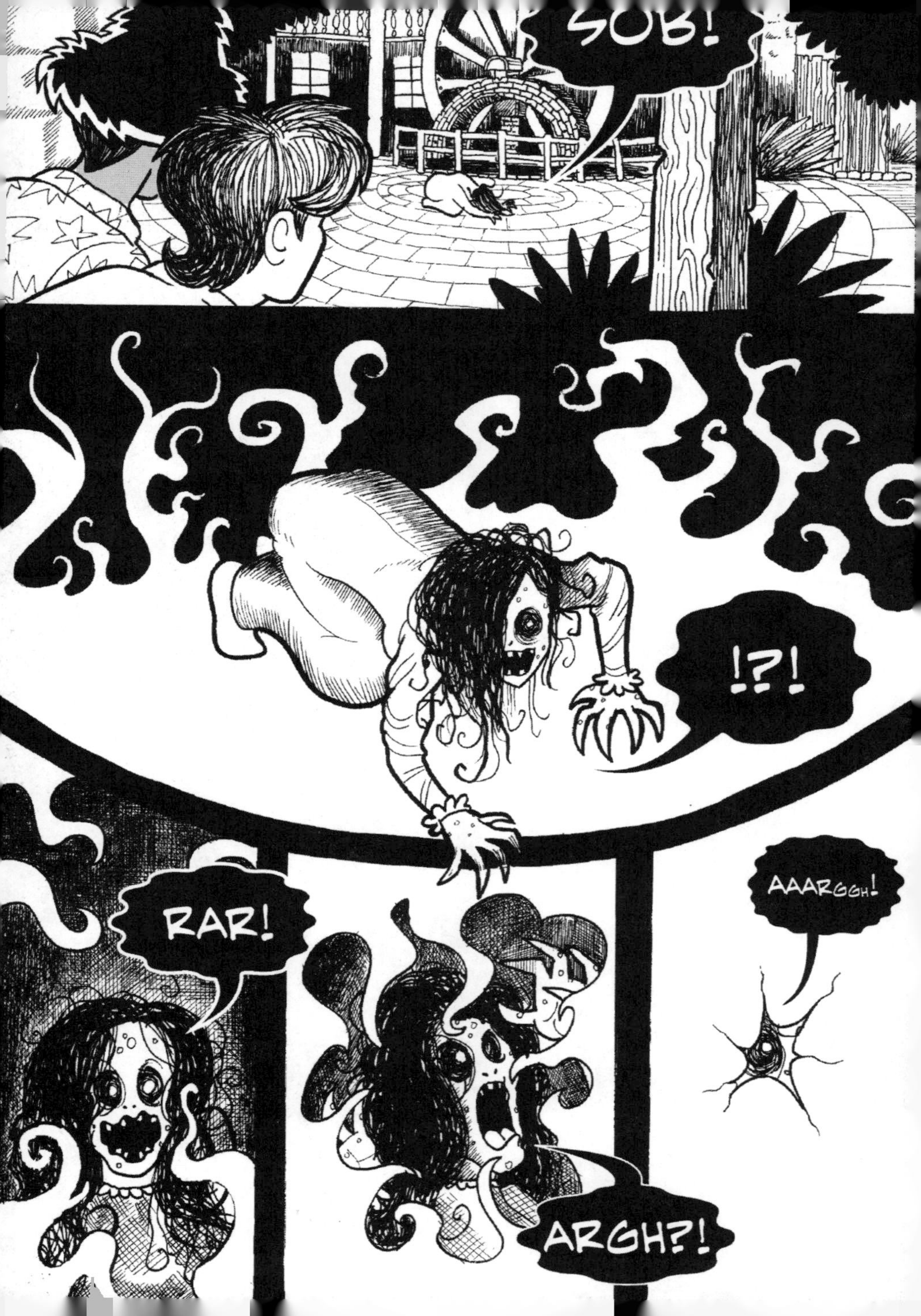
SOB!
!?!
RAR!
ARGH?!
AAARGGH!

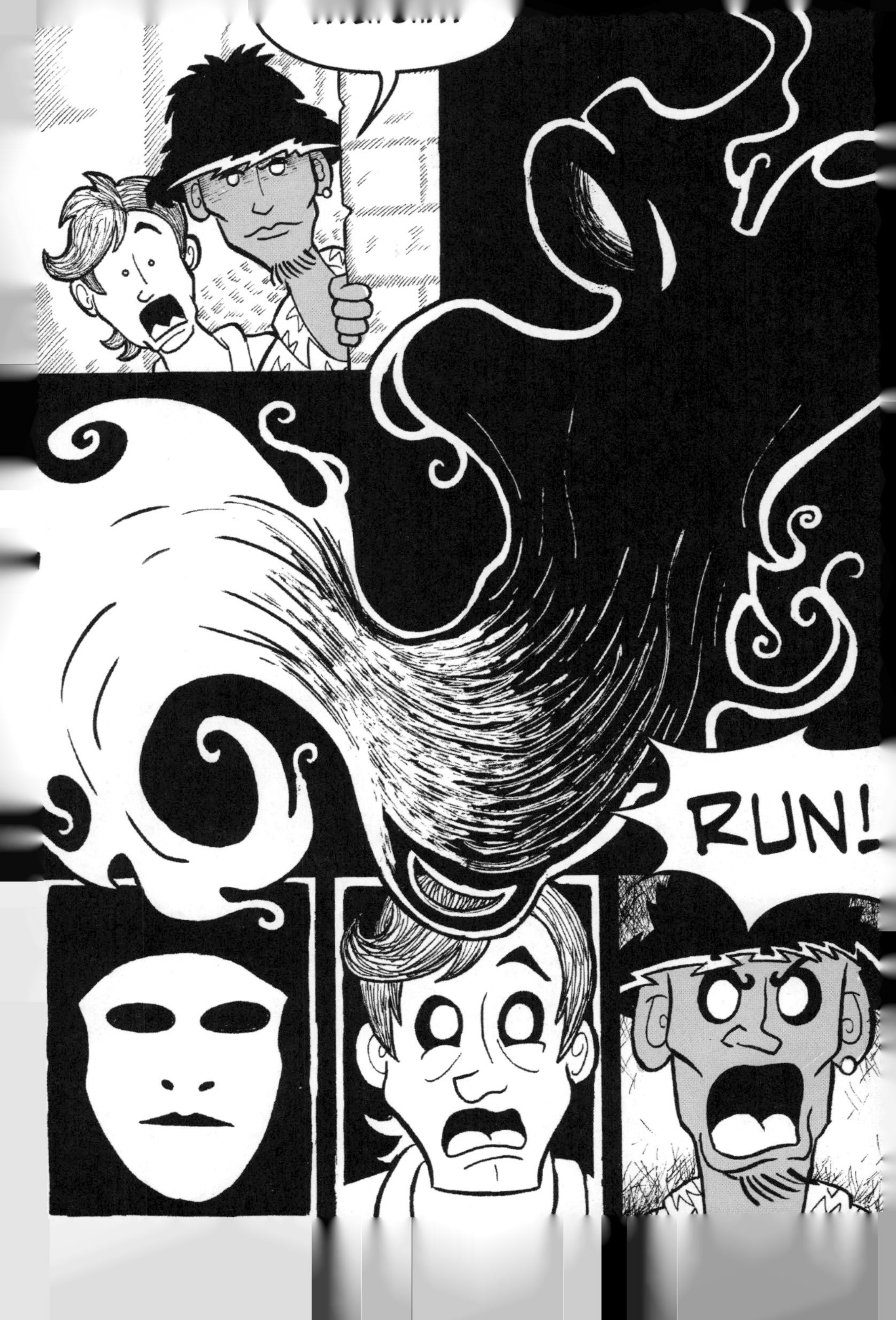
RUN!

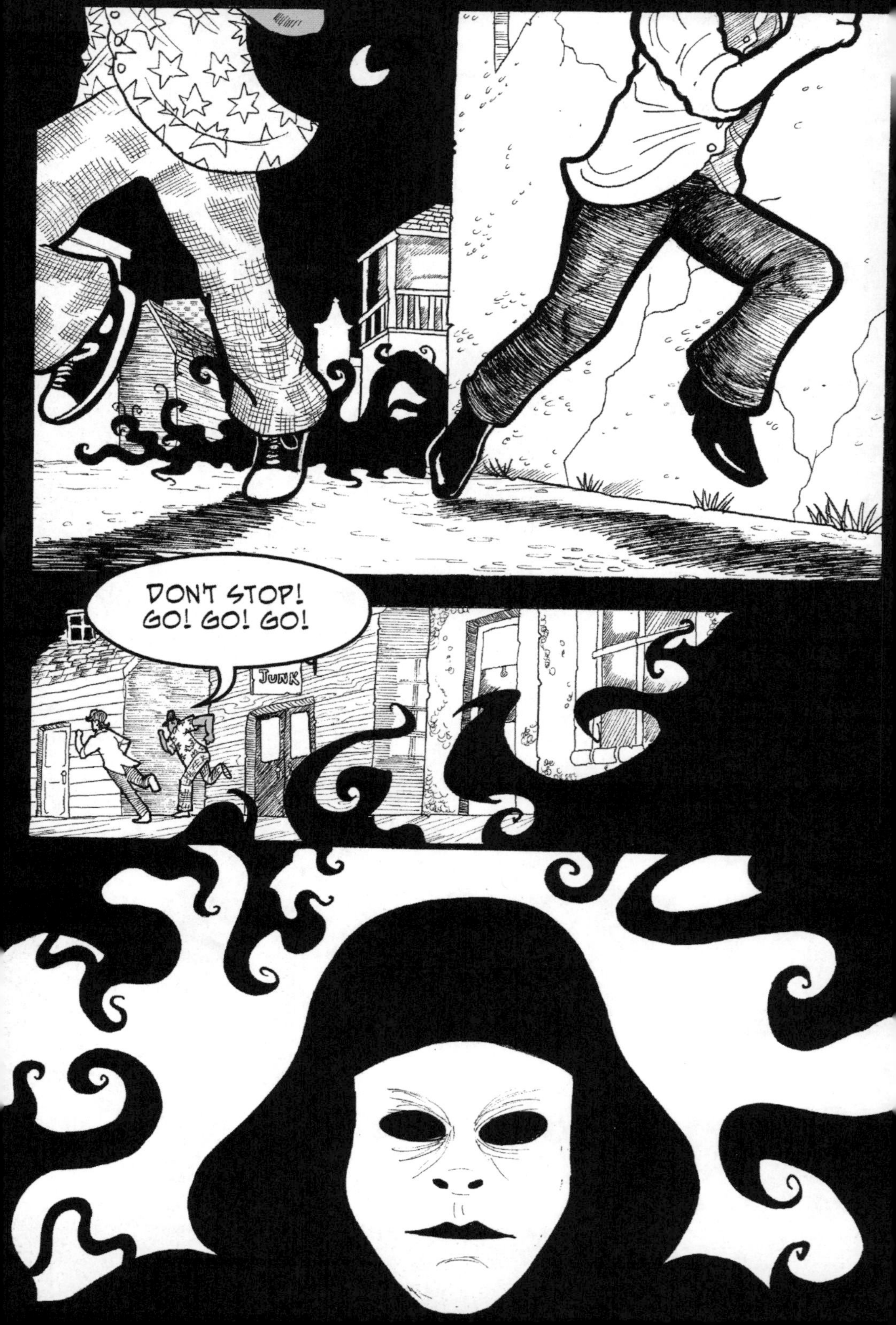
DON'T STOP! GO! GO! GO!
JUNK

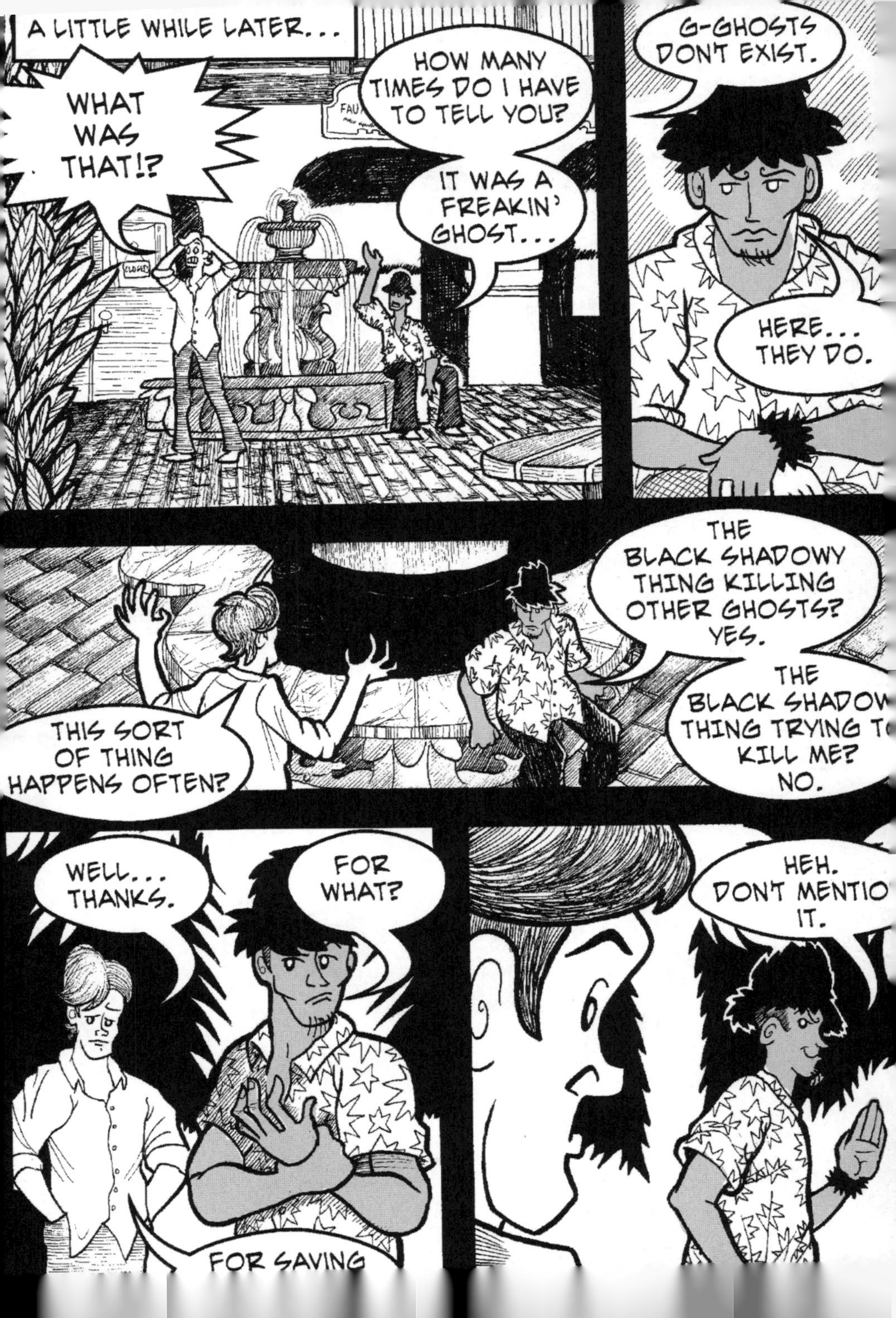
A LITTLE WHILE LATER...
WHAT WAS THAT!?
HOW MANY TIMES DO I HAVE TO TELL YOU?
IT WAS A FREAKIN' GHOST...
G-GHOSTS DON'T EXIST.
HERE... THEY DO.
THIS SORT OF THING HAPPENS OFTEN?
THE BLACK SHADOWY THING KILLING OTHER GHOSTS? YES.
THE BLACK SHADOW
THING TRYING T
KILL ME? NO.
WELL... THANKS.
FOR WHAT?
FOR SAVING
HEH. DON'T MENTIO
IT.

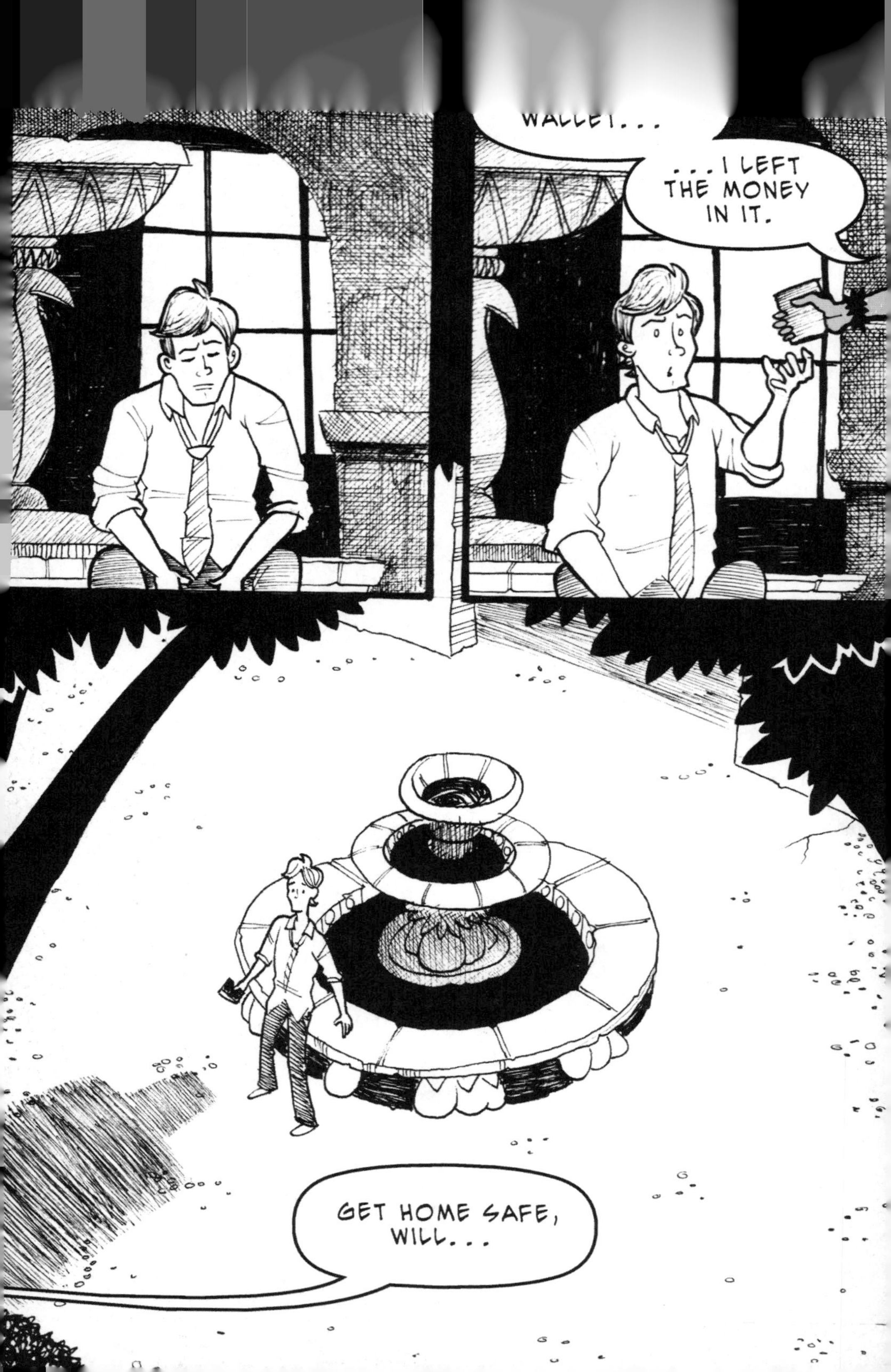
...I LEFT THE MONEY IN IT.
GET HOME SAFE, WILL...

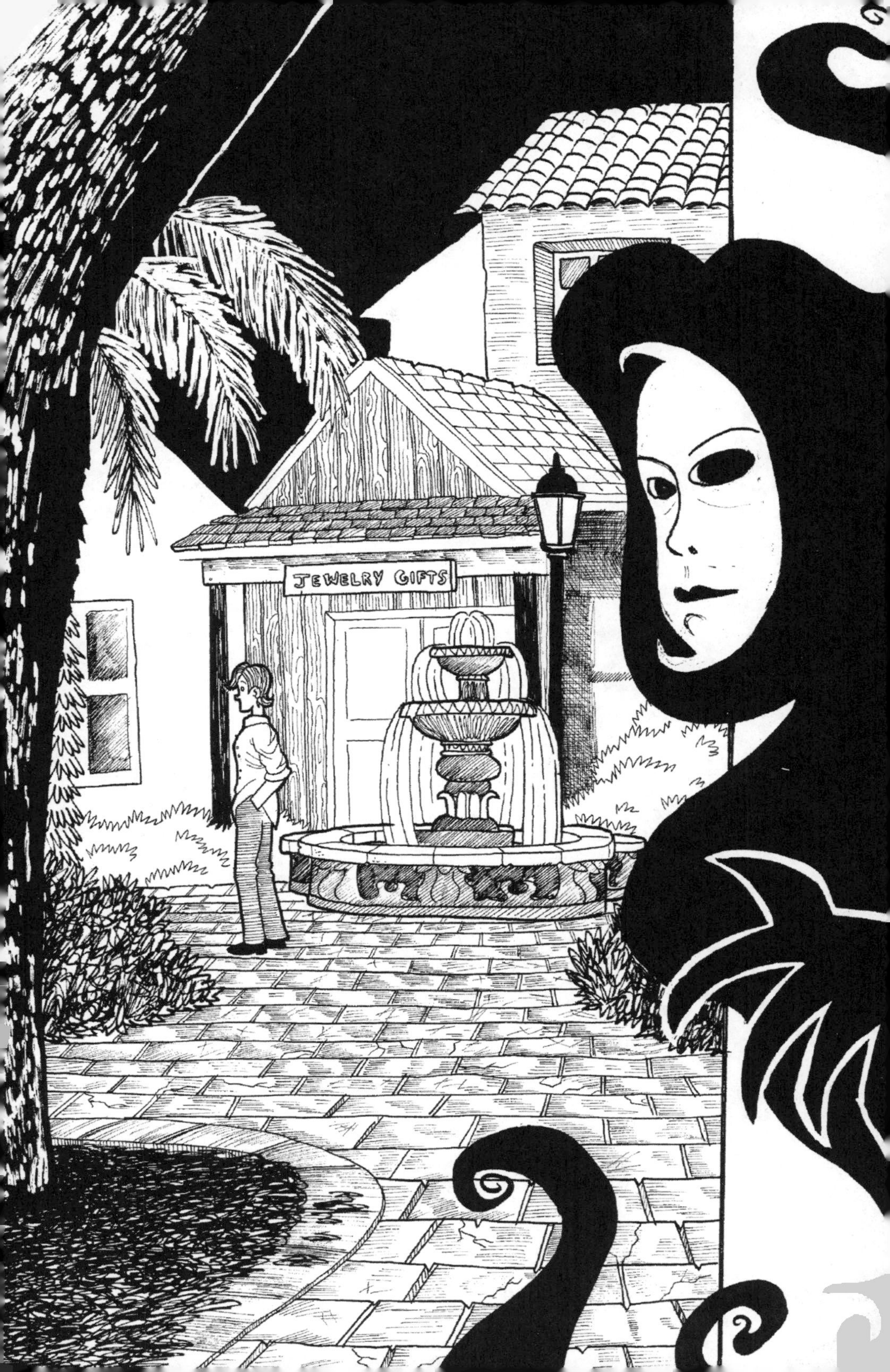
JEWELRY GIFTS

CHAPTER

6

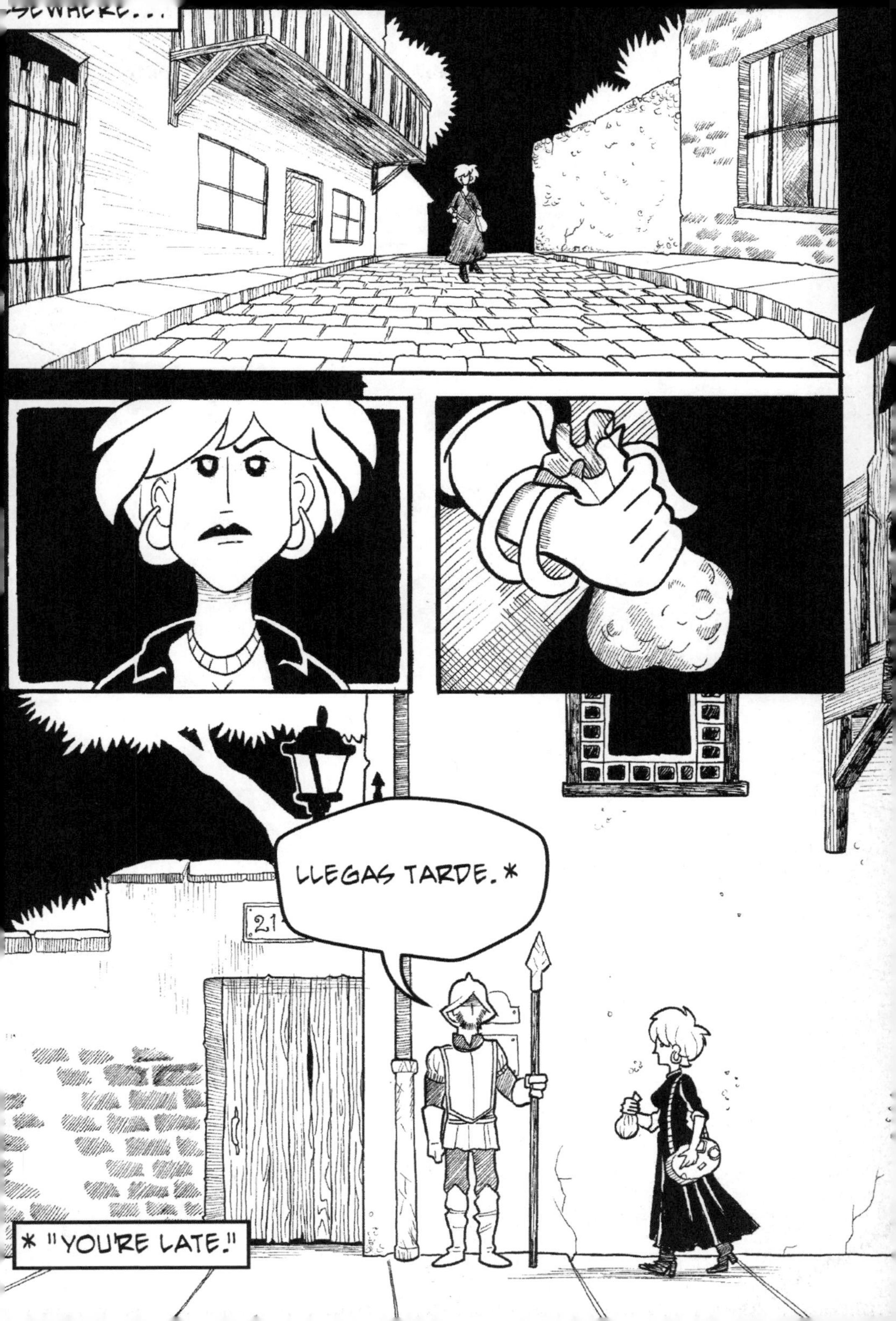
SEWHERE...
LLEGAS TARDE.*
21
* "YOU'RE LATE."

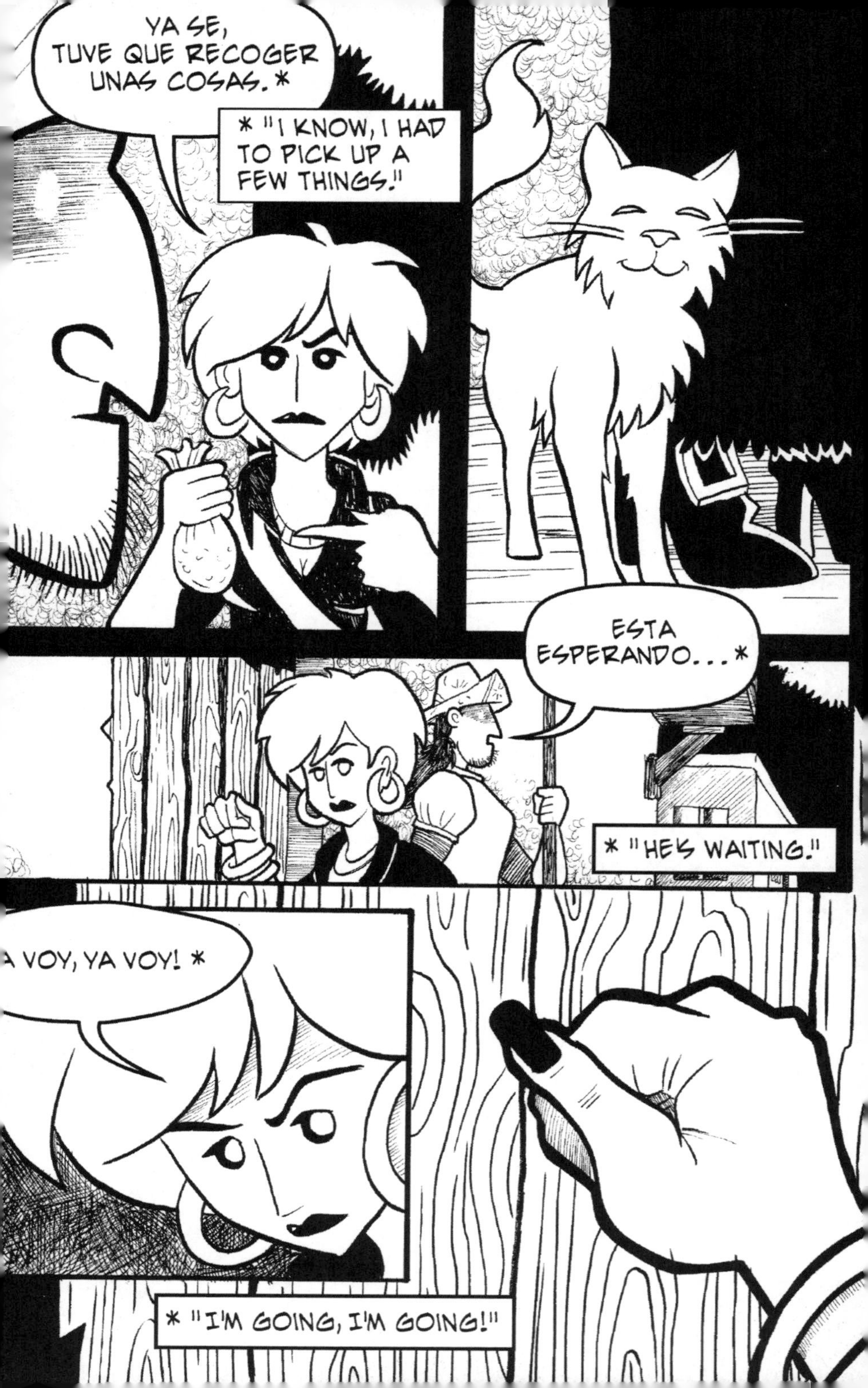
YA SE, TUVE QUE RECOGER UNAS COSAS. *
* "I KNOW, I HAD TO PICK UP A FEW THINGS."
ESTA ESPERANDO... *
* "HE'S WAITING."
A VOY, YA VOY! *
* "I'M GOING, I'M GOING!"

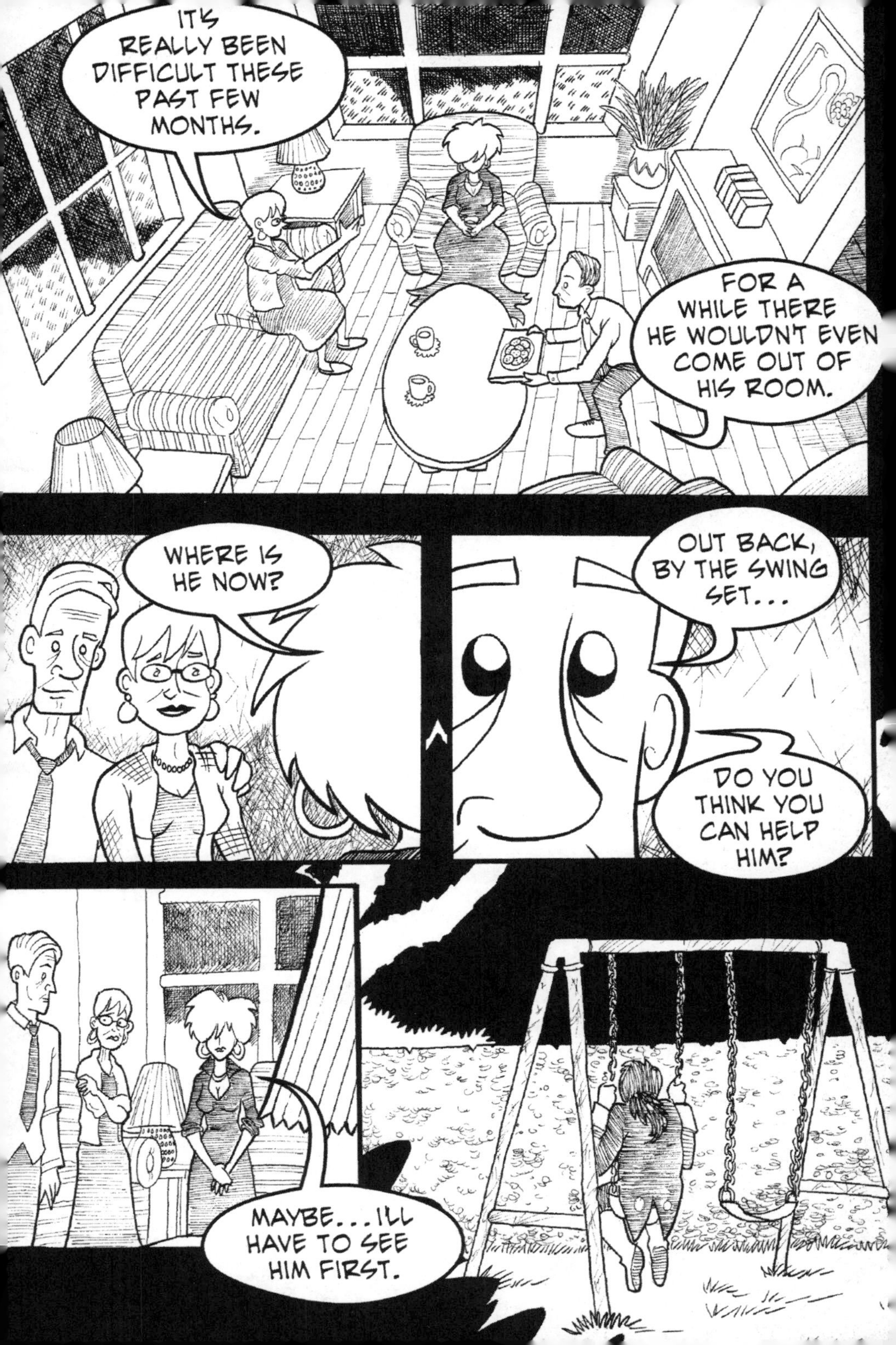
IT'S REALLY BEEN DIFFICULT THESE PAST FEW MONTHS.
FOR A WHILE THERE HE WOULDN'T EVEN COME OUT OF HIS ROOM.
WHERE IS HE NOW?
OUT BACK, BY THE SWING SET...
DO YOU THINK YOU CAN HELP HIM?
MAYBE...I'LL HAVE TO SEE HIM FIRST.

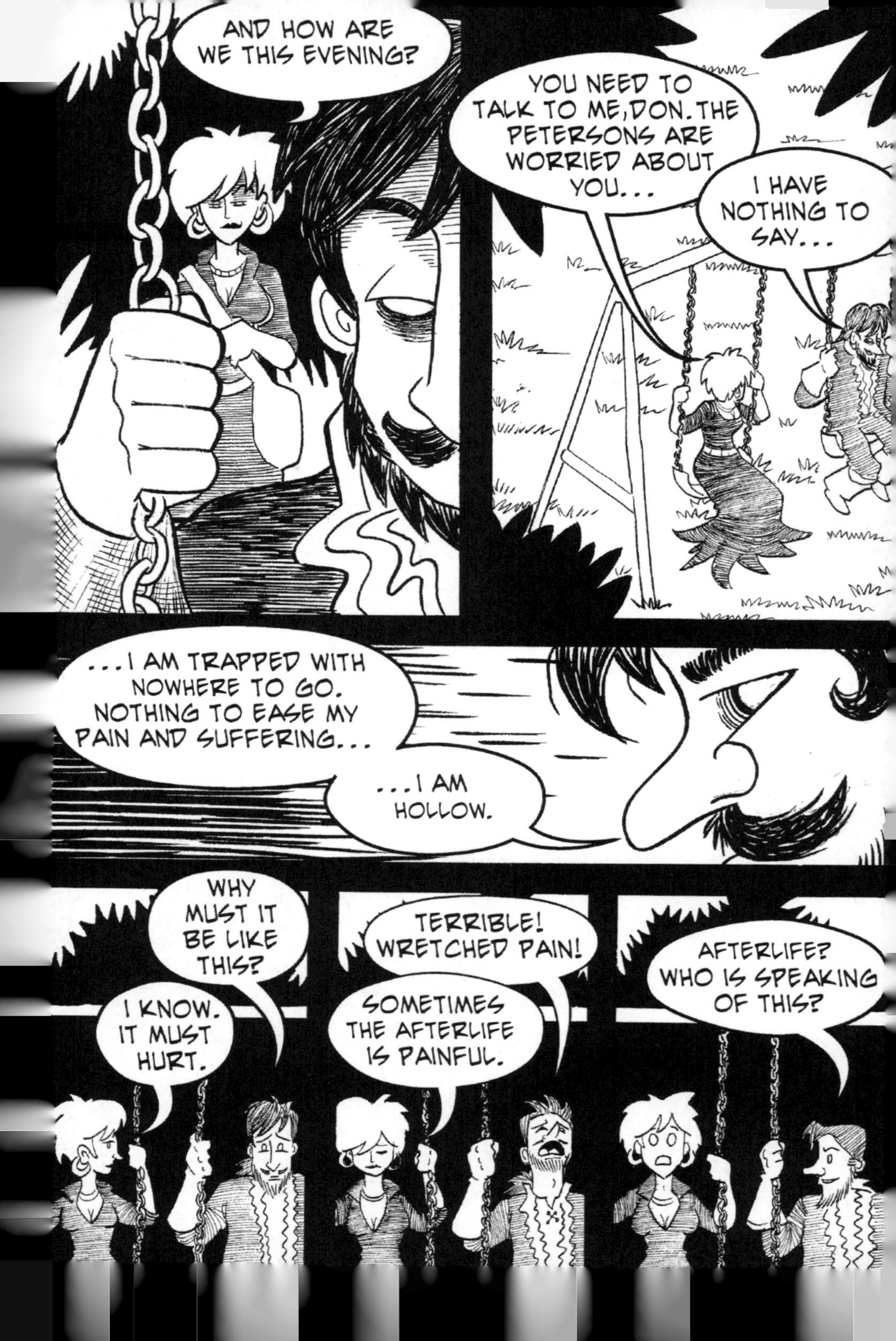
AND HOW ARE WE THIS EVENING?
YOU NEED TO TALK TO ME, DON. THE PETERSONS ARE WORRIED ABOUT YOU...
I HAVE NOTHING TO SAY...
...I AM TRAPPED WITH NOWHERE TO GO. NOTHING TO EASE MY PAIN AND SUFFERING...
...I AM HOLLOW.
I KNOW. IT MUST HURT.
WHY MUST IT BE LIKE THIS?
SOMETIMES THE AFTERLIFE IS PAINFUL.
TERRIBLE! WRETCHED PAIN!
AFTERLIFE? WHO IS SPEAKING OF THIS?

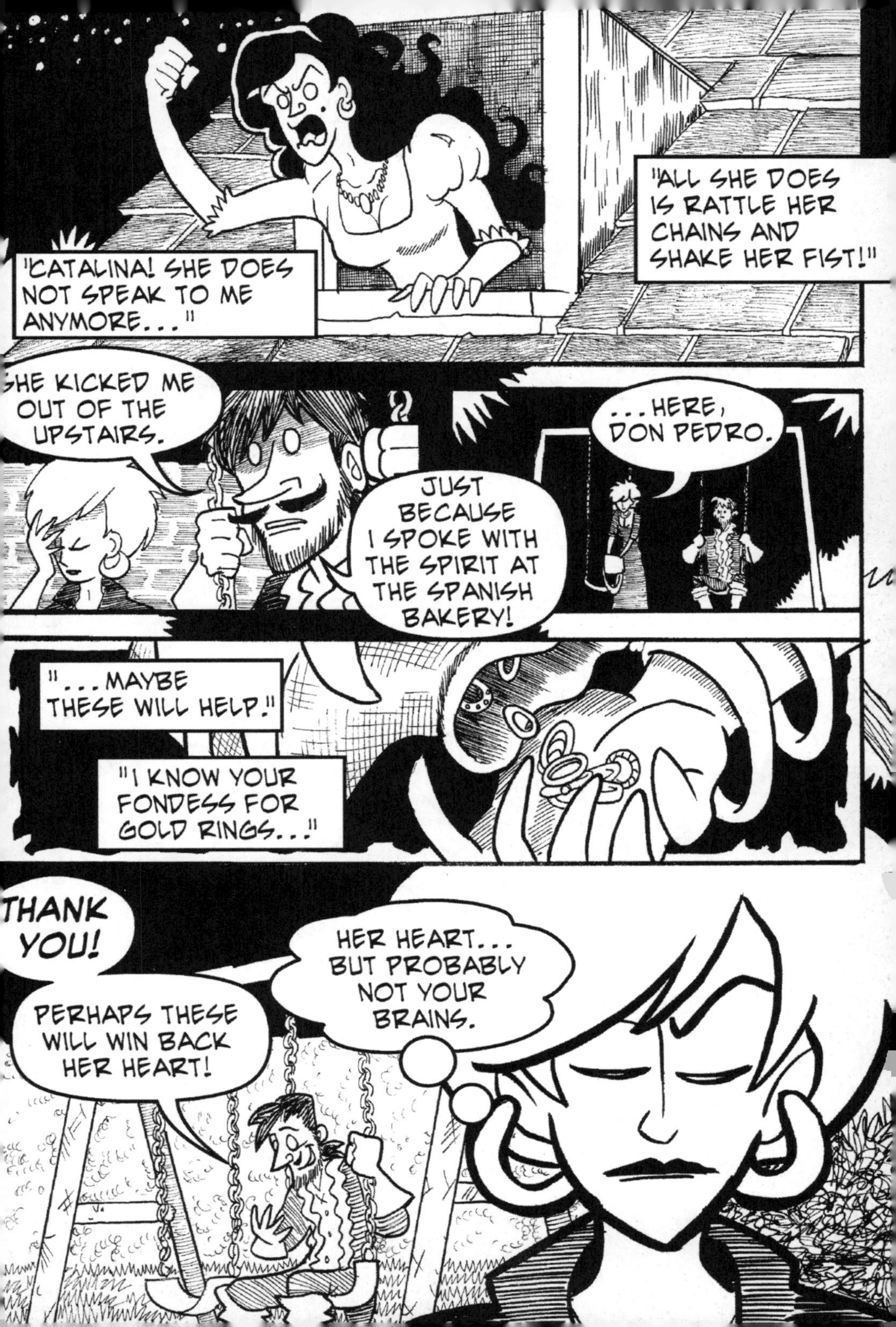
"CATALINA! SHE DOES NOT SPEAK TO ME ANYMORE..."
"ALL SHE DOES IS RATTLE HER CHAINS AND SHAKE HER FIST!"
SHE KICKED ME OUT OF THE UPSTAIRS.
JUST BECAUSE I SPOKE WITH THE SPIRIT AT THE SPANISH BAKERY!
...HERE, DON PEDRO.
"...MAYBE THESE WILL HELP."
"I KNOW YOUR FONDESS FOR GOLD RINGS..."
THANK YOU!
PERHAPS THESE WILL WIN BACK HER HEART!
HER HEART... BUT PROBABLY NOT YOUR BRAINS.

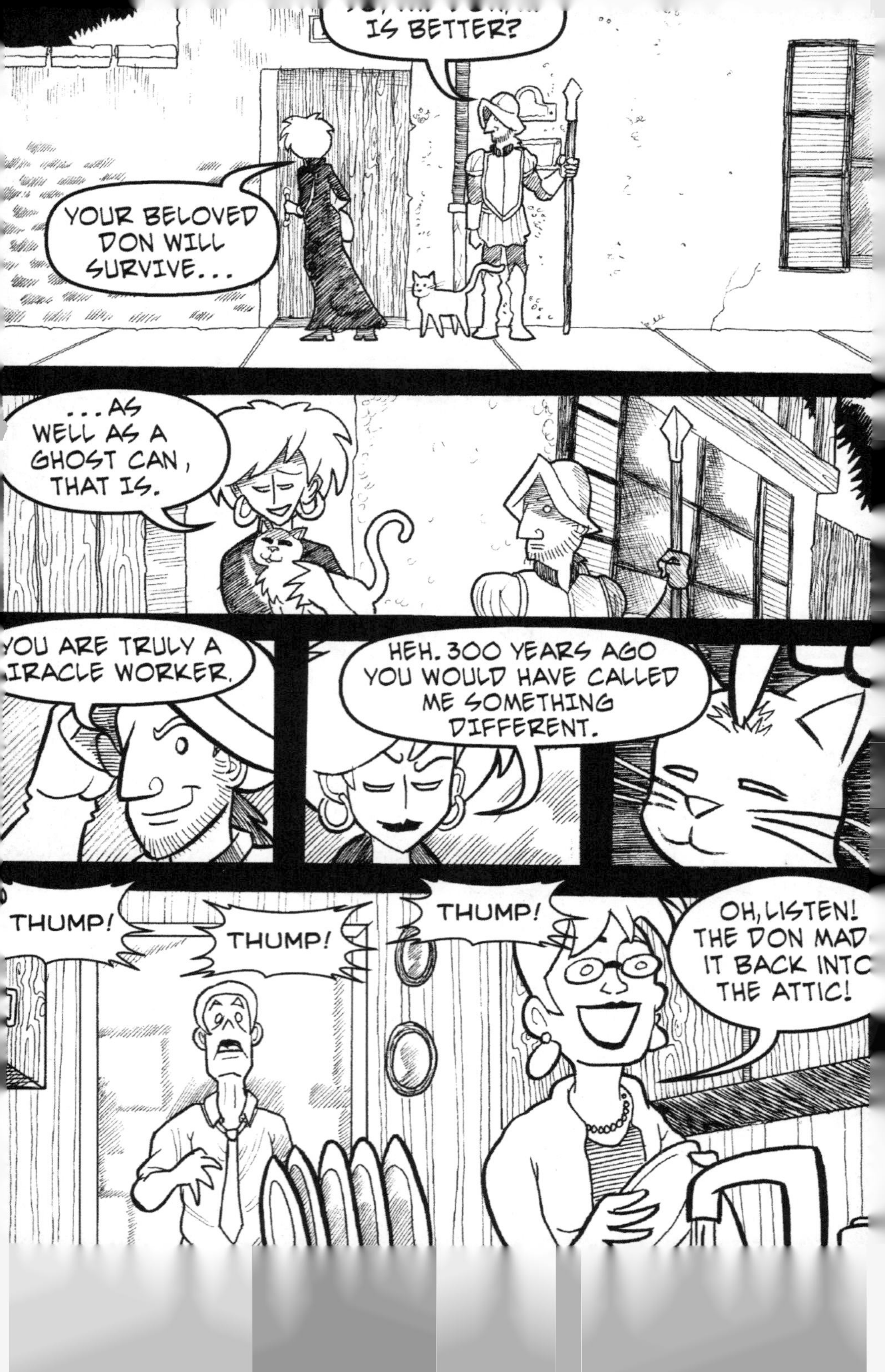

IS BETTER?
YOUR BELOVED DON WILL SURVIVE...
...AS WELL AS A GHOST CAN, THAT IS.
YOU ARE TRULY A IRACLE WORKER.
HEH. 300 YEARS AGO YOU WOULD HAVE CALLED ME SOMETHING DIFFERENT.
THUMP!
THUMP!
THUMP!
OH, LISTEN! THE DON MAD IT BACK INTO THE ATTIC!

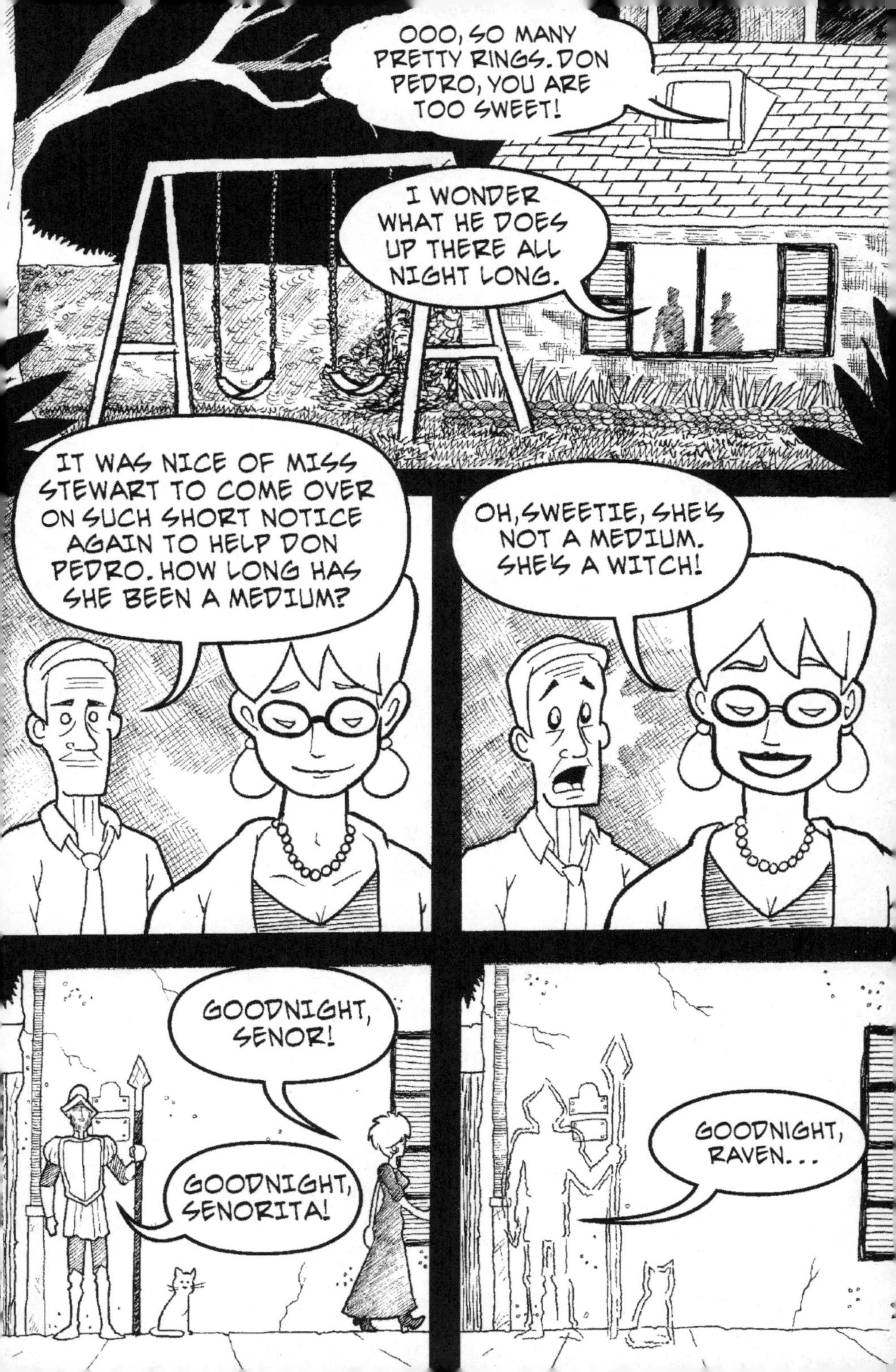
OOO, SO MANY PRETTY RINGS. DON PEDRO, YOU ARE TOO SWEET!
I WONDER WHAT HE DOES UP THERE ALL NIGHT LONG.
IT WAS NICE OF MISS STEWART TO COME OVER ON SUCH SHORT NOTICE AGAIN TO HELP DON PEDRO. HOW LONG HAS SHE BEEN A MEDIUM?
OH, SWEETIE, SHE'S NOT A MEDIUM. SHE'S A WITCH!
GOODNIGHT, SENOR!
GOODNIGHT, SENORITA!
GOODNIGHT, RAVEN...

CHAPTER
7

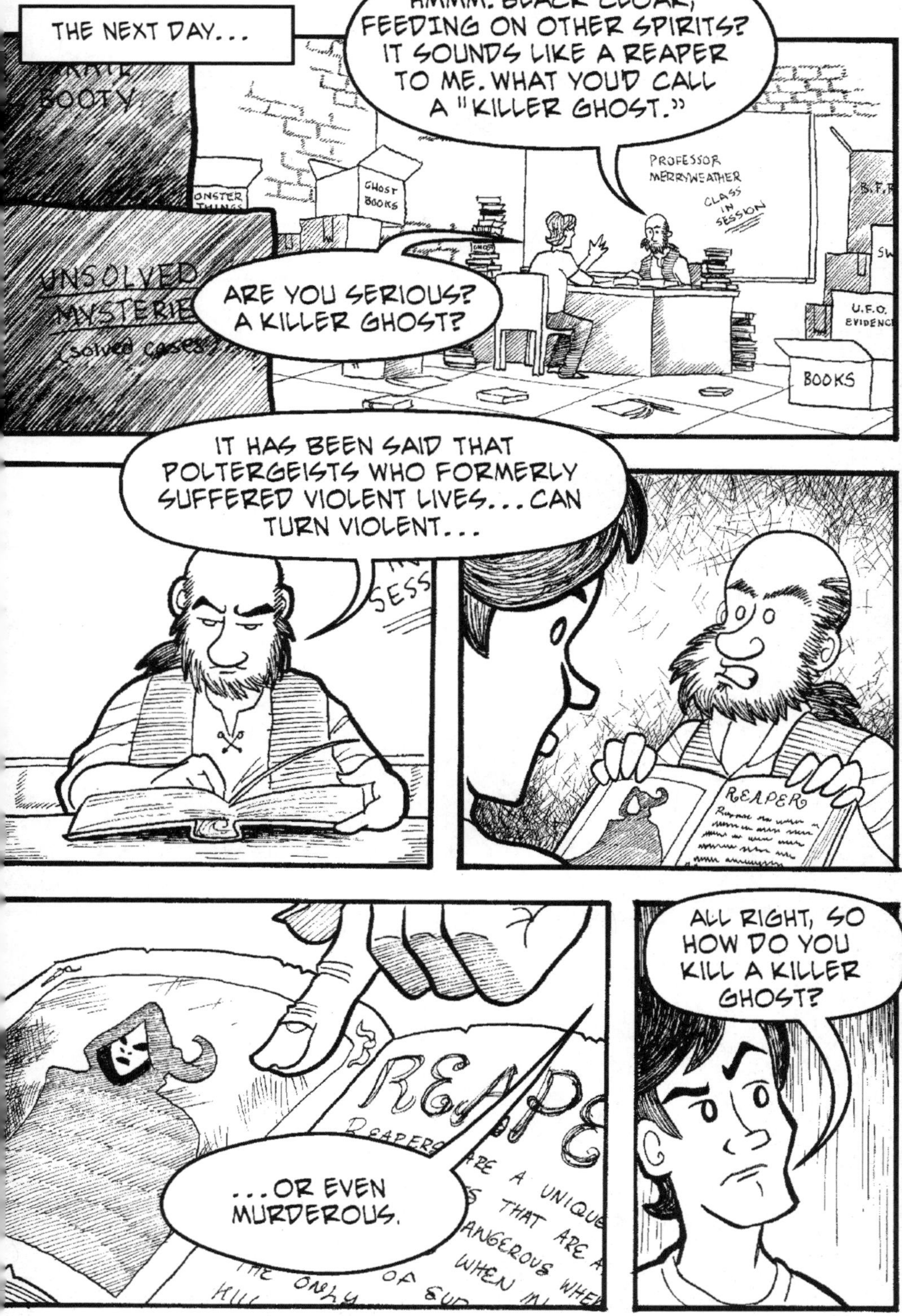
THE NEXT DAY...
PIRATE BOOTY
MONSTER THINGS
GHOST BOOKS
UNSOLVED MYSTERIES (solved cases)
HMMM. BLACK CLOAK, FEEDING ON OTHER SPIRITS? IT SOUNDS LIKE A REAPER TO ME. WHAT YOU'D CALL A "KILLER GHOST."
PROFESSOR MERRYWEATHER
CLASS IN SESSION
U.F.O. EVIDENCE
BOOKS
ARE YOU SERIOUS? A KILLER GHOST?
IT HAS BEEN SAID THAT POLTERGEISTS WHO FORMERLY SUFFERED VIOLENT LIVES... CAN TURN VIOLENT...
REAPER
...OR EVEN MURDEROUS.
ALL RIGHT, SO HOW DO YOU KILL A KILLER GHOST?

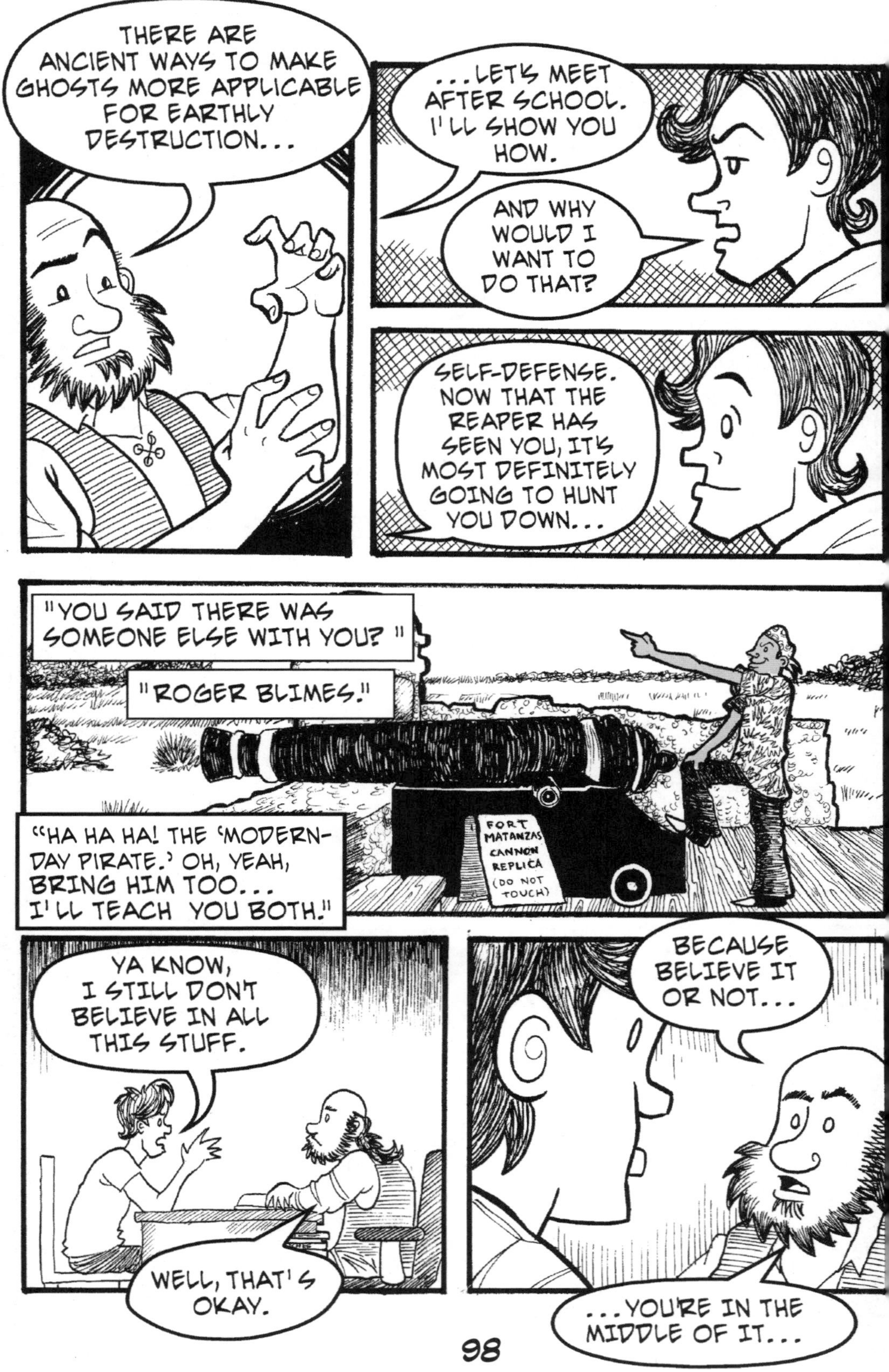

THERE ARE ANCIENT WAYS TO MAKE GHOSTS MORE APPLICABLE FOR EARTHLY DESTRUCTION...
...LET'S MEET AFTER SCHOOL. I'LL SHOW YOU HOW.
AND WHY WOULD I WANT TO DO THAT?
SELF-DEFENSE. NOW THAT THE REAPER HAS SEEN YOU, IT'S MOST DEFINITELY GOING TO HUNT YOU DOWN...
"YOU SAID THERE WAS SOMEONE ELSE WITH YOU?"
"ROGER BLIMES."
"HA HA HA! THE 'MODERN-DAY PIRATE.' OH, YEAH, BRING HIM TOO... I'LL TEACH YOU BOTH."
FORT MATANZAS CANNON REPLICA (DO NOT TOUCH)
YA KNOW, I STILL DON'T BELIEVE IN ALL THIS STUFF.
WELL, THAT'S OKAY.
BECAUSE BELIEVE IT OR NOT...
...YOU'RE IN THE MIDDLE OF IT...

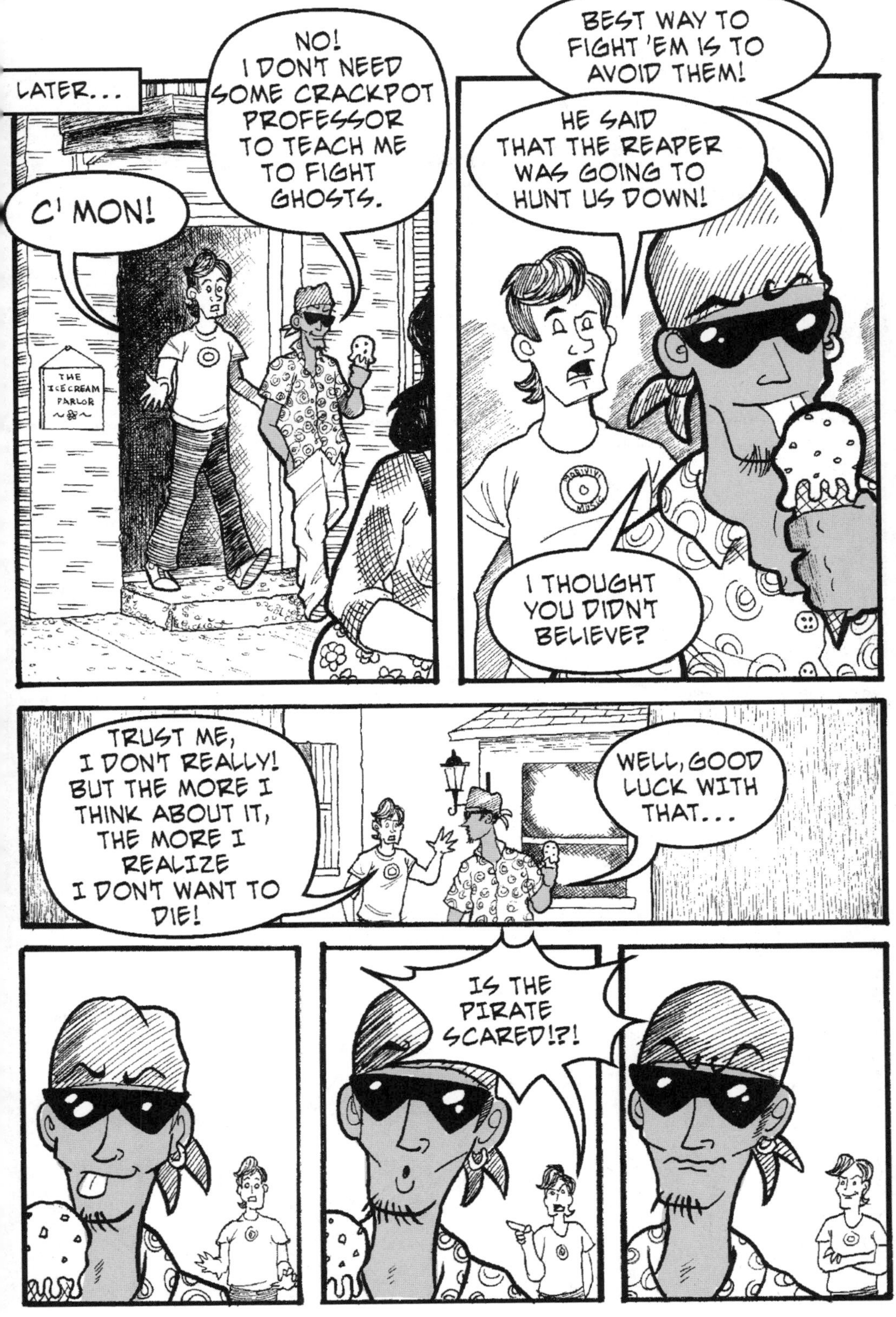
LATER...
C' MON!
NO! I DON'T NEED SOME CRACKPOT PROFESSOR TO TEACH ME TO FIGHT GHOSTS.
THE ICE CREAM PARLOR
BEST WAY TO FIGHT 'EM IS TO AVOID THEM!
HE SAID THAT THE REAPER WAS GOING TO HUNT US DOWN!
I THOUGHT YOU DIDN'T BELIEVE?
TRUST ME, I DON'T REALLY! BUT THE MORE I THINK ABOUT IT, THE MORE I REALIZE I DON'T WANT TO DIE!
WELL, GOOD LUCK WITH THAT...
IS THE PIRATE SCARED!?!

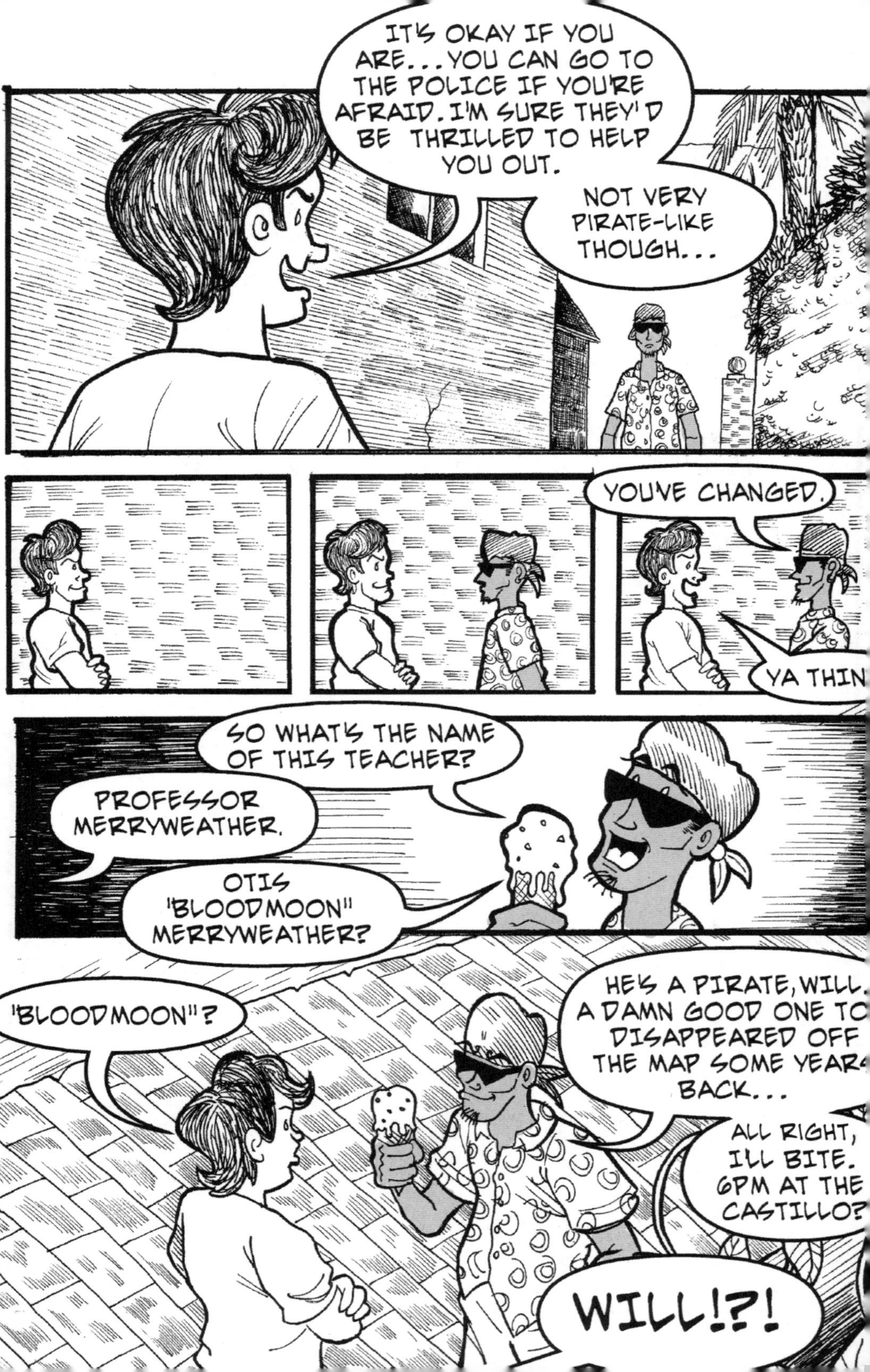
IT'S OKAY IF YOU ARE...YOU CAN GO TO THE POLICE IF YOU'RE AFRAID. I'M SURE THEY'D BE THRILLED TO HELP YOU OUT.
NOT VERY PIRATE-LIKE THOUGH...
YOU'VE CHANGED.
YA THIN
SO WHAT'S THE NAME OF THIS TEACHER?
PROFESSOR MERRYWEATHER.
OTIS "BLOODMOON" MERRYWEATHER?
"BLOODMOON"?
HE'S A PIRATE, WILL. A DAMN GOOD ONE TO DISAPPEARED OFF THE MAP SOME YEAR BACK...
ALL RIGHT, I'LL BITE. 6PM AT THE CASTILLO?
WILL!?!

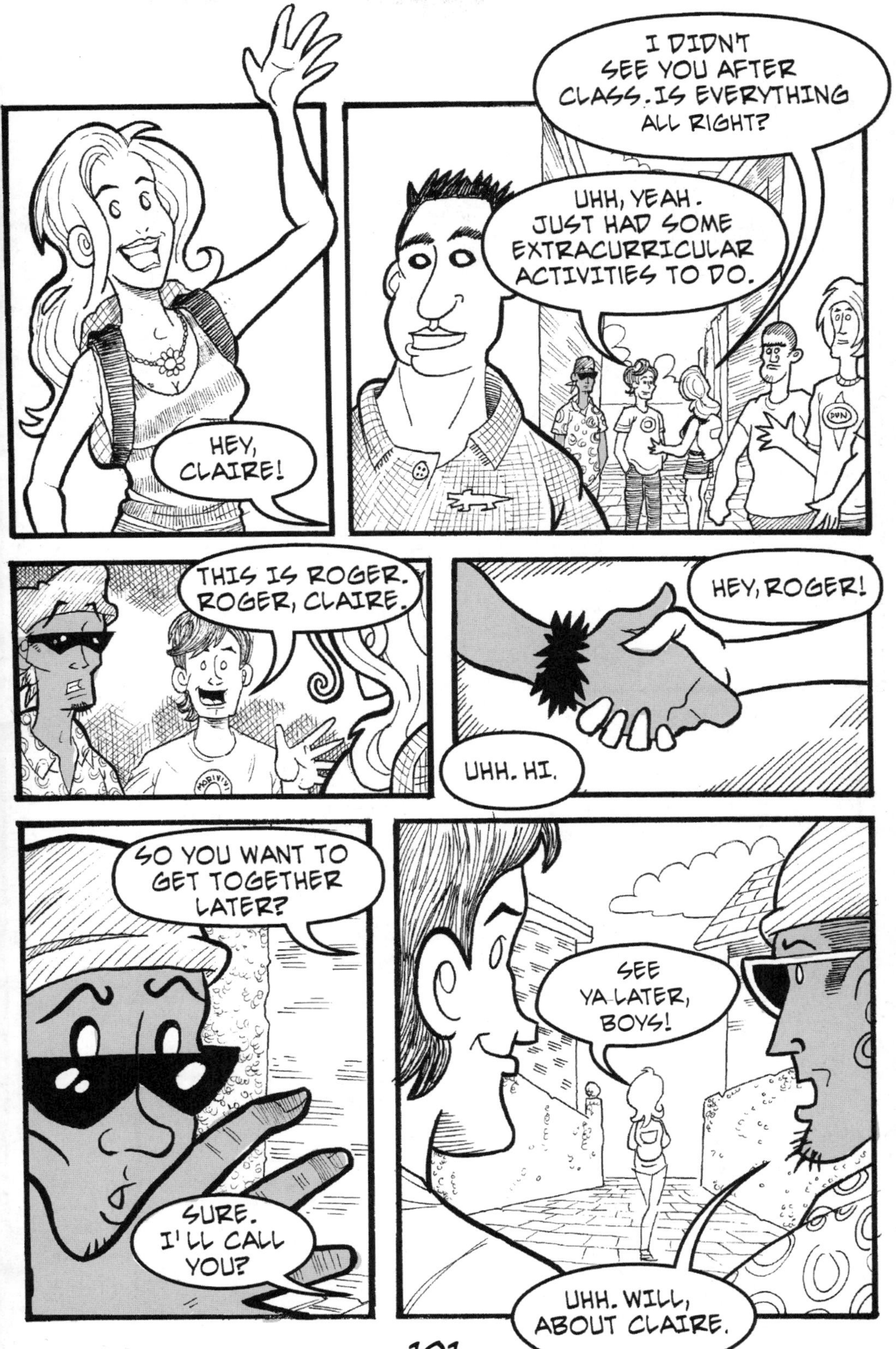
HEY, CLAIRE!
I DIDN'T SEE YOU AFTER CLASS. IS EVERYTHING ALL RIGHT?
UHH, YEAH. JUST HAD SOME EXTRACURRICULAR ACTIVITIES TO DO.
THIS IS ROGER. ROGER, CLAIRE.
HEY, ROGER!
UHH. HI.
SO YOU WANT TO GET TOGETHER LATER?
SURE. I'LL CALL YOU?
SEE YA LATER, BOYS!
UHH. WILL, ABOUT CLAIRE.

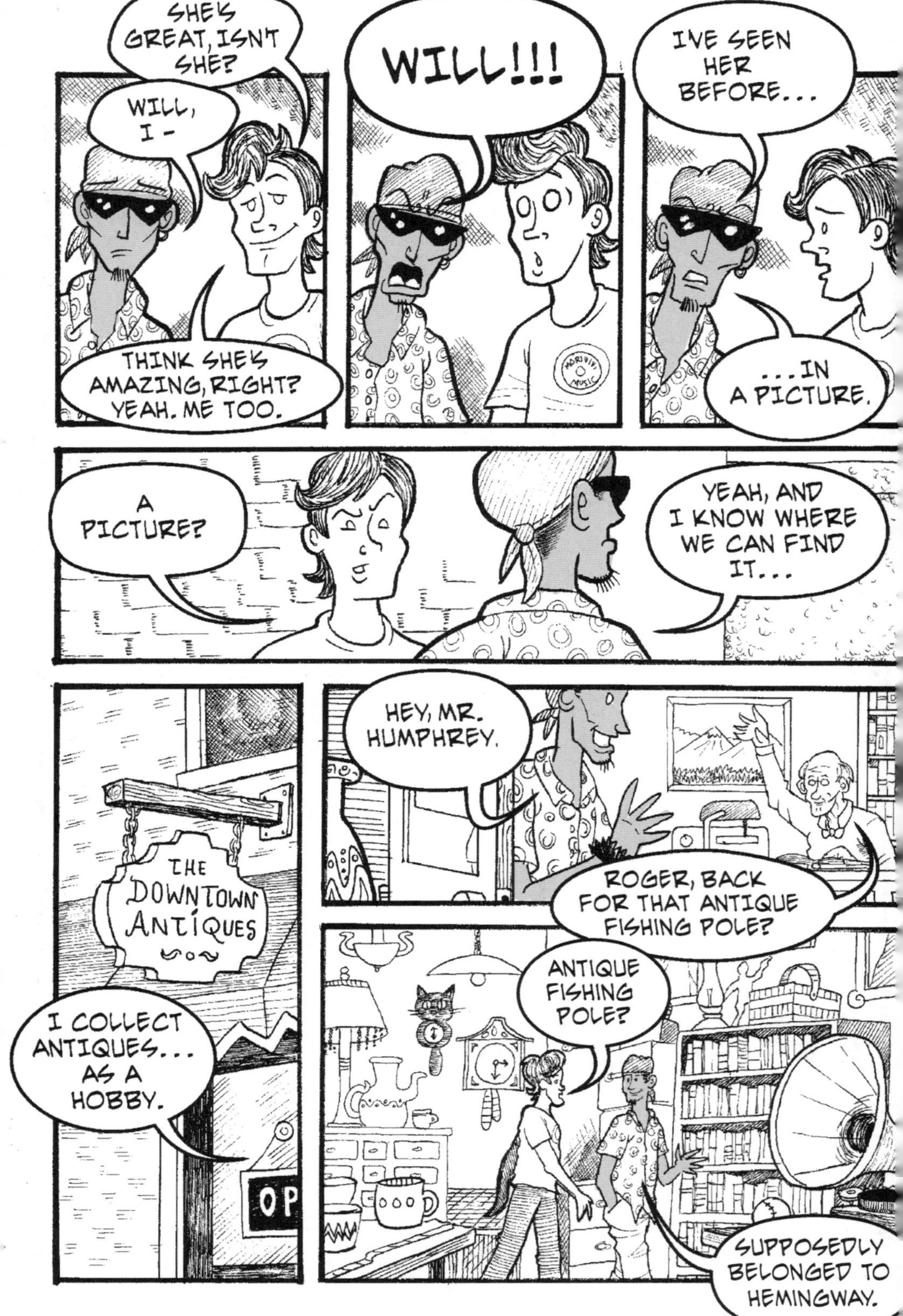
SHE'S GREAT, ISN'T SHE?
WILL, I -
THINK SHE'S AMAZING, RIGHT? YEAH. ME TOO.
WILL!!!
I'VE SEEN HER BEFORE...
...IN A PICTURE.
A PICTURE?
YEAH, AND I KNOW WHERE WE CAN FIND IT...
THE DOWNTOWN ANTIQUES
I COLLECT ANTIQUES... AS A HOBBY.
HEY, MR. HUMPHREY.
ROGER, BACK FOR THAT ANTIQUE FISHING POLE?
ANTIQUE FISHING POLE?
SUPPOSEDLY BELONGED TO HEMINGWAY.

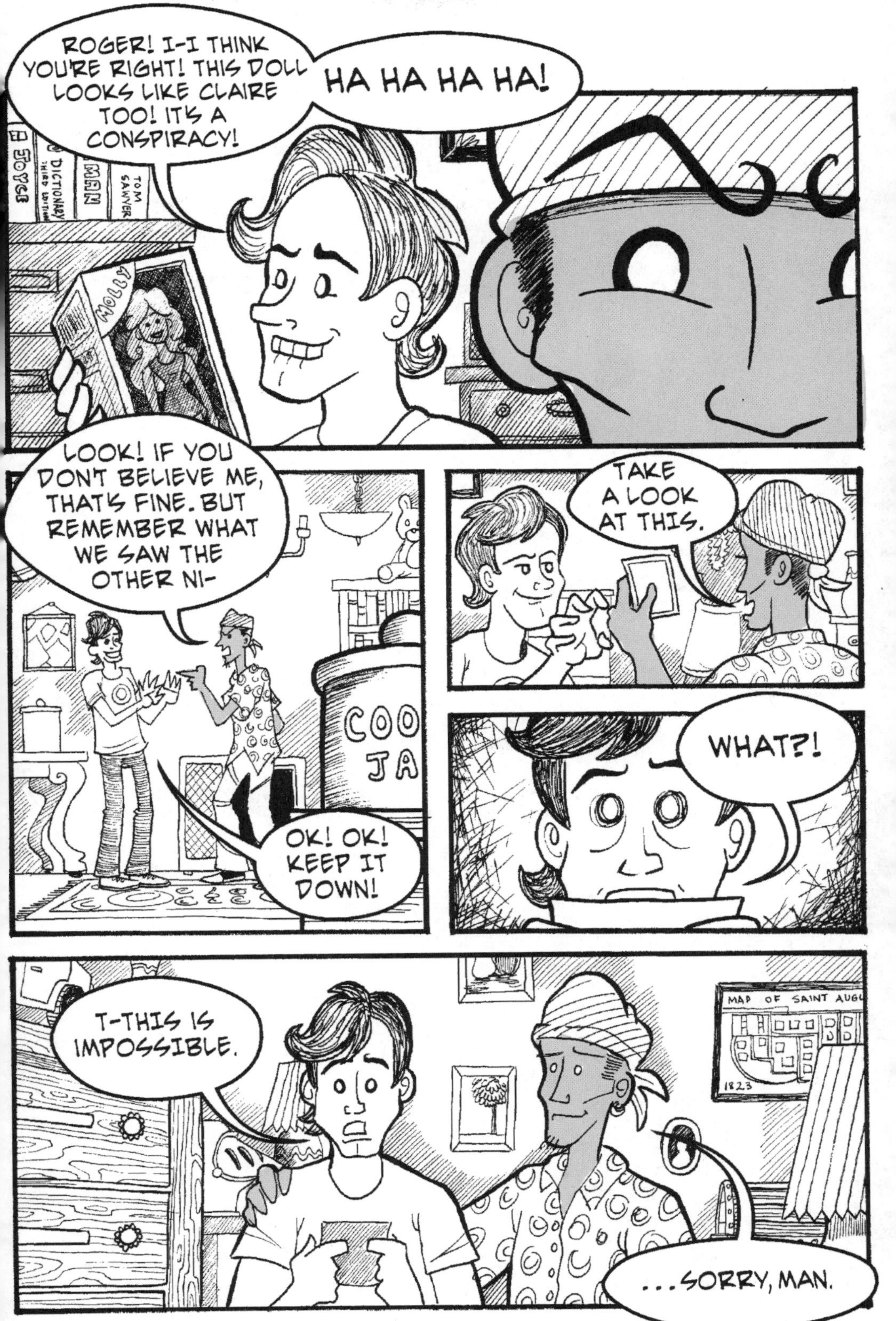
ROGER! I-I THINK YOU'RE RIGHT! THIS DOLL LOOKS LIKE CLAIRE TOO! IT'S A CONSPIRACY!
HA HA HA HA!
JOYCE
DICTIONARY THIRD EDITION
MAN
TOM SAWYER
MOLLY
LOOK! IF YOU DON'T BELIEVE ME, THAT'S FINE. BUT REMEMBER WHAT WE SAW THE OTHER NI-
OK! OK! KEEP IT DOWN!
COO JA
TAKE A LOOK AT THIS.
WHAT?!
T-THIS IS IMPOSSIBLE.
MAP OF SAINT AUG
1823
...SORRY, MAN.

CHAPTER

8

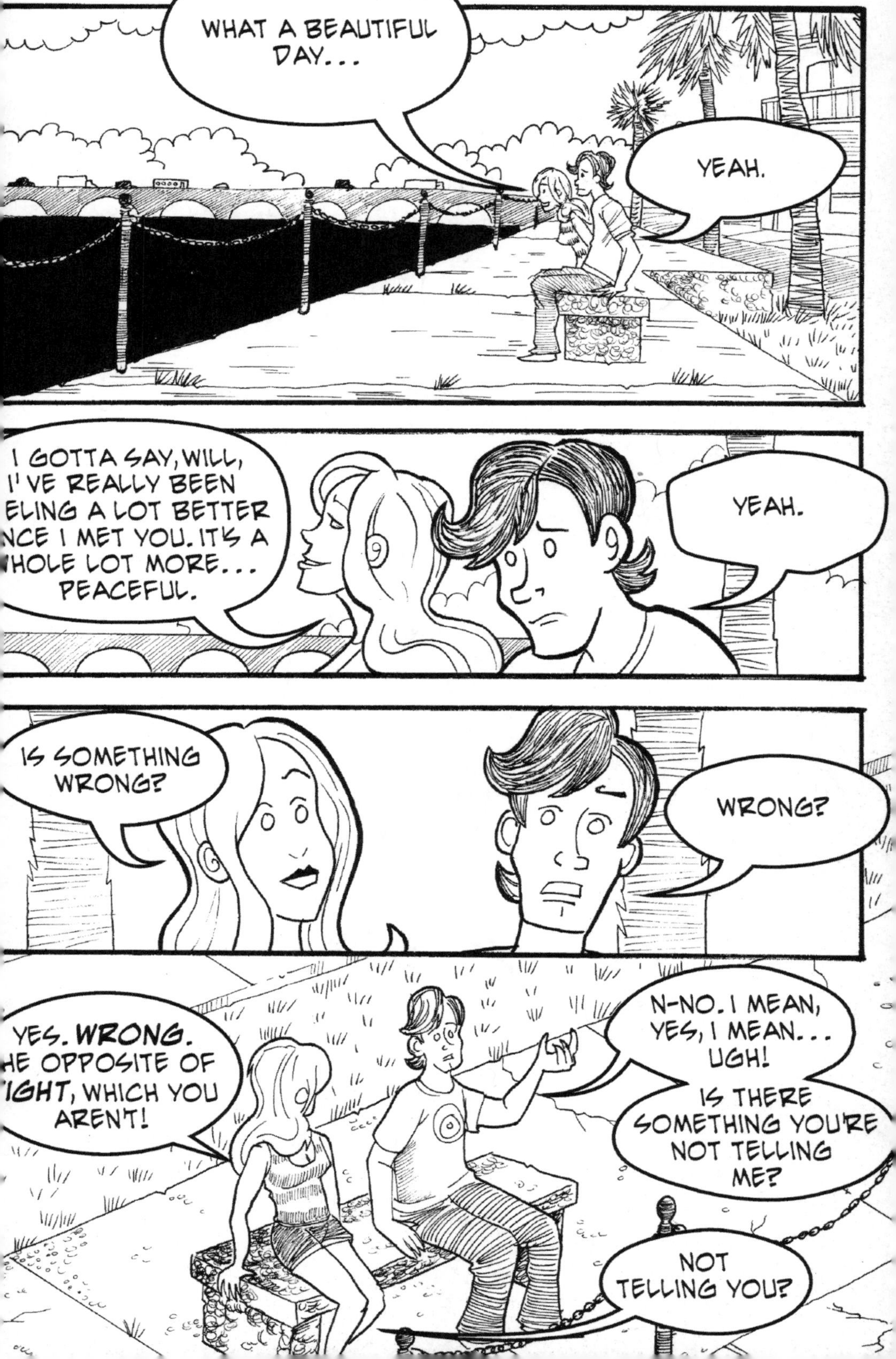
WHAT A BEAUTIFUL DAY...
YEAH.
I GOTTA SAY, WILL, I'VE REALLY BEEN ELING A LOT BETTER NCE I MET YOU. IT'S A HOLE LOT MORE... PEACEFUL.
YEAH.
IS SOMETHING WRONG?
WRONG?
YES. WRONG. HE OPPOSITE OF IGHT, WHICH YOU AREN'T!
N-NO. I MEAN, YES, I MEAN... UGH!
IS THERE SOMETHING YOU'RE NOT TELLING ME?
NOT TELLING YOU?

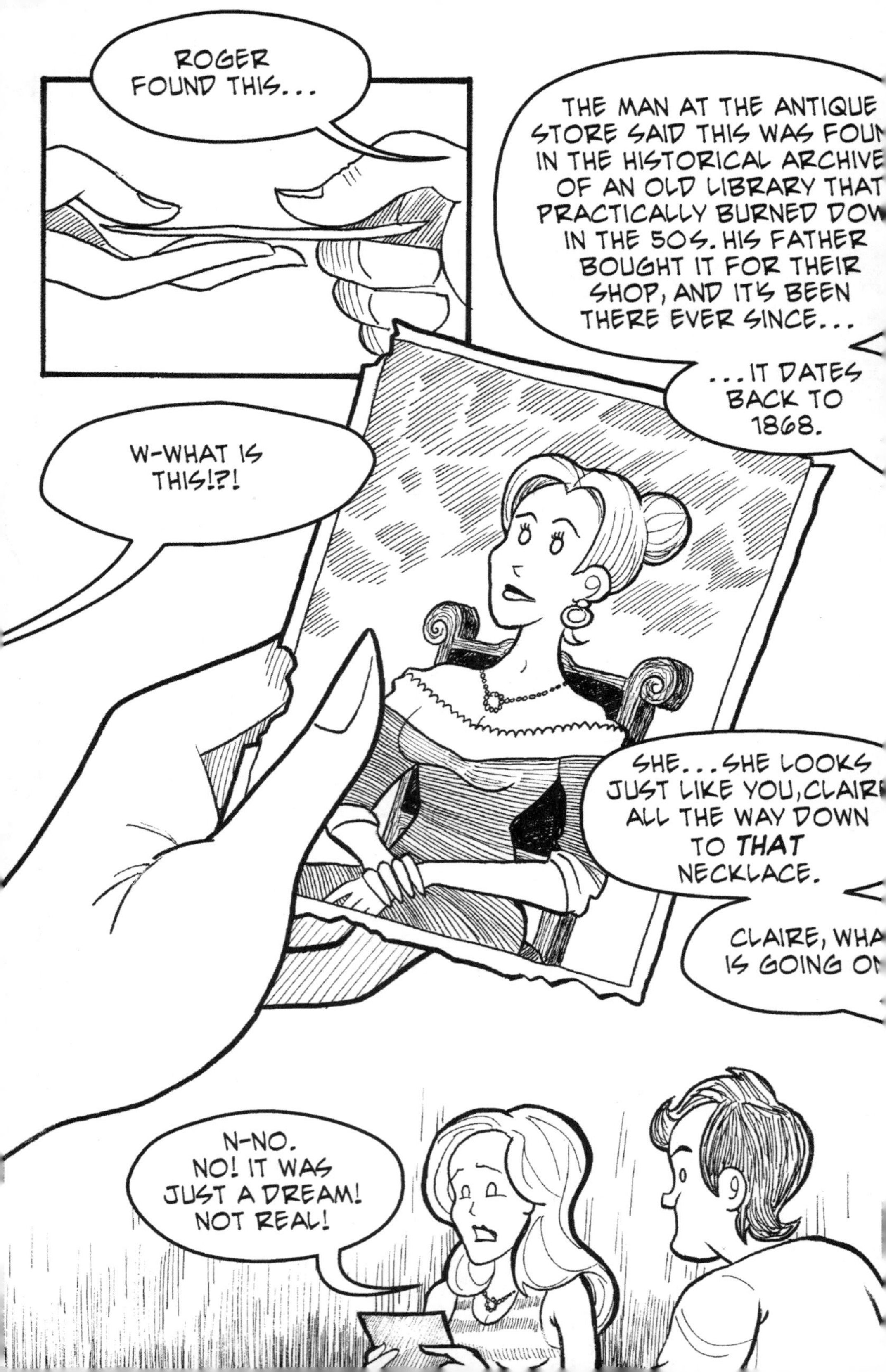
ROGER FOUND THIS...
THE MAN AT THE ANTIQUE STORE SAID THIS WAS FOUN IN THE HISTORICAL ARCHIVE OF AN OLD LIBRARY THAT PRACTICALLY BURNED DOW IN THE 50S. HIS FATHER BOUGHT IT FOR THEIR SHOP, AND IT'S BEEN THERE EVER SINCE...
...IT DATES BACK TO 1868.
W-WHAT IS THIS!?!
SHE...SHE LOOKS JUST LIKE YOU, CLAIR ALL THE WAY DOWN TO *THAT* NECKLACE.
CLAIRE, WHA IS GOING O
N-NO. NO! IT WAS JUST A DREAM! NOT REAL!

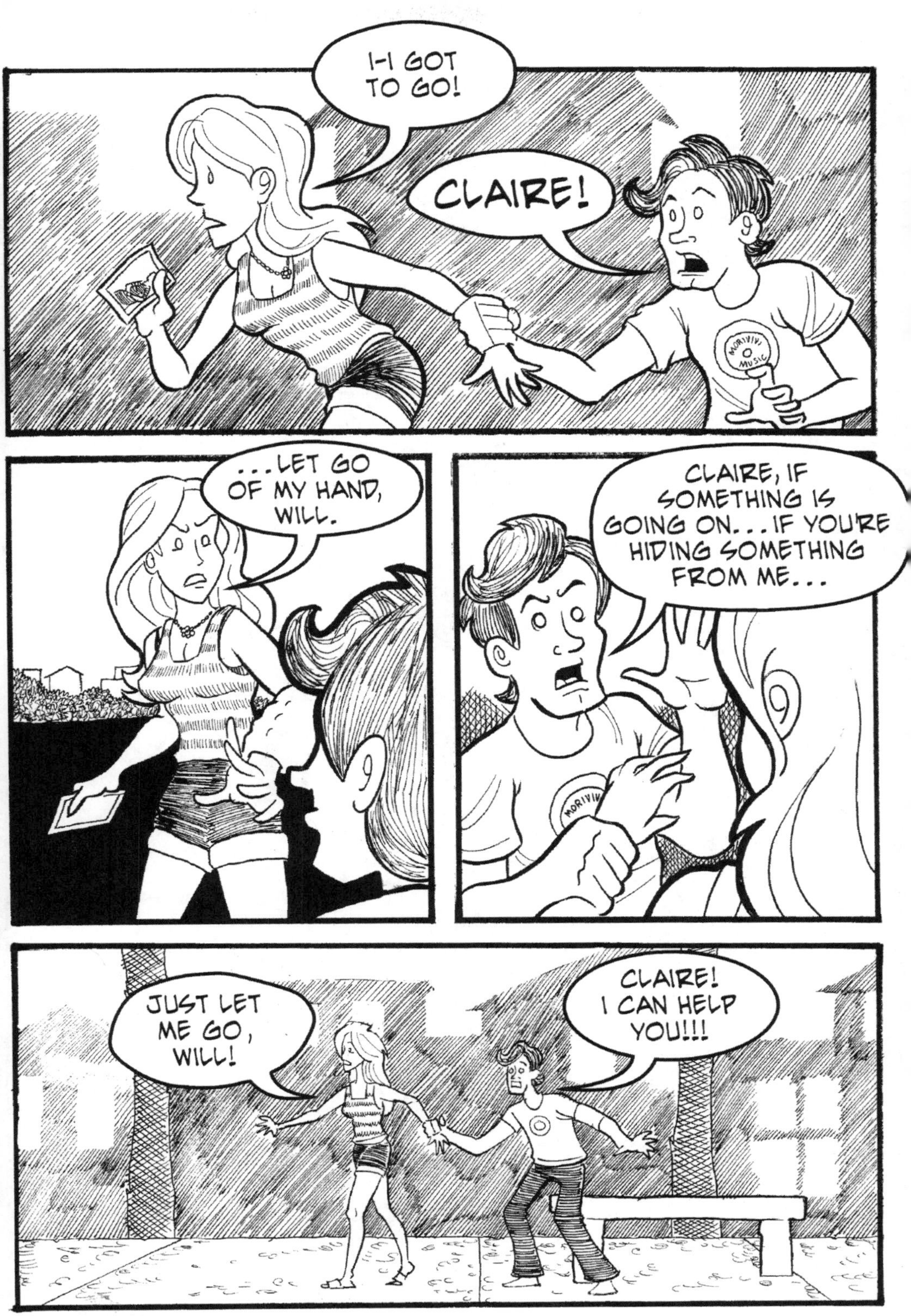
I-I GOT TO GO!
CLAIRE!
MORIVIVI MUSIC
...LET GO OF MY HAND, WILL.
CLAIRE, IF SOMETHING IS GOING ON... IF YOU'RE HIDING SOMETHING FROM ME...
JUST LET ME GO, WILL!
CLAIRE! I CAN HELP YOU!!!

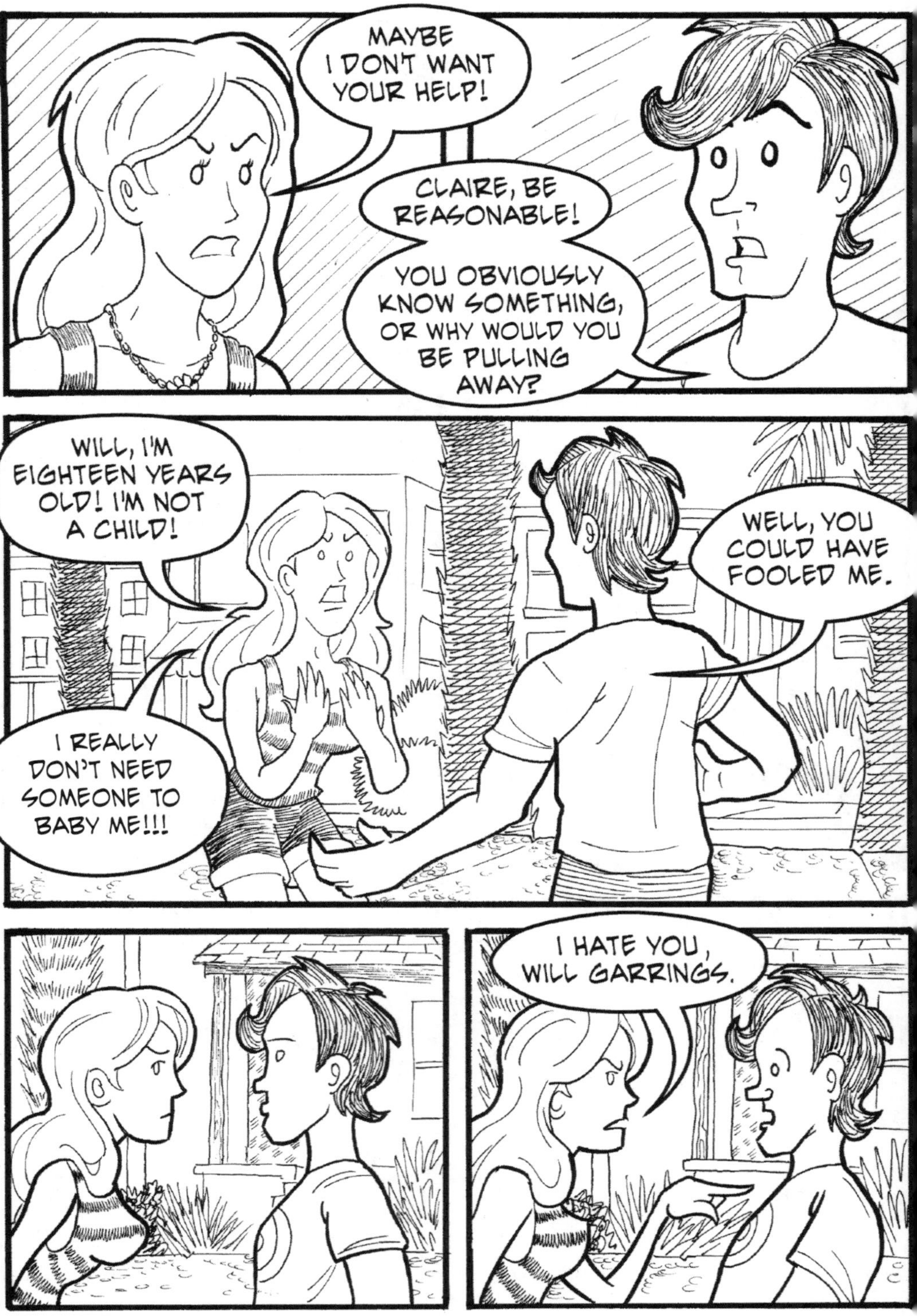
MAYBE I DON'T WANT YOUR HELP!
CLAIRE, BE REASONABLE!
YOU OBVIOUSLY KNOW SOMETHING, OR WHY WOULD YOU BE PULLING AWAY?
WILL, I'M EIGHTEEN YEARS OLD! I'M NOT A CHILD!
I REALLY DON'T NEED SOMEONE TO BABY ME!!!
WELL, YOU COULD HAVE FOOLED ME.
I HATE YOU, WILL GARRINGS.

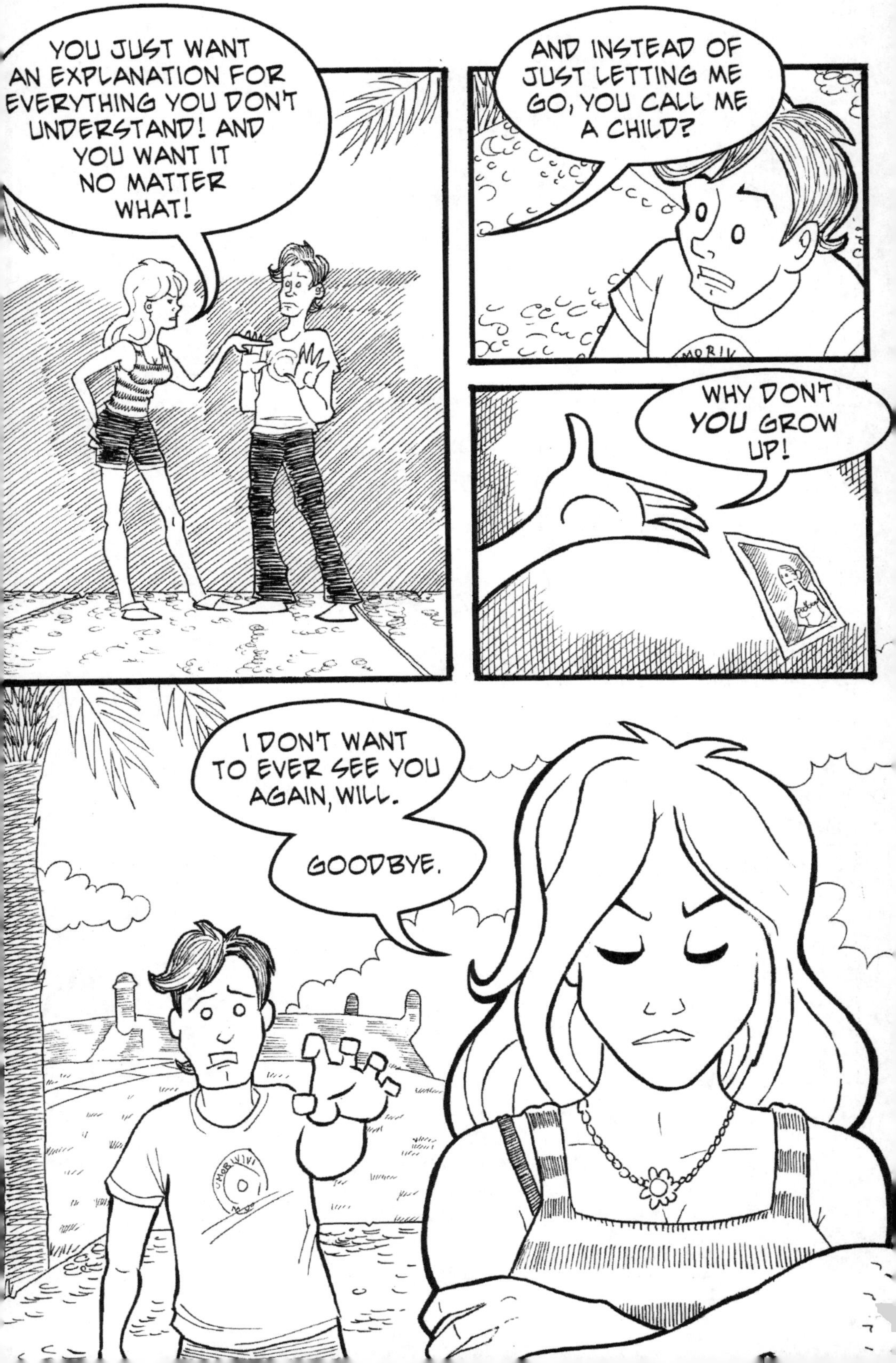
YOU JUST WANT AN EXPLANATION FOR EVERYTHING YOU DON'T UNDERSTAND! AND YOU WANT IT NO MATTER WHAT!
AND INSTEAD OF JUST LETTING ME GO, YOU CALL ME A CHILD?
WHY DON'T YOU GROW UP!
I DON'T WANT TO EVER SEE YOU AGAIN, WILL.
GOODBYE.

CHAPTER

9

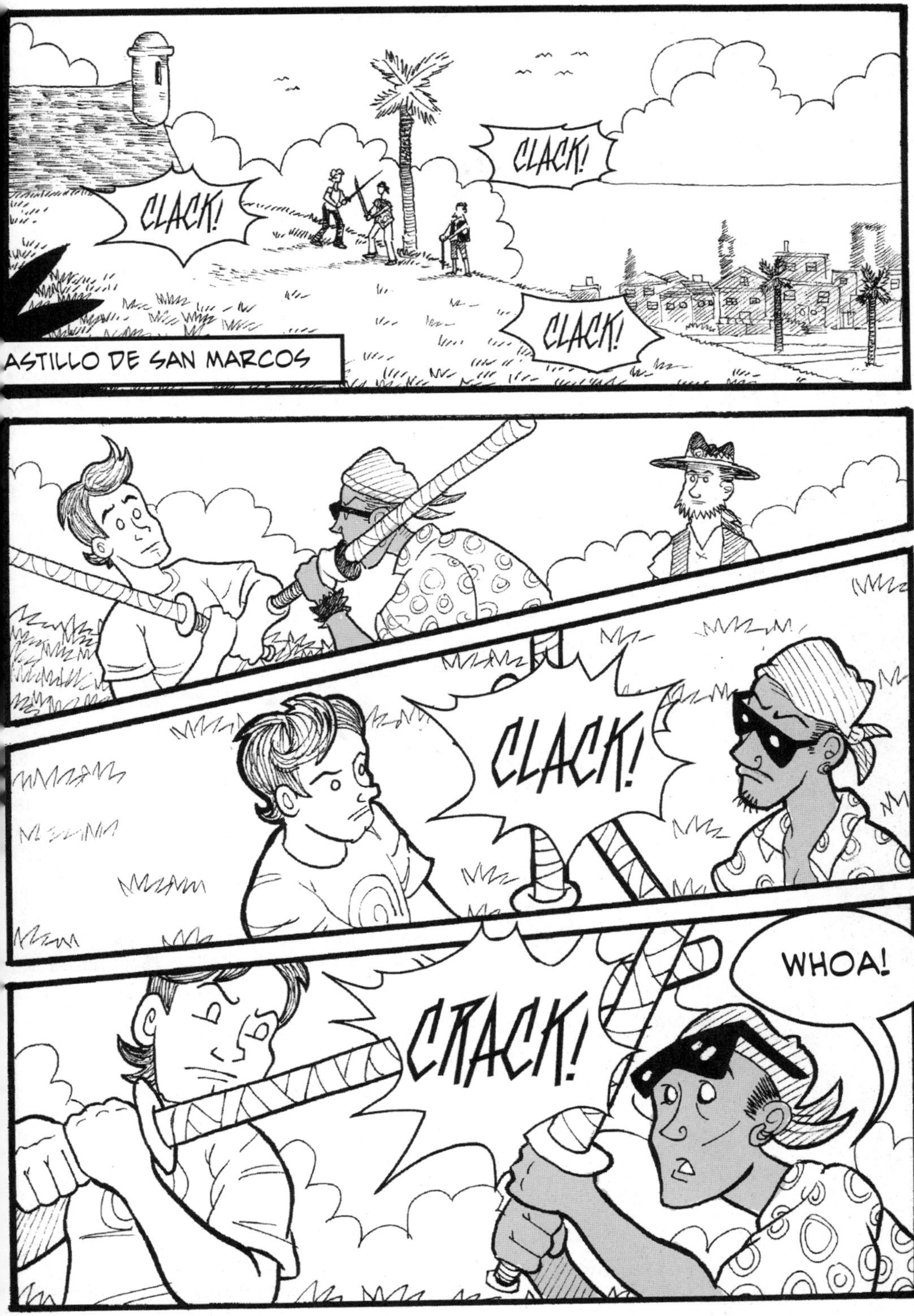

ASTILLO DE SAN MARCOS
CLACK!
CLACK!
CLACK!
CLACK!
CRACK!
WHOA!

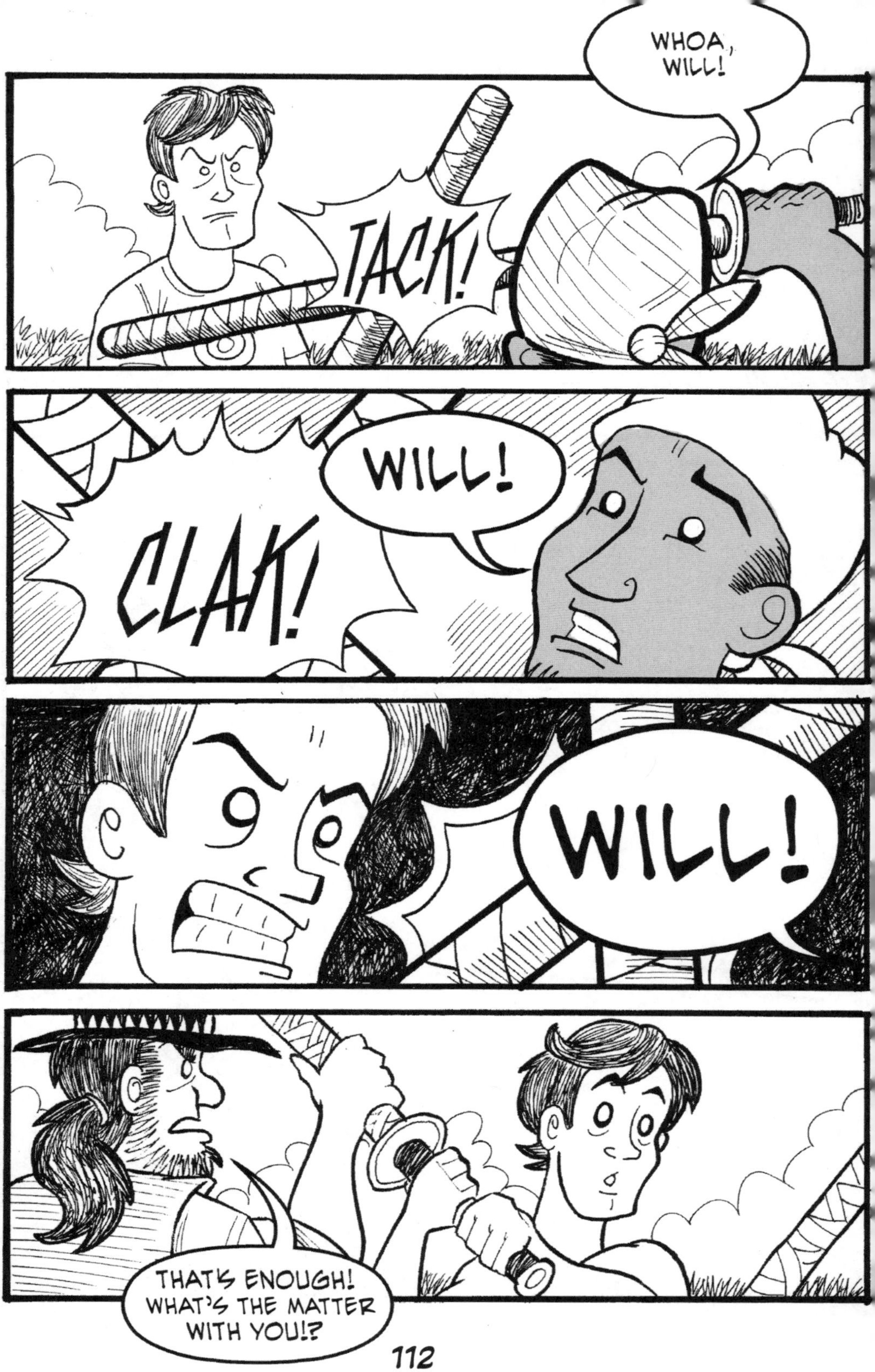
WHOA, WILL!
TACK!
WILL!
CLAK!
WILL!
THAT'S ENOUGH! WHAT'S THE MATTER WITH YOU!?

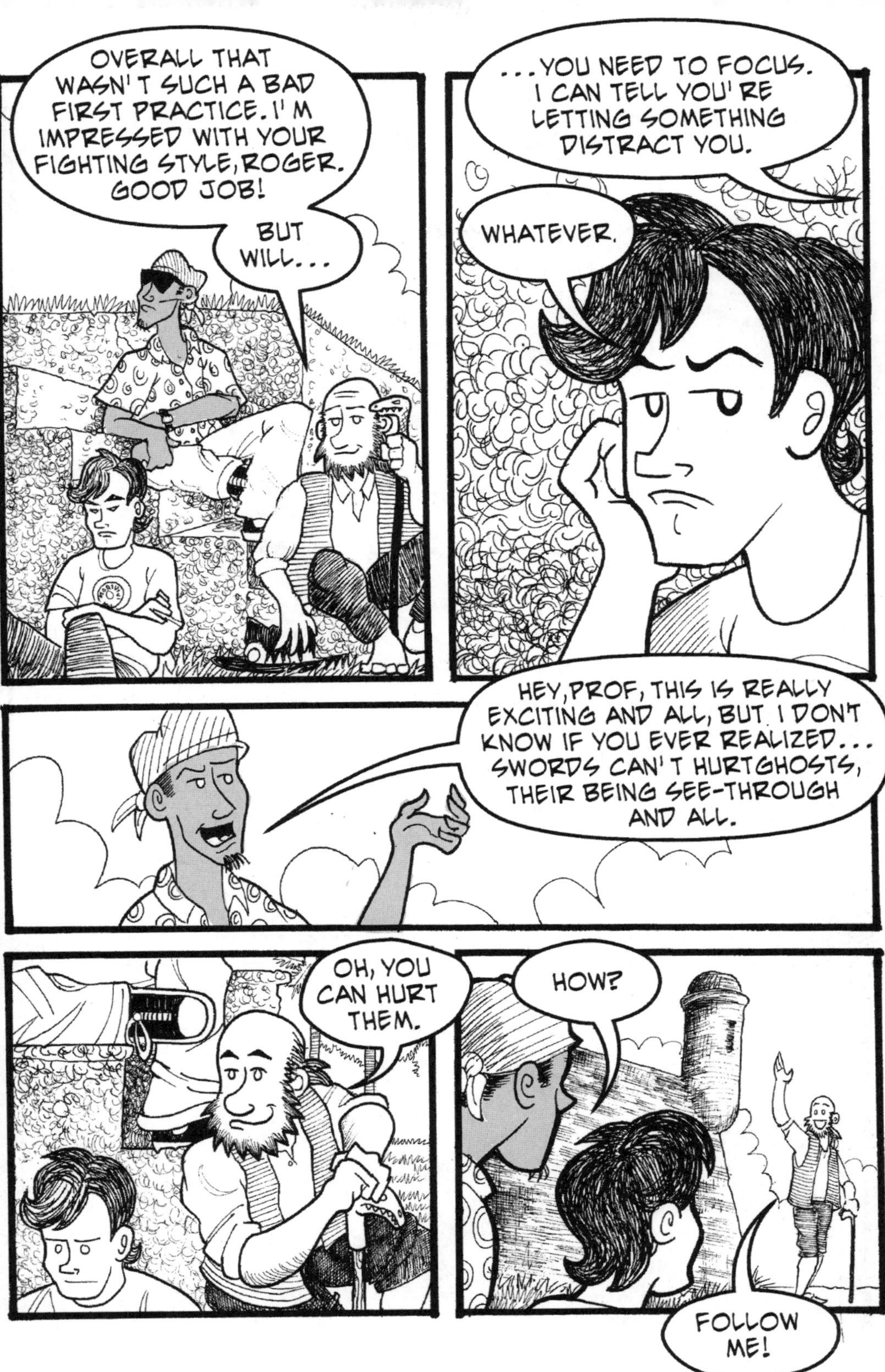
OVERALL THAT WASN'T SUCH A BAD FIRST PRACTICE. I'M IMPRESSED WITH YOUR FIGHTING STYLE, ROGER. GOOD JOB!
BUT WILL...
...YOU NEED TO FOCUS. I CAN TELL YOU'RE LETTING SOMETHING DISTRACT YOU.
WHATEVER.
HEY, PROF, THIS IS REALLY EXCITING AND ALL, BUT I DON'T KNOW IF YOU EVER REALIZED... SWORDS CAN'T HURTGHOSTS, THEIR BEING SEE-THROUGH AND ALL.
OH, YOU CAN HURT THEM.
HOW?
FOLLOW ME!

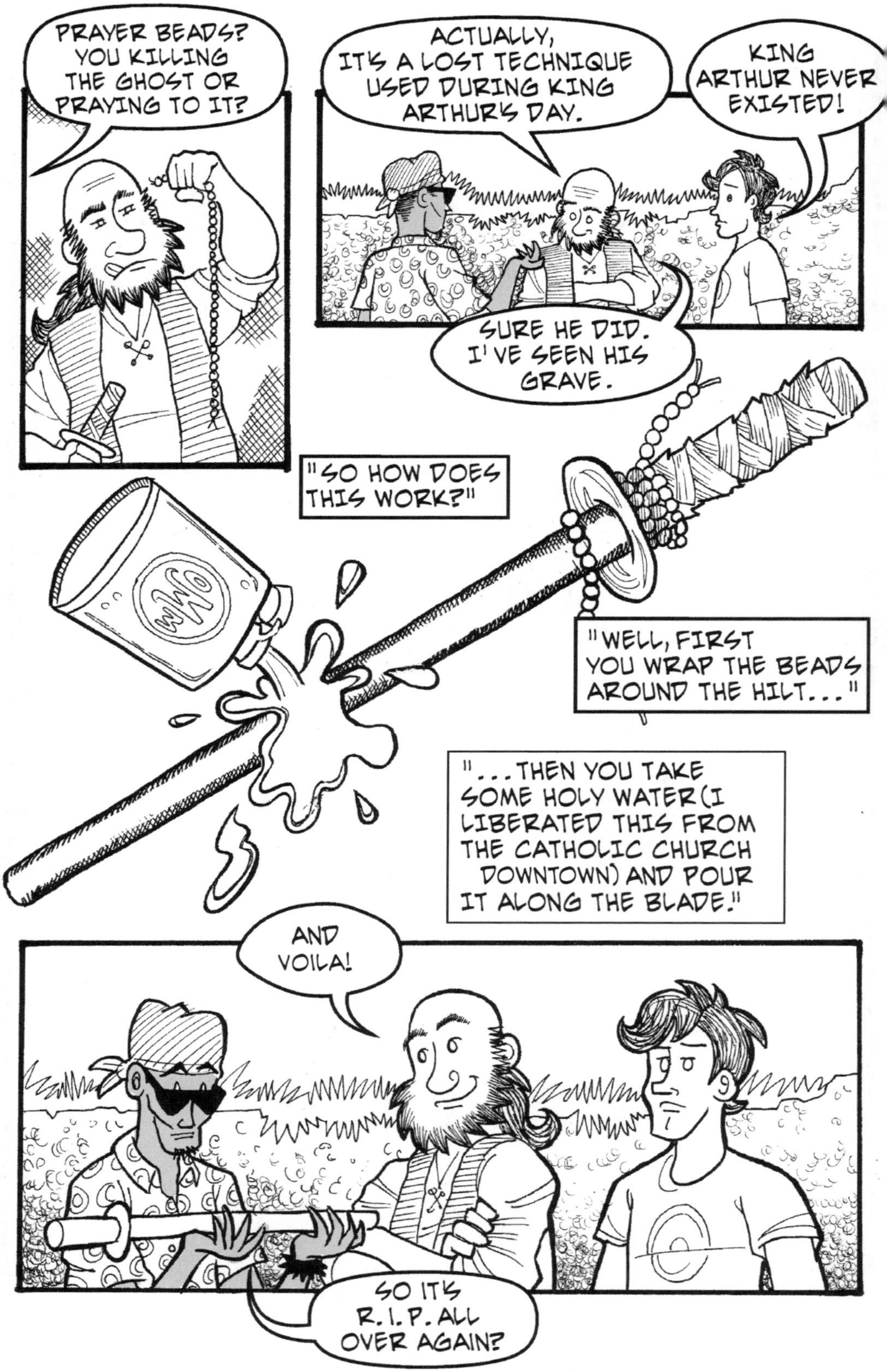
PRAYER BEADS? YOU KILLING THE GHOST OR PRAYING TO IT?
ACTUALLY, IT'S A LOST TECHNIQUE USED DURING KING ARTHUR'S DAY.
KING ARTHUR NEVER EXISTED!
SURE HE DID. I'VE SEEN HIS GRAVE.
"SO HOW DOES THIS WORK?"
"WELL, FIRST YOU WRAP THE BEADS AROUND THE HILT..."
"...THEN YOU TAKE SOME HOLY WATER (I LIBERATED THIS FROM THE CATHOLIC CHURCH DOWNTOWN) AND POUR IT ALONG THE BLADE."
AND VOILA!
SO IT'S R.I.P. ALL OVER AGAIN?

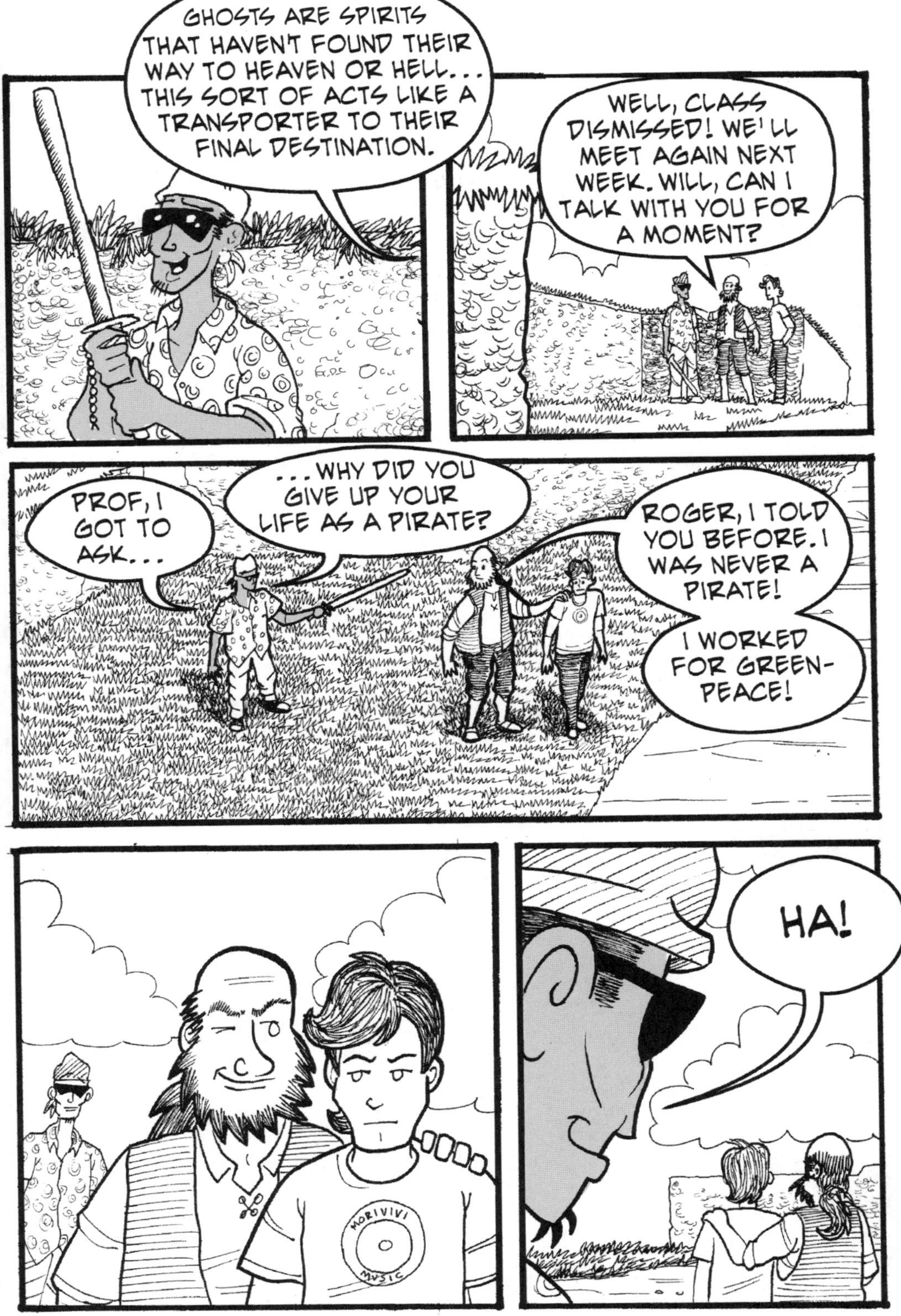
GHOSTS ARE SPIRITS THAT HAVEN'T FOUND THEIR WAY TO HEAVEN OR HELL... THIS SORT OF ACTS LIKE A TRANSPORTER TO THEIR FINAL DESTINATION.
WELL, CLASS DISMISSED! WE'LL MEET AGAIN NEXT WEEK. WILL, CAN I TALK WITH YOU FOR A MOMENT?
PROF, I GOT TO ASK...
...WHY DID YOU GIVE UP YOUR LIFE AS A PIRATE?
ROGER, I TOLD YOU BEFORE. I WAS NEVER A PIRATE!
I WORKED FOR GREEN-PEACE!
MORIVIVI MUSIC
HA!

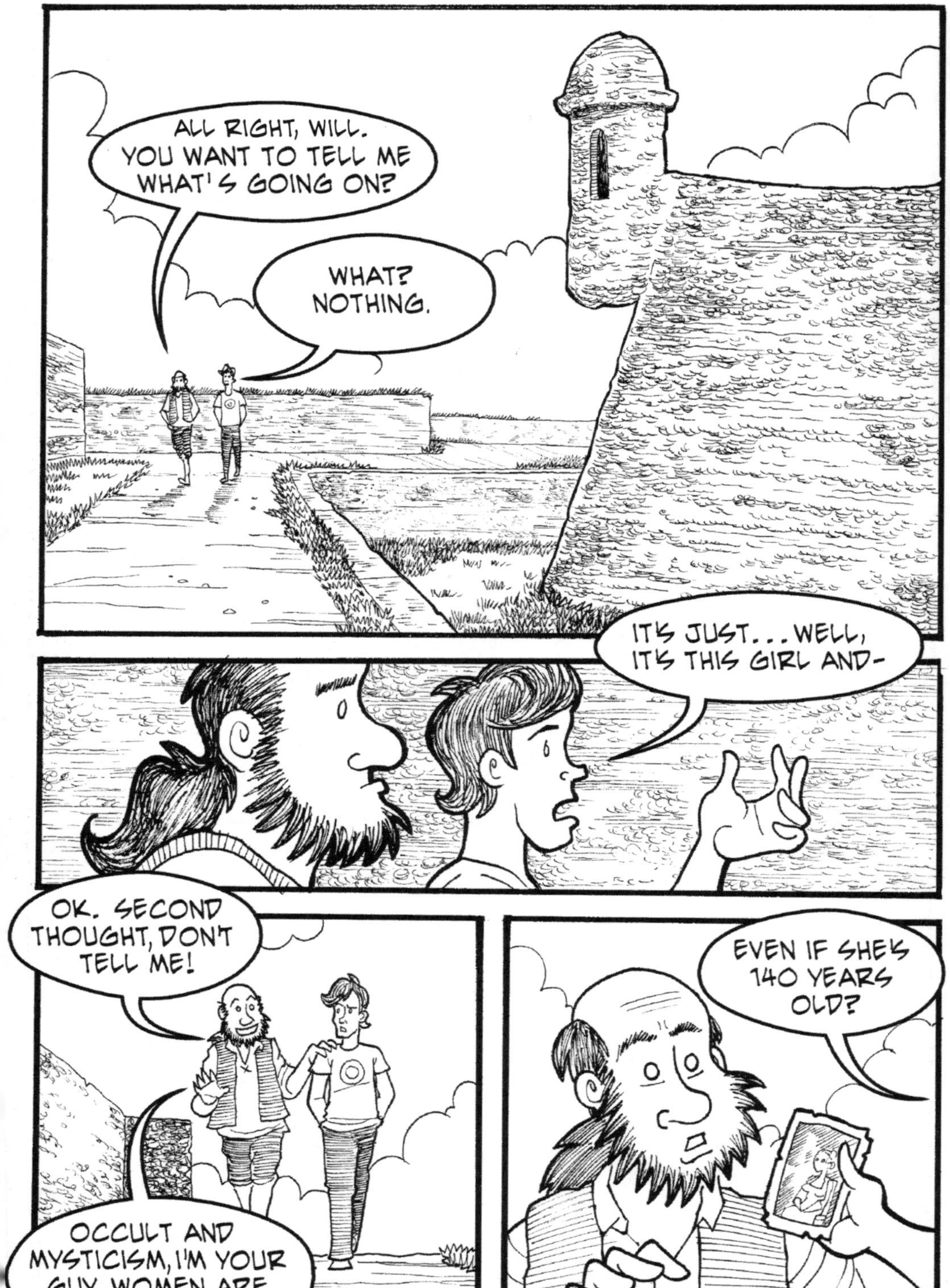
ALL RIGHT, WILL. YOU WANT TO TELL ME WHAT'S GOING ON?
WHAT? NOTHING.
IT'S JUST... WELL, IT'S THIS GIRL AND-
OK. SECOND THOUGHT, DON'T TELL ME!
OCCULT AND MYSTICISM, I'M YOUR GUY. WOMEN ARE OUT OF MY FIELD.
EVEN IF SHE'S 140 YEARS OLD?

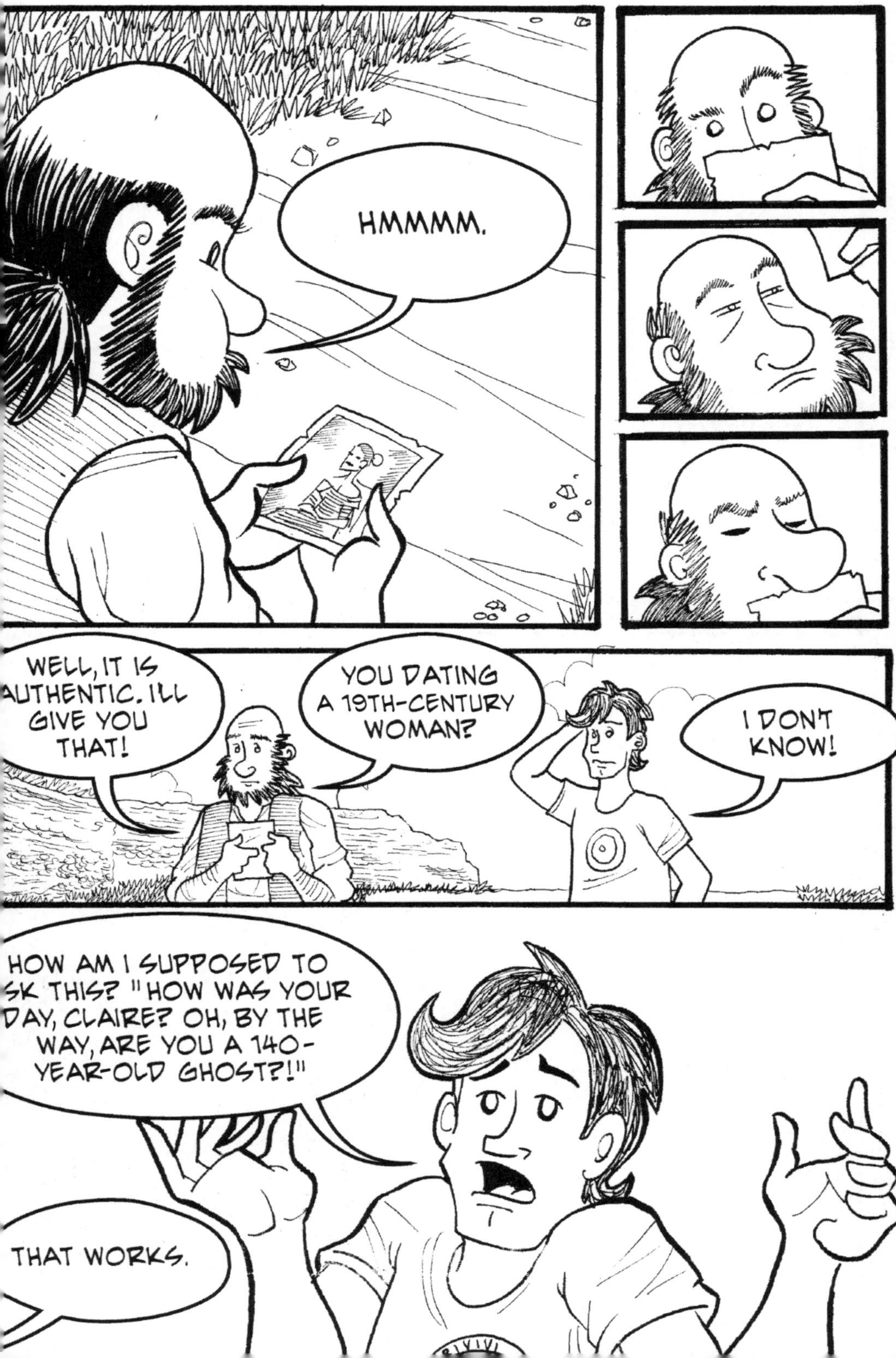
HMMMM.
WELL, IT IS AUTHENTIC. I'LL GIVE YOU THAT!
YOU DATING A 19TH-CENTURY WOMAN?
I DON'T KNOW!
HOW AM I SUPPOSED TO ASK THIS? "HOW WAS YOUR DAY, CLAIRE? OH, BY THE WAY, ARE YOU A 140-YEAR-OLD GHOST?!"
THAT WORKS.

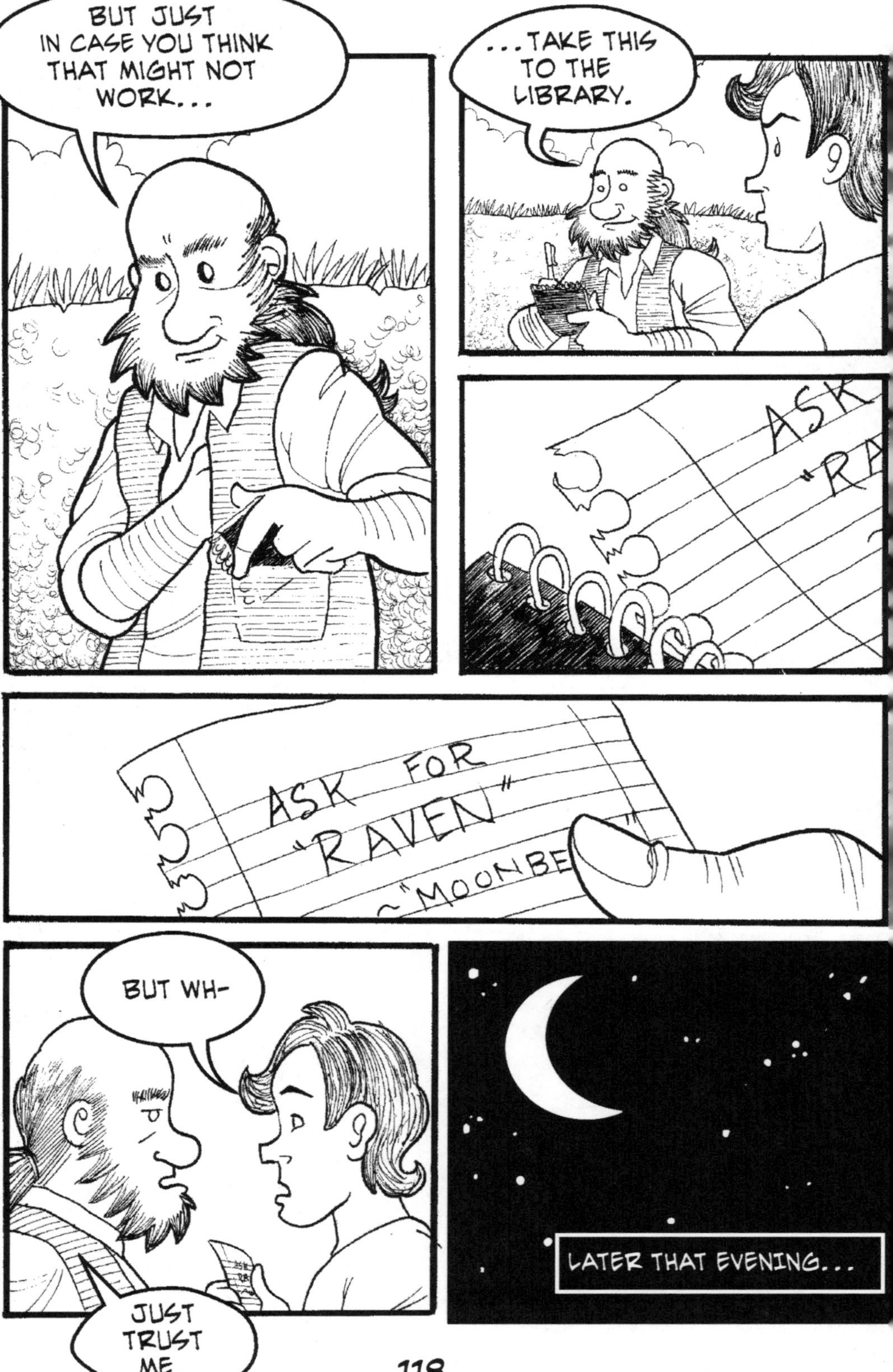
BUT JUST IN CASE YOU THINK THAT MIGHT NOT WORK...
...TAKE THIS TO THE LIBRARY.
ASK FOR "RAVEN"
"MOONBE
BUT WH-
JUST TRUST ME.
LATER THAT EVENING...

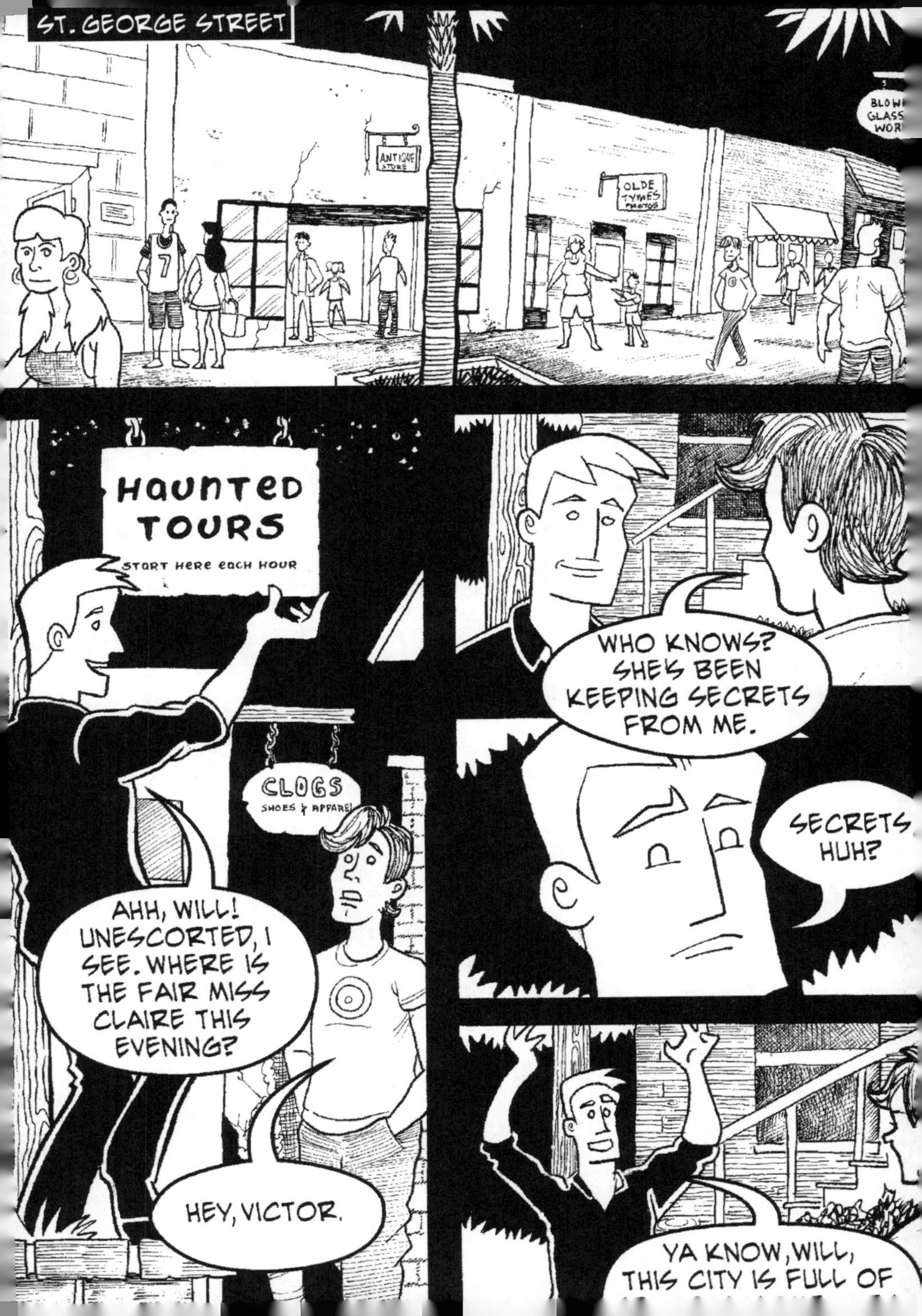
ST. GEORGE STREET
ANTIQUE STORE
OLDE TYMES PHOTOS
HAUNTED TOURS
START HERE EACH HOUR
CLOGS
SHOES & APPAREL
AHH, WILL! UNESCORTED, I SEE. WHERE IS THE FAIR MISS CLAIRE THIS EVENING?
HEY, VICTOR.
WHO KNOWS? SHE'S BEEN KEEPING SECRETS FROM ME.
SECRETS HUH?
YA KNOW, WILL, THIS CITY IS FULL OF

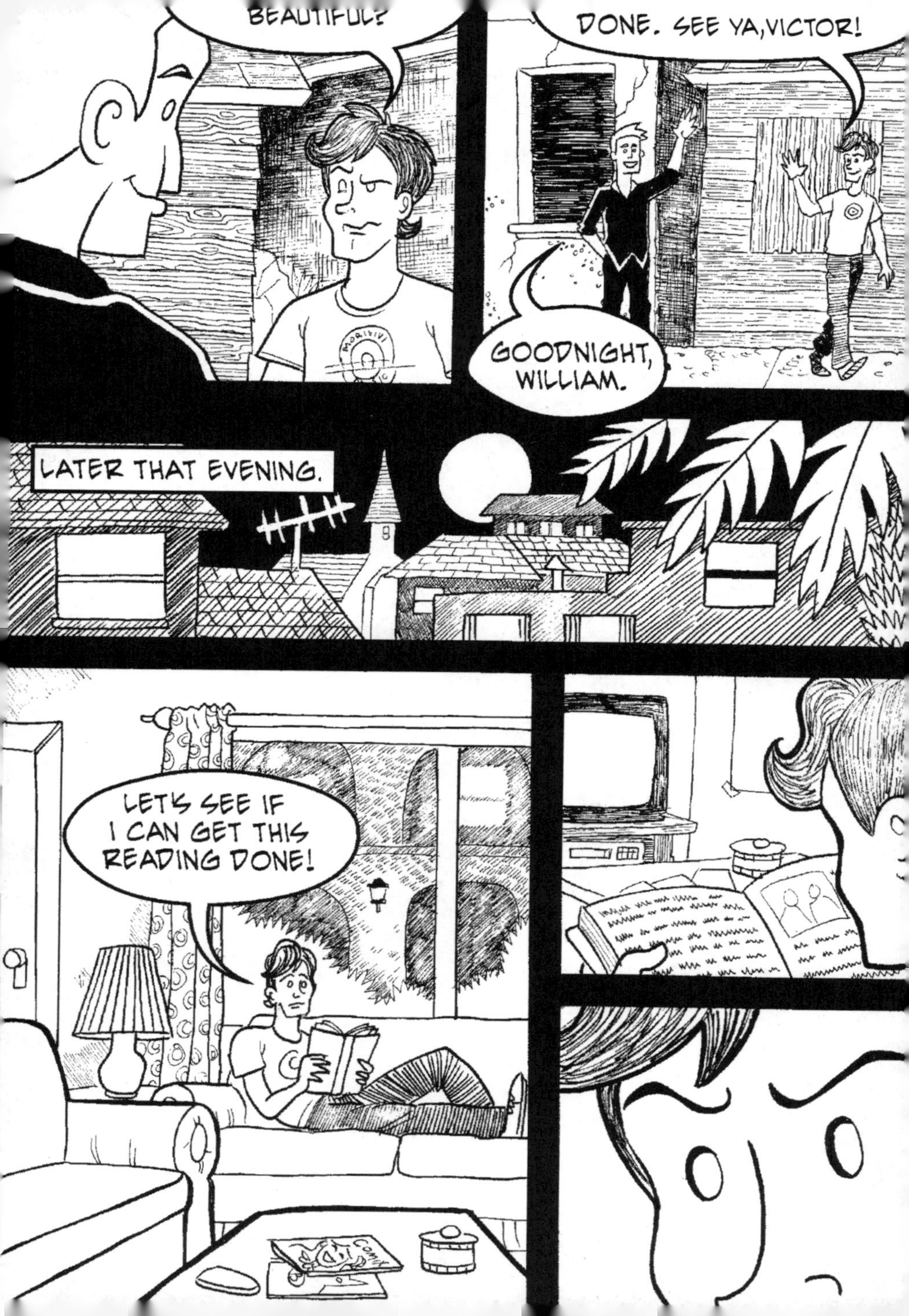
BEAUTIFUL?
DONE. SEE YA, VICTOR!
GOODNIGHT, WILLIAM.
LATER THAT EVENING.
LET'S SEE IF I CAN GET THIS READING DONE!

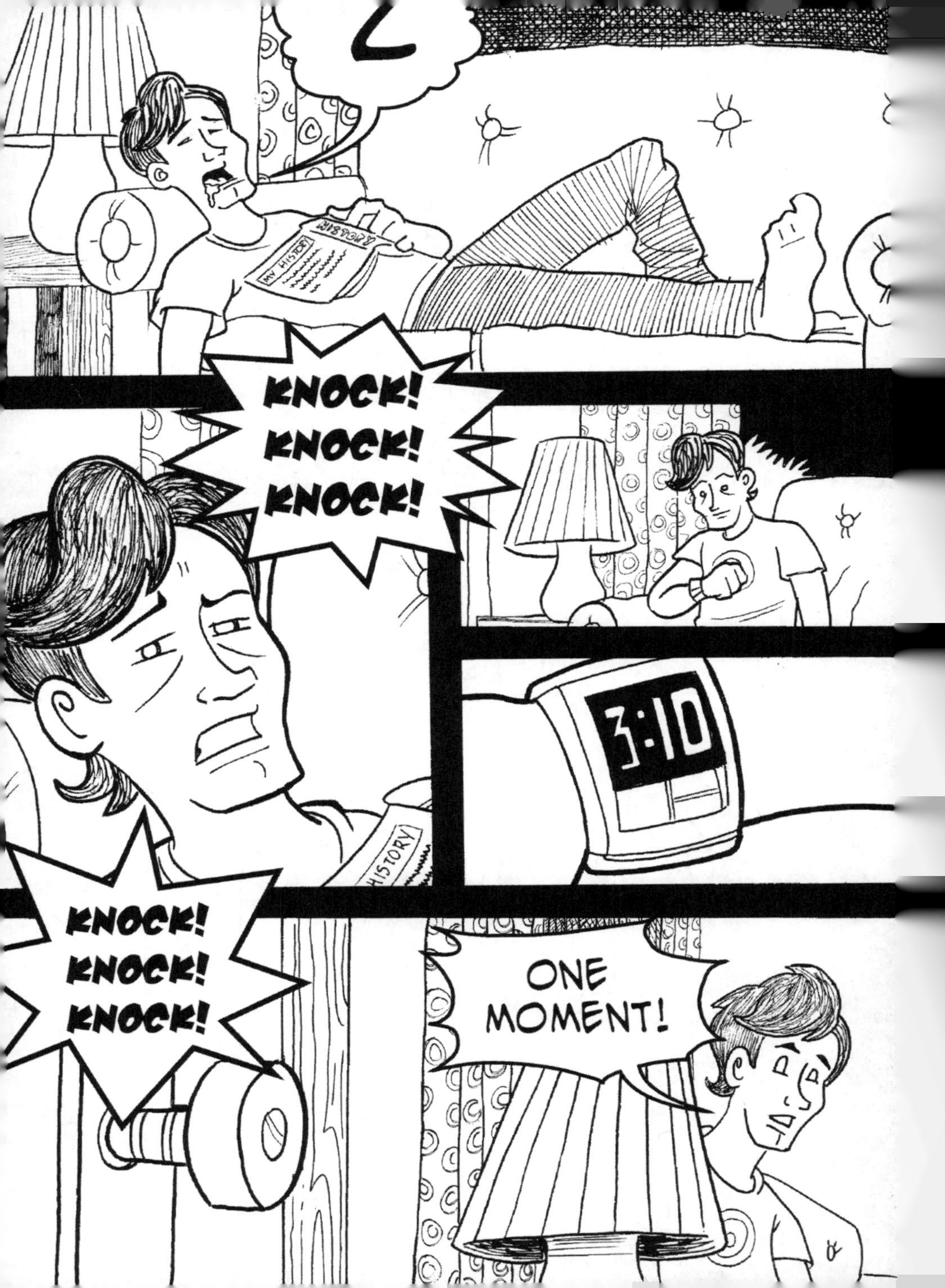

MY HISTORY
HISTORY
KNOCK! KNOCK! KNOCK!
3:10
HISTORY
KNOCK! KNOCK! KNOCK!
ONE MOMENT!

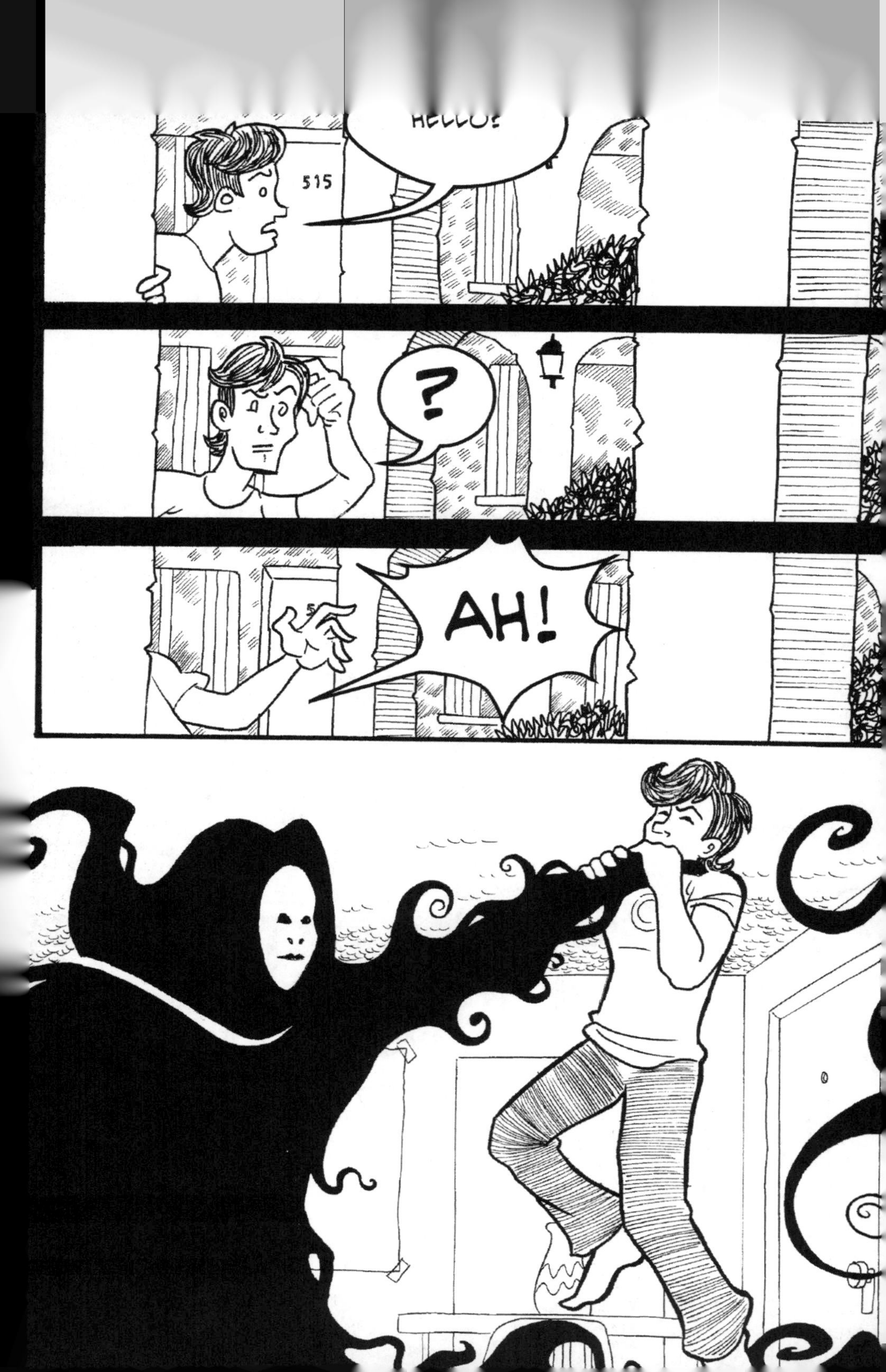
HELLO
515
?
AH!

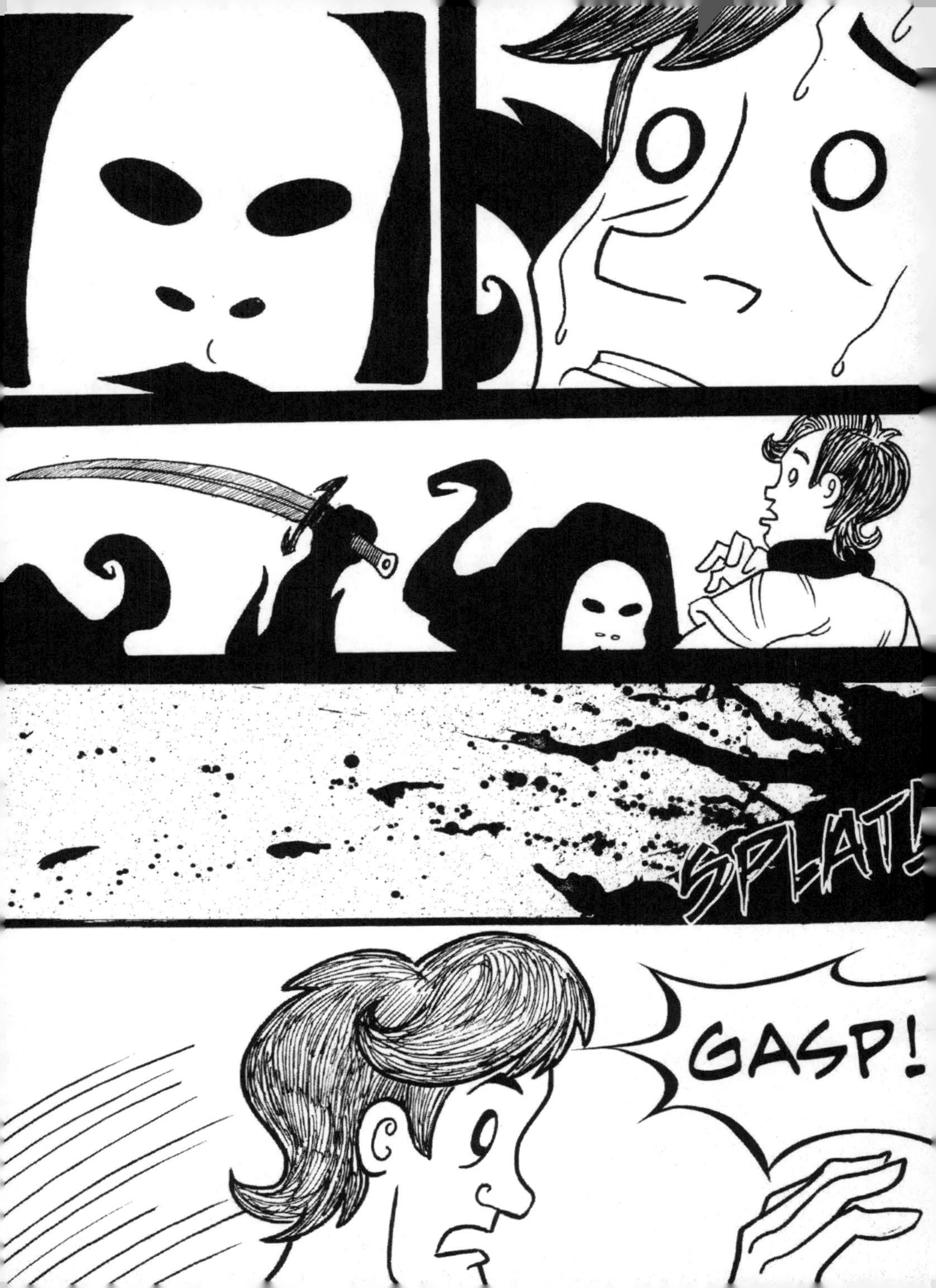
SPLAT!
GASP!

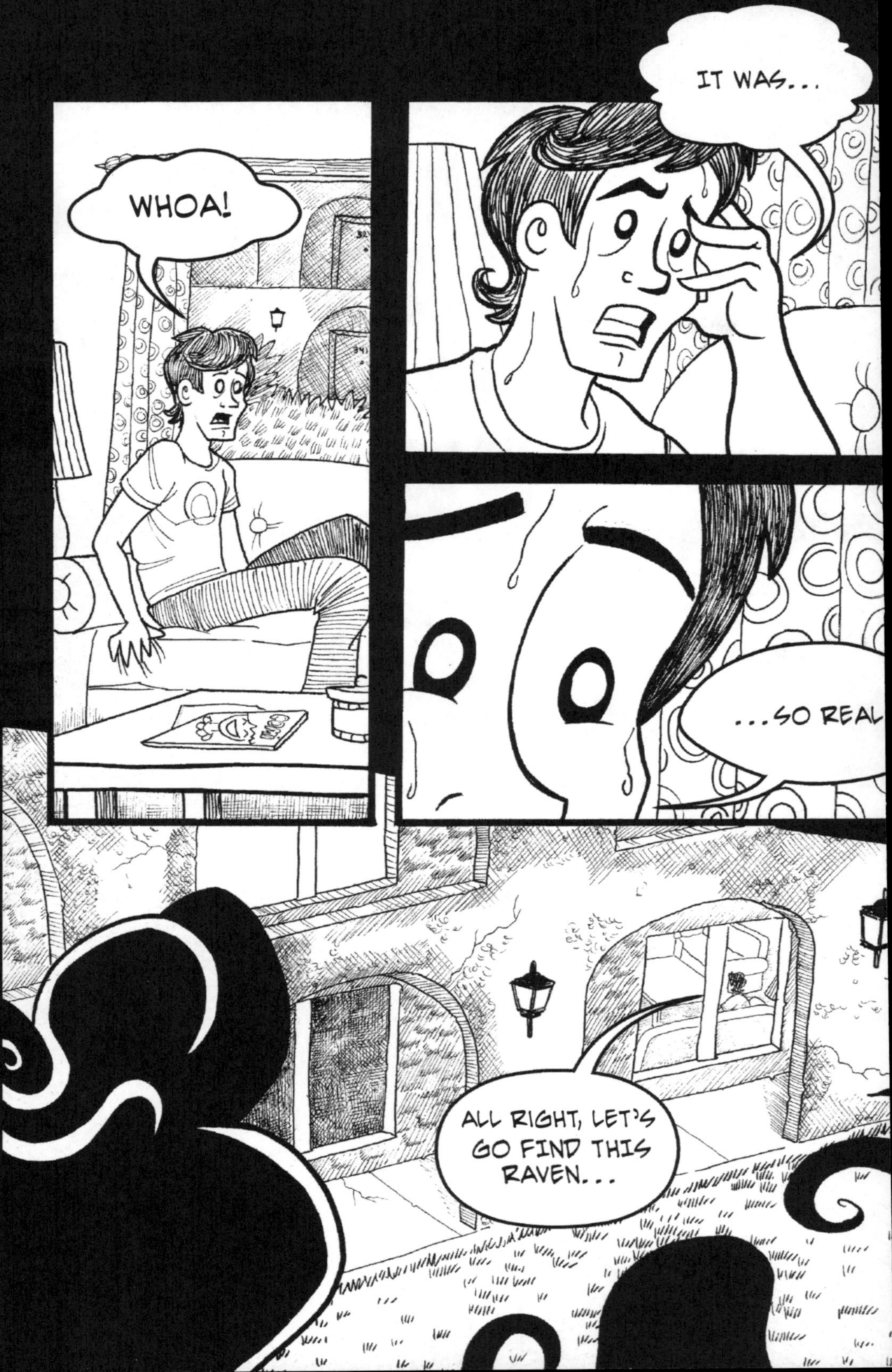
WHOA!
IT WAS...
...SO REAL
ALL RIGHT, LET'S GO FIND THIS RAVEN...

CHAPTER 10

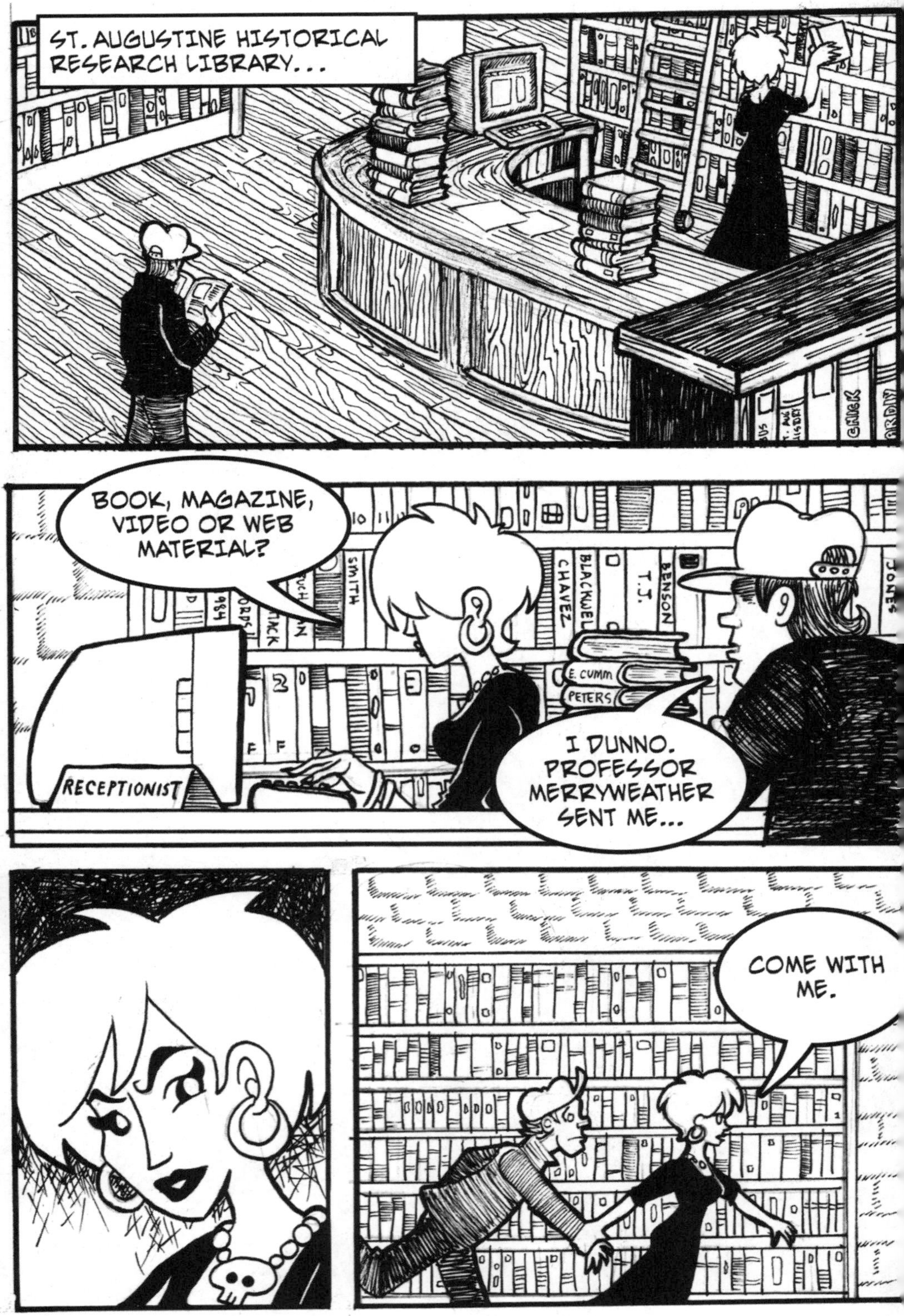
ST. AUGUSTINE HISTORICAL RESEARCH LIBRARY...
BOOK, MAGAZINE, VIDEO OR WEB MATERIAL?
RECEPTIONIST
I DUNNO. PROFESSOR MERRYWEATHER SENT ME...
COME WITH ME.

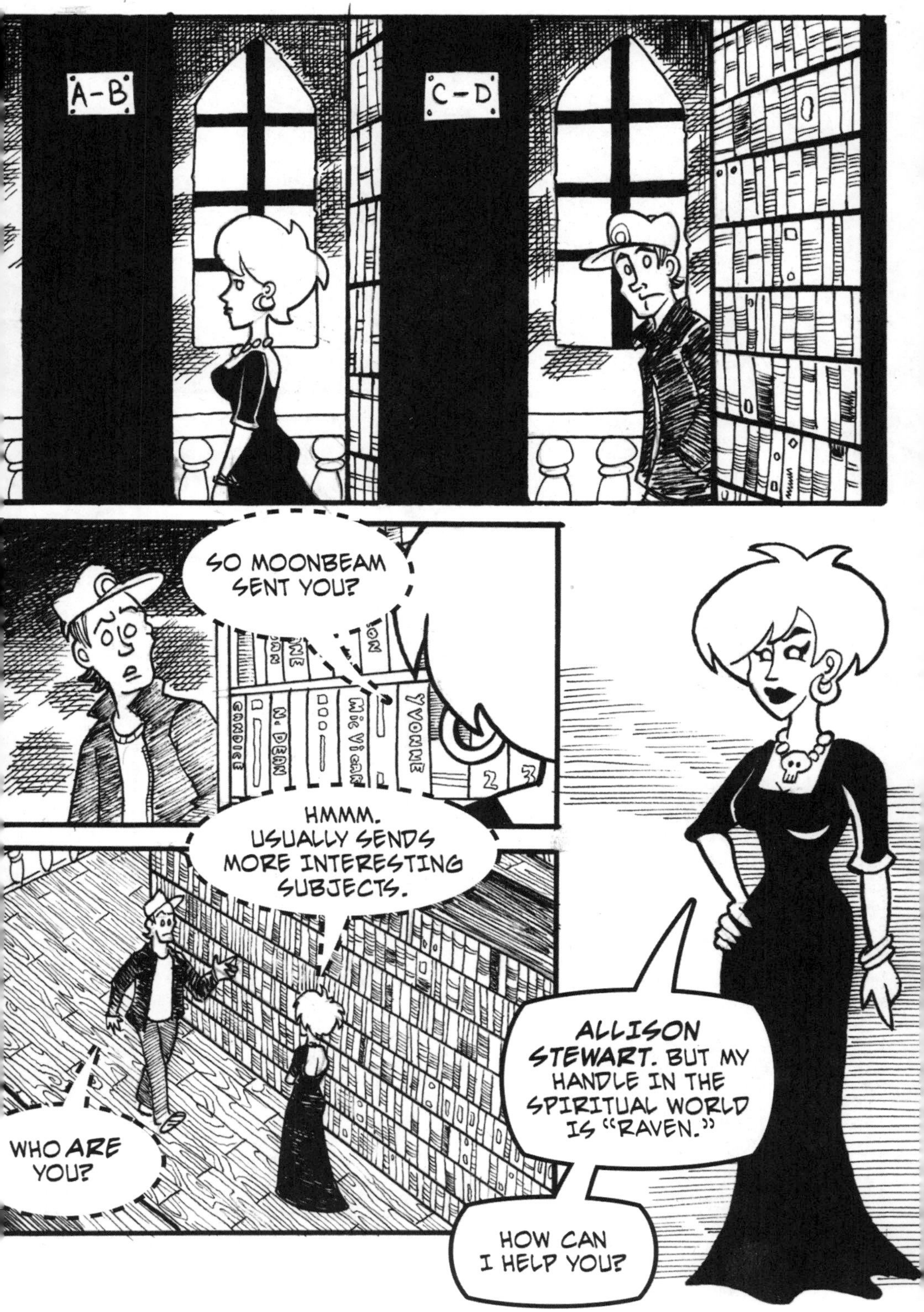
A-B
C-D
SO MOONBEAM SENT YOU?
HMMM. USUALLY SENDS MORE INTERESTING SUBJECTS.
WHO ARE YOU?
ALLISON STEWART. BUT MY HANDLE IN THE SPIRITUAL WORLD IS "RAVEN."
HOW CAN I HELP YOU?

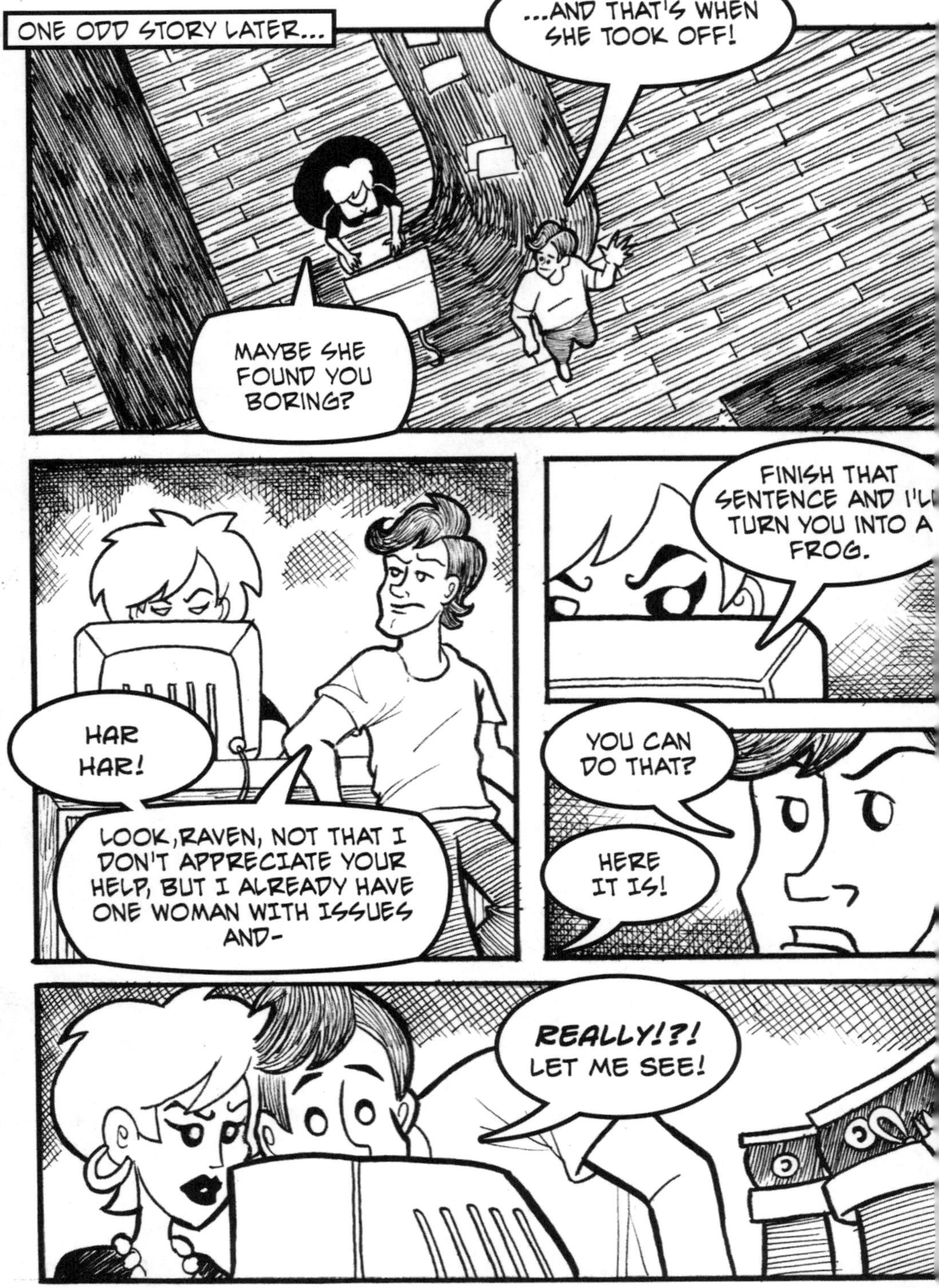
ONE ODD STORY LATER...
...AND THAT'S WHEN SHE TOOK OFF!
MAYBE SHE FOUND YOU BORING?
HAR HAR!
LOOK, RAVEN, NOT THAT I DON'T APPRECIATE YOUR HELP, BUT I ALREADY HAVE ONE WOMAN WITH ISSUES AND-
FINISH THAT SENTENCE AND I'LL TURN YOU INTO A FROG.
YOU CAN DO THAT?
HERE IT IS!
REALLY!?! LET ME SEE!

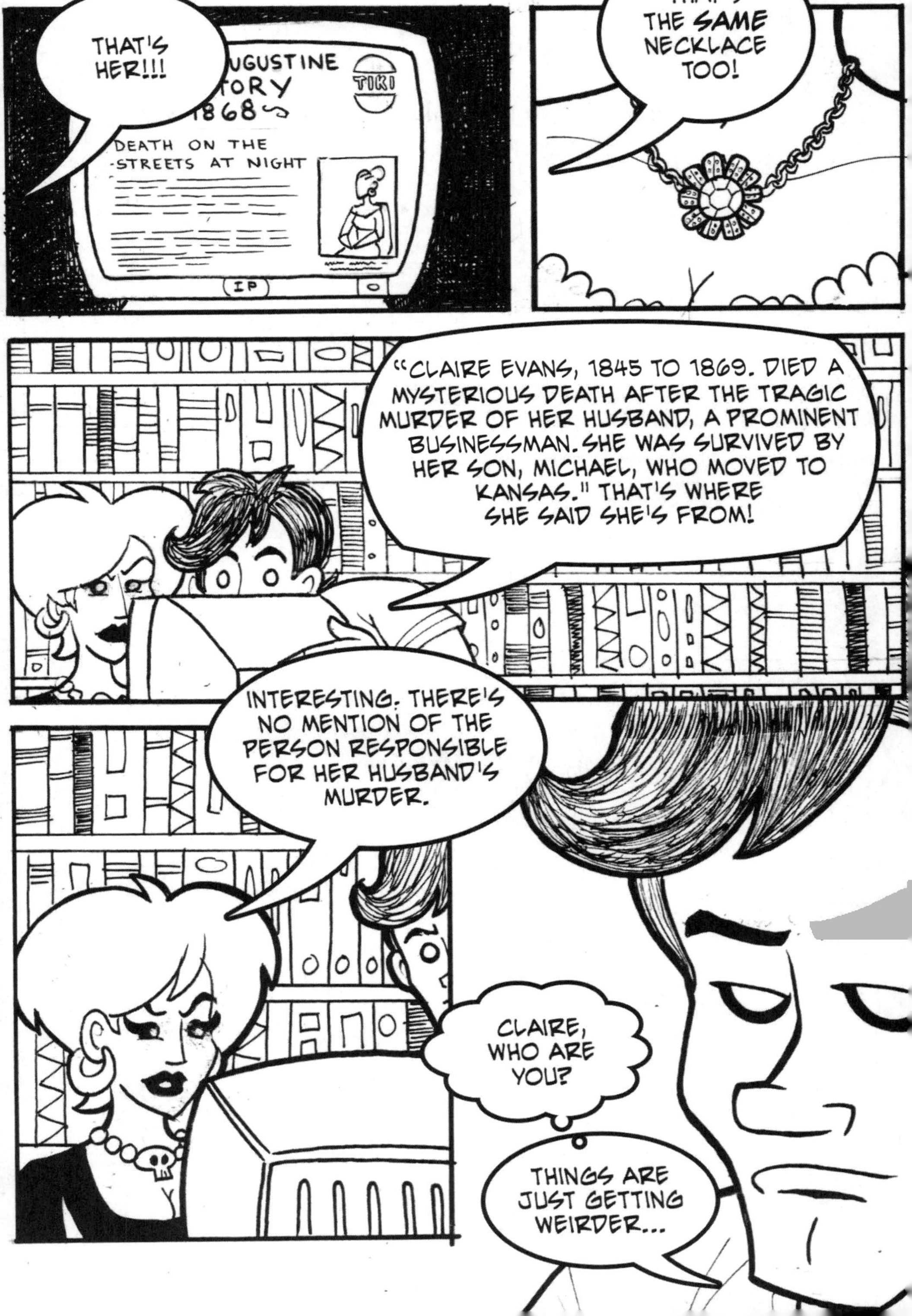
THAT'S HER!!!
UGUSTINE
TORY
1868
TIKI
DEATH ON THE
STREETS AT NIGHT
IP
THAT'S THE SAME NECKLACE TOO!
"CLAIRE EVANS, 1845 TO 1869. DIED A MYSTERIOUS DEATH AFTER THE TRAGIC MURDER OF HER HUSBAND, A PROMINENT BUSINESSMAN. SHE WAS SURVIVED BY HER SON, MICHAEL, WHO MOVED TO KANSAS." THAT'S WHERE SHE SAID SHE'S FROM!
INTERESTING. THERE'S NO MENTION OF THE PERSON RESPONSIBLE FOR HER HUSBAND'S MURDER.
CLAIRE, WHO ARE YOU?
THINGS ARE JUST GETTING WEIRDER...

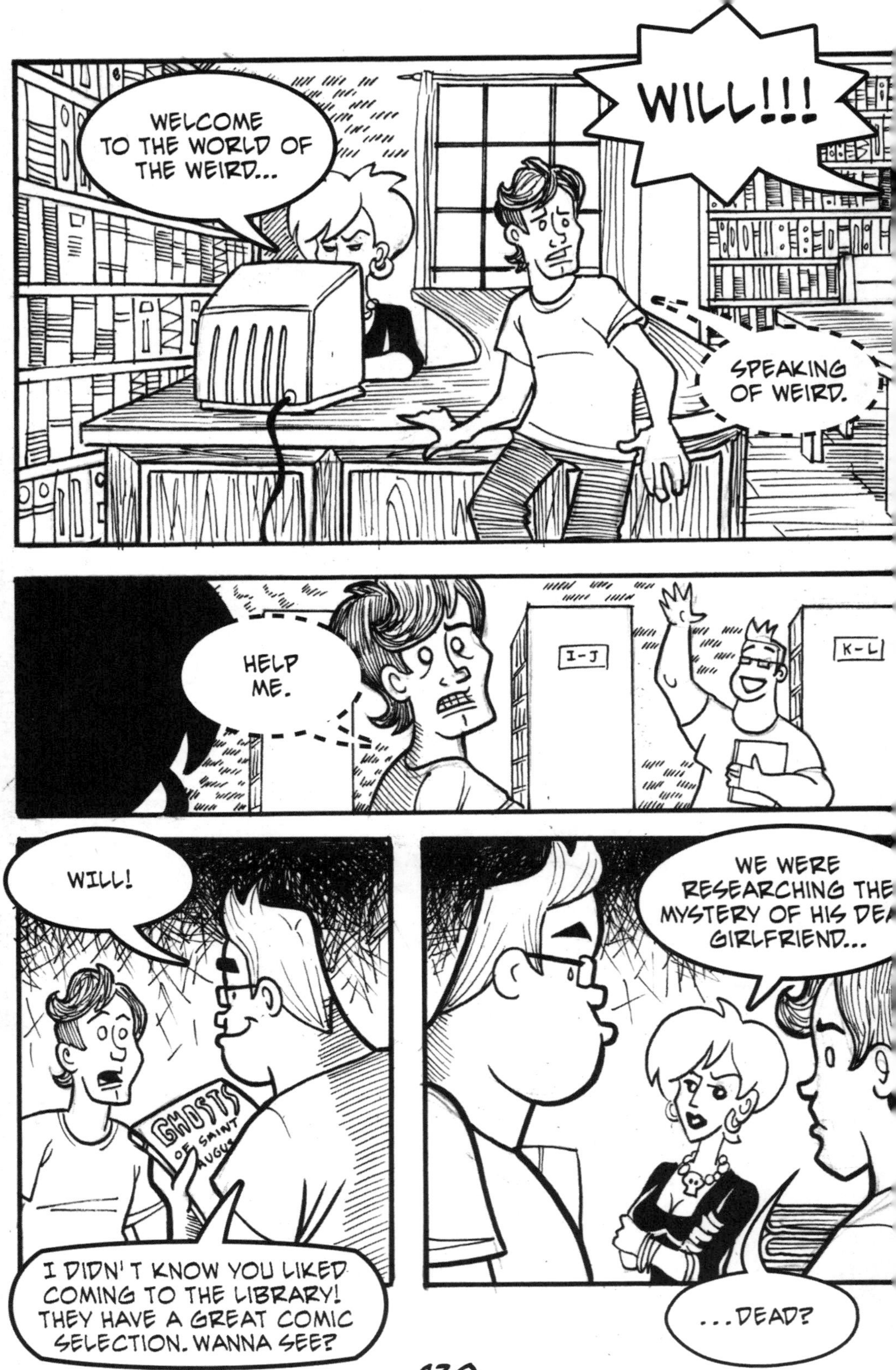
WELCOME TO THE WORLD OF THE WEIRD...
WILL!!!
SPEAKING OF WEIRD.
HELP ME.
I-J
K-L
WILL!
GHOSTS OF SAINT AUGUS
I DIDN'T KNOW YOU LIKED COMING TO THE LIBRARY! THEY HAVE A GREAT COMIC SELECTION. WANNA SEE?
WE WERE RESEARCHING THE MYSTERY OF HIS DEA GIRLFRIEND...
...DEAD?

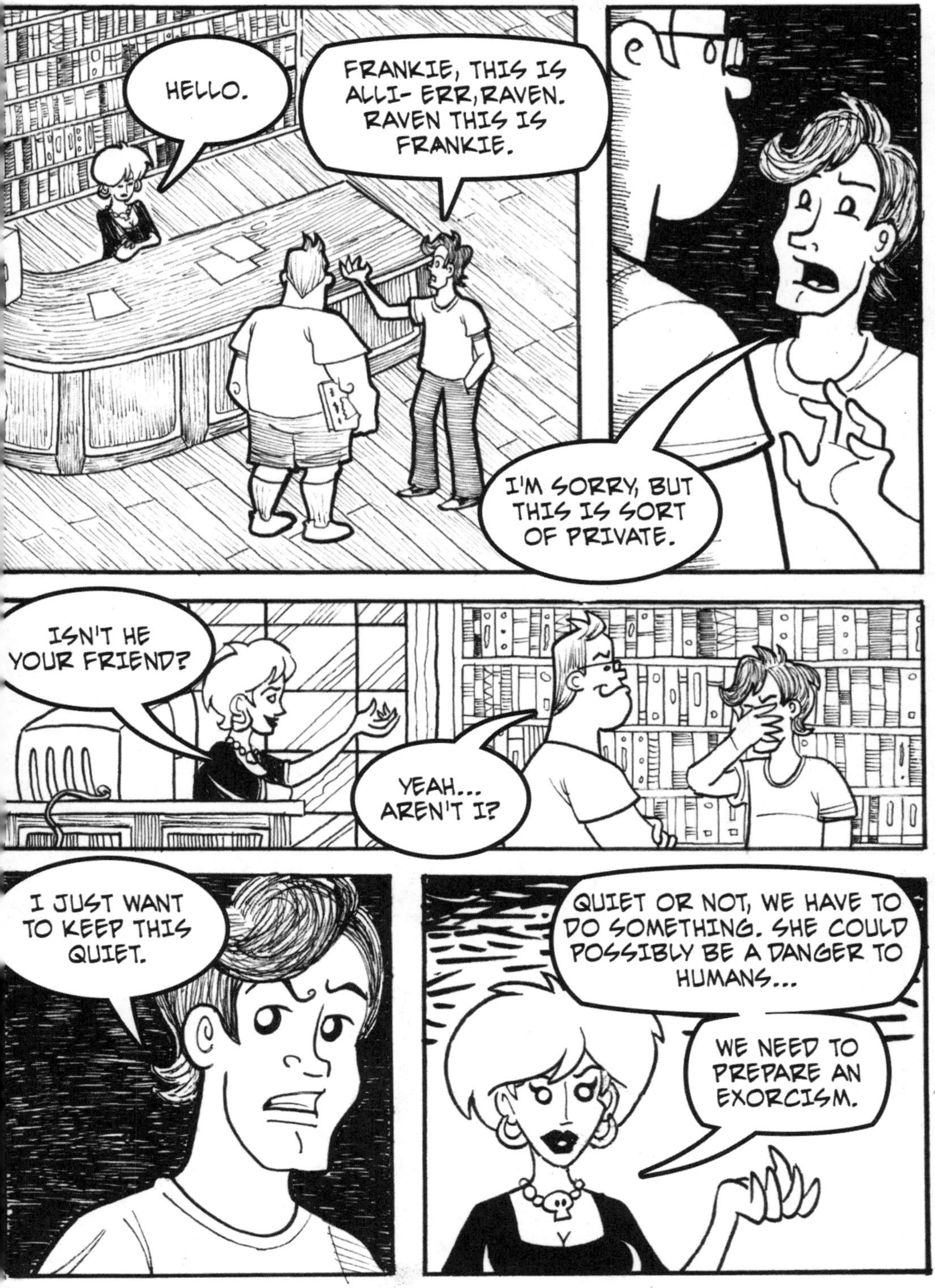
HELLO.
FRANKIE, THIS IS ALLI- ERR, RAVEN. RAVEN THIS IS FRANKIE.
I'M SORRY, BUT THIS IS SORT OF PRIVATE.
ISN'T HE YOUR FRIEND?
YEAH... AREN'T I?
I JUST WANT TO KEEP THIS QUIET.
QUIET OR NOT, WE HAVE TO DO SOMETHING. SHE COULD POSSIBLY BE A DANGER TO HUMANS...
WE NEED TO PREPARE AN EXORCISM.

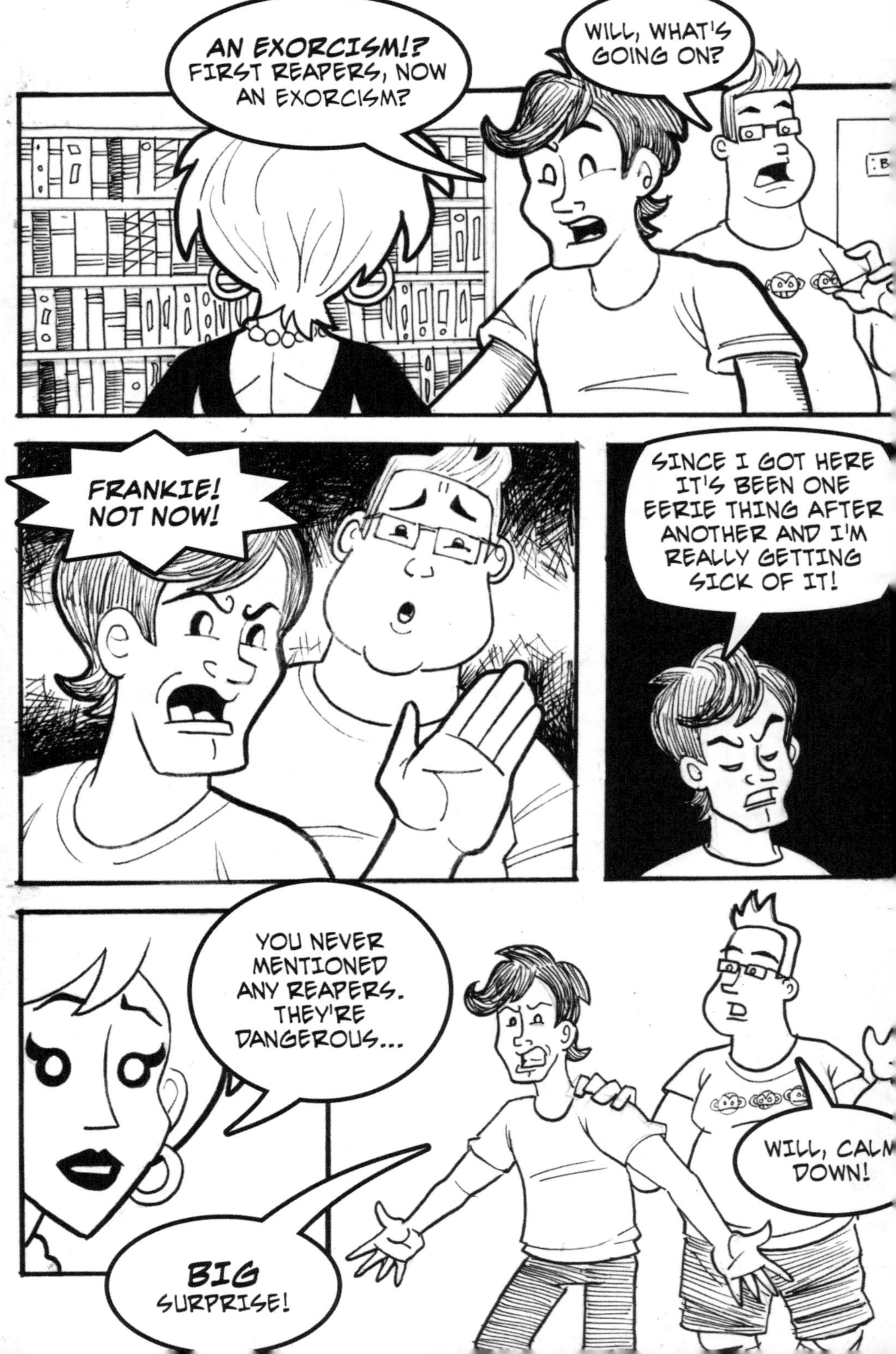
AN EXORCISM!? FIRST REAPERS, NOW AN EXORCISM?
WILL, WHAT'S GOING ON?
FRANKIE! NOT NOW!
SINCE I GOT HERE IT'S BEEN ONE EERIE THING AFTER ANOTHER AND I'M REALLY GETTING SICK OF IT!
YOU NEVER MENTIONED ANY REAPERS. THEY'RE DANGEROUS...
BIG SURPRISE!
WILL, CALM DOWN!

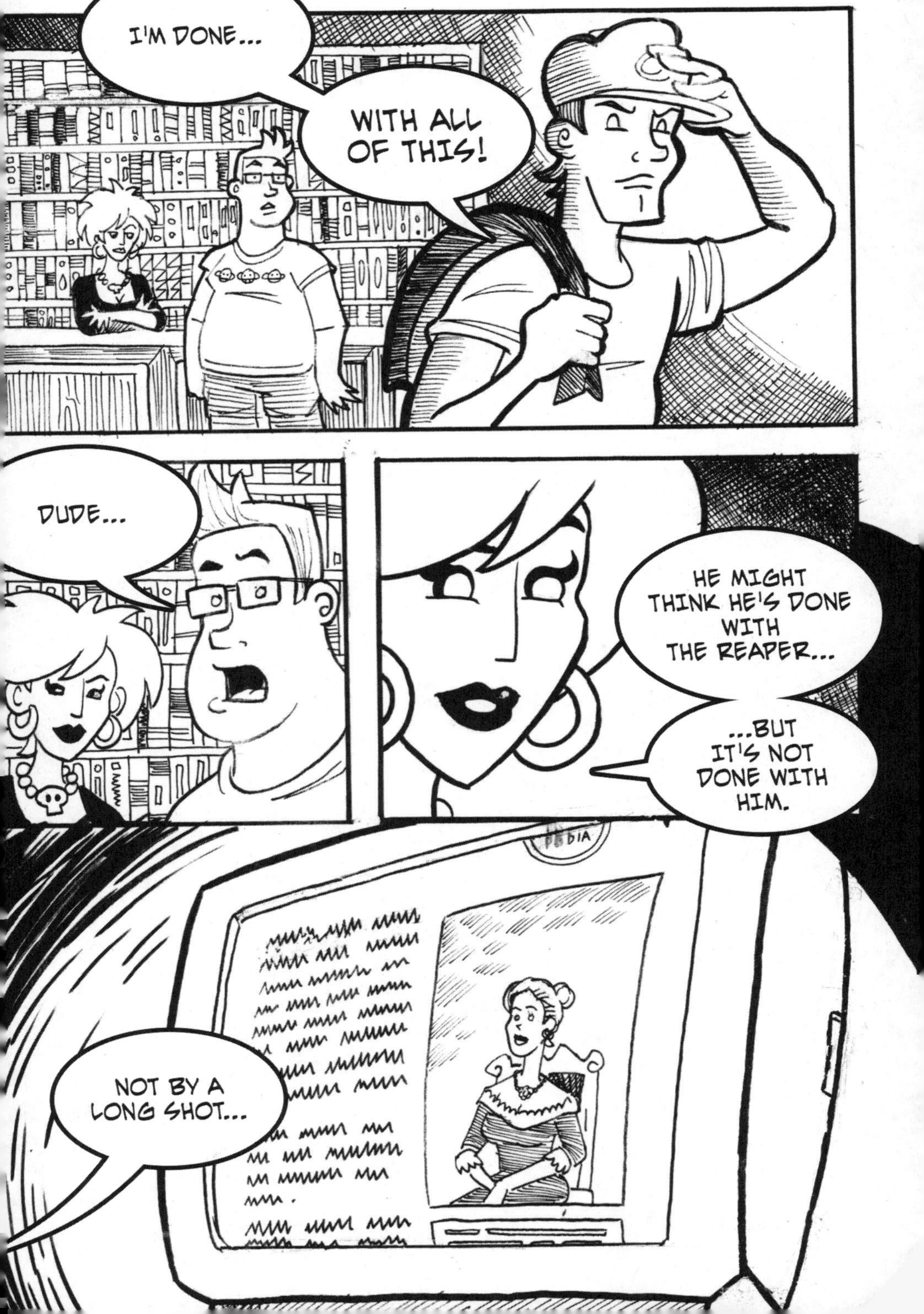
I'M DONE...
WITH ALL OF THIS!
DUDE...
HE MIGHT THINK HE'S DONE WITH THE REAPER...
...BUT IT'S NOT DONE WITH HIM.
NOT BY A LONG SHOT...

CHAPTER

11

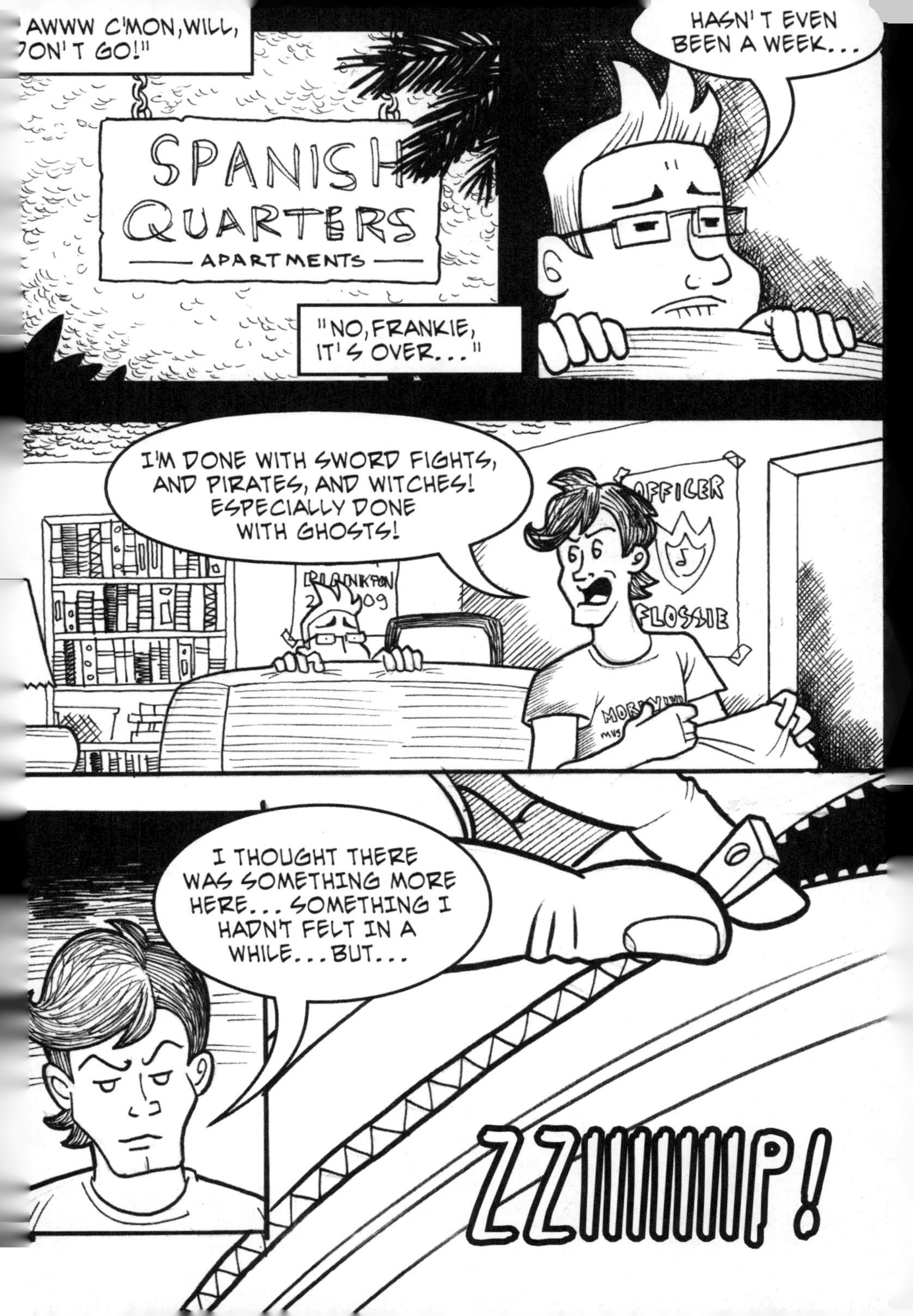
"AWWW C'MON, WILL, DON'T GO!"
SPANISH QUARTERS APARTMENTS
"NO, FRANKIE, IT'S OVER..."
HASN'T EVEN BEEN A WEEK...
I'M DONE WITH SWORD FIGHTS, AND PIRATES, AND WITCHES! ESPECIALLY DONE WITH GHOSTS!
OFFICER FLOSSIE
I THOUGHT THERE WAS SOMETHING MORE HERE... SOMETHING I HADN'T FELT IN A WHILE... BUT...
ZZIIIIIIIP!

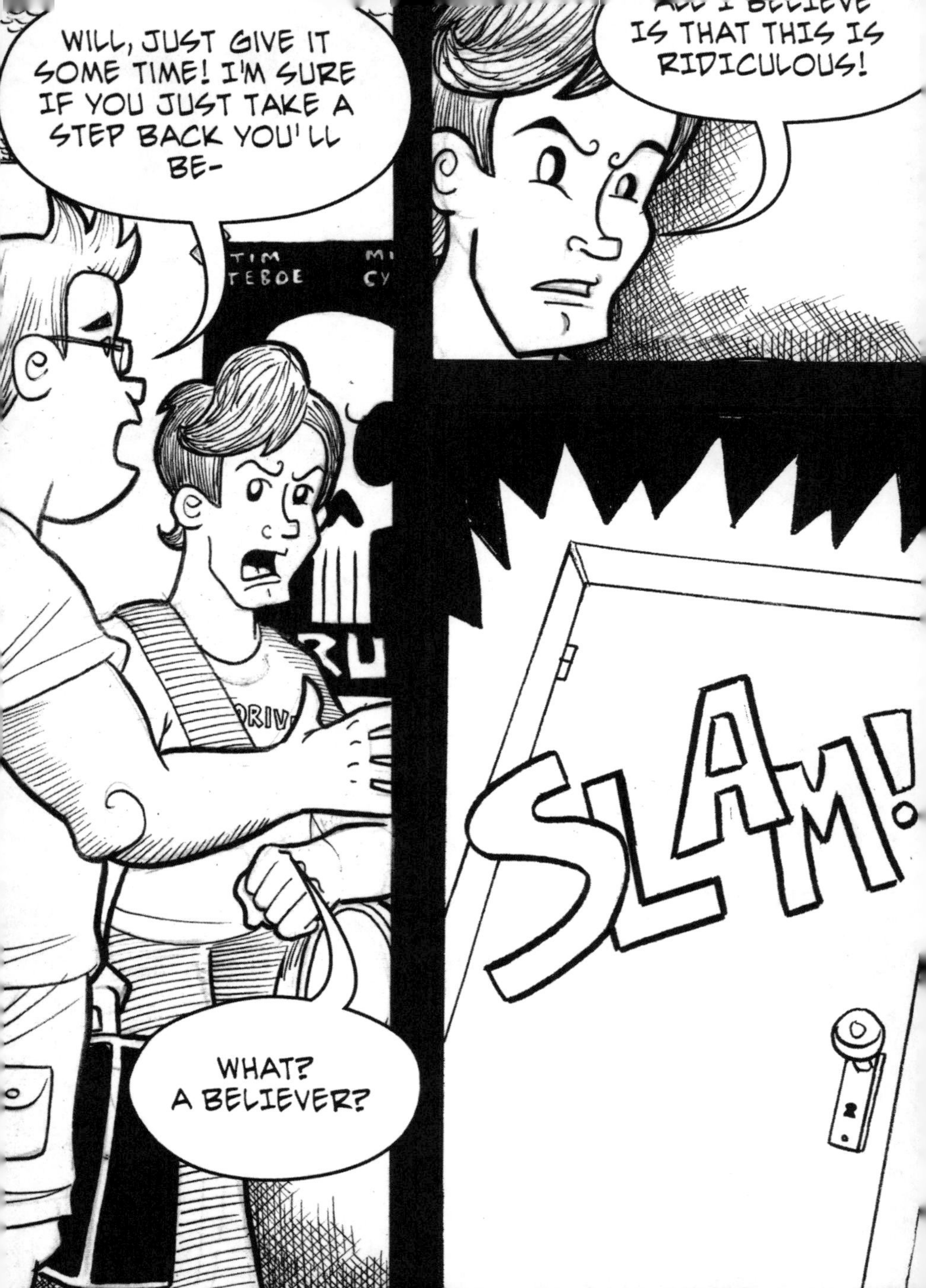
WILL, JUST GIVE IT SOME TIME! I'M SURE IF YOU JUST TAKE A STEP BACK YOU'LL BE-
WHAT? A BELIEVER?
IS THAT THIS IS RIDICULOUS!
SLAM!

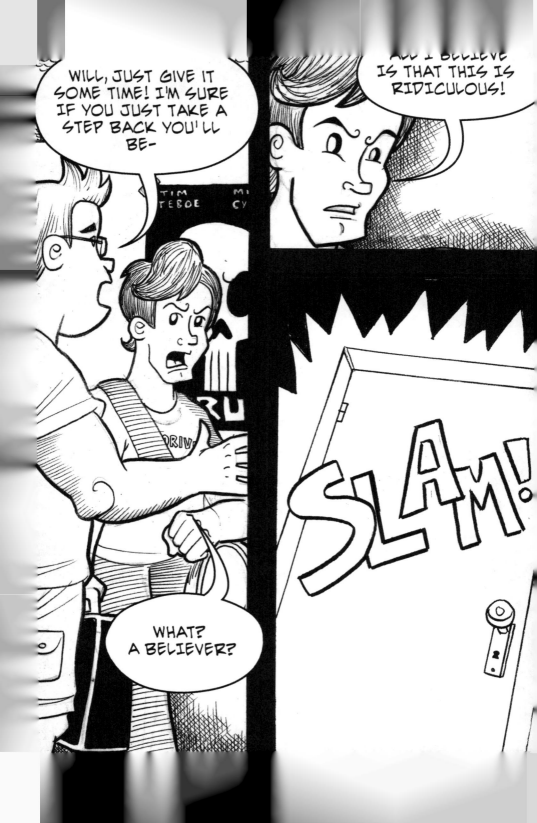

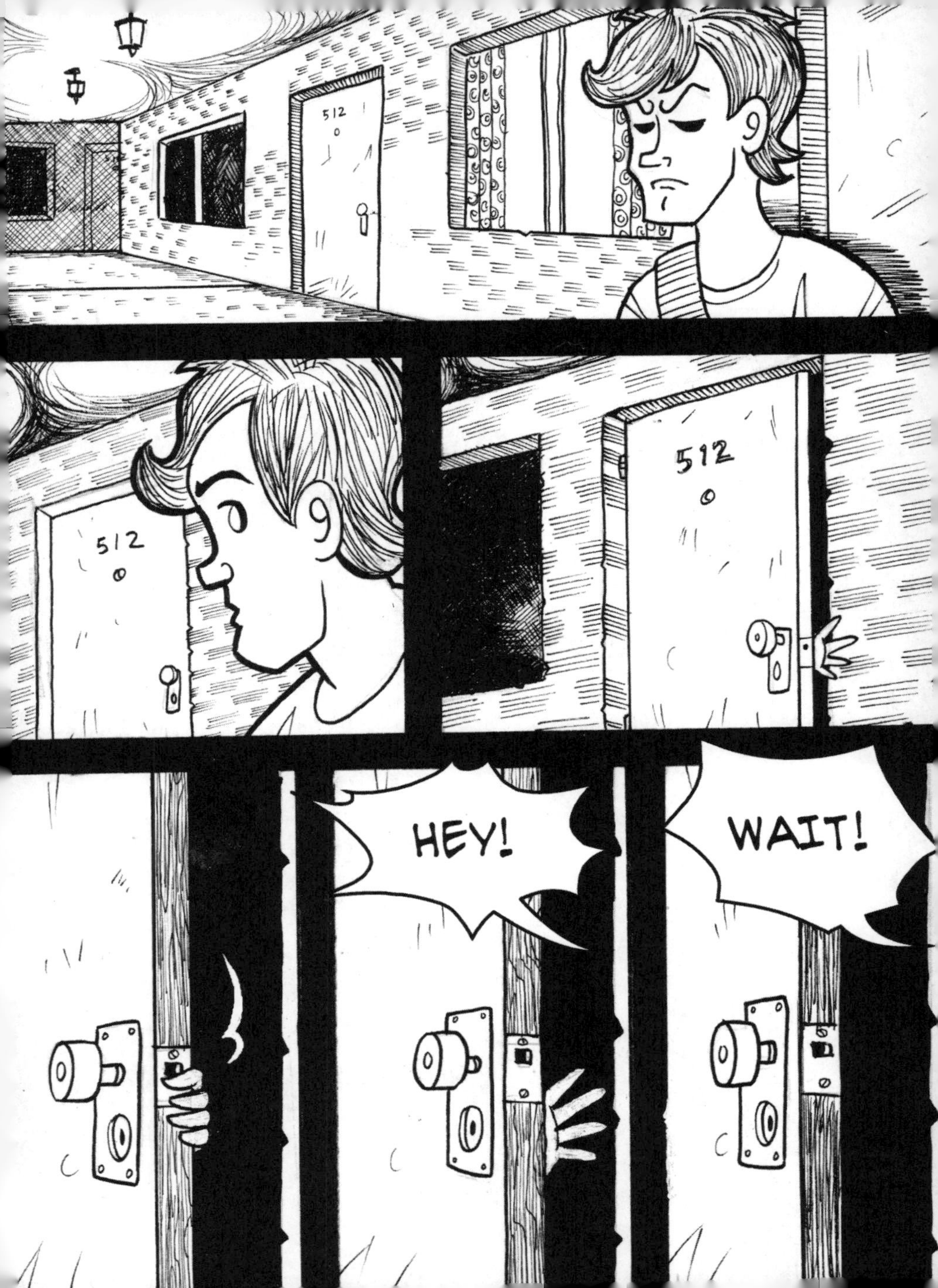

512
512
512
HEY!
WAIT!

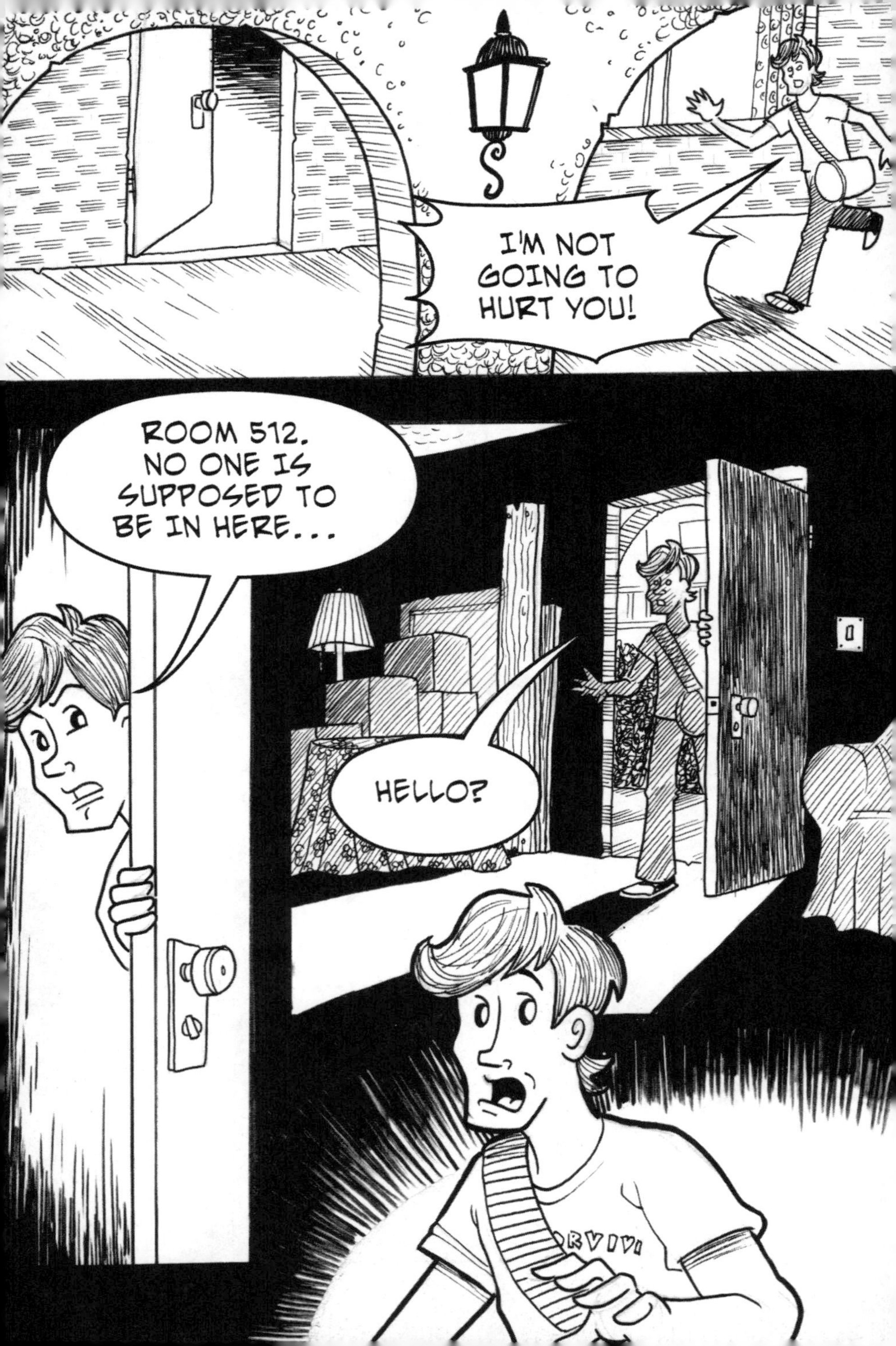
I'M NOT GOING TO HURT YOU!
ROOM 512. NO ONE IS SUPPOSED TO BE IN HERE...
HELLO?

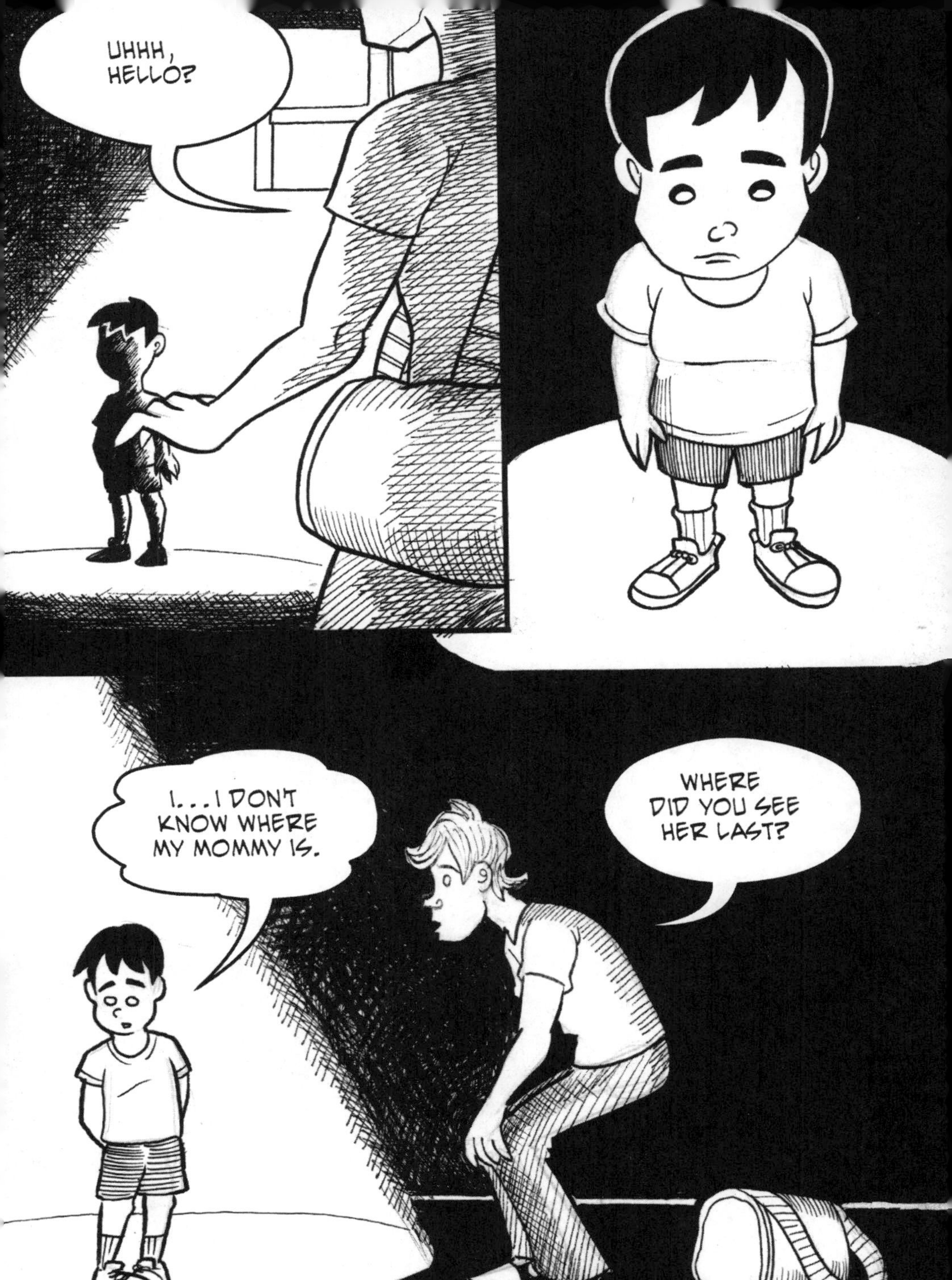
UHHH, HELLO?
I...I DON'T KNOW WHERE MY MOMMY IS.
WHERE DID YOU SEE HER LAST?

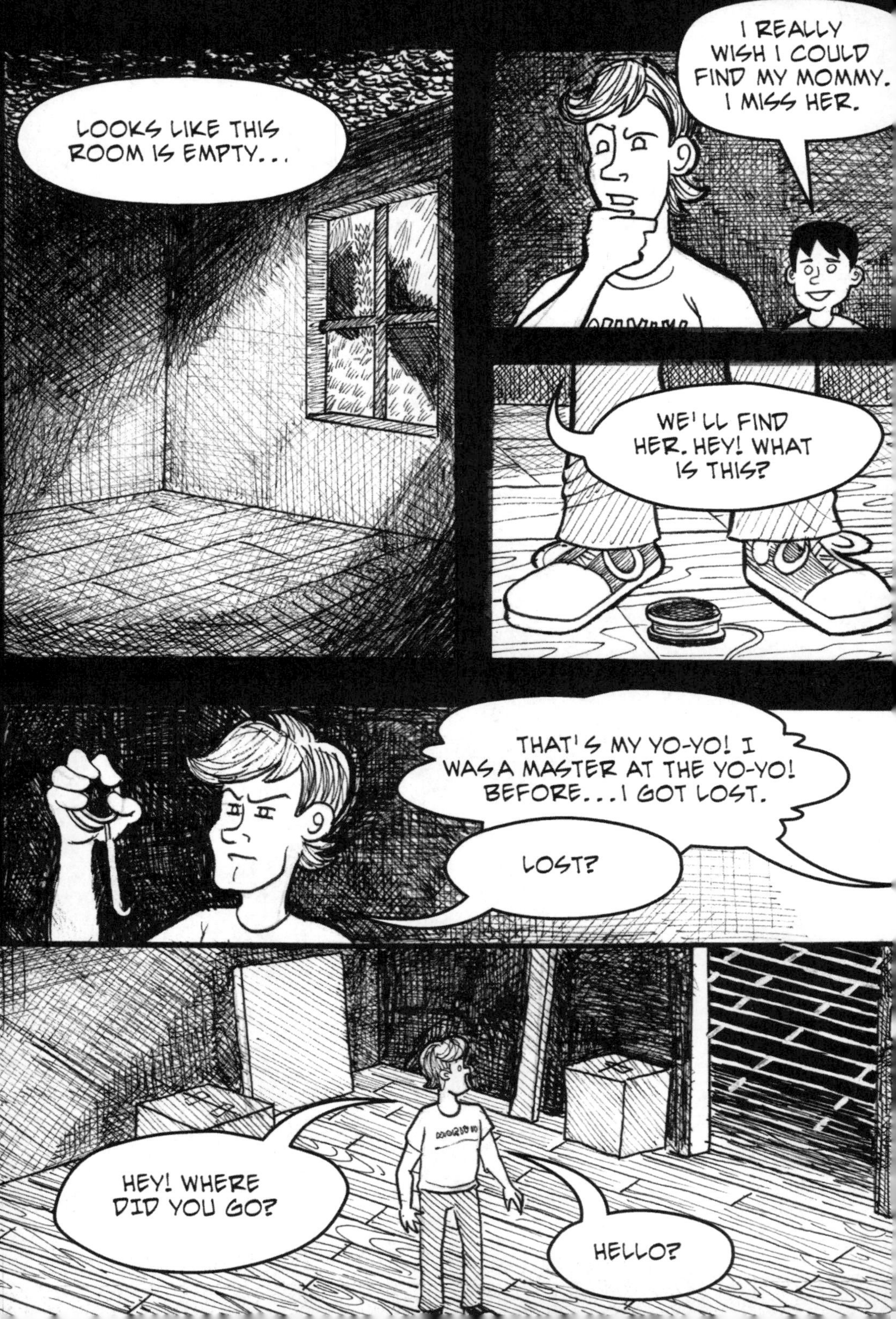
LOOKS LIKE THIS ROOM IS EMPTY...
I REALLY WISH I COULD FIND MY MOMMY. I MISS HER.
WE'LL FIND HER. HEY! WHAT IS THIS?
THAT'S MY YO-YO! I WAS A MASTER AT THE YO-YO! BEFORE...I GOT LOST.
LOST?
HEY! WHERE DID YOU GO?
HELLO?

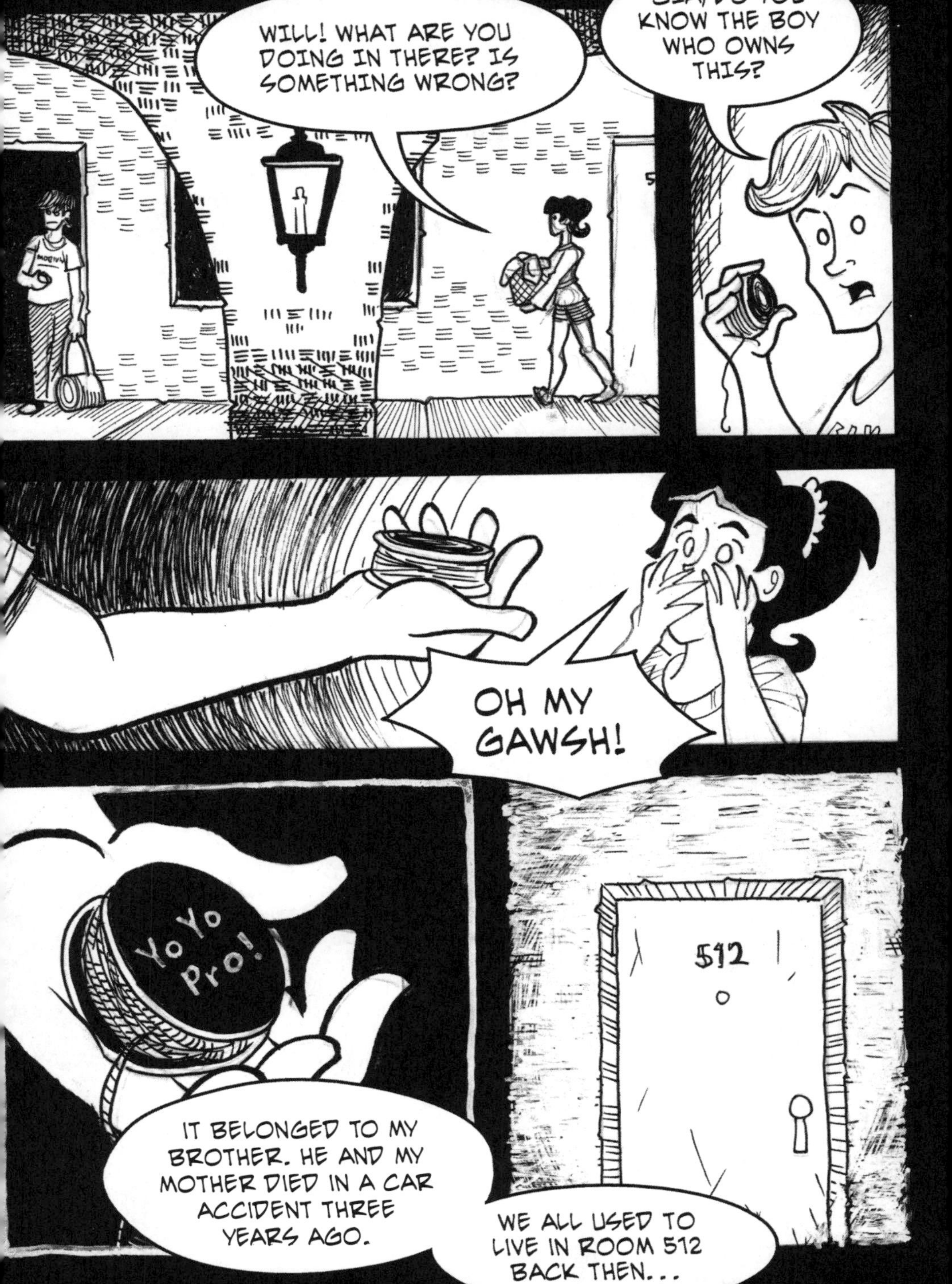
WILL! WHAT ARE YOU DOING IN THERE? IS SOMETHING WRONG?
GIA, DO YOU KNOW THE BOY WHO OWNS THIS?
OH MY GAWSH!
Yo Yo Pro!
512
IT BELONGED TO MY BROTHER. HE AND MY MOTHER DIED IN A CAR ACCIDENT THREE YEARS AGO.
WE ALL USED TO LIVE IN ROOM 512 BACK THEN...

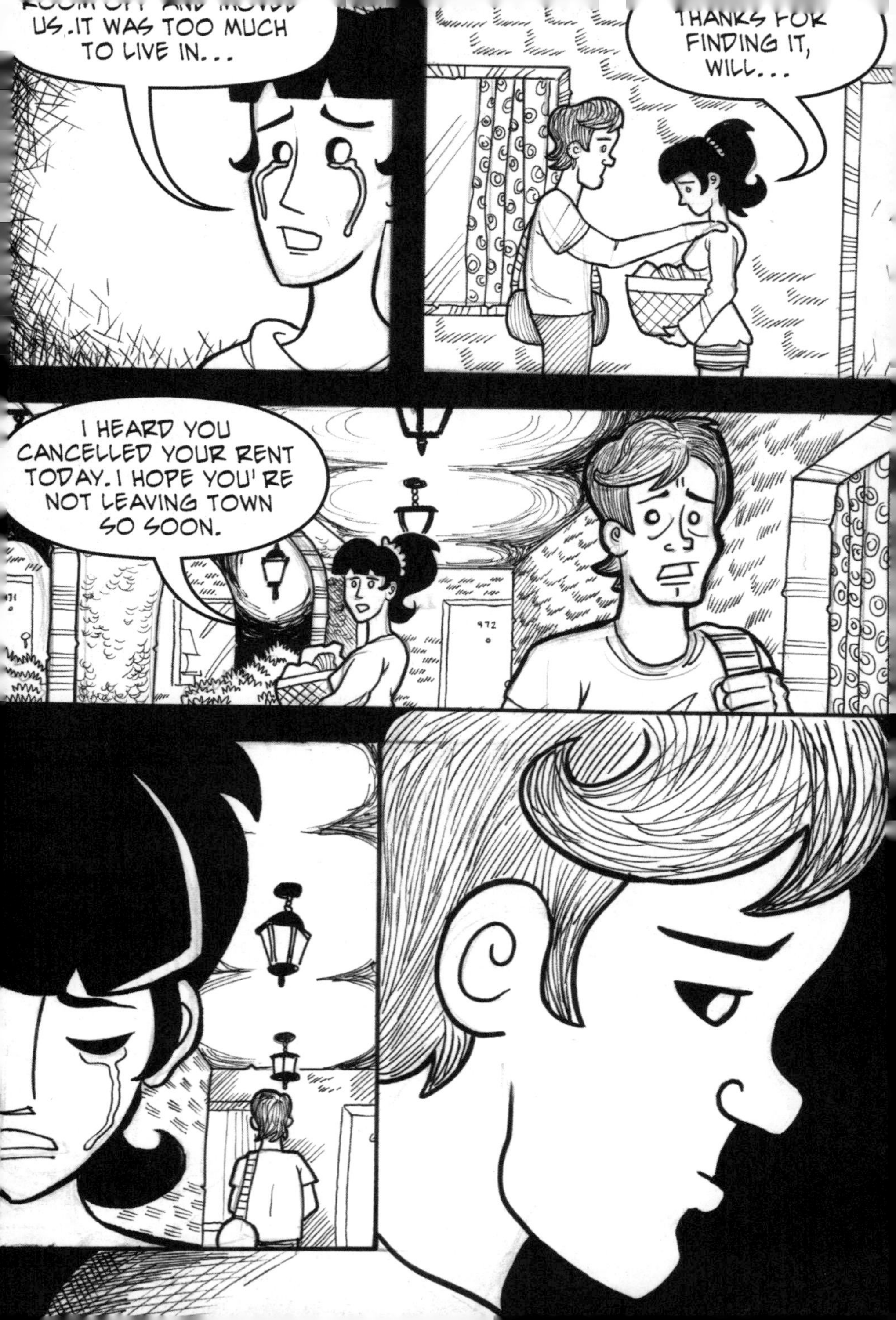
US. IT WAS TOO MUCH TO LIVE IN...
THANKS FOR FINDING IT, WILL...
I HEARD YOU CANCELLED YOUR RENT TODAY. I HOPE YOU'RE NOT LEAVING TOWN SO SOON.
472

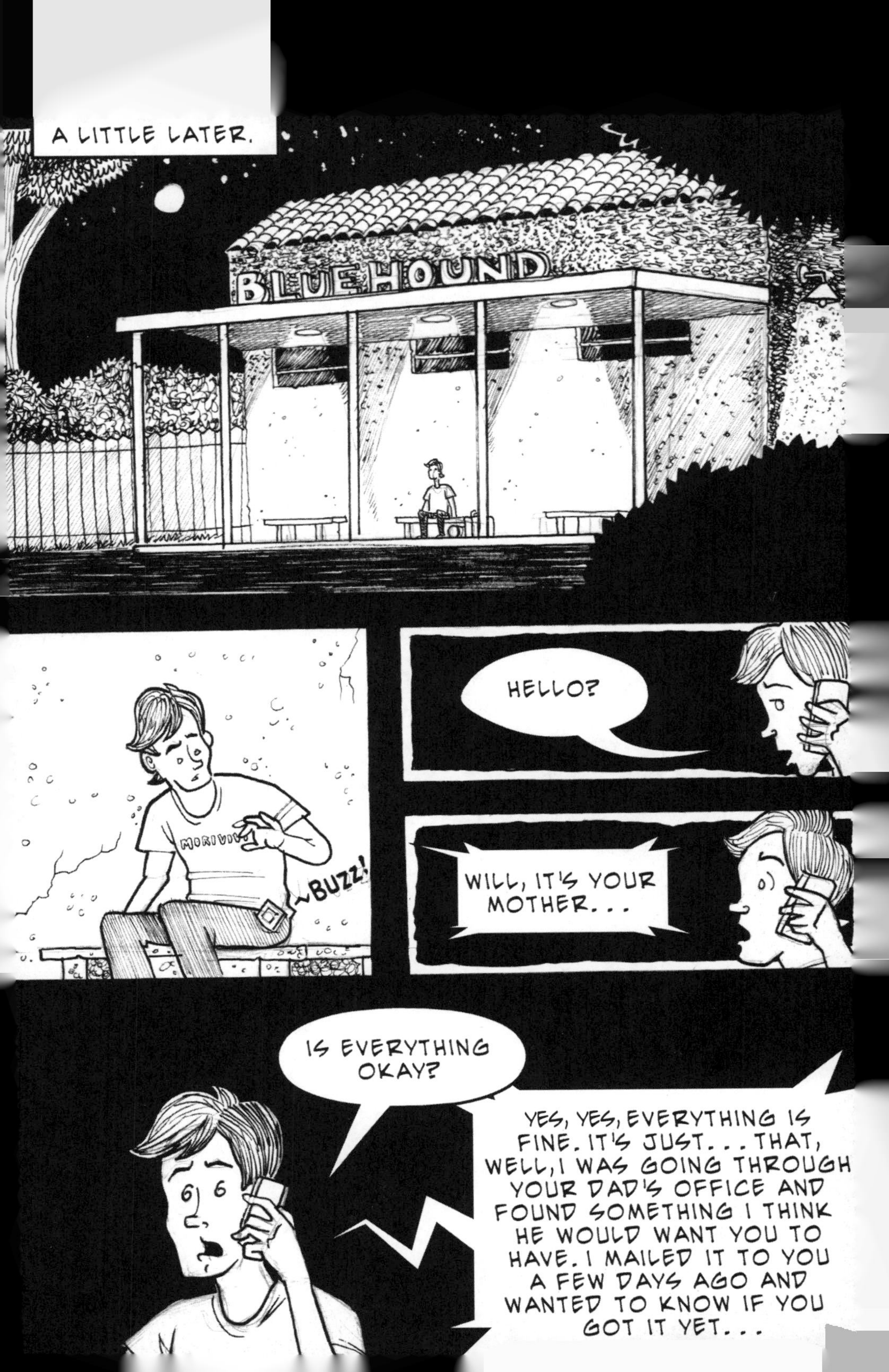
A LITTLE LATER.
BLUEHOUND
MORIVIV
BUZZ!
HELLO?
WILL, IT'S YOUR MOTHER...
IS EVERYTHING OKAY?
YES, YES, EVERYTHING IS FINE. IT'S JUST... THAT, WELL, I WAS GOING THROUGH YOUR DAD'S OFFICE AND FOUND SOMETHING I THINK HE WOULD WANT YOU TO HAVE. I MAILED IT TO YOU A FEW DAYS AGO AND WANTED TO KNOW IF YOU GOT IT YET...

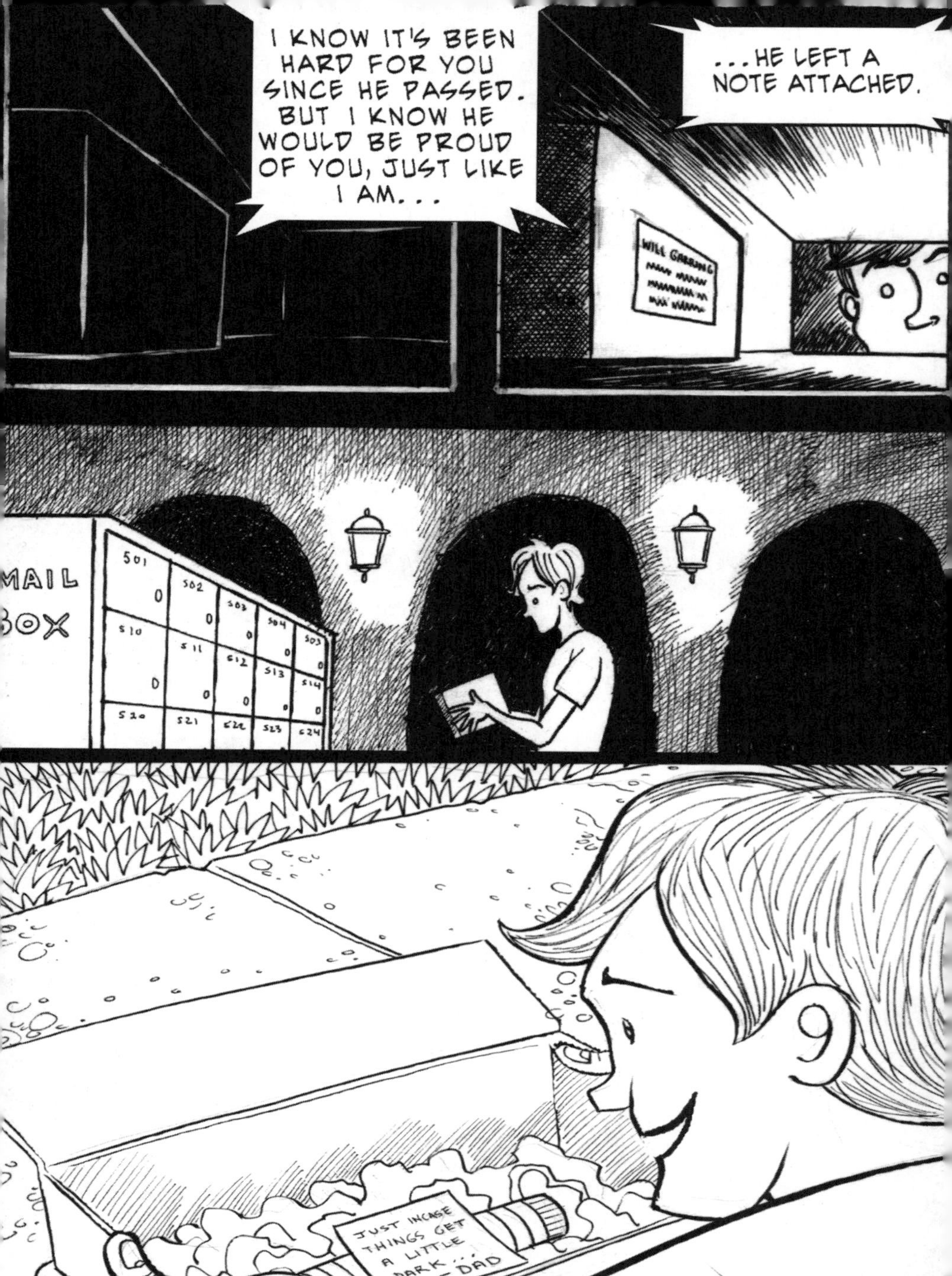
I KNOW IT'S BEEN HARD FOR YOU SINCE HE PASSED. BUT I KNOW HE WOULD BE PROUD OF YOU, JUST LIKE I AM...
...HE LEFT A NOTE ATTACHED.
MAIL
JUST INCASE THINGS GET A LITTLE DARK... —DAD

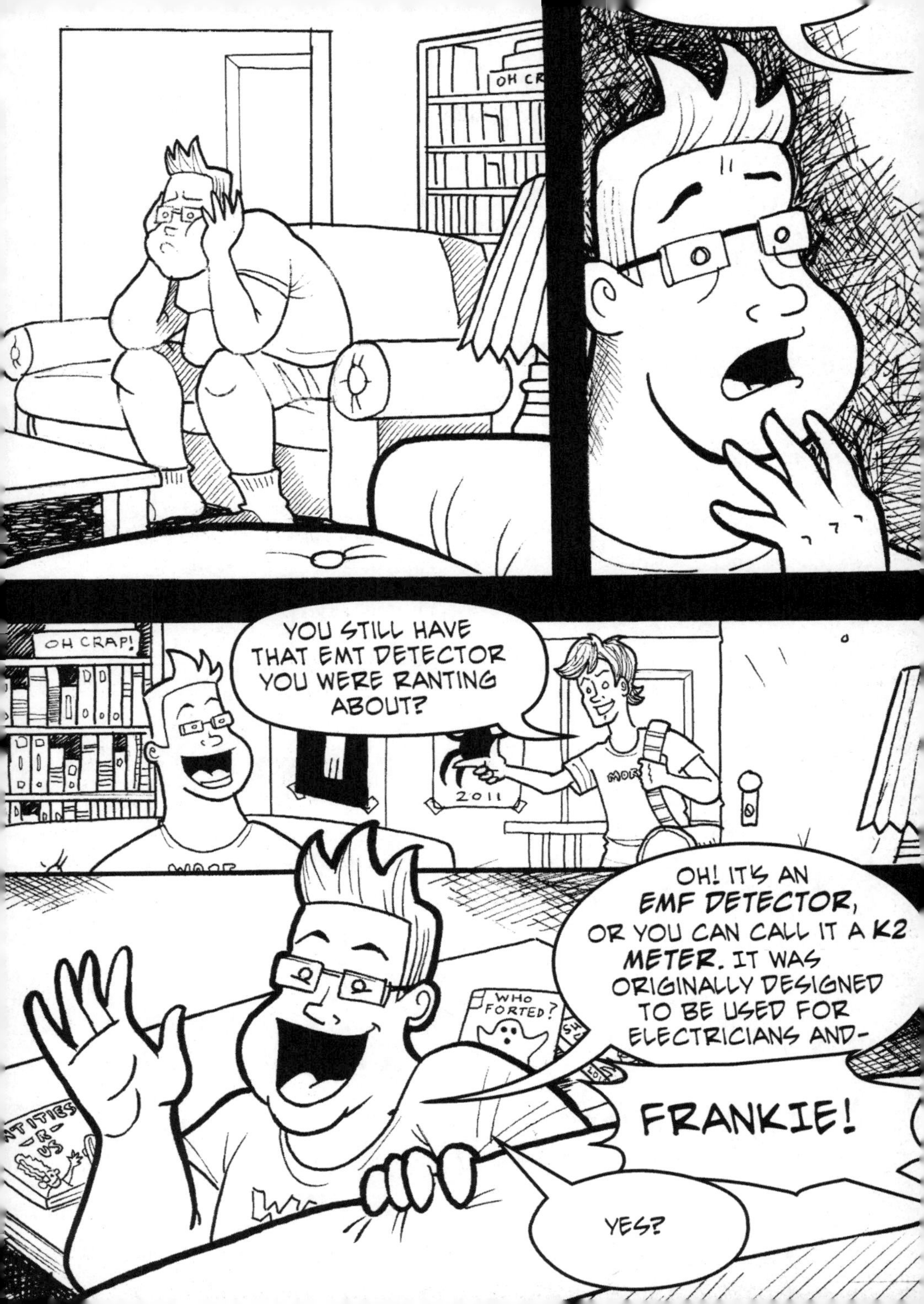
OH CR
OH CRAP!
YOU STILL HAVE THAT EMT DETECTOR YOU WERE RANTING ABOUT?
2011
OH! IT'S AN EMF DETECTOR, OR YOU CAN CALL IT A K2 METER. IT WAS ORIGINALLY DESIGNED TO BE USED FOR ELECTRICIANS AND-
WHO FORTED?
FRANKIE!
YES?

CHAPTER

12

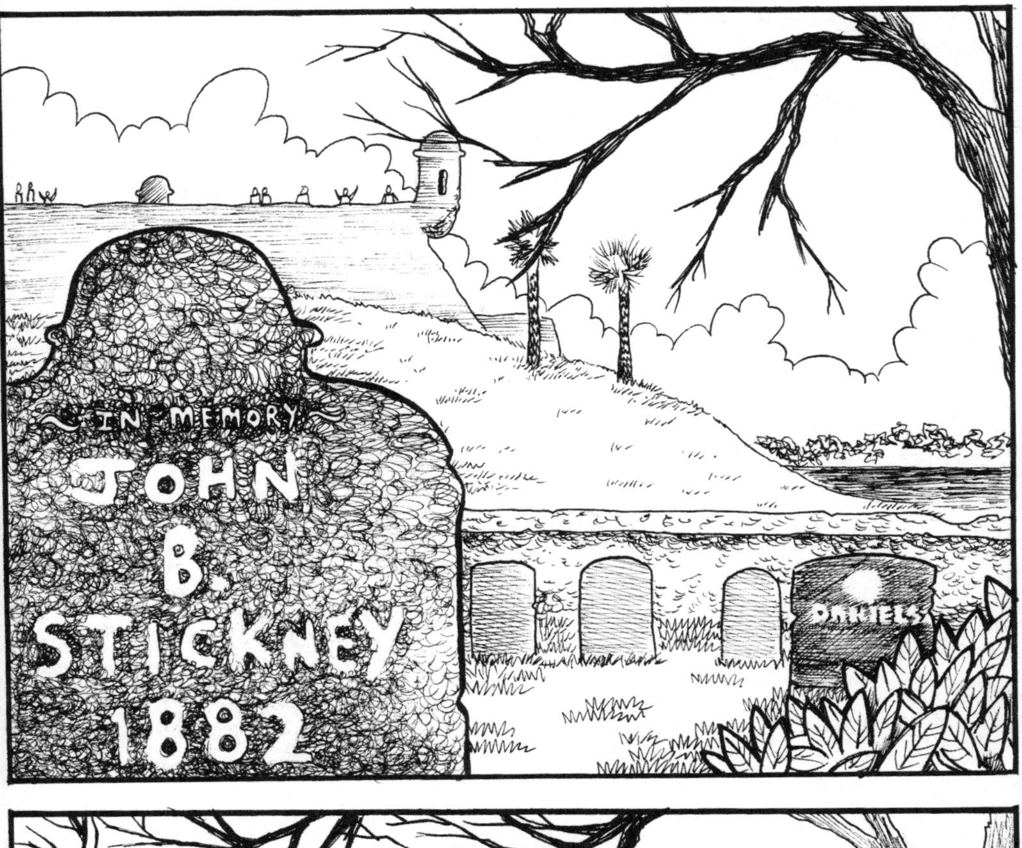
IN MEMORY
JOHN
B.
STICKNEY
1882
DANIELS

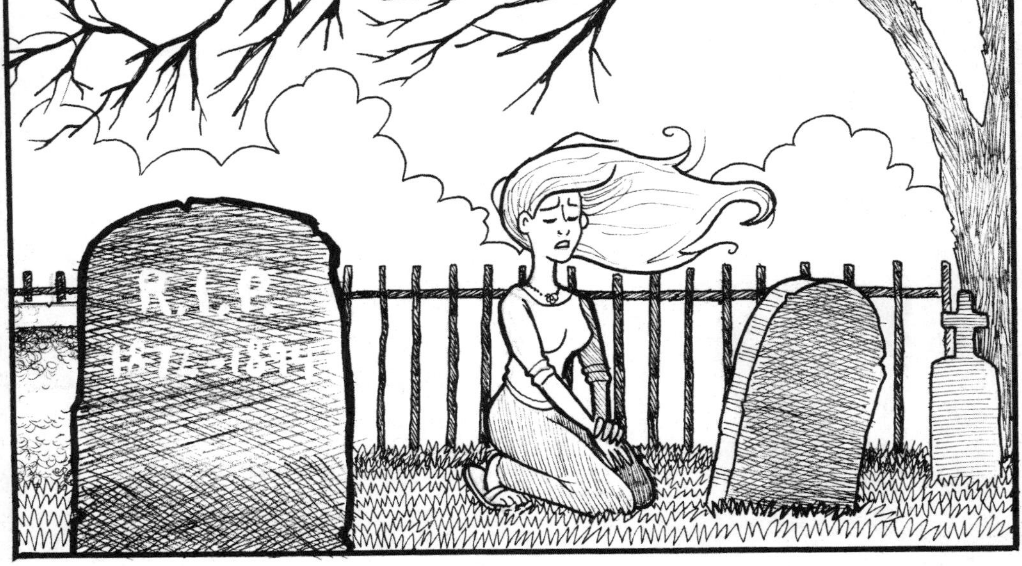
R.I.P.

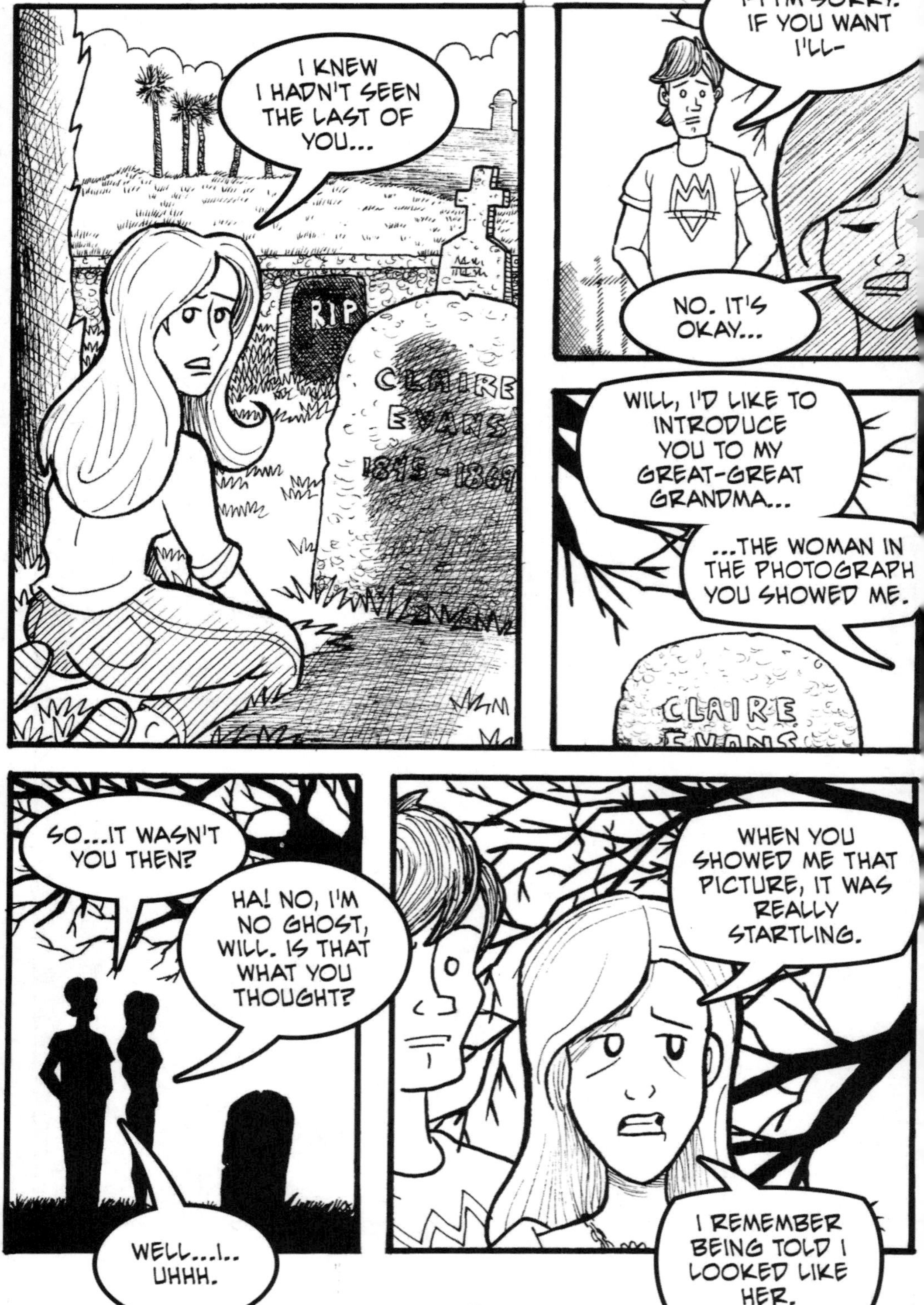

I KNEW I HADN'T SEEN THE LAST OF YOU...
RIP
CLAIRE EVANS
I-I I'M SORRY. IF YOU WANT I'LL-
NO. IT'S OKAY...
WILL, I'D LIKE TO INTRODUCE YOU TO MY GREAT-GREAT GRANDMA...
...THE WOMAN IN THE PHOTOGRAPH YOU SHOWED ME.
CLAIRE
SO...IT WASN'T YOU THEN?
HA! NO, I'M NO GHOST, WILL. IS THAT WHAT YOU THOUGHT?
WELL...I.. UHHH.
WHEN YOU SHOWED ME THAT PICTURE, IT WAS REALLY STARTLING.
I REMEMBER BEING TOLD I LOOKED LIKE HER.

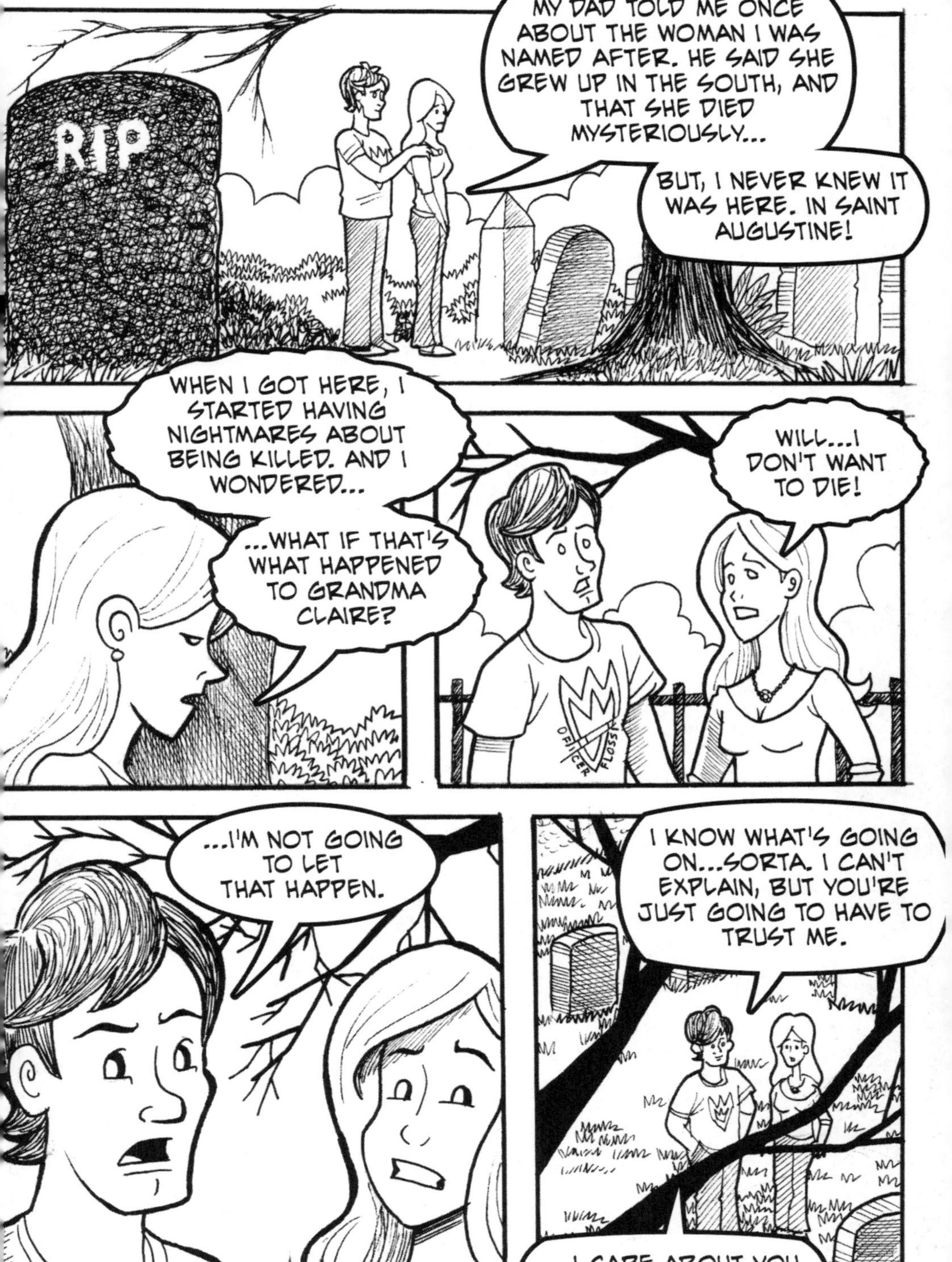
MY DAD TOLD ME ONCE ABOUT THE WOMAN I WAS NAMED AFTER. HE SAID SHE GREW UP IN THE SOUTH, AND THAT SHE DIED MYSTERIOUSLY...
BUT, I NEVER KNEW IT WAS HERE. IN SAINT AUGUSTINE!
RIP
WHEN I GOT HERE, I STARTED HAVING NIGHTMARES ABOUT BEING KILLED. AND I WONDERED...
...WHAT IF THAT'S WHAT HAPPENED TO GRANDMA CLAIRE?
WILL...I DON'T WANT TO DIE!
OFFICER FLOSS
...I'M NOT GOING TO LET THAT HAPPEN.
I KNOW WHAT'S GOING ON...SORTA. I CAN'T EXPLAIN, BUT YOU'RE JUST GOING TO HAVE TO TRUST ME.
...I CARE ABOUT YOU, CLAIRE, A LOT.

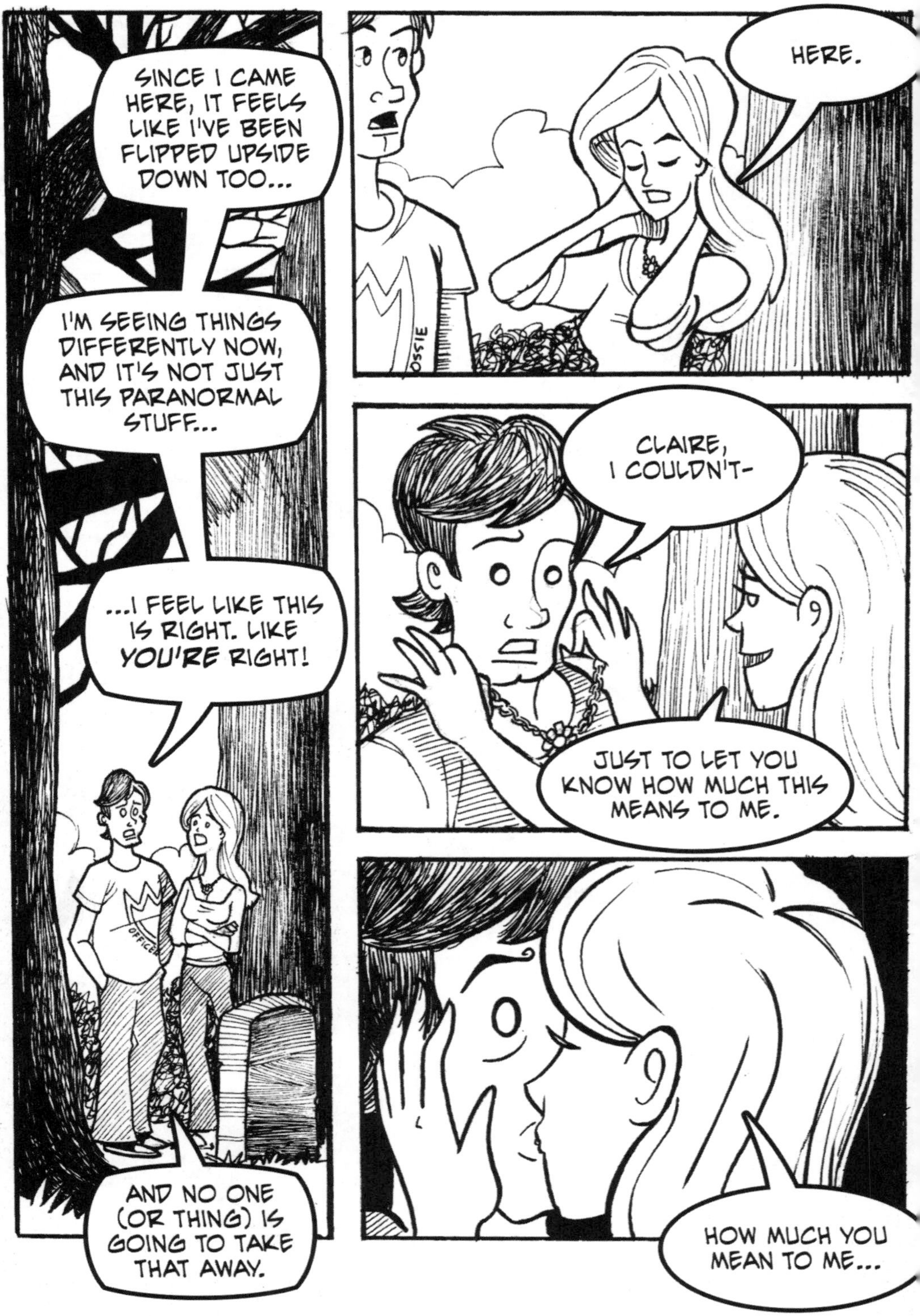
SINCE I CAME HERE, IT FEELS LIKE I'VE BEEN FLIPPED UPSIDE DOWN TOO...
I'M SEEING THINGS DIFFERENTLY NOW, AND IT'S NOT JUST THIS PARANORMAL STUFF...
...I FEEL LIKE THIS IS RIGHT. LIKE *YOU'RE* RIGHT!
OFFICE
AND NO ONE (OR THING) IS GOING TO TAKE THAT AWAY.
HERE.
OSSIE
CLAIRE, I COULDN'T-
JUST TO LET YOU KNOW HOW MUCH THIS MEANS TO ME.
HOW MUCH YOU MEAN TO ME...

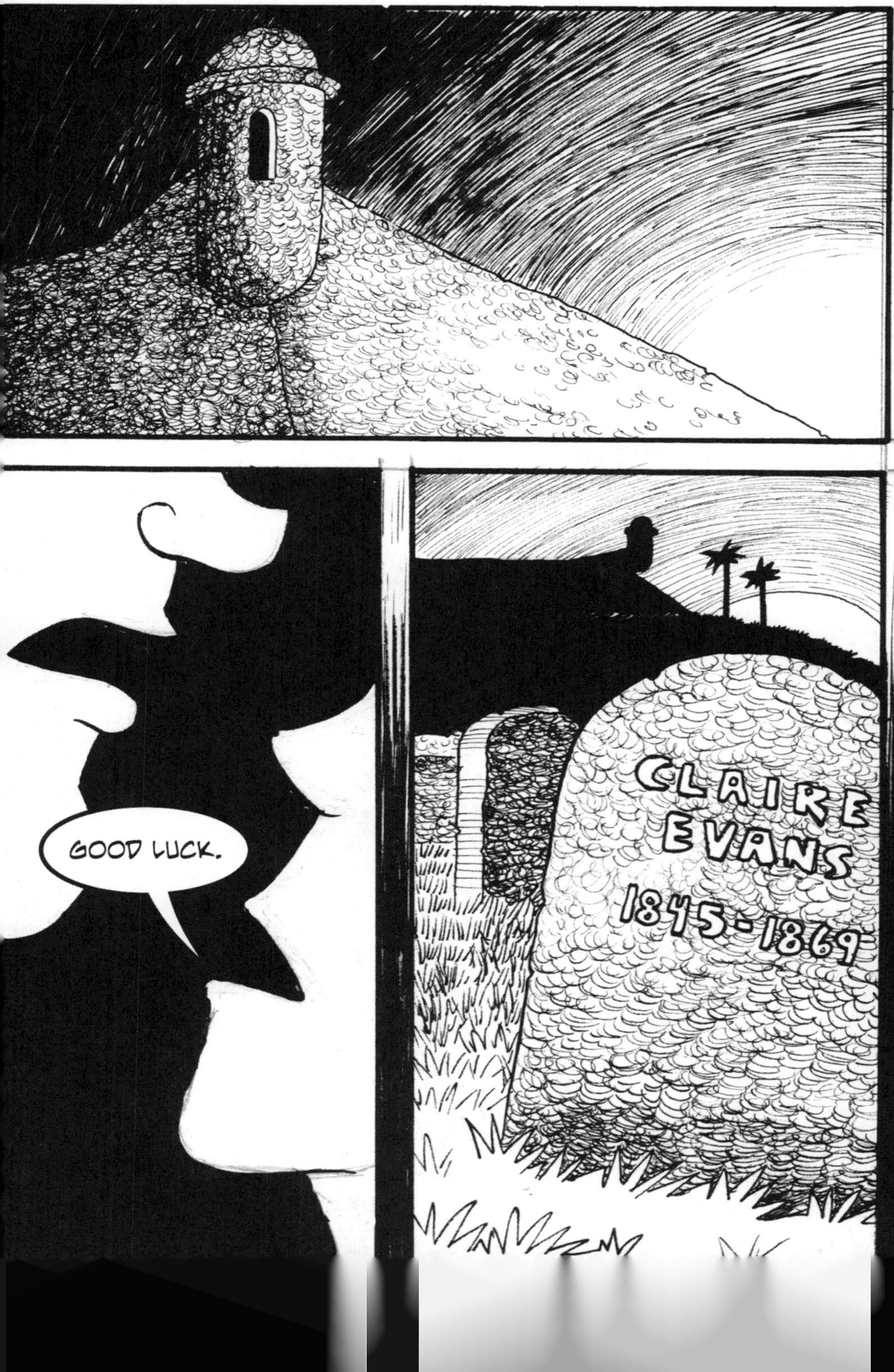
GOOD LUCK.
CLAIRE EVANS
1845-1869

CHAPTER

13

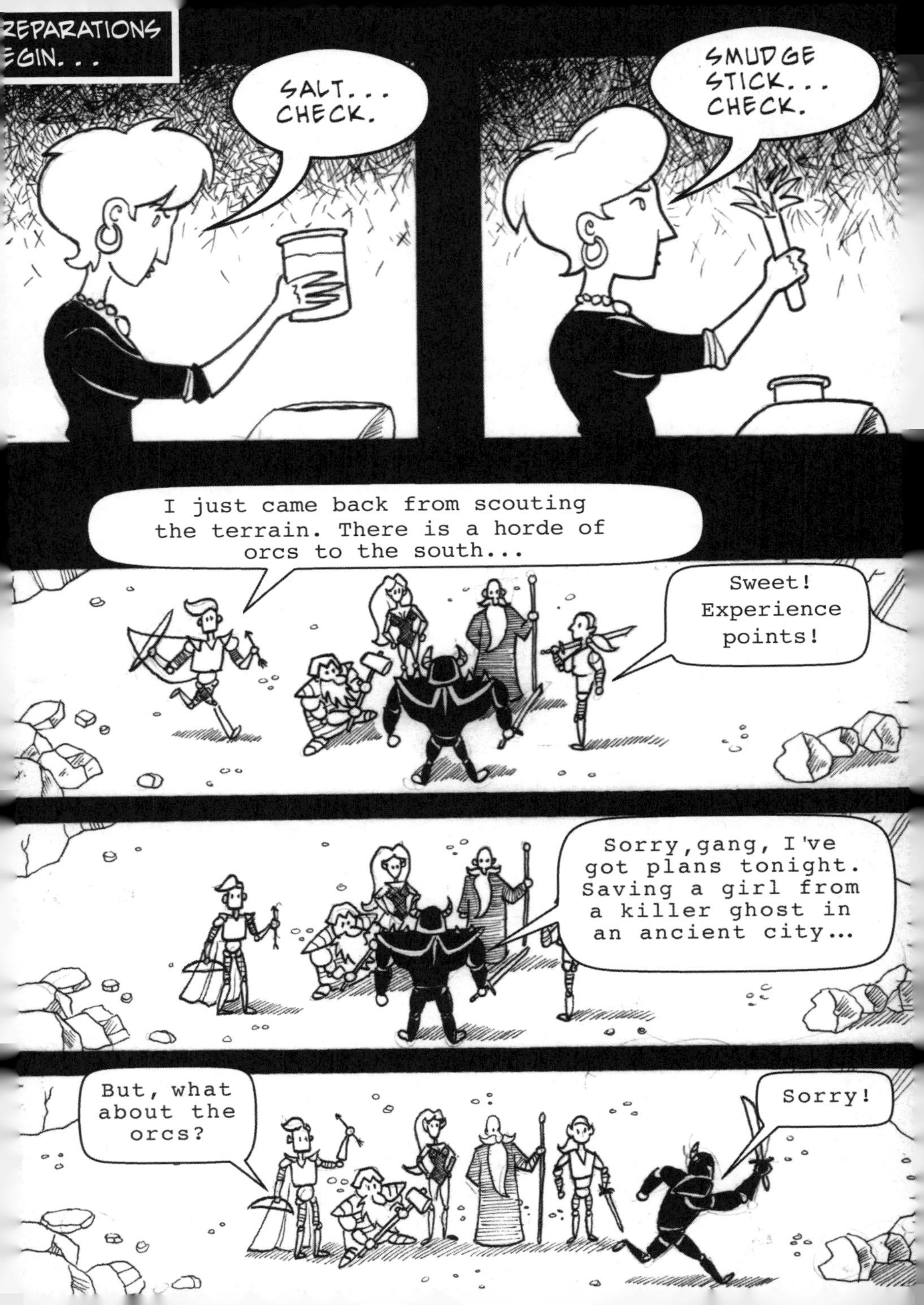

REPARATIONS
EGIN...
SALT... CHECK.
SMUDGE STICK... CHECK.
I just came back from scouting the terrain. There is a horde of orcs to the south...
Sweet! Experience points!
Sorry, gang, I've got plans tonight. Saving a girl from a killer ghost in an ancient city...
But, what about the orcs?
Sorry!

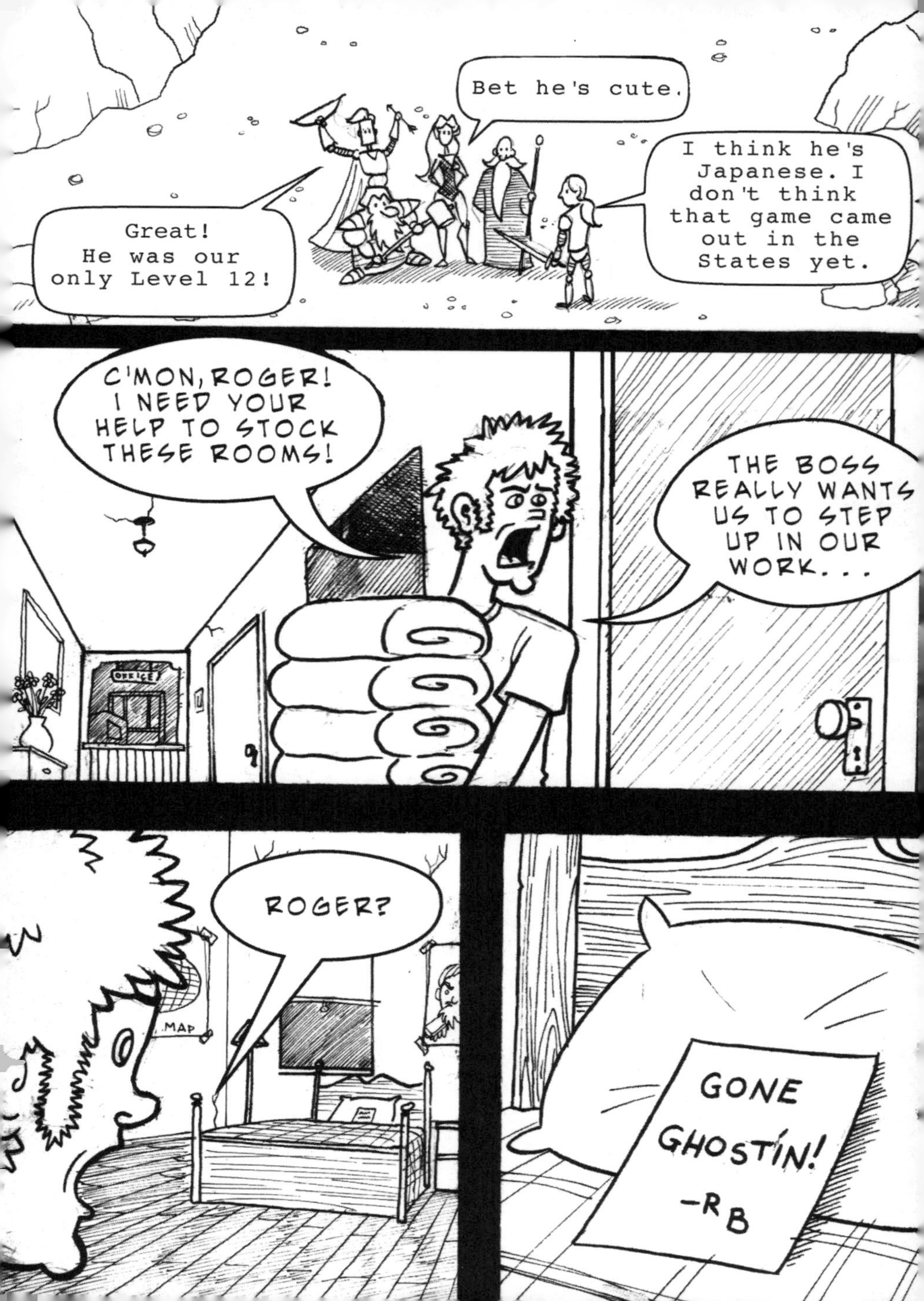
Bet he's cute.
Great! He was our only Level 12!
I think he's Japanese. I don't think that game came out in the States yet.
C'MON, ROGER! I NEED YOUR HELP TO STOCK THESE ROOMS!
THE BOSS REALLY WANTS US TO STEP UP IN OUR WORK...
ROGER?
MAP
GONE GHOSTIN! -RB

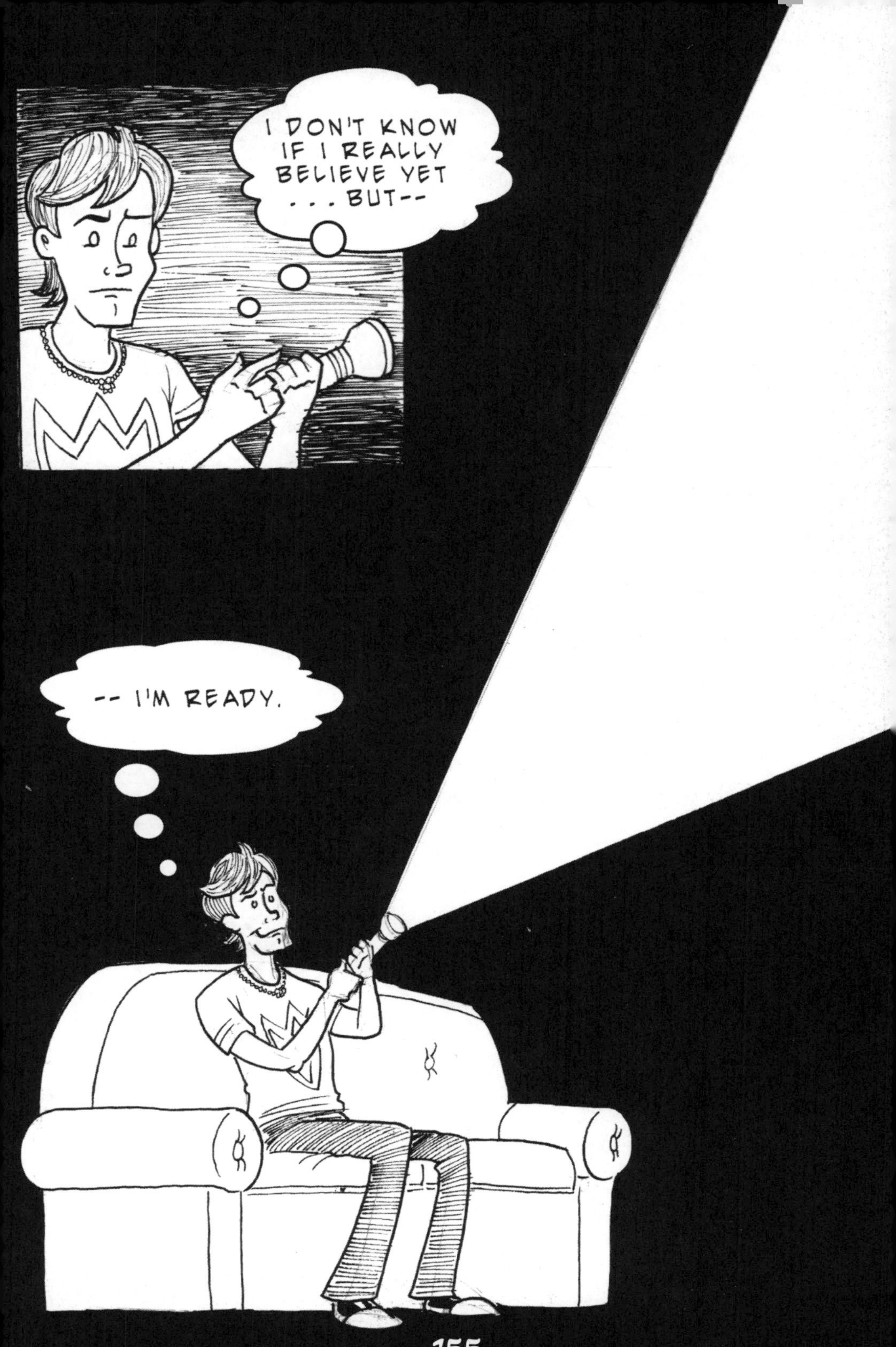
I DON'T KNOW IF I REALLY BELIEVE YET . . . BUT--
-- I'M READY.

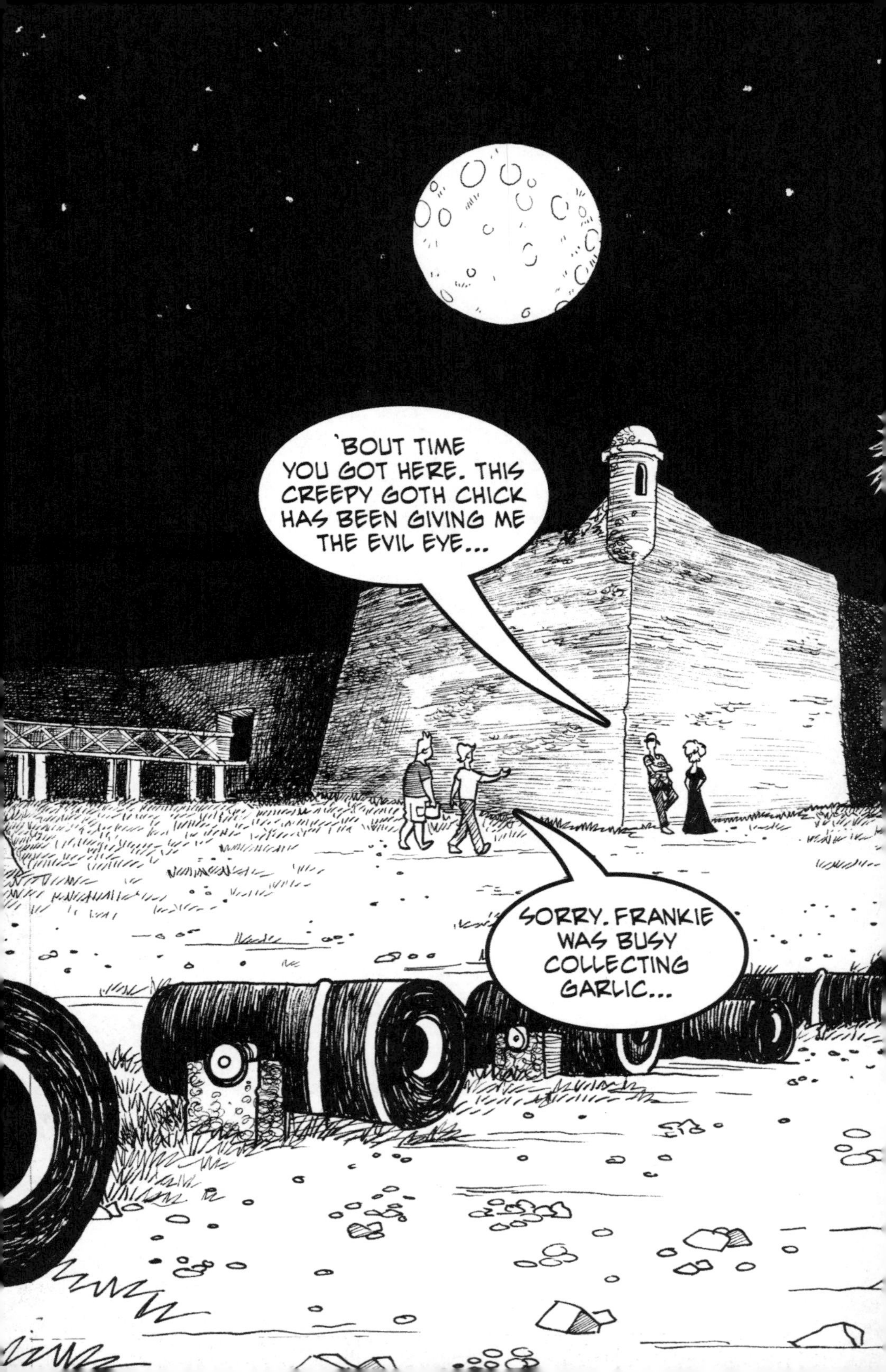
'BOUT TIME YOU GOT HERE. THIS CREEPY GOTH CHICK HAS BEEN GIVING ME THE EVIL EYE...
SORRY. FRANKIE WAS BUSY COLLECTING GARLIC...

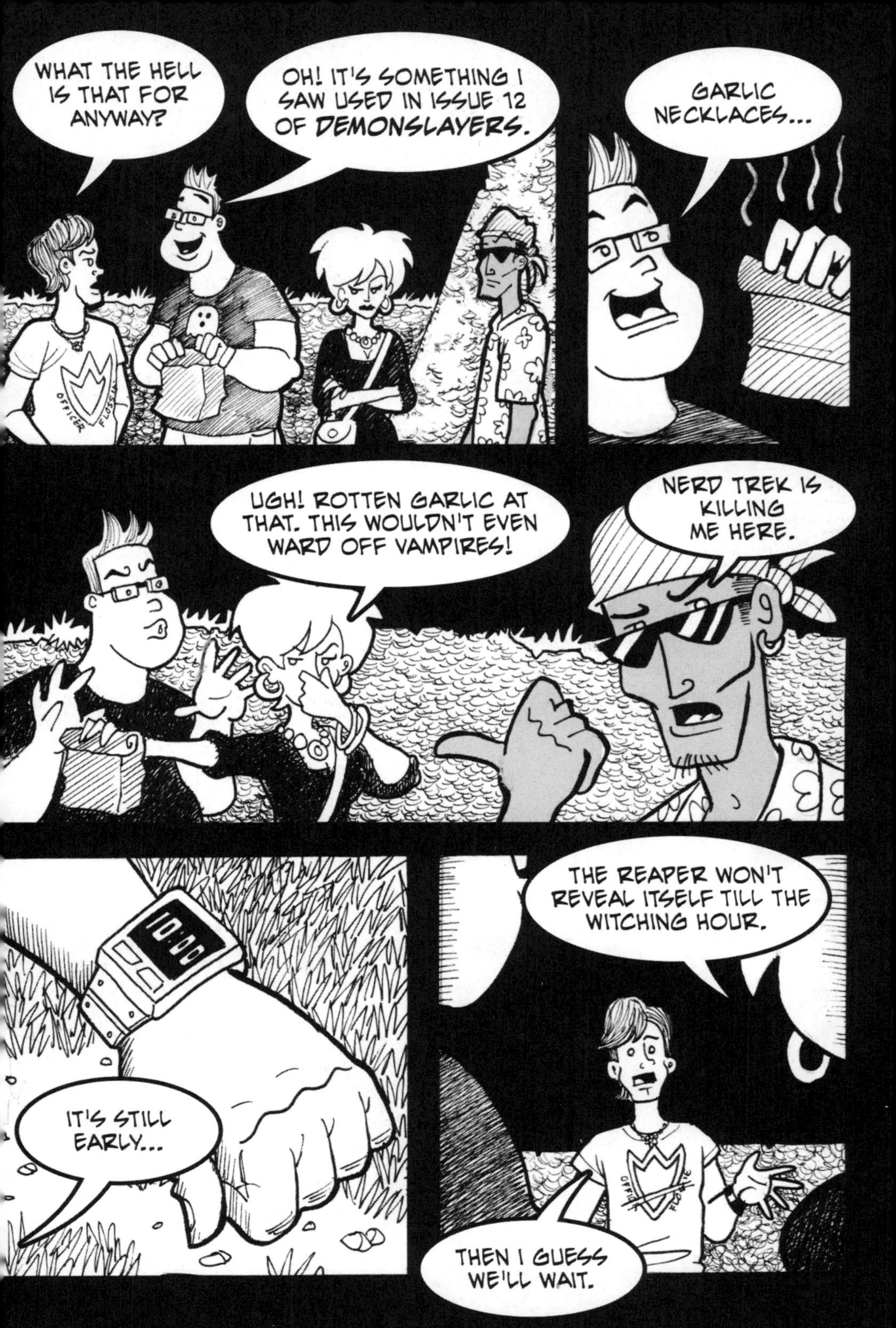
WHAT THE HELL IS THAT FOR ANYWAY?
OH! IT'S SOMETHING I SAW USED IN ISSUE 12 OF DEMONSLAYERS.
GARLIC NECKLACES...
UGH! ROTTEN GARLIC AT THAT. THIS WOULDN'T EVEN WARD OFF VAMPIRES!
NERD TREK IS KILLING ME HERE.
IT'S STILL EARLY...
THE REAPER WON'T REVEAL ITSELF TILL THE WITCHING HOUR.
THEN I GUESS WE'LL WAIT.

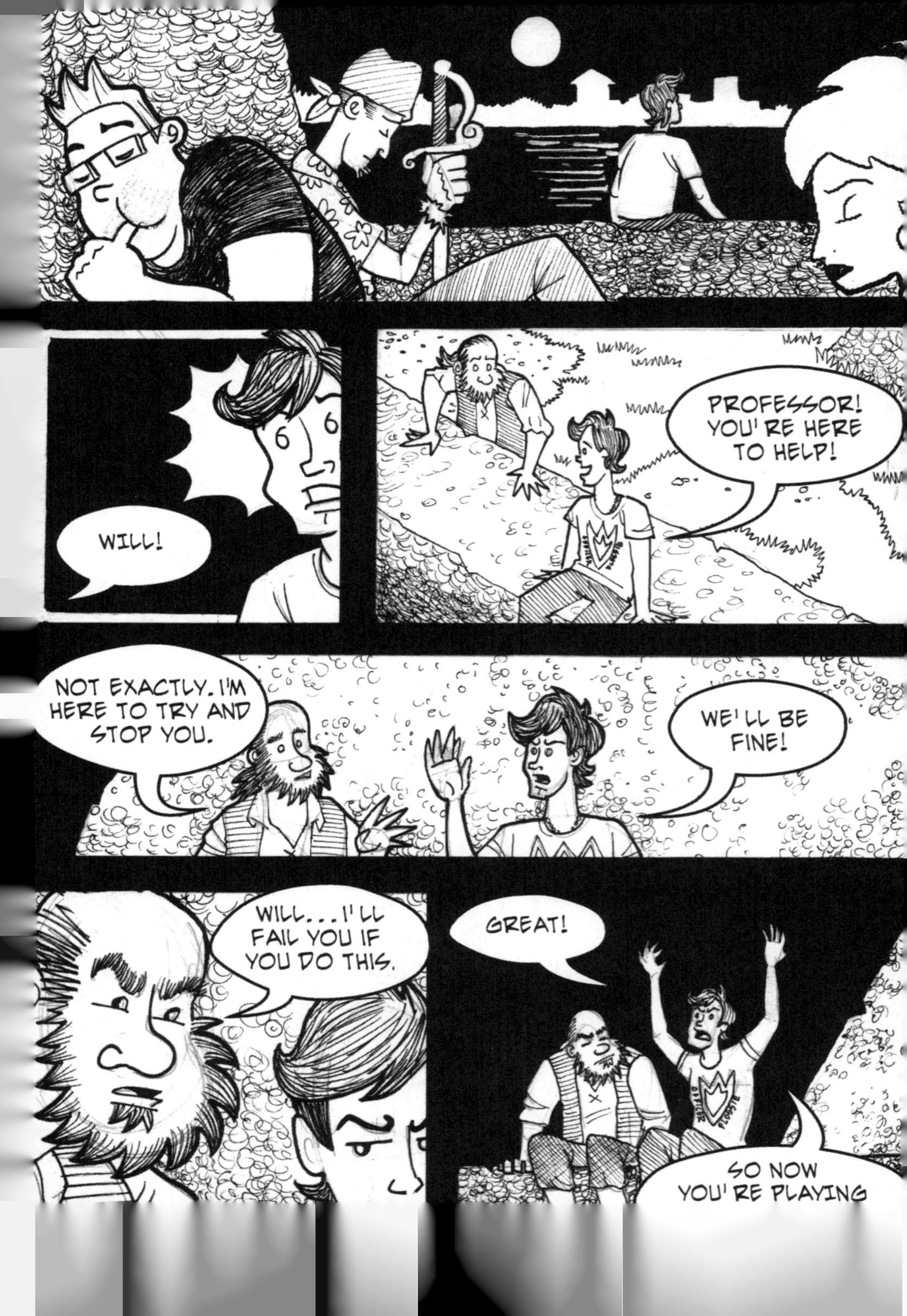
WILL!
PROFESSOR! YOU'RE HERE TO HELP!
NOT EXACTLY. I'M HERE TO TRY AND STOP YOU.
WE'LL BE FINE!
WILL... I'LL FAIL YOU IF YOU DO THIS.
GREAT!
SO NOW YOU'RE PLAYING

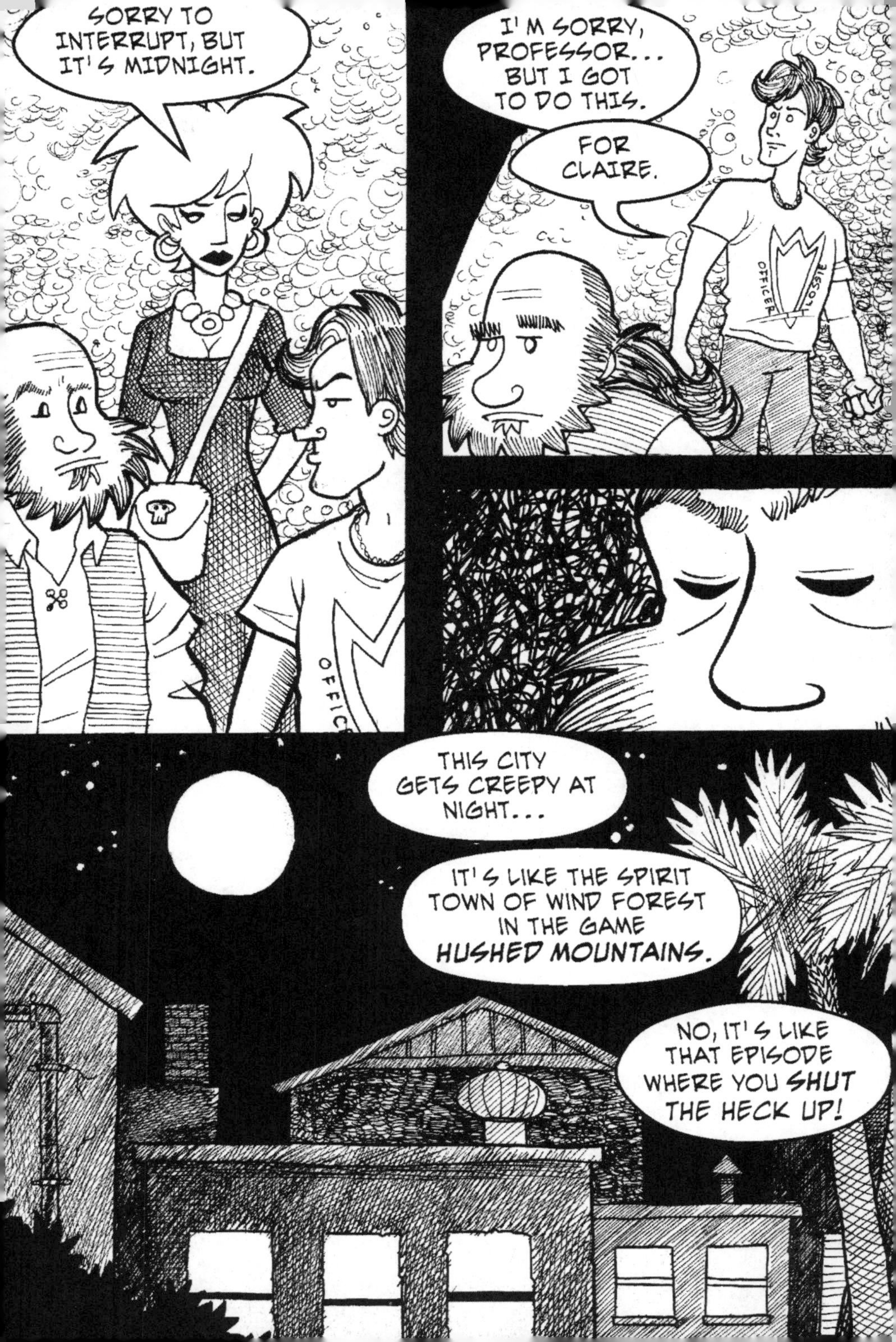
SORRY TO INTERRUPT, BUT IT'S MIDNIGHT.
I'M SORRY, PROFESSOR... BUT I GOT TO DO THIS.
FOR CLAIRE.
OFFICER
THIS CITY GETS CREEPY AT NIGHT...
IT'S LIKE THE SPIRIT TOWN OF WIND FOREST IN THE GAME *HUSHED MOUNTAINS*.
NO, IT'S LIKE THAT EPISODE WHERE YOU *SHUT THE HECK UP!*

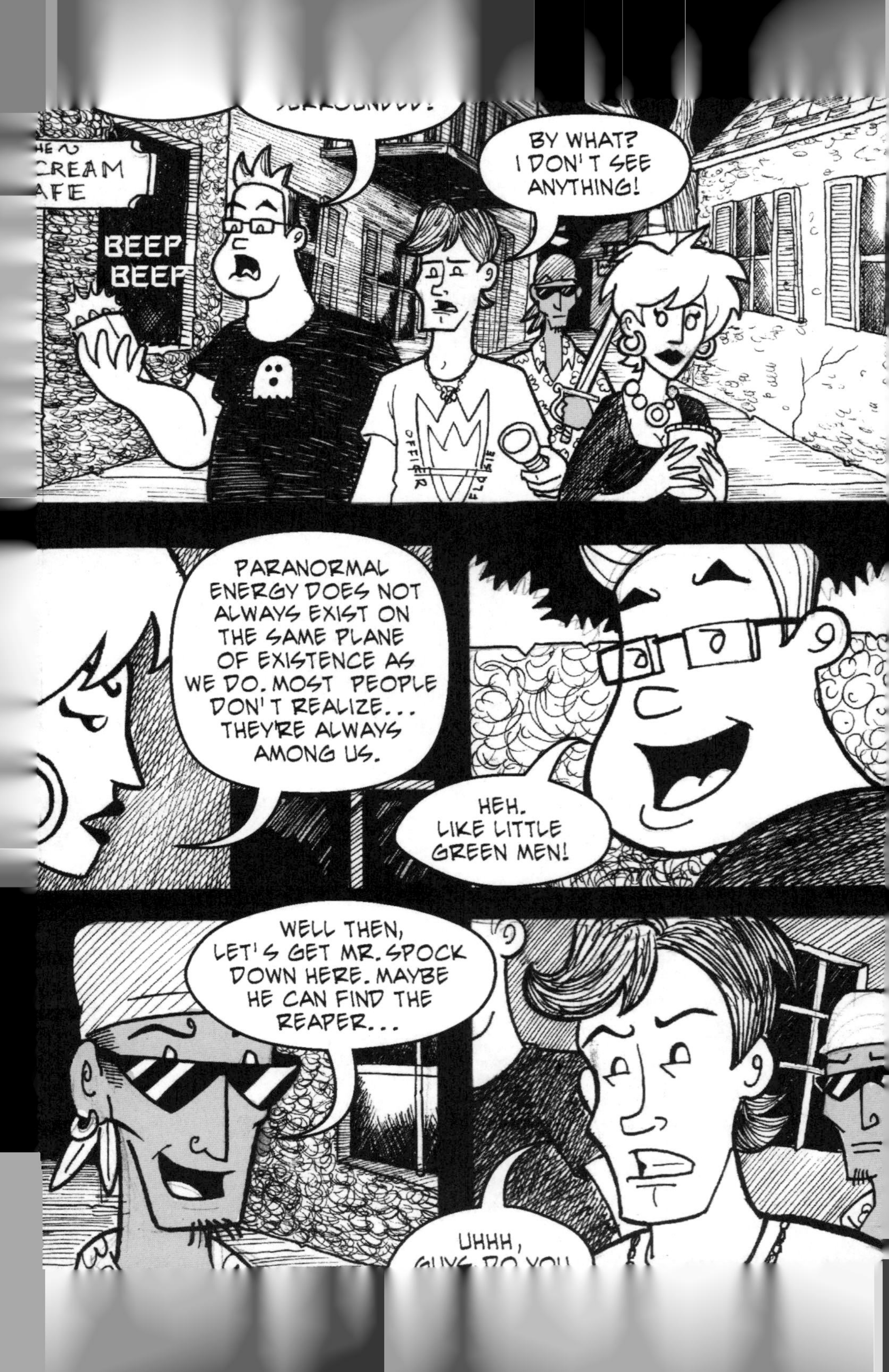
CREAM
BEEP BEEP
BY WHAT? I DON'T SEE ANYTHING!
PARANORMAL ENERGY DOES NOT ALWAYS EXIST ON THE SAME PLANE OF EXISTENCE AS WE DO. MOST PEOPLE DON'T REALIZE... THEY'RE ALWAYS AMONG US.
HEH. LIKE LITTLE GREEN MEN!
WELL THEN, LET'S GET MR. SPOCK DOWN HERE. MAYBE HE CAN FIND THE REAPER...
UHHH,

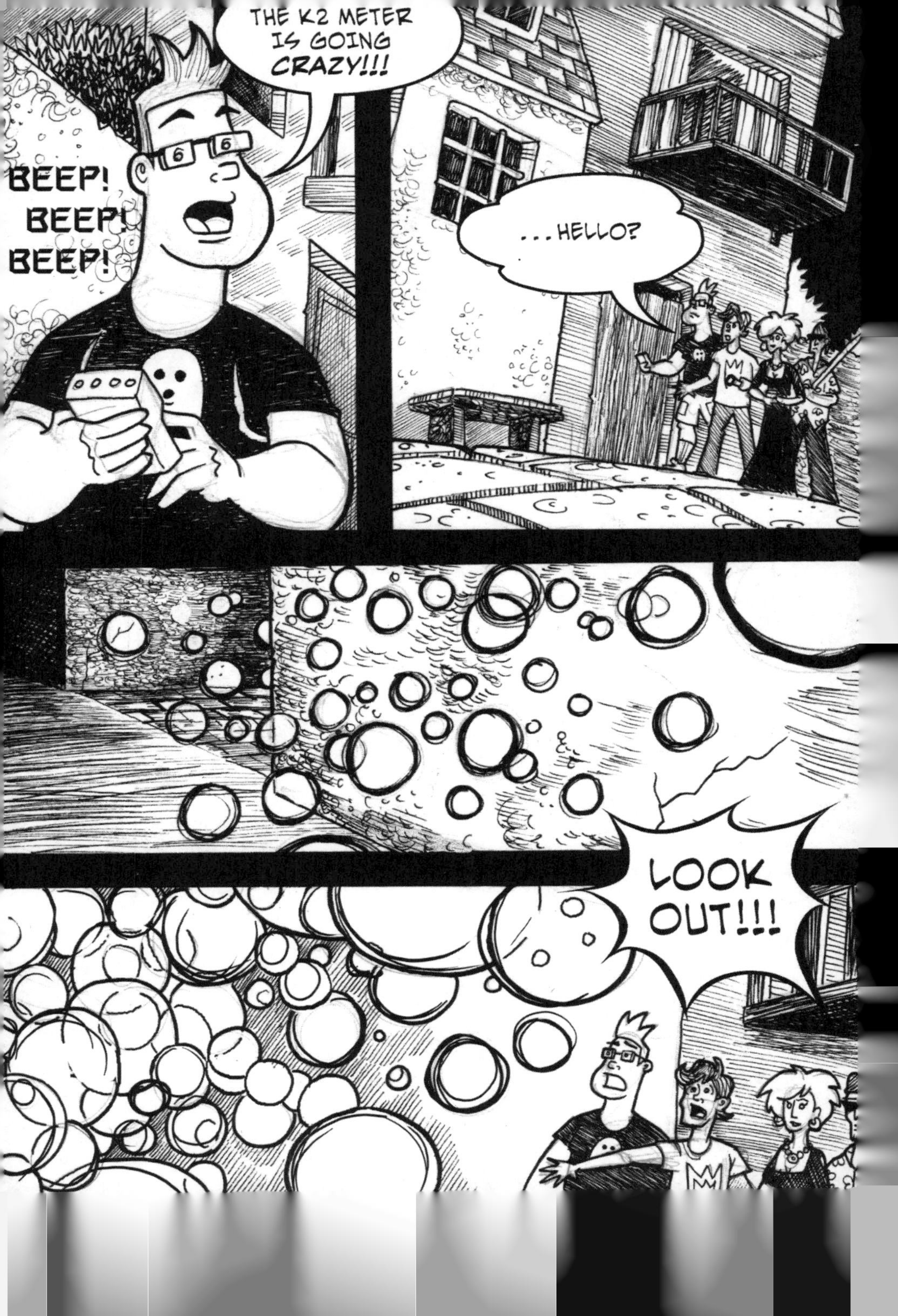
THE K2 METER IS GOING CRAZY!!!
BEEP! BEEP! BEEP!
...HELLO?
LOOK OUT!!!

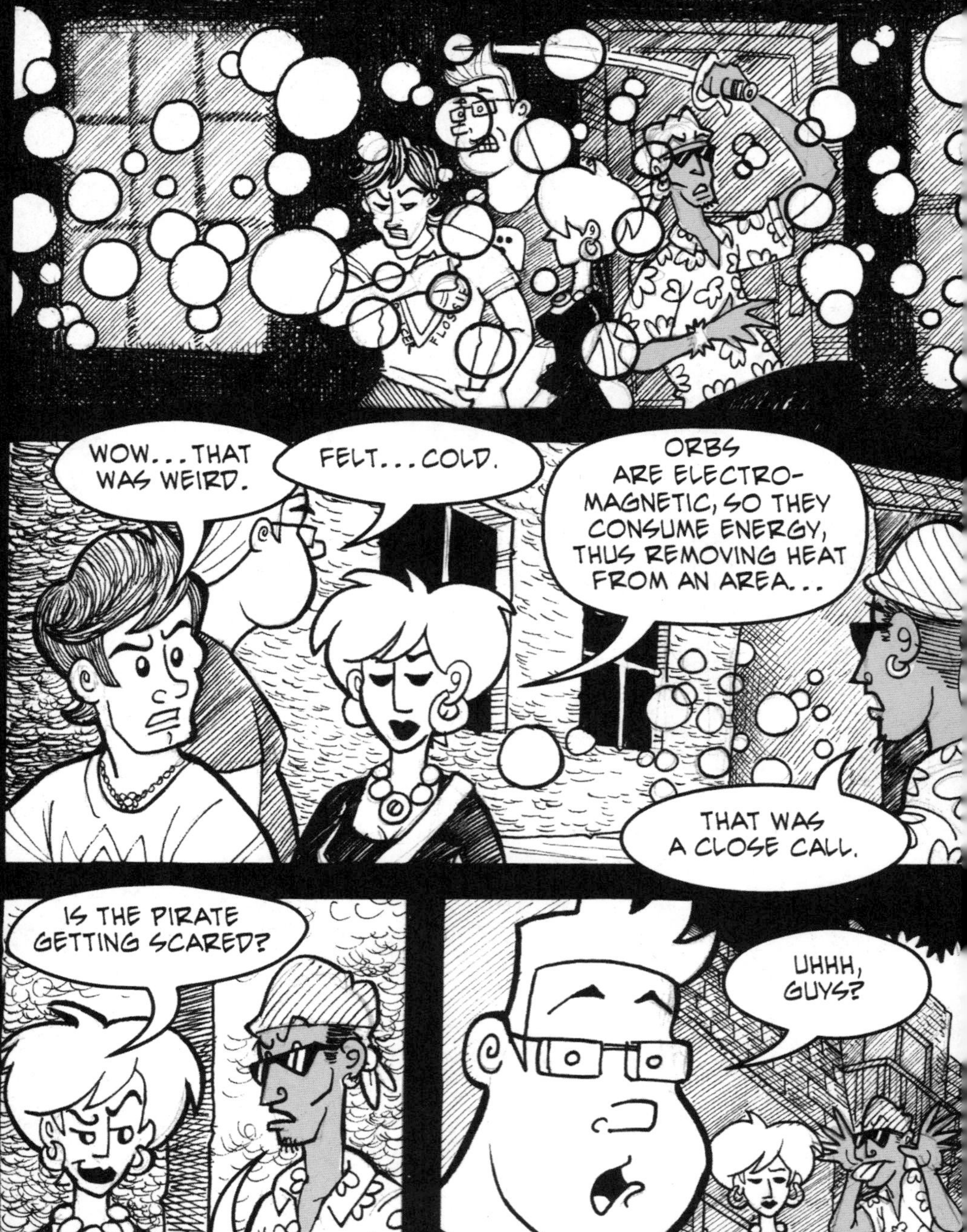
WOW...THAT WAS WEIRD.
FELT...COLD.
ORBS ARE ELECTRO-MAGNETIC, SO THEY CONSUME ENERGY, THUS REMOVING HEAT FROM AN AREA...
THAT WAS A CLOSE CALL.
IS THE PIRATE GETTING SCARED?
PHSSH! YOU WISH.
UHHH, GUYS?

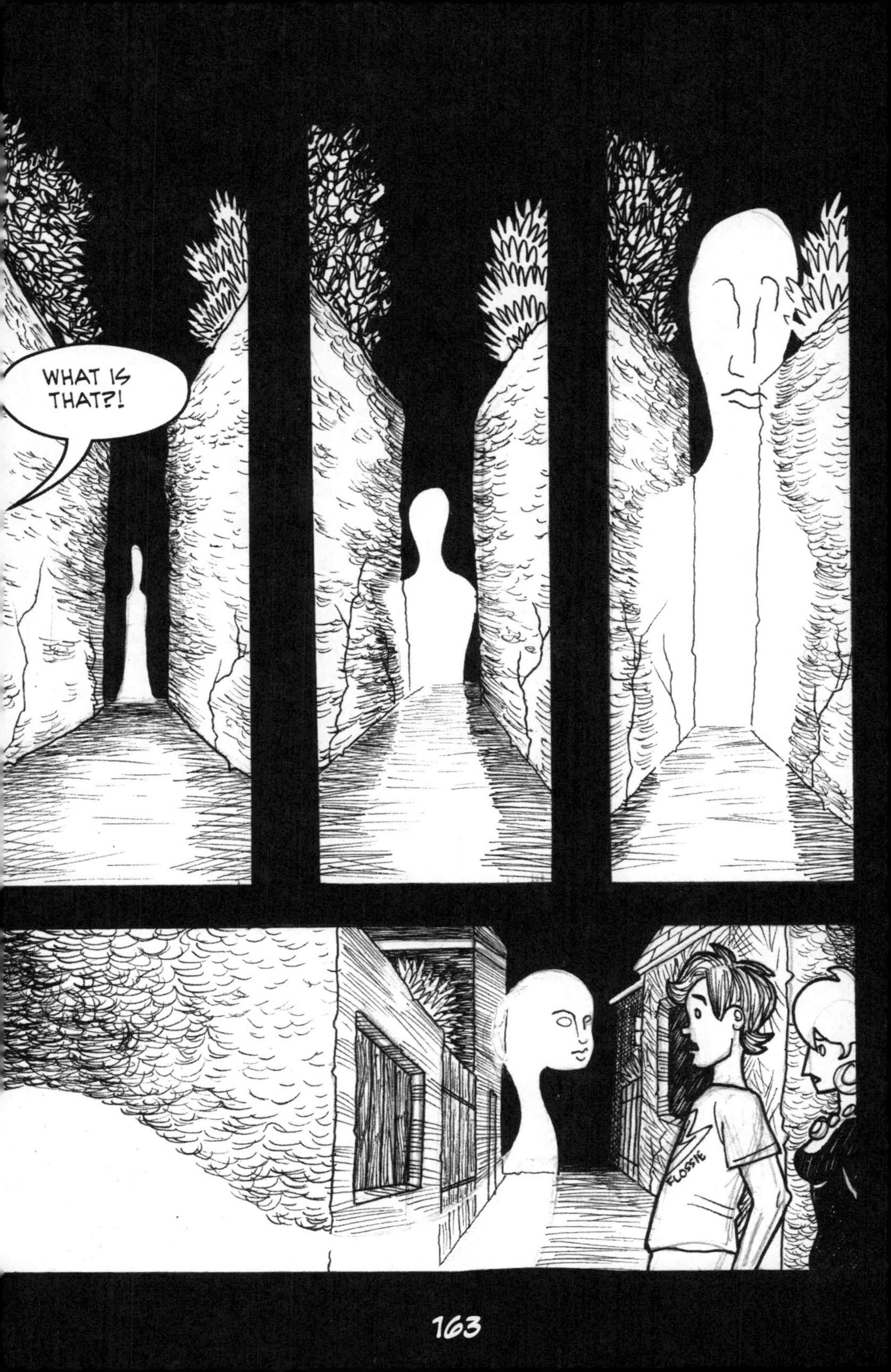
WHAT IS
THAT?!
FLOSSIE

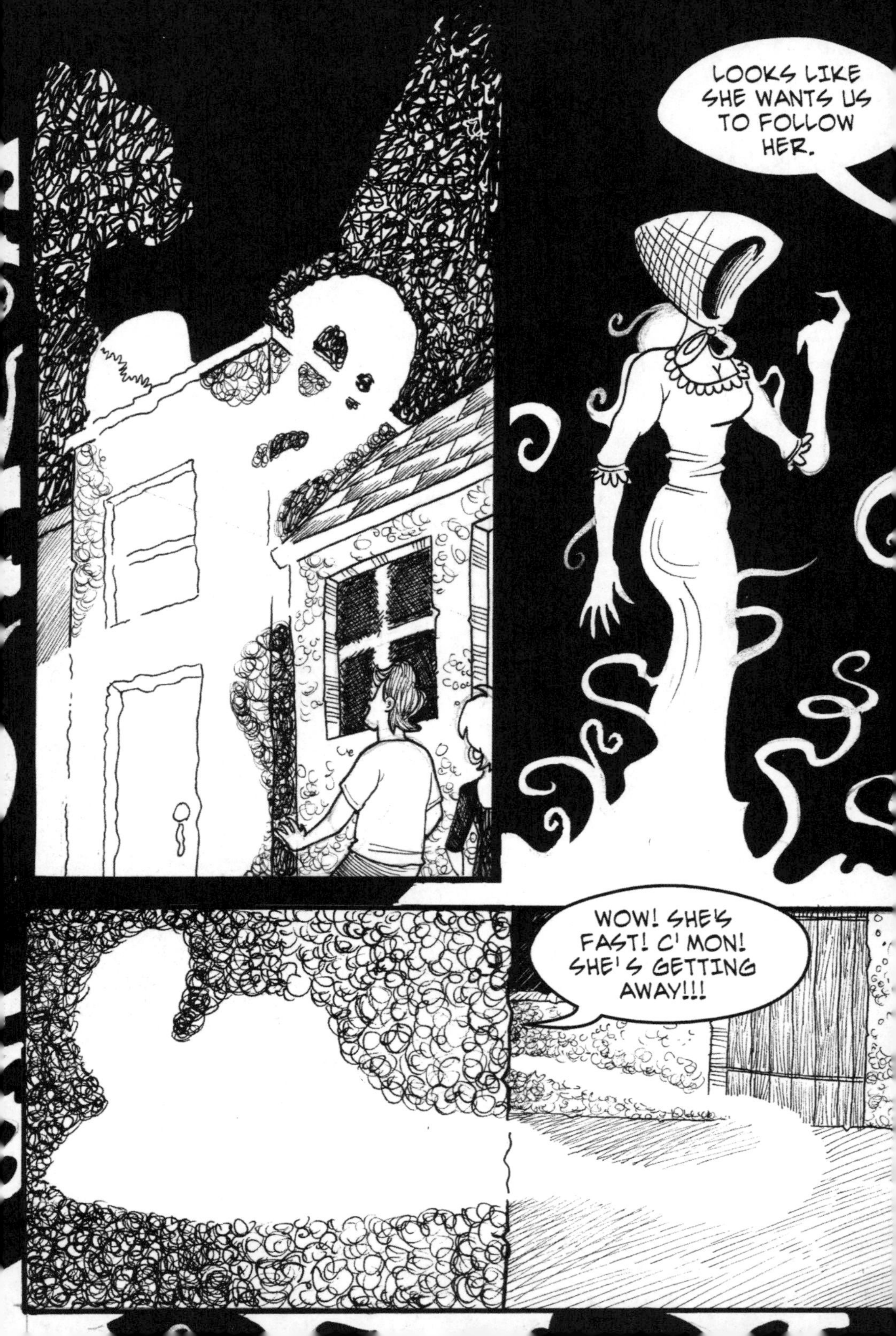
LOOKS LIKE SHE WANTS US TO FOLLOW HER.
WOW! SHE'S FAST! C'MON! SHE'S GETTING AWAY!!!

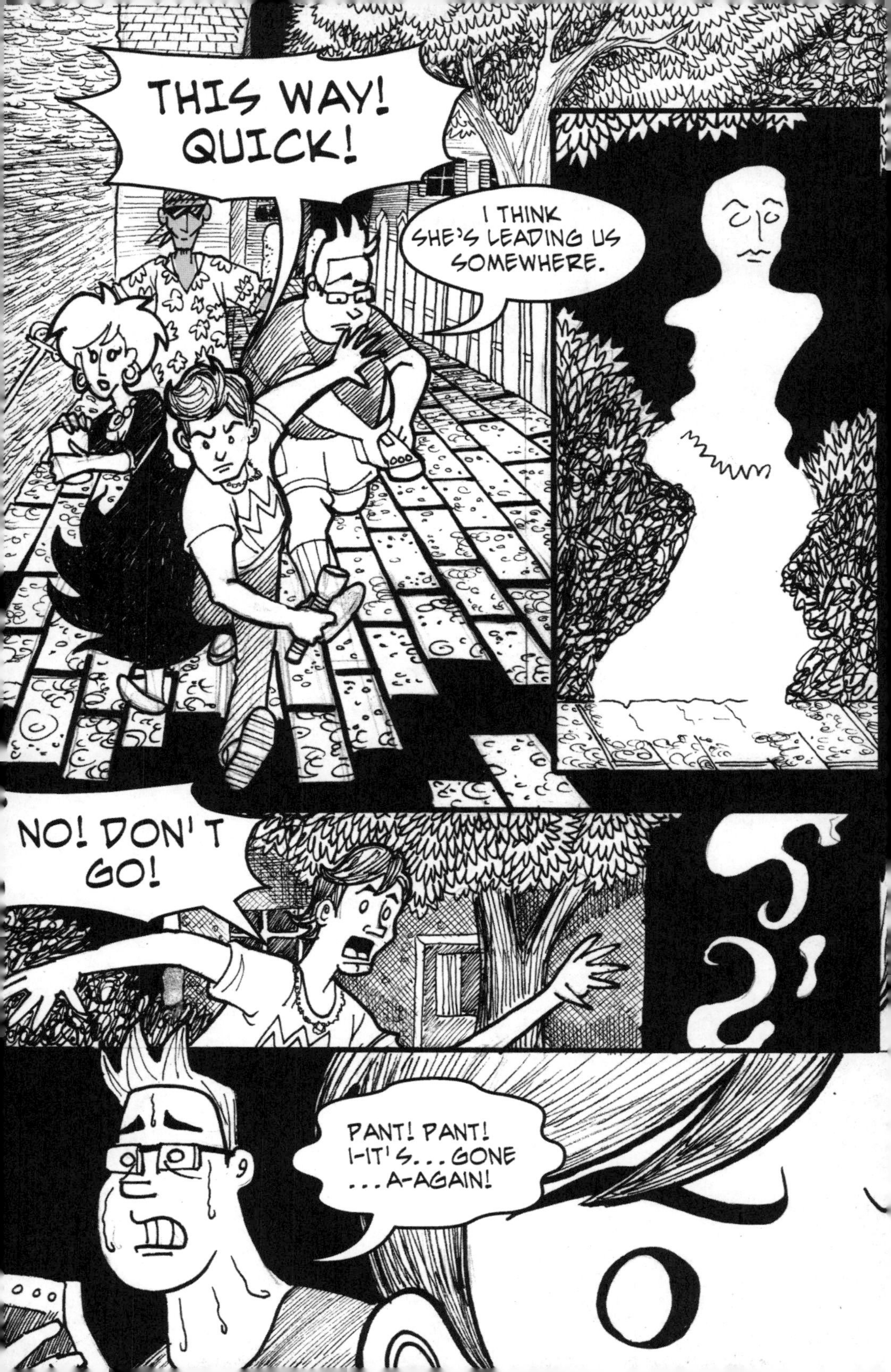
THIS WAY! QUICK!
I THINK SHE'S LEADING US SOMEWHERE.
NO! DON'T GO!
PANT! PANT! I-IT'S... GONE ...A-AGAIN!

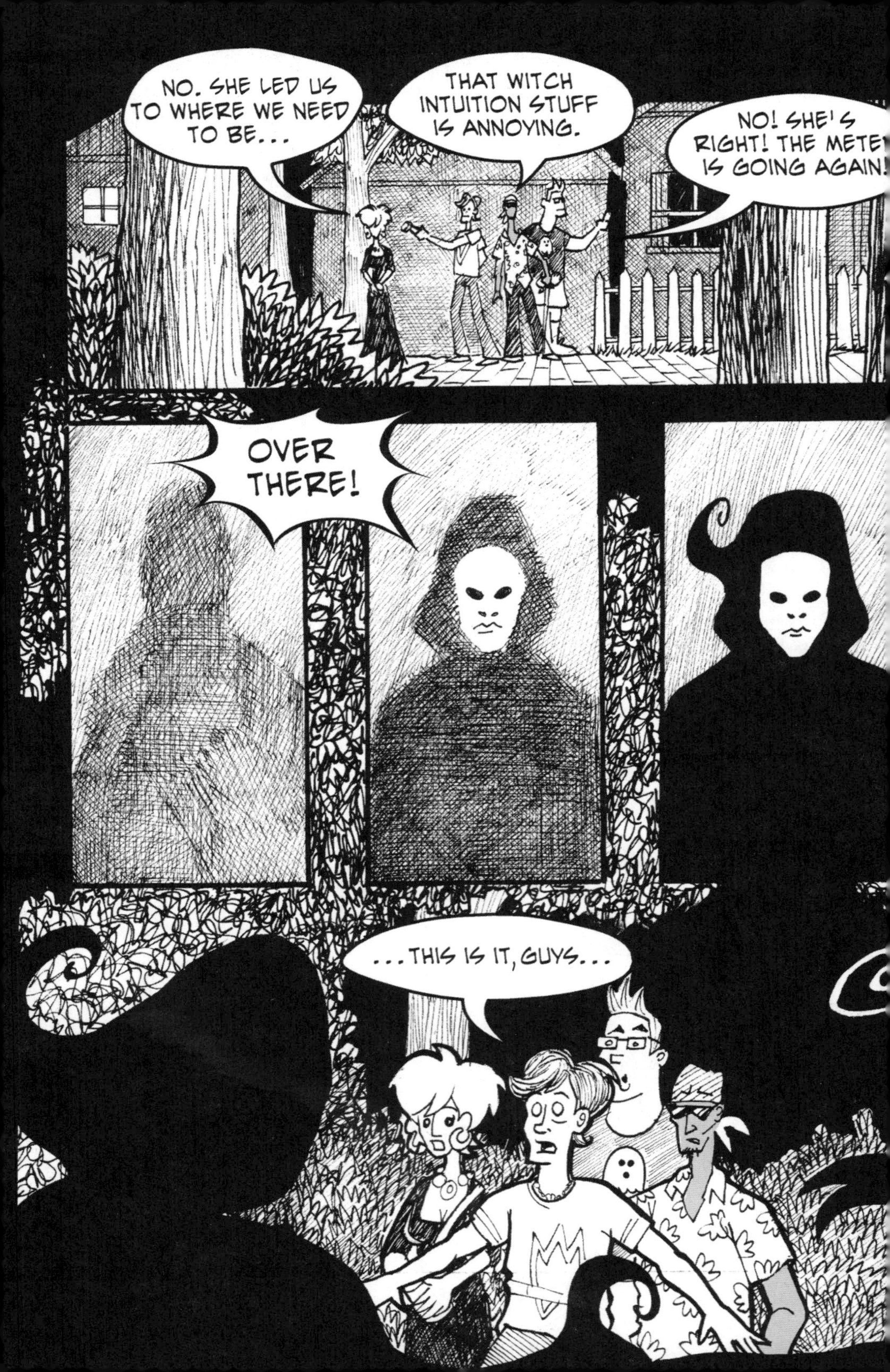
NO. SHE LED US TO WHERE WE NEED TO BE...
THAT WITCH INTUITION STUFF IS ANNOYING.
NO! SHE'S RIGHT! THE METE IS GOING AGAIN!
OVER THERE!
...THIS IS IT, GUYS...

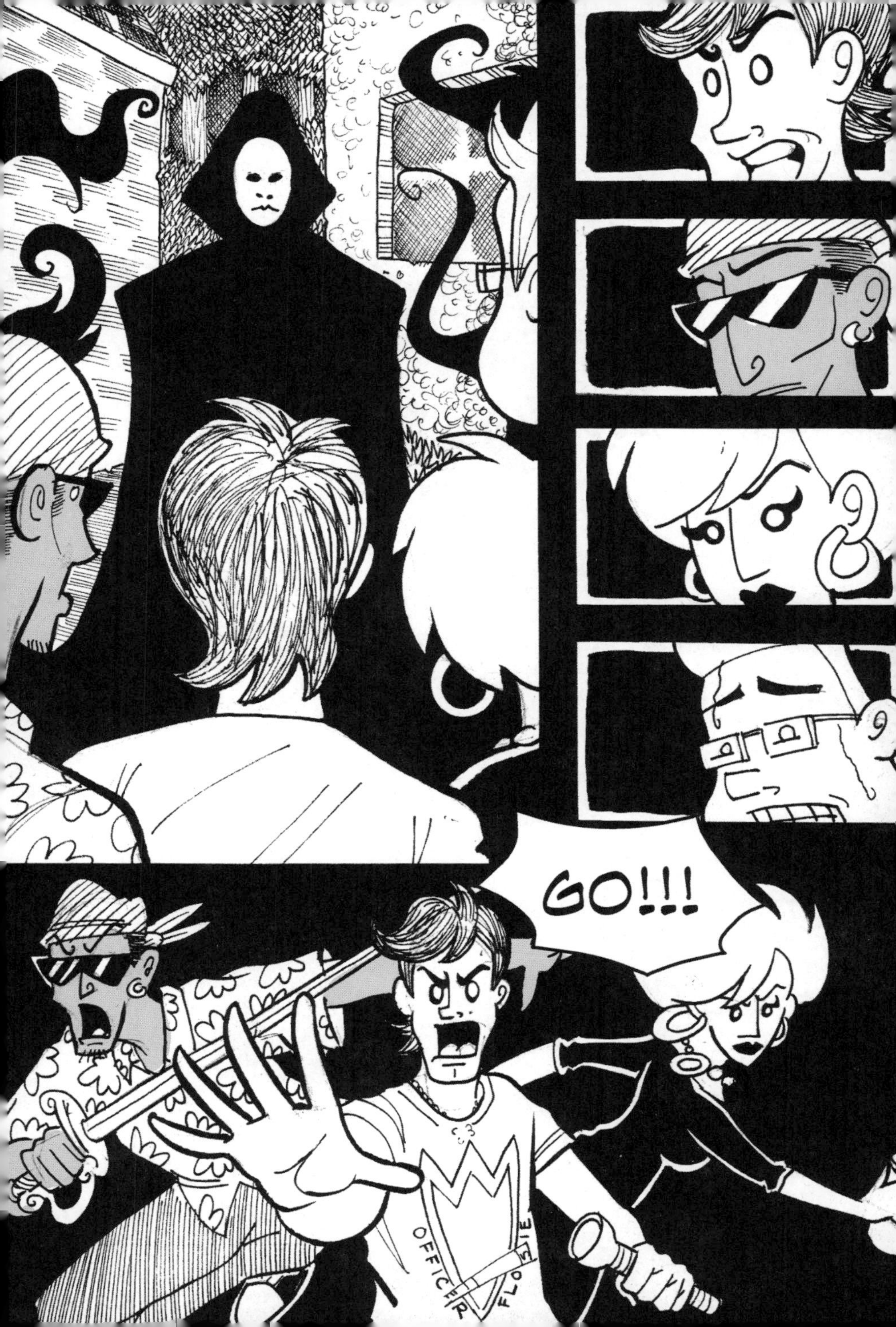
GO!!!

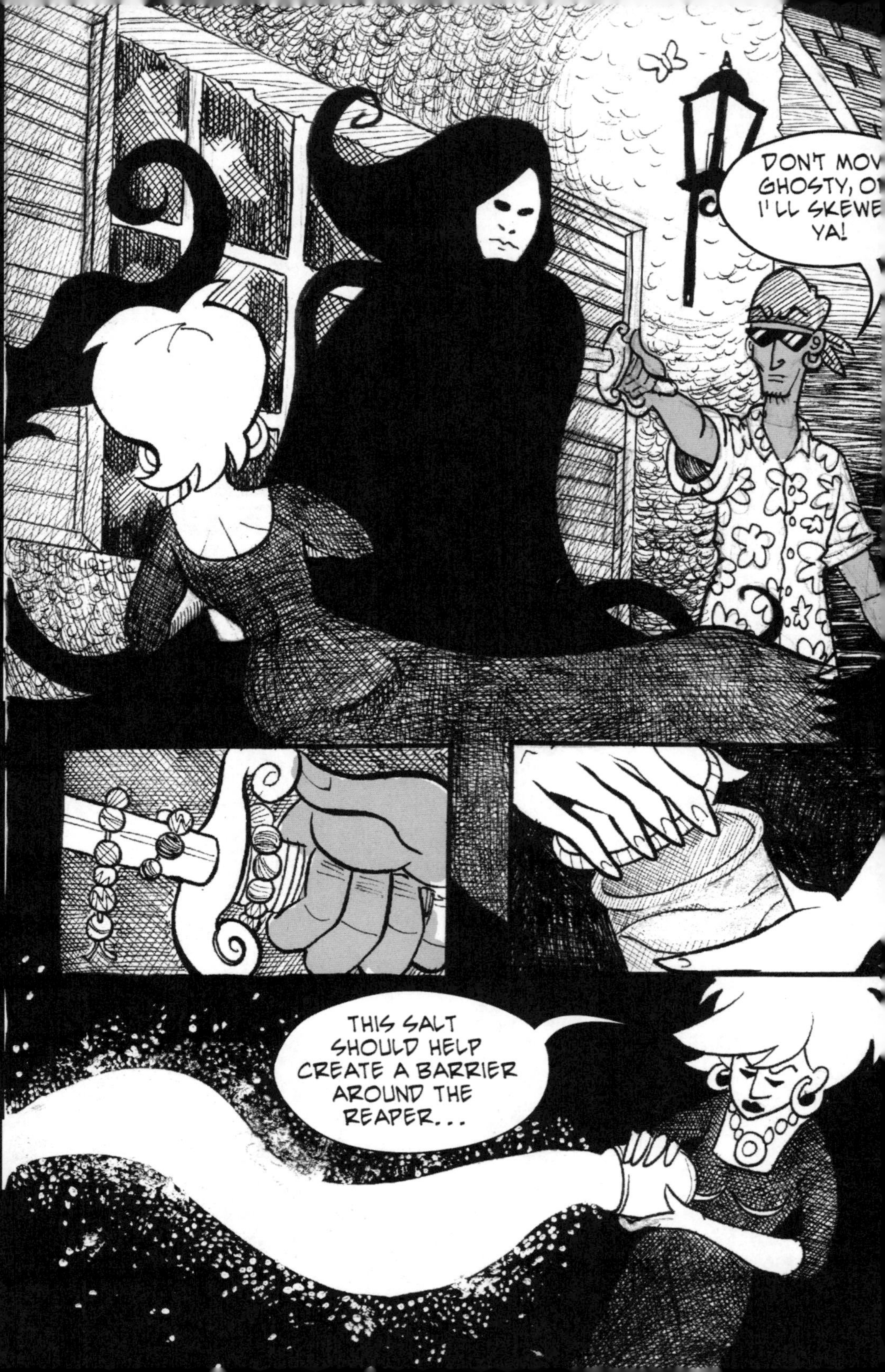
DON'T MOV
GHOSTY, O
I'LL SKEWE
YA!
THIS SALT SHOULD HELP CREATE A BARRIER AROUND THE REAPER...

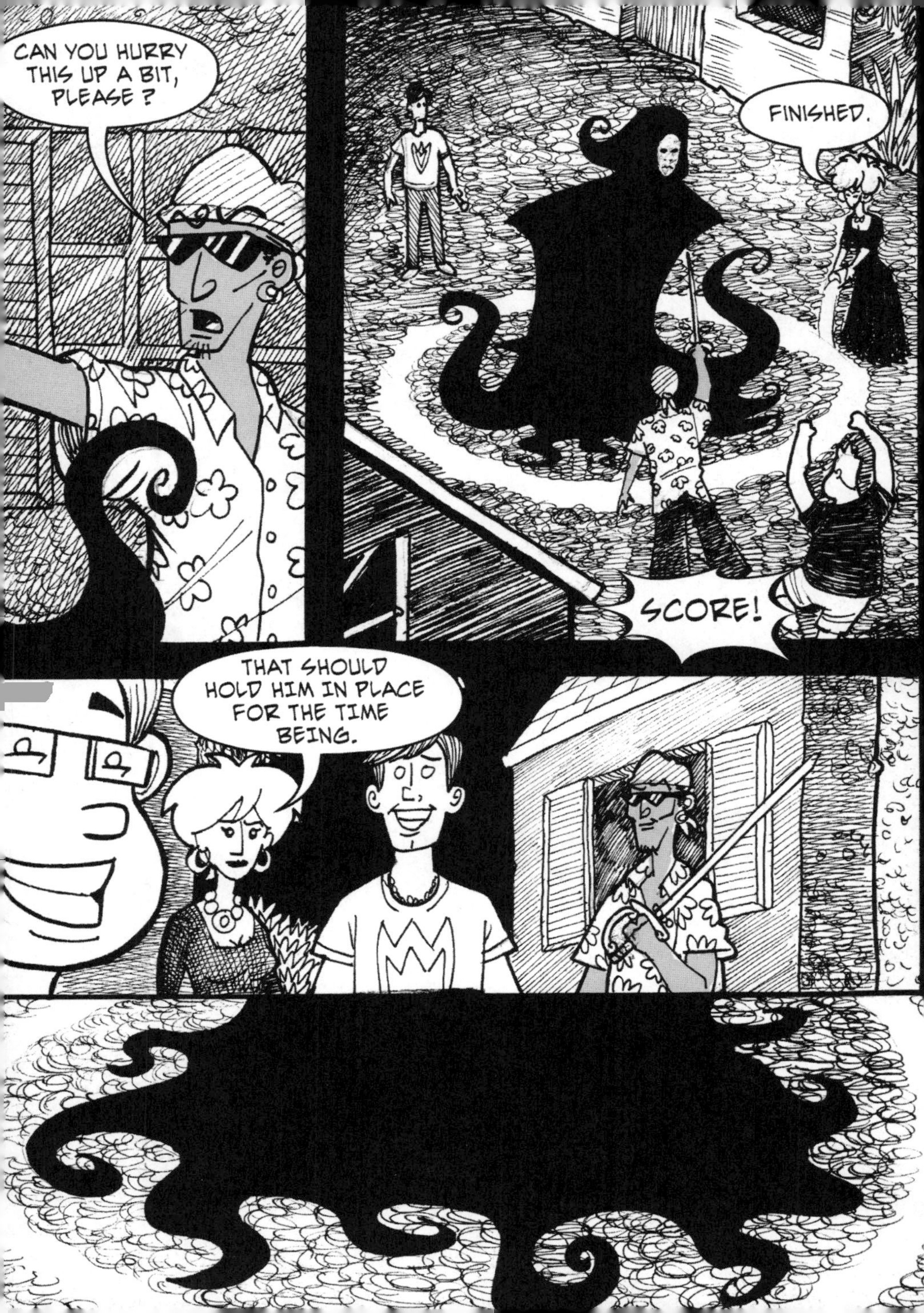
CAN YOU HURRY THIS UP A BIT, PLEASE ?
FINISHED.
SCORE!
THAT SHOULD HOLD HIM IN PLACE FOR THE TIME BEING.

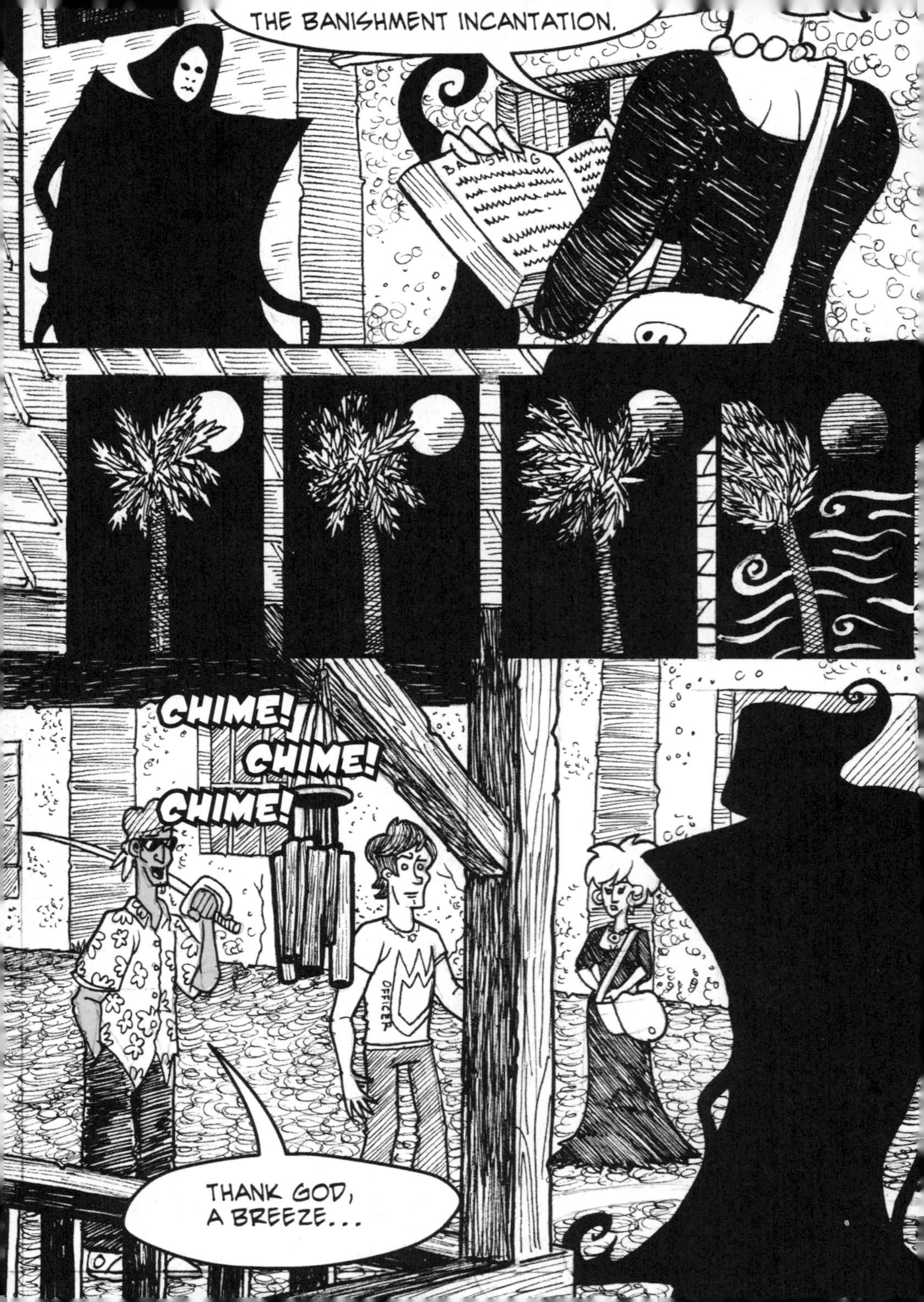
THE BANISHMENT INCANTATION.
BANISHING
CHIME!
CHIME!
CHIME!
OFFICER
THANK GOD,
A BREEZE...

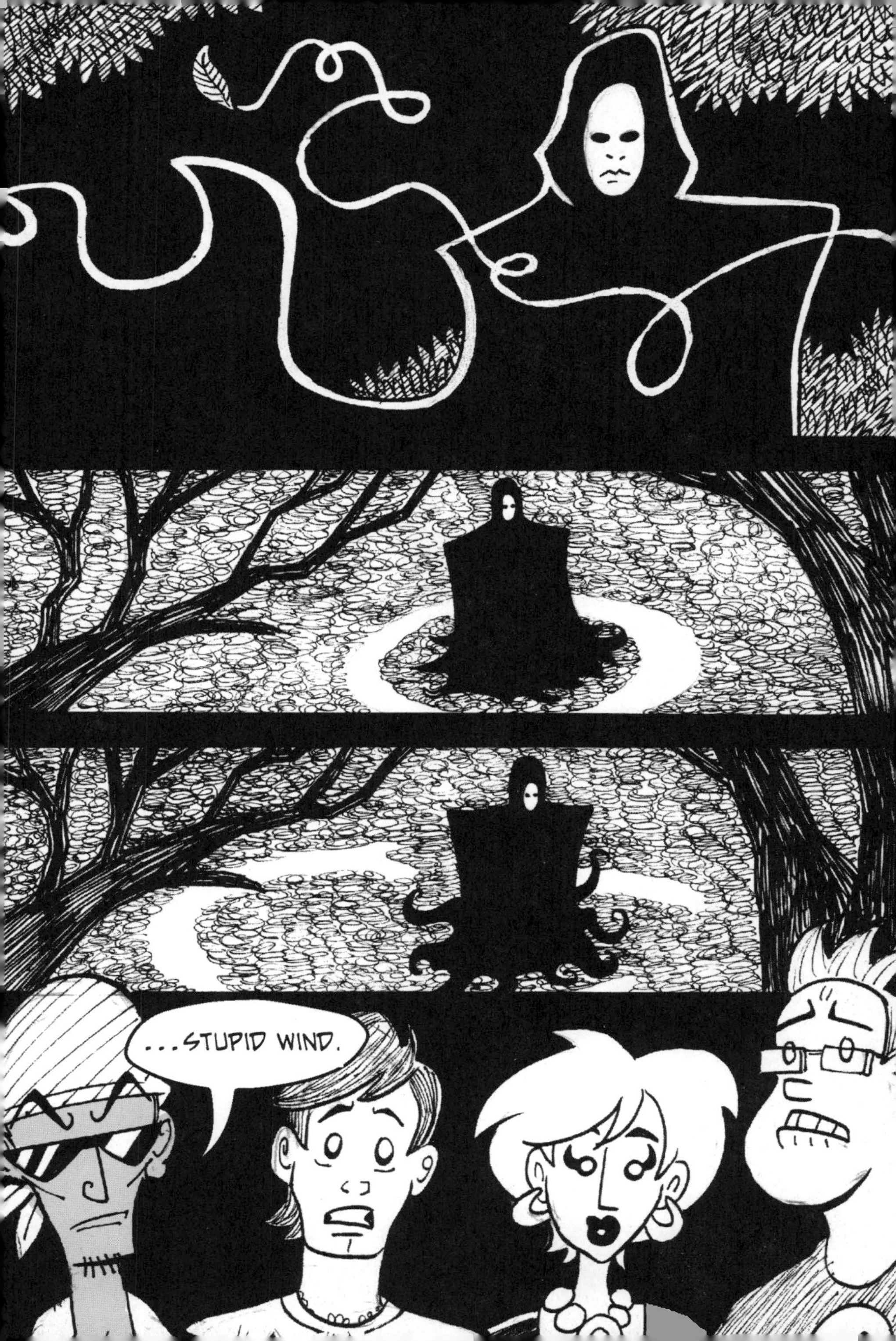
...STUPID WIND.

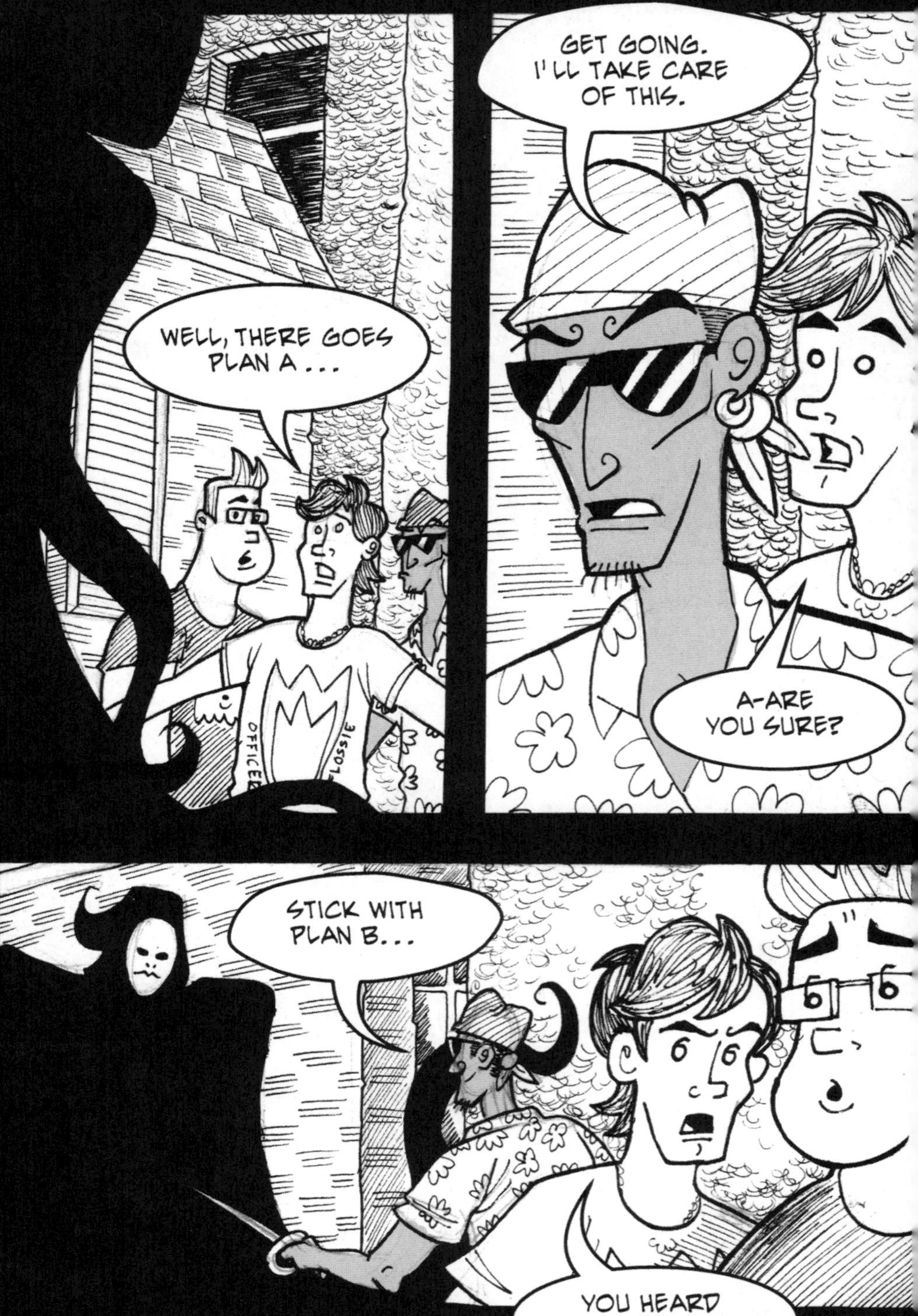
WELL, THERE GOES PLAN A . . .
GET GOING. I'LL TAKE CARE OF THIS.
A-ARE YOU SURE?
STICK WITH PLAN B. . .
YOU HEARD THE PIRATE!

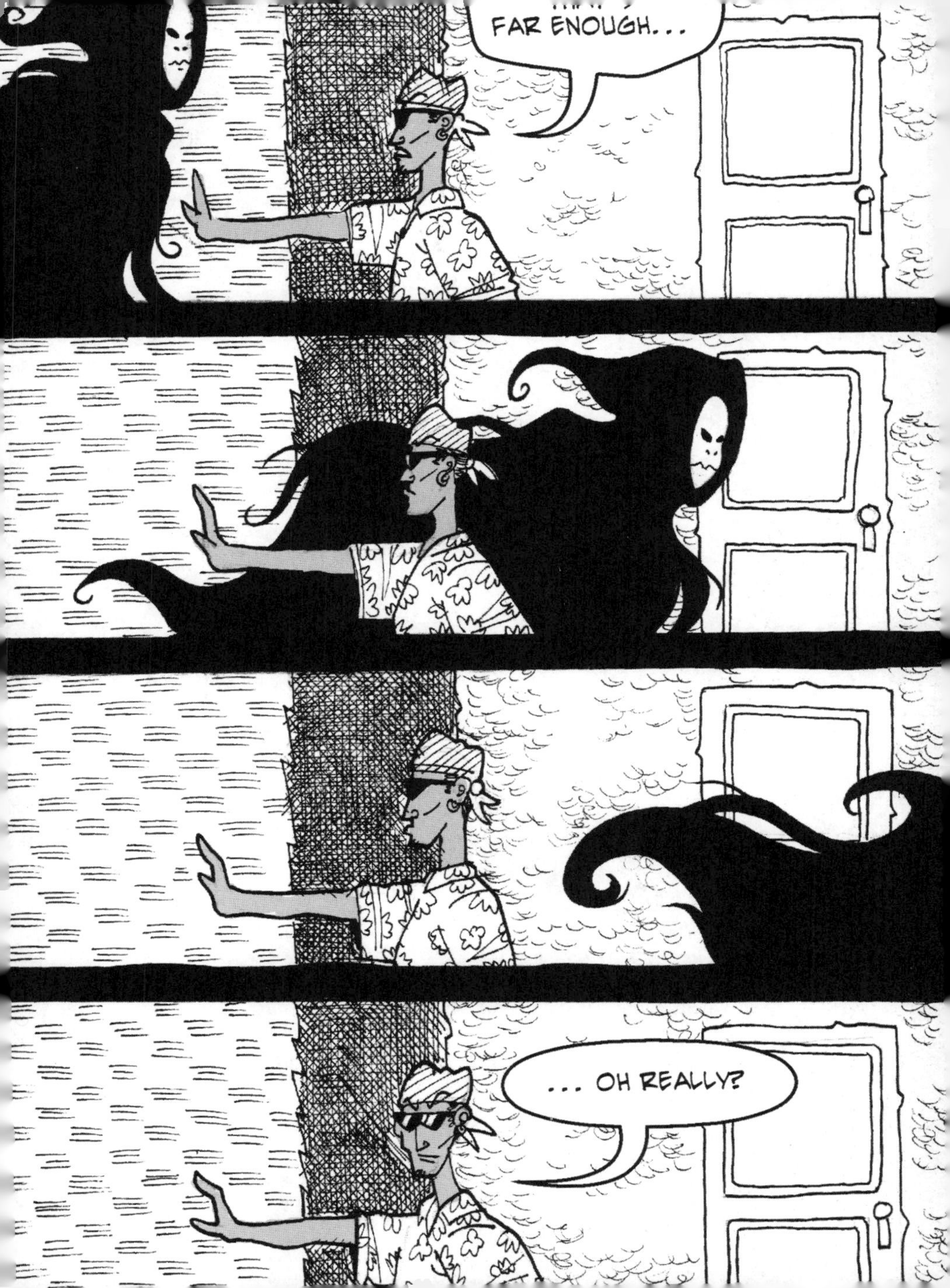
FAR ENOUGH...
... OH REALLY?

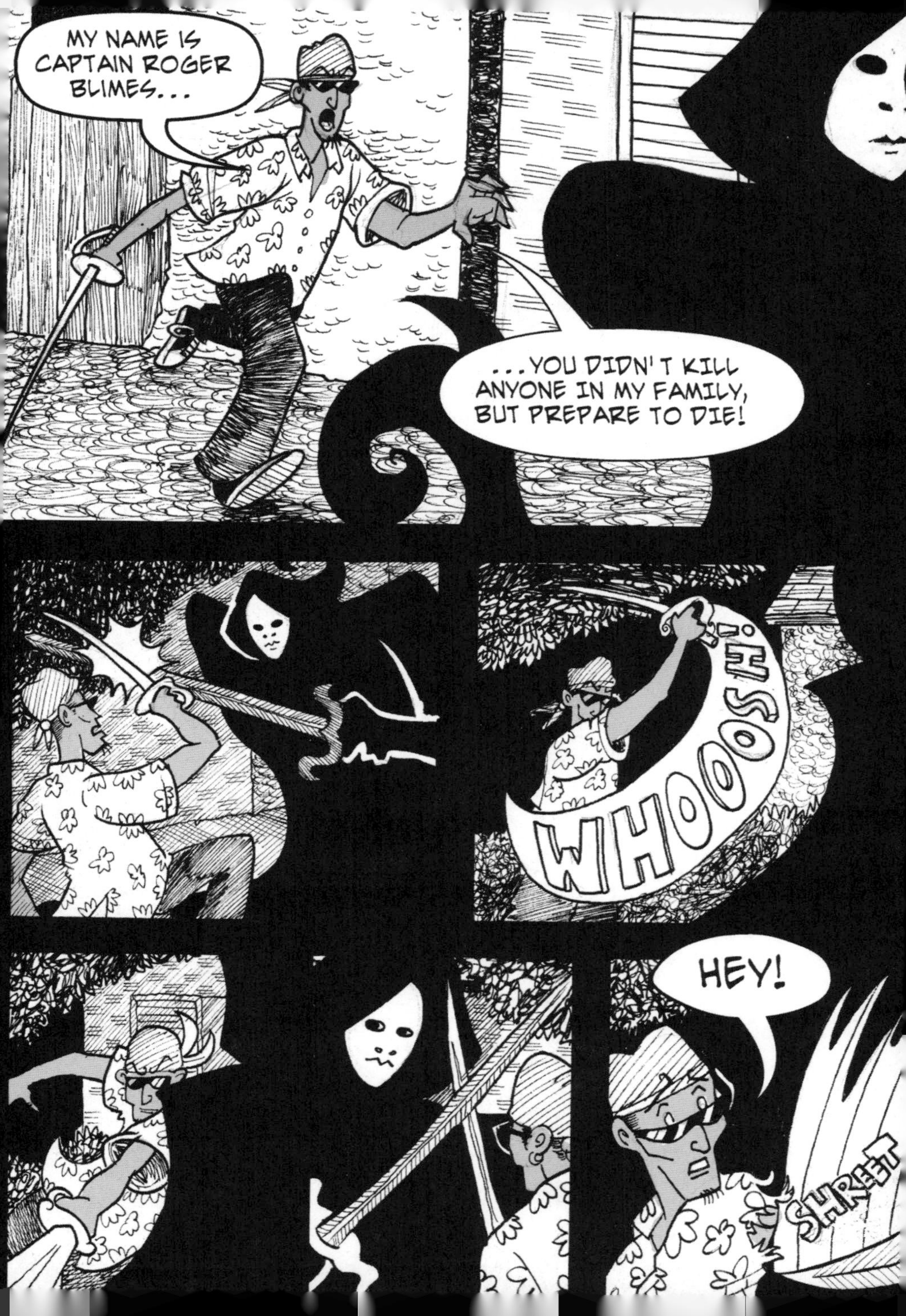
MY NAME IS CAPTAIN ROGER BLIMES...
...YOU DIDN'T KILL ANYONE IN MY FAMILY, BUT PREPARE TO DIE!
WHOOOSH!
HEY!
SHREET

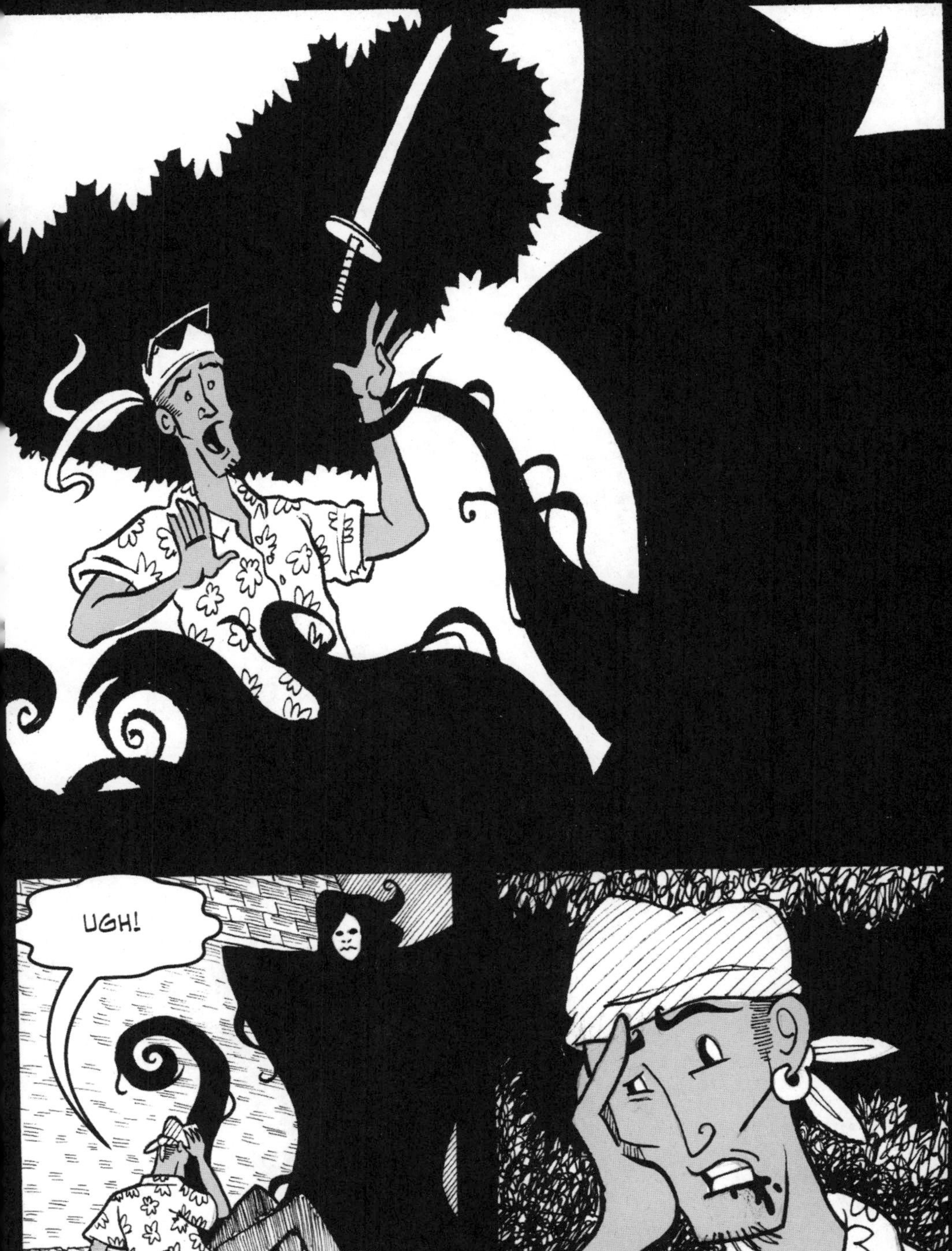
UGH!

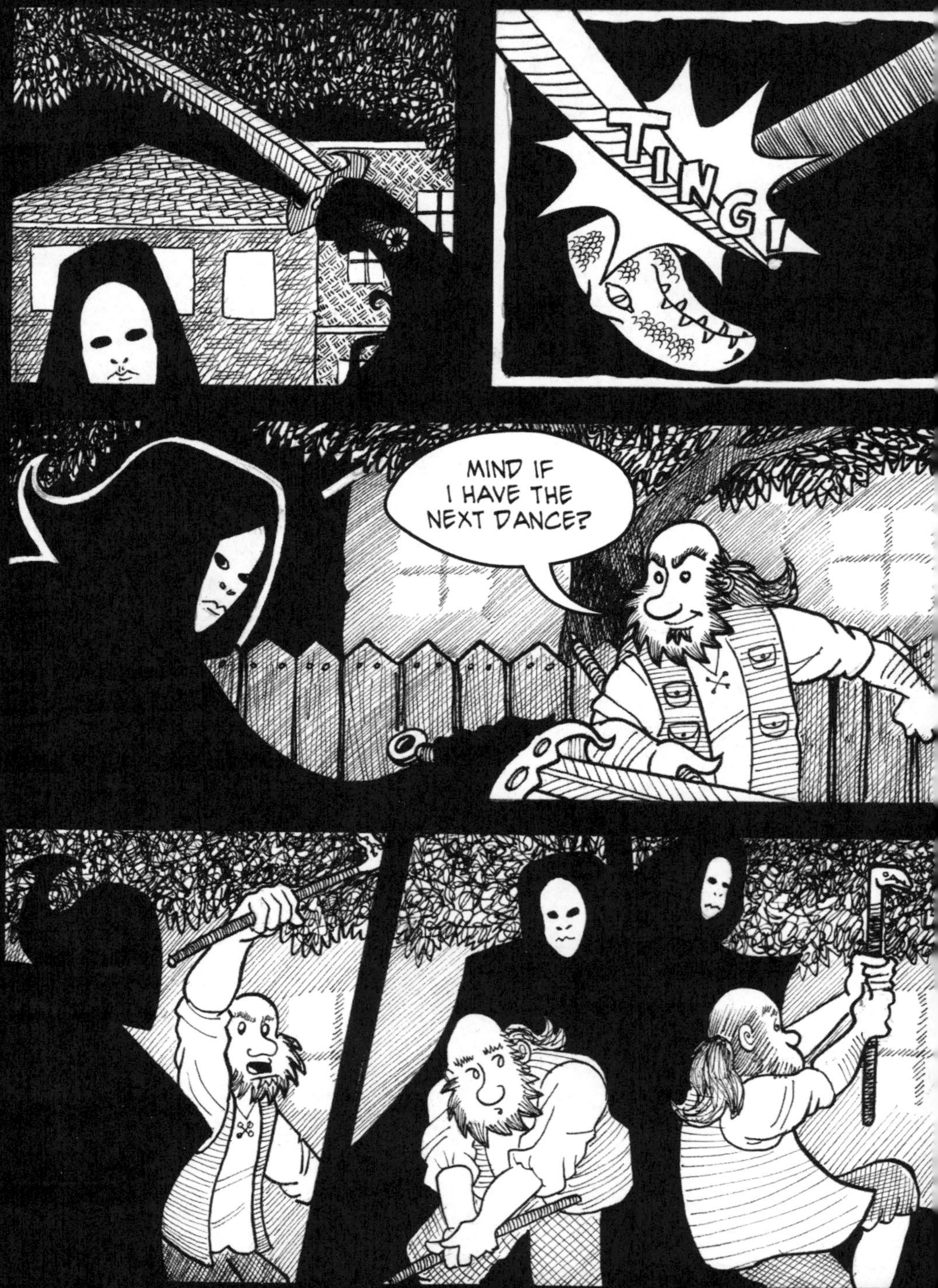
TING!
MIND IF I HAVE THE NEXT DANCE?

UHHH, YEAH. JUST FINE.
ROGER!!

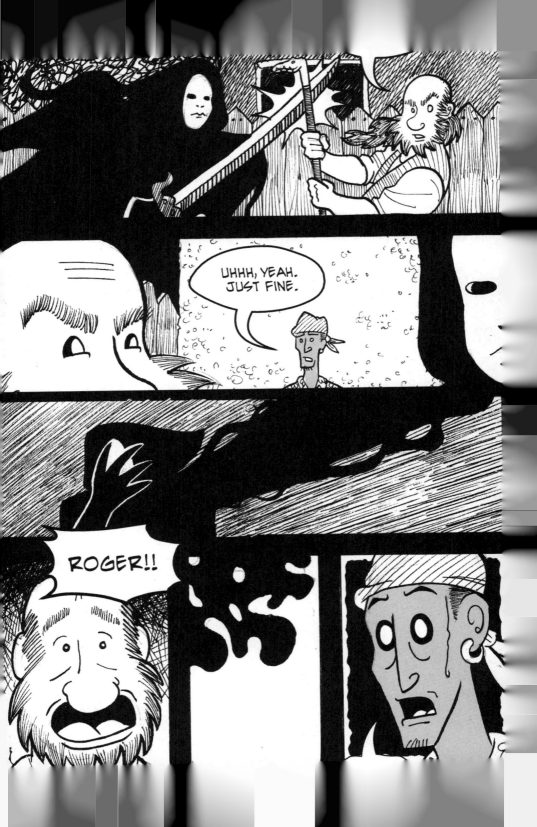

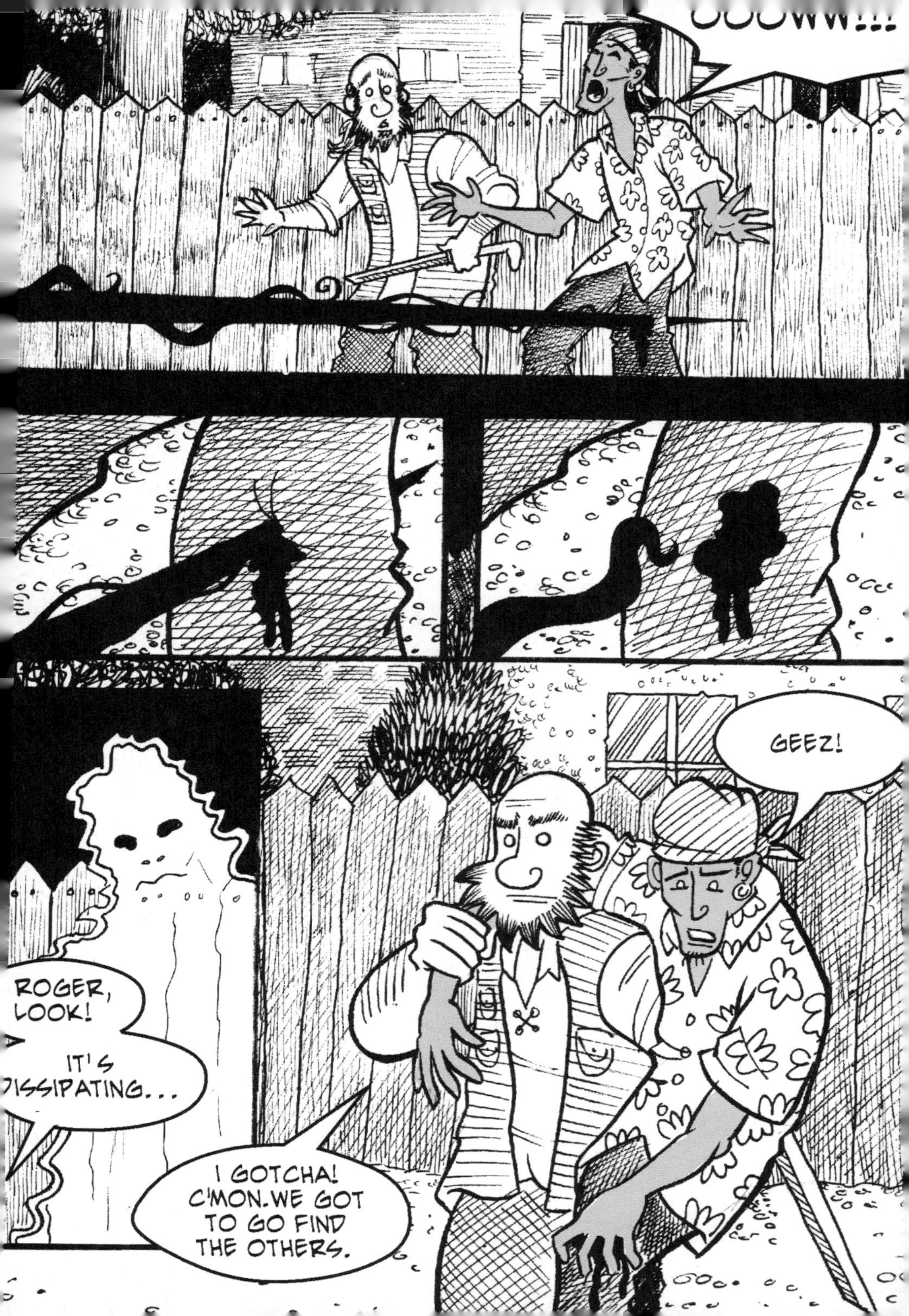
OOOWW!!!
GEEZ!
ROGER, LOOK!
IT'S DISSIPATING...
I GOTCHA! C'MON. WE GOT TO GO FIND THE OTHERS.

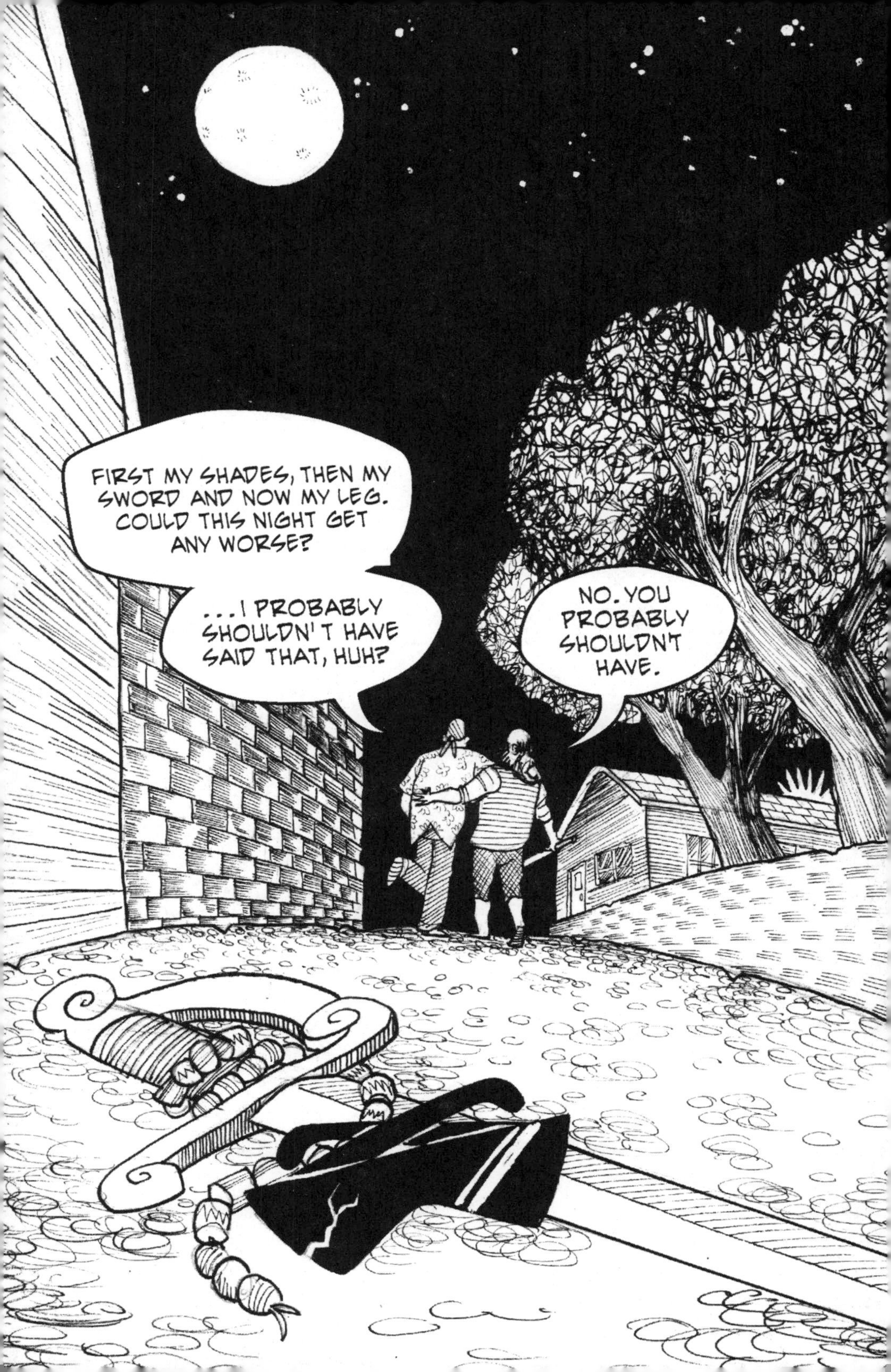
FIRST MY SHADES, THEN MY SWORD AND NOW MY LEG. COULD THIS NIGHT GET ANY WORSE?
...I PROBABLY SHOULDN'T HAVE SAID THAT, HUH?
NO. YOU PROBABLY SHOULDN'T HAVE.

CHAPTER

14

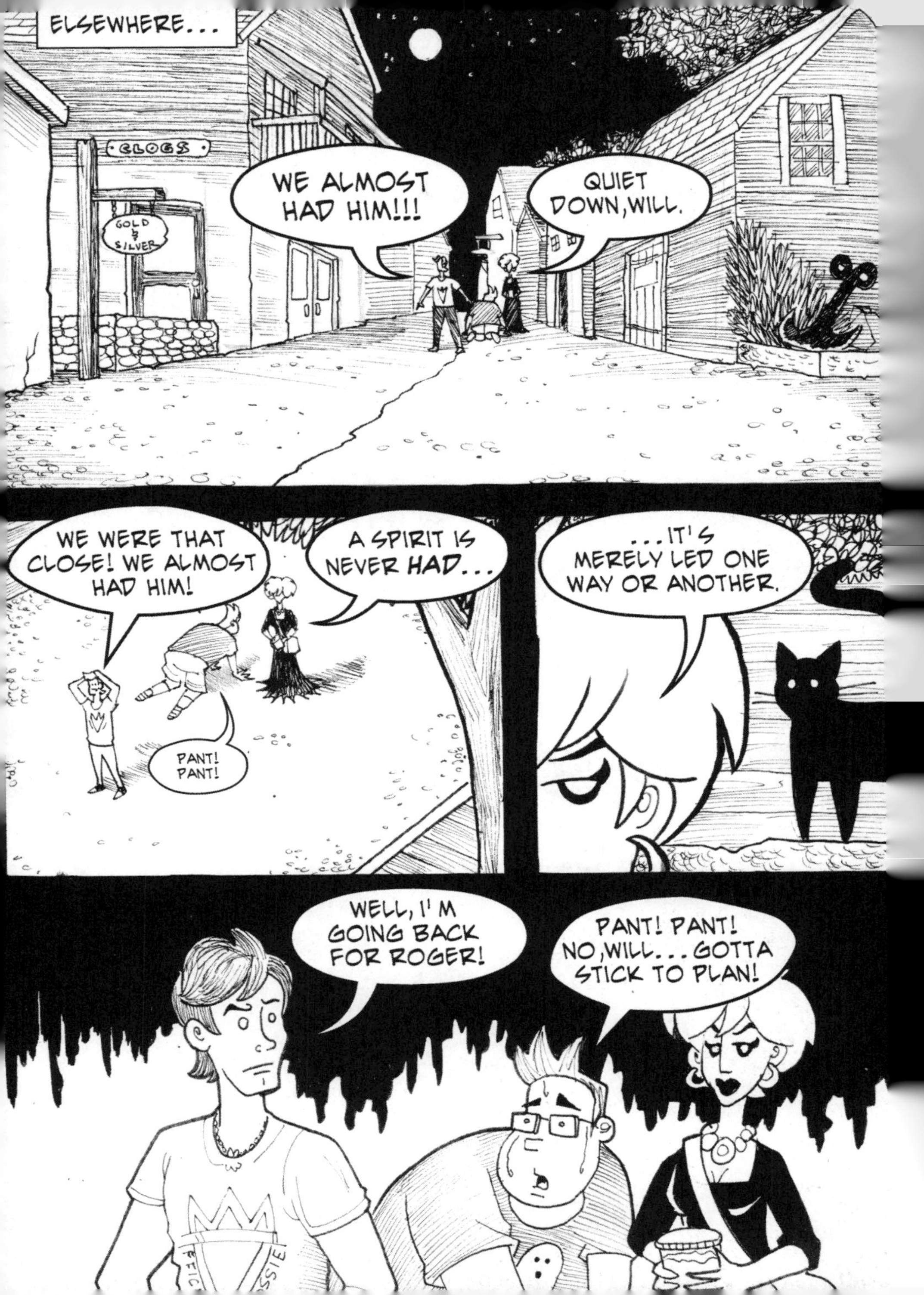
ELSEWHERE...
CLOGS
GOLD & SILVER
WE ALMOST HAD HIM!!!
QUIET DOWN, WILL.
WE WERE THAT CLOSE! WE ALMOST HAD HIM!
A SPIRIT IS NEVER HAD...
PANT! PANT!
...IT'S MERELY LED ONE WAY OR ANOTHER.
WELL, I'M GOING BACK FOR ROGER!
PANT! PANT! NO, WILL... GOTTA STICK TO PLAN!

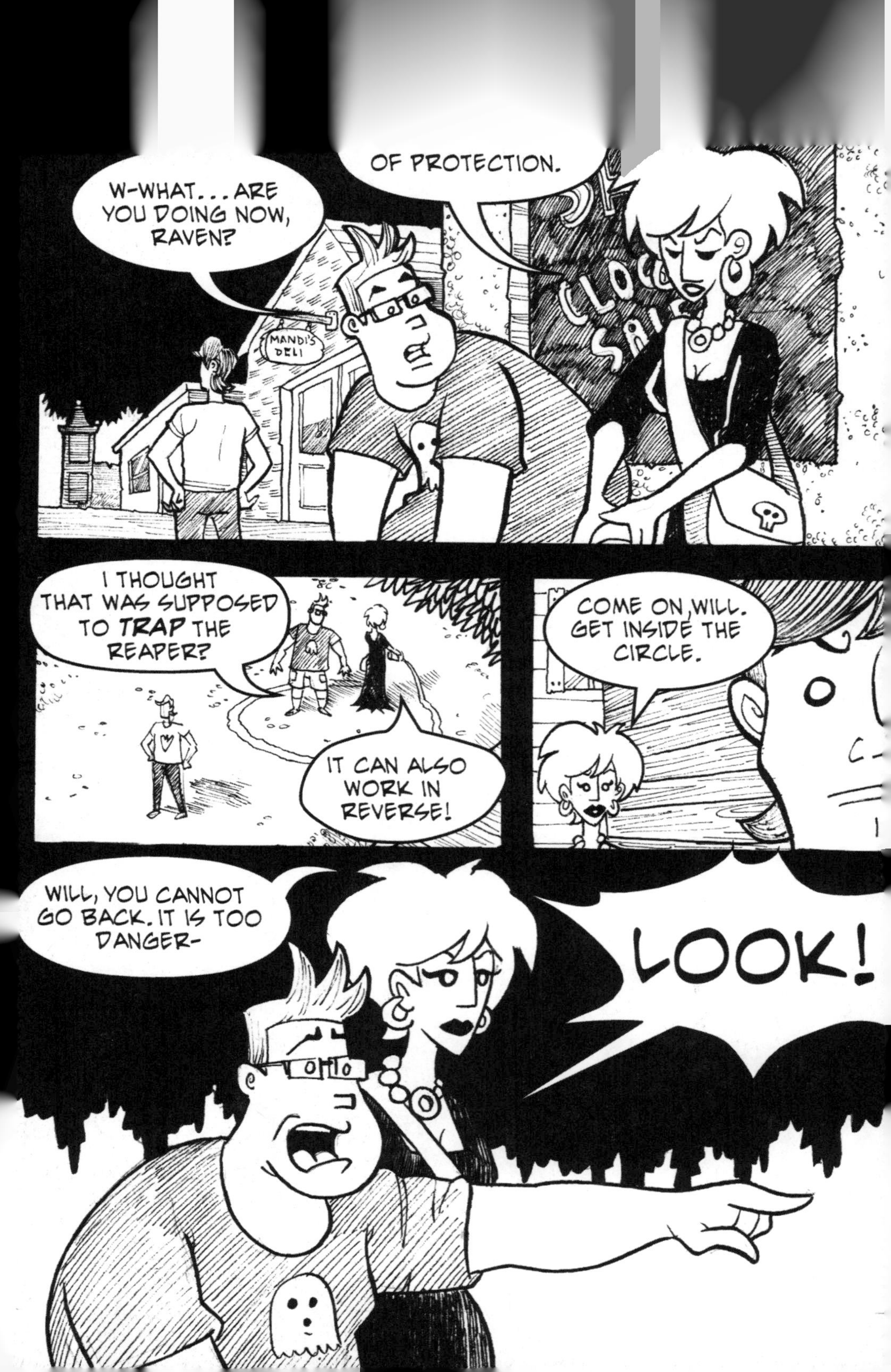
W-WHAT... ARE YOU DOING NOW, RAVEN?
OF PROTECTION.
MANDI'S DELI
I THOUGHT THAT WAS SUPPOSED TO *TRAP* THE REAPER?
IT CAN ALSO WORK IN REVERSE!
COME ON, WILL. GET INSIDE THE CIRCLE.
WILL, YOU CANNOT GO BACK. IT IS TOO DANGER-
LOOK!

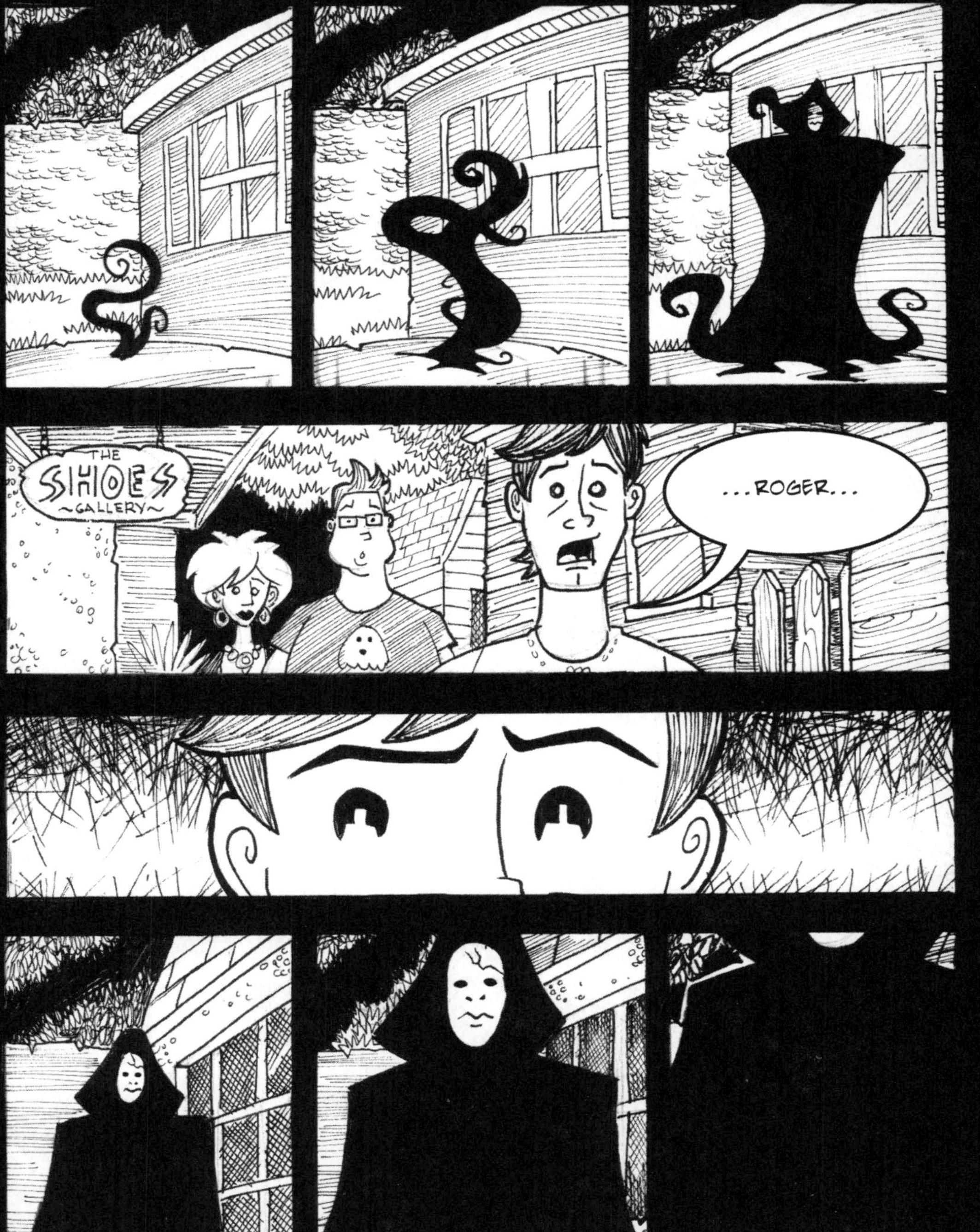
THE SHOES ~GALLERY~
...ROGER...

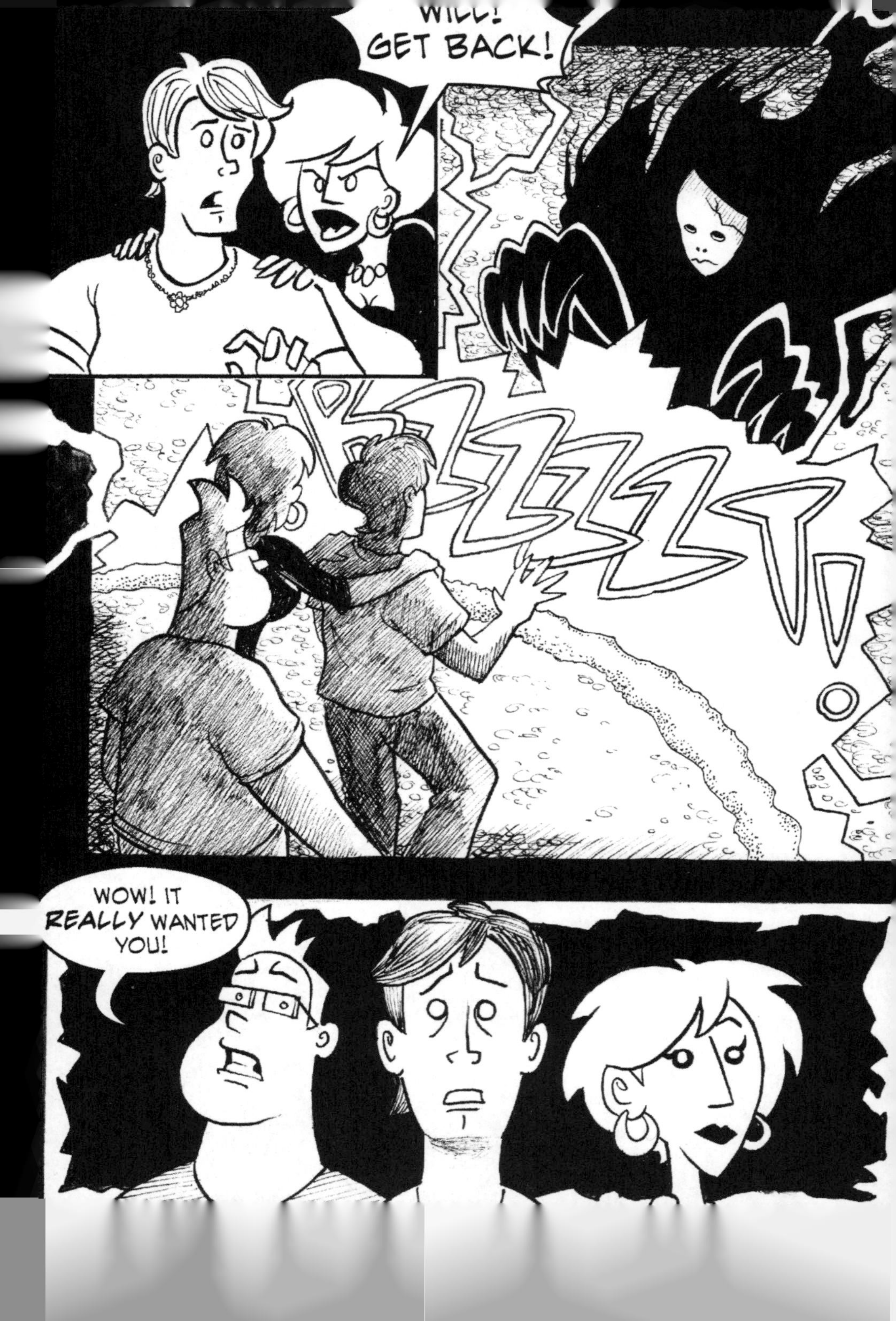
WILL! GET BACK!
BZZZZZT!
WOW! IT REALLY WANTED YOU!

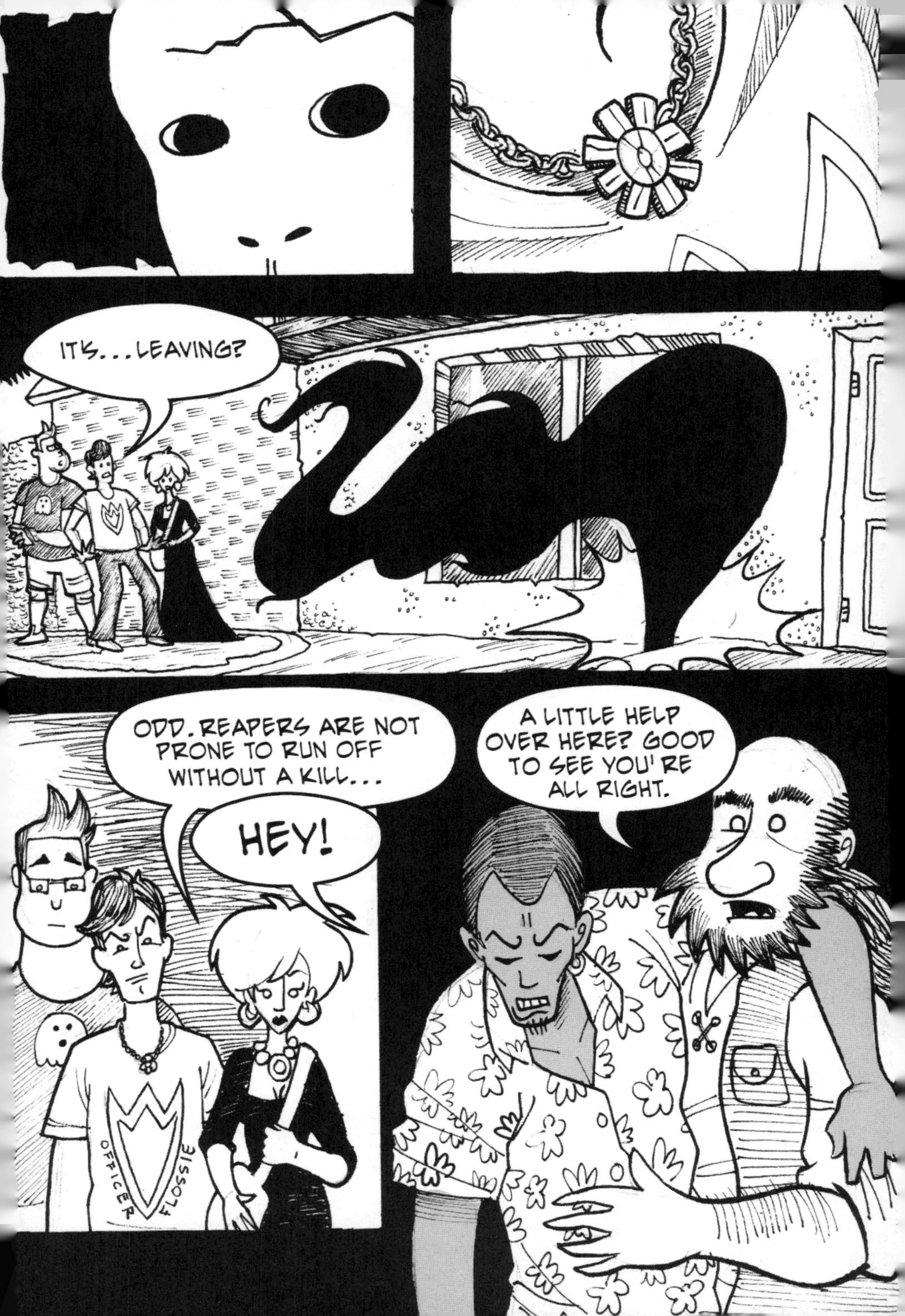
IT'S...LEAVING?
ODD. REAPERS ARE NOT PRONE TO RUN OFF WITHOUT A KILL...
HEY!
A LITTLE HELP OVER HERE? GOOD TO SEE YOU'RE ALL RIGHT.
OFFICER FLOSSIE

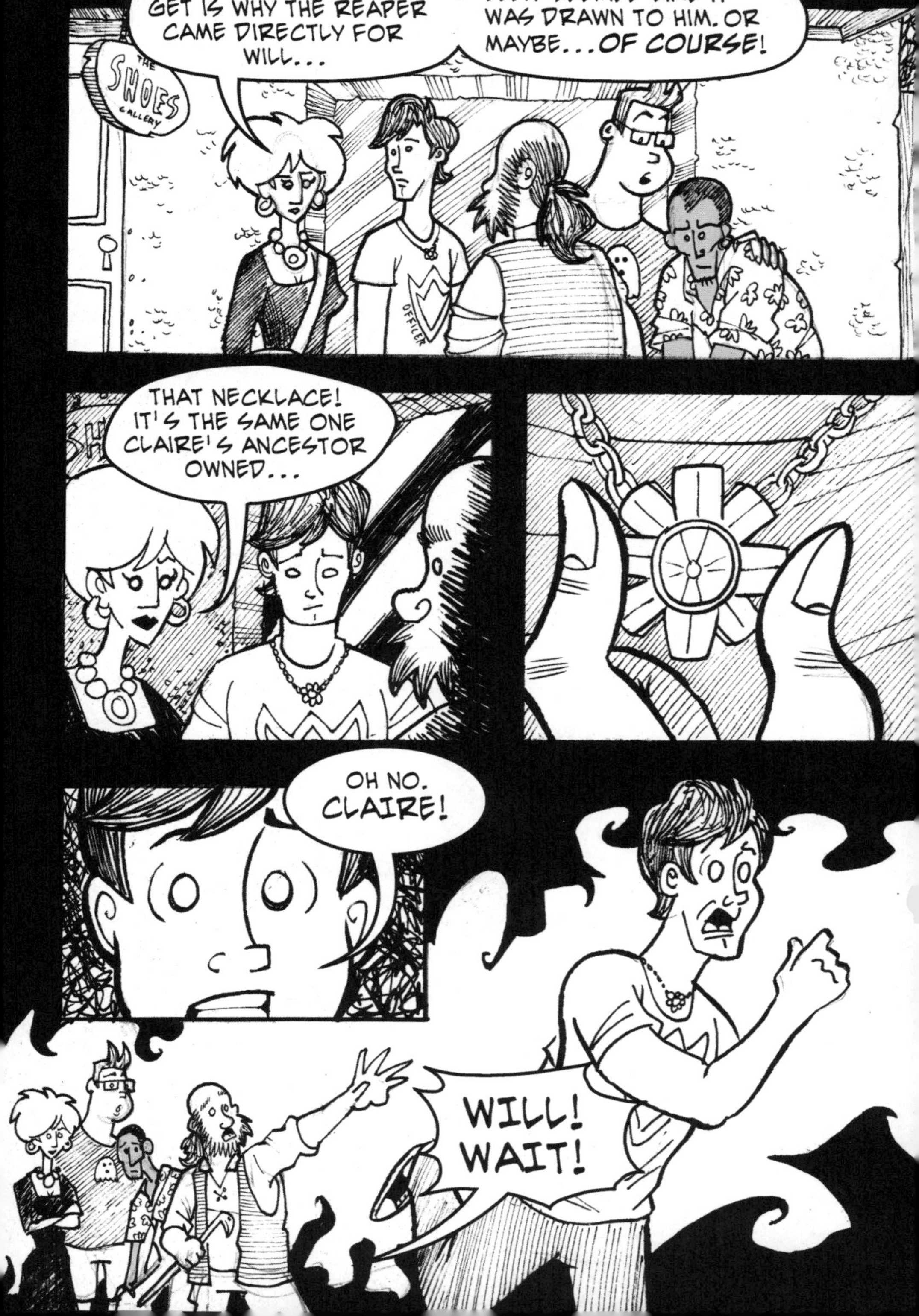
WHAT I DON'T GET IS WHY THE REAPER CAME DIRECTLY FOR WILL...
...IT SEEMED LIKE IT WAS DRAWN TO HIM. OR MAYBE...OF COURSE!
THE SHOES GALLERY
OFFICER
THAT NECKLACE! IT'S THE SAME ONE CLAIRE'S ANCESTOR OWNED...
OH NO. CLAIRE!
WILL! WAIT!

CHAPTER 15

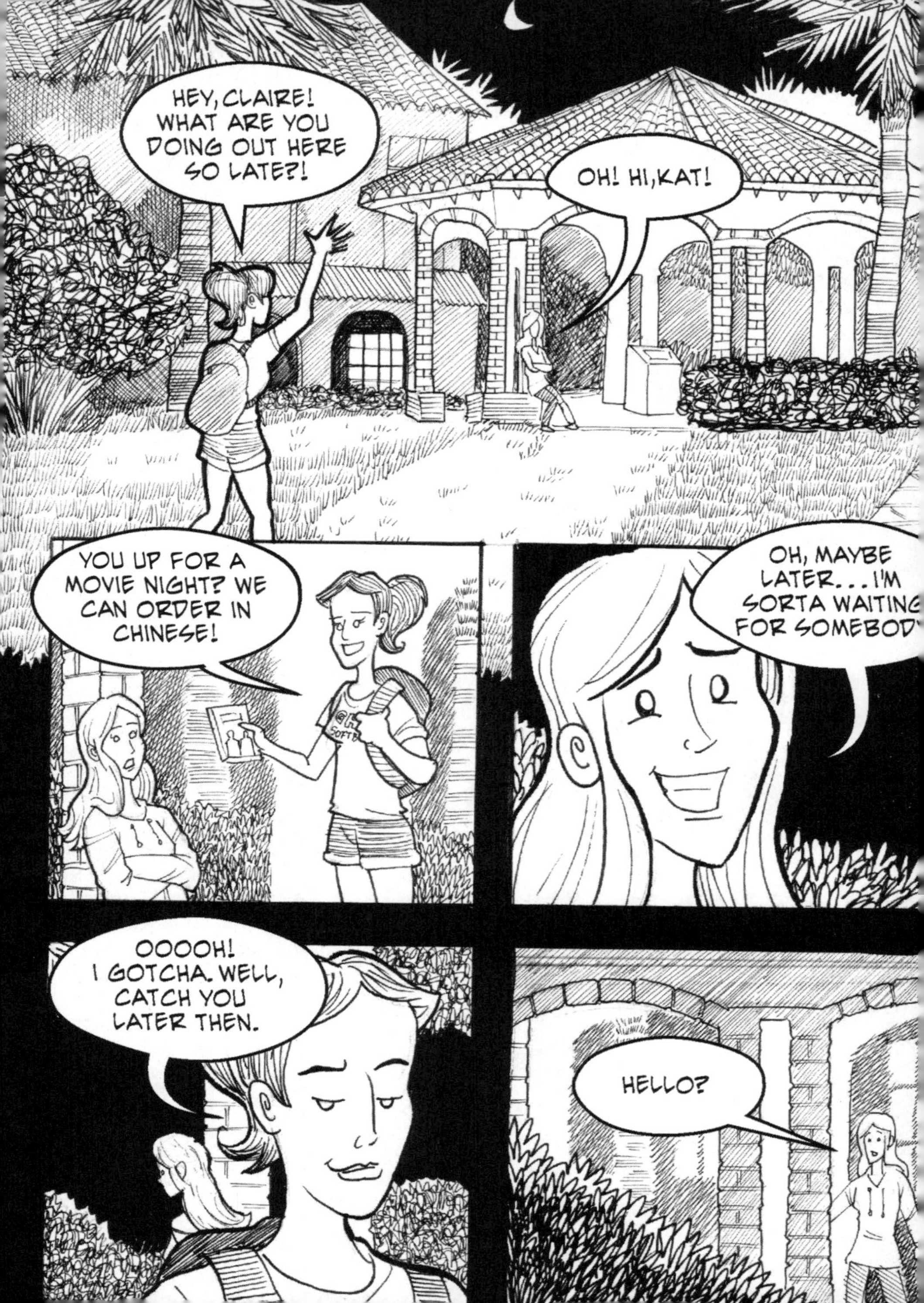
HEY, CLAIRE! WHAT ARE YOU DOING OUT HERE SO LATE?!
OH! HI, KAT!
YOU UP FOR A MOVIE NIGHT? WE CAN ORDER IN CHINESE!
OH, MAYBE LATER... I'M SORTA WAITING FOR SOMEBODY
OOOOH! I GOTCHA. WELL, CATCH YOU LATER THEN.
HELLO?

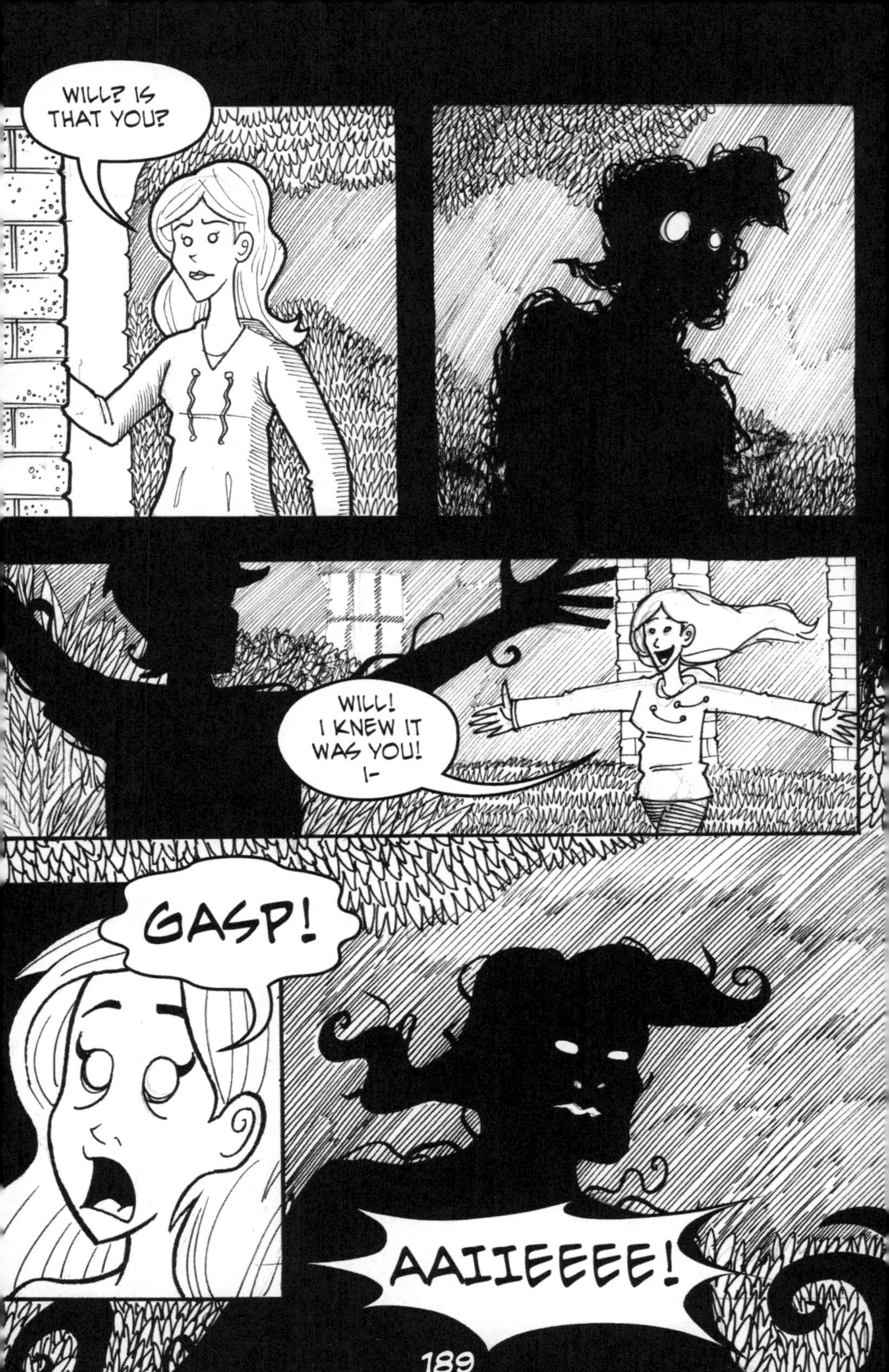
WILL? IS THAT YOU?
WILL! I KNEW IT WAS YOU! I-
GASP!
AAIIEEEE!

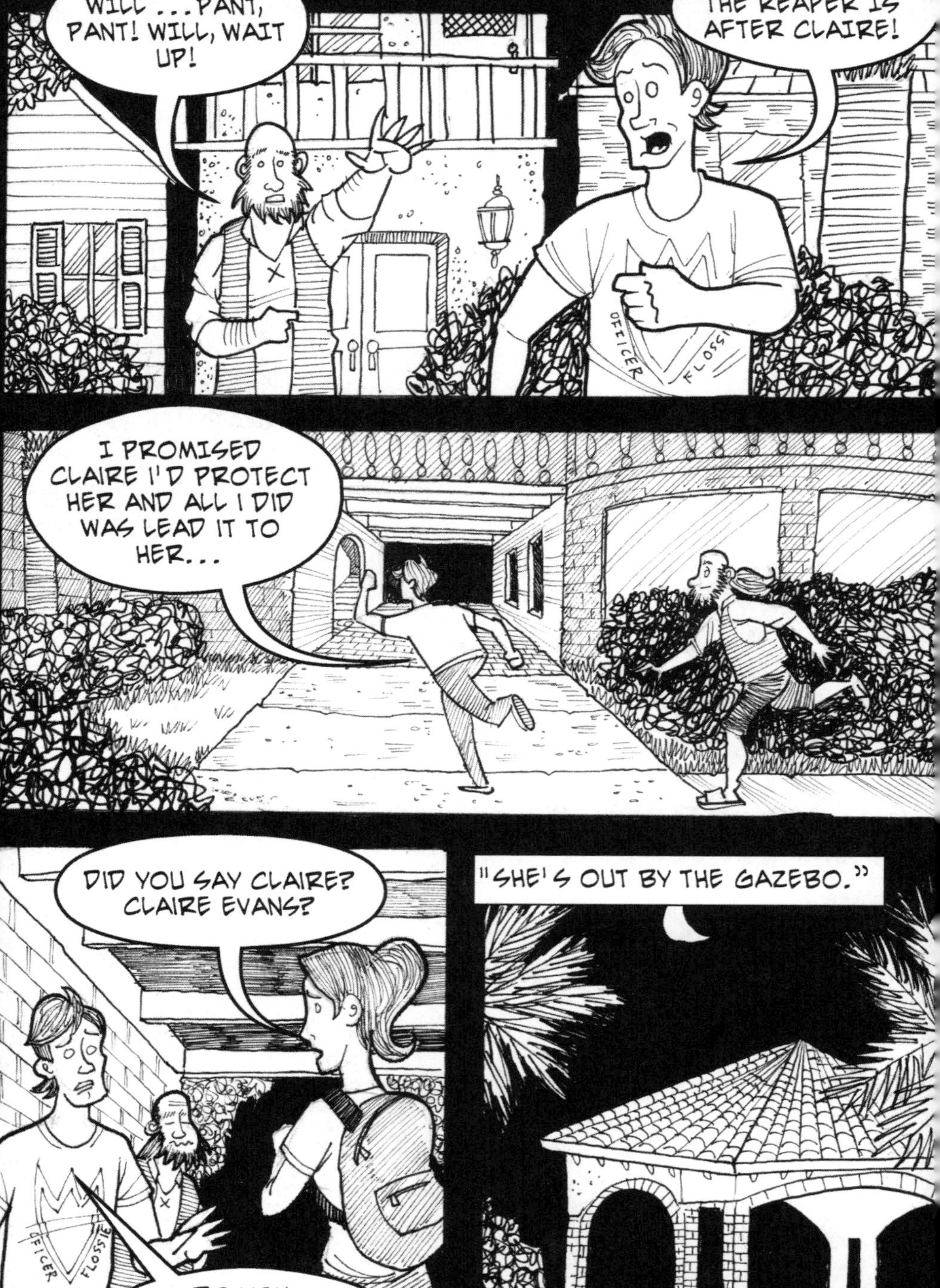
WILL ... PANT, PANT! WILL, WAIT UP!
IT'S CLAIRE! THE REAPER IS AFTER CLAIRE!
OFFICER FLOSSIE
I PROMISED CLAIRE I'D PROTECT HER AND ALL I DID WAS LEAD IT TO HER...
DID YOU SAY CLAIRE? CLAIRE EVANS?
OFFICER FLOSSIE
DO YOU KNOW WHERE SHE IS?!
"SHE'S OUT BY THE GAZEBO."

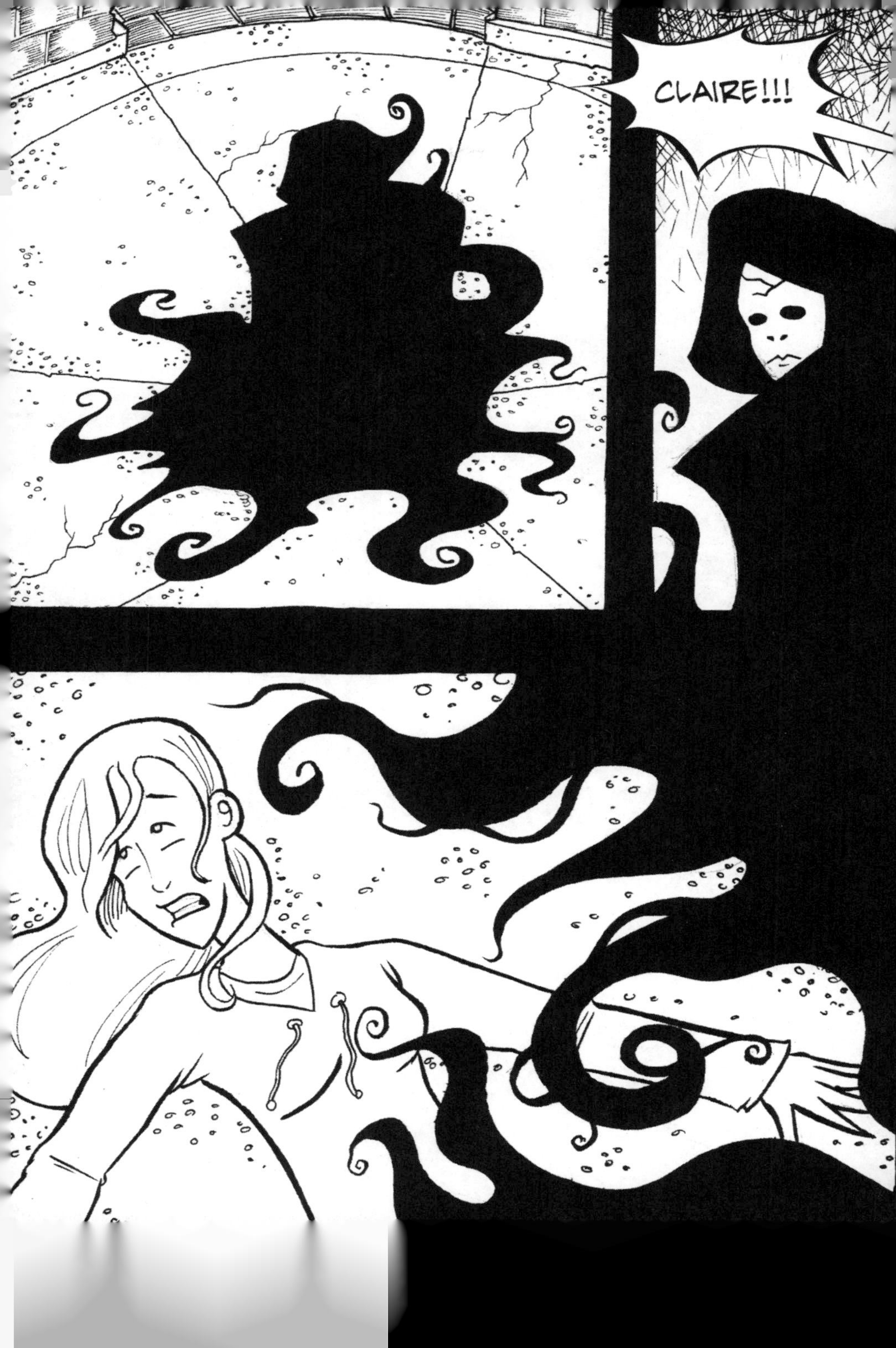
CLAIRE!!!

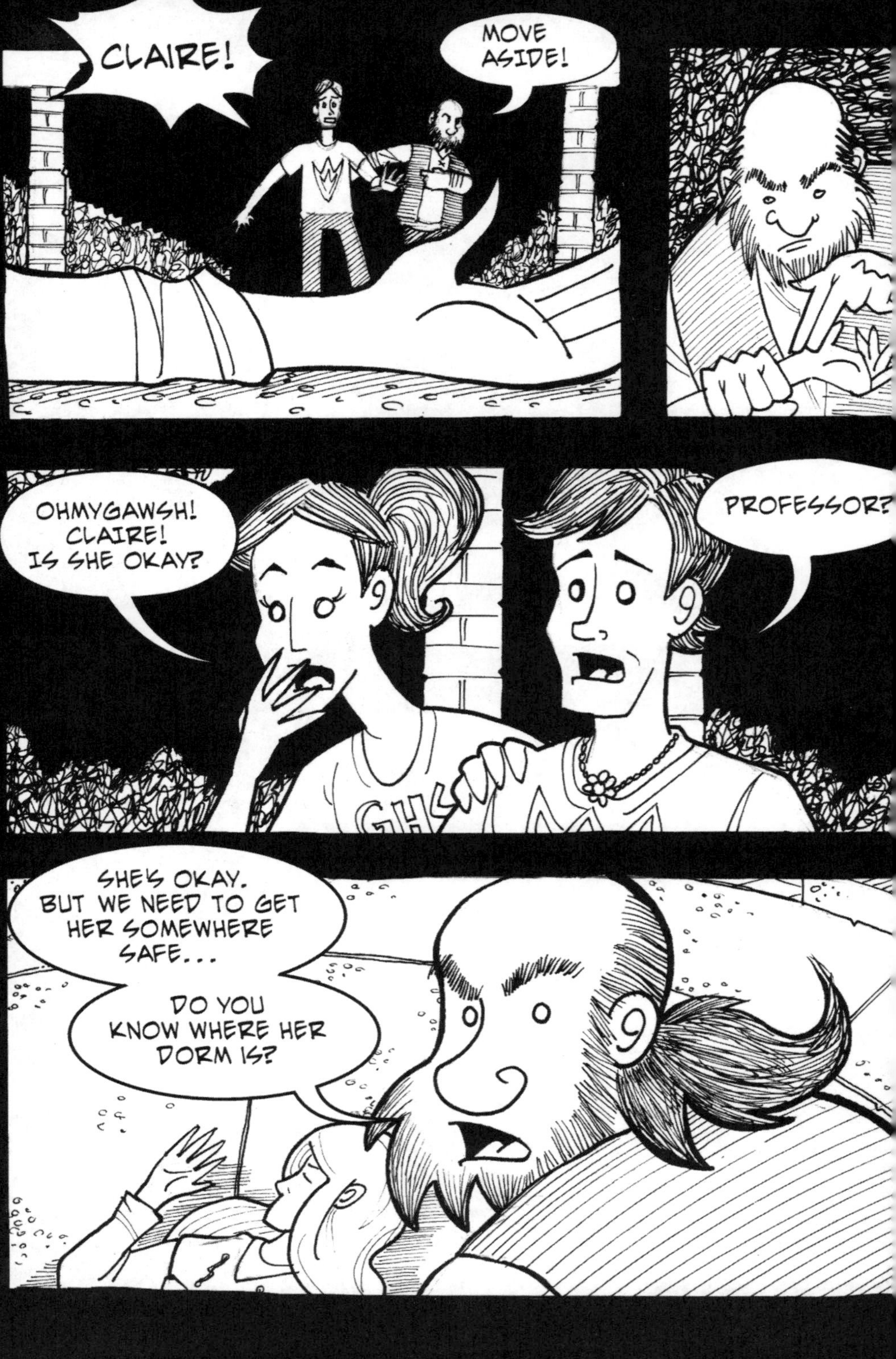
CLAIRE!
MOVE ASIDE!
OHMYGAWSH! CLAIRE! IS SHE OKAY?
PROFESSOR?
SHE'S OKAY. BUT WE NEED TO GET HER SOMEWHERE SAFE...
DO YOU KNOW WHERE HER DORM IS?

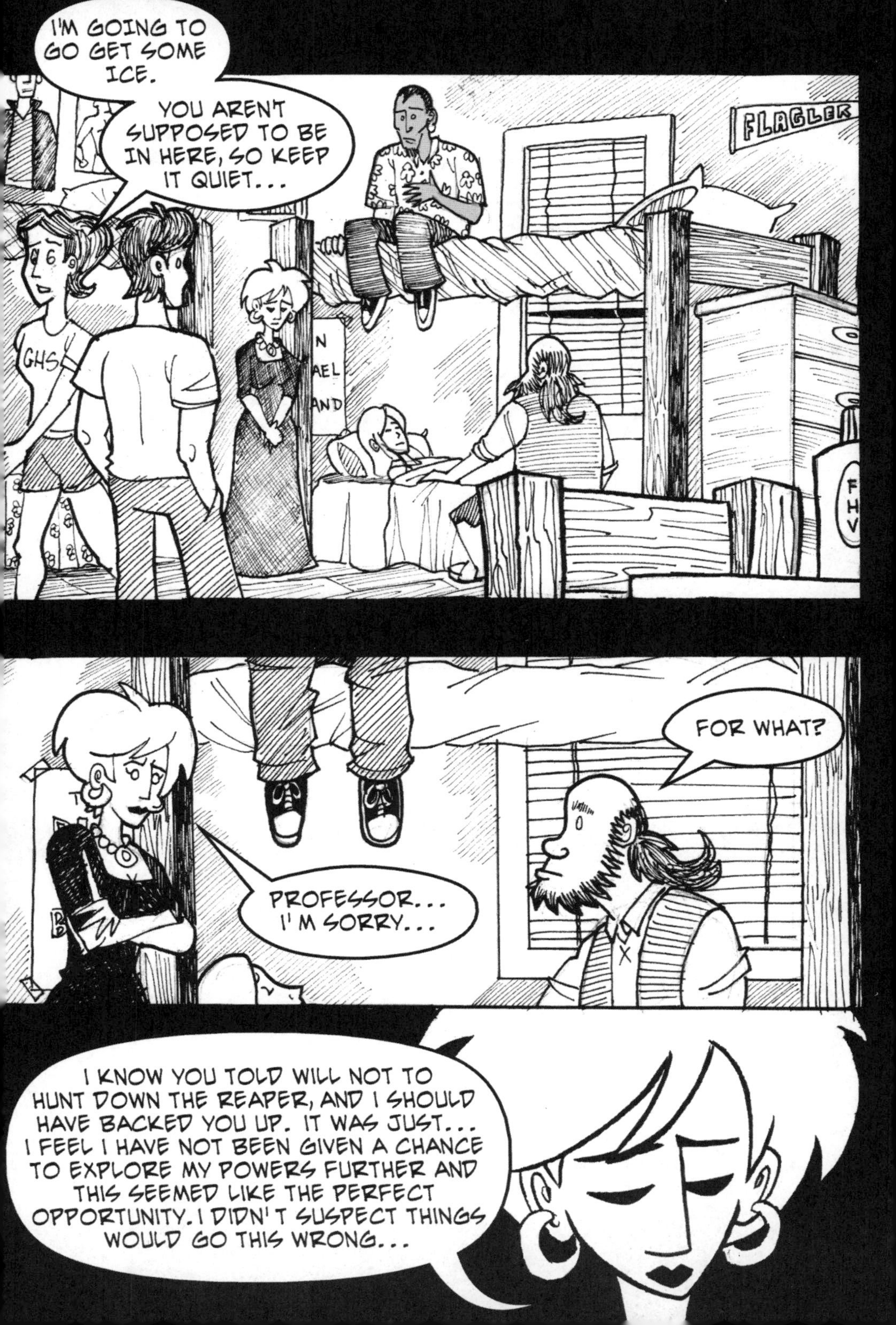
I'M GOING TO GO GET SOME ICE.
YOU AREN'T SUPPOSED TO BE IN HERE, SO KEEP IT QUIET...
FLAGLER
GHS
PROFESSOR... I'M SORRY...
FOR WHAT?
I KNOW YOU TOLD WILL NOT TO HUNT DOWN THE REAPER, AND I SHOULD HAVE BACKED YOU UP. IT WAS JUST... I FEEL I HAVE NOT BEEN GIVEN A CHANCE TO EXPLORE MY POWERS FURTHER AND THIS SEEMED LIKE THE PERFECT OPPORTUNITY. I DIDN'T SUSPECT THINGS WOULD GO THIS WRONG...

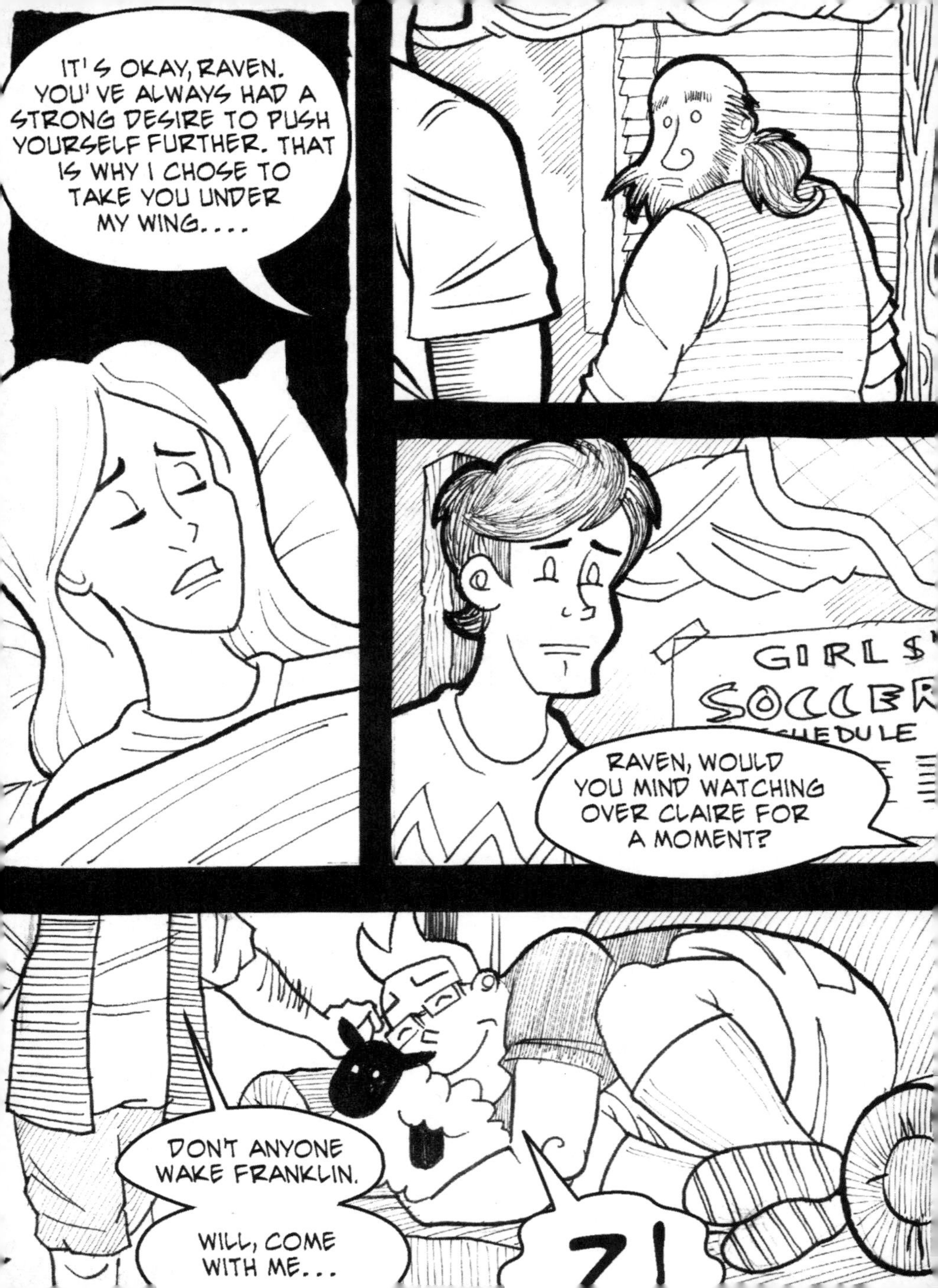
IT'S OKAY, RAVEN. YOU'VE ALWAYS HAD A STRONG DESIRE TO PUSH YOURSELF FURTHER. THAT IS WHY I CHOSE TO TAKE YOU UNDER MY WING....
GIRLS'
SOCCER
SCHEDULE
RAVEN, WOULD YOU MIND WATCHING OVER CLAIRE FOR A MOMENT?
DON'T ANYONE WAKE FRANKLIN.
WILL, COME WITH ME...
Z!

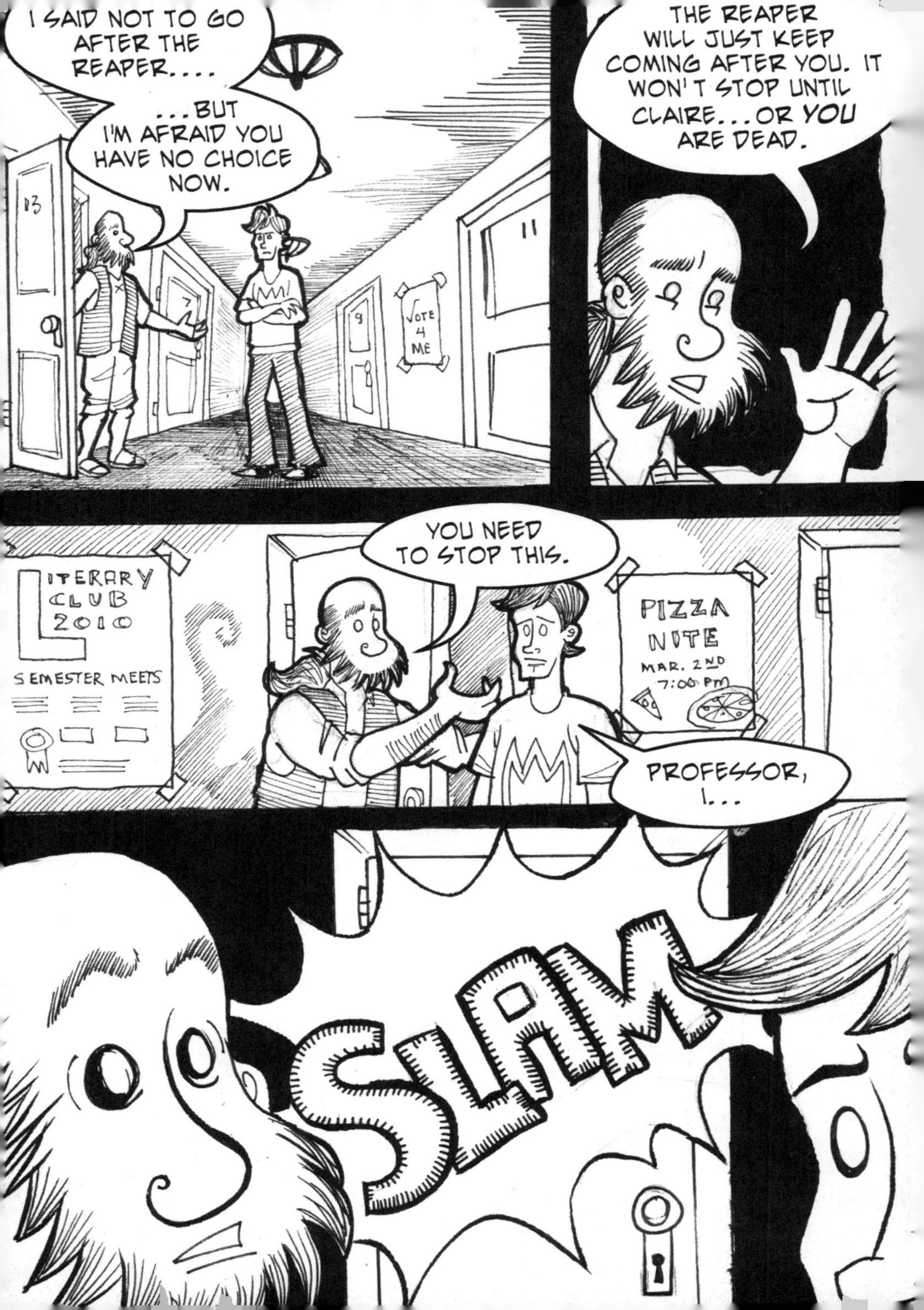
I SAID NOT TO GO AFTER THE REAPER....
...BUT I'M AFRAID YOU HAVE NO CHOICE NOW.
13
7
9
11
VOTE 4 ME
THE REAPER WILL JUST KEEP COMING AFTER YOU. IT WON'T STOP UNTIL CLAIRE...OR YOU ARE DEAD.
LITERARY CLUB 2010
SEMESTER MEETS
YOU NEED TO STOP THIS.
PIZZA NITE
MAR. 2ND
7:00 PM
PROFESSOR, I...
SLAM

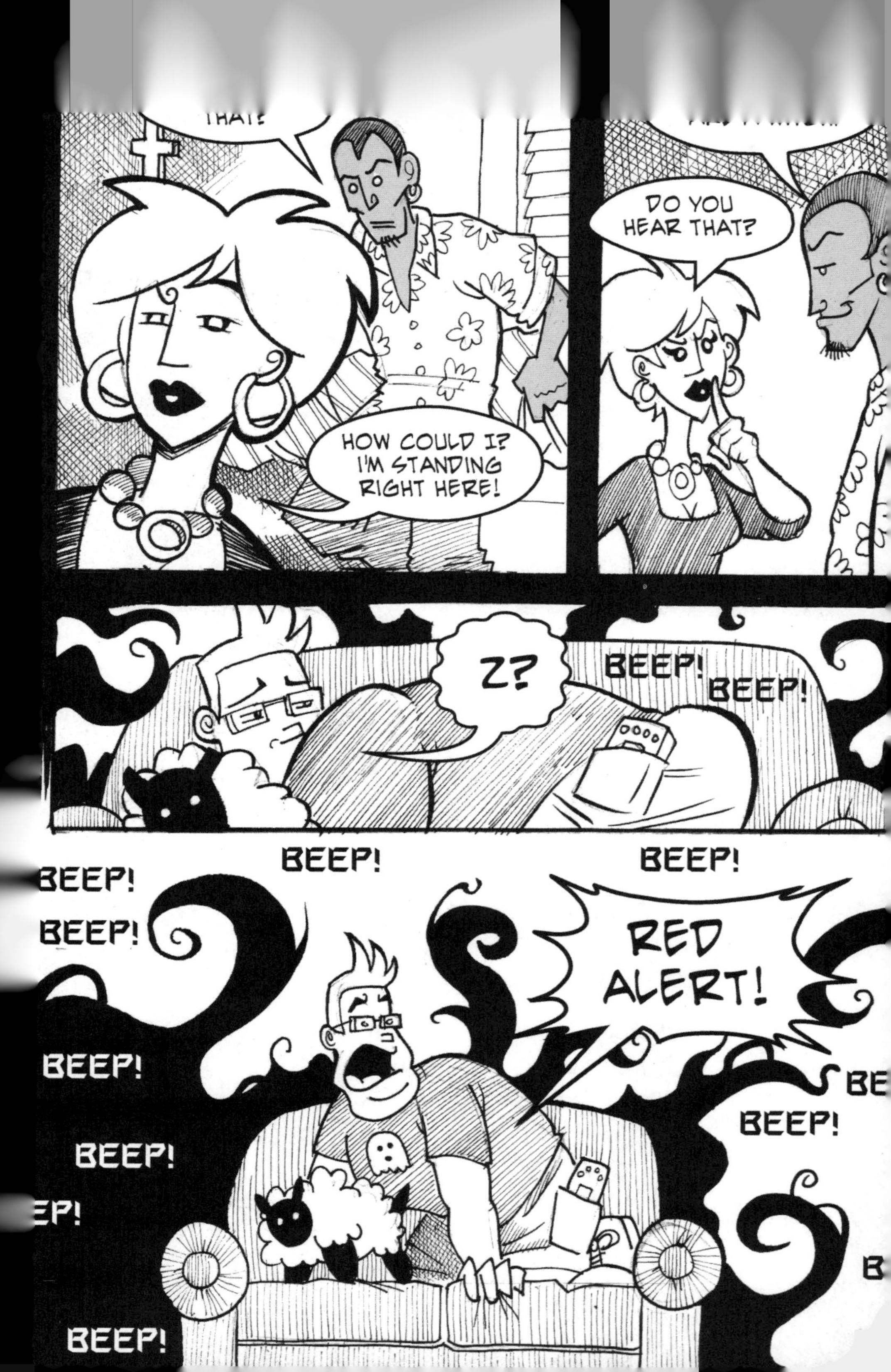

HOW COULD I? I'M STANDING RIGHT HERE!
DO YOU HEAR THAT?
Z?
BEEP! BEEP!
BEEP!
BEEP!
BEEP!
BEEP!
RED ALERT!
BEEP!
BEEP!
BEEP!
BEEP!

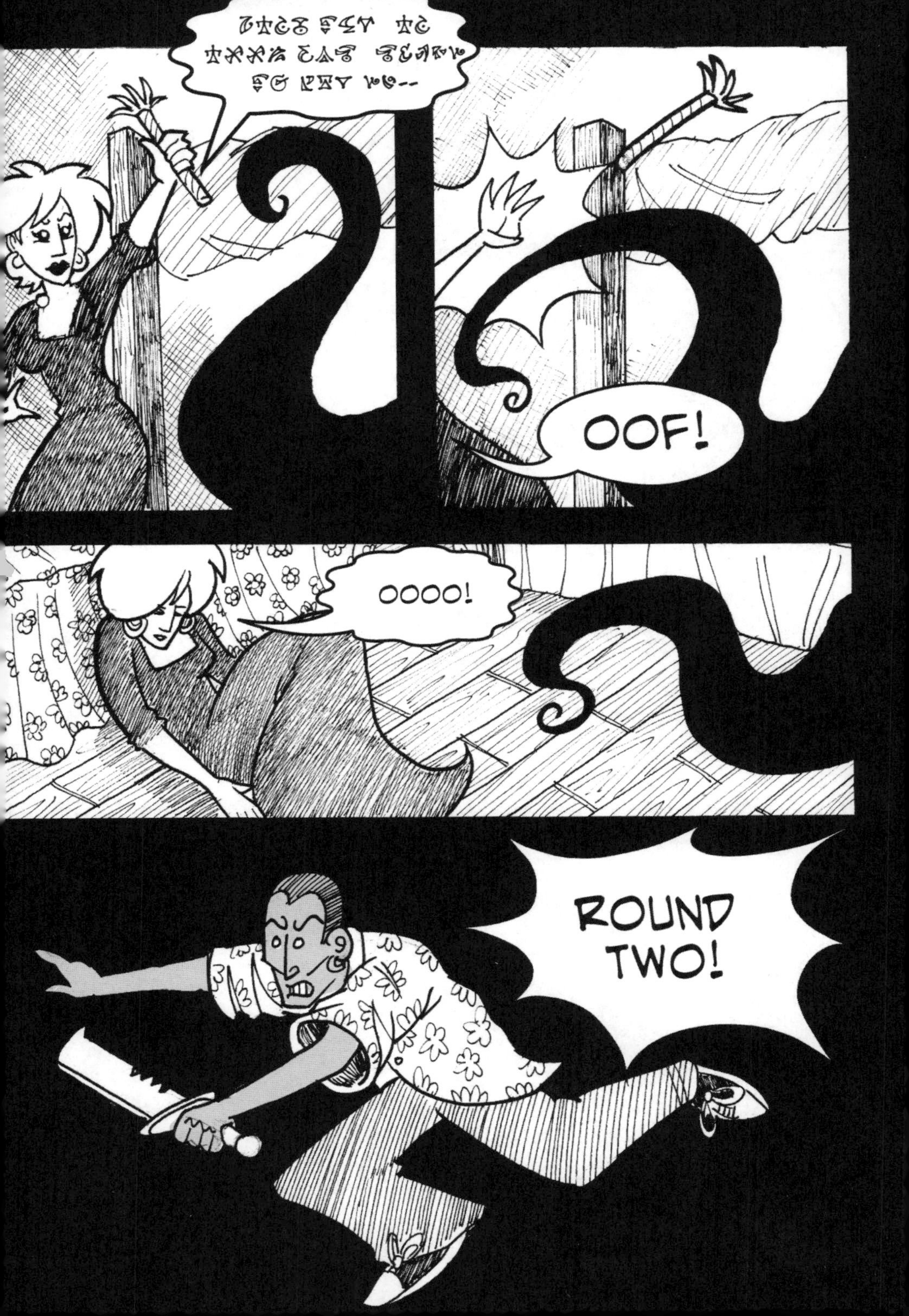
OOF!
OOOO!
ROUND TWO!

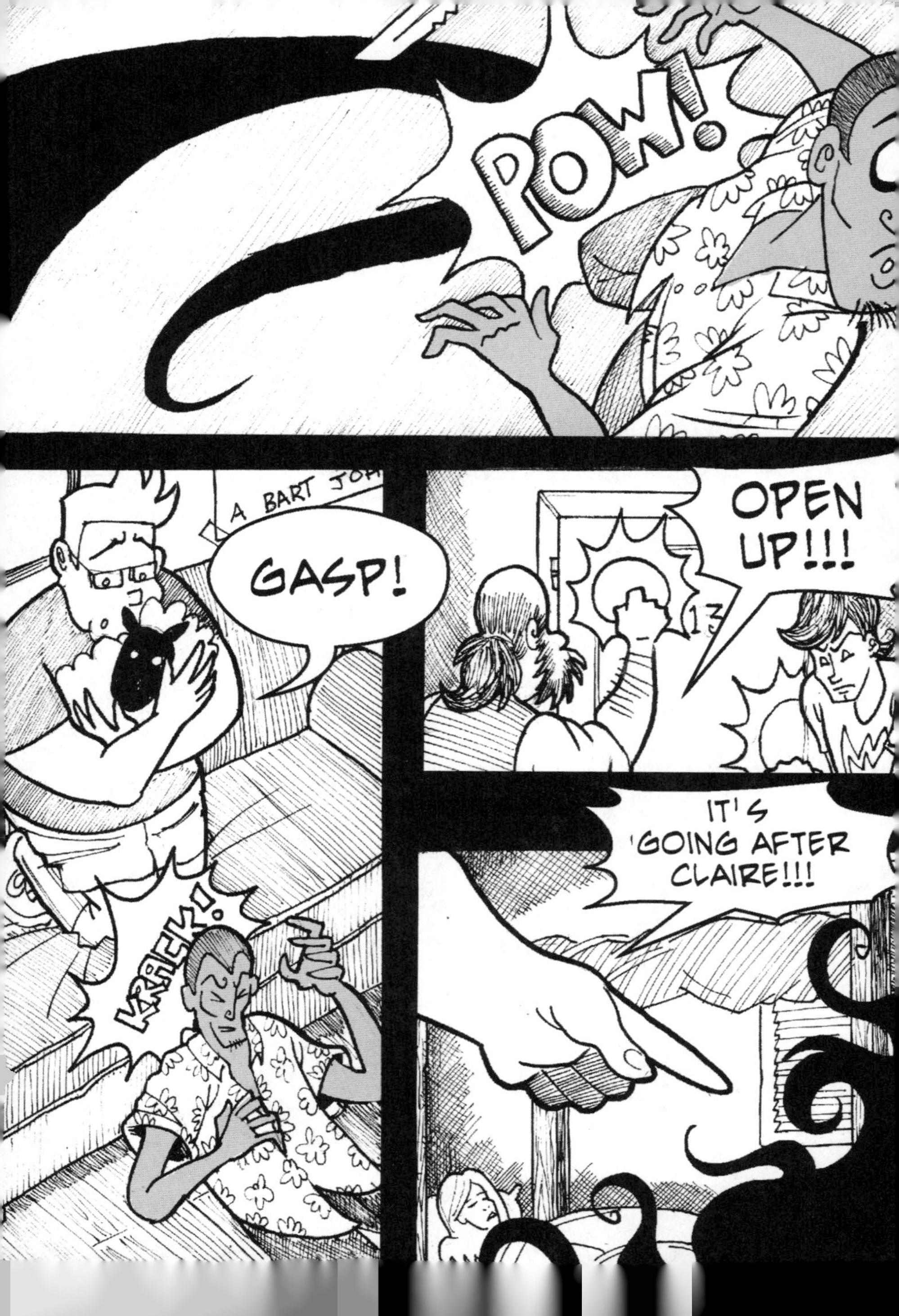
POW!
GASP!
KRAACK!
OPEN UP!!!
13
IT'S GOING AFTER CLAIRE!!!

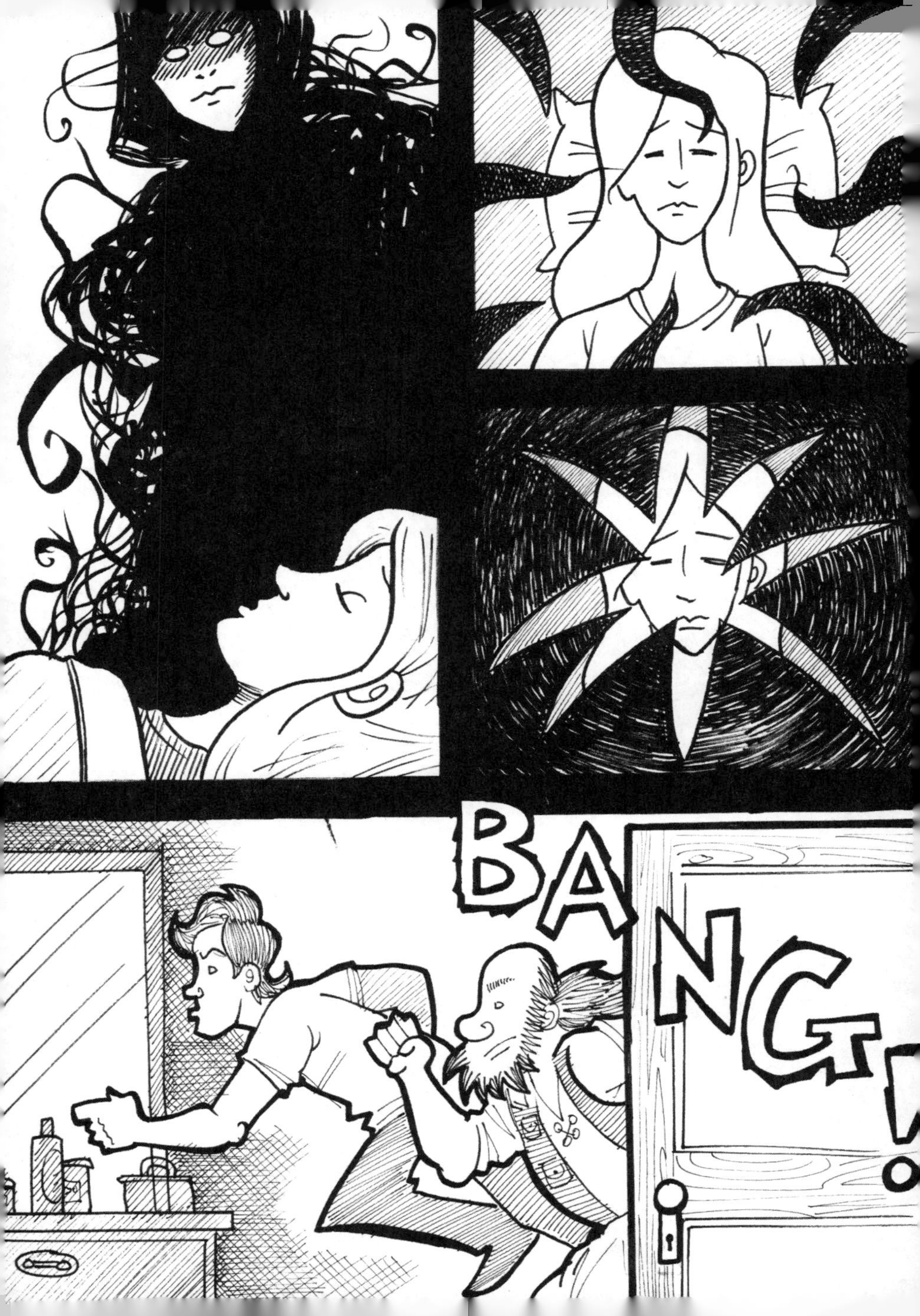
BANG!

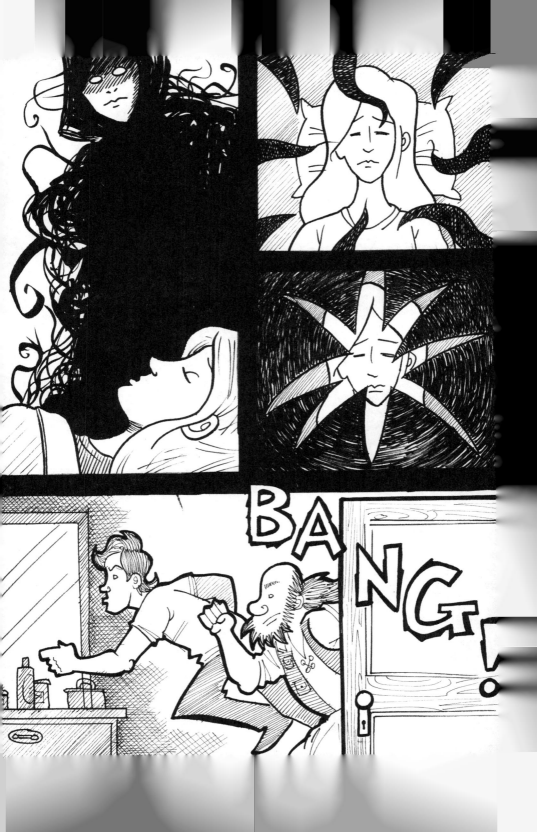

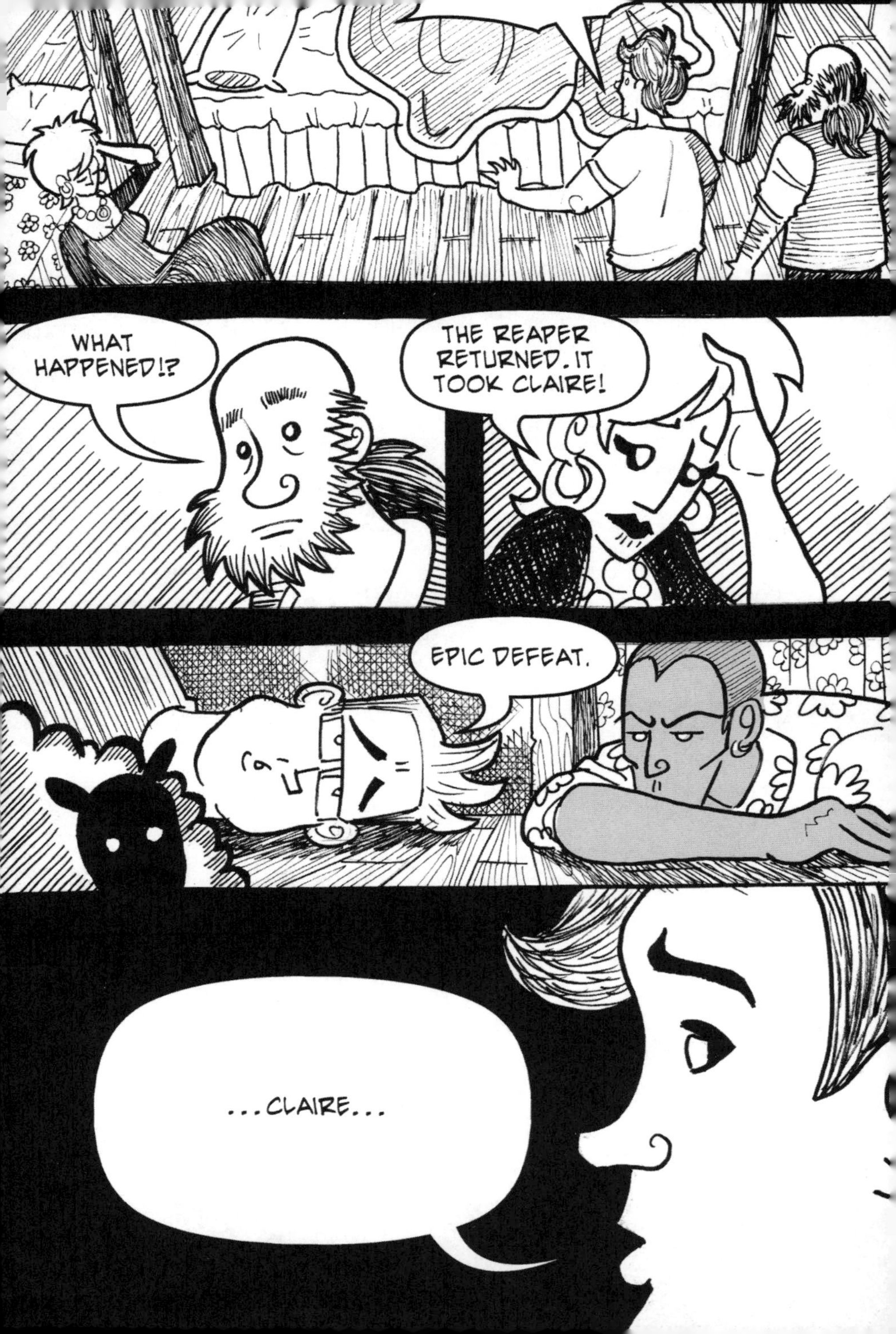
WHAT HAPPENED!?
THE REAPER RETURNED. IT TOOK CLAIRE!
EPIC DEFEAT.
...CLAIRE...

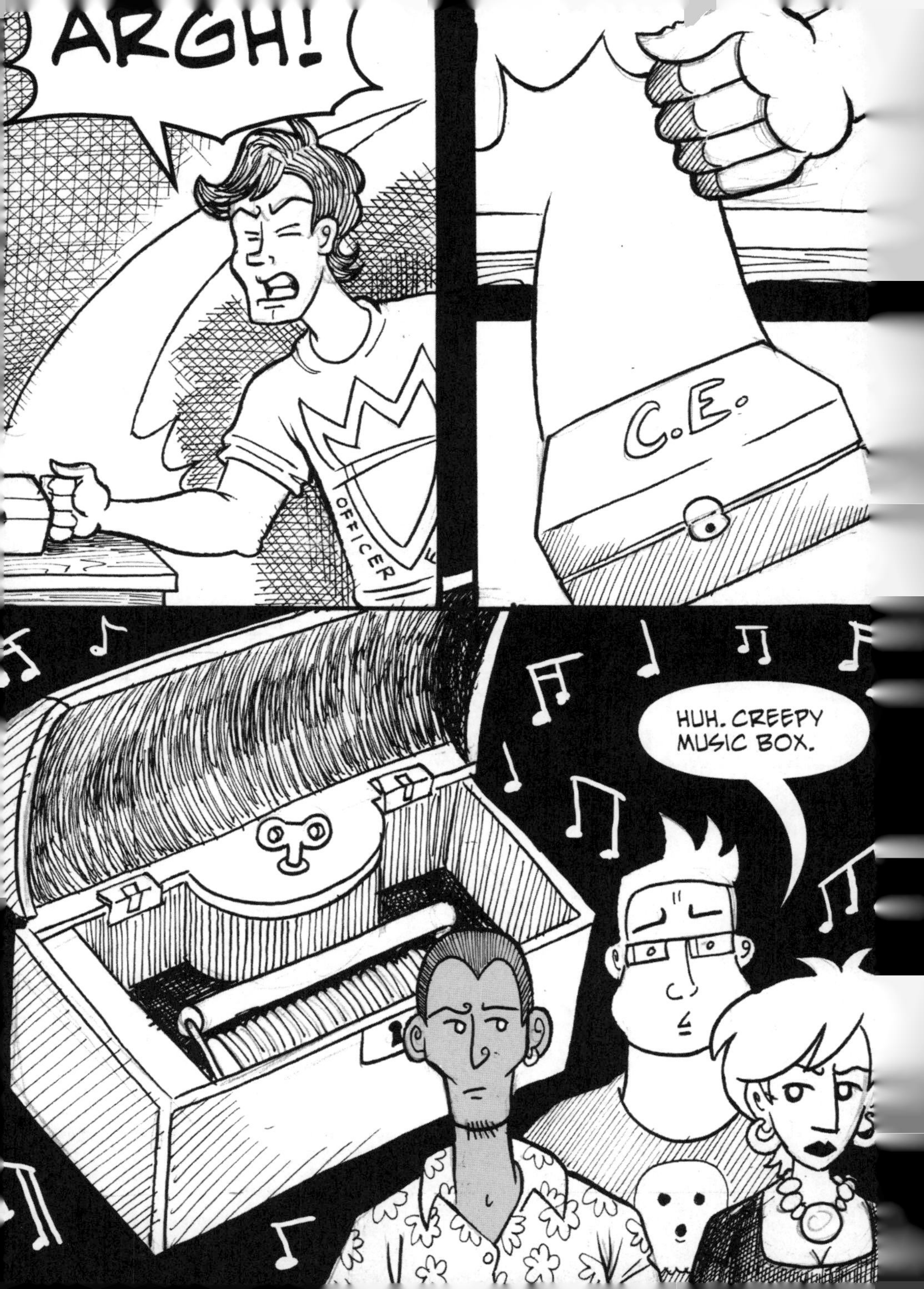
ARGH!
C.E.
OFFICER
HUH. CREEPY MUSIC BOX.

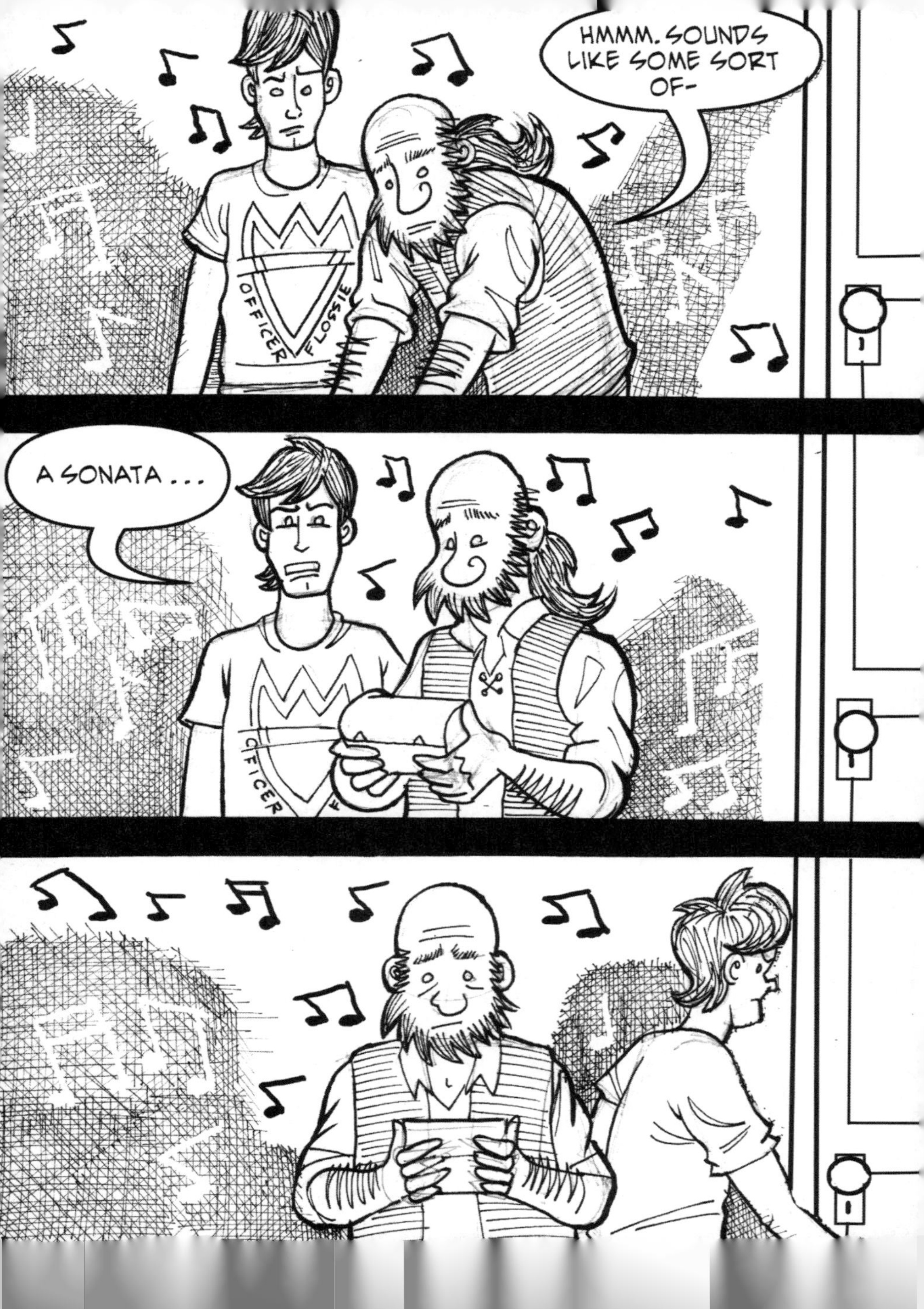
HMMM. SOUNDS LIKE SOME SORT OF-
A SONATA . . .

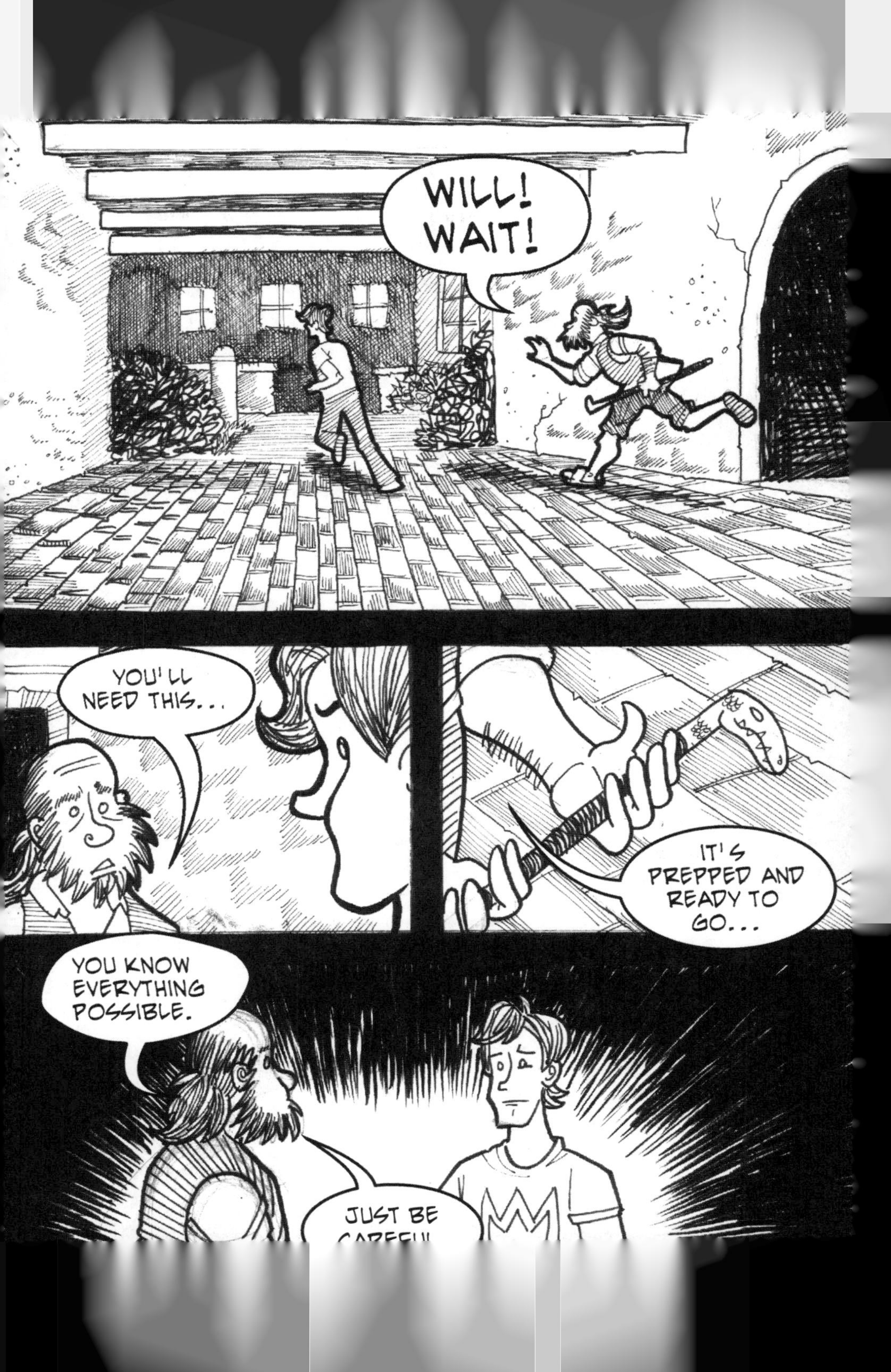
WILL! WAIT!
YOU'LL NEED THIS...
IT'S PREPPED AND READY TO GO...
YOU KNOW EVERYTHING POSSIBLE.
JUST BE

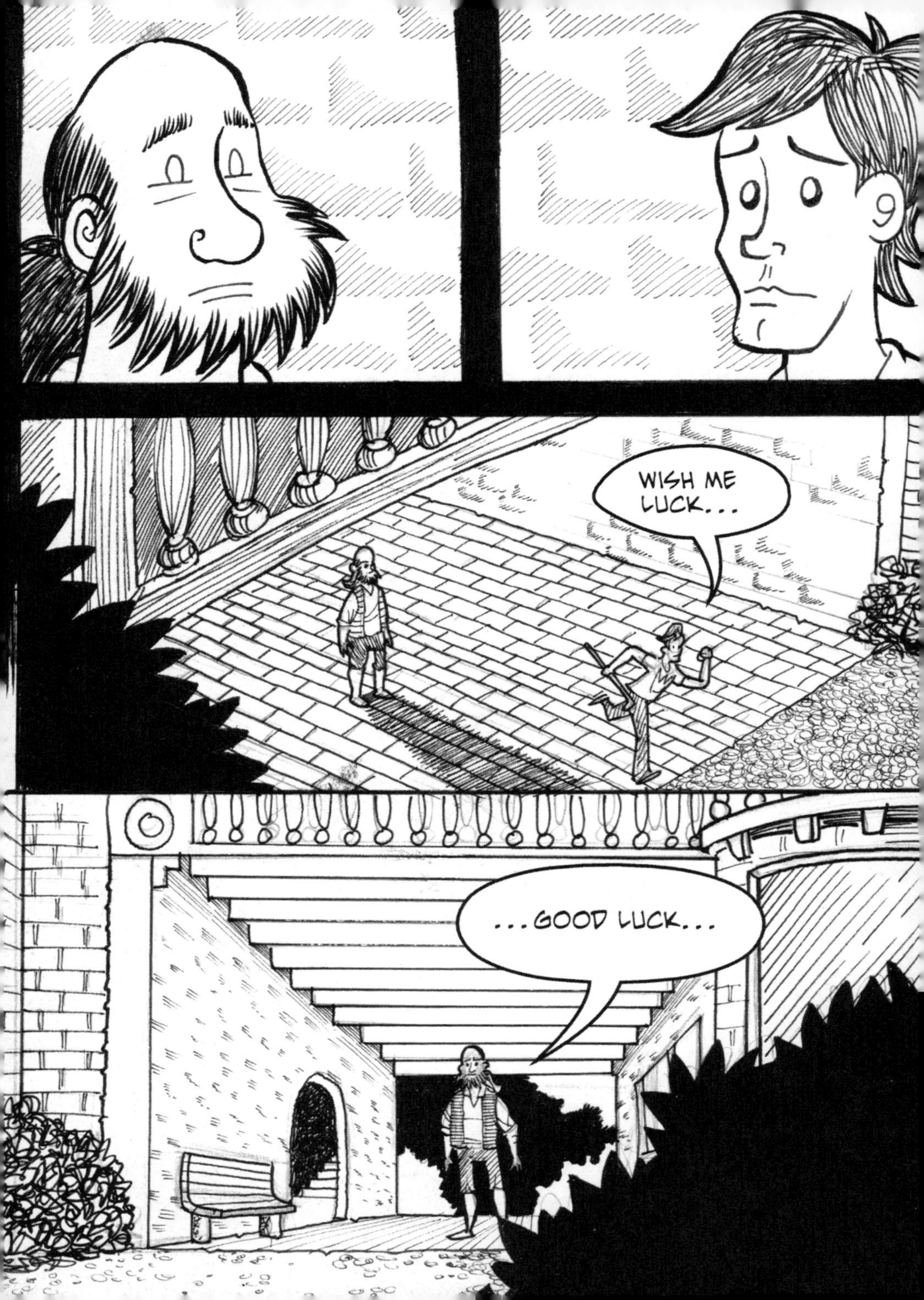
WISH ME LUCK...
...GOOD LUCK...

CHAPTER
16

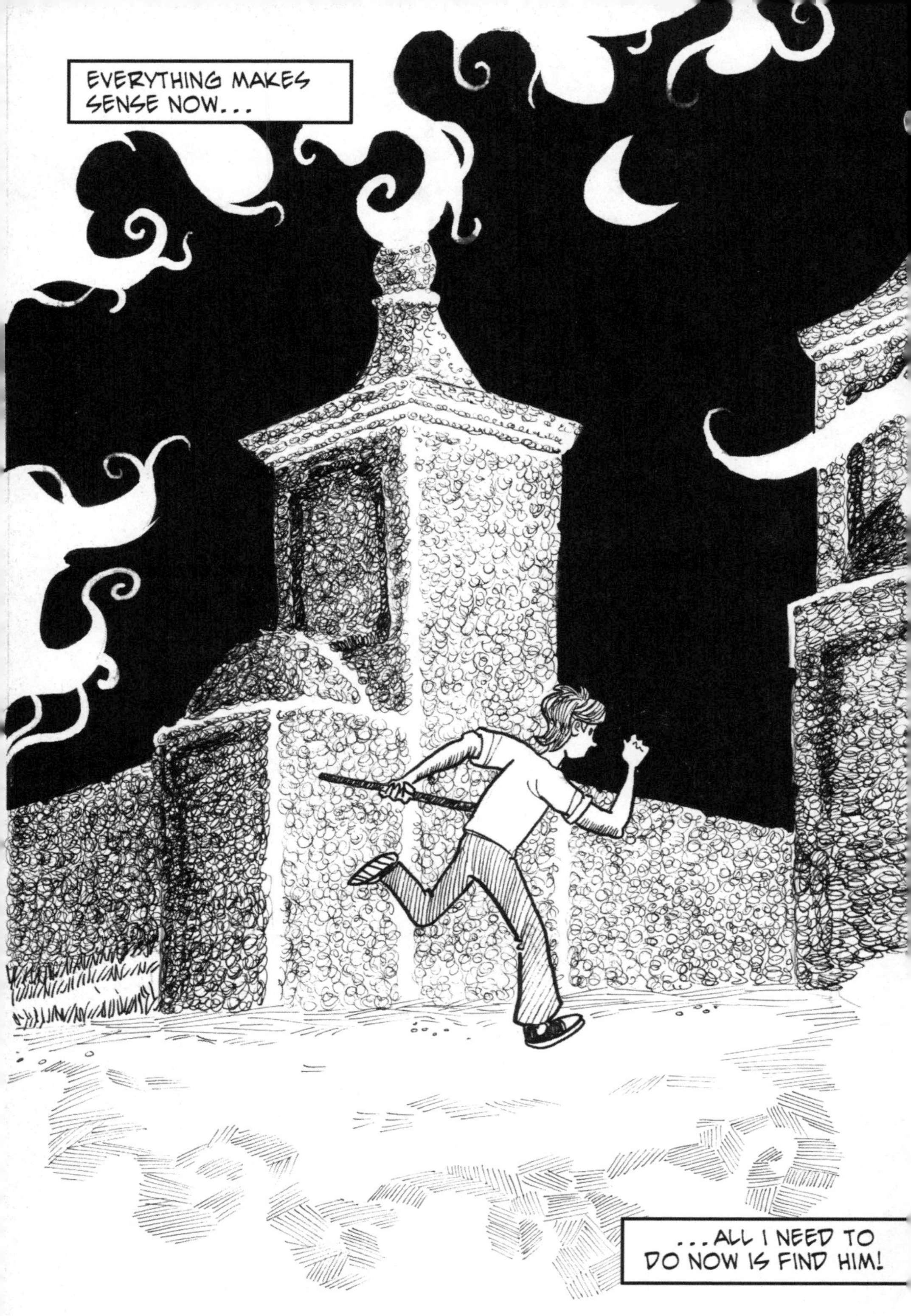
EVERYTHING MAKES SENSE NOW...
...ALL I NEED TO DO NOW IS FIND HIM!

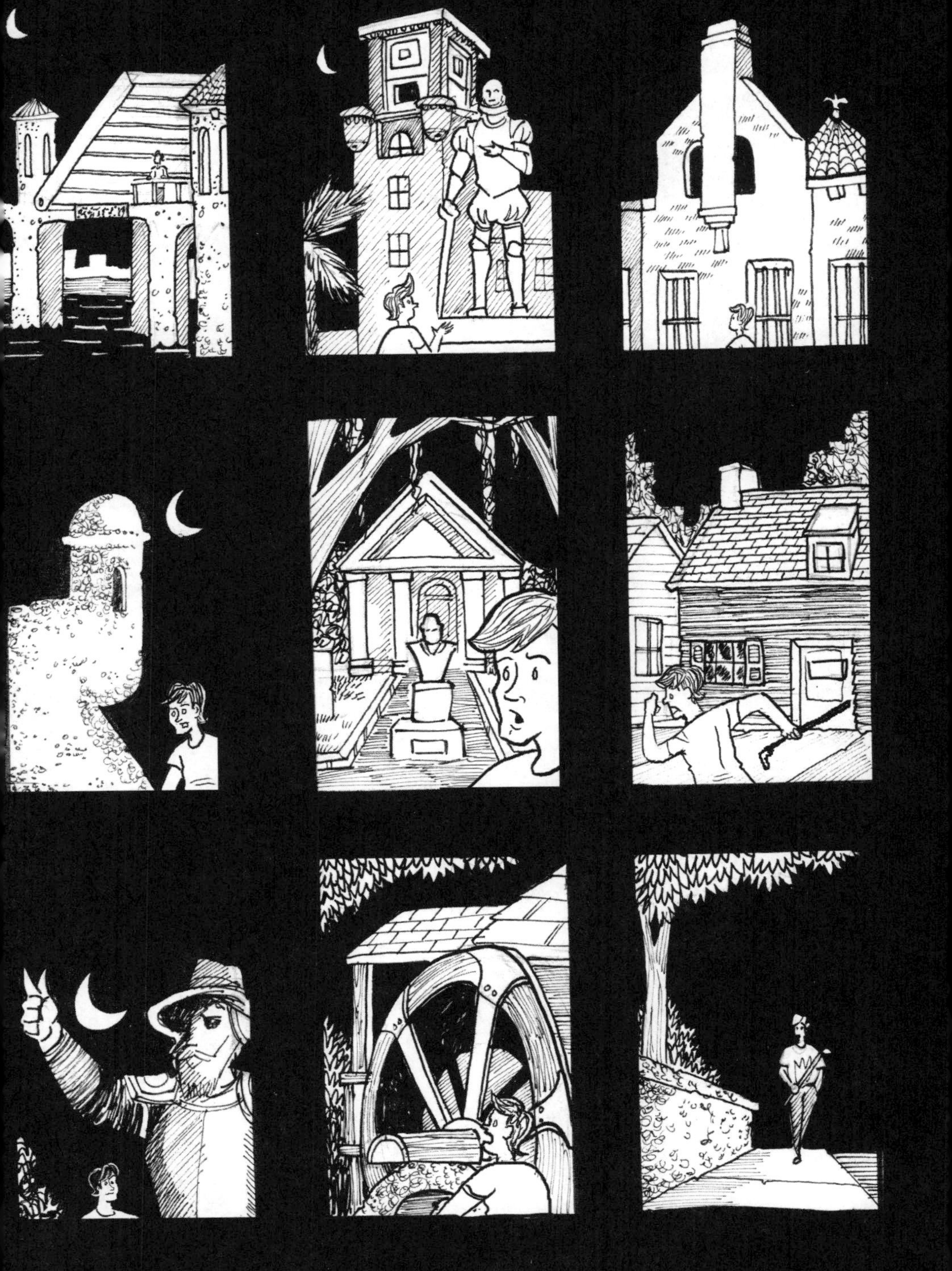

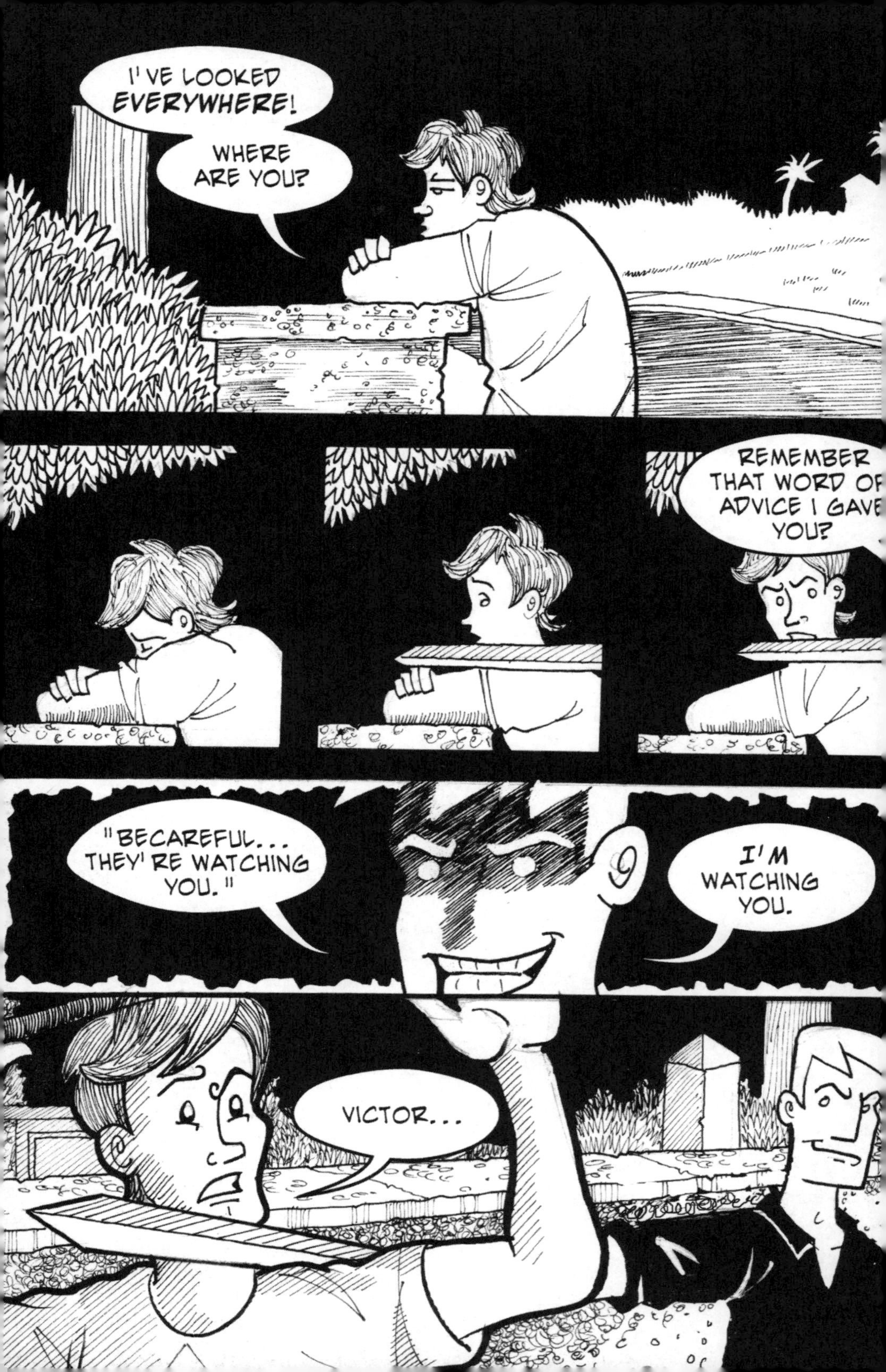

I'VE LOOKED EVERYWHERE!
WHERE ARE YOU?
REMEMBER THAT WORD OF ADVICE I GAVE YOU?
"BECAREFUL... THEY'RE WATCHING YOU."
I'M WATCHING YOU.
VICTOR...

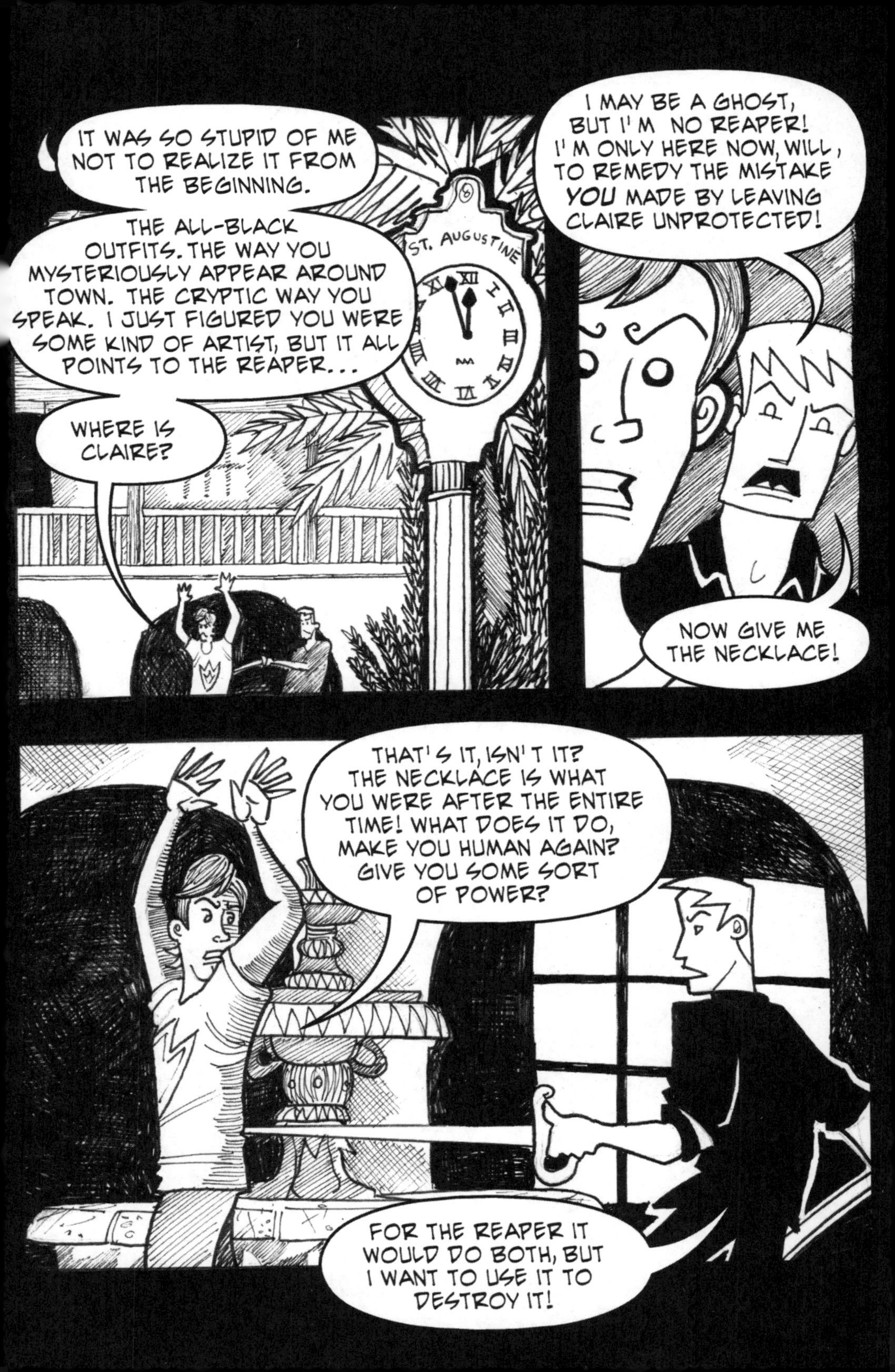
IT WAS SO STUPID OF ME NOT TO REALIZE IT FROM THE BEGINNING.
THE ALL-BLACK OUTFITS. THE WAY YOU MYSTERIOUSLY APPEAR AROUND TOWN. THE CRYPTIC WAY YOU SPEAK. I JUST FIGURED YOU WERE SOME KIND OF ARTIST, BUT IT ALL POINTS TO THE REAPER...
WHERE IS CLAIRE?
ST. AUGUSTINE
I MAY BE A GHOST, BUT I'M NO REAPER! I'M ONLY HERE NOW, WILL, TO REMEDY THE MISTAKE *YOU* MADE BY LEAVING CLAIRE UNPROTECTED!
NOW GIVE ME THE NECKLACE!
THAT'S IT, ISN'T IT? THE NECKLACE IS WHAT YOU WERE AFTER THE ENTIRE TIME! WHAT DOES IT DO, MAKE YOU HUMAN AGAIN? GIVE YOU SOME SORT OF POWER?
FOR THE REAPER IT WOULD DO BOTH, BUT I WANT TO USE IT TO DESTROY IT!

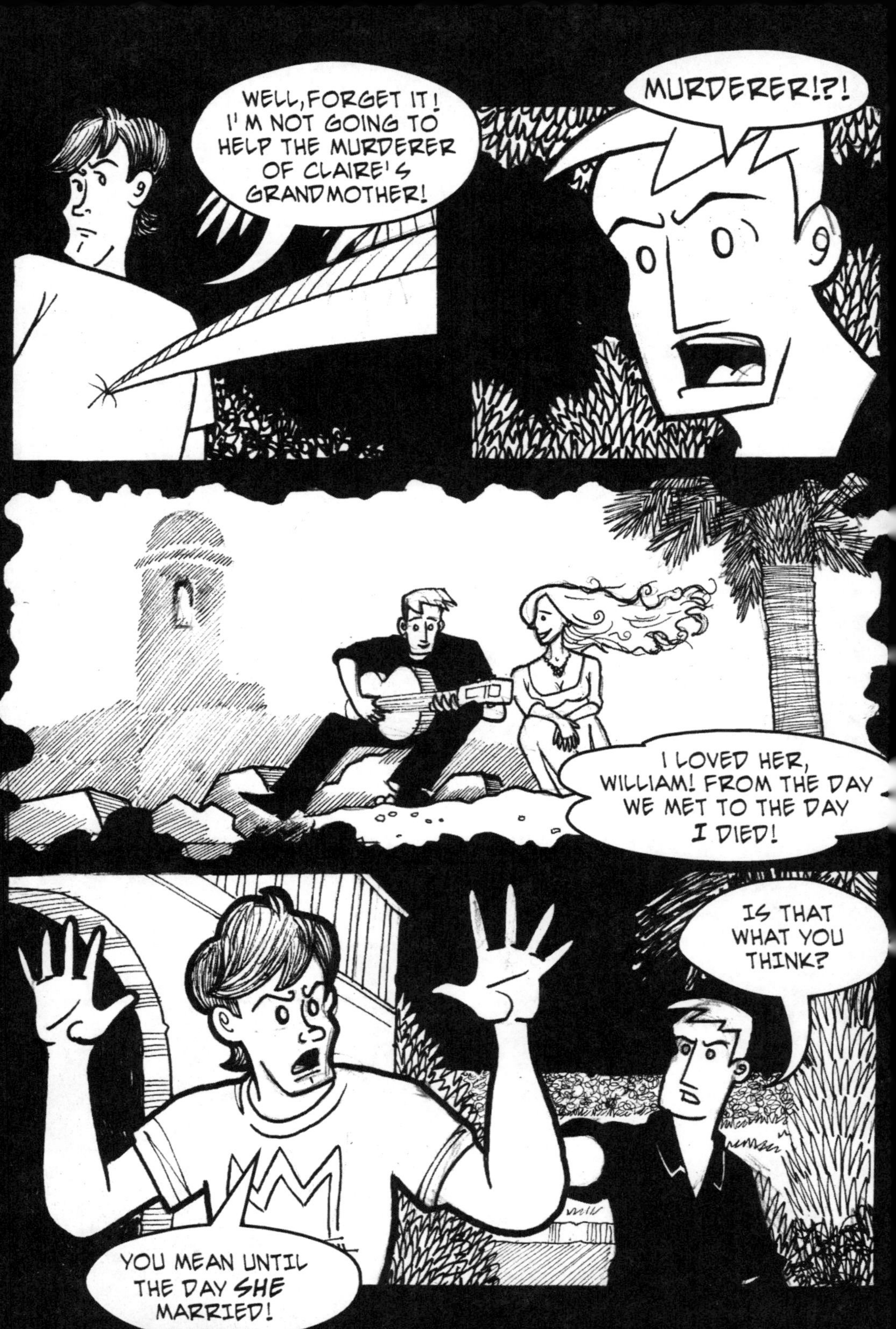
WELL, FORGET IT! I'M NOT GOING TO HELP THE MURDERER OF CLAIRE'S GRANDMOTHER!
MURDERER!?!
I LOVED HER, WILLIAM! FROM THE DAY WE MET TO THE DAY I DIED!
YOU MEAN UNTIL THE DAY SHE MARRIED!
IS THAT WHAT YOU THINK?

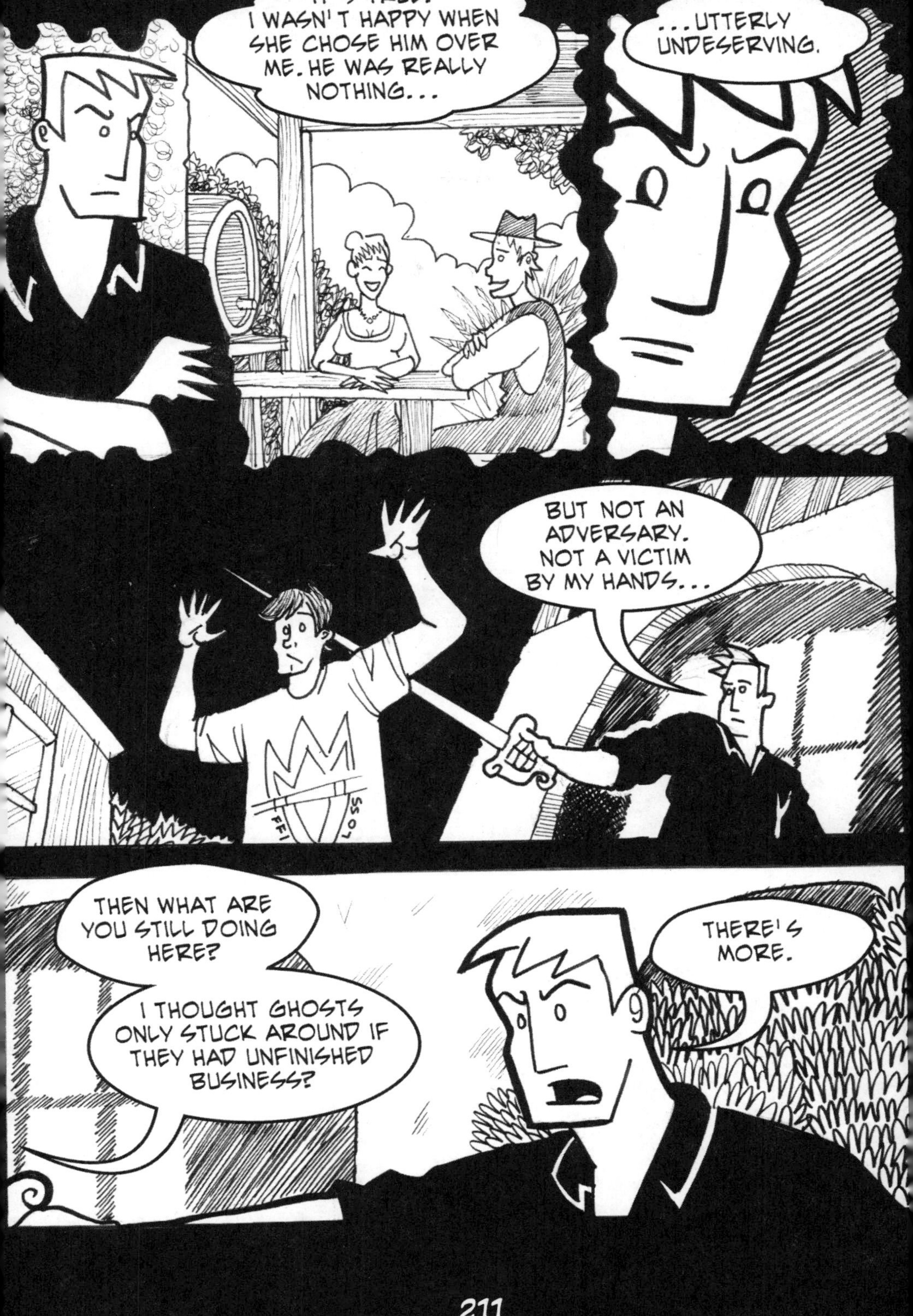
IT'S TRUE. I WASN'T HAPPY WHEN SHE CHOSE HIM OVER ME. HE WAS REALLY NOTHING...
...UTTERLY UNDESERVING.
BUT NOT AN ADVERSARY. NOT A VICTIM BY MY HANDS...
THEN WHAT ARE YOU STILL DOING HERE?
I THOUGHT GHOSTS ONLY STUCK AROUND IF THEY HAD UNFINISHED BUSINESS?
THERE'S MORE.

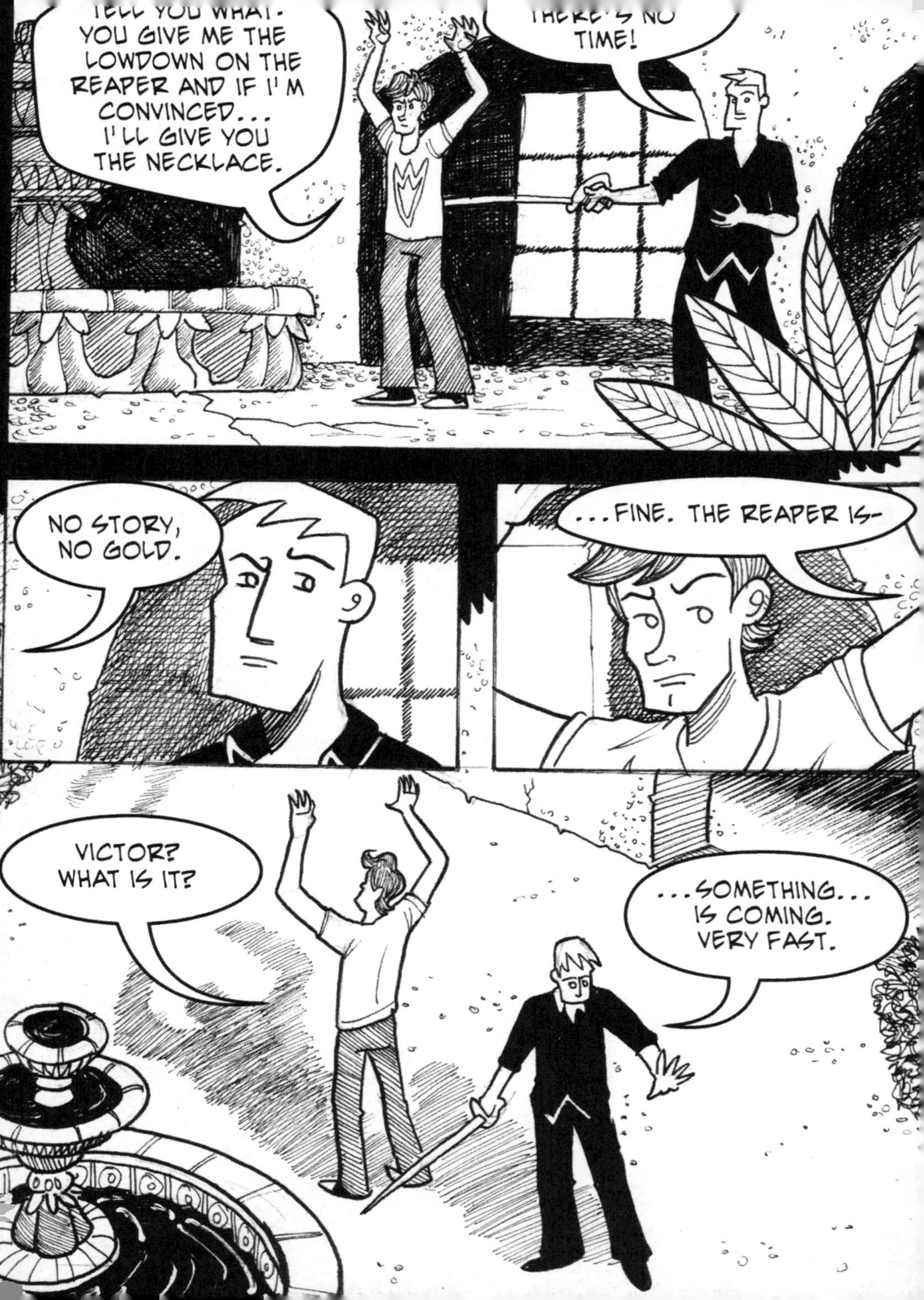

YOU GIVE ME THE LOWDOWN ON THE REAPER AND IF I'M CONVINCED... I'LL GIVE YOU THE NECKLACE.
TIME!
NO STORY, NO GOLD.
...FINE. THE REAPER IS-
VICTOR? WHAT IS IT?
...SOMETHING... IS COMING. VERY FAST.

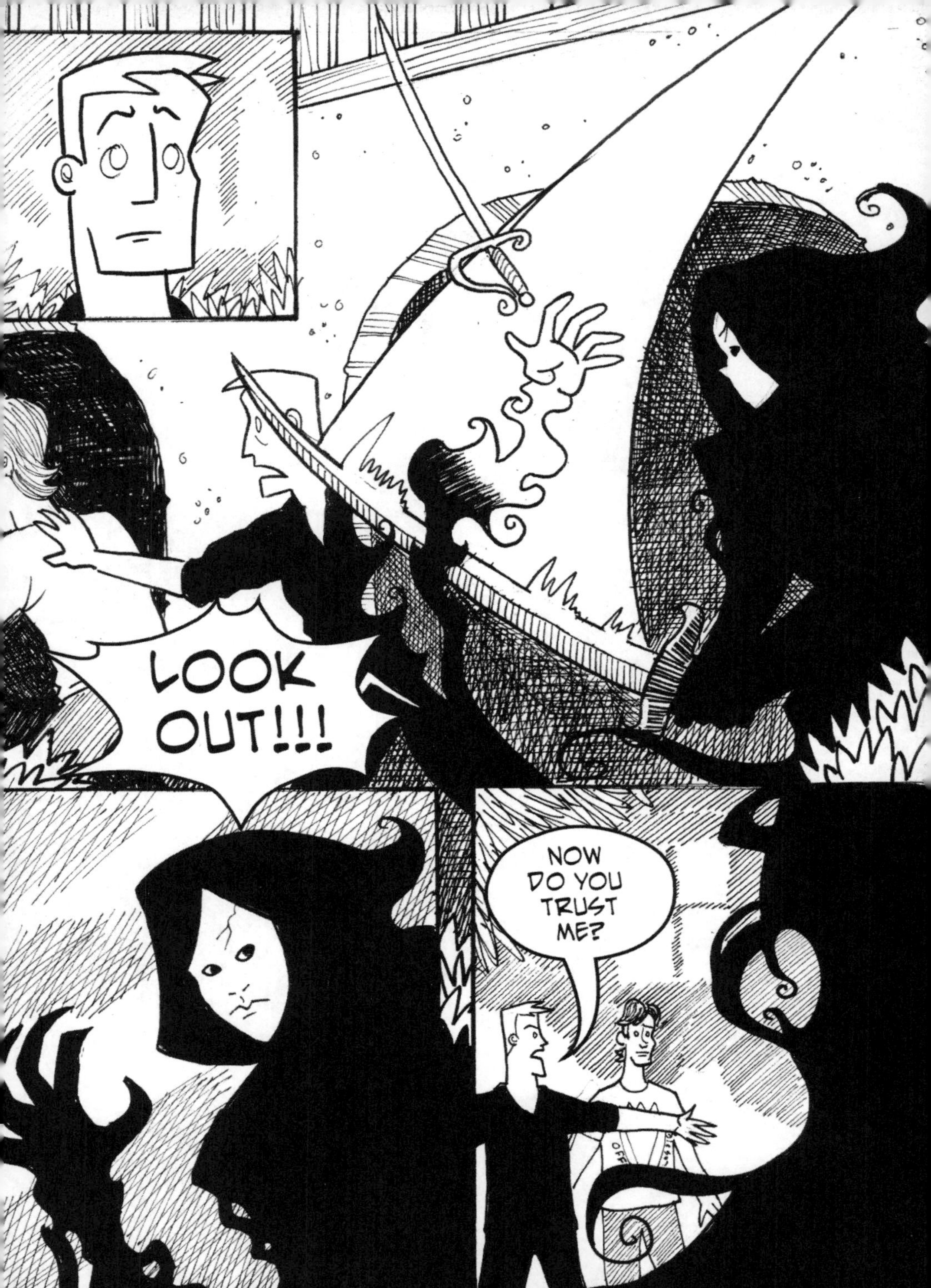
LOOK OUT!!!
NOW DO YOU TRUST ME?

LOOK, WILL, GO! GET OUT OF HERE! GO FIND CLAIRE!
WHAT ABOUT YOU?
I'LL BE FINE... NOT LIKE I'M GOING TO DIE OR ANYTHING.
CHING!

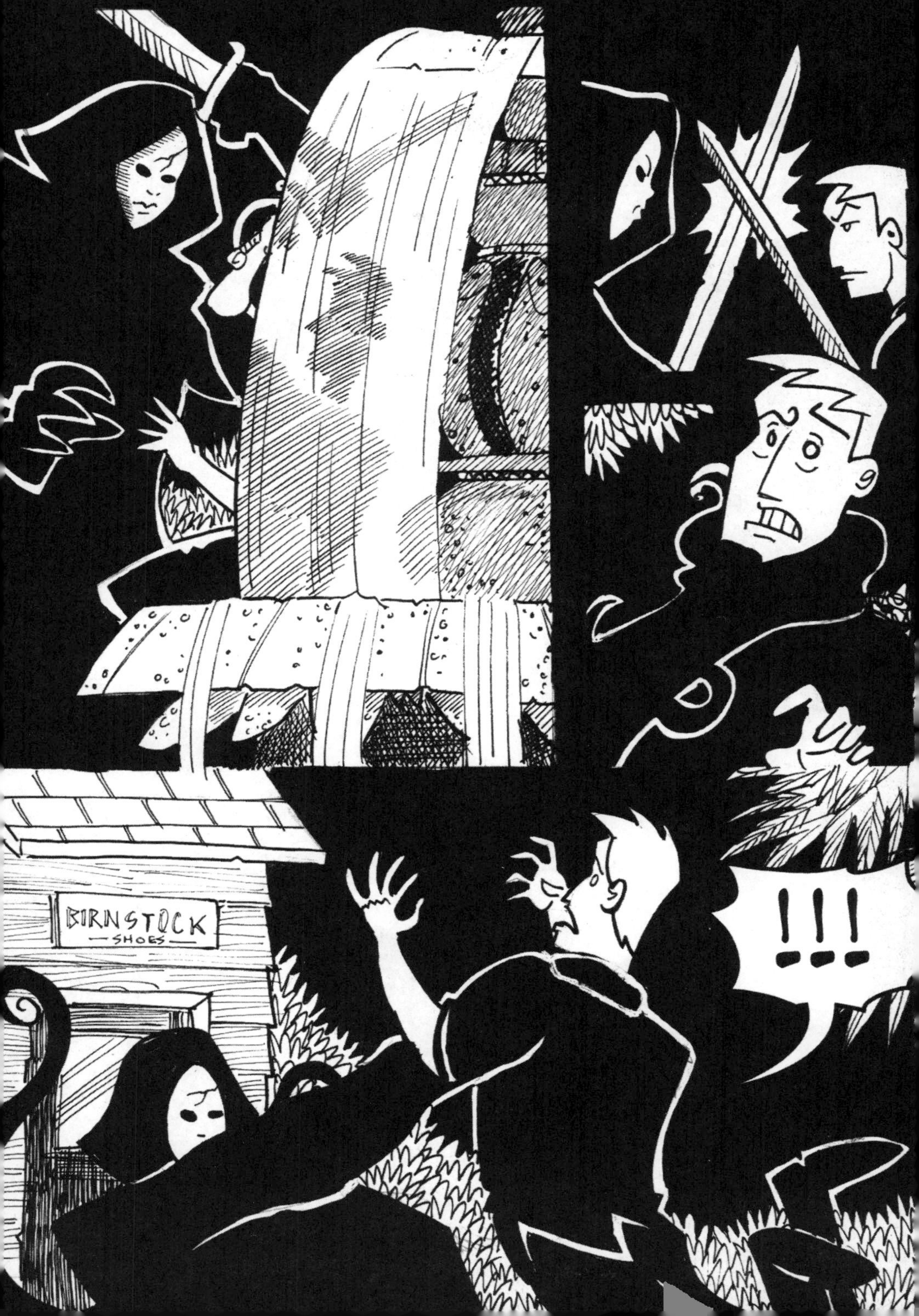
BIRNSTOCK
SHOES
!!!

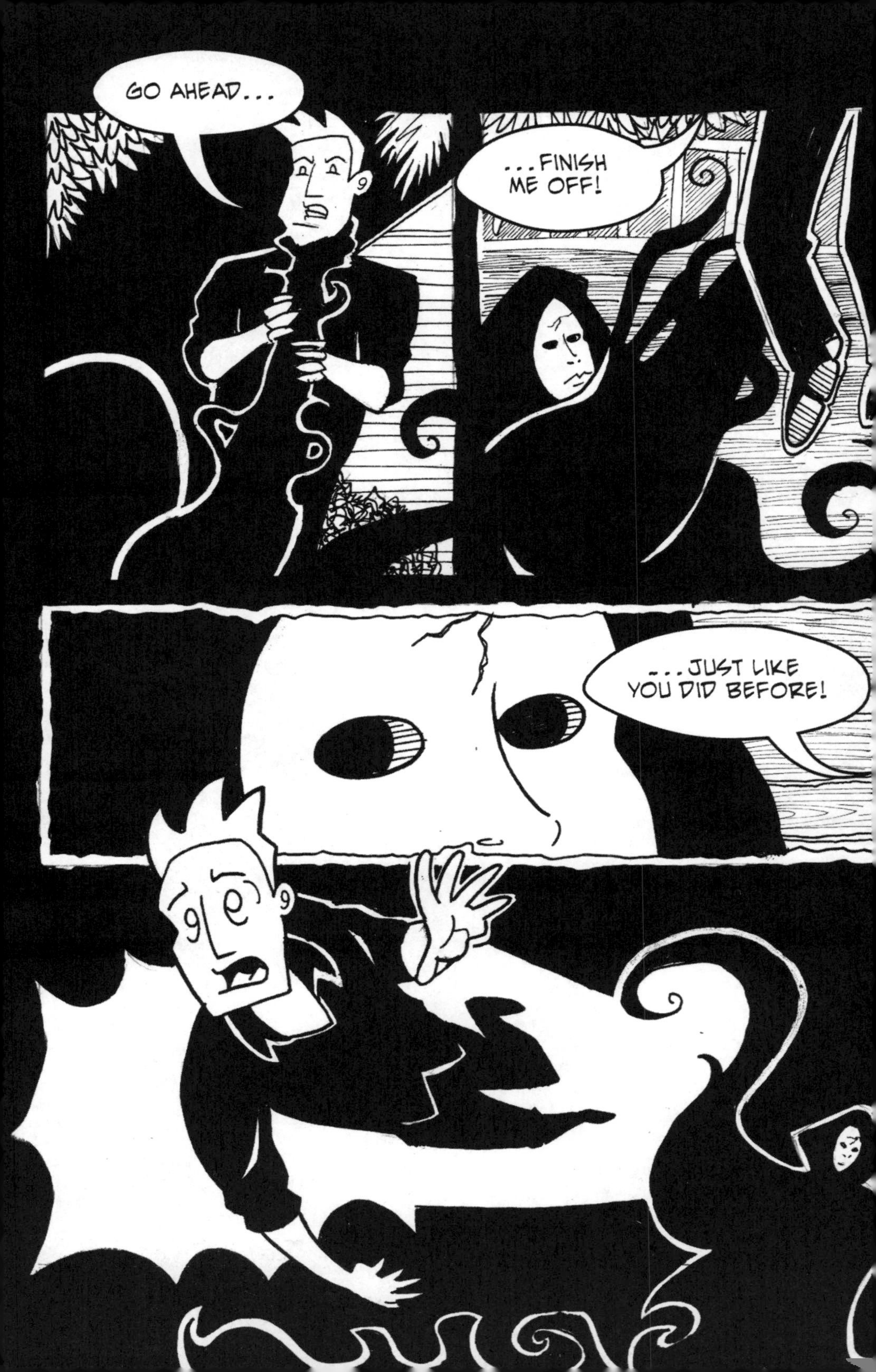
GO AHEAD...
...FINISH ME OFF!
...JUST LIKE YOU DID BEFORE!

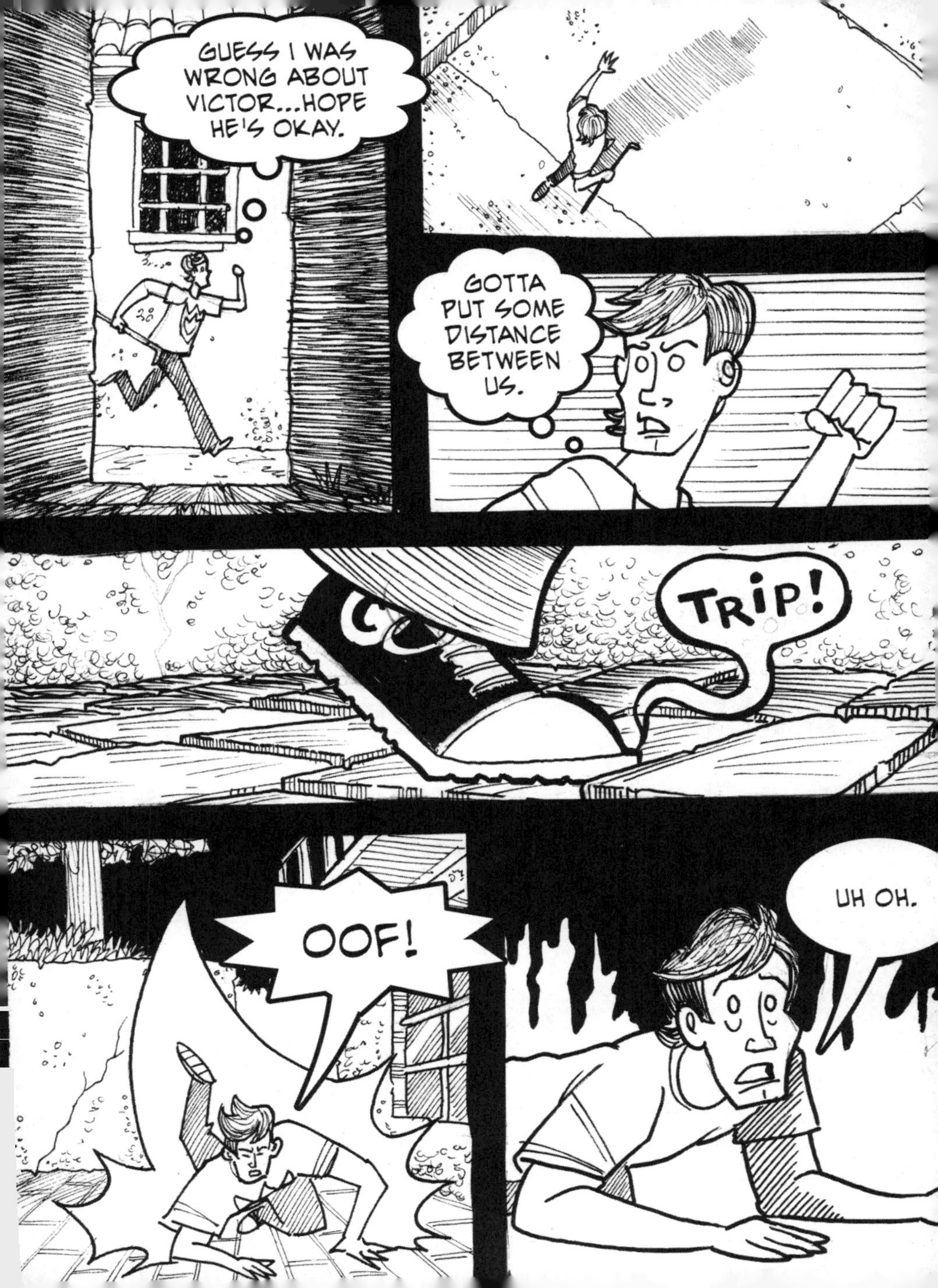
GUESS I WAS WRONG ABOUT VICTOR...HOPE HE'S OKAY.
GOTTA PUT SOME DISTANCE BETWEEN US.
TRIP!
OOF!
UH OH.

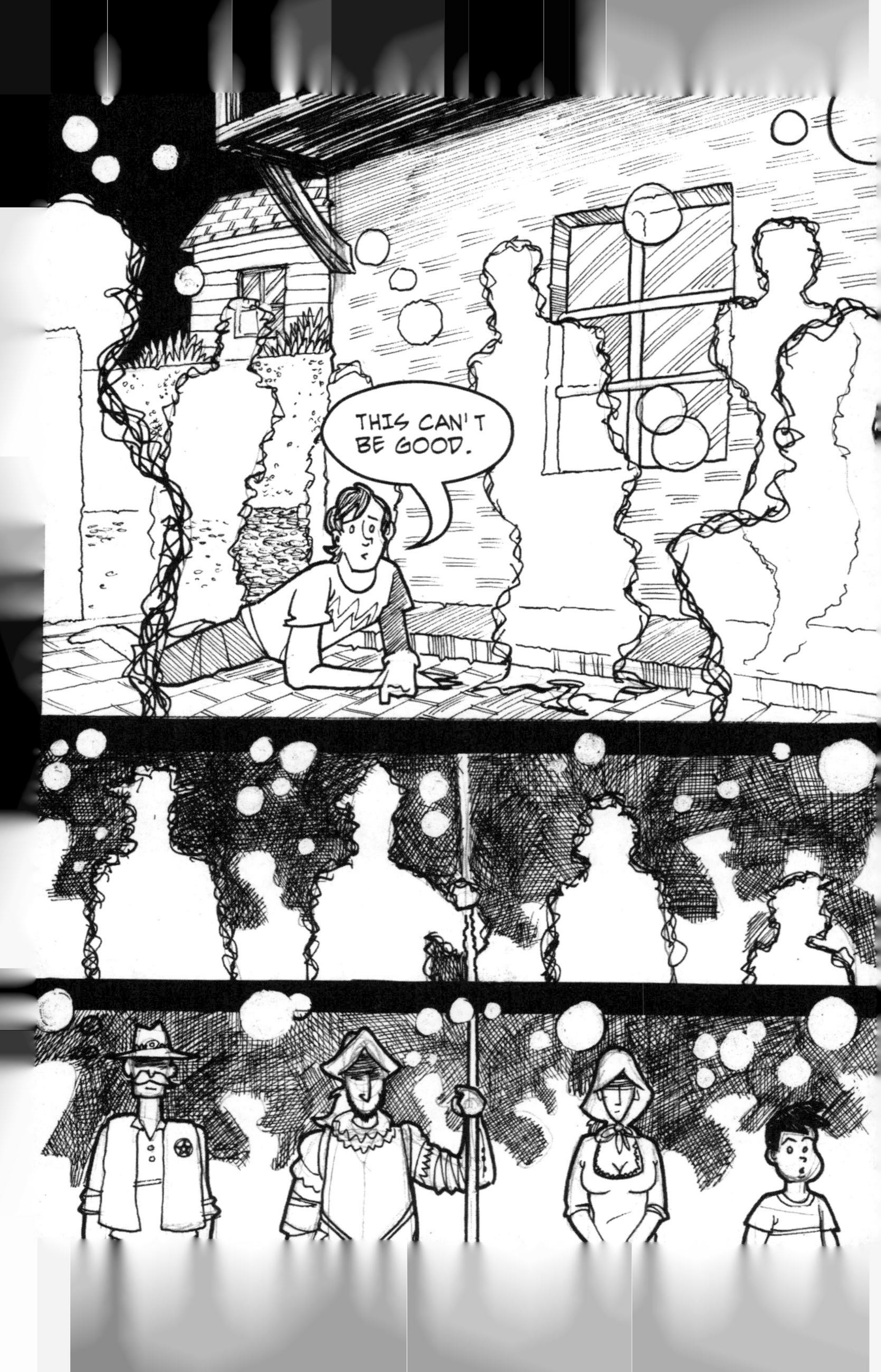
THIS CAN'T BE GOOD.

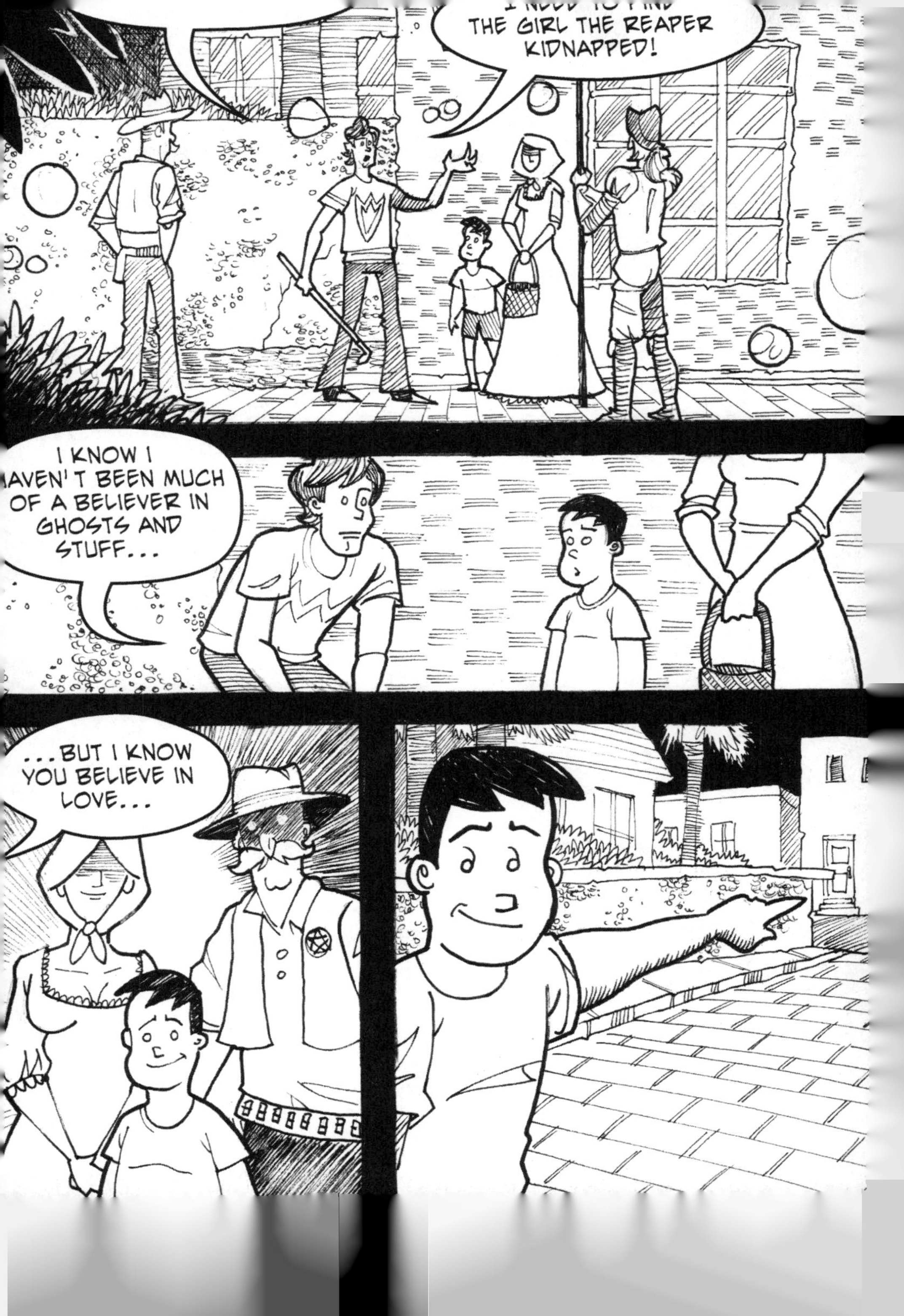
THE GIRL THE REAPER KIDNAPPED!
I KNOW I AVEN'T BEEN MUCH OF A BELIEVER IN GHOSTS AND STUFF...
...BUT I KNOW YOU BELIEVE IN LOVE...

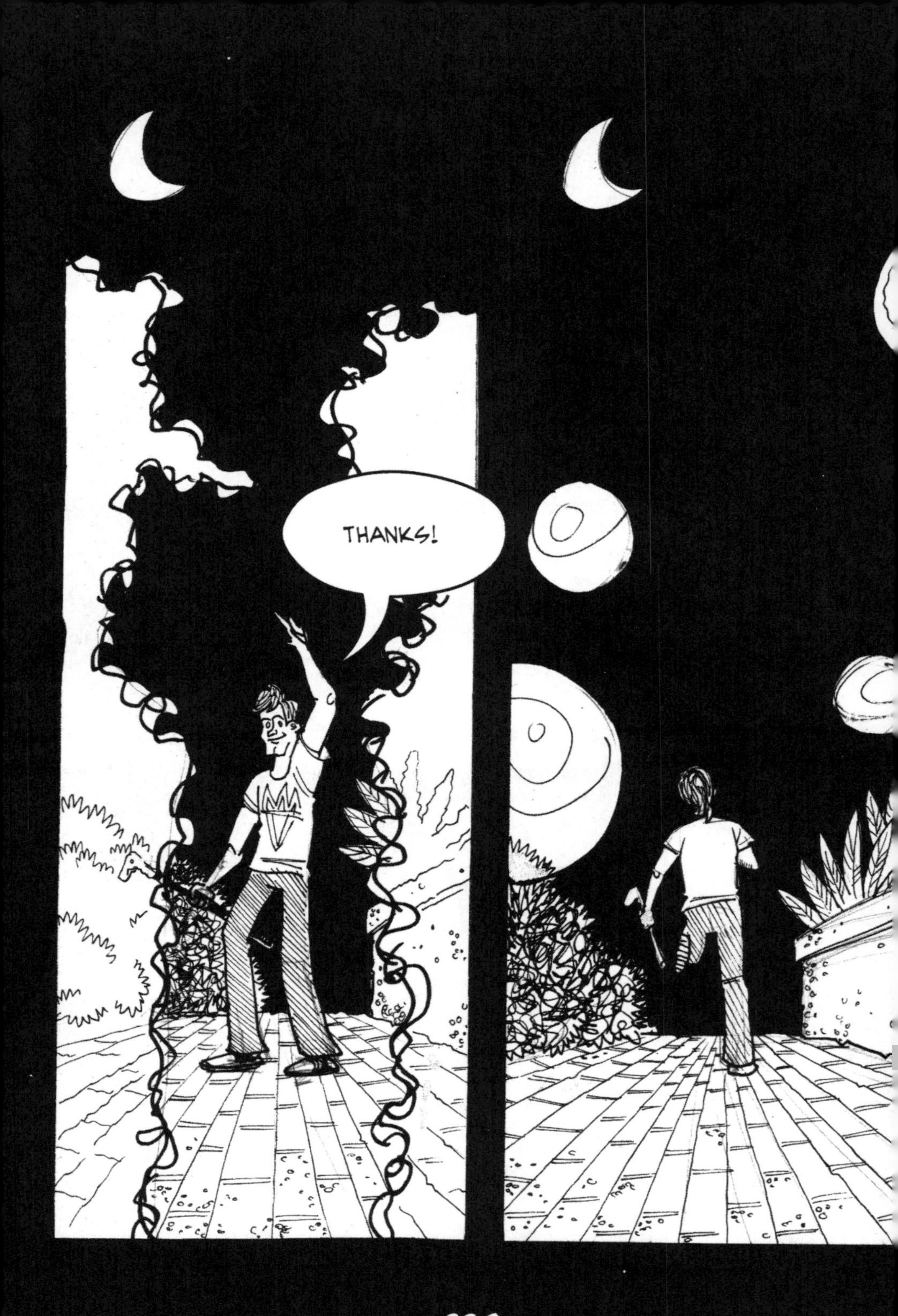
THANKS!

CHAPTER
17

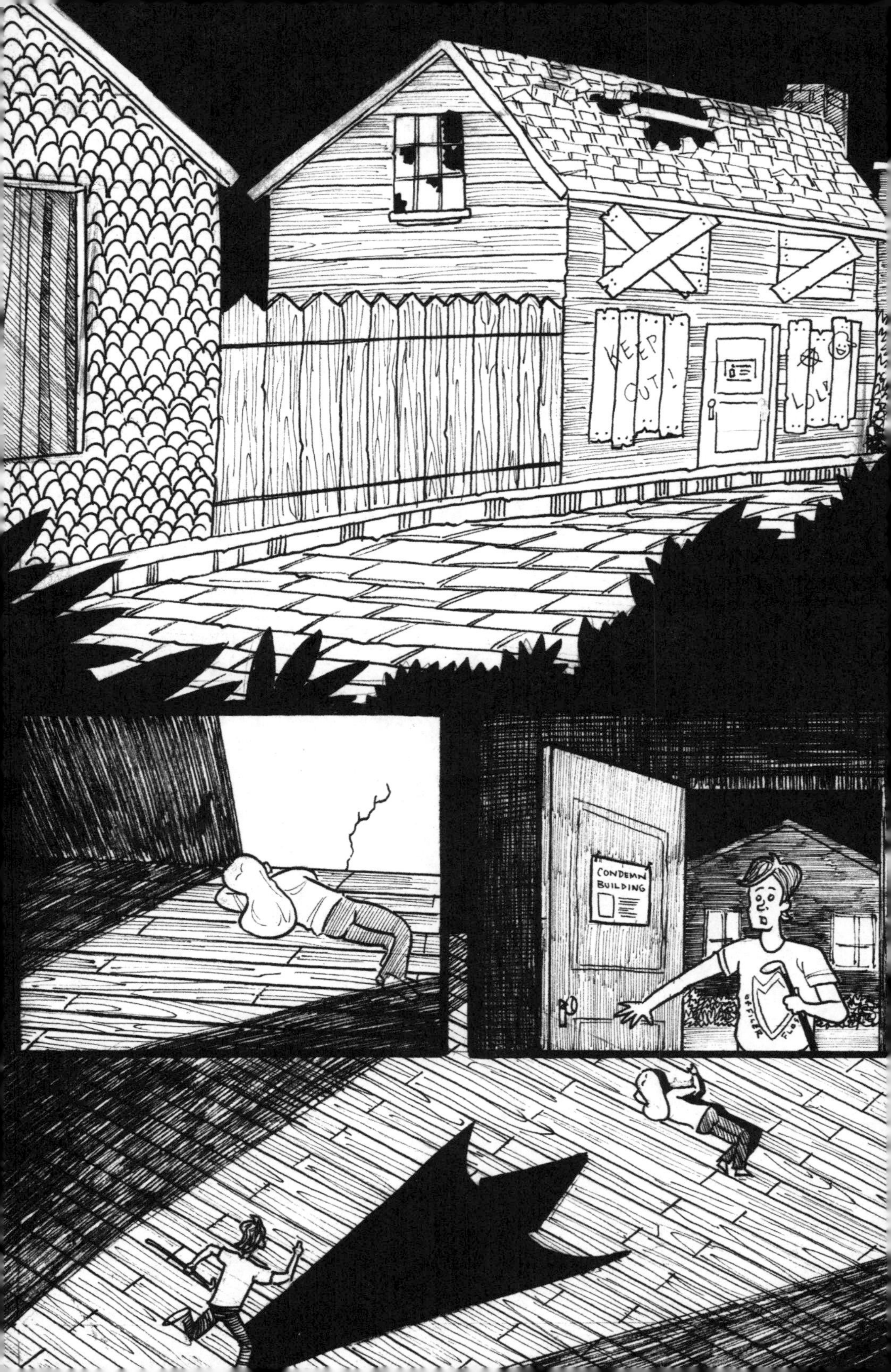
KEEP OUT!
LOL!
CONDEMN BUILDING

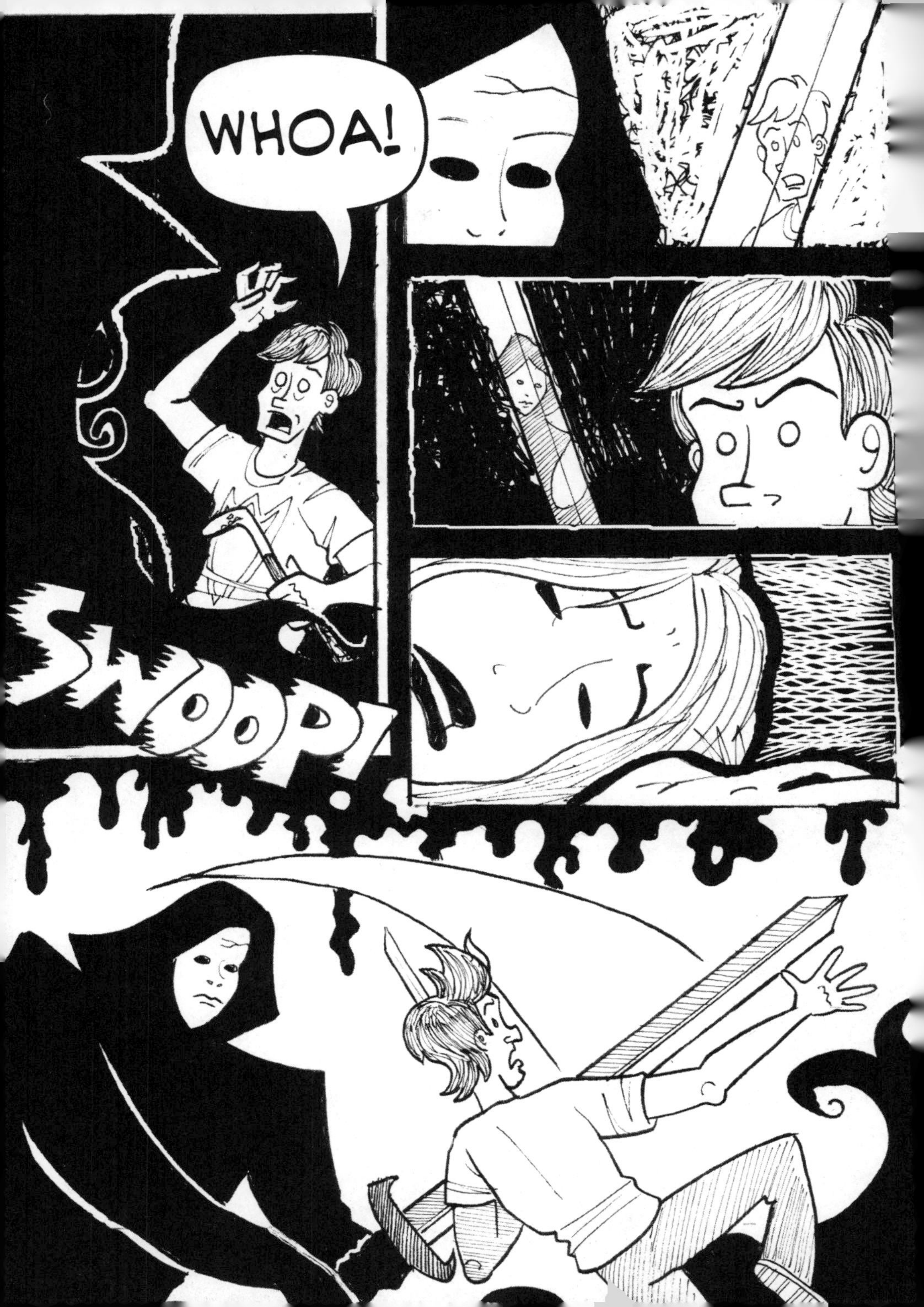
WHOA!
SWOOP!

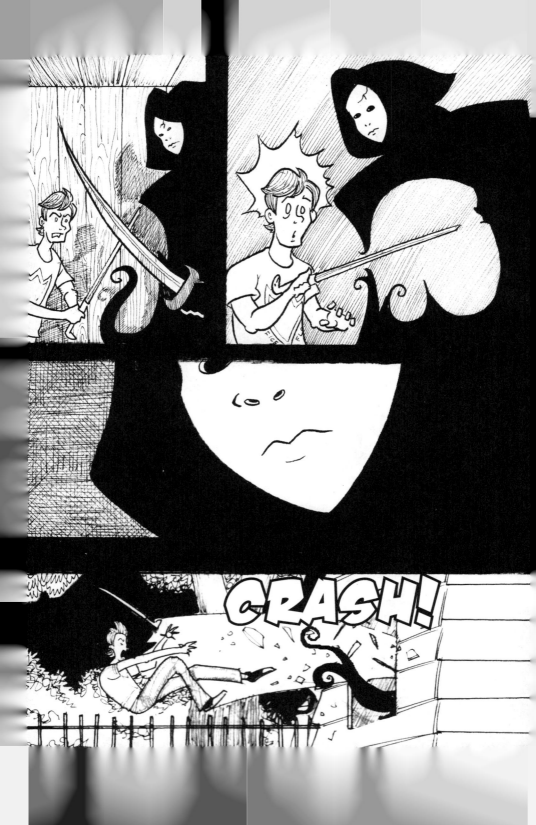

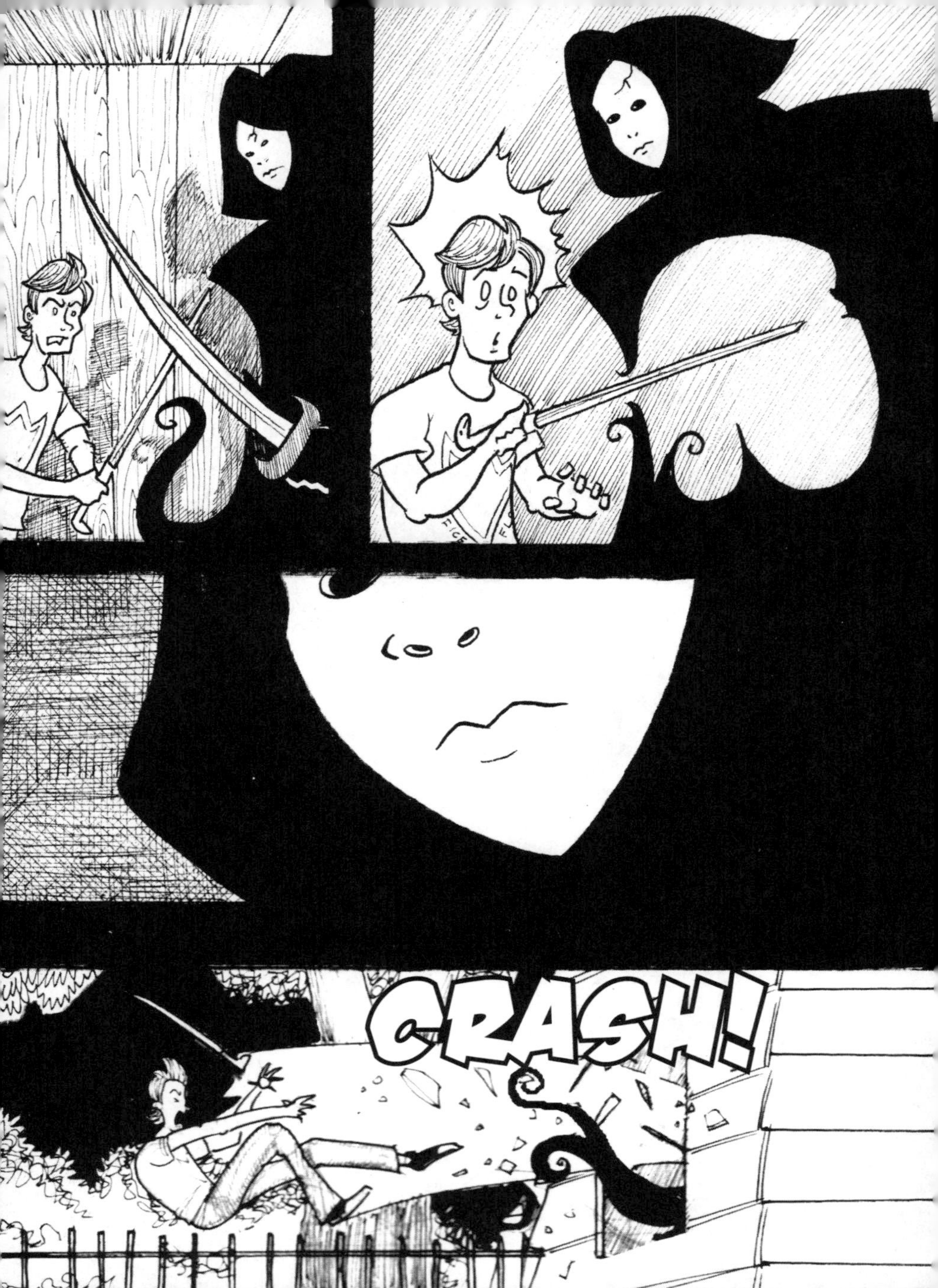
CRASH!

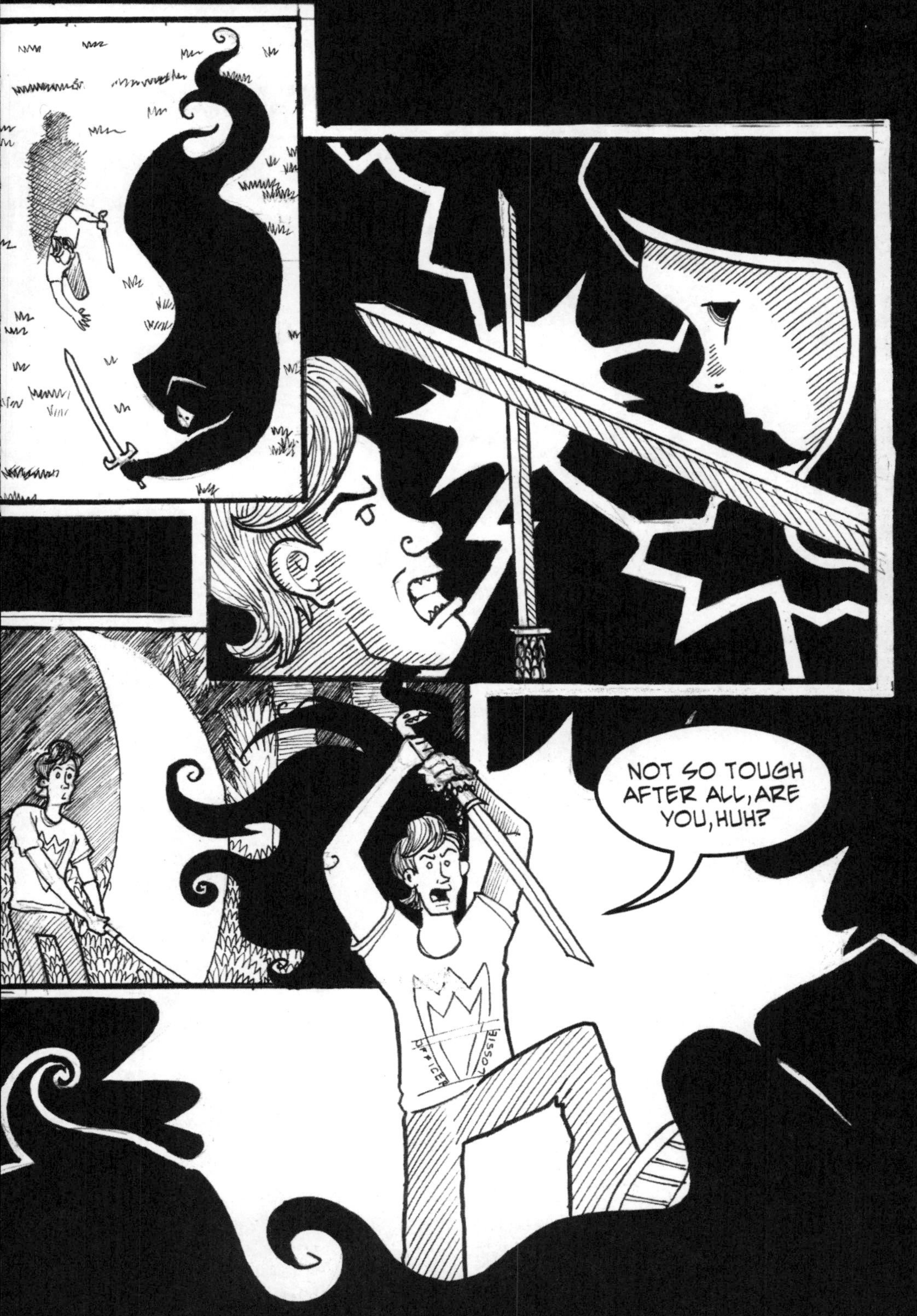
NOT SO TOUGH AFTER ALL, ARE YOU, HUH?
OFFICER

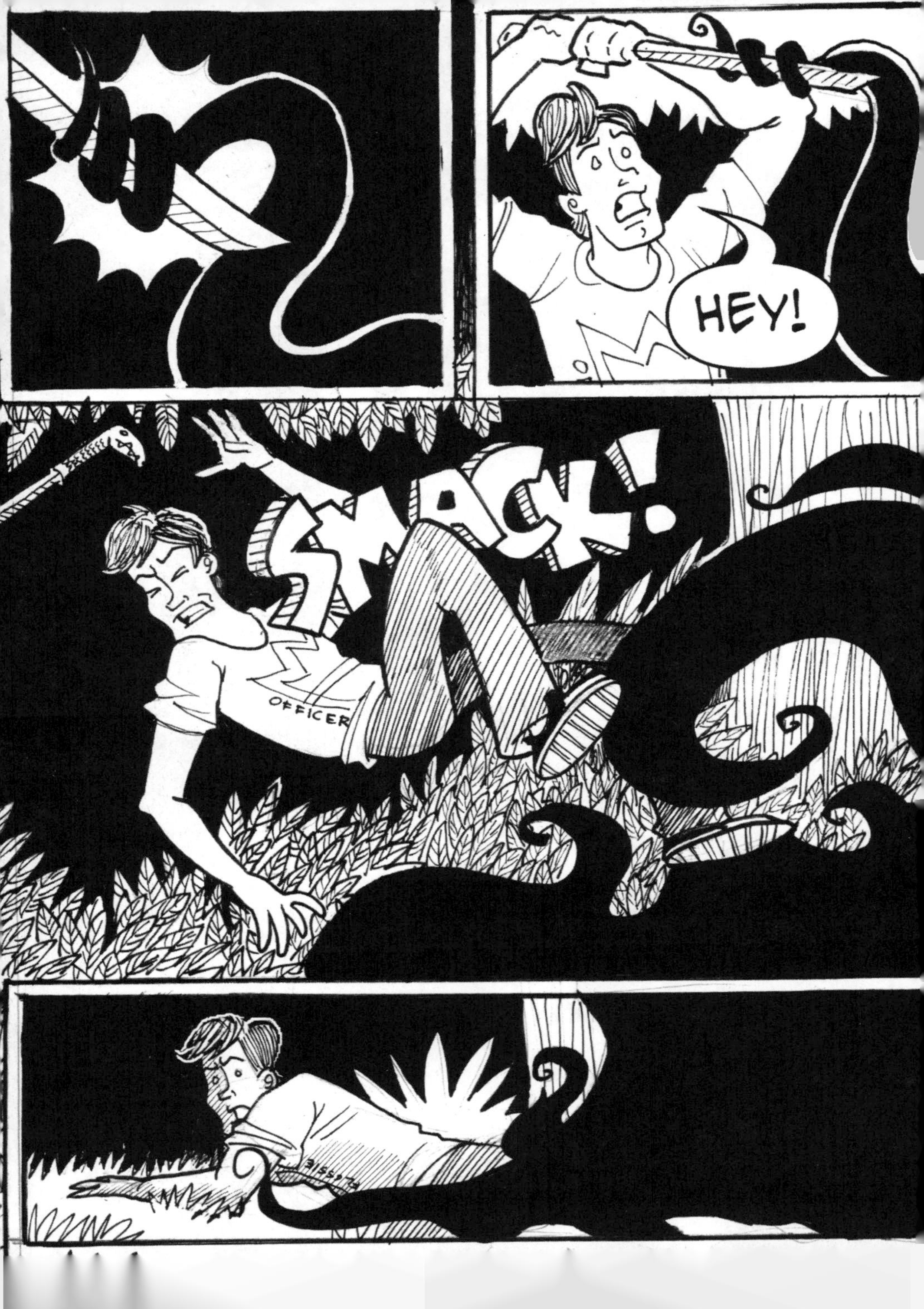
HEY!
SMACK!
OFFICER

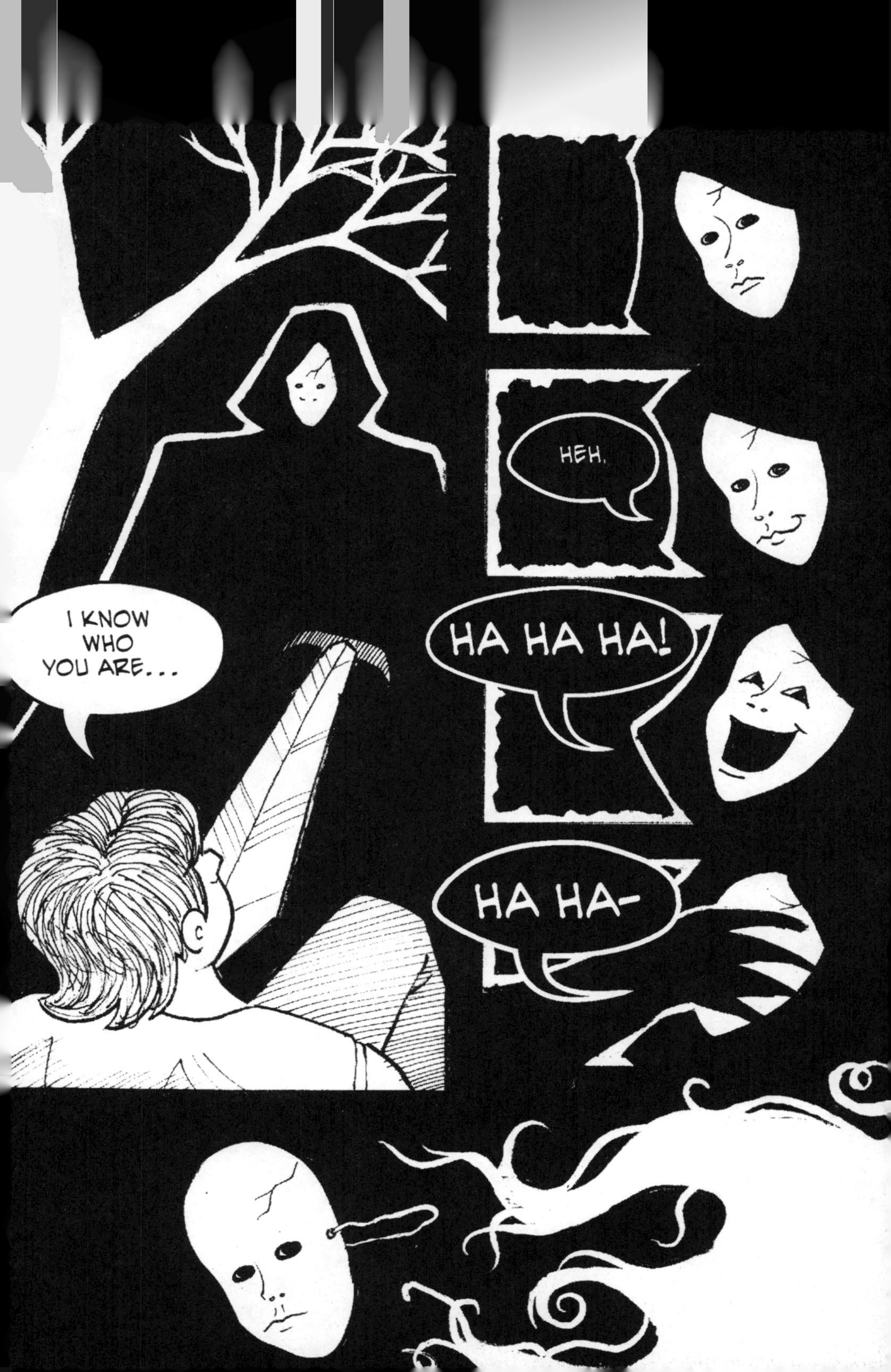
I KNOW WHO YOU ARE...
HEH.
HA HA HA!
HA HA-

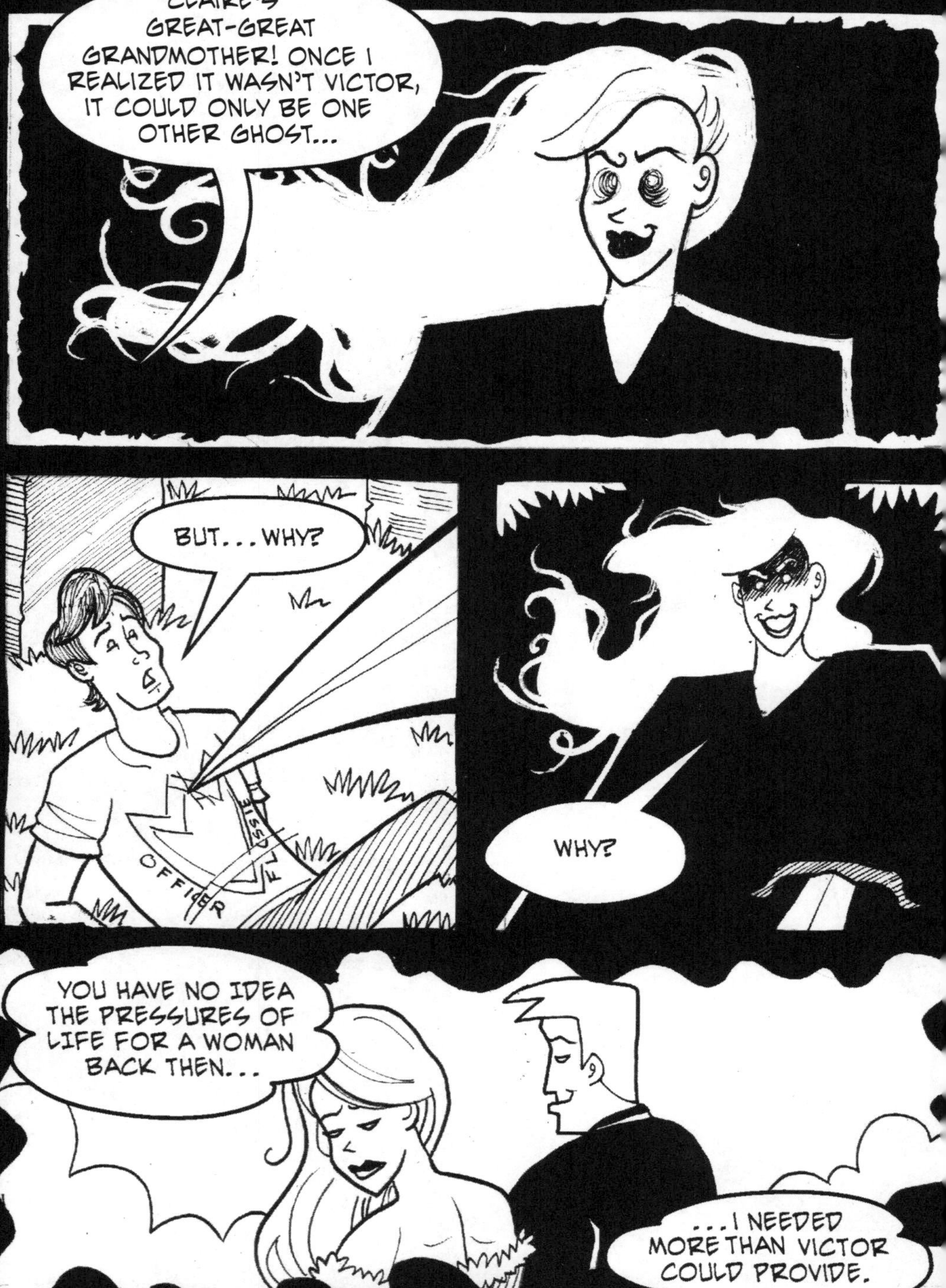
CLAIRE'S GREAT-GREAT GRANDMOTHER! ONCE I REALIZED IT WASN'T VICTOR, IT COULD ONLY BE ONE OTHER GHOST...
BUT... WHY?
OFFICER
WHY?
YOU HAVE NO IDEA THE PRESSURES OF LIFE FOR A WOMAN BACK THEN...
...I NEEDED MORE THAN VICTOR COULD PROVIDE.

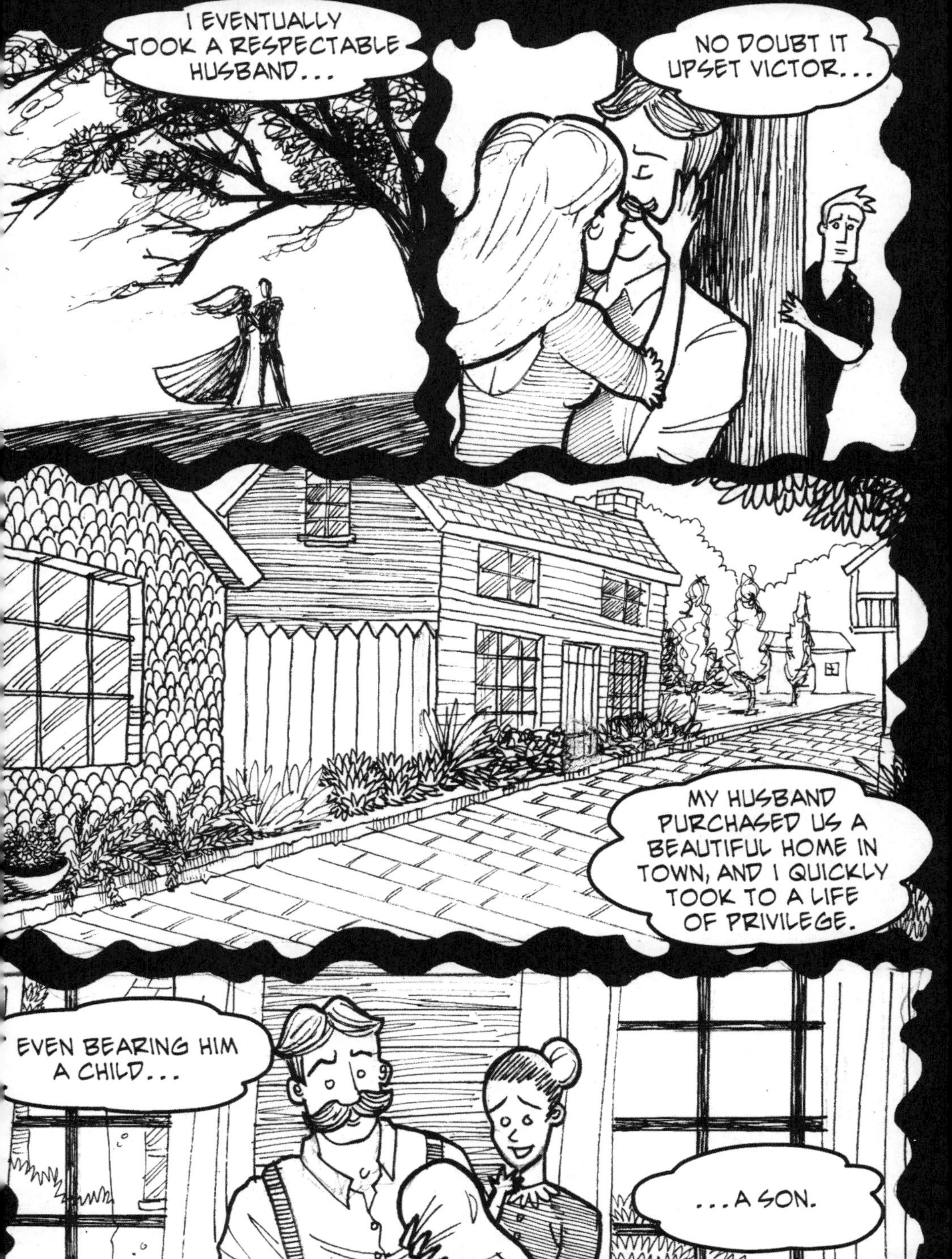
I EVENTUALLY TOOK A RESPECTABLE HUSBAND...
NO DOUBT IT UPSET VICTOR...
MY HUSBAND PURCHASED US A BEAUTIFUL HOME IN TOWN, AND I QUICKLY TOOK TO A LIFE OF PRIVILEGE.
EVEN BEARING HIM A CHILD...
...A SON.

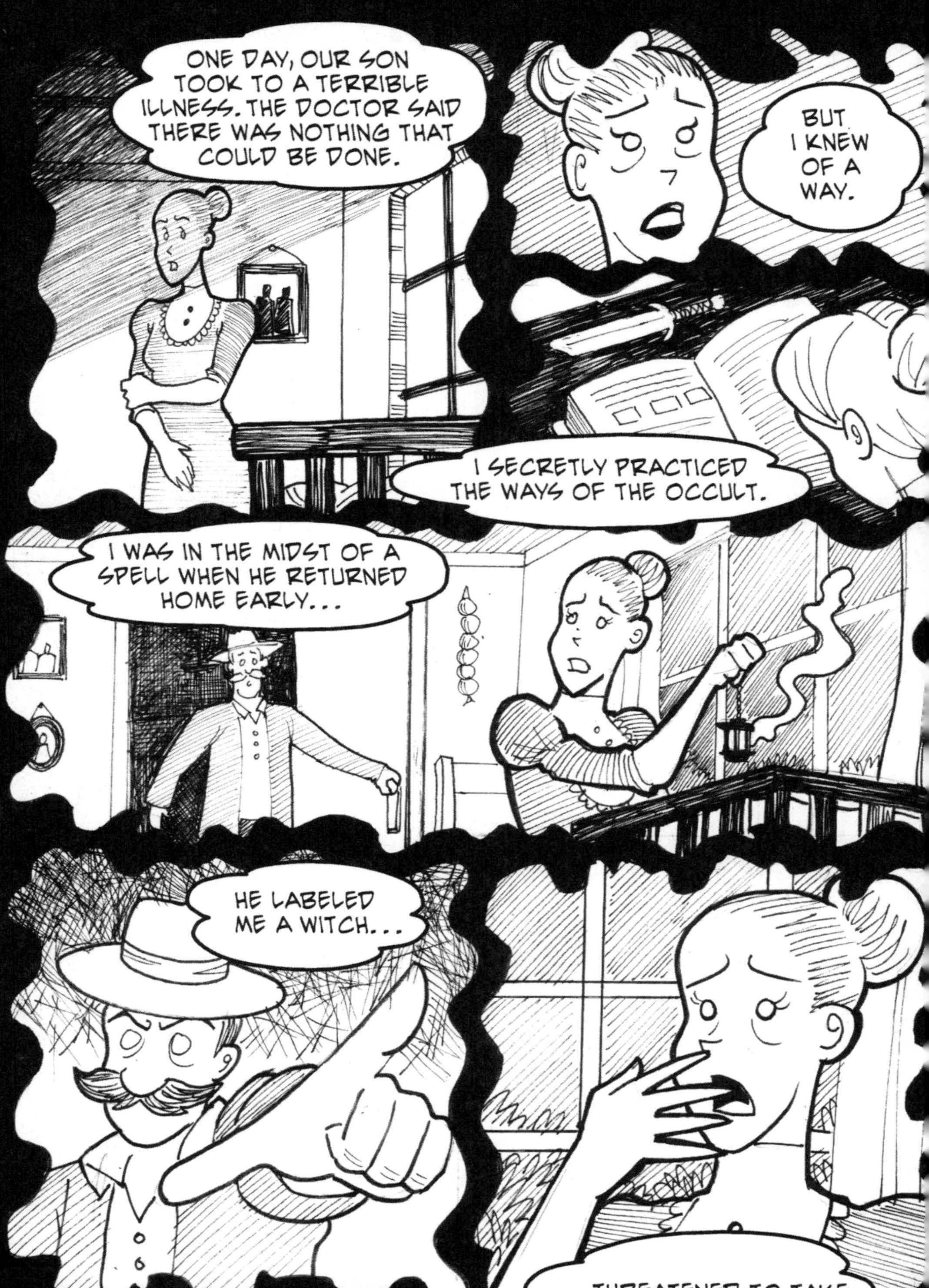
ONE DAY, OUR SON TOOK TO A TERRIBLE ILLNESS. THE DOCTOR SAID THERE WAS NOTHING THAT COULD BE DONE.
BUT I KNEW OF A WAY.
I SECRETLY PRACTICED THE WAYS OF THE OCCULT.
I WAS IN THE MIDST OF A SPELL WHEN HE RETURNED HOME EARLY...
HE LABELED ME A WITCH...
...THREATENED TO TAKE OUR CHILD AWAY!

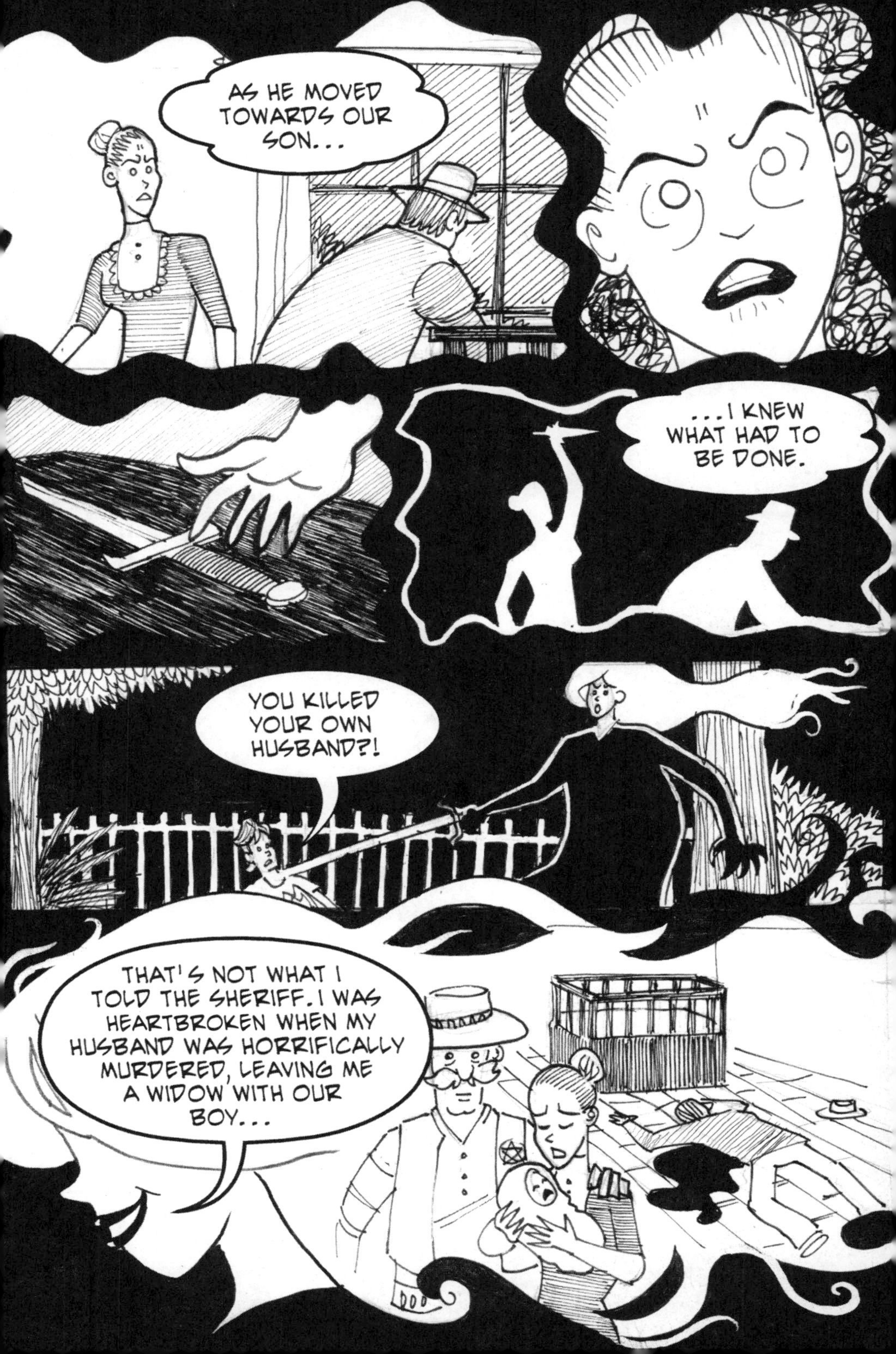
AS HE MOVED TOWARDS OUR SON...
...I KNEW WHAT HAD TO BE DONE.
YOU KILLED YOUR OWN HUSBAND?!
THAT'S NOT WHAT I TOLD THE SHERIFF. I WAS HEARTBROKEN WHEN MY HUSBAND WAS HORRIFICALLY MURDERED, LEAVING ME A WIDOW WITH OUR BOY...

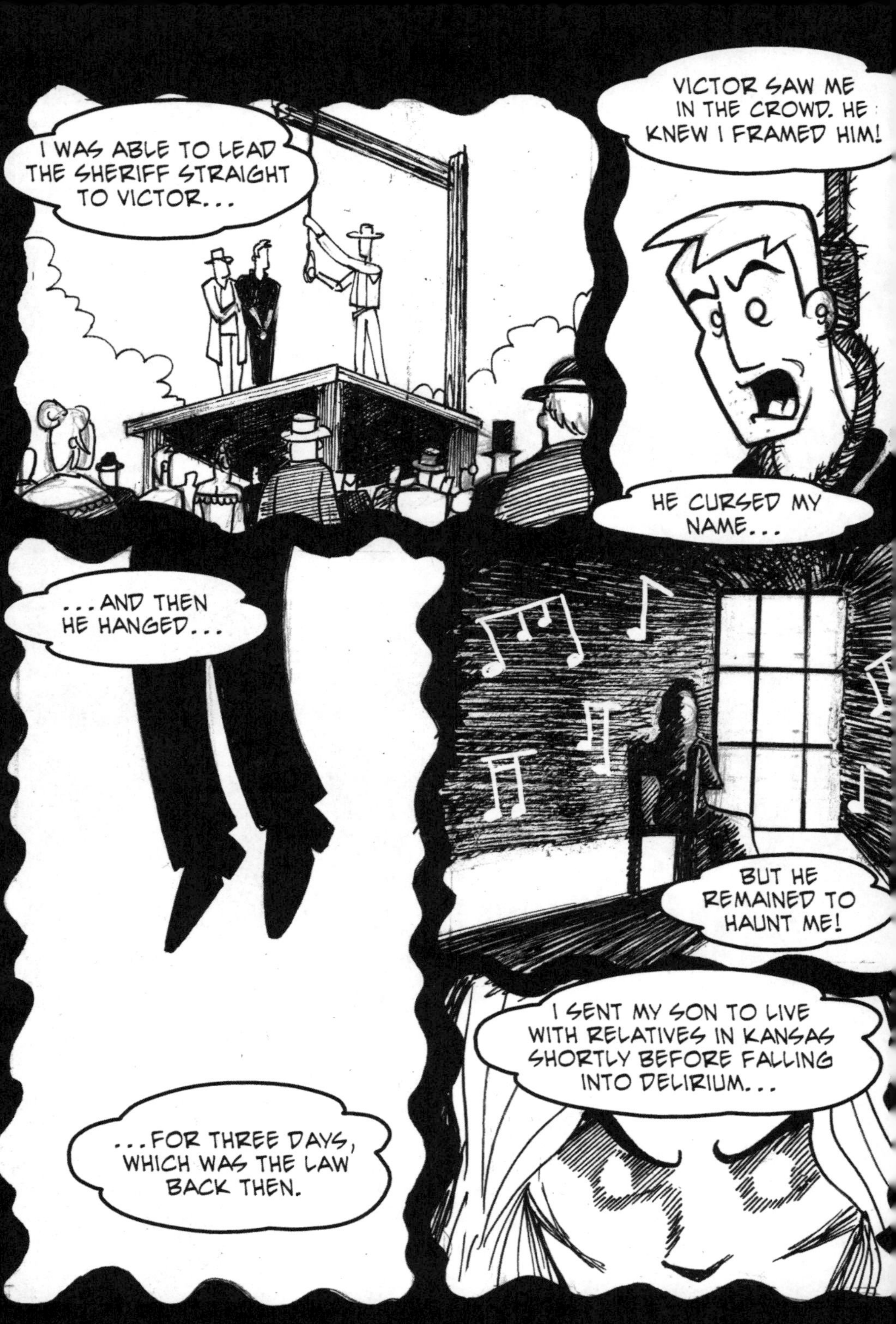
I WAS ABLE TO LEAD THE SHERIFF STRAIGHT TO VICTOR...
VICTOR SAW ME IN THE CROWD. HE KNEW I FRAMED HIM!
HE CURSED MY NAME...
...AND THEN HE HANGED...
...FOR THREE DAYS, WHICH WAS THE LAW BACK THEN.
BUT HE REMAINED TO HAUNT ME!
I SENT MY SON TO LIVE WITH RELATIVES IN KANSAS SHORTLY BEFORE FALLING INTO DELIRIUM...

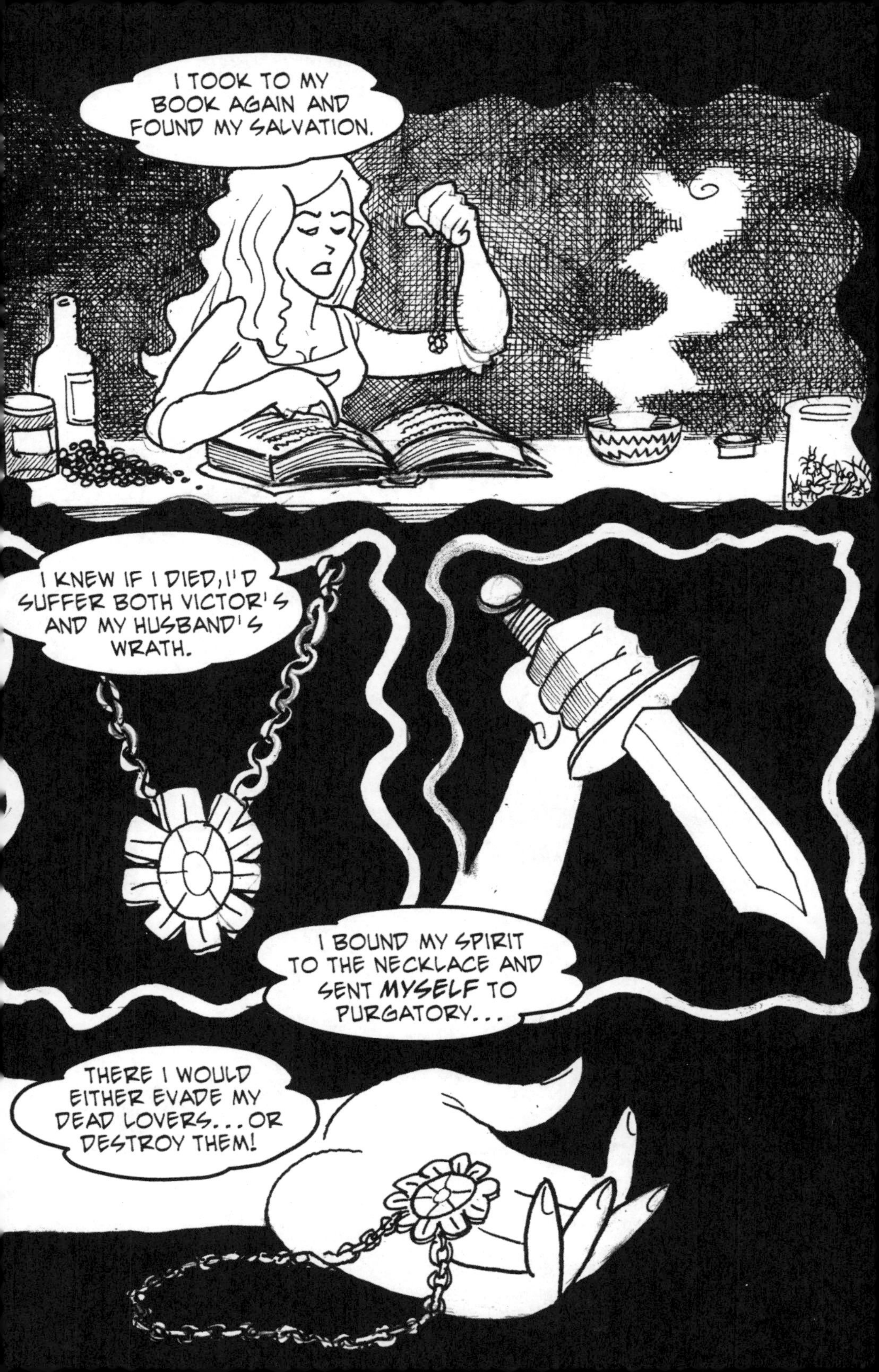
I TOOK TO MY BOOK AGAIN AND FOUND MY SALVATION.
I KNEW IF I DIED, I'D SUFFER BOTH VICTOR'S AND MY HUSBAND'S WRATH.
I BOUND MY SPIRIT TO THE NECKLACE AND SENT MYSELF TO PURGATORY...
THERE I WOULD EITHER EVADE MY DEAD LOVERS...OR DESTROY THEM!

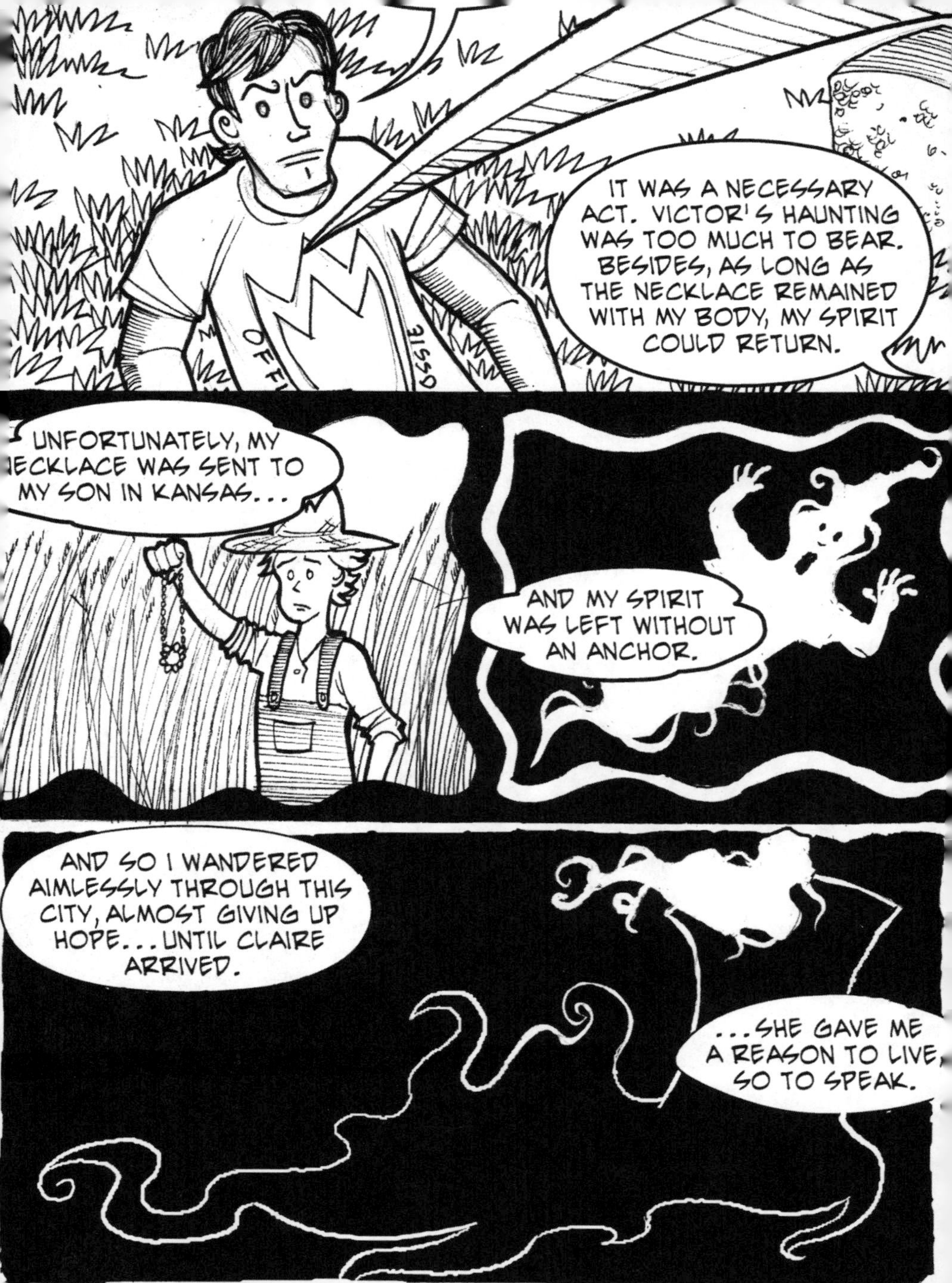
IT WAS A NECESSARY ACT. VICTOR'S HAUNTING WAS TOO MUCH TO BEAR. BESIDES, AS LONG AS THE NECKLACE REMAINED WITH MY BODY, MY SPIRIT COULD RETURN.
UNFORTUNATELY, MY NECKLACE WAS SENT TO MY SON IN KANSAS...
AND MY SPIRIT WAS LEFT WITHOUT AN ANCHOR.
AND SO I WANDERED AIMLESSLY THROUGH THIS CITY, ALMOST GIVING UP HOPE... UNTIL CLAIRE ARRIVED.
...SHE GAVE ME A REASON TO LIVE, SO TO SPEAK.

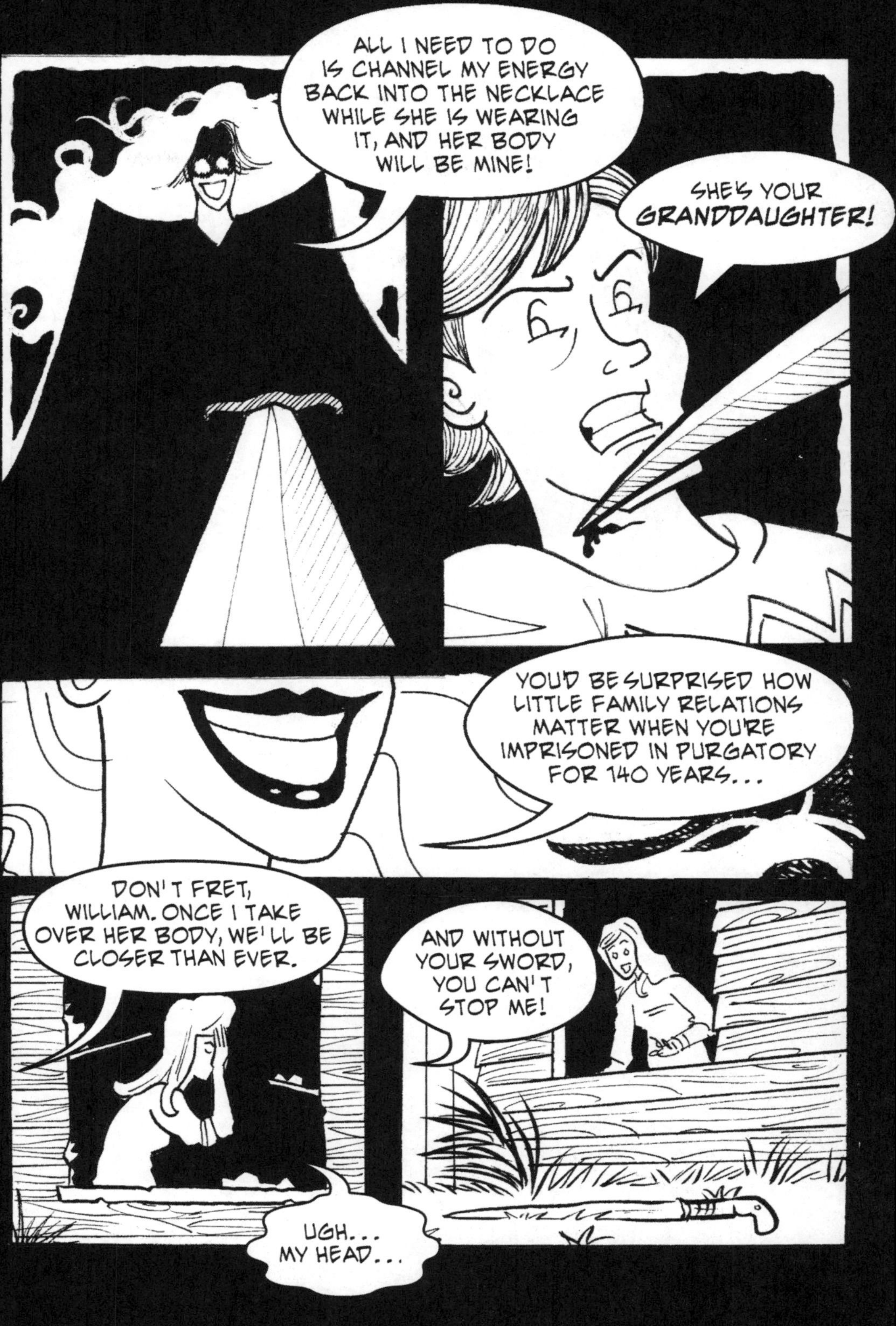
ALL I NEED TO DO IS CHANNEL MY ENERGY BACK INTO THE NECKLACE WHILE SHE IS WEARING IT, AND HER BODY WILL BE MINE!
SHE'S YOUR GRANDDAUGHTER!
YOU'D BE SURPRISED HOW LITTLE FAMILY RELATIONS MATTER WHEN YOU'RE IMPRISONED IN PURGATORY FOR 140 YEARS...
DON'T FRET, WILLIAM. ONCE I TAKE OVER HER BODY, WE'LL BE CLOSER THAN EVER.
UGH... MY HEAD...
AND WITHOUT YOUR SWORD, YOU CAN'T STOP ME!

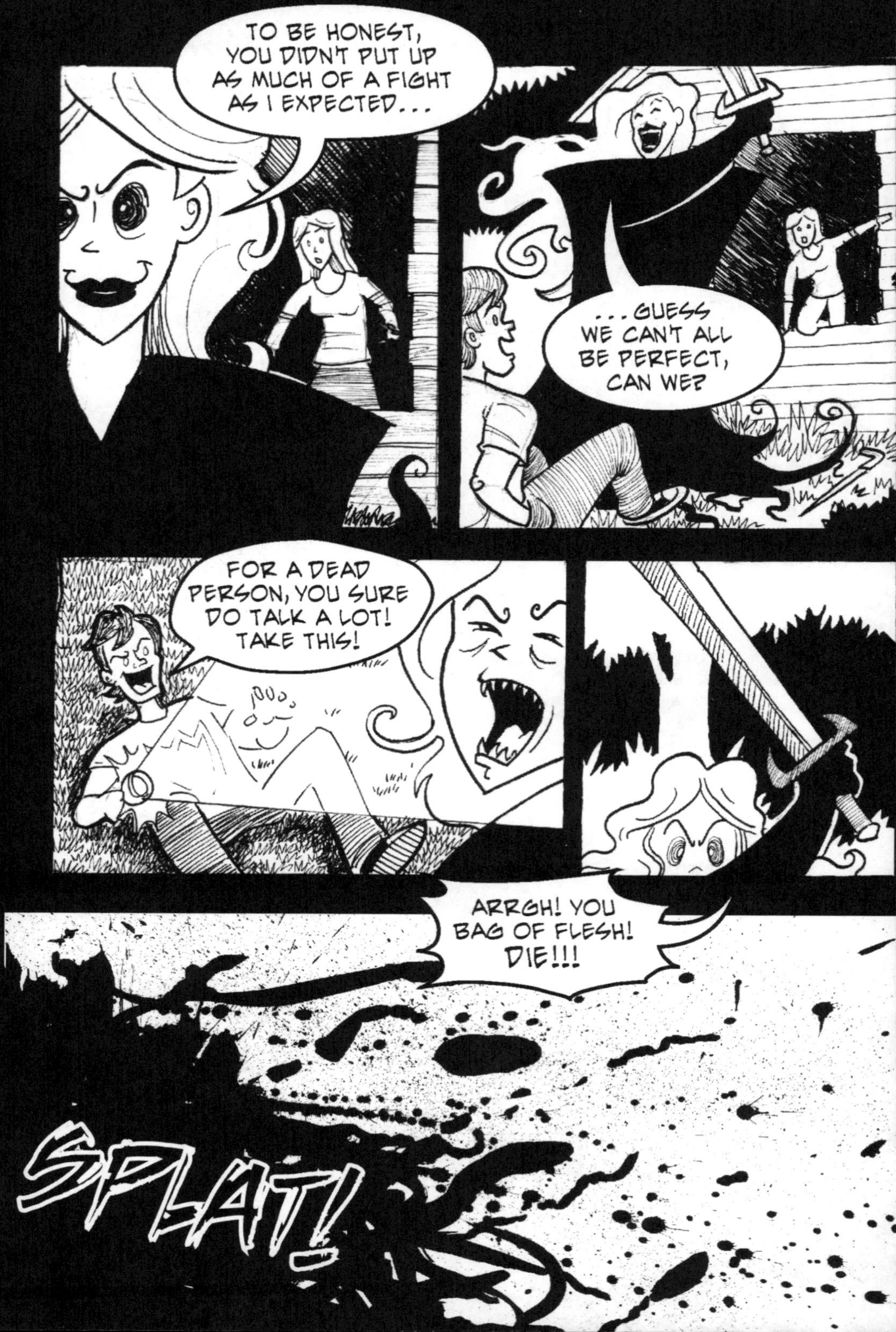
TO BE HONEST, YOU DIDN'T PUT UP AS MUCH OF A FIGHT AS I EXPECTED...
...GUESS WE CAN'T ALL BE PERFECT, CAN WE?
FOR A DEAD PERSON, YOU SURE DO TALK A LOT! TAKE THIS!
ARRGH! YOU BAG OF FLESH! DIE!!!
SPLAT!

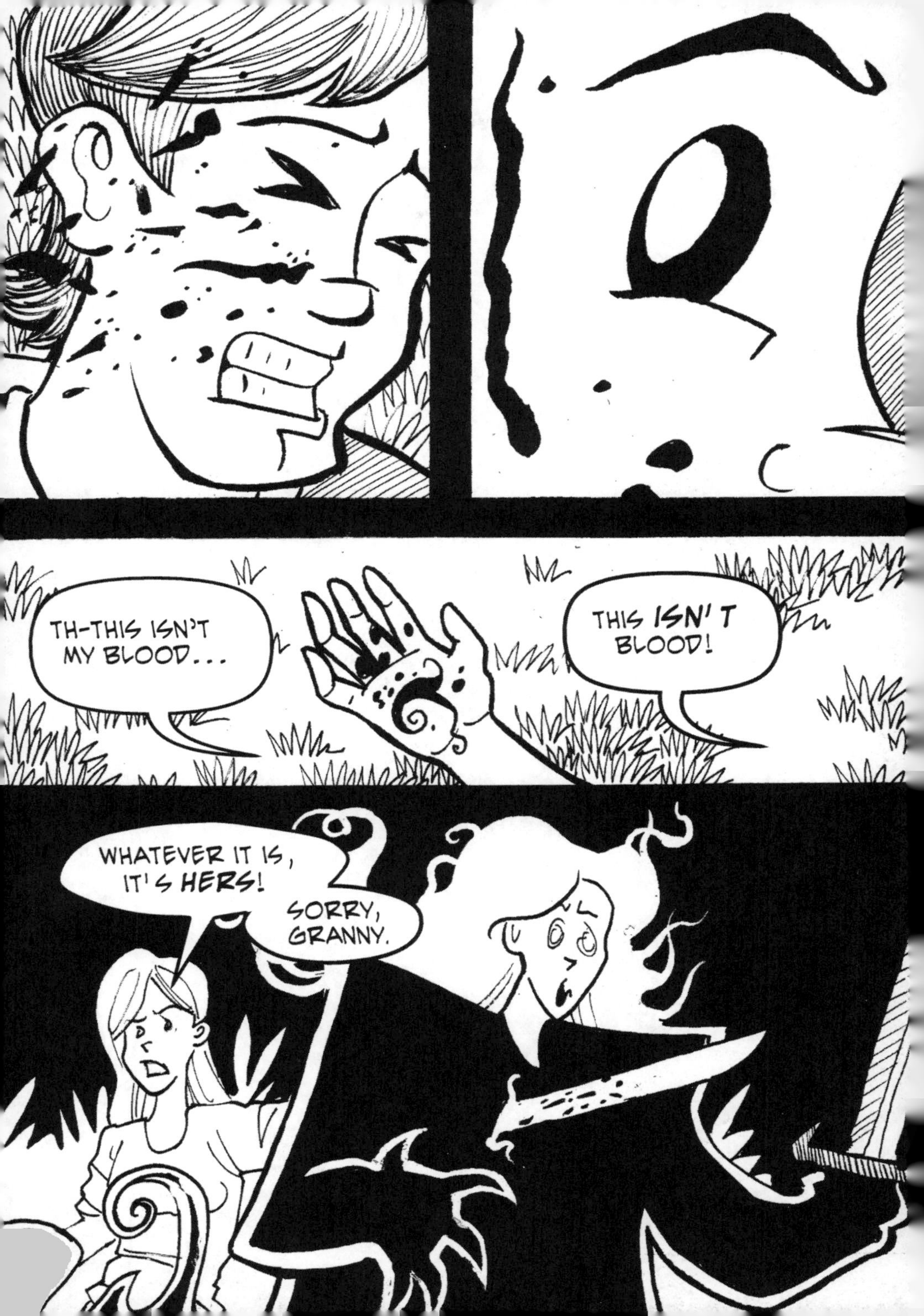
TH-THIS ISN'T MY BLOOD...
THIS ISN'T BLOOD!
WHATEVER IT IS, IT'S HERS!
SORRY, GRANNY.

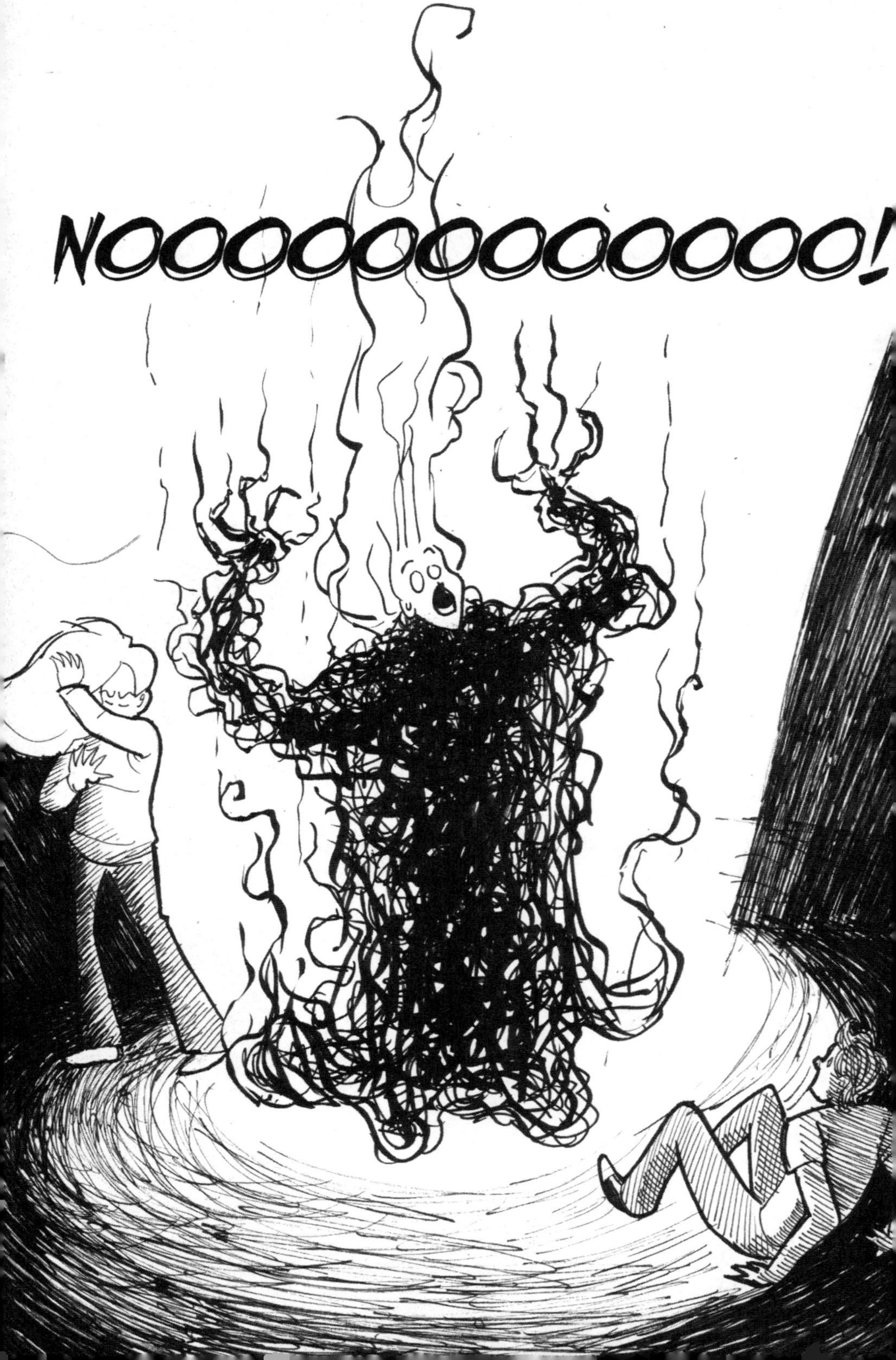
NOOOOOOOOOOOO!

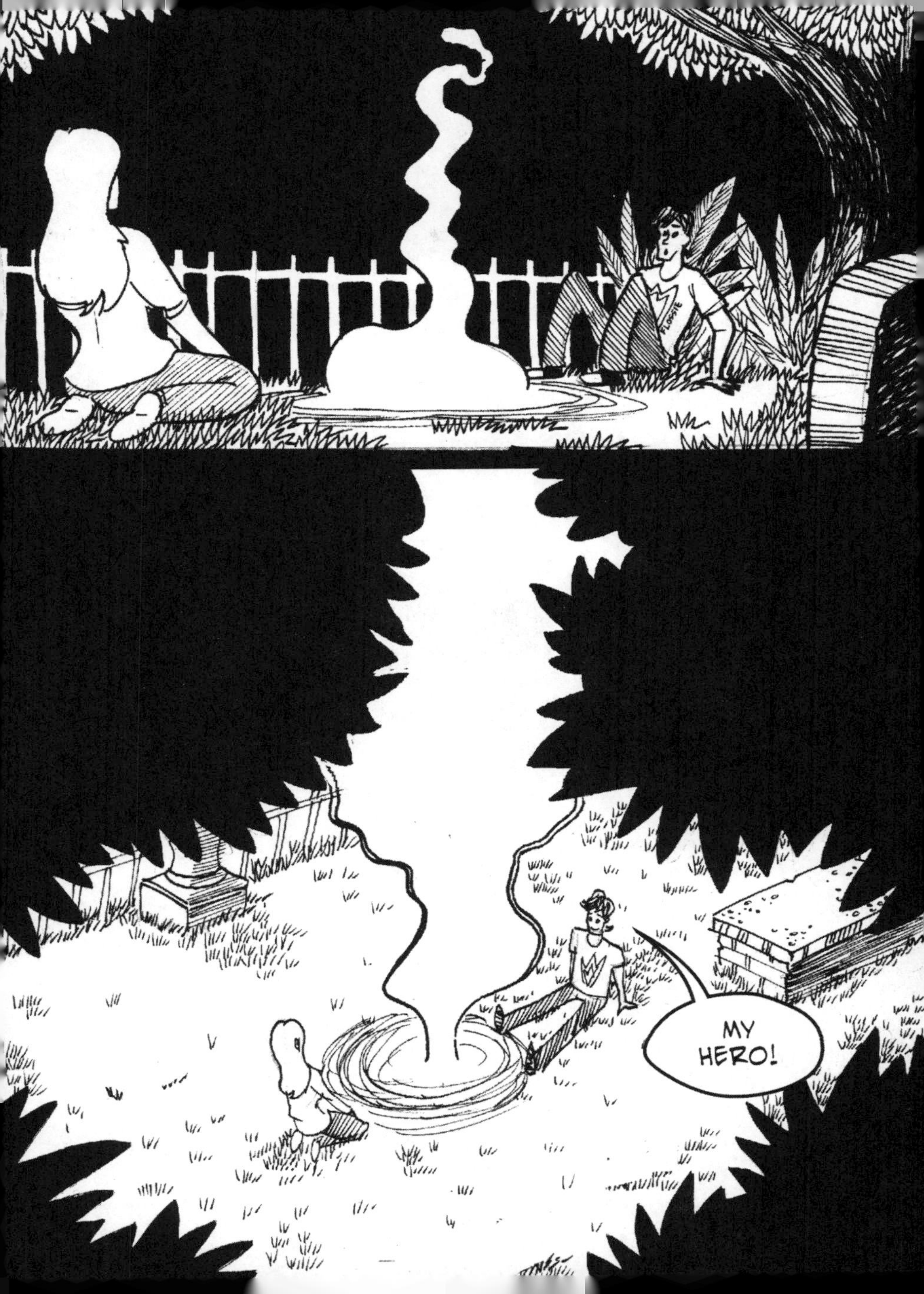
FLOSSIE
MY HERO!

CHAPTER 18

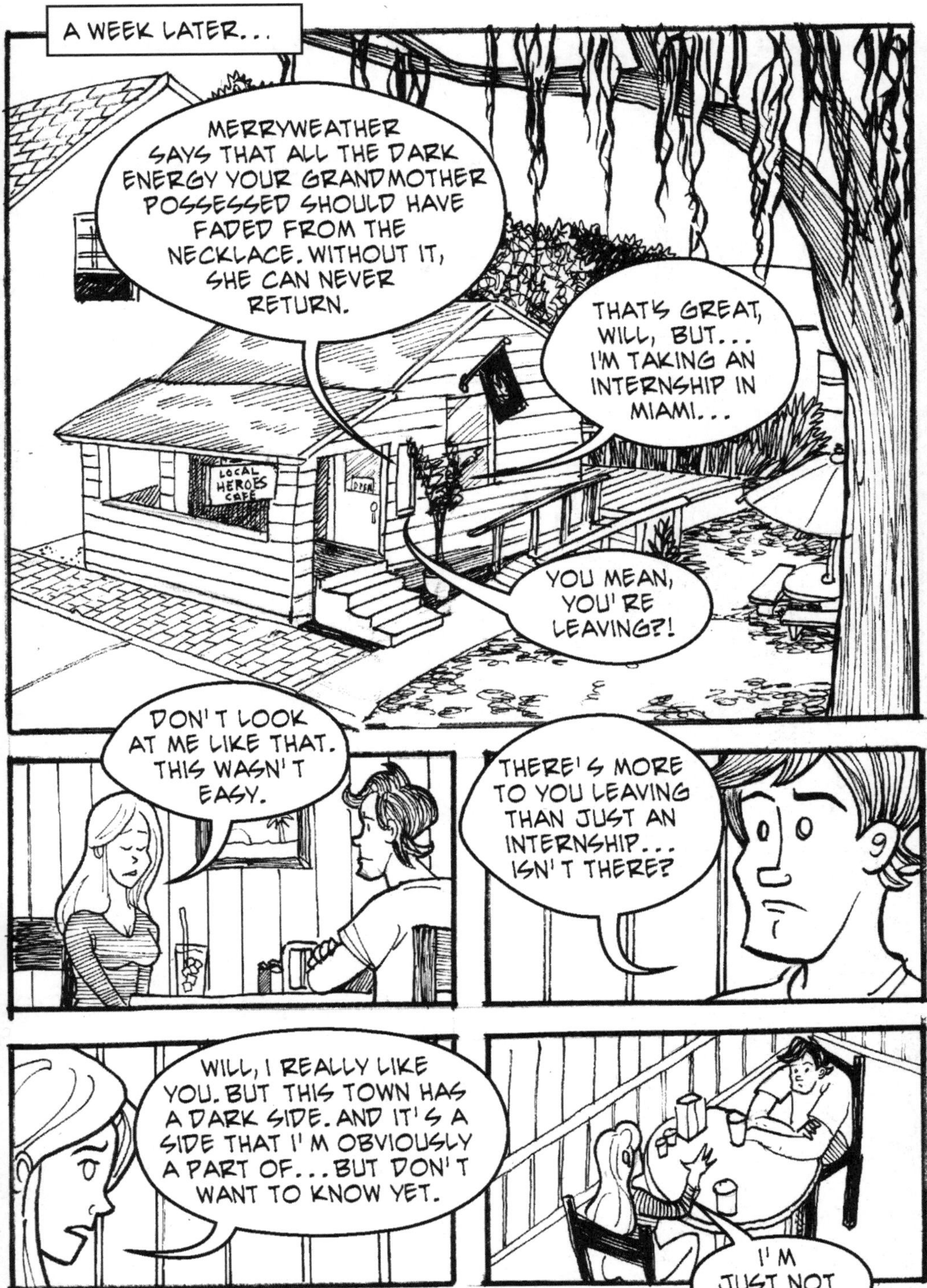
A WEEK LATER...
MERRYWEATHER SAYS THAT ALL THE DARK ENERGY YOUR GRANDMOTHER POSSESSED SHOULD HAVE FADED FROM THE NECKLACE. WITHOUT IT, SHE CAN NEVER RETURN.
THAT'S GREAT, WILL, BUT... I'M TAKING AN INTERNSHIP IN MIAMI...
LOCAL HEROES CAFE
OPEN
YOU MEAN, YOU'RE LEAVING?!
DON'T LOOK AT ME LIKE THAT. THIS WASN'T EASY.
THERE'S MORE TO YOU LEAVING THAN JUST AN INTERNSHIP... ISN'T THERE?
WILL, I REALLY LIKE YOU. BUT THIS TOWN HAS A DARK SIDE. AND IT'S A SIDE THAT I'M OBVIOUSLY A PART OF... BUT DON'T WANT TO KNOW YET.
I'M JUST NOT READY.

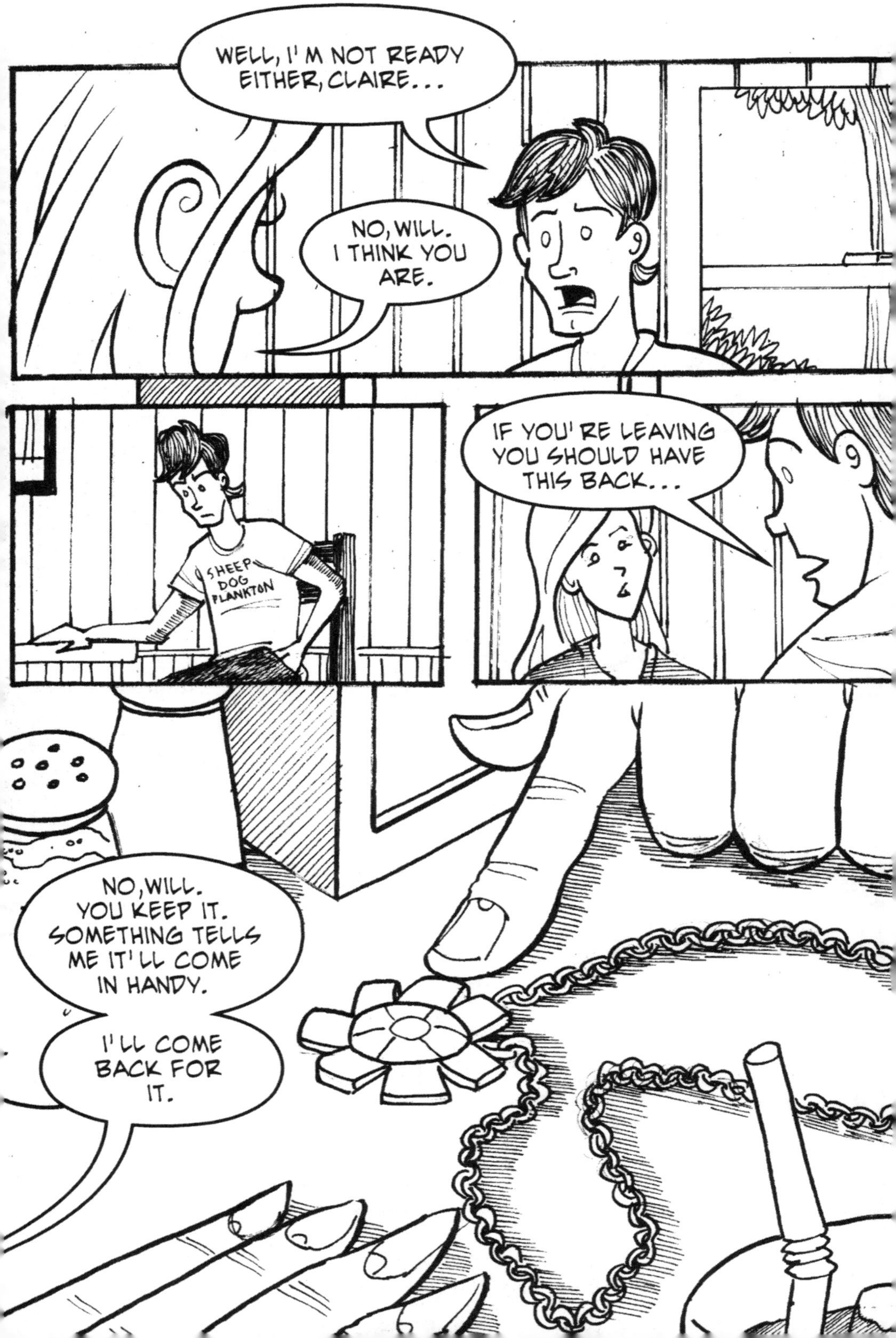
WELL, I'M NOT READY EITHER, CLAIRE...
NO, WILL. I THINK YOU ARE.
SHEEP DOG PLANKTON
IF YOU'RE LEAVING YOU SHOULD HAVE THIS BACK...
NO, WILL. YOU KEEP IT. SOMETHING TELLS ME IT'LL COME IN HANDY.
I'LL COME BACK FOR IT.

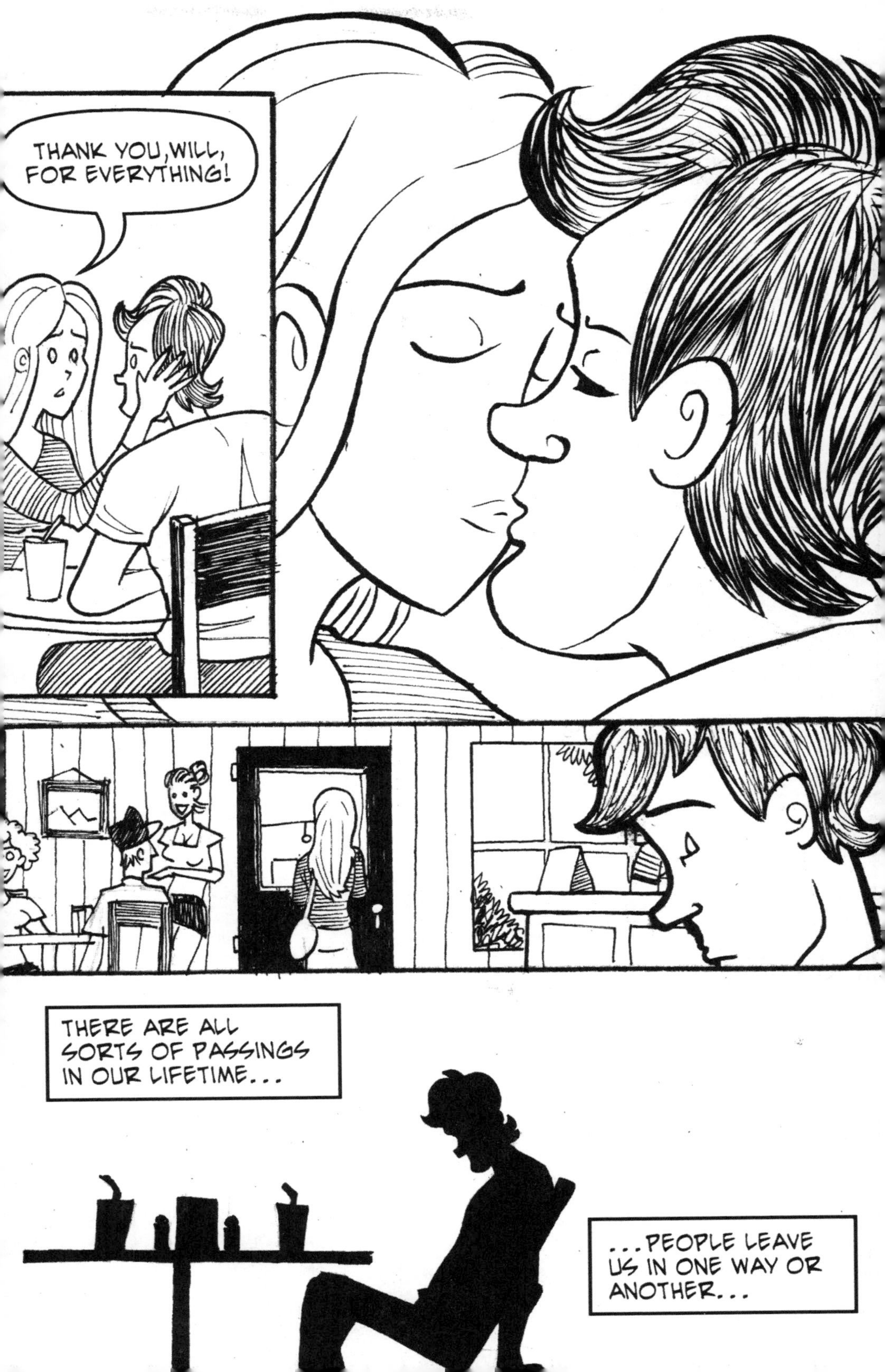
THANK YOU, WILL, FOR EVERYTHING!
THERE ARE ALL SORTS OF PASSINGS IN OUR LIFETIME...
...PEOPLE LEAVE US IN ONE WAY OR ANOTHER...

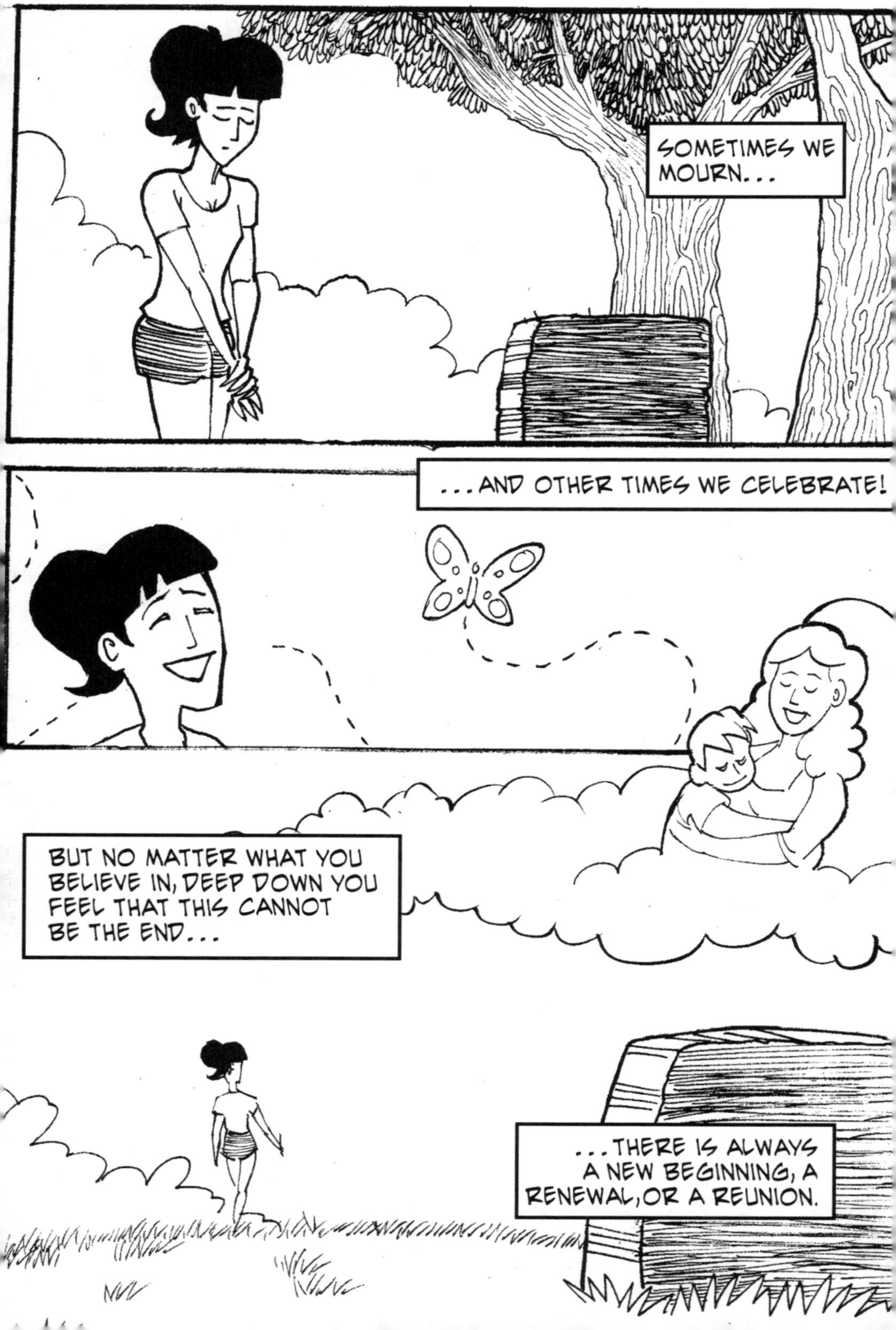
SOMETIMES WE MOURN...
...AND OTHER TIMES WE CELEBRATE!
BUT NO MATTER WHAT YOU BELIEVE IN, DEEP DOWN YOU FEEL THAT THIS CANNOT BE THE END...
...THERE IS ALWAYS A NEW BEGINNING, A RENEWAL, OR A REUNION.

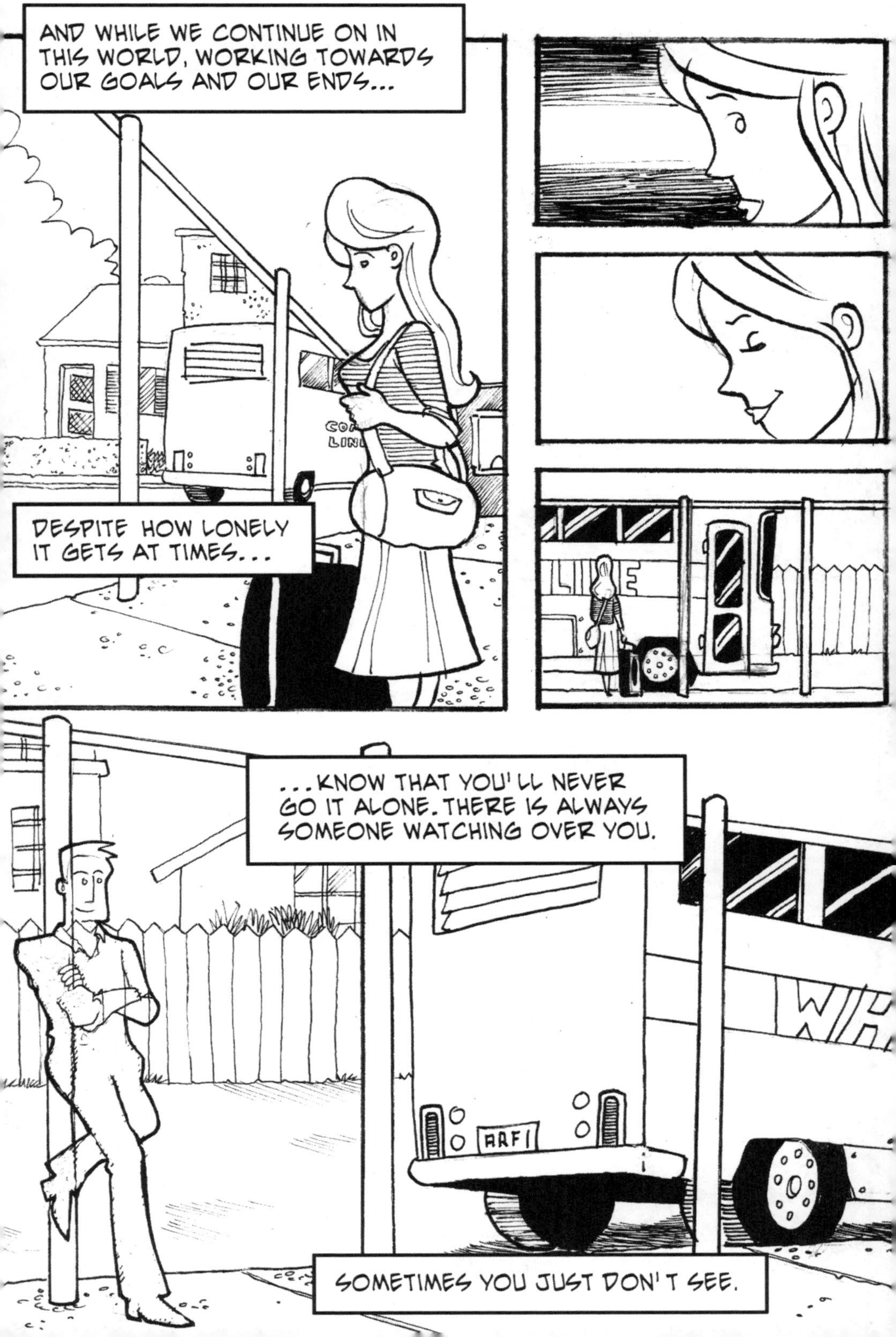

AND WHILE WE CONTINUE ON IN THIS WORLD, WORKING TOWARDS OUR GOALS AND OUR ENDS...
DESPITE HOW LONELY IT GETS AT TIMES...
...KNOW THAT YOU'LL NEVER GO IT ALONE. THERE IS ALWAYS SOMEONE WATCHING OVER YOU.
AAF1
SOMETIMES YOU JUST DON'T SEE.

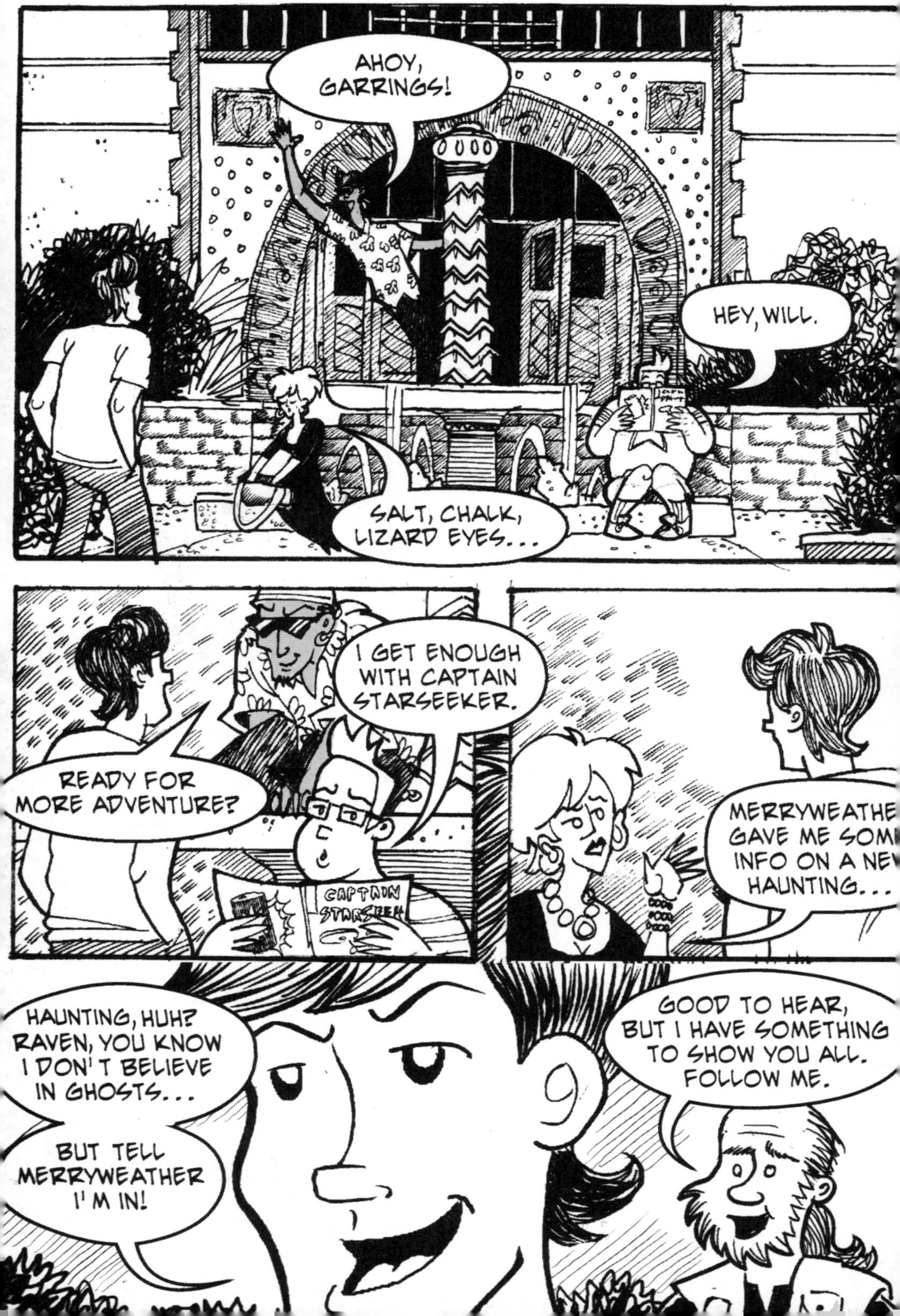
AHOY, GARRINGS!
HEY, WILL.
SALT, CHALK, LIZARD EYES...
READY FOR MORE ADVENTURE?
I GET ENOUGH WITH CAPTAIN STARSEEKER.
CAPTAIN STARSEEKER
MERRYWEATHE GAVE ME SOM INFO ON A NEW HAUNTING...
HAUNTING, HUH? RAVEN, YOU KNOW I DON'T BELIEVE IN GHOSTS...
BUT TELL MERRYWEATHER I'M IN!
GOOD TO HEAR, BUT I HAVE SOMETHING TO SHOW YOU ALL. FOLLOW ME.

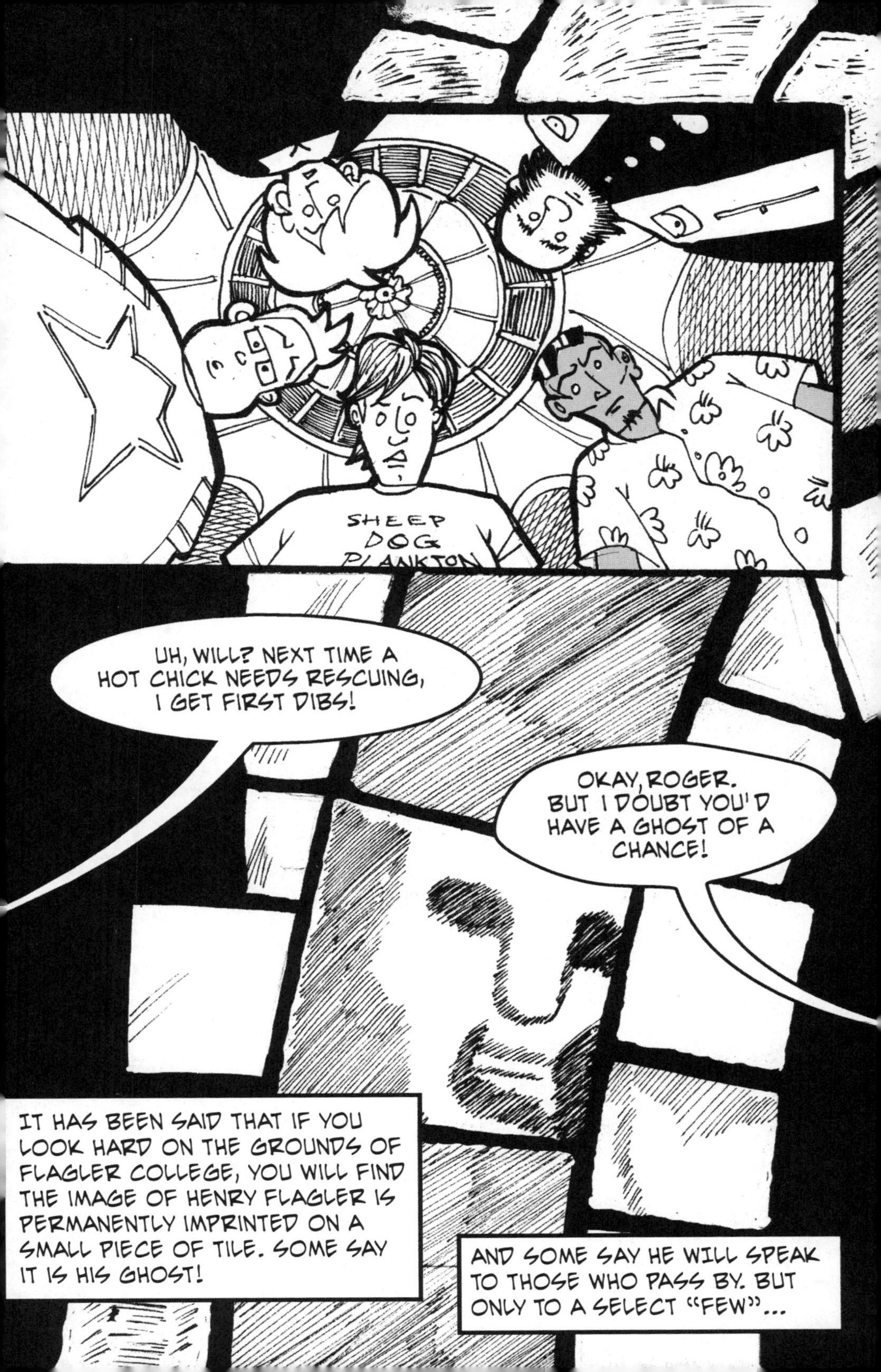
SHEEP DOG PLANKTON
UH, WILL? NEXT TIME A HOT CHICK NEEDS RESCUING, I GET FIRST DIBS!
OKAY, ROGER. BUT I DOUBT YOU'D HAVE A GHOST OF A CHANCE!
IT HAS BEEN SAID THAT IF YOU LOOK HARD ON THE GROUNDS OF FLAGLER COLLEGE, YOU WILL FIND THE IMAGE OF HENRY FLAGLER IS PERMANENTLY IMPRINTED ON A SMALL PIECE OF TILE. SOME SAY IT IS HIS GHOST!
AND SOME SAY HE WILL SPEAK TO THOSE WHO PASS BY. BUT ONLY TO A SELECT "FEW"...

THE

END

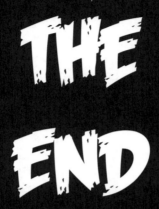

Bibliography

Cain, Suzy. *A Ghostly Experience: Tales of Saint Augustine*.
Tour St. Augustine, Inc., 1997.

Canwell, Jonathan Sutherland, and Diane. *Witches of the World*.
Edison, NJ: Chartwell Books, Inc., 2007.

Carpenter, John Reeve. *Pirates: Scourge of the Seas*.
New York, NY: Sterling Publishing Co., 2008.

Cribbs, Randy. *Tales from the Oldest City*.
Jacksonville, FL: OCRS, 2003.

Harvey, Karen. *Oldest Ghosts: St. Augustine Haunts*.
Sarasota, FL: Pineapple Press, 2000.

Lapham, David. *Ghosts of Saint Augustine*.
Sarasota, FL: Pineapple Press, 1997.

Lapham, David. *Ancient City Hauntings*.
Sarasota, FL: Pineapple Press, 2004.

Mack, Carol, and Dinah Mack. *A Field Guide to Demons,
Fairies, Fallen Angels, and Other Subversive Spirits*.
New York, NY: Henry Holt, 1998.

Moore, Joyce Elson. *Haunt Hunter's Guide to Florida*.
Sarasota, FL: Pineapple Press, 1998.

Nolan, David. *The Houses of Saint Augustine*.
Sarasota, FL: Pineapple Press, 1995.

About the Author

Andre Frattino was born and raised in Gainesville, Florida. Having spent most of his summers since he was a child on the beaches of St. Augustine, he has gained a deep love for the city and its history. Besides his devotion to the arts, Andre's other passion is the paranormal. He has conducted more than fifty haunting investigations across the East Coast and even had an opportunity to work as a consultant for SyFy's *Ghosthunters*.

Andre graduated from Savannah College of Art and Design in 2009 with a BFA in Sequential Art. He has worked steadily as an illustrator for various clients. His works include the children's novel *Here Comes Julie Jack* and graphic novels *Poe Twisted* and *Azteca*. He is an active contributor to the *Independent Florida Alligator*.

Andre currently resides in Gainesville, where he is pursuing a master's degree in Fine Arts at the University of Florida. He continues his pursuit of both the arts and the paranormal and hopes to continue to bridge the gap between them.